W9-DEV-371

THE LIVELY LADY
and
CAPTAIN CAUTION

TWO NOVELS COMPLETE IN ONE VOLUME

"It is a maxim, founded on the universal experience of mankind, that no nation is to be trusted further than it is bound by its interest; and no prudent statesman or politician will venture to depart from it."

—*George Washington.*

THE LIVELY LADY
and
CAPTAIN CAUTION
Two Novels Complete in One Volume

KENNETH ROBERTS

Doubleday & Company, Inc.
Garden City, New York

THE LIVELY LADY

"*The Lively Lady* is the best historical novel we have read in years. After considering soberly the works of William Stearns Davis and S. Weir Mitchell and Rafael Sabatini and the earlier Robert W. Chambers, we'll go even further. We have read no better book of its type than *The Lively Lady*, anywhere, any time. It drives, full-sailed and rail under, logging a yarn of the War of 1812 and the privateers that were America's chief substitute for a navy. There is a mighty gusto in the book, controlled and disciplined by writing of high merit. It hurries you along through frothing sea and pungent powder smoke and the grim ordeal of Dartmoor Prison with no respite in its traction. Its people are real, its situations plausible, its style a delight. To this reviewer *The Lively Lady* stands quite as high in the aristocracy of historical romance as *Hugh Wynne,* and it is quite possible that the patina of years will make it seem even finer."

—FREDERIC V. VAN DE WATER, *New York Evening Post*

PRINTINGS

First published .... April 7, 1931
Revised, replated and reprinted .... December, 1935
Reset, replated and reprinted .... September, 1958
U.S., 1933; 1934; 1935; 1937 twice; 1938 three times; 1939 twice;
   1940; 1941; 1942; 1943; 1945 twice; 1946; 1948; 1950; 1953; 1956
Braille, Library of Congress .... April, 1936
Armed Services Edition .... March, 1945
Family Reading Club .... March, 1958
  Reprinted .... September, 1958
Peoples Book Club .... September, 1958
Doubleday Dollar Book Club .... March, 1959
England (Bodley Head) .... October, 1935
Germany (Holle) .... March, 1938
Spain (Janes) .... November, 1945
Czechoslovakia (Odeon) .... August, 1946
Sweden (Bonniers) .... May, 1947
Finland (Gummerus) .... January, 1948
Rumania (Boema) .... January, 1948
Italy (Aldo Martello) .... December, 1949
France (Editions de la Paix) .... July, 1950
Germany (Diana) .... June, 1952

CAPTAIN CAUTION

"It is such powerful writing as that in *Captain Caution* describing the British hulks, the prisoners and their escape that sets Mr. Roberts' work apart from that of most historical novelists."

—Saturday Review of Literature

PRINTINGS

First published .... November 7, 1934
U.S., 1934 twice; 1937; 1938 twice; 1939; 1940; 1941; 1942; 1943; 1944; 1945 twice; 1946; 1948; 1950; 1953; 1957
Braille, Library of Congress .... March, 1935
Talking Books, American Foundation for Blind ...... December, 1939
Armed Services Edition .... April, 1944
Family Reading Club .... March, 1958
    Reprinted .... September, 1958
Peoples Book Club .... September, 1958
Doubleday Dollar Book Club .... March, 1959
Spain (Janes) .... May, 1946
Czechoslovakia (Odeon) .... Suppressed: Iron curtain
Switzerland (Diana: German) .... February, 1948
Sweden (Bonniers) .... October, 1948
England (Collins) .... January, 1949
Hungary (Konyvkiado) .... March, 1949
Italy (Mondadori) .... September, 1951
Norway (Cappelens) .... October, 1951
Sweden (Bonniers, Folkbibliotek) .... March, 1953
Iran (Gotemburg, Tehran) .... April, 1956

THE LIVELY LADY

TO
A. M. R.

Our town of Arundel, at the mouth of the Arundel River in the Province of Maine, halfway between Portsmouth and Portland, is a small place; and those who live there think that nothing happens in it, ever. It is to escape from that dullness, no doubt, that so many of my townsmen have taken to the sea, knowing it and using it as landsmen know and use their front yards and back yards and farms and warehouses and highways.

Yet there is more curiosity among Arundel folk concerning the small things of life than concerning events commonly called great and romantic; and they are less interested in knowing how wars are won than in hearing how soup is cooked by the French and the English with whom Jeddy Tucker and I had so many dealings, some of them savory and some not so savory.

Therefore I shall put into this tale the small things that happened to me on the high seas and in various ports of this and other countries, and within the cruel bell-topped walls of Dartmoor Prison during our struggle with England's ships in the War of Impressments.

Jeddy Tucker, who was a school teacher and a scholar before he became a mariner, has said often that if he had the time, he could write more entertainingly than I of our adventures, putting in flowery language and noteworthy deeds and making a history out of it, whereas I can set down nothing but the simple truth and our own unimportant endeavors—though God knows they seemed important to us.

Yet, since he never had the time, being busy with conversation concerning his experiments with gambling games and the drinking of liquor, or concerning his uncle John Burbank, who was master at arms on the *Bonhomme Richard* under John Paul Jones, there was no way of getting it done unless I did it myself.

It seems strange that John Burbank, uncle to Jeddy Tucker, should have had an influence on me, considering that he died in 1793, which was three years after my birth. But it was because of him that Jeddy and I set out from Portland on a warm March day in 1812 and took the road down Bramhall's hill toward Arundel, and that journey profoundly affected my life.

This walk is a pleasant one under ordinary circumstances, what with the White Hills lying off to the northward, the vast flocks of ducks in the marshes near Dunstan's, and the sweet smells of young grass, moist earth and pine forests that blend with the fresh perfume of the sea between Biddeford and Arundel. Yet it is no walk for a man just ashore from a long cruise, lacking the feel of the land in his feet and legs; and if I had done as I wished I would have ridden home in state in a cushioned coach, for we were newly returned in our brig *Neutrality* from Cadiz in Spain and had not yet adjusted our clumsy sea legs to the hellish ruts and mire holes that are left in all our roads when the frost goes out of them in the spring.

But I couldn't ride; for when I went ashore from the *Neutrality* and turned into Fore Street with my small white dog, the one my father brought me from England when he last sailed there with my mother, I saw Jeddy waiting near the door of the Weather Rail Tavern. He came to me immediately with a serious expression on his face, which was small and innocent-looking, a little like a child's, but impudent.

I knew from the way he frowned and covered his lips with his hand that he had been splicing the main brace; for although this attitude gave him an air of thoughtfulness, it was only adopted to divert the smell of liquor from my nose. I wouldn't like to say Jeddy never spoke of his uncle John Burbank except when drunk; but it seemed to be a fact that whenever he devoted himself seriously to drinking, his uncle automatically entered the conversation—as a result of which there was immediate and overwhelming trouble. It seems that when his uncle was master at arms on the *Bonhomme Richard,* she had fought a desperate engagement with the *Serapis* and the *Countess of Scarborough;* and when the *Bonhomme Richard* was sinking, Jeddy's uncle had loosed the prisoners to let them escape with their lives. For doing it he was censured by John Paul Jones, who was a great captain, but hard. It was over this that the fighting began; for Jeddy, having stated his case, would at once offer to remove the hide from any man who would not admit that Paul Jones was a flint-hearted Scotch snake. Always, it seemed to me, there was someone to defend Paul Jones, which obliged Jeddy to fly at him without further formalities.

"Captain," Jeddy said, behind the shelter of his hand, "I'd think it a great favor if you'd take my bag to Arundel with you, seeing as how I might be delayed."

"Why might you?" I asked, mindful of his feelings. Men can do as they like for all of me, and I won't ask why they do it; but with

Jeddy it was different. I didn't wish to lose sight of him, because he was quick to see the meaning in printed words and figures, which is a great help on shipboard to a new-made captain, young and forgetful of the many wordy problems in Bowditch's Navigator. Also, being skilled at card games, he was a pleasant companion on long voyages.

"Well, Captain," said Jeddy, moving quickly on his feet to keep from settling back on his heels, "it so happened I met two men, mariners from Halifax, looking for loads of potatoes for the British armies. They play piquet."

"So," I said, "you met two herring chokers, did you? Ten to one they're Scotch and hard losers."

"I'll make it as easy for 'em as I can," he said, drawing a deep breath and blowing it from the side of his mouth.

I saw there was nothing for it but to walk him to Arundel; for if I left him with two Scotchmen, and he inflamed them by winning their money, they would fall on him together when he maligned Paul Jones, which was inevitable.

That was how we came to be plodding along the road together, with my small white dog Pinky running ahead of us, sniffling into every stone wall and ditch and old stump, and covering twenty miles for each one of ours. He was a good dog, this Pinky, called by that name because he was small and short, rising to a point at bow and stern, like the vessel known to us as a pink, a craft able to wriggle in and out of anything. When he came suddenly into a field he would behave like a pink in a choppy sea, leaping smoothly up and down, and seeing everything around him with a minimum of fuss and wild antics. He had small, high ears and black eyes, and important bristly white whiskers like those of Mr. Cutts the shipowner in Saco. He swaggered and rolled in his gait, his short tail bent upward, taut and jaunty; and he was high-and-mighty with other dogs, walking on his toes in their vicinity and seeming to fling oaths at them.

We traveled light, for I had given our dunnage, all but my mother's shawl, to Tommy Bickford, our cabin boy, the son of the Thomas Bickford who saved my father's life at the battle of Valcour Island; and Tommy, though only fourteen years old, would carry it safely to Arundel by coach, so that we needed to give it no further thought. The shawl, a white silk one embroidered with blue and pink flowers and bright green leaves, very rich and Spanish, was from Cadiz; and I had wrapped it around my waist under my jacket so I could give it to my mother on entering the house.

Between Dunstan's and Saco there is a dip in the road, with a meandering brook running through the meadow at the bottom. On the slopes are groves of birches, wild cherries and hawthorns, among which stand pines and tall elms. Even a man with half an eye would recognize it as the best of cover for partridges or woodcock.

When we came up from this dip we found a light coach standing by the side of the road, the driver asleep in the sun, and the body of the coach filled with expensive dunnage: hat boxes and coach robes and cloaks and small trunks, and atop the pile a man's beaver hat and an empty gun case.

While we stood looking at it, wondering whether to wake the driver, we heard a faint scream from a field nearby; then a ripple of laughter, soft and exciting laughter, unlike the sort I was accustomed to hear along the waterfronts of Havana and Lisbon. Close on the laughter came the sharp bark Pinky makes when waiting permission to accept food.

I left Jeddy, pushed through the shrubbery into the field and at once came on two women. They were on rising ground, a heavy stand of pines at their backs and the warm noonday sun shining down on them. One was an oldish woman, pleasant enough looking, but with an air of grayness about her, as if she had worn nothing but gray all her life and busied herself in colorless pursuits. The other was young and the opposite of her companion in appearance, for she had the look of never having worn gray and of never having done anything that didn't give her pleasure. She was kneeling on a robe, offering food to Pinky, who was sitting straight on his stub of a tail, as I had taught him when he was small; and her cloak, which had been placed around her shoulders, had fallen a little away, so I could see her dress was green, with ruffles on it, and her pretty arms bare below the elbow.

When Pinky looked around at me and barked, impatient to be allowed to accept the proffered food, the younger woman looked up. Her hair was the color of a copper rivet worn by rubbing, and her eyes seemed to mirror the greenness of her bonnet, though I could not make sure without staring overlong.

"Oh, la!" she said, prim and disdainful, "such a stubborn little wretch I never saw, never! Such a darling! Is he yours?" She turned from me at once, but I knew she had missed nothing of my clay-covered shoes, and the tie I had loosened at my throat, and the thickness at my waist where my mother's shawl was hid.

"Yes, ma'am," I said, wishing I had worn my varnished boots and my new baggy pantaloons and my blue silk shirt from Cadiz. "Take, Pinky." With that Pinky leaped up and took the food from the lady's

fingers. She screamed again, a faint, affected scream, and sank back
on her robe, drawing her cloak around her. Pinky moved a little, so
to be immediately before her, and, after glancing at me apologetically, threw himself upright once more; nor could I blame him, for if
he was as empty as I he could have eaten a whole ox tongue and
then looked around for something filling.

"You should feed your dog, sir!" she said to me severely.

It was then that Jeddy came up beside me and stood staring at
the green-clad lady. When she held out more food to Pinky, Jeddy
stepped forward and took it from her fingers.

"Is it fitten and proper for him to have such food as this?" he asked
doubtfully. He held it out to me inquiringly; then popped it into his
own mouth. He rolled his eyes upward, seemingly in contemplation.
"You better taste it," he told me. "It might be bad for little dogs."

He burst into a rapid series of laughs, elevating his pale eyebrows
until they almost vanished beneath his cap; and with that the lady
in green, who had put on a dubious and distant look, glanced up at
us and laughed herself. Her eyes, I then saw, were not green at all,
but a sort of smoke color.

"La!" she said, rising to her knees to slice delicately at sausages
and cheese that she took from a basket, "how thoughtless I am! I
had it in mind you were on your way to your dinner, but perhaps
you don't live hereabouts at all."

"No, ma'am," I said. "We live in Arundel, fifteen miles from here."

She looked at me blankly. "In a Rundle?" she asked, saying the
name of our town as I had said it. "You live in a Rundle?" Then
understanding seemed to come to her. "Lud!" she cried, "what a way
to pronounce it! You should know it's Arun Del. We have an Arun
Del in England, on the Arun River. You mustn't call it as you do,
'a Rundle'!"

"Well," I said, "there's no Arun River in Maine, and goodness
knows what port you'll make if you go around asking for Arun Del."

She laughed lightly. "Small loss if we miss it! I remember the place
too well!" She turned to her companion, the gray woman. "It was a
Rundle where we stopped last night," she said, with an air of having
suffered martyrdom. Then she turned back to me. "The food swam
in grease, and we dared not rest in our beds. A terrible place! How
do you stay there all winter without dying?"

"You'd say no such thing if you stopped with us!" I protested.
"None of our food swims in grease! My aunt Cynthy's the best cook
in the world, and I'd rather have our food than anything you can
find in any country! Where do you live, ma'am?"

"I?" she asked, looking at me haughtily. "I live in London and at Ransome Hall, near Exeter and Plymouth in England."

"Those are terrible places," I told her. "London's a rabbit warren of filthy houses filled with drabs and slatterns and paupers, and Plymouth has fishwives and boozing kens enough to supply all America, I do believe."

"Ooh!" she said, tossing her head. "There was never such an untruth! Plymouth has the greenest hills and the fairest houses of all Devon; and there's no city anywhere with such fashionable people and lovely shops and entrancing routs as London!"

"Well, ma'am," I said, "I've been in London and Plymouth, and seen the things I tell you of."

"I don't care!" she cried, seizing Pinky in her arms and kissing the top of his head. "It isn't true! I've never seen such things in my life, and I've spent all of it in London or near Exeter."

"We've spent a good part of our lives in Arundel," Jeddy said, "and we don't recognize your description of the place."

The lady in green looked closely into Pinky's glazed eyes and ruffled his bristly whiskers with a small white hand, at which he sighed, throwing himself back voluptuously in her lap and raising his chin in the hope of having it scratched.

"Where is it you live in Arun Del?" she asked.

"I live in the garrison house at the mouth of the river. It was an inn when I left, and for all I know it's an inn still. If you'll come there, my aunt Cynthy'll bake beans for you such as you'll get nowhere in England."

"Why did you leave it if you're so fond of it?"

"Because it's my trade to follow the sea."

"Oh, la!" she cried. "To follow the sea! What an expression! To follow the sea! Where do you follow it to?"

"Why, to Spain," I told her, "or Portugal or Havana, or wherever there's cargoes to be carried."

She rubbed Pinky's head idly. "Do sailors have sweethearts in every port?" She glanced at me from the corners of her eyes.

"As many as they want," I said, "and a nuisance it is, too, carrying presents from each port to the next port for the sweethearts. Here's what I mean." I unbuttoned my jacket and unrolled my mother's Spanish shawl from around my waist, spreading it out in the bright March sunshine so that its pinks and greens and blues flashed wonderfully brilliant by contrast with the dead grasses and somber pines.

She squealed like a little girl, spilling Pinky from her lap and rising quickly to her knees to get her hands on the shawl. I saw she was

younger than I had first thought, because of her hoity-toity air and
her fine lady's dress.

"There never was anything so lovely! How did you come by it?"
She jumped to her feet, letting her cloak fall from her shoulders and
pushing off her bonnet with a quick sweep of her hand. She took the
shawl from me, whipping it about her so that it bound her tightly,
making her beautifully smooth and slender.

"I got it in Spain."

She put her hands on her hips and flung me a look over her shoulder. "Is your sweetheart a fine lady?" I could see from the way she
asked the question that she had a slatternly wench in mind. "Do
you think she'll take the pleasure in this shawl that she ought, or will
she fold it away in a drawer and be afraid to touch it for fear of
soiling it?"

"How do I know?" I asked. "She suits me, and I've learned many
things from her; and if she hid it away in a drawer she'd probably
get as much pleasure from it as though she wore it at her work."

"At what does she work?" the lady inquired, smoothing the shawl
over her hips.

"At anything that comes to hand." Then because there seemed to
be a look of distaste about her small nose, I added quickly that she'd
find few folk in New England who did no work, and that most of us
worked because we liked to be busy.

"Oh, la!" the lady cried. "Teach your grandmother to suck eggs!
You can't tell me anything about work, only I was thinking—I was
thinking——"

"It's a difficult art!" Jeddy Tucker said with his best schoolmaster's
air.

"I was thinking," she said, casting a scornful glance at Jeddy, "that
your sweetheart might prefer another sort of present: a dress, or—or
—or a sum of money. My husband, S'Roth, would pay well for this
shawl."

That was how she called her husband—S'Roth; and it took me some
time to realize it was her English way of saying Sir Arthur.

"Where is your husband?" I asked.

Instantly she was all smiles, so I could see she thought I would
sell the shawl; nor, indeed, was I sure I wouldn't.

"He's gone into the fields," she said. "He saw some fine coverts
and thought to shoot a few pheasant or woodcock." She seized the
gray woman by the arm and shook her a little. "Give these good
men a glass of wine, Annie," she added; and I knew she wished to
keep us near at hand until the shawl was hers.

"Well," I said, while the gray woman rummaged for glasses and a bottle in the basket, "he'll get no pheasant, for we have no pheasant here, only partridges, which are better to eat and shoot than any pheasant; but it may be he'll find a woodcock, though it'll be luck if he does."

"Are they so hard to get?"

"No, but they're queer birds, vanishing like ghosts from where they were an hour before, and never to be seen in their flights, and shutting off their scent when they wish, so dogs can't smell them."

"Lud!" she said, laughing merrily, "you Americans can't be happy unless you're drawing the long bow! Shutting off their scent, indeed!"

"Why, so they do," I said. "There's no scent to them when they're nesting, and none when they're moulting, though a smart dog can track them by their footsteps."

She plumped herself down on her knees before me, wide eyed.

"What else do they do?" But there was no way of telling whether or not she was making game of me.

"Well," I said, when Jeddy and I had taken a glass of port from Annie's hands, and Jeddy had pledged all of us by raising his glass and saying, "Down the hatch!" as was his custom before drinking, "well, if they find there's too much passing near their nests, they take their chicks between their knees, one by one, and fly with them to a safer place."

"They never do!" she cried.

"Yes, they do! I've seen them."

"It's strange," she said, "that Sir Arthur has never told me of any such marvelous matters as these."

Pinky raised himself from where he had been drowsing with his head on my boot. He made a sound in his throat a little like a pump when it sucks, a malevolent sound to come from so small a dog. I looked around quickly to see what was amiss. Just this side of the young pines that screened us from the road stood a tall man with a fowling piece under his arm. He was a thin, glum-looking man with a pale face. There seemed to be an upward twist to his eyebrows and ears and hair, and a downward twist to his mouth, so that there was a flavor of old Diavolo about him that would have set me to growling like Pinky if I had been given to growling, even if the gentleman had not had a mislikable air of having listened to what we were saying.

II

SIR ARTHUR RANSOME, I saw at once, would be forever free, where I was concerned, from any demonstration of devotion or affection; for when he joined us, he stooped over and brought out the bottle of port from the basket, held it against the light to see how much was gone, then looked coldly at the glasses Jeddy and I still held. It was in his face that if the giving had lain with him we would have tasted none of his wine.

It may be his wife was accustomed to finding a gray glumness in him, for she jumped to her feet, caught his arm, and swung herself close to him, looking gaily up into his face. "Look, Arthur!" she said, leaning back so he might see how she was encased in my shawl. "He bought it in Spain for his sweetheart, and I've asked him to sell it to us."

Sir Arthur examined her, back and front, as he might look at a chair he was minded to buy. "Not a bad shawl," he admitted. "Have one like it at Ransome Hall. Black though. How much did you pay for it?"

"Forty dollars," I told him.

"Ow! Did you now! That's rather high for a shawl! I'll take it off your hands for thirty."

"That's little short of princely!" Jeddy whispered.

Sir Arthur rounded on him. "Aren't you getting a bit above yourself, my man?"

I feared Jeddy would either cackle derisively or fly at the Englishman like a kingbird at an owl; and I knew whatever he did would prove disquieting to Lady Ransome, who had done nothing to deserve disquiet. Therefore I shouted his name, harsh and quick, as I might shout it on shipboard. "Set off up the road!" I said. "I've made this trip to keep you company, and I'll have no more delay."

When he looked at me uncertainly, I added that I'd catch up with him in five minutes. At this he made a pretense of pulling his forelock, saying in an obsequious voice, "Yes, sir, Captain, sir!"

He raised his eyebrows at Sir Arthur and laughed twice, glanced with broad and open admiration at Lady Ransome, and went strutting off through the brush like an impudent little gamecock. I half expected Sir Arthur to rebuke him again for his insulting laughter, but he only peered hard at me, as though he had forgotten Jeddy's very existence, which no doubt he had.

"Captain!" he exclaimed. "Surely you can't be a captain at your age: not of anything large enough to go out of sight of land!"

It has seemed to me that over-many Englishmen of my acquaintance pride themselves on what they call their frankness, and are seldom moved to be frank concerning the pleasant things that come to their notice, so that their frankness has much the flavor of rudeness. At such frankness Sir Arthur seemed a master.

"Well," I said, "it's true our brig's no great shakes in size, but she's a sweet sailer, and minds me as well as my dog Pinky. As for going out of sight of land, I've been in no Spanish harbor these two years past without seeing twenty Yankee craft for every Britisher; and eight out of ten of the Yankees were as small as our brig: yes, and smaller, too, though she tons only two hundred and sixteen."

"Haw!" Sir Arthur said. "Two hundred and sixteen! One must feel highly important, being captain of such a vessel!"

"There's no time aboard our brig to feel important," I told him. "Many people from Arundel follow the sea, but nobody does it to fatten his feelings."

"I see! You mean you do it for money!"

Now I have small love for folk who go up and down the land squabbling and fighting for no reason except to coddle their own vanity. Yet every word this man spoke seemed somehow to exasperate me; and I would gladly have squabbled with him except that his lady, wrapped tight in my shawl, stood staring thoughtfully at him with one finger on her lower lip, which was as red as though newly wet with French wine.

"It's true," I said, "we must work for our living and, as you imply, have no leisure class like your own, which does nothing except for its own pleasure. This reminds me—I'm taking more leisure than I should; so if the lady'll return my shawl I'll be off on my business."

At this she clasped her hands before her and hopped a little on her toes, as children hop when teasing their mothers for cookies. "Arthur!" she cried, "you'll never let him go away without buying the shawl, Arthur!"

Sir Arthur said, "Ow!" again, as if he had forgotten about the shawl. Then he looked at me distantly. "I think the price was forty dollars," he said. "Of course, that's high, but I'll not argue. We'll take it at that price."

"The shawl's not for sale."

"My good man!" Sir Arthur said, "these trading tricks will do you no good, you know!"

I looked down at my knuckles, at a loss what to say to such a man; but while I still considered the matter I felt Lady Ransome's hand on my arm. "You wouldn't keep me from it, would you," she asked, "when you know how much I want it?"

I think it must have been Sir Arthur's talk of trading tricks that put an idea into my head as I looked at her standing straight and slender in the flowered shawl against the brown grass and the blue-green pines.

"No," I said, "I can't sell it to you, because it's for someone else; but if you'll stop to see her when you return from where you're going, she may exchange with you."

The lady laughed gaily. "La!" she cried, "I think I'll have no more chance of getting the shawl from your sweetheart than of getting the moon!"

"She thinks highly of me," I said.

Lady Ransome crowed with delight. "Such modesty!" she cried. "Or a skillful lover from having a sweetheart in every port! How shall I find this maid who's made you so trustful of her affections? Where does she live and what's her name?"

"She's my mother," I said. "Her name's the same as mine, and my name is Nason—Richard Nason."

"Oh," she said. She examined the flowers on the shawl. "It's beautifully worked," she added thoughtfully. "The shadings seem almost real." She whipped it off and handed it to me, turning to Sir Arthur as she did so. "He lives at an inn at the mouth of the river in Arun Del," she said. She clung to Sir Arthur's arm. "We could stop there on our way back from the Lygonia Patent."

Sir Arthur looked over my head contemptuously and ejaculated, "Tah!" or some word that sounded like it. "You must learn from experience, Emily! Do you really wish to return to Arun Del at the cost to ourselves of a meal of rancid pork, in company as unsavory? Do you know what these taverns are, my dear?"

"But the young man claims it's not so at his mother's inn," she persisted. "He spoke of some tasty dishes." She tossed her head at me impatiently. "What were they?"

"Lobster stew," I said quickly. "Corned beef hash moist in the middle and browned on both sides. Toasted brown bread spread with fresh butter, and with cream poured over it."

"Ow!" Sir Arthur said, rather more weakly than he had yet spoken.

"Every traveler reports the inns of New England vile, with a few exceptions—which are viler."

Upon this, for a moment, I was near open profanity, but controlled myself by coughing and gave him a mild answer.

"Sir, you may have listened to the wrong travelers."

"I beg pardon?" Sir Arthur returned, looking at me from under drooping lids.

"Not all travelers say the inns of New England are vile," I said. "There was a French gentleman, Charles Maurice de Talleyrand-Périgord, who stopped more than once at our inn a few years ago. He was so taken with our chocolate custards that my aunt Cynthy had to teach him how to make them."

"Chocolate custards!" Lady Ransome exclaimed, clasping her hands at her throat and staring at me with eyes that seemed to glisten.

Sir Arthur favored her with a gesture of reproof. "What a pretty picture!" he exclaimed. "The great Talleyrand hovering over an oven in Arun Dell!" He laughed an abrupt, unpleasant laugh, looking a little like a horse, and sounding somewhat like one. "You country folk are too credulous! I could tell you I was Talleyrand, and you'd believe me."

I thought of saying I would do no such thing, since all America knew Talleyrand to be a gentleman and a diplomat, whereas anyone could see Sir Arthur Ransome was neither; but I busied myself with my mother's shawl, adjusting it around my waist once more.

"I'm amazed," Sir Arthur continued in a thin and reedy voice, "that Talleyrand hasn't returned from France to Arun Del and brought the French emperor with him, if he found the cookery and the company so diverting! There'd have been a sight for sore eyes, my dear Emily —Boney eating with these fishermen! Highly congenial, I fancy!"

"Let me tell you something," I said. "Talleyrand never came back with the emperor, and that's the emperor's loss; but he did something almost as good. When Louis Philippe, Duke of Orleans, came to America three years after Talleyrand went home, he had been told by Talleyrand to come to our inn. Not only did Louis Philippe do this, but he brought with him his two brothers, the Duke of Montpensier and the Count of Beaujolais."

Seeing Sir Arthur again preparing to neigh like a horse, I raised my voice and hurried my speech. "They professed themselves well enough entertained. My mother says my father showed Louis Philippe and his brothers how to shoot an entire covey of partridges out of a tree, one by one, without frightening them away, and won fifteen dollars in so doing. There's no use saying they were impostors, for when Louis Philippe returned to Sicily he sent my mother ten silver skewers engraved with the royal crest."

Sir Arthur drew the fingers of his right hand across his forehead, as if to wipe a horrible vision from his mind. "Sitting!" he exclaimed, staring at me. "You shoot them sitting!" He raised his eyes to the sky with an appearance of helpless despair. "What a country!" he gasped. "What a country!"

"What gives him this trouble?" I asked Lady Ransome, who had crouched near me to pull Pinky's ears.

"The partridges," she said quickly. "You spoke of shooting them out of a tree, and it's not sporting to shoot a sitting bird. Everyone knows that."

"Oh," I objected, "there's some sport to it! It takes a good eye to find a partridge in a tree; and it only ceases to be sport when you hit one without killing it and then try to find it without the help of a dog."

"Dear me, dear me," Sir Arthur said, "they shoot sitting birds!"

"Well, we don't——"

"Tut, tut, young man!" the Englishman cut me off. "I had a grandfather, it happens, who purchased what was called the Lygonia Patent, and I'm on my way now to prove my ownership of all your province; but I think, though I might own it, I'd be pained to live in it if it's the habit here to shoot sitting birds."

"Well, sir," I said, "I've heard people in these parts speak of how your countrymen are forever trying to get away the Lygonia Patent from those who now live on it, and I can tell you you're wasting your time."

Sir Arthur looked at me icily, and turned to his wife. "Pick up this litter," he said. With that he stalked through the bushes toward his coach.

Lady Ransome jumped to her feet, knotting her bonnet strings beneath her chin. When I would have helped her with the rugs and luncheon basket, she pushed me away with a hand that looked a little like a child's, dimpled at the knuckles. "You should never be truthful with travelers," she said, "if you wish them to taste your chocolate custards."

I would have been glad to see her in Arundel if she could have come alone; but since I couldn't tell her this, I whistled to Pinky and set off after Jeddy Tucker, wondering how any woman could endure being the wife of an Englishman.

III

I F EVER there was a haven for a retired seafarer, it was our house at the mouth of the Arundel River; for it stood on a twenty-acre oblong of fertile ground, with the river running snug along the easterly end of it, a sheltered creek for its northern boundary, and the ocean and a long beach of hard gray sand bordering the side to the southwest. Within sight of its windows was everything a mariner could wish to occupy his attention. There were cows and hens, and fields of corn, beans, potatoes and pumpkins, large enough to keep our cellar stocked with food during the longest winters. In addition there were ducks, geese, wild pigeons and fish to be had for the taking; and best of all, from a seaman's viewpoint, there were eight shipyards between our house and the new toll bridge, all busily engaged in turning out the schooners, sloops and brigs that made our town of Arundel the busiest and the wealthiest in the province of Maine, next to Portland. It was the custom of large vessels to load the last of their cargoes while lying out beyond the bar that obstructed the river mouth, and never a day passed but what a brig or a snow or a ship entered the river at high water with a cargo from Spain or Portugal or Denmark or the Indies, or stood off and on, waiting for tide or wind.

There was a quickened thumping under the shawl that bound my waist when Jeddy Tucker and I came down the path between the tall pines, that evening, and saw our house, low and gray, against the ragged dunes and the darkening seas beyond. I could not blame Pinky for the yapping he set up, nor for the dash he made across the narrow foot bridge and along the path to the house, scuttling into the dusk so rapidly that he might have been the ghost of a dog.

The front door opened; a stream of yellow light flooded out, and in the midst of it stood my mother. I had no more than kissed her when my aunt Cynthy, my sister Sarah and my older brother Nathan came at me with their greetings. Nathan's was brotherly but a little envious; for he had not followed the sea since the embargo, he being color blind and therefore unable to tell one flag from another—a dangerous affliction indeed in days when a mistake of that sort may result in a twelve-pound shot between wind and water.

We went at once into the large front room, which had changed during my absence. In place of the sanded floor and the trestle table there were braided rugs underfoot, brightly colored, and against the wall the long sofa inlaid with satinwood, and the tall secretary made for us by Benjamin Frothingham in Boston. Not only had my mother enriched the room with her carved chairs in the Chinese taste, bought when she sailed with my father to England, but she had covered the pine walls with wall paper depicting scenes in distant cities to which I had never been, so that to be in the room was as good as traveling to foreign parts.

"Quick!" said my mother, taking my arm and shaking me, "say how you like it!"

My mother was small and dark, with a back as flat as a board, though it was a mystery to me how she kept as straight as she did; for when I was young she had gone overboard in a gale to help my father, and had been pounded on a ledge by a heavy surf so that her lower half was somehow weakened. Above she was as strong as ever, and perhaps even stronger; as I was reminded when she thumped me on the chest to emphasize what she was saying.

I said at once that it was no sort of room for an inn, since Jeddy Tucker would use the sofa to heave at the head of any man who stood up for Paul Jones.

"Yes," my mother said, "that's what would happen if this house should continue to be an inn. Our inn-keeping days are over, however, for I'm fond of my furniture; and things are going to be worse instead of better, with all this talk of war, and our people ready to throw chairs at any man who says a good word for the rights of America."

"Well, and why not?" I asked her. "What rights do we have, and what have we got to demand them with?"

My mother twisted her fingers in the string of cat's-eyes she had worn at her throat since I was able to remember, and I knew I was on the verge of hearing something that might not please me. Declaring hurriedly, therefore, that I was dying for lack of food, I unwrapped the shawl from my waist. "Look here," I said, tossing it over her head so she was muffled in it, "I brought this from Spain, and all I ask in return is that I sha'n't be talked to of war or anything else till I've had supper."

It was on my mind, while eating, that I might have been overhasty in speaking to Lady Ransome and her husband about our inn and the food to be had there. After a time I asked my mother whether a traveler could be accommodated as in the old days if there seemed to be some special reason for it. When she was silent, I looked up under my eyebrows at her, and saw her fingers at work again on her cat's-eyes.

At length she nodded. "I think so," she said, "especially since she's young and pretty and took such a fancy to my shawl."

I gave Jeddy Tucker a glance of some severity, but he, with unbuckled belt, was busy on his third helping of corned beef and looked entirely guiltless. Puzzled as to where my mother had her information, "She?" I inquired. "What 'She' took any fancy to your shawl? She?"

My mother, exasperated at my stupidity, rolled her eyes toward the ceiling. "There's the odor of a fine perfumery on the shawl," she said. "Would it last all the way from Spain? I think not! It's been somewhere, my son, and I think the where was young and pretty."

Perhaps I got a little red. "Maybe so. Maybe so; I admit it," I said, "but you might guess too much; for she was traveling with her maid and her husband——"

"Oh, her husband! And traveling? On foot, perhaps?"

"No, in their own coach."

"Ah! Then you thought the husband an unpleasant fellow, didn't you, and too old for her?"

"You've seen them!" I exclaimed. "They must have passed through here!"

My mother shook her head. "You must learn to draw conclusions, or you'll go through life not seeing half the things that lie before you. If the lady's young and pretty and traveling besides, it's quite certain she didn't marry a man younger than herself. And when a young lady marries an older man, he soon learns to be unpleasant toward the younger men who meet his wife; and to them he appears ancient and decrepit."

"If you're trying to accuse me of paying undue attention to the lady," I said, "you're making a mistake. There was some talk of the evils of our Arundel inns and our Arundel food, and her husband declared that all travelers invariably pronounced them vile."

"I see! And after that you were on such friendly terms that the lady tried on the shawl?"

"No," I said, conscious that my sister Sarah was casting sidewise glances at my brother Nathan, "the shawl came up in another way."

"Ah," my mother said, twisting her fingers in the string of cat's-eyes.

"The Englishman," I continued hurriedly, "wouldn't believe I was a captain, or that our brig was large enough to get out of sight of

land; and he wished to buy your shawl for less than I paid for it.
I told him it wasn't mine to sell; and since he had such a fine opinion
of himself I added that if he'd visit our inn, it might be you'd trade
him for it. I knew if you'd take the matter in hand he'd think twice
before trading for Spanish shawls in New England again."

My mother lifted an eyebrow. "My son, I'm too old a bee to be
caught with that sort of sugared water! Any traveler who wishes
hospitality in this house will always have it as long as I'm alive, unless he's the sort who doesn't deserve hospitality—and it seems to me
our country is producing more and more persons of this sort, thanks
to the preachments of that madman, Thomas Jefferson!"

Now one thing the sea had done for me was to give me relief from
the daily cursing of Thomas Jefferson that resounded through all our
province from morning until night, even though three years had
passed since James Madison had replaced him as president. So great
was my abhorrence of Jefferson that I preferred, for the benefit of
my digestion and my peace of mind, never to hear him mentioned.
Like nearly every other New Englander, I detested him for his petty
meannesses, his economies that proved to be dreadful extravagances,
his aping of the leaders of the French mob, his supplanting of our
fine navy with little gunboats that sank in a capful of wind and could
no more stand against a frigate than a jellyfish could fight a shark. I
couldn't endure his hatred of cities and city folk, and his desire to
rid the nation of manufacturers and artisans, so there might be nobody to cast votes except farmers; and I was fairly sickened by his
strange belief that all people are perfectly equal: not to be called by
any title whatever—a belief he could never have held if he had spent
less time examining the manners and customs of vegetables and
more time on a deep-water brig.

It was this last belief that most often turned the stomachs of our
seafaring people, who know disaster is bound to overtake any craft
on which the captain is not respected and instantly obeyed.

"What," I asked her, happy the conversation had at last turned
from Lady Ransome, "is this talk of war? Is it anything new, or is
it the same old war talk we've been hearing since I was knee-high
to a duck?"

My mother rapped her knuckles on the table to emphasize her
words. "It's new, because the crazy fools in Washington who've been
trying to sell their country's services to either England or France,
whichever would pay them best, haven't been smart enough to avoid
being cheated. They struck a bargain with Bonaparte, who's as great
a thief as a Barbary pirate. Bonaparte swindled them, and England's

in a rage because we trafficked with him; so now there's nothing to be done but fight England. What wearies me is that if we had anybody in Washington but a pack of sawdust dolls, we'd have fought both of them a dozen years ago. We should have fought at once, as soon as they began telling us where we could trade and where we could sail our ships, as if they owned all the oceans of the earth, and taking our seamen from our own vessels as if we were black slaves in Africa."

"To be frank," I said, "I see no sense to this talk of war. We're making a living out of our brig; but if we fight England, we'll have no living at all, for we'll have to lay her up. You'll never get me into a war with England. England's the only nation that defends the world's freedom against Bonaparte."

My mother stood up, her hands on her hips and her new shawl clinging to her arms and her flat shoulders as if she had backed her topsail to give us a chance to come up with her.

"Yes, indeed!" she said ironically. "England's always been a great hand to defend freedom! She's as eager to defend freedom as to cut her own throat!" She made a derisive sound in her nose. "Can't you tell the difference between right and wrong? Can't you get in a rage when the British and French do things to us that they shouldn't?"

"They never did anything to me."

"Oh, my Land, Richard! The French never did anything to your grandfather, but he fought them at Louisburg! The English never did anything to your father, but he fought them at Quebec and Saratoga; and a good thing for you and all of us that he did!"

"There might be two ways of looking at that," I said. "Not even the English could have sent us worse governors than Jefferson and Madison with their damned embargoes and shilly-shallying. I can't see how my father gained much by his fighting if you now say we must fight again. How many people in this town want to fight England, anyway?"

"How many? How many? Probably four out of every four hundred. The other three hundred and ninety-six are making a little money, and it blinds 'em. That's the way people are down here. You've caught it from 'em, Richard."

She came around the table to tap me on the chest. "Richard," she said, "you look a little like a sleepy pirate, with your gray eyes and your black side-whiskers. That's how your father and grandfather looked; so I have hopes that you, like them, may wake up at last."

I V

Fretted by this talk of war, it seemed best to me, after a few days of our good Arundel food and feather beds, to get back to Portland and hasten the sale of our Spanish wine and hides, so we might be off to sea once more.

It was late afternoon when I set out to find Jeddy and let him hear my plans. I knew I would probably come across him at one of the taverns, hobnobbing with the men from the shipyards over their daily four o'clock rum.

Therefore I went to John Patten's inn on our own side of the river, but Patten had seen nothing of Jeddy for more than two hours. He had dropped in, Patten said, peaceful and elegant spoken, and taken a few glasses of rum with Job Averill; then left for Ward's shipyard to look at the new brig Ward was building.

I crossed the river to Ward's shipyard, where Dominicus Weeks, the rigger, told me he had seen Jeddy going toward Nathan Wildes' public house with Pelatiah Ham, Keziah Gooch, and Rowlandson Drown. I was not pleased to hear this. Rowlandson Drown was a chair maker, more quarrelsome than an old bull whale with a sore nose. Once, indeed, he had fallen out with his brother-in-law and tried his best to drown him in the river.

I hurried to Wildes' public house, fearful that Rowlandson Drown might take a sudden dislike to Jeddy; and even before I entered I could hear Jeddy and Keziah and several others saying their say against a war with England. I heard Drown whine that if there was a war there wouldn't be a chair made in Arundel in five years; while Keziah Gooch was bawling that not a man from Arundel would lift a finger against England; and Jeddy was shouting that he could use his time more profitably than in fighting.

I pushed open the door and went into Wildes' dark little front room, where you could either sit on kegs or stand up, as suited your convenience. No sooner had I set foot inside than Drown, a bull-necked man with a face all gray and blotched like the sides of a young sculpin, tossed off a glass of rum and complained that if we had a few seamen like Paul Jones there might be some sense in this talk of fighting England, but as it was we'd get nowhere.

There was a growl of assent from the caulkers and adze-men; but
Jeddy came off his keg like a squirrel, peering into Drown's mottled
face.

"Jones!" he exclaimed. "That piece of Scotch pudding! Why, we've
got ten men that can sail rings around Jones!"

"Who are they?" growled Keziah Gooch, while Rowlandson
Drown's face darkened as though the rum he had drunk were coming to the surface.

"Who?" Jeddy shouted. "Why, Bainbridge and Decatur and Hull
and Perry and every man jack that helped lick the Pasha of Tripoli!
Jones! He was a Scotchman, and there ain't a Scotchman on earth
that can sail with our Yankee captains! Jones! Jones, hell! There's a
dozen men in this town that can outsail Jones! Why, Richard Nason
can outsail Jones! Why, my God, I can outsail Jones!"

Rowlandson Drown made a ripping sound between his tightly
closed lips, whereupon Jeddy pushed closer to him, his spine so
straight that he seemed to lean backward.

"Listen," he said, "I want to tell you about Jones! My uncle, John
Burbank—John Burbank of Arundel—was master at arms under Paul
Jones! Don't try to tell me about Paul Jones! I know all there is to
know about Paul Jones! He was nothing but a big lucky bag of Scotch
porridge, that's what he was! Master at arms under Jones, my uncle
was! Don't you try to Jones me!"

Rowlandson Drown made a snarling sound, took Jeddy's small face
suddenly in his tremendous hand, and pushed him backward over
the keg. I started forward when I saw this; but before I could reach
Rowlandson, Jeddy had slipped from beneath his hand, bounded upward as though shot from a mortar, and seized Drown by the ears.
Drown's huge body seemed to float upward from the keg, and an
instant later his head was driven against the top of the barrel with a
hollow clang. Seeing that Keziah Gooch was making ready to kick
Jeddy from behind, I hit him on the chin, knocking him between
two kegs; and then, although Pelatiah Ham had made no move, I
drove my fist into his stomach for fear he might take it into his head
to leap at Jeddy. Pelatiah went down on top of Keziah and lay quiet,
except for a slight choking sound; and Jeddy and I had a little space
in which to move.

It was well we did; for Rowlandson, though his head was still
being thumped against the keg top, had recovered from the first surprise of the attack and got his big hands under Jeddy's arms. I
shouted to the little bantam to leave go and come away; but even
as I did so Rowlandson heaved hard, and Jeddy turned a slow and

majestic somersault over Rowlandson and the keg. Since he kept hold of Rowlandson's ears the keg was displaced and the two of them fell over on the floor, scuffling and panting.

By this time the adze-men and caulkers were shouting and milling around. It was plain they hadn't relished Jeddy's words about Paul Jones and hoped Jeddy would be killed. I jumped over to pull him away from Rowlandson, and I think we might have got out of it without further difficulty if Nathan Wildes had not come running in from the back of the house, a bung starter in his hand, shouting, "I'll get the little weasel!" Seeing this would never do, I took the bung starter from Wildes and hit him lightly with it on top of his head. Even as he fell, I saw, out of the tail of my eye, one of the caulkers coming for me. It is bad, in such a case, to wait for an attack; so I felled the caulker with the bung starter: then dropped it, for fear of spattering someone's brains on the floor, and went after the rest of the caulker's friends with my fists. I felt two go down before me. Then the room was full of noise and confusion, and over my left shoulder I saw a bottle coming hard at my head. The floor seemed to fall out from under my feet, letting me drop miles into a black pit.

* * *

We were lying outside in the dusk when my senses returned. My skull seemed stuffed with sea urchins; and when I opened my eyes they stung and smarted until I said to myself they must have been knocked from their sockets. The smarting, I found, was caused by brandy that had been poured on my head, whence it had run into my eyes and over my clothes, so that I smelled like a distillery. Keziah Gooch was standing over me, a brandy bottle in his hand; and when he saw my eyes were open, he asked what should be done about Jeddy's ear. "Drown got his teeth in it," he said, "and kind of frayed it. Mebbe we ought to heat a poker and sear it off."

I sat up and looked at Jeddy. His left ear was torn in two or three places, but there was nothing about it that couldn't be remedied with stout thread and a sail maker's needle. None the less, he was so still and white that he worried me.

"What happened to him?" I asked. "Is his back broken?"

"Not to speak of," Keziah said. "He was all right when they carried Rowlandson home with his knee out of joint and four teeth missing. Then we saw this ear and started to put brandy on it. He told us an ear was no place for brandy, and before we could stop him he took the bottle and drank the whole of it. That's his trouble."

I paid Keziah for two bottles of brandy, shoving the partly used bottle into my trousers pocket; and after I had tied a handkerchief around my head so no more blood could spatter on my shirt, I picked Jeddy up, slung him over my shoulder, and went hunting for a punt to carry us down river. It was dark by the time I found one, and still darker when the punt grated on the sand at the river end of our farm. I held Jeddy by the feet and dipped his head in the cold river water; but since he seemed to derive no benefit from it I hung him over my shoulder once more and carried him through the potato patch to our house. When I kicked open the back door, there was nobody in the kitchen, which seemed strange to me; so I opened the door into our new big room, the one that was our gathering room in the old days. Every candle around the wall was lit, and as I staggered forward, carrying Jeddy toward my mother's sofa, there seemed to me to be a hundred people standing in the room, all of them blurred and indistinct in the brilliant light. My mother's face came out clear from the muddle, and then my sister's and my aunt Cynthy's. They were staring at me, and I could see horror in their eyes. With my left coat sleeve I wiped away the blood that was seeping through the bandage round my head; and then I saw, beyond Sir Arthur Ransome and, at the height of his shoulder, looking at me out of a haze, the startled face of his young wife.

I stared at her hard, not even shifting my gaze from her as I let Jeddy slip down upon the sofa. She was in brown, and not in green, as I had seen her in the field near Saco.

"You changed your dress," I said.

At that I heard my mother laugh. "Was it a good fight, Richard?" she asked as she put her arm about me and turned me toward the stairway.

*   *   *

By good fortune the next day was one of those fine unseasonable March days especially made for the loosening of the bands of ice that bind our Maine fields and streams. There was a sweet, warm, smoky breeze out of the northwest, a breeze that flattened the ocean near to shore, so that the waves were small and weak, dropping wearily on the sand as though they lacked the strength to press onward to the high-tide mark. I might have slept the clock around if my aunt Cynthy had not stood by my bed, smiling her gentle smile and holding in her hands a cup of clam broth to which she added a generous portion of horseradish juice—an excellent drink for relieving an aching head. When I told her about our fight at Wildes' public house, she clucked her tongue sympathetically and sat on the edge of my bed to wash the cut over my ear. It was a little tender, this cut, but nothing to think about unless a boom should swing against it.

While she stitched a neat band of old linen around my head, she told me how Sir Arthur had gone with Nathan to Batson's River to shoot teal, and how Lady Ransome was with my mother, asking a thousand questions concerning America.

When I came downstairs I found Lady Ransome beside my mother on our long sofa inlaid with satinwood. I thought she looked pale, though this may have been caused by the black dress she was wearing, a fetching dress that billowed out from her like a doll's dress, making her seem too small to be a grown woman and a wife. She was at work on a piece of needlework, a white thing on a round frame, entirely useless-looking, to my mind, more for appearance than anything else; and she was telling my mother about her father, who, if I correctly understood the little I heard, was a man who considered it demeaning to work, but wholly respectable to permit his wife and children to toil like Barbary galley slaves. She was so interested, seemingly, in what she was saying that she was oblivious to my entrance; and when she had finished she went at her needlework as if she intended never to look up from it.

My mother lifted an eyebrow at me but spoke to Lady Ransome. "My child, here's Richard himself come to tell you that you need distress yourself no more about him."

Lady Ransome dropped her hands in her lap. "Oh, lud!" she exclaimed, looking up at me as if in despair, "your mother calls me 'child' out of meanness, I do believe! I remembered you spoke of chocolate custards, and because I asked for them she calls me 'child'!"

"How many was it you ate?" my mother asked. "Five, it seems to me."

"I tell you that was *not* the reason I went early to bed!" Lady Ransome declared. "It was because I was weary!"

My mother's knitting needles clicked busily for a time, while Lady Ransome looked loftily from the window, wholly indifferent.

"Richard," my mother asked, "is it too early for woodcock to be nesting?"

Lady Ransome tossed her head a little. "La! I fear it's too warm for walking, and Sir Arthur will return shortly!"

"Do as you wish, my child," my mother said. "You spoke so much of them, I thought you wished to see one."

I could think of better ways to spend an afternoon than to walk in the woods with a girl who didn't know her own mind two minutes running; so I was turning away with no further words when Lady Ransome shot a quick glance at me without lifting her head from her sewing—a glance so fleeting I couldn't have sworn I saw it. Yet it left in my mind an impression of stifled hopefulness, such as I sometimes have from Pinky when I leave him lying in a corner of my cabin and he rolls an eye at me in the vain and momentary hope I may relent and invite him to come. Therefore I turned back and said that if her husband had never shot teal in our marshes he would be gone till sundown; for it would take him till then to learn he couldn't kill them as they came down on a northwest wind unless he led them, as our duck hunters say, from here to Scarborough. As for the woodcock, I told her, there was no way of telling whether they were nesting until we looked, and the place to look was an is-land of pines and birches in the marsh where they had always nested since I was able to find my way about. If there was none, I said, I could show her something in the marsh pools that she had never before seen—sticklebacks building round nests under water and slashing at each other out of cussedness with the rows of bayonets on their backs.

"I don't believe a word of it!" she said, proud and lofty. Then she dropped her needlework and hugged my mother's arm to her. "When can we go?" she asked. "Is it true, what he says? And shall we see bears and Indians?"

"You'll see no bears," my mother said, "because there are none hereabouts; and even if there were, they'd run for miles to escape a man or a woman, being timid creatures. Neither will you see an Indian unless you go around by Perkins' wharf, where there's an Abenaki working on Westbrook Hopping's sloop. You'll know him, if you see him, by the way he wears his shirt tails outside his trousers. You can't go walking in that dress, so you must change it: then you can go as soon as you like."

Lady Ransome jumped to her feet, smiled up at me as gaily as though she had never learned how to be stiff or haughty, and ran from the room. We could hear her calling to Annie that she wanted her green dress.

"She'd be better off to stay here," I said, "because she'll get her feet wet and turn up her nose at the things she thinks she wishes to see."

My mother shook her head and smiled her one-sided smile. "She's like a puppy taught to stay quietly in a house with old people and not bark or chew shoes. She wants to play but doesn't know how."

Her knitting needles darted in and out of the stocking yarn. "Besides," she added, "her lot may be pleasanter if this husband of hers should find some man willing and able to throw her a kind word."

I went out in the sun to wait for her. A clean, soothing smell came from the hot sea sand. In the northwest wind the ocean was like ruffled dark blue velvet; and on the far side of Wells Bay the slopes of Mount Agamenticus rose sharp and smoothly curved. It came to me suddenly that there might be worse things than talk of war; and that, given the proper companions, another day or two on land could be mighty pleasant.

V

Tʜᴇʀᴇ is a wide-spreading beech tree with silvery bark in a clearing near the edge of the marsh that borders the tide creek on the northerly side of our farm; and when I set off with Lady Ransome we crossed the creek and struck in past this tree, which is covered with the initials of all the young folk who have kept company together since the earliest days of our town; for it stands in a pleasant spot, sweet with marsh odors and sheltered from the tang of unseasonable winds, and cursed only with mosquitoes, which are never troublesome to lovers.

She stared at this tree from every side, reading the initials and marveling at the hearts and arrows with which some of the initials were embellished, and asking about the people who carved them. I told her how a beech tree was always planted in every New England town by the first settlers in it, even before they planted corn, because without a beech tree the lovers would have no place to carve their initials and do their courting properly—and lacking this, there might be a dearth of marriages and consequently an insufficient increase in the size of the town. That was the trouble, I told her, with the earliest settlers in our province under the Lygonia Patent: they brought no beech trees with them from England, and therefore their settlements were not successful.

"You never tell me anything that isn't a wild tale for children," she complained. Then she begged for the loan of my knife so she could cut her own initials on the tree.

"You mustn't do that!" I told her.

She stamped her foot. "Indeed," she cried, "and why not? Give me your knife this minute, sir!"

"Well," I said, "you won't believe it, but this is the truth: when a person cuts his initials on that tree he can never be content to live in any place but Arundel."

She laughed lightly. "La!" she said. "I'd rather have your knife than hear about the strange weaknesses of your countrymen!"

Seeing she was bound to have her way I gave her the knife, and she went to hacking her initials in the bark, irregular and slovenly. I might have done it for her and carved an English crown over the letters, but she had been so hoity-toity about it that I said to myself she could make the whole tree into kindling wood without help from me. Nor was I sorry I had let her do it alone, for she was pleasing to look at as she stood pressed against the twisted trunk of the old beech, slim and straight in her bright green dress, cutting away at the bark with both her small hands clasped around the handle of my knife, and her bonnet fallen back from the copper-colored hair so that the braids in which it was twisted seemed like fillets of ruddy gold.

"There," she said, when she stepped back to look proudly at the malformed E. R. that had resulted from her labors, "when you tell your tales to other girls, don't forget to tell them Emily Ransome put her initials here and never came back again."

She seemed to wait for me to speak, but since I could think of nothing I took my knife from her and pocketed it. "Of course," she added, looking at me scornfully, "you'll be glad to tell them this."

"No," I said, "we don't talk of such things to other girls." With that, when I had shown her the path, which ran in and out of the pines and bayberry bushes at the edge of the marsh, I went ahead so she would pester me no more with her notions.

When we came to the brook that runs into the marsh, making a sort of bight in the pines, I showed her, close under the bank, one of the round pools cut in the marsh as though the earth had been removed by an enormous doughnut punch. It was near the brook, and I knew it must have been recently filled by the tides, so that sticklebacks would come up into it from the ocean. I told her to sit quietly on the bank and stare into the pool, and soon she would see sticklebacks fighting.

We sat together on the smooth carpet of pine needles, peering down into the clear water, and when we had sat a while, dark arrows began to shoot from the sides of the pool toward the center and return again to the banks like streaks of darkness. "Those," I told her, "are male sticklebacks driving the females from their nests."

She clutched my arm as two streaks of crimson rose to the surface and slashed at each other. They were giants among sticklebacks, three inches long and shaped like mackerel, and the belly of each was blood red because of the mating season. As they slashed and fought, we could see the stiff spines, erect and murderous, along their backs. When one of them turned and ran, the other caught him by the tail, brought him to the surface, and shook him as a dog shakes a rat, slapping him about on the water.

"Why," said Lady Ransome, as pleased as a small girl, "it's wonderful! What else do they do?"

"They weave nests the size of crab apples out of soft pieces of water plants. There's a hole at the bottom and top of each nest, and after the female lays her eggs, the male drives her away and stands guard beneath it, staring up at the eggs like a lovesick zany, and wriggling his fins to drive fresh water through the nest. When an egg falls out he picks it up in his mouth and blows it back, like a boy blowing a bean through an open window."

"Then what?" she asked, her eyes as round as my mother's blue beads.

"Then the eggs hatch out, and the faithful father eats all he can. When the marsh is flooded at the next spring tide he goes back to sea and forgets about them."

"Like a sailor?" she asked.

I had nothing to say to this, so she smiled at me pleasantly enough and said, "La! I didn't mean it! I'm sure no good sailor would eat little children!"

She leaned over and peered more intently into the pool. "Do you suppose you could find a nest?"

I lowered myself over the interlaced roots that held the bank intact, tossed my coat to her, and began to fumble among the growing things under water. I could feel the sticklebacks dashing themselves against my hands in a frenzy of rage, and soon I came across one of the loose nests. I passed my cap beneath it and drew it out; then turned back to Lady Ransome.

"Now," I said, "you can never again say I don't speak the truth." I seized a bush at the edge of the bank and sprang onto the tangle of roots. The bush pulled loose, and somehow my foot turned under me. As I pitched slowly backward I heard Lady Ransome scream and saw her reach for my arm. The thought came to me that I would land on the cut made by the bottle during last night's fight. Even as I thought it, the thing itself occurred. The little soreness in my head blazed into a mighty, all-pervading stab: then there was nothingness.

*   *   *

I was conscious, when consciousness returned, of a cold wetness, coming and going, on the side of my head. A voice, close to my ear, said often and often, "Richard, Richard, can you hear me, Richard?" Water, cold salt water from the feel of it, dripped on my head, which seemed to be solid, like a twelve-pound shot.

Lady Ransome was kneeling beside me. When I rolled over she held a wet cloth against the cut.

"I thought you'd lie there all night," she said. "Does it hurt?"

The air was cold, and there was a greenish pinkness in the west, so I knew the sun was down.

"No," I said. "I'm all right."

"I thought you'd bleed forever," she whispered.

I looked over the bank and saw a splotch of blood on a bit of driftwood near the pool. I wondered, considering her slenderness, that she had been able to drag me up over the tangled roots.

"I'm not as helpless as you may think," she said, answering my look. "If it hadn't been for the bleeding I believe I could have dragged you home."

My mind cleared. "You shouldn't be here at this hour," I told her. "Start back, and I'll follow as soon as I can. Your husband will be angry."

"Probably," she said. "I'll wait for you."

"Go home at once," I insisted.

She took the handkerchief from my head, and jumped down over the bank to wet it in the brook. When she returned, I rose to my feet, feeling as though my head had been beneath a log for days.

"Now we can tie this against the cut," she told me. "Bend down."

I bent down, and she fixed the pad in place. I could feel her soft arm against my cheek.

It was no great while before I was able to walk and disgusted to think of myself having fainting spells like a half-fed girl. By the time we reached the foot bridge across the creek Lady Ransome was clinging to my sleeve, trotting a little, every few steps, to keep up with me.

I had felt in my bones there'd be trouble when we reached our house, and so there was. It was dark when we came to the door. Lady Ransome ran into the front room before me and caught my mother by the arm. "He fell and struck his head again," she said, "but it's nothing."

I kept my eyes on Sir Arthur, who sat close beside the whale-oil lamp on our center table, reading or pretending to read some papers that filled his lap and his hands. He threw her one hard, cold look, I saw: then seemed to have no further interest in her.

When Lady Ransome had told my mother, she went to her husband and stood behind him, pressing her cheek to his.

"I'm sorry to be late, Arthur," she said, "but I couldn't leave Richard until he got his senses back. Did you shoot many ducks?"

He moved his shoulders petulantly under her hands. "I think you

knew I'd finish shooting by mid-afternoon, and that we might need
to press on at once."

"I thought I'd be back much earlier, Arthur."

He moved his head a little to one side, as if to avoid the touch of
her cheek against his, and at that she stood straight. "I supposed
you understood you weren't to leave, since there was a possibility
we might move on. You're not to be trusted, I fear."

At this it may be I made some slight movement, for he eyed me
frigidly.

"See here!" he said, "didn't you know better than to permit Lady
Ransome to go gallivanting about, miles from any house? I can't afford to be detained in a place like this! I should think even an inn-
keeper's son would show more intelligence."

I looked from Lady Ransome to my mother, who gave me a warning glance and went hastily from the room; and at the same time
my brother Nathan came in. I turned from Ransome and spoke to
Nathan. "Did you have any luck with the teal?" But it was Sir Arthur
who took it upon himself to reply.

"Ow!" he said, hitching himself petulantly in his chair, "I never
saw such birds! Really, you know, it's fearful, they're so nervous,
always on the go! I could scarcely see them, they'd go by so fast! And
they'd never sit down for a moment!"

"We got thirty-two," my brother Nathan told me.

"Well, upon my word," Sir Arthur said in his thin, fretful voice, "I
think you shot all of them! Very humiliating, I assure you!"

I must admit that although Sir Arthur was as disagreeable a man
in his speech, almost, as any man I ever knew, he was just and fair
according to his lights. I can only say he seemed detestable to me.
It was plain to be seen he considered me in the light of a groom or a
footman and thought I should keep myself in another part of the
house, well removed from his sight.

When my mother returned, she brought with her two glasses of
hot buttered rum, a drink favorably known in our province, where it
is thought the blandness of the butter softens the action of the rum
and produces a kindlier and more genial glow than does the raw
liquor. Yet it is little used, not only because butter is dearer than rum,
but because of a general belief that the mixture may so soften the
drinker as to lead him into dangerous generosities.

"Drink this," she said to me, "so you won't catch cold from loss of
blood." She held out the other to Sir Arthur. "It would never do," she
told him, "for you to go back to England without tasting the great

New England drink that made it possible for us to win our freedom from England."

Sir Arthur thanked her and tasted it. "Ow!" he exclaimed. "It's a trifle greasy, isn't it!" He tasted it again: then looked coolly at my mother. "I can't for the life of me see how Britain lost to such a rabble as your people must have been. Scarcely an officer in all your armies, I've heard it said, was trained to the profession of arms."

My mother looked up at the ceiling, as if trying to recall something about the war.

"I remember," she said, "that one of our officers before Quebec was a barber."

"Think of it!" Sir Arthur marvelled. He drank heartily of his buttered rum. "You were handsomely beaten at Quebec, I recall."

My mother nodded thoughtfully. "Yes, the English were unexpectedly helped by the French at Quebec, so they gave a tolerable account of themselves. The tale might have been different if we'd had food and clothes and dry powder."

Sir Arthur took another drink and eyed my mother warily.

"It was later at Saratoga," she added, "when we'd been able to get another barber or two, that we put an end to the nonsense and captured the entire British army, including your Hessian friends."

My mother sighed gently. Sir Arthur stared morosely into his glass, which was empty.

At length my mother took it from him. "I'll get you one more before supper."

Sir Arthur roused himself. "It's greasy," he admitted, "but not a bad drink."

"You seem almost like a New Englander," my mother said, "you're so quick to fall in with our ways of eating and drinking, and so hearty with your approval."

"Ow!" Sir Arthur said, somewhat uncertainly.

"We only learn these things about each other," my mother added, "as we become more intimate. When I know you understand our feelings, I realize you may at heart be as excitable and sentimental as we, in spite of your imperturbable exterior. About my shawl, for example. If you feel as strongly about my shawl as I do, it may be I've made a mistake in refusing to sell it to you. Of course, we have no great need of money, but we might be able to find some ground for exchange."

Sir Arthur almost glowed. "By all means!" he exclaimed immediately. "To be quite frank with you, my wife took a liking to your shawl when she first saw it. I'm sure we've a number of things in our boxes you'd be happy to possess—Ow! a great number of things."

My mother seemed surprised. "Oh," she said, "so it wasn't for yourself you wanted the shawl!"

"No, no!" Sir Arthur replied. "It's for my wife."

"I see!" my mother said, as though a new aspect of the situation had dawned on her. She looked down at the glass in her hand. "I must fill this," she added. She glanced up at me suddenly, "Don't stand there gawking!" she cried. "Go along upstairs; get a clean bandage on your head and make yourself proper for supper!"

I said to myself, as I climbed the steep stairs to my easterly room, that if I were fifty years old and the captain of a thousand-ton ship, there'd be times when my mother would still think of me as a small, stupid boy, and speak to me as if I were that, and make me feel so into the bargain.

When I came down again I found my mother had been up to her old tricks, she having been master of her own sloop for years, trading in Boston and Portsmouth and Portland, where a trader needs smartness if he hopes to come out of a trade without losing his breeches.

Beside her on the sofa sat Lady Ransome, wrapped tight in my Spanish shawl. Across my mother's lap was the finest fowling piece I had ever seen—a beautiful gun with two barrels and a raised ridge between them to permit of a sight being taken, and locks and hammers so delicate that the first discharge, it almost seemed, would break them. Also she had around her neck, in place of her cat's-eyes, a string of carved green stones, and on her shoes two new buckles set with brilliants. I knew nothing about the necklace and the buckles: but I had trafficked a little in guns, and knew a fowling piece such as my mother held was worth four times what I had paid for the shawl.

The mellowness of the buttered rum, I saw, had done its work on Sir Arthur; for when he addressed my mother, he was all loquaciousness and spoke as though his mouth were half filled with hot mush.

"You prob'ly don't know what you got in that gun," he told her. "You never saw one like it, I'll venture to say. There ain't a gunsmith in Belgium nor Spain nor Italy nor this whole America of yours that can make a gun like that fowling piece. A Joseph Manton, that gun is! Deadliest li'l' thing y'ever saw! Load her up with slugs and she'll kill a stag at a hundred paces!"

"Foxes too?" my mother asked.

"Fockshes!" Sir Arthur exclaimed, his face a horrified mask. "Shoot fockshes!" Then he laughed. "Thought you meant it! 'Pon my word, one must watch you Americans every moment to find out whether you mean a thing. You're very shavage here, but you wouldn't shoot fockshes! You're wigging me, eh?"

I could see my mother had an answer on the tip of her tongue, and I suspected she wished to say that fox hunting was not much sport: that we only shot them when there were no Englishmen to shoot. She kept silent, however, so I felt Sir Arthur was so easy for her that she took no further pleasure in baiting him.

"You're wigging me!" Sir Arthur repeated thickly. "Talking about war and shooting fockshes! War, indeed! Fancy you making war on England!"

"Well, there's this about it," my mother told him. "People who deal in ships belong to a brotherhood and have ways of knowing things. I'll say this much to you and no more: get your young wife down to Boston or New York as soon as you can, and take her home with no loss of time."

Sir Arthur stared hazily at my mother. "I think it's nothing but moonshine!" he said at length. "The thing's absurd on the face of it! Why, your country's helpless! Your army ain't worth mentioning; and where's your navy, hey? You ain't got one!"

"You're right," I said, though I disliked siding with anybody against my mother. "We have no ships to fight England, and no desire, either! I've no reason for fighting England, and I won't do it. Neither will any man in this town. Our living comes from the sea! Why should we let ourselves be driven off the ocean because a lot of fools in Washington who never smelled salt water say we must fight?"

Sir Arthur nodded. "You've more sense than I thought," he said. "We've a hundred ships, and more too, for every one of yours, and our soldiers are the finest in the world, able to whip the strongest nations of Europe. What could you do against our ships and our armies?" He laughed shrilly. "Did you ever hear of Dartmoor Prison, where we've shut up thousands and thousands of Frenchmen since they set out to fight us? It's the stoutest prison ever built; and within a month after you declared war on us, your cockleshells would be blown to pieces and your men behind the walls of Dartmoor."

My mother, slender and small and straight, rose suddenly to walk across the room and back. This, I had learned, she only did when boiling with words and fearful of exploding with the press of them inside her. She stood behind her chair, picked it up and thumped it down again.

"I believe it's the custom for a mother to be older than her son," she said. "In my time, too, I've done a fair amount of sailing, so maybe I can tell you things neither you nor my son would otherwise hear.

You English are a great people, good sailors and brave fighters; but you've done things in certain ways for too many years. You're slow to realize other methods may be better than your own. I know the best ships on the seas, once, were English; but that's past. The best and fastest ships to-day are built by French and Americans, who've been driven by necessity to build better than you. I know there was a time when English mariners were the ablest of all the world's seamen, but that time has gone, too. To-day the greatest seamen in the world are Americans."

Sir Arthur threw back his head and crowed.

"I know how you feel," my mother told him. "The Englishmen who came over here during our revolution were scornful of our manner of fighting; and even when they found themselves disarmed and made prisoners, they thought it was all a terrible mistake. I'll say that for your countrymen: they're obstinate, especially about admitting defeats."

"Not at all! Not at all!" Sir Arthur protested.

"Well, I'm glad they've changed," my mother told him, "because soon they may have opportunity to admit another defeat. What you don't know, and what may mean nothing to you if you do know it, is that there's no house in this town—not one house—that hasn't a seaman living in it. There are more master mariners along our river road and the Saco road than there are Frenchmen in your English town of Quebec. In some houses you'll find five and six and seven sons, all captains. What's more, they're deep-water captains, born with salt in their noses and the feel of the sea in their bones; and you can believe it or not, but it's the truth: there's something about these New Englanders that makes it possible for them to sail their craft into places where the captains of other nations won't go. All up and down our coast it's the same—in Wiscasset and Damariscotta and Portland and York and Portsmouth and Newburyport and Salem and Boston and New Bedford, and in the little towns between; all the length of Cape Cod, and farther south, along the Connecticut and Rhode Island shore, and in New York and New Jersey and in every creek on Chesapeake Bay and in a hundred other places: everywhere you'll find master mariners who can handle craft as they've seldom been handled before, and seamen who are wild and rampageous."

Sir Arthur made as though to speak, but my mother thumped her chair on the floor again and wouldn't hear him. "I've seen our people go out like hornets against the French and Indians," she told him. "I've seen 'em drop their hoes and plows to pour out in rivers against your great Burgoyne, when he and his fine army proposed to batter the last of our resistance from us. You may think you can crush us with your hundreds of great ships; that we'll let ourselves be swallowed up without a struggle by this dark monster of a Dartmoor you talk about; but I tell you these New England mariners aren't easy to crush! They'll sting you and outrun you and sting you and outrun you until you're as fuddled as a horse with a foot through a beehive."

Even then she would listen to no reply from Sir Arthur, but suddenly declared Lady Ransome was half dead with sleepiness, and so hurried the two of them upstairs.

"Remember what I tell you," I heard her saying to Sir Arthur. "Get yourself over to New York and on your way to England."

Sir Arthur assured her, in his reediest voice, that he'd make every effort to do so, not because he feared a war but because he feared to hear further talk of it.

*   *   *

When my mother returned, she closed the door carefully and took a letter from the front of her dress. "I'd have told you sooner," she said, "but I wanted you all together and these English people out of the way. This letter is from Captain Callender in Boston. It came by express this afternoon. Here's what he says:

"'We have to-day received advices from Washington that Congress will immediately pass an act of embargo for ninety days. This will become a law on the 4th April, after which date no vessel will be allowed to clear from an American port. This is in anticipation of war with England and is designed to prevent American ships and seamen from falling into the hands of the enemy, as well as to prevent the carriage of necessary supplies to the British armies in Spain.

"'It is my duty to inform you that the shipowners of this section are nearly unanimous in refusing to submit to this embargo, the feeling being that supplies furnished to the British armies in Spain will not materially affect any military operations which may take place in America. Kindly feel free to pass on this information to any interested parties.'"

My mother folded the letter and tapped it on the table. "Well," she said, looking from one to the other of us, "there it is! Pretty advice, I must say! The shipowners of Boston setting up to know more than the government of their own country! Advising us to dodge out ahead of the embargo so the embargo can't do what it's intended to do!"

"It's intended to ruin us!" I reminded her.

"It's intended to keep food from the British!" my mother protested.

"Nonsense!" I said. "If they don't get it from us, they'll get it somewhere else! I'll set out for Portland to-night, and be off for Spain as quick as you could skin an eel."

"I say No!" my mother cried, shaking the table to emphasize her words. "If we're going to fight 'em, let's fight 'em: not trade with 'em!"

"Let those fight 'em who declare war," I said. "I won't fight Englishmen, who've done nothing to me, just because some damned old landlubber from South Carolina votes to have me do it! Why should I? Didn't my grandfather buy French rum from the French while we were fighting the French?"

My mother turned to Nathan. "You'll stand by me, won't you?"

"It appears to me," Nathan said, moving his fingers clumsily, "it would be a sin if we let every other shipowner beat the embargo and just laid and rotted in harbor ourselves."

My sister Sarah squirmed in her chair. "Me too," she cried. "Bring me a shawl when you come back from Spain, will you, Richard?"

My mother stared at the table before her for a time. At length she looked up at me. "Is there anything you need, Richard?"

Since there wasn't, I left it to her to send my dunnage by Jeddy and Tommy Bickford on the morning stagecoach, after which I said good-bye to her and Sarah and aunt Cynthy and set out to walk the twenty-six miles to Portland, Nathan going with me for company, and Pinky sticking his nose in every stump along the road and fluttering his tail with delight at being off once more.

VI

THERE was never anything seen, on the Portland docks, to equal the happenings of the next four days; and word reached us that the self-same things went on in Philadelphia and Alexandria and Baltimore and New York and Boston and every other port in America.

When we came up Fore Street in the early morning, the docks lay quiet, smelling of tarred rope and lumber and sacking and fish, no different from any other morning. By mid-afternoon, when news of the embargo had spread through the city, every dock was alive with men, howling and sweating, and hauling at flour barrels, grain bags, salted beef, bread boxes and God knows what. Drays were backing up to all the docks, laden with provisions, and clattering empty to the warehouses for fresh supplies. Men came out from stores and counting houses, eager to have a hand in forestalling the embargo, and worked, adrip with perspiration, alongside stevedores and wharf rats and seamen and teamsters and farmers.

Never since ships were built did supplies tumble into holds with such speed. The work went on after darkness fell, by the light of smoking torches that gave the workmen, wrestling at their piles of provisions, the appearance of demons clambering over the lava heaps of hell. It continued until the pinkness of dawn came into the sky over Peak's Island, and on through the day and around through the night again. There was a sort of madness among the people against the embargo and against a war—such a frenzy to defy the government that a stranger might have thought us engaged in a revolution.

There was free rum for the workers, and free food; and whenever a vessel left her dock and set her sails, there was as much hullabalooing and cheering as though a victory had been won.

Only for one departure was there no cheering, that being in the case of the brig *Riddle*, said to be bound for Nova Scotia with food for the British in Canada. Because of this the captain, Eli Bagley, a Portsmouth man, had fought five fights in Fore Street taverns, there being a feeling that there was something wrong in dealing with the British on our own continent.

Eli Bagley was an opinionated man with a thin face and great prominent jaw bones. His whiskers grew like a hairy frill underneath his clean-shaved chin, and extended from ear to ear. This is a style of whisker I mislike, since all those on whom I have seen it have been sanctimonious men, tyrannical and churlish, always able to consider themselves right and everyone else wrong. Those who knew him said he was a vain man, fond of fighting but not good at it, since he couldn't keep his head when he fought, and so shipped only smallish, timid men on the *Riddle,* in order to indulge his fancy for fighting with no danger to himself.

Eli was opinionated enough, God knows, in this matter, declaring it was no worse to sell in Canada than in Spain, which seemed unreasonable on the face of it, and I, being bound for Spain, felt obliged to give him a black eye in return for his belief.

When the *Riddle* moved out into the harbor along toward dusk of the second day, a sort of snarling growl followed her from every dock; and showers of rocks and bolts flew toward her, bouncing harmlessly from her sides.

Thanks to a good agent and a good crew, all from Arundel, and thanks, also, to my early knowledge of the embargo, we were loaded and set off late on the third of April, a bright, cloudless day with the wind still in the northwest and blowing great guns, as it often does off our Maine coast in the spring of the year.

When I packed away my good blue coat in my chest that night I did a thing I had been in two minds about doing since Jeddy and Tommy Bickford had brought my dunnage from Arundel. In this dunnage was my good blue coat, which I had last worn when I walked with Lady Ransome in the pines by the marsh; and when I took it out there was a thin disk, something like a silver dollar, caught in the lining. In the bottom of the pocket was a slit that looked to me to have been cut with scissors. I worked my fingers through the slit and fished out the disk. It was a plaque of ivory surrounded by a band of gold in which brilliants and colored stones were countersunk, and the plaque was painted clear and beautiful with a miniature of Lady Ransome—a portrait so delicate and fine that I could almost count each strand of her copper-colored hair and the black lashes that seemed to shade a little the smoky color of her eyes. The lips were so fresh and warmly red in appearance that I feared to touch them, lest the paint be as new and wet as it seemed.

It was true this lady had wearied me somewhat with her changeableness, being first hoity-toity and then friendly: yet I had hunted for an excuse, on the night of my departure from Arundel, to bid her farewell. More than once after I had left, I had regretted my failure to have a final word with her; and now this miniature called her to

my mind once more and left me puzzled as to how it had come in
my coat. I thought of asking Jeddy whether he knew how it got
there, since he had brought the coat from Arundel. I was reluctant
to speak of the matter to him, but I was even more eager; so in the
end I sent Tommy Bickford to bring Jeddy to my cabin.

When he came in, his knee-long pea-jacket unbuttoned, I unlocked the small oak chest my father bought in Ireland, the one with
the large eight-sided bottle and the two six-sided bottles and the four
four-sided bottles, and we hooked our feet around the table leg and
had a thimbleful of red rum to a quick trip.

At length I asked Jeddy whether he had seen Lady Ransome before he left Arundel. He said he had. She had come down to breakfast
with her husband, he said, seeming to be in a fret, most likely over
the embargo, and in a twitter to be gone from the house. For a time
I held the picture of her in my hand under the table, and finally
brought it up and showed it to him. He whistled when he saw it,
and I could tell he had never seen it before.

"There's a tidy craft!" he said, taking it gingerly between his salt-
hardened fingers. "Fine sweeping sheer to her and no foolish top-
hamper. Sweet bows, and as nice a tumble home to her dead-works
as you'll find anywhere!"

There were times when Jeddy became so nautical in his talk that
a porpoise might have sickened to hear him run on, though he had
often enough heard my mother declare that no man with a thought
for the comfort of others would speak constantly in terms of his
calling. "Just because you set out to be a mariner," she said, "don't
forget the manner of speech of those who can't understand sea
terms." But it may be that Jeddy, having been a school teacher for so
many years, was impelled by the very dullness of his former occupation to express himself in the terms of his new one.

"You talk like a ship chandler," I said, taking the picture from him.
"I'm not blind! What I want to know is what to do with it. I don't
know how it got in my dunnage nor anything about it."

Jeddy squinted at me knowingly. "I'll tell you this much! That
picture's worth something! It's not one of those things done by a
swab-artist out of a bumboat for eight dollars. You'd pay fifty pounds
for a picture like this in London, even without any copper bottom
or binnacle lights around it! Stow it away, Richard! Findings keep-
ings! If ever you're without money in a foreign port, a little bauble
like that would keep you for a month."

This was good advice, so I put the picture on top of the striped
silk shirts in my chest, and Jeddy and I played piquet and had an-

other thimbleful of red rum to fair winds and a smooth passage before turning in. But after he left me I took the miniature from the
chest and dropped it in a pocket of my shirt, determined always
to have it near in case there was need, as Jeddy had said, to sell it.

I was happy to be back on the old *Neutrality* once more, for she
was a good brig and comfortable, having been planned by my
mother. I have heard it said in Arundel that many masters plan their
own vessels, but they are built the way the shipbuilders think they
ought to be built—except in my mother's case. Where my mother
was concerned it was not so; and either the vessel was built the way
she drew it, or the shipbuilder was tongue-lashed into going away
and living in another town. The bulkheads creaked, in a heavy sea,
like a whole flock of crow-blackbirds walking in an oatfield; but the
chairs and the bunks were big and comfortable, and a man could
move around without having his head caved in by the bottom of a
whale-oil lamp, they being out of the way and so fixed that they
reeked less than most; though to my mind there is a homey scent to
burning whale oil, perhaps because I was born aboard the *Orestes*
in Copenhagen harbor and so learned to know the smell before I
had formed other tastes.

* * *

It was a little before sunrise the next morning when Cephas Cluff,
the first mate, banged on the door to say there was a sail to leeward,
maybe two miles away, and that she had just hauled her wind to
cross our course. A ship, Cephas said she was, probably homeward
bound and wishful of speaking us to get news or bearings.

The wind had dropped, and the water was tolerably smooth; so,
mindful of the embargo, I told Cephas we must warn her. With that
I hustled into my clothes and pea-jacket and went on deck.

She had come up fast, a sturdy black ship with a white streak; too
sturdy, it seemed to me—and in a breath it dawned on me that here
was no merchantman at all, but a sloop-of-war. In that very moment she triced up a port, fired a gun, hoisted the British flag, hauled
up her courses, hauled down her jib, took in her topgallant sails, and
backed her maintopsail, all with a speed impossible for a merchantman.

Here was a fine mess, I thought to myself, feeling as though someone had stuffed my mouth with cotton—a fine mess, and never so
much as a rat hole through which we could dodge.

The men stood looking from me to the sloop and back again, knowing well that one or more of them, before nightfall, would be wearing

a British seaman's uniform; and I could hear Jeddy cursing a set of curses he never learned out of the Fifth Reader or Bowditch's Navigator.

She was pierced for eight carronades to a side and had long guns forward and amidships, so I knew we would be torn to shreds with grape if we tried to run for it, or overhauled in this breeze, even though we got through the grape unscathed. There was nothing to do but come into the wind, and bring-to under the lee of this damned sloop.

The captain, a portly man, stood on one of the carronades, looking at us. "This is His Britannic Majesty's sloop *Gorgon!*" he bawled through a trumpet, "I'm sending a boat!" and send it he did, with twelve men besides the oarsmen, and a thin, red-faced lieutenant important in the stern sheets.

There was no formality about this officer when he came aboard, except for his uniform, which was a natty blue affair with tight net breeches, and with a gold swab as big as my mother's mop on one of his shoulders. It made me uncomfortable to look at him, what with my pea-jacket and my red-flannel shirt and the high leather boots I found most comfortable at sea. Ten men came over the side behind him, hard-looking broad-shouldered men, blue jackets to their knees and cutlasses and pistols at their waists.

"Who's master here?" he snapped, looking at Cephas Cluff, who was as tall as I, but broader in the beam, and important looking.

"I am," I said. "Step in the cabin and look at my papers."

He whirled and stood staring at me for a moment, his head lowered a little. Then he flashed a quick glance at Cephas and Jeddy and turned his attention to me again.

"Call all hands on deck!" he ordered, without so much as a "sir" or "if you please." I think if I had met this lieutenant under other circumstances I might have felt a liking for him; but there was something about the hard roundness of the blue eyes in his thin red face, and the fixed, contented smile on his down-curved mouth, that soured everything in me.

Every last one of our crew was in the waist, watching us. "The men are on deck," I said, "and you'll find no Britisher among 'em. They're all from the same town: the town of Arundel. There isn't one of 'em you can touch."

"Call 'em aft!" he said. "I've heard that story before! I know more than to let any Yankee skipper pick men for me."

The men came aft silently. The lieutenant turned to me with more politeness than he had yet shown. "Was there any talk of an embargo when you cleared?" he asked.

I pretended ignorance. "What embargo is that?"

His smile hardened on his face, and his eyes, fixed on mine, were cold as those of a halibut. "You say you're master of this brig, and you ask what embargo! You Yankees think you're pretty smart, but we know a thing or two ourselves! We know you're a lot of tricky rascals, quick as snakes to turn against your own country or against the country that provided spawning grounds for your people!"

I had heard all I could stand. "Do what you've come to do and get off this quarter-deck," I said, keeping as quiet as I could, because of the long guns slewed around on the sloop to bear on us.

He turned and looked at the men. They were staring at the mastheads, or at the deck seams, mild and harmless appearing as though no word of what had been said had penetrated their skulls.

The lieutenant went down among them. When he came to Tommy Bickford, he stopped. Now, Tommy was like his father, who carried my father to shore when he was hurt aboard the Congress galley, on the day General Arnold outthought and outfought the British at the Battle of Valcour Island, though outnumbered ten times over. He was flat backed and handsome, with wavy light hair and cheeks like a girl, and so soft-spoken and pleasant and willing that he was no more like the ordinary run of boy than a tapering spar is like an alder fish pole. There was no man on our brig or in all Arundel for that matter who wasn't perpetually pleased with Tommy and forever going out of the way to coddle him; and it was my guess he would be master of his own ship at eighteen.

The lieutenant laughed. "You can't breed 'em like this in your filthy country!" He motioned to his line of waiting seamen. "Take this one!"

"Hold on," I told him. "That's Tommy Bickford from Arundel. His father was a soldier in the Revolution!"

"Gammon!" the lieutenant said, watching me closely, so it came to me he had a reason for speaking roughly. "There never was an American that told the truth about that tuppenny ha'penny business you call a war!" He motioned to his seamen again. "Take him!"

The slatting of the running rigging, the yawping of the chickens in the coops that filled our boats, and the creaking of the rudder sounded as loud in my ears as though I had never heard them before. There was an aching in the muscles of my upper arms. The corvette, no doubt impatient at the lieutenant's slowness, fired another gun. We stood like figureheads.

Two of the Britishers closed in on Tommy, taking him by the shoul-

ders and wrists. At that my little white dog Pinky whipped out from
behind me like the end of a parted tow rope; and with his whiskers
bristling so they hid his furious little black eyes he went to haggling
at the ankle of the nearest sailor, all the time making a hellish sucking
noise in his throat.

The man kicked at him, shouting, and strove to draw his cutlass
without loosing Tommy's wrist. At that the lieutenant shouted as
well, and stooped to slap Pinky with his open hand. Somehow the
little dog released himself like a chronometer spring, whipping up
and turning in mid-air; and in a second he had slashed the soft, mus-
cular edge of the lieutenant's hand, cutting it to the bone. The lieutenant yelled and kicked at him, and all our Arundel men shouted
together. Pinky, whirling, ran between them and stood partly behind
the mainmast, peering out at the lieutenant with his stump of a tail
bent up over his back as though on the verge of breaking, his whiskers bristling fiercely, and his legs planted as stubby and straight as
a brace of whitened hitching posts.

The lieutenant stared at his hand, flipping it in the air so that
drops of blood fell on the scoured deck; then in a flash he reached
in the bosom of his coat and drew a pistol, which he leveled at Pinky.

Now, I well knew my business, which was to take our brig and its
cargo safe to Cadiz, regardless of the acts of British lieutenants who
exceeded their authority, or of the misfortunes of our crew, or even
of my dog, who was a better friend to me than most of the humans
I had met. Yet it is impossible, as I must often say, to lay out a course
in this life and stick to it. Much as I hated the British lieutenant for
his treatment of us, I would have laid no hand on him or any of his
men, but would have steered clear of his determined spite. Our un-
doing came because I couldn't see my little Pinky shot down without
protest. Neither, as luck would have it, could Jeddy Tucker. I have
no doubt, in view of what I later learned, that if our downfall had
not come through this, it would certainly have come somehow; for
the officers of the war sloop knew what they were about.

However that may be, I struck at the leveled pistol with a belaying
pin that had got into my hands God knows how; and a fraction of a
second later Jeddy Tucker, on the lieutenant's other side, undertook
to do the same. The force of my blow must have been greater than
I thought, for when I hit the pistol the lieutenant pitched forward
as though he had stumbled, and the pistol exploded. It was then
that Jeddy's belaying pin came down. He was able to soften the blow,
he told me, but he couldn't stop it, and so the pin rapped the lieu-

tenant lightly on the back of the head. He dropped to one knee and was up again immediately.

"All right! Keep back there!" he shouted to his men, who had their cutlasses out and were spreading toward us. He felt the overhang of his head with his good hand and looked from Jeddy to me. "Whose dog is that?" he asked.

Half inarticulate from apprehension, I said it was mine, where-upon the down-curving smile deepened on his lips, as if there were something about the fact that gave him malicious pleasure.

A faint angry bellow came down wind to us. I could see the captain of the corvette standing on a carronade, clutching a shroud, and I knew he was bawling to his lieutenant to come back.

"Under the circumstances," the lieutenant said, "I shall have to ask you to return with me and explain to the captain about this boy."

"My God, man!" I said, "this is an American vessel! You can't do a thing like that!"

The lieutenant indicated Jeddy. "This man one of your mates?" he asked.

"Second mate."

"Bring him, too. You'll want someone to corroborate your statements." He motioned to his men. They signaled their boat, and two of them went over the side with Tommy Bickford.

The lieutenant laughed at my irresolution. "Hurry along, Captain," he said, his voice seeming to mock me, "or I'll bring over the gig and press your whole crew. God knows we need 'em, and anybody with half an eye can see they're all Englishmen!"

He had us, and there was no way out. "We'll come in our own boat," I said.

"Suit yourself," he replied, grinning sardonically.

"Lower away a boat!" I shouted, thinking to have a moment to say a word to Jeddy and Cephas.

"I'll send two men with you," the lieutenant added, "to guard against Yankee tricks."

I could feel my muscles move under my pea-jacket. For the first time in my life I felt an ugly, coppery hatred, a great powerful bitterness surging through me, from head to foot, like the wave of heat from a tumbler of bad brandy, against men who would use their strength to change the lives of defenseless people. I hated this sneering lieutenant; I hated his ship; above all I hated the country that had sent him out to rob us of our rights and our freedom.

We went into our boat, Jeddy and I, followed by two English sailors; and Gideon Lassel and Seth Tarbox pulled us over to the sloop. The lieutenant, waiting for us when we came over the side, led us aft at once.

The captain, a walrus-like man, leaned against the weather rail and looked at us from under heavy eyebrows, each as big as a field mouse.

"Sir," the lieutenant told him, "this man claimed to be the master, but the whole thing was too fishy. No master would have assaulted a king's officer, as this man did. There's no doubt the affair was hocus-pocused to screen the real captain, who must have been English. This man admitted ownership of a terrier that bit me, sir, and the dog's an English dog, no fear of that!"

He had hardly finished before the captain snapped at him, "Pass the word to get under way, and turn these men over to the bos'n."

"My God, sir!" I exclaimed, "you can't press the officers of a merchant vessel!" The captain looked up to see the fore-topsail braced aback. I could hear the orders being given in the waist of the ship and see the men, swarms of them compared with our little crew, hoisting and sheeting home the sails. I thought for a moment of going overboard and swimming for it, but two red-coated marines stood near at hand, their muskets slanted toward us. As the sloop fell off, Gideon and Seth set up a shouting from our boat below; but before I could answer them the captain turned sharply on us.

"Oh, indeed!" He clasped his hands behind his back and teetered on his toes. "I can't, eh? And what's to stop me, if I may ask?"

"The customs of civilized nations," I said.

"Tchah!" The captain worked his bushy eyebrows up and down. "Tchah! Save your exalted sentiment for the marines!" He brandished his finger in my face. "We spoke the ship *Clio* out of New York yesterday. She told us every port on the Atlantic coast had been warned of to-day's embargo against England. Yes, by God, and here you are dodging out with a full cargo! Customs of civilized nations, indeed! You say you're an American, and yet you're doing your best to embarrass your own country!"

He bellowed with laughter. "Doesn't that seem a bit contradictory, Mr. Doyle?"

"It puzzles me completely, sir," the lieutenant answered.

"There you are!" bawled this red-faced walrus. "You *can't* be Americans if you're turning against your country! All Americans are noble heroes, willing to die for their glorious nation—eh, Mr. Doyle?"

"Yes, sir: so we've always heard."

The captain turned to look back at the *Neutrality*. A stretch of tumbling blue water lay between us. She had gone off on her course, flirting her taffrail in the air as if glad to be rid of us.

"Certainly!" the captain said, and he spoke jovially, as though doing us a favor. "That's what makes us sure you're Englishmen; but whether you're Englishmen or runaway Americans, here's your chance! War'll follow the embargo, and this is the cruiser that'll put the Yankees in their places."

He looked at us hard and sharp. We stood silent before him. God knows there was no fitting answer to be made to what he had said; and besides that, the captain of a British man-of-war is a harder and more dangerous taskmaster than any king and therefore no man with whom to argue.

"I have a word for you before you enter on your duties in this king's cruiser," he growled. "Play the man and keep out of trouble, and there'll be prize money coming to you and shore leave aplenty. Go to playing the fool with your fists or your mouth, and you'll get the cat at the gratings. As for this talk about being Americans, belay it, or I'll lay you a course for a haven that'll rot the skin off your bones. That's the tidy stone prison up among the Dartmoor snows that we built for those who try to trip us in our little wars!" He glowered at us from under his beetling, mouse-like brows; then nodded to his lieutenant. "Take 'em forward, Mr. Doyle."

VII

Wʜᴇɴ I had heard from the captain of the corvette, Sir Mungo Bullard-Jones, that I was a tricky Yankee, and from Lieutenant Drake Doyle that I was full of Yankee tricks, and from the bos'n that he was sick of seeing bloody Yankees brought aboard a decent ship, knowing he would have to set a watch to keep the tricky rats from stealing the copper sheathing from the corvette's bottom; and when these fine Britishers had played us the foulest trick that had ever been done me, and lashed the both of us like black slaves or baulky horses into the bargain, and set us to carrying slops and tarring ropes and messing with rabbit-toothed, twist-brained beasts out of the filthy cellars of the world's filthiest cities—Dublin and Liverpool . . . When all these things had happened, I said to myself that while I had so far had no training in trickiness, it was never too late to begin; and since they expected trickiness, I'd give them as much of it as I could rake and scrape together, and see them all in hell if ever I could.

Yet I also determined that never, while I remained on the corvette, would I show anything but a smiling and contented face to any Englishman, whether officer or sailor; for I knew that if I could trick them into thinking me harmless and not worth watching, all subsequent trickeries would be easier of accomplishment.

I was at home on a brig, whether full-rigged or jackass: consequently I was equally easy on a schooner or a barkentine or a ship. As to a cruiser such as the one into which we had been pressed, I could have sailed her with no trouble, for she was ship-rigged; but when it came to fitting in with her crew of some sixscore men, I was in a state of befuddlement for days, what with gun stations and bevies of half-baked midshipmen to issue senseless orders, and a half-dozen numbers to answer to, and captains of a score of different parts of the craft, and droves of marines to keep an eye on the movements of the seamen, and food that nobody on the *Neutrality* would have fed to Pinky for fear of poisoning him, and all the rules and regulations and officials and divisions and subdivisions that are necessary to keep an unwieldy body of men, most of them worthless, from turning a vessel into a madhouse in time of stress.

I made out after a fashion, and so escaped further rope-endings, largely through the help of a Wiscasset seaman in the next mess to mine, John Cromwell, a cat-footed man not overly tall, but quick and powerful. He walked with his stomach pushed a little forward, so that he looked fattish; but he was not, and his upper arm, where it joined his shoulder, was near as wide as his thigh. He came to me on the pretense of showing me how to ticket a bag of food for dropping into the great mess kettles called the coppers. The first thing he said was "Where you from?" I told him Arundel and he nodded his head, eyeing me covertly.

"I watched you come aboard. Captain, wa'n't you?"

"I suppose you might say so, but they say not," I told him.

"There's talk in the tops," he said, speaking from the side of his mouth, "that a captain wouldn't never have been took if we wasn't close to a war with——" He left the sentence unfinished, canting his head quickly in a half circle that seemed to include the entire British navy.

He narrowed his mouth still more. "There's eleven Yankees on this ship, all of 'em pressed. Three of 'em's waisters and don't count. Two of 'em's boys. One works for the master at arms, and he'd tattle on himself in his sleep, so to hell with him. There's the three of you, and me, and 'Lisha Lord."

"Who's 'Lisha Lord?" I asked.

Cromwell snorted as though I had asked who Bonaparte might be. "'Lisha Lord's captain of the maintop," he said. "He comes from Bath. There ain't anywheres he ain't been. He can shoot the ear off a horsefly with a musket or a long twenty-four. He knows all there is to know about this corvette."

"Why don't you let *him* tell you about the war, if he knows so much?" I asked, though satisfied Cromwell would do me no harm.

"You York County folks always was suspicious of us Down-Easters," he said angrily. "'Lisha Lord wants to know what there is in this war talk, and I want to know too. How long you think we'd stay on this damned weevil box in case of—in case of——" He canted his head again and worked a shoulder under his shirt. I suspected he, like many another American, must have had his back made into hash by a British nine-tailed cat.

"You're right," I said. "There was a three months' embargo put on, starting the fourth of April."

"And on the fourth of July we fight?" he asked.

"Looks so," I said.

"Well I declare!" he drawled; and with that he hurried away, light as a fox to the roll of the ship.

As a result of this, Cromwell passed the word to me at noon the next day to go into the maintop. It was a fine big top with rope railings, and when I came over the edge I found two men in it, one a tall man with black whiskers whose sheen gave them the look of having been rubbed with an oily rag. At sight of me, the man with the glossy whiskers rounded suddenly on the other. "Look at that breast backstay!" he growled. "Look at the way she's chafed! Anybody'd think this was a Portygee fisherman instead of a king's cruiser! Spratt, you hop down to the first luff and tell him I say to get somebody up here to serve that backstay with leather." The other immediately lowered himself through the lubber hole.

The whiskered man, I saw, must be 'Lisha Lord. Turning his attention to me, he went on growling. "My good gravy! I don't know what the world's coming to when they put boys in command of merchantmen! Had either of your mates been weaned, by any chance?"

"Both of 'em," I said, "and on good New England rum, what's more! Maybe you can tell me whether there's any talk of discontinuing the use of old women in the maintops of British sloops-of-war?"

He sniffed and peered down through the lubber hole; then sat at the edge of the top, his legs doubled under him and his glossy beard pointing between his knees at the slender canted deck far below, on which seamen moved as slow and maggot-like as sheep in a meadow seen from a mountain side.

"If I'm any judge," he said, "you're madder'n I was when they pressed me, and I was pretty gol-blamed mad."

I saw no reason to answer. When he twisted his head over his shoulder and looked at my face, he seemed to need no reply. "Yes," he continued, "me and John cal'late to cut loose from this durned old scow."

"How did you figure on leaving her?" I asked.

"Well," he said, "we figured you'd figure out a way; and we figured on hauling our wind when you do."

He leaned backward to peer through the lubber hole once more. "You figure we'd have trouble getting off?" I asked.

He laughed shortly. "Brother," he said, "you ain't had dealings with these dirty sea soldiers on a British ship! Some folks think they have 'em aboard to fight; but what they have 'em for is to put a bullet between our shoulders if we make a move to slip our moorings. You can lay to it Jonah wouldn't have got out of the whale so easy if he'd swallered a few lobster-backs."

"Seems to me you and Cromwell could have left the ship long before this if you'd wanted to," I told him, wishing to be sure of him.

He laughed again. "Listen," he said. "The British never pay off except in home ports for fear the crews of their whole damned navy'd desert; and I'll bet you they would, too. They always hold back six months' pay and prize money for the same reason. They got a way of turning men over from ship to ship so you stay away from England for about three years—ten, sometimes—and then get back with a sheaf of pay notes fit to choke a swordfish! Then they got a lot of lunatics running their pay section, and you couldn't get your notes cashed if you spent all your shore leave in the paymaster's office. If you want money, you sell your notes to the Jews. They allow you six shillings to the pound."

"That's less than thirty cents on the dollar," I protested.

"Yes, by gravy!" 'Lisha Lord returned, "and that's why some of us New Englanders kept hanging on. Well, we're ready to quit now. I've got more than seventeen hundred dollars in pay and prize money coming to me, but I'll quit any minute."

"Well, there's this about it," I said: "I know Tucker and I know Bickford, and they'll do as I tell 'em; but you might find me too young to take orders from."

"Don't worry about that," he assured me. "I take orders from some of these half-grown midshipmen, don't I?"

"All right," I said, "only I'm no midshipman."

'Lisha Lord nodded. "You're the old man."

"See if you can find out where we're bound," I told him, "and contrive for Tucker and Bickford to get to know something about long guns."

"Hell," he said, "I can show 'em all there is to a long gun in half an hour, and we're bound for the Banks to chase Frenchies away from our fishing fleet. After that we'll make Halifax." He gave me a quick push. "Down you go—lee side: here comes the bos'n."

*　　*　　*

Lord and Cromwell, being old hands and used to English ways, were one thing; but Jeddy, who found a new grievance wherever he turned, was another thing altogether. He couldn't keep his feelings from his face when he spoke with me, but looked so murderous that any officer would have been justified in clapping him in the Black Hole on general principles.

"Wipe that look off your face!" I told him when he caught me alone one day. "Keep smiling if you don't want to get us all shipped to England for the next ten years!"

He grinned a horrible, blood-curdling grin, worse than the malevolent stare it replaced. "Dried peas!" he whispered. "Nothing but dried peas and pork for mess twice in a week! You know what pea soup does to me, Richard! I'm blown up like a bladder!"

He seemed to ooze profanity.

"Forget these things," I told him. "They're nothing."

"Oh, are they!" he snarled. "How about having to hang over a yard and take in sail when you're blown up like a bladder? I'd rather teach the rule of three to all the idiot children in Arundel than fold myself over a yard when I'm like that!"

"Look pleasant!" I told him.

He contorted his face in a ghastly simper. "If that's nothing," he persisted, "how about having to sling my hammock between two jailbirds so filthy I'm afraid of being poisoned, just sleeping beside 'em. You know what they do? They call me a damned Yankee! And I can't answer 'em, because it's the simple truth."

"Look here," I said to him as fiercely as I could say it in a whisper, "shut up! Wait! This won't last forever!"

"It'll be forever for me if they give me any more pea soup!" he growled. There were times, indeed, when I feared that Jeddy, unable to express his bitter rancor against the British, would die of an apoplexy.

*   *   *

We cruised for a week off the Banks, handing out medicine and rum to English fishermen; and though we wallowed through a gurry of fog and rain for a great part of the time, there was not enough of a grog allowance, so that we were half sick, all of us, and as full of coughs and whoops as a ledge full of seals.

Our red-faced captain was given, according to the crew, to a heavy consumption of port wine, and I think his liver or his stomach was affected by his anger and by days of inaction; for he was touchy while we lay in the fog. He watched the men continually, and had them flogged whenever he saw one of them so much as looking cross-eyed. He caught Jeddy at some sort of facial contortion one sticky, shivery afternoon. At once he began to bellow that Jeddy had malingered at the polishing of the monkey tail on a carronade; and the next second he ordered him to the after gangway for a catting.

I wanted to go below when they peeled off Jeddy's shirt, lashed his wrists to the hammock nettings over his head and made his feet fast to a hatch grating; but I dared not move, not even to shut my eyes, not only because the English require a flogging to be witnessed by all hands, so to teach them a lesson, but because I knew the captain would see me, which might have proved unpleasant, since he was aching to serve everyone the same way if he could find an excuse.

While Jeddy stood there, waiting, his eyes flicked over us who were watching in the waist and caught at mine for a second. Then he faced to the front with a small pale smile. When the bos'n's mate swung the cat against him, his head snapped a little and his eyelids flickered: the skin on his back jerked up as though drawn by halyards and then slipped slowly down; but in spite of the red wales that grew and grew across his muscles and crawled into the deep groove over his backbone, his lips were still curved upward, as though he faintly contemplated a pleasure yet to come. To me that smile meant more than all his profanity and scowling, and I thought to myself there were squalls ahead for any Englishman Jeddy might later encounter.

When, after his flogging, I came across him in the rigging or at the coppers, he said nothing, but he smiled that same pale smile; and his eyes looked red, like those of a weasel making up his mind to go down after a rabbit.

It was late in May when we raised the high hill of Halifax in Nova Scotia and stood into long, narrow Chebucto Bay, as fine a harbor as there is in the world, but the dreariest looking place I know, with one exception.

I knew, as we went through the western channel into the harbor, that this was where we must escape from the *Gorgon* if ever we hoped to escape at all; and while I racked my brains for a means by which the five of us could leave the ship, I caught sight of a brig that seemed familiar. As we came abeam of her, I saw a nick in the edge of the smoke pipe that stuck from the galley; and there came into my mind, suddenly, how I had stood on the end of the dock in Portland and thrown the half of a brick at just such a brig with just such a nick in the edge of her smoke pipe.

She was the *Riddle*, captained by Eli Bagley; and I felt, somehow, she was manna sent from heaven, though I could not see at the moment how it would nourish us.

I knew, however, that Eli Bagley, famous in every Maine seaport for being meaner than all get-out, would be aching to pay me for the black eye I had given him in Portland and, even without that score to settle, was not a man to help a distressed fellow countryman at the price of any risk to himself.

Nevertheless, I looked hard at the little *Riddle* and began to think about her even harder.

VIII

THE officers of the *Gorgon* watched us like hawks in Halifax harbor; for it was plain to them that every American aboard would cut and run if he had the chance. Therefore no American was given shore leave. Wherever we moved, from bowsprit to taffrail, there was always a marine with his eyes fixed upon us; and I, eager to devise a method of escape that would harm no one but myself if it failed, was near desperate before my plans at last were made.

There was a constant passing of bumboats between the shore and the *Gorgon* at all hours of the day and night, and a great hurroaring and screaming on the part of drunken seamen and their equally drunken women; for women come aboard British men-of-war when they are in port, do what they please, and stay as long as a seaman has a shilling to spend on them.

Always there were traders somewhere about the decks, dealing in trinkets and food, and illicitly in rum; and through the night drunken sailors were perpetually returning, some of them carried, and some still able to sing unmelodiously and fight each other.

With all these things in mind I had 'Lisha Lord get me two bottles of brandy, a long knife, a curved marlinspike, and a ball of spun yarn. At sundown on our second day in Halifax harbor, I gave out instructions and stations to Lord, so that he could pass them on to Jeddy and Cromwell and Tommy Bickford.

The noisiest and busiest time on the *Gorgon's* decks during the preceding evening had been at nine o'clock; and immediately after that hour on the night of our attempt, Jeddy Tucker came reeling around the deck, seemingly as full as a tick. He had a bottle of brandy stuck in the waistband of his trousers; and almost at once he laid hold of a girl, whipped out the bottle, and went to hullooing about everybody being shipmates together. At this the seaman on whose knee the girl had been sitting began to roar and bellow, but Jeddy took her by the arm and ran forward with her, the outraged seaman pelting after him.

They stopped by the starboard sheet anchor. Here Jeddy, dodging behind the girl as if for protection, worried the cork from the bottle

and offered it to the willing Nova Scotia damsel. The seaman seized
it, and he and Jeddy wrestled together, the girl pinched between
them. Some of the brandy spilled upon her from the bottle. She
squealed, and the sentry in the bow walked over to look at the trouble. Having been waiting for this, I moved forward, slid over the
bulwarks by the larboard sheet anchor, went down the cable until I
could go no farther, kicked off my shoes and dropped feet first into
the water.

The water was as cold as though pumped fresh from the bilge of
the North Pole: so cold I near opened my mouth under water to
suck in my breath against the shock. I swam a few strokes; then
came up with the back of my head toward the corvette, so the white
glimmer of my face might not be seen in the bright starlight.

I moved slowly away. Two boatloads of drunken sailors passed
within twenty yards. A little later a boat, returning to shore, came
toward me, its oars thumping cheerily in the rowlocks. I could see
there was only one man in it. When I had taken three quick strokes
toward him I stopped, groaning and thrashing. He backed his oars
and swore, startled. I threw up an arm and went under: then rolled
to the top and gurgled; and at that the boatman sculled over to me
quickly and thrust an oar beneath my stomach.

I groaned again and caught at the oar. The boatman took me by
the hair and upper arm, heaving at me; and with his heaving and
my scrambling I rolled over the thwart and into the bottom of the
boat, lying there with chattering teeth and quietly freeing the marlinspike from its resting place along the seam of my trouser leg, where
I had tied it with spun yarn.

"Man!" he said, "ye must be froze! What are ye, fey or only drunk?"
He turned the boat toward the corvette.

I thanked God for a Scotch blue-nose; for though the Scotch have
no use for Americans, neither are they inclined to waste love on the
English, though they will fight for them against Americans. From
what I have seen of the Scotch, they hate the English, but hate everyone else worse.

"Not there," I whispered hoarsely, to hide my accent from the
boatman, "not to that dirty box of slave-drivers! They'll press you
and cut your hide off!" I pulled up my shirt and showed him my
back, where the welts from my colting still showed blue when I was
cold.

"The bloody lobsters!" he said, pulling the boat around again.
"What'll I do with ye? Ye'll freeze in the fields; and there's a raft
of sentries on the docks."

"There's a brig lying there," I whispered, pointing to the eastward. "If I can get aboard quiet, they'll ship me."

"Losh!" he said, "there's *thirty* brigs off there! What'll ye do: try 'em all?"

"I know her," I told him. "Let me at the oars to keep from freezing, and I'll be there before you could down a gill of rum."

When he had made way for me to come up on the seat he fumbled in a stern-locker and brought out a bottle. After sucking at it with melodious gurglings, he passed it to me. I think I let a pint slip down my throat; then, when I had given the bottle back, I fished in my soggy breeches and handed the boatman a dollar.

"Na! I dinna want this!" he said. He took it quickly, nevertheless.

"It's worth something to find a friend," I whispered, "who'll help a poor sailor out of a pickle and keep his trap closed in the bargain."

"Dinna fear!" he said, pocketing the dollar. "I never saw ye."

When we had found the *Riddle* at last and nosed our way to her bow, I went up the anchor cable hand over hand and clung to the cat-head for a while, to let the thudding of my heart die down.

The brig, except for the lap-lap under her counter and the faint clacking of a piece of loose gear, seemed heavy and dull, like a house filled with sleeping people. I went over the bulwarks at last and crept to the capstan, holding my knife and marlinspike in my left hand. Peer down the deck as I would, I could see nobody; so at length, knowing it must be done, I stepped softly toward the stern. As I passed the mainmast, I made out a figure, a small figure, leaning against the larboard rail by the cabin. I went for him, making no sound in my stocking feet. I heard him say, "What the hell you want?" Then I got my hand on his jacket and the point of my knife against his throat.

"Easy now," I told him. "It's all right, only don't talk or move."

"Git away!" he squeaked.

"One more like that and I'll slit your hawse hole," I said, pricking him a little.

He stayed as he was, bent rigidly backward in the attitude of a girl seeking to escape a kiss.

"All right," I said. "Now we'll go see the old man. Walk down to the cabin, open the door and pull him out of his bunk."

"He'll kill me!"

"He won't kill anyone! I'll look after you as long as you do what I say." I prodded him. With an anxious grunt he stepped toward the captain's quarters.

She was a slovenly brig, with a foul smell about her, as if she had never been cleaned. The cabin, lighted by a dirty little pewter whale-oil lamp, was fouler still. We had no sooner opened the door than Bagley thrust his head from his berth, making chewing motions with his lips. He had on a red knitted nightcap; and what with his thin bluish face and his protuberant jaw bones, he looked like somebody thrown out of hell for meanness.

"Knock before you come in, dum ye!" he protested; but the mate's only answer was to lay hold of his arm and haul him over the side of the bunk. He bounced upright, a raging fury in a red flannel nightshirt.

"Here!" he yelped at me, "what you doing here? Who be you?"

"A fellow countryman," I said, "in trouble and needing help."

He peered at me, moving his chin whiskers. "Nason!" he snarled. "You set up to be pretty high and mighty down in Portland! Better'n me, you was! You wun't get no help here!"

I took the ball of spun yarn from my pocket and tossed it to the mate. "Tie his hands," I said, "then light the big lamp."

"By gorry!" Bagley said. "I'll have the law on you!"

When his hands were tied and the big lamp lit, I took the yarn and tied the mate's hands as well.

"You'll have a fine time doing it," I reminded Bagley. "You're carrying cargoes to the British!"

He eyed me venomously. "You're dretful pious, you are! I s'pose *you* ain't doing it, nor nothing like that!" He paused uncertainly. "I thought you cleared for Spain."

"I did, but something happened, and I've seen a light. Where's your Bible?"

I knew Bagley to be as superstitiously religious as he was mean, so that the Bible would bind him more securely than any spun yarn.

"Bible!" he exclaimed, watching me warily out of little pig eyes as hard as snail shells. "I wun't trust ye, Nason: not even with a Bible!"

I found it, at last, in a pocket beside his bunk. "All right," I said, pushing it against his tied hands. "I'm leaving this brig: leaving it in your boat. Swear on this to lower it away for me, help me off, and keep your mouth shut for two days, so help you God."

Bagley glared at me. "What you think I am!"

"A traitor!" I told him. "Hurry up and swear! I haven't got all night!"

"Gol dum ye!" he said. "I wun't!"

I pulled the whale-oil lamp from the wall, kicked the wood box from behind the stove, and smashed the lamp over it with a chunk of pine. "You've got one minute before I set her afire!"

"Gimme that Bible!" the mate said.

They took their oaths, the both of them; and half an hour later I was under the *Gorgon's* bow in the *Riddle's* boat.

* * *

I was pleased to hear from the deck above a prodigious drunken singing of hoarse voices. The chorus was so loud that Jeddy, peering down at me, could have spoken in his natural tones, I think, without fear of detection; and the disorder was so happily useful that four figures slid down the anchor cable and into my borrowed boat with what I might almost call comfort.

We sculled softly away from that well detested vessel, then, under cover of dark, pulled hard for safety. Almost in the harbor mouth we had a great fright and an astounding piece of luck, even while we wrangled among ourselves as to whether we should set out afoot for Annapolis or capture a pink by boarding. The American schooner *Nancy* of Kittery, Captain Rich, which had cleared at sundown for her home port, but lay a little inside, becalmed, had caught a breeze and was running out, and in so doing almost ran us down. Captain Rich took us on board, was astounded to find men from a town neighboring his in such a plight, showed himself a hearty patriot, swore by Job's Turkey he'd land us safe on our mutually native soil, and kept the potent Maine oath. On the second afternoon after he made it we stepped again on Arundel ground.

* * *

There was nobody in sight when we crossed the creek and came again to our comfortable gray farmhouse nestled above the dunes and the curving crescent of beach: nobody, that is to say, except Rowlandson Drown, that violent-tempered man, who sat beside the front door in the golden rays of the late afternoon sun, his mottled gray face and his bull neck hunched over a chair he was mending.

"Hey!" he said, working at the turnings of a rung with a draw shave, "you're back quick!"

"Yes," I said, feeling quarrelsome inside, and glad for the opportunity of letting out on one who was against a war because it would hurt the chair trade. "Yes, thanks to the English, who have more friends around here than they rightly ought to have."

Rowlandson Drown picked a sliver of hickory from his draw shave. "Do tell!" he said, looking quickly at 'Lisha Lord and Cromwell and then fastening his eyes on Jeddy.

"You're damned right," Jeddy said, watching Rowlandson with

round, unblinking eyes. "They licked me twice, once with a cat. You'd be real friendly with the British, I suppose, if they took a cat to that fat back of yours!"

"You keep out of this," I warned Jeddy. Then I turned to Rowlandson. His face had grown darker, so I knew violence was rising in him.

"Jeddy was whipped," I told him, "and I was whipped too. That isn't much. We can pay 'em back for that. But you know what they did to me, Drown? They came aboard my brig and called me a lying, tricky Yankee. They tried to kill my little dog Pinky. Then they pressed me; me, her master! Took me right off my own vessel, by God! Said I was a Britisher! Said my dog Pinky was British! Said Tommy Bickford was British because we couldn't breed people like Tommy in our filthy country. Maybe you'd like to say a word or two for the English, Drown."

His face grew darker, and he grunted at me, a groaning sort of grunt that made his shoulders heave.

"Now," I said, wagging my finger in his face and marking the little lump on the side of his jaw where I proposed to hit him, "I'm going to take out a privateer against the British; and if God's good to me, I'll pay 'em back for what they did; and what's more, I'll take every opportunity to deal harshly with any man who tries to tell me the British are friends of ours. That's what Caleb Strong, the Governor of Massachusetts, has been telling us for years, Drown, and I've believed him. Now I know he's a liar, and as much my enemy as the English. All the ministers and merchants of Boston have been talking like Strong, Drown, and I was fool enough to trust 'em! I trusted the Timothy Pickerings and the John Lowells and the Francis Blakes and the Harrison Gray Otises, Drown; but now I've got the welts of a British colt on my back, and I know better! I know they're all liars; and if you hold with Caleb Strong and the Boston Federalists, Drown, you're a liar as well!"

Just as I was about to hit him he dropped his head. "Your little white dog? They tried to kill your little white dog?"

"Yes," I said, hoping he'd have to be carried home on a shutter.

He turned back to the chair and picked up his draw shave. "Well," he growled, "I'm a good cabinet worker, which is a more valuable trade than carpenter, and I'm as good a carpenter as any man, and a damned sight better than most I can name, so I'll ship as carpenter on your privateer."

"Carpenter?" I said, taken aback by the suddenness with which his sentiments seemed to have altered. "I don't want a carpenter!"

He turned on me, snarling. "You *got* to have a carpenter," he said violently. "You got to cooper and uncooper your water barrels and fish your busted masts, ain't you?"

"Yes," I admitted. "I guess I have."

"I guess you *have!*" Rowlandson Drown sneered. "I can carpenter and I can fight. If you got any good reason why I shouldn't ship as carpenter, I got some money saved, and I'll buy some shares in your privateer! I'll buy 'em anyway, by gosh!"

The five of us stared at Rowlandson, who growled and grumbled to himself, wobbling the chair on its front legs to make sure it was stout and rigid. Before I could say anything I heard a familiar clicking sound. I looked up to see my mother standing in the front yard, one hand on her hip and the other rattling the string of cat's-eyes at her throat. She smiled a pleasant, one-sided smile.

"Welcome home," she said.

IX

People knew nothing about vessels, my mother told me when we got to arguing about the proper sort of craft for privateering. "You can't expect a man who hasn't been to sea," she said, "to know or care that a sloop-of-war isn't a sloop at all, but a brig or a ship, and that she's a corvette at the same time because her guns are all on one deck, whereas those of a frigate are on two decks, and those of a line-of-battle ship on three. I tell you that for every man who knows a full-rigged brig has two masts with square sails on both, whereas a brigantine is square rigged on the foremast and fore-and-aft rigged on the mainmast, there are twenty thousand who can tell you nothing about a brig except that she's a ship, which she isn't. Who knows, do you think, that a corvette carries a crew of a hundred and fifty, and a frigate a crew of five hundred, and a line-of-battle ship a crew of a thousand, whereas a 700-ton armed merchant ship carries only twenty-five or thirty? Nobody, or next to nobody!"

"I thought we were speaking of a proper vessel to be a privateer," I ventured to remind her.

"So we were. Let me repeat you're aiming too high when you think to use a brig for a privateer. Also a Baltimore clipper schooner's no good, because she'll crush like an eggshell if you undertake to lay her alongside a heavy ship in any kind of sea. They're too delicate, these Baltimore clipper schooners. Furthermore——"

"But if we wait for the *Neutrality* to come home," I interrupted, "we can add to her speed. She's familiar to me, and it'll be a great saving of money."

My mother snorted. "It won't be a saving of money if a British sloop-of-war makes sail in chase of you and your topmast carries away. Listen to my arguments, now, and remember I know more about sailing and war than you do. No doubt you consider yourself almost better than Stephen Decatur; but you must bear in mind it was little longer ago than yesterday that I was paddling you with a hairbrush to keep you out of the cooky jar."

"Go ahead," I told her. "You'll be telling me I'm still a child when I'm sixty years old."

"It may be," she admitted, smiling her one-sided smile, "but let's stick to the matter in hand. You say you care less about taking prizes than about harrying the British and sinking their ships."

"Yes," I said, "but at the same time I wish to overlook no opportunities to enrich ourselves at their expense."

"Certainly not," my mother said. "You'd be a fool if you did! At any rate, you wish to capture and sink Britishers. Now I've marched with fine fighters in my day; and they've all persisted in saying that the true art of war is the art of ambushing and surprising your enemy, and of inflicting the greatest possible loss on him at the least cost to yourself.

"If you attempt to carry this theory into sea fighting, you'll find few ways to ambush and surprise an enemy. You can do it by night attacks, which are dangerous unless you're sure of the enemy's strength. You can do it by sending your boats into a harbor under cover of dark and cutting out an enemy craft; but that's even more dangerous. I've given the matter some thought, and it seems to me the surest method of surprising British ships would be to lead them to hold you in contempt—to underestimate your strength. I think it's the surest method, because the British have always underrated us as opponents and always will, so it'll take no great skill to lead them astray.

"Suppose, now, you privateer in our own brig. In the first place she must be rerigged, so to be speedier. Then you must raise a crew of a hundred men for her, or a hundred and twenty; for it's impossible to do with less if she's to be properly fought; and you must find supplies for these men, which is no child's play. Then, when you've got to sea, you'll be the prey of every British frigate and sloop-of-war that sights you; for any brig is a good prize, and they'll chase even a small one as long as they can keep her in sight.

"On the other hand, if you go out in a smaller craft—a sloop, say— you can get along with fewer men; you can come down all unsuspected on some lordly merchantman and blow him out of water just as he's preparing to be gracious and give you your latitude and longitude. You can tack three times, if you're caught in a box, to anybody else's once. You can sweep out of gunshot if you blunder into an enemy in a calm. You can depend on prizes for much of your supplies; and frigates and sloops-of-war won't waste time on you if they see you have any chance at all of getting away."

"Then you give the word I must use a sloop?" I asked.

"I think so," she said, working her fingers in and out of her cat's-eyes. "Go somewhere and get a strong, fast sloop of about sixty tons burden, and you'll have a craft that can be handled by a few men.

Thirty or forty can fight her as well as a hundred and twenty could fight our brig, and she can be made to look as harmless and unimportant as a porgy fisherman. Yet she'll carry enough guns, and there'll be room for all of you as well as for a fair load of prisoners in case of need; and if she's the right sort of sloop there's no British-built vessel of any size whatever that can catch her."

So the end of our argument was that I was to get a sloop; and we had no sooner decided on it than I took Jeddy and 'Lisha Lord and Cromwell, and started off toward Salem and Boston to see what we could find.

I thought to leave Tommy Bickford in Arundel; but he spoke his mind to my mother to such good purpose that she told me to take him along, she having a weakness for the boy because of the manner in which his father had dragged my father ashore through a shower of bullets at Valcour Island, and also because he was a handsome, polite boy with a broad smile that won the women, and the men too, for that matter.

With me I carried fifty-five hundred dollars, forty-two hundred being my mother's money and my own, and two hundred belonging to my aunt Cynthy, she having made it in a venture of twenty dollars during my first year as captain of the *Neutrality*. Four hundred and sixty belonged to that violent man, Rowlandson Drown, seventy to Jeddy, and five hundred to Dominicus Lord, the shipowner. Fifty-seven dollars of it was the sole wealth of Tommy Bickford's widowed mother, and I wouldn't have taken it if my mother had not insisted, saying it was a good thing to have a responsibility like that on my mind.

In Portsmouth and Newburyport we found only the regular run of brigs and snows and sloops laid up by the embargo, none of them fit for our purpose. All through the taverns and along the waterfront the people were talking against the war, which was fairly on us, since the President on the first of June had sent a message to the Congress, telling of the wrongs we had suffered at England's hands.

Much of this hatred of the war was due to the knowledge that there would be fighting in Canada, Thomas Jefferson having said in one of his frequent moments of lunacy that the capture of Quebec was merely a matter of marching, and that we would therefore invade Canada to take it from the British. Having no dislike for Canada or the Canadians, and being with good reason suspicious of Thomas Jefferson, our New Englanders declared hotly that any war fought in Canada would be fought without them.

When we reached Salem, we found little outcry against the war and no argument in favor of a Canadian campaign; but everywhere there was talk of privateering and privateers: how the Crowninshields would take off the upper deck of the ship *America* and fill her sides solid between planking and ceiling, like a man-of-war, and fit her for a privateer; how Holton Breed would take out a privateer for the leading merchants of the place as soon as a fast enough brig could be found; how twenty-four Salem captains had formed a company to go out in their own vessel against the British.

At Crowninshield's wharf, by good fortune, I found Captain William Webb, who had helped me buy the shawl for my mother in Cadiz. He was superintending changes in a pink little larger than a ship's longboat. She had two six-pounder carronades, one mounted aft of her mainmast, and one between the main and foremast, so arranged that both could be pivoted and fired from either side. There were twelve or fifteen men crowded on her deck, working at this and that, and it took no more than a glance to see they were not common seamen.

"Hey!" Webb said, when I nudged his elbow, "what you doing here?"

"Looking," I told him.

Webb scanned the drifting white clouds overhead. "If you're looking to sign on with me," he said, "it can't be done. She's all divided: twenty-four owners. All masters. We're taking her out ourselves."

"I'm looking for one of my own," I said.

Webb studied the sky to the westward: then to the eastward. "What you think of this craft?" he asked.

"Good for her size," I said. "She'd make a nice cutter for my brig."

"Yes," Webb said. "She'd run all the way around your brig twice while you were shaking the reefs out of your topsails. Built in Chebacco in 1804. There's a pink that *is* a pink! Thirty tons burden, and I'd take her to Canton as quick as to Boston."

"What's her name?" I asked.

"*Fame*," he told me, smiling affectionately at the little craft. "That's her name, and I hope it'll be her nature. Fame for her, fortune for us, and hell for the British."

Never was there a vessel, it seems to me, so aptly named; for there was no American privateer afloat who didn't learn, before the war was five months old, how the *Fame*, in spite of her diminutive size and her thirty tons and her two little sparrow guns, took eight British prizes in no time at all, one an armed British ship of 300 tons, and another a 200-ton brig, and all of them together representing a loss of two hundred thousand dollars to the English.

"Well," I said, "I've had something the same idea, only I want a sloop."

"You're making a mistake," he said gravely. "Everybody in Salem tells me I'm crazy, going to sea in a toy like this. What I ought to have is a Baltimore clipper schooner."

"Yes," I said, "I've heard there's nothing like a Baltimore clipper schooner. I want a sloop."

Webb laughed. "Good sloops are scarce. You'll find plenty of sloops laid up here but none that I'd——"

A thought came to him. "By gum!" he exclaimed, "how big a sloop can you do with?"

"Well," I said, "I don't rightly know till I've seen her. Fifty tons. Sixty maybe. Maybe more. I figure on thirty men, and I guess I could scare up thirty-five."

"Then I guess this won't interest you," he said. "A North River sloop slid in here yesterday, loaded with grain, and clumsy-looking as they come; but she had an old h'ister of a stick in her. Prob'ly she's too big for you. Seventy tons—eighty, maybe: it's hard to tell about those North River sloops."

"Where is she?"

"She's up toward Whipple's Wharf," he said.

In ten minutes the five of us were scattered along Whipple's Wharf, scanning, with apparent indifference, the towering mast of the *Lottie Green*. It was the tallest stick I ever saw on a craft of her size, ninety feet high if an inch, with so few shrouds and stays that it seemed likely to whip out of her at the first blow. She was broad beamed; and a litter of hen coops, old sails, and lumber up forward distracted the eye from her flush and level decks. A part of her seeming clumsiness was due to her heavy bowsprit and her solid bulwarks, as well as to the manner in which she was daubed with paint, as though the owner's money had run out and he had borrowed some light green here and some dark green there. As soon as I had looked hard at her I knew she was worth thinking about.

"But," I said to myself, as I stood staring at her, "she'll never be the *Lottie Green* if I should come to be part owner of her, and her master."

Straightway I fell to thinking how I should name her, and thereupon a curious little thing happened. The green of her sides made me think suddenly and with little relevancy of a green dress I had seen; and unconsciously I put my hand to my breast pocket and felt the round contour of the miniature I carried there as a provision against poverty.

In that very moment I renamed the sloop: the words came murmuring upon my lips without my knowing well just how they got there.

"The Lively Lady!" I whispered. "The Lively Lady!"

That was how the *Lively Lady* got her name.

*   *   *

I turned to 'Lisha Lord. "What about guns?"

"She'll carry anything," he said confidently.

I went down onto the sloop's deck, where a tall man with a large stomach was wearily supervising the unloading of grain from her hold. "You cap'n?" I asked him. This was flattery; for we merchant captains are masters in theory, and only the captain of a war vessel is supposed to be called a captain.

"Yes, I be," he said, shifting a straw in his mouth.

"War's going to catch you, isn't it?" I asked, thinking to pave the way for a trade by frightening him.

"No, it ain't. There ain't nothing going to catch me. You looking for a privateer?"

"Well," I admitted, "I might be and I mightn't be. If I got a fast craft cheap, I might."

"Listen, mister," said the large-stomached man, blowing the straw from his mouth, "this sloop come off the ways at Newburgh in 1809. She's staunch and she's gentle and she's fast. You might not think it to look at her, but this sloop can do thirteen knots."

"Thirteen knots your grandmother!" I said, for thirteen knots is better than any of His Britannic Majesty's frigates can do, even if they throw over all their guns, their reefers, and their bos'n's mates.

"Thirteen knots and nobody's grandmother," he said impressively. "She can do better than ten knots for twenty-four hours on end, and she ain't never been pushed. This little old sloop, she's sweet as a nut and sound as a bell; and what she'd do if she was pushed I'd hate to say."

"If she was pushed," I said, "she'd carry away the top of that coach whip you've got in her." From the inward movement of his eyes I could tell I had touched him on a tender spot.

"Mister," he said, "you're all fouled up! She's sweet as a bell and sound as a nut from stem to stern, blow high, blow low. She's ninety-six tons, and you know the rule for masting North River sloops: a foot of length for every ton."

"She looks about seventy-five tons to me," I said, for the sake of saying something. "How many men you carry, and what you asking for her?"

The large-stomached man waved his hand toward the three men who were swaying up the grain. "There they be, and I got to get sixty dollars a ton for a craft like this."

"Good grief!" I said, "that's nearly six thousand dollars figuring at ninety-six tons. I see now why you claim she's ninety-six. I'll bet she's not an ounce over eighty; and no sloop afloat's worth more than forty dollars a ton."

"Mister," he assured me, "you New Englanders beat anything I ever see! Durned if you wouldn't turn your back on a dollar to hunt for a copper. This sloop'll make you a hundred thousand dollars—a million, if you know how to handle her—and yet you're shaking in your boots at spending fifty-seven hundred and sixty for her. Well, there ain't nothing mean about me! I'll knock off the sixty and make it an even fifty-seven hundred."

The upshot was that I gave him four thousand dollars for his sloop, which may have been a whisker less than she was worth; and as soon as her grain was out we took her in hand, slipped away from Salem and scudded up the coast with as little fuss as a loon moving out of gunshot.

Thanks to General Dearborn, with whom my mother had marched to Quebec in her youth, we had an order on the Portsmouth Navy Yard for guns, so we ran up the Piscataqua that afternoon and anchored off Kittery.

"Our order calls for six thirty-six-pound carronades," 'Lisha Lord told me. "I don't know how you feel about carronades, but I wouldn't give 'em house room. They ain't bad for clearing an enemy's decks at close range; but at long range their shot just bounces. If you want to take vessels without boarding, you want long guns that'll throw a shot clear through a ship."

"I'm afraid of long guns," I objected. "Their pivots are too high and they weigh too much. They'd make us top heavy and slow."

"Not if you mount 'em on carriages," 'Lisha said. "We'll fire 'em through ports; and if she blows too hard, we can sway 'em into the hold in five minutes."

'Lisha, being from Bath, would, I knew, have profited by all the mistakes as well as the wisdom of the British under whom he had learned about guns.

"If you want to know what I think," he said, "I'd ask for two long eighteens—traversing pieces. For carronades I'd take two eighteen pounders, so I could use my long-gun ammunition in 'em if there's need, and a twenty-four pounder betwixt my bow ports to throw langrage wherever it's handiest. Then I wouldn't be over-gunned, and there'd be few craft as dangerous."

By langrage Lord meant the old iron and scraps of lead and odd bullets that are loaded into guns at close range to chop up stays and shrouds and clear the decks of an enemy vessel.

We got our guns the next day, and in addition to them our barrels of powder, pistols, forty cutlasses, forty boarding axes, twenty boarding pikes; round shot, grapeshot, and double-head shot; musket and pistol cartridges aplenty, cartridge boxes, rammers, and sponges; worms and ladles; tubes, priming wires, lanthorns, blue lights, wads, cartridge paper, gun tackles, gun aprons, bed and quoins, gun hand spikes, tompions, gun breechings, kegs of manila rope, hooks for breeching; and a mighty mess our sloop was when we had all this aboard.

We had only a part of it stowed when a pleasant young lieutenant came down to tell me war had been formally declared. "The British'll be down from Halifax like hornets," he said, "and all our ships are in New York; so if you see a frigate or a sloop-of-war, cut and run, for she'll be British."

Fortunately we had not far to go, yet in the short distance after we had scudded between Boon Island and Cape Neddick and stood away across Wells Bay for home, we sighted eleven brigs, all of them back from foreign parts—and all of them, as I knew from my own caution and watchfulness, feeling as hurried and harried as a dog that scuttles past a master wishful of kicking him.

From far off we could see the squat chimneys of our house behind the Arundel dunes, rising against the green slope of the high land across the river. Behind the house, as we skirted the half circle of brown reefs that guard our river and beaches from the sea, we spied a brig's topgallant sails moving slowly upstream with the tide. We rounded Mile Ledge, slipped easily over the bar and followed the topgallant sails around the bend.

They belonged to the *Neutrality;* and on her quarter-deck, his feet on the taffrail and his stump of a tail cocked over his back as if hoisted up and sheeted home, barking and barking in a sort of ecstasy, as if he knew he'd find me on our river, was my little white dog Pinky.

X

No MAN, I have learned, is qualified to say what brings joy or sorrow to another. There was a man in our town of Arundel whose home and worldly goods were entirely destroyed by fire, and two of his children as well; yet the one lost thing for which he mourned loudest and longest was a snuffbox made from a cow's horn.

We should have been in a state of excitement because Cephas Cluff had brought the *Neutrality* safe home, laden with salt as instructed, so that we not only had our brig, together with her crew to join with us aboard our sloop, but a handsome profit on our cargo —a profit so large that my mother would be well fixed, no matter how long the war might last; for salt had shot up in price as the war came close. Yet the thing that stirred me was neither of these things, but the knowledge that I had my little white dog Pinky again; whereas my mother seemed to have no thoughts for the brig because of her interest in the sloop.

She had me row her from one side to the other and back again, and she climbed around the deck and in and out of the cabin until I was in a mind to order her home so we could set to work undisturbed. When I spoke of this she set her hands on her hips and stared up the mast as though looking for a twist in it, and said nothing could be done until she had gone out in her and got the feel of her.

"Look here," I said, "I won't have it; not with your back apt to be lamed again. Besides that, this country's at war. We've no time for pleasure cruises."

Her eyes seemed to scoff at me. "I suppose not," she said. "I suppose you only have time for a trip to Dartmoor Prison. You're saving all your time for that, no doubt."

"Stop fretting about how she feels," I told her. "She feels good. There's nothing to worry about, and I'd like to get out and pick up a couple of Britishers before they're all gone."

"Try to contain yourself," she said. "This war won't be over in a week or two. If it lasts till we get an army, I think it may even last two or three hundred years. What I want to find out is this: Is that stick of yours all right?"

"Well," I said, "to tell the truth, I think it's a trifle long."

"I see." Smiling a faint one-sided smile, she twisted her fingers rapidly in her string of cat's-eyes. "That was something you'd forgotten to mention! You thought it was too long, and you were willing to go to sea without making sure! Richard, Richard! Haven't I taught you better than that?"

"She logged over ten knots coming down here," I told her, which would have been enough of a defense to satisfy anyone except my mother. She only turned her shoulder to me and lifted it a little; then scanned the sky and sniffed the wind. "It'll come in from the southwest this afternoon," she said. "We'll take her out and see about this."

*   *   *

There were times, that afternoon, after my mother had all sail cracked on and was conning the sloop around the ledges off the southerly tip of the point we call Hell's Two Acres, when I wished we had left our gunners' stores on the river bank, being sure we must rip off our bends against the barnacle-covered rocks.

My mother was in high spirits, humming constantly with her lips tight closed, and seldom opening them except to call, "Luff!" or, "Nothing off!" to John Cromwell, who was steering. The wind holding constant, we logged her again and again. She showed always just short of eleven knots.

"Let's reef that mainsail," my mother said at length.

I saw what was in her mind, so we reefed it. "Now," she said to me, "work her!" I took the wheel from John and worked her. There was a lift to her, as though a whale were fast to us, drawing us forward; and she hissed in the water, so there was a noise beneath her counter like streams from a dozen pumps pouring overside.

We logged her again. This time she showed eleven knots and two fathoms.

"There you are, Richard," my mother said. "I suspected it, and now I know it! She's got too much mast and too tall a sail. It forces her head down. I say take off ten feet of mast and ten feet of canvas. If you do, she'll sail as well as most Baltimore clippers and keep you twice as dry."

We went to work on her the next day, Rowlandson Drown in charge of the carpenters, and 'Lisha Lord supervising the mounting of the guns.

On this little sloop of ours, only sixty-eight feet over all, we made living quarters for forty men, and a cabin and a gun room aft, if you want to call it a gun room, though I think Jeddy Tucker was nearer the truth when he called it the popgun room; for it was about as big, Jeddy said, as a pint of rum half poured out.

Also we had to allow for water casks and gunners' stores and a place for prisoners; because, though I wanted no prisoners, we well knew the day might come when willy-nilly we'd have them. And, finally, we needed plenty of space in the hold for whatever we might take from prizes, though I'm not ashamed to say now that none of us spoke of making prizes without knocking on wood or spitting over our left shoulders, these two precautions having long been known, in our province of Maine, as sure preventives of disaster.

It was not until late July that a commission was brought to me by post. It bore the signature of James Madison and authorized the private armed vessel *Lively Lady* to cruise against the enemies of the United States under the command of Captain Richard Nason. With that we made more haste, laying in supplies and rounding out our crew, which was not easy because nine tenths of the folk in Arundel and neighboring towns were bitter against the war and those who had forced them into it. It would put an end to their prosperity, they said, and they wanted nothing to do with it.

What I most needed were men handy with small arms; and by bribery and arguments of one sort and another I got eight of the best marksmen the town afforded, among them Moody Haley, who in a morning could shoot enough Eskimo plover to fill a hogshead; and Moses Burnham, whose rifle, though carrying a ball no larger than a pea, would kill rabbits and moose with equal thoroughness; and Pendleton Quint, who could drop a flying partridge without raising his fowling piece above his hip, he having learned to shoot in this fashion, he said, because of the weight of his weapon, which made it a nuisance to lift; also Bezaleel Bird, whose eyes were so keen he could distinguish goslings from ganders in a flock of geese and kill only goslings. I was fortunate in signing Jotham Carr, he having worked at rolling pills and holding forceps in Dr. Wiswall's office, so that we wouldn't be without a doctor. With him came Alley Mc-Alley, an Irish tailor who had appeared in our town from some place to the south and been cured of the itch by Jotham, so that he was Jotham's ardent follower, and glad for the opportunity to ship with him.

Also, in a cabin near Durrell's Bridge on the river road lived two black men named Pomp and Sip, which are names given to all black men in our part of New England, and these two I persuaded to sign on the *Lively Lady,* both of them being good-natured and handy at fishing, snaring, or shooting, as well as at cooking simple messes such as lobscouse and fish chowder.

By the end of August, thanks to the defeat of the *Guerrière* by our splendid frigate *Constitution,* and the news of the privateering successes of the little *Fame* out of Salem, our Arundel folk had become heartier for the war, so that we had more than enough men from whom to choose when our work was completed. Nevertheless, I held the crew to thirty men, over and above Jeddy and Cephas Cluff and 'Lisha Lord and Cromwell and myself, for I figured this number would answer my needs.

If we were lucky, the smaller the crew, the richer they'd be; for the owners were to receive one half of our taking, the other half going to the officers and crew. In this, there was matter to trouble the mind of any conscientious privateer captain, especially that of a young one; for the swelling of the shares by the taking of rich prizes was all too likely to become the main object with the crew, to the exclusion of what was more patriotic and important.

* * *

The crickets were loud the night before we sailed. I sat with my mother in the large room; and since then I have never heard a cricket's monotonous plaint without recalling the fragrant perfume of a Maine August—sweet grass and pines and wet sea sand and uncovered ledges—and without seeing quick pictures in my brain: the sharp current riffles in our river; a distant sail on the horizon; a handful of men standing silent and staring by the side of a long gun, their mouths hanging open against the explosion; and other pictures not so pleasant.

"There's a number of things I've had it in mind to tell you," she said, rounding off the toe of a white woolen stocking she was knitting. "War's a dirty business. They talk a lot about chivalrous enemies and land knows what-all; but chivalry doesn't help much if you have to be sewed up in a topsail and dropped overboard with an eighteen-pound shot at your feet. The chief idea in war is to kill and destroy. If you feel a bit of chivalry coming on, I'd recommend fighting it off till there's no chance of being killed and destroyed yourself."

"Don't worry about me," I told her.

"Privateering," she persisted, "has its bad points. Any Britisher that gets an opportunity will treat you like a pirate. You'll find, oftentimes, they'll keep on firing after one of our privateersmen strikes his colors. They did in the Revolution, in between some of their talk about chivalry. You needn't look for much mercy."

"I don't figure on giving 'em the chance to show me any."

"Weight of metal's a thing you can't do much against," she continued. "It may look cowardly, but don't lose time in running when you see a big one after you. Do what damage you can, and take as little as may be."

"That's why I shipped Moody Haley and Bezaleel Bird and the others."

"That's right," she said absently. "Pick 'em off at the top. That's how we won at Saratoga. The British don't like it, but that's because they aren't as good at it as we are." Her needles clicked rapidly. "Were you figuring on leaving her that dirty green color?"

"Yes," I said.

"I thought you might be planning to paint her a nice fresh green, like that green dress of Lady Ransome's." She eyed me sharply.

"I hadn't thought of it," I said. I had, but there seemed to be no reason to say so to my mother; and I had decided, finally, that the very dirtiness of the green was an advantage, since it might make us less easily visible to enemy craft. Once or twice, too, I had been tempted to speak to her of the miniature I had found in the pocket of my coat; but I knew nothing would be gained by idle chatter on the subject, so I remained silent about that as well.

She moved restlessly in her chair and sighed. "Get your charts," she said, not looking up from her knitting. "I've been thinking about the British trade routes. It's easiest to go to the Grand Banks and so intercept the merchantmen bound to Halifax from Britain and the Indies; but I'm beginning to suspicion it would be a mistake."

"I've been thinking," I said, unrolling a chart for her, "that all our privateers will run for the Grand Banks at the same time."

"That's been my thought," my mother said. "If I were captain of the *Lively Lady*, I'd head out across the Gulf Stream and bear south to the sugar trade route." She tapped her finger on the point that coffee and sugar traders from the West Indies must cross in sailing to England: the same point where there are always slow-moving merchantmen laden with English goods, heading for the West Indian markets. "It'll be hot down there," she said, "but you can't let a little heat stop you. What's more, I think you'll find next to no enemy war craft and few enough of our own privateers to compete with you."

"That's what I'll do, though I'd mislike to be caught by one of those tidy little hurricanes."

My mother lifted her shoulder. "They won't hurt you," she said. "You're lucky. They'll only stave up the merchantmen so you can take 'em easier."

Again we sat in silence. The crickets chirped on and on. I stared
at a picture of Rome on the wall paper, a picture showing a sheep
herder putting his arm around a handsome, dressy girl, though from
what I had seen of sheep herders in Spain and Portugal they'd be
given a wide berth by any girl not weak in the head.

My mother finished the stocking. "There," she said, "that's the
fastest knitting ever done in this town! If you're going out on the
flood tide you'd better get forty winks."

We stood in the door, listening to the soft, slow, irregular plunge
and murmur of the surf on the hard beach, and to the chirping of
the crickets. Then she patted me gently on the shoulder, and we
went upstairs.

I've heard it said we New Englanders are cold folk, taking no
pleasure in life or love. I don't know how such beliefs spring up, for
there's as much marrying among us as among people said to be more
passionate; and our families couldn't conveniently be larger. And I,
at least, knew that although my mother failed to scream and burst
into tears because of my departure, as more excitable and less sensible mothers might have done, she took no pleasure in my going and
would be happy when I came back.

XI

It was early on the fifth day out that Pendleton Quint sighted the first sail, bearing north with the Gulf Stream. We made sail in pursuit; and since it was our first chase the men were excited and in high spirits, though they made an effort to remain calm, leaning over the bulwarks and spitting when asked a question, and looking always at the sky before answering, though there was no cloud in sight and no chance of a change in wind.

As we drew up on this first sail of ours we cleared for action. The muskets, except those for the sharpshooters, were ranged in a rack by the main hatchway; each man was at his post, a cutlass buckled around him, the two long guns were cleared of their screens, the hatchway coamings were set with eighteen-pound shot; and ready on the decks were boxes of grape and langrage, water buckets, tubs of wadding, rammers and sponges, among which Pinky sniffed as though they were there for the sole purpose of letting him locate the rat that had made free with them.

She was a slow brig of some three hundred tons. The closer we came, the more Jeddy Tucker licked his lips, pleased and eager at what was about to happen. Just then the brig hove-to and hoisted Russian colors, so I was certain she was a neutral and our first chase a vain one. All around the deck the men settled back on their heels, growling and swearing; while I, wishing to make no mistake, spoke her and found her to be the Russian brig *Moskva*, Captain John Blanton, eight days out from Havana bound to St. Petersburg with a full cargo of sugar, logwood, and coffee. Jeddy Tucker went on board to examine her papers, log book, letters, crew and passengers. All was in order, as I had felt sure would be the case; and from Blanton, a Louisianian, Jeddy picked up intelligence that did us little good—that he had been boarded five days before by His Majesty's brig *Scorpion* but had sighted no other sail; that there were many British vessels at Havana, several ready for sea, and that a convoy was expected to set out within the month.

We sent the *Moskva* on her way and made sail to the southwest. Finding only light airs and calms, such as are often found in this section of the Gulf Stream in the month of September, we got out our lines and trolled, which I do whenever I can in the Gulf Stream because of the innumerable fish that cruise on its surface—ferocious fighters and as good eating, or better, than halibut.

When the breeze picked up we moved along to the southwestward. Toward evening of the second day we sighted another sail, but darkness fell. Jeddy was exasperated by this disappointment. We were, he said, carrying a Jonah aboard, one that soured our luck; and from various of his phrases having to do with chair makers and grayfaced wild men, I gathered he had somehow got it in his head that Rowlandson Drown would be at the bottom of any ill success we might have.

We laid a course, that night, calculated to hold us in the neighborhood of the sail we pursued; and when dawn came, the lookout spied it four miles astern. She was a brigantine, a clumsy, slow thing; and when we ran down toward her and fired a gun, she hove-to and hoisted the American flag. She seemed to have a familiar look; so when we boarded her I went myself with Jeddy to see what it was that stirred my memory. As our boat came up to her side, I saw a nick in the galley stove pipe. A moment later the lean face of Eli Bagley stared over the rail, as inflamed and congested as when I had bound him in his cabin in Halifax harbor.

"Well, Captain," I said, as I came aboard, "this seems like old times."

He smiled a sick smile, and I suddenly remembered he was what we call a fish-chowder sailor: one who lacks the courage or the skill to navigate out of sight of the coast.

"Aren't you a little far from home?"

"Oh, a leetle; a leetle. I—I got me a sailing master."

"Well, well! You're coming up in the world! You'll be working a tea ship before you know it! Let's look at this sailing master of yours."

Bagley hesitated, his jaw bones moving like the gills of a fish. I could see he wanted to question my authority, but felt he might be treading on delicate ground. "I hold a commission from President Madison," I told him, "to capture, burn, sink, or destroy all enemy craft."

"Gosh," he said, "I ain't no enemy craft! You know me: I'm out of Portsmouth."

"Where's that sailing master?"

He hesitated: then pointed to a lean, red-nosed man who stood at the lee rail, looking fixedly at nothing and chewing busily.

"What's your name?" I asked him.

"His name's Thomas," Bagley said hurriedly.

"Tammas *McAndrew*," said the red-nosed man, a hint of sourness in his voice.

"A herring choker!" I said. "I don't like it. Let's see your papers."

"There ain't nothing wrong," Bagley said. "You know me, Nason. You won't find nothing out of the way."

"Let's see your papers."

We went into his smelly little cabin. The pewter whale-oil lamp, unmended, had been hung back on its hook beside the door.

"Well," I said, when I had finally wormed his papers from him, "you're bound from a British port to a British port with lumber for the British. You're as good as a Britisher yourself."

Bagley's lumpy jaw bones moved convulsively. "Why, that ain't so! I'm just a poor man with a living to make! Why, Halifax harbor's full of New Englanders running flour to the Canadians! Gosh almighty, Nason, them poor Canadians couldn't live a week if we didn't run flour to 'em!"

"Nor the British army in Canada," I said.

"No," he agreed uncertainly.

He seemed to have no idea he was doing anything out of the way. "Will you tell me how in hell we're going to whip the British if we keep feeding 'em before we fight 'em?"

"We got to live, ain't we?"

"I don't see what's gained by it. I'll keep these papers, and you can make for the nearest port in the United States."

"No," he protested, "I'm going to Jamaica! I got to have those papers."

"You'll never hit Jamaica in a thousand years. I'm taking your sailing master with me, so you'd better head for more familiar waters."

"You *can't!*" he shouted, his face a mottled green and crimson, like a half-ripe apple. "I can't find my way without McAndrew."

"Yes, you can," I said. "All you need to do is steer west. You've got to hit land if you do that. Columbus did it, and so can you, if you know where west is."

"Gosh!" he said, his eyes round and staring, "what'll I do if a British frigate chases me?"

"It ought to be worth watching," I said. "Maybe you can outmaneuver her."

We threw overboard his deckload of lumber. As an afterthought I sent Jeddy to the cabin to hunt for rum. He found a keg; but after tasting it I left it with Bagley, fearful it might poison my crew if I took it with me.

McAndrew made no protest when I ordered him into the boat.

"Accept my apologies," I said, "for taking you off that tidy little craft;
but this is a war, even though some haven't sensed it."

He spat over the side. I saw he was chewing slippery elm. "Tidy!"
he ejaculated.

"Didn't he set a good table?" I asked.

"Ghastly!" McAndrew said.

I shook my head at Jeddy. "Life can be very disappointing. Under
the circumstances we'll have to let Mr. McAndrew mess in the gun
room—at least until we take other prisoners to keep him company."

*   *   *

We were not long in doing that. On the third of November we
came up with a brig flying the Spanish flag. We brought her to, for
I hoped to buy a few pipes of Spanish wine from her, so our crew
might not brood over our failure to take prizes. She was the *Dos
Hermanos* from Pernambuco to Portsmouth—a fine craft, coppered
to the bends and clean as the inside of a mussel shell, which isn't
usual with Spanish vessels, all those I have seen being thickly crusted
with dirt and smelling villainously of rancid oil, garlic and mold. To
add to these suspicious circumstances, she had two Englishmen
aboard as passengers, one of whom was standing with the captain
at the rail as we came up; and her cargo was composed entirely of
India goods: silks, guavas, opium, indigo, tea, ivory, carpets, and
spices, chief among these being ginger and turmeric. Now it seemed
unreasonable to me that this brig out of Pernambuco should be laden
with India goods, rather than with sugar or coffee or aguardiente or
cigarros, which are Pernambuco products.

The captain was a Spaniard and held the backs of his thumbs
against his breast when I sought to question him, flapping his fingers
limply in the air and looking stupid as a goat.

"All right," I told Jeddy, "bring down those two Englishmen."

They came down, polite and affable, and we had a glass of Spanish
wine together.

"You gentlemen took passage from Pernambuco?" I asked them.
They said that was the case.

Jeddy walked around them and around the captain, looking at
them front and rear. I could see he made the Englishmen uneasy.

"You gentlemen have lived in Pernambuco for some time?" I asked.

One of them, a squatty red-faced man, looked helplessly at the
other, a small man with the protruding upper front teeth that seem
almost a fashion with so many of the inhabitants of mighty Albion.
He said quickly they had been traveling.

"For business or for pleasure?"

"Pleasure," he answered readily enough. The squatty man, I thought, relaxed gently in his chair.

"And where have you traveled?"

"Oh," said the man with the teeth, waving his hand loosely as if to indicate far-off lands, "China, India, Ceylon, Madagascar, Brazil——"

Jeddy laughed, his eyes as wide and blue as those of a china doll. The glance of the buck-toothed man shifted and wavered.

I poured him another glass of wine, and we drank, all of us.

"A pleasant trip, indeed," I said. "You make it often?"

"No, we've worked hard for a number of years, and now we feel it's time we enjoyed ourselves."

"Of course," I said. "And what may your business have been?"

The squatty red-faced man, I could see, had grown tense once more.

"Really," said his buck-toothed friend, thoroughly English in his manner but smiling sweetly none the less, "such interest in our affairs is complimentary, I assure you."

"A natural interest," I told him, "for I recently spent some little time among English people and became almost excited about them. Now for a few more questions—after I learn your business?"

"Land," said the buck-toothed man sourly. "We dealt in land."

"Where?"

"London, of course. Land and houses."

"Your families didn't accompany you?"

"No; my wife is dead—ah—my children are too young to travel."

"So you left them with relatives?"

"Here!" he protested, "you've no right to ask these things!" His lips were tight across his teeth; but when I looked at him without speaking and Jeddy laughed under his breath, he smiled again, albeit a trifle weakly.

"Of course," he said, "I left them with my sister: two sweet little girls and a little boy."

"And you learned to speak Spanish while selling land in London?"

"Why, yes; that is, no. I don't speak Spanish."

"Probably you were talking to the captain in Russian when we came up, then, or was it Malay?"

He glowered at me, and Jeddy laughed again.

"Oh, well," I said, "that doesn't matter. Suppose you show me the trinkets you picked up in China and Ceylon and Madagascar for your two sweet little girls. And for the little boy. And for the kind sister who has been caring for this lonely little family."

Both Englishmen stared at me.

"Well," I said at length, "I'm waiting. Let me see some of the things you bought somewhere except India."

"This is a damned outrage," the red-faced man said huskily.

"No doubt," I returned, "but if we start exchanging outrages, we'll be here all night, and we must be on our way. This is an English brig carrying English goods to an English port, and it's as plain as the nose on my face that the captain's no captain at all, but a cat's-paw put aboard for you to hide behind. Get your dunnage together. We'll shift you to the sloop."

"I protest," said the man with the buck-teeth, though it was plain he knew he was caught. "What's to become of the brig?"

"Well, it's a shame to harm this fine new English vessel, even though she does masquerade under the Spanish flag; but I'm going to shift her cargo to the sloop and burn her." With that I told him to tell the Spanish captain that if all of them would help shift cargo, we would put them aboard a smaller prize some day, so they could sell it and have the money: otherwise they would be ordinary prisoners of war with the chance of being carried to America.

We laid the sloop alongside and worked at shifting cargo all that afternoon and through the hot, calm night. An hour after sunup the next day we had what Cephas Cluff and Jeddy and I figured was close to eighty thousand dollars' worth of the best India goods under hatches, to say nothing of a lot of new spars and sails, kegs of Spanish wine, and barrels of powder to replace that shot away in practice; and the crew were sluicing themselves with buckets of clear cool water from the blue Gulf Stream.

At eight o'clock we hoisted her sails, lashed her helm, and set her afire. Ten minutes later we ran up to windward and used her as a target. There was an oval keg of Spanish wine at the foot of the musket rack by the main hatch; and when the crew had given her a few rounds out of long guns double shotted with grape and ball, there were so many white splinters showing around her bends and bulwarks, and so much gear at loose ends, that Jeddy went down and told the crews to have a small tot all around. With that we wore ship under her stern and let her have both long guns through the cabin windows. The grape and solid shot went in with a crash that could be heard above the roar of the guns—such a crash as might be made by a horse falling through a roof. Her mainmast was cut four feet above the deck and her foremast halfway up; so that in less than five minutes she had become a torn and shattered hulk, belching a column of smoke amidships, and trailing masts, sails and shrouds over her sides.

'Lisha Lord turned from this sad wreck to shake his fist threateningly at the crews. "By Ory!" he shouted, "I told you to keep that fire low, and here you've gone halfway up the foremast with your shot! What the hell you think you're shooting at? Angels?"

XII

W₍ HAD worked well down toward the trade route when Pomp, seated at the masthead like a black cloud, shiny and happy from the heat of the noonday sun, caught the flash of a distant sail on our starboard quarter. We put about, and when we drew up on it in the late afternoon, we made her out to be a ship: a good one; partly laden so that she rode high out of water, and pierced for twelve guns, five on a side and two in the stern. We stared hard at her, but could find no trace of a long gun.

"I tell you," 'Lisha said, "she carries carronades and nothing else, like most running vessels."

The men in the waist of the ship were shouting "Take her! Take her!" so we piped to quarters and loaded and double-shotted the long guns. Tommy Bickford brought me the double-barreled fowling piece my mother had traded out of Sir Arthur Ransome, placing it on the deck where it would be handy; and my little dog Pinky came and lay beside it, helpful and obliging, his whiskers resting on its stock.

We ran up the British flag and bore off to windward of her. Her ports were open, and we could see men at the guns, but not many, and I was sure there would not be enough of a crew to damage us with musketry fire when we closed with her.

She hoisted no answering flag, so we hauled down the British flag, ran up the American flag, and fired a gun. She ran on as silently as before, a beautiful, high-sided ship, her mass of sails ruddy in the late afternoon sun. A cloud of pink smoke puffed from her stern; and a spout of water shot into the air two hundred yards ahead of us well off line.

"Hell," 'Lisha told me, "that's a twenty-four pound carronade! We can outrange her and take her from here."

"Go ahead," I said, having determined long ago never to risk losing a man if I could avoid it.

'Lisha sighted his long eighteen. The deck jerked; the gun roared; the white smoke came down around us. There was a distant crackle, like a dog crunching a stick between his jaws. The boat at the after davits seemed to fall apart reluctantly.

'Lisha cursed bitterly while the gun crew sponged and rammed, moving with seeming laziness, as they had been taught, but having the gun ready almost before the smoke from Pendleton Quint's gun had blown into our throats.

"There, by gravy!" said 'Lisha, squinting after Pendleton's shot. "Caught her that time!" A star-shaped patch of white splinters appeared at the stranger's water line.

'Lisha pulled his lanyard, and the ship's mizzenmast swayed drunkenly, just as she turned slowly into the wind. She ran up the British flag, only to haul it down instantly.

She was the ship *Auchterlonie*, Gilbert Lubbock, master, from St. Thomas for Bermuda, 518 tons and twenty-four men, armed with two twenty-four pound carronades and ten nine-pound carronades, and half laden with sugar and rum. I went aboard with Jeddy and found Lubbock feeling unhappy, as well he might.

"Here," I told him, "it's not your fault. If I didn't take you, somebody else would."

"Aye," he said, gazing bitterly at the *Lively Lady*, which seemed too small and battered, lying off to windward, to be anything but a tender for his splendid vessel, "but I could have stayed with the convoy another day or so."

Here was news indeed—news that might, if our luck held, result happily for us and sadly for the British. "That's true," I said, hoping to lead him into giving me further information, "but doubtless we'd have caught you in the end; for it's probably a small convoy, and weakly guarded, like most we find in these waters."

Lubbock nodded angrily. "Weakly!" he growled. "The word's as weak as the guard! If the Governors of the Bank of England followed the methods of the fools in the Admiralty, they'd toss their money in the street and set a sleepy midget to guard it! Thirty-two sail there were in our convoy when I hauled away, and no protection save the *Turnstone* sloop-of-war."

Delighted at what he told me, I assured him we would do all we could for him.

"Aye," he groaned, "in America."

"No," I said, "we'll try to get you another vessel somewhere. Anyway, America isn't so bad. All our prisoners are paroled."

"I dinna like the place," he growled. "It's either too hot or too cold, always, and not too bonnie, neither." As an afterthought he added, "But bonnier than the stone box the British have for prisoners. *They'll* give ye no parole!"

"I know," I said hastily, having heard enough of Dartmoor. "Where's your specie, Captain?"

He shrugged his shoulders and pressed his lips together stubbornly; then, evidently figuring on making the best of a bad bargain, he showed me the panel behind which he kept his specie kegs, they being made and marked to look like nail kegs. We rolled out twelve, containing thirty-five hundred English pounds, or in the neighborhood of eighteen thousand dollars. We took out some rum and small articles from the *Auchterlonie,* and bales of pink flamingo skins— birds that must look like patches of Maine sunsets, so beautifully rosy are their feathers. Then, though I disliked the thought of so many prisoners, we sent the captain and the crew to the *Lively Lady,* wheeled a carronade to the *Auchterlonie's* main hatch, and blew a hole in her bottom—though I couldn't help but hear the men growling while they did it.

We had brought Rowlandson Drown with us, in anticipation of needing a carpenter's help in scuttling her; and I think his grumbling was loudest. "We'd get forty thousand dollars for this ship if she was manned out for home," he told Seth Tarbox, his face dark with sourness; and unfortunately he was right.

* * *

It was dark when we set her afire and tumbled into our boat; and we wasted no time on rum or Spanish wine, for every last one of us panted to see the convoy of which Lubbock had spoken.

We paroled Captain Lubbock, the two Englishmen from the *Dos Hermanos,* the Spanish captain and McAndrew from Eli Bagley's brig; but we had to be watchful of the seamen lest they rise against us and seize the *Lively Lady* for themselves, which was why I disliked taking prisoners if I could avoid it; yet I couldn't turn them loose in a good ship when it was my purpose to distress the enemy in the greatest possible degree.

We bore off to the eastward, hunting for the convoy, and cruised for three days, with the weather what it so often is in those parts— bright blue overhead, fleecy beds of cloud near the horizon, and occasionally a sharp squall banging past with a thunderstorm in its arms. Toward mid-afternoon on the third day there was a bellowing of "Sail ho!" from the bow and the masthead at the same time, a distant squall having uncovered a white speck like the tip of a hen feather.

Hoping we had found the convoy, we held on our course, and soon discovered the stranger had hauled her wind and was bearing straight for us. Since there was no other sail in sight, we concluded she was in chase of us. We ran off on the other tack, figuring on getting to windward of her, whereupon she went off on the other tack herself, and we saw she was a schooner with a raking stern and bow and almost no freeboard, so that she seemed plastered to the water. She had tremendously tall raking masts and next to no top-hamper, there being only two shrouds to the foremast and one to the mainmast; and the masts, bending like fishing rods, seemed to spring the schooner ahead as though she were alive and being whipped along. She had a beautiful clean run, and she slipped over the waves, rather than through them, seeming to have no keel at all to hold her back.

"Well," I said, "there's only one place where they build schooners like that, and that's Baltimore." The others agreed, but we manned the long guns for the sake of safety and watched her whisk through the water. We saw she could weather us with no difficulty. Indeed, she was the fastest schooner I had ever seen. If we were logging twelve knots, which I think we were, she must have been logging thirteen and a half. I even think she was doing a knot or so better than that, but I am reluctant to say it for fear there will be folk to snort and declare no craft afloat can travel with such speed. I knew no Britisher could have overhauled her in a chase, so it seemed to me that she must be an American privateer. If I had not felt sure, I would have run from her long before; and I think I could have kept ahead of her until dark and then given her the slip.

We ran up the American flag, and I maneuvered to get under her lee; but a hen might as well have maneuvered to get under the lee of a kingfisher.

She came about and ran down on us. We could see she carried fourteen guns—two of them long guns—and had a sizable crew on deck. She hoisted the American flag and slipped alongside, not a half pistol shot away; and since there were no muskets leveled at us we knew her captain was certain of our nationality. None the less, her gun crews were at their stations, and a dark, slender man with a small black mustache, flashing white teeth, and elegant-seeming clothes clung to the ratlines, one hand on his hip, and shouted down wind, "What sloop is that?"

I rapped Pinky on the snout to stop his barking, he being beside me with his forepaws on the rail, considerably affronted by this stranger's question. "Private armed sloop *Lively Lady*, Nason, out of Arundel," I called back.

The dark man took off his gray beaver hat and made me a polite bow. "Schooner *Comet*," he shouted, "out of Baltimore; Boyle commanding. Would you do me the honor?"

We hove to, and I was rowed over to the *Comet,* where Boyle met me, hat in hand, as mannerly as though Commodore Truxton himself were coming over the side.

This Captain Thomas Boyle of Baltimore was the most affable man I have ever known, and the gentlest-seeming. Indeed, if I had not seen more of him at a later date, I might have thought his deference assumed; for it seemed to me, at times, that no man could be as gracious as he and still be serious about it. Yet he was always courteous, even to his men and prisoners; though there are captains of a score of British war craft and masters of almost a thousand British merchantmen who have declared he was the most tantalizing and troublesome man that ever lived.

He was, as I have said, gentle—so gentle, almost, as to seem harmless—and appreciative of things said by others. I noticed early in our acquaintance that if I was speaking with him and he was forced, for some reason, to interrupt the conversation, he would apologize profoundly at the earliest opportunity and ask me to be kind enough to proceed from the point where he had, as he put it, so rudely broken in on me.

He was quiet, too: the most deceptive man, it seems to me, that ever lived. His seamanship was a thing for seamen to marvel at, and I have never seen his equal for boldness. It was this boldness that so addled and fuddled the British; and it was common talk in French ports at one time that the captain of a British frigate had been so infuriated at Captain Boyle's behavior in the Channel that he had wept openly on his own quarter-deck from rage.

He took me below to a neat small cabin as pleasant to look at as his beautifully fitting broadcloth coat and pale-colored trousers buckled under his boots, and had out a mahogany chest inlaid with a satinwood lion and unicorn.

"I *do* hope you'll like this, Captain," he said, drawing out a five-sided bottle made from purple glass—the prettiest bottle I had ever seen. "It seems to me not half bad. I took it from a ship with a delightful captain: thirteen pipes of old Madeira wine, he had. This is from the oldest, and I find it passable, but I'm eager to have your opinion."

He took a goblet from the slots in the cover—a purple goblet, like the bottle—filled it for me, and watched me anxiously while I sipped. If the wine had been sea water and sour milk I would have praised it, because of his eager hospitality, but it seemed to be a blend of delicious fruits and faint perfumes and the essences of tropical nuts.

"Well," he said, when I spoke enthusiastically of it, "that is very kind of you. *Very* kind. Let us have another glass. Then you must tell me about your cruise. I hope and trust, Captain, that your cruise has been successful. Your idea of a small boat is excellent—excellent! Next year you may find a larger craft advisable; but what we need now is speed. I think you're exactly right."

"She's a tub beside yours," I said.

"No, your sloop is very fast, Captain Nason. You're too modest by far. You could have lost me in the dark if you'd tried."

"Yes, and if I'd tried, I might have been raked with a long twenty-four around midnight."

Captain Boyle laughed, a musical Southern laugh, quite in keeping with his voice, which, being soft and flat, was easy on the ear. "No, sir; I always talk things over with an enemy before I shoot, if it's possible."

"Well," I said, "I saw she was a Baltimore schooner, so I suspicioned you were American, but I never saw a Baltimore schooner behave like this. Sometimes she gets right up out of the water and flies."

"It's a pleasure to hear such appreciation from a seaman like yourself, Captain Nason," Captain Boyle assured me. He held up his purple goblet and stared through it at the scuttle overhead. "Now that you mention it, I feel free to tell you that so far as I know the *Comet* is the fastest Baltimore clipper ever built. She's faster than the little Baltimore-built government sloop *Enterprise*. Doubtless you remember her, Captain Nason. Before the navy cut down her masts and made her into an unbreakable brig she was said to be the fastest craft afloat. I'm *very* averse to saying it, sir; for I might be misunderstood; but you've seen the *Comet*, sir, from the deck of a fast sloop; so I'll tell you she's logged over fifteen knots."

I could make no reply to this except to whistle, which I did; and we had a drink on it.

"Well," I said, "I've had fair luck, but I hope to have better. There's a convoy of thirty-two sail bound for England under the sloop-of-war *Turnstone*."

"A convoy!" Boyle exclaimed, and his eyes, velvety brown eyes, seemed to glow with yellow lights. "A convoy! And only one sloop-of-war to guard it!"

We sipped our Madeira silently. I knew he was thinking longingly, as was I, of that diversity of vessels with the sloop-of-war fussing around them like a hen with a family of addle-pated chicks.

Finally Boyle shook his head. "I should be off about my business. I've taken nine prizes on this cruise and manned out six for American ports. My crew's reduced to forty-two men instead of the hundred and twenty with which I started; and I've a swarm of prisoners aboard, eating me out of house and home."

I asked him whether many privateers were putting to sea.

"Lord!" he said, chuckling a rich Southern chuckle, "the sea's full of 'em!" He threw himself back in his chair, hung a fawn-colored leg over its arm, looked up at the scuttle, and checked them off on his fingers. "Out of Baltimore alone there's Barney in the *Rossie* with a hundred and twenty men and fourteen guns, Grant in the *High Flyer*, Richardson in the *America*, Miller in the *Revenge* with sixteen guns and a hundred and forty men, Dooley in the *Rolla*, Wilson in the *Tom*. That's six. There's the *Dolphin*, the *Nonsuch*, the *Globe*, the *Wasp*, the *Hornet*, the *Liberty*: twelve. There's the *Sparrow*, thirteen, and the *Sarah Ann*, fourteen, all out of Baltimore. There must be three thousand Baltimore men at sea in privateers and letters-of-marque: all fast vessels, sir; fast and well armed; commanded by able men. Speaking of able men, Dominique Diron's out of Charleston in the *Decatur*. He's a Frenchman and a pirate, but he's able! There's some out of New York that you'll hear from, too: fast and dangerous—the *Governor Tompkins*, and the *General Armstrong*—by jolly, Captain Nason, there's a brig, the *General Armstrong*, with nineteen guns and a hundred and forty men, that would make trouble for any British sloop-of-war! There's the *Yorktown* and the *Holkar* and the *Anaconda*, each with a hundred and sixty men: there's the *Saratoga* and the *Orders in Council* and the *Benjamin Franklin*—and over a dozen more I'll call to mind in a minute. Why, they're coming out of the Chesapeake like a swarm of bees and pouring out of New York; and I've heard, Captain Nason, that New England's not being backward in the matter."

"They must be coming out of Salem and Boston almost as fast," I told him, "and they'll be out of Portsmouth and Newburyport in fair numbers, if they haven't started already."

He nodded. "If I knew how to do it, I'd bet a thousand dollars to a pipe of old Madeira that American privateers will capture or destroy five hundred British merchantmen in a year's time, and do more than a hundred million dollars' worth of damage."

"Don't you ever bet?" I asked him.

"Whenever I get the chance," Captain Boyle replied politely, "but I can't find anyone to take me up on that one."

"This convoy, now," I reminded him: "It would be an education to watch you in chase of it."

"That's very kind of you, sir: very kind," Captain Boyle said. "Not only kind, but gracefully expressed." He meditatively touched his small black mustache with his finger tips. "I should be getting home with my prisoners and refitting for another cruise." He stared at me thoughtfully. "But it would be mighty pleasant," he added, "to keep company with you against that flight of doves."

"I must get rid of my prisoners, too," I reminded him, "and I'll refit from one of the convoy if my luck holds." At this both of us rapped the table top with our knuckles.

He sighed gently. "I don't like to sail short-handed. It's an uncomfortable feeling if you have a sudden need to fight. Still, we may find a few Britishers who'll prefer our service to their own. It *has* been known to happen—" he smiled at me gaily—"so I'll go along with you a little way, though we can't expect to do much unless we get a bit of dirty weather."

I knew that here was a rare piece of good fortune, running into a seaman like Boyle and finding him willing to keep company with me against a convoy; for while it's not overdifficult to harry a convoy alone, provided you have luck, it's easier and surer when two together make the attack. None the less, I didn't begin to know how fortunate I was; for all I knew of Boyle was that he was a good seaman.

We arranged that the first to sight the convoy should run down to the other so that plans might be made, and that if the convoy should be sighted by one while we were separated, the discoverer should hang astern of it for three days before attacking, in the hope that the other would come up.

So we cruised off to the northwest, being already on the trade route; and I was almost discouraged at the manner in which the *Comet* outsailed us, even though we cracked on all we had. Yet we hung together by dint of Boyle making long reaches to windward and to leeward, and so worked up in the general direction of the Azores.

The bright blue sky that had favored us so long was filmed with a loose gray veil on the second or third day, and the wind had started to pick the tops from the waves, shake them to pieces and toss them against our mainsail, when Pomp, riding high and darksome at the masthead, shouted that the *Comet* had put about. We made her out shortly, bearing down on us like a distant gull; and ten minutes later, when she had taken on size, Pomp went to shouting, "Sail ho! Sail ho! Sail ho!" until I thought he had lost his mind.

But the men in the bow moved excitedly and looked back at us, so I knew we had sighted the convoy. With that I put the sloop into the wind, hoping we had escaped their notice; and in the southwest I saw, faint and far off, a small gray dot that came and went, and then another, and then two more close together. I didn't bother to hunt for others, for they couldn't be far away, I knew, and it was a pleasant thought that within our reach were more than thirty West Indiamen laden with millions of dollars' worth of rum and sugar and India goods, and God knows how many kegs of specie.

The *Comet* came slipping up under our lee as easy and graceful as a seal, and Boyle waved his gray beaver to me, affable and polite and anxious to please.

The men crowded up to look at him when he came aboard; and I could tell from this how they felt toward him; for our Maine men won't stir two feet to see a person like the Dey of Algiers, who has nothing but wealth and position to his credit.

He glanced around at them and smiled a bashful smile, very friendly. "Well, Captain," he said, bowing a quick little bow to me, but speaking, I was sure, for the benefit of the crew, "it looks as though England might find herself somewhat poorer by dawn to-morrow."

XIII

Wᴇɴ we had made our plans, we payed off to the southward till dusk; then turned to the northeast in the track of the convoy. It was a night of pale darkness with a smart wind from the east; yet it was not bad, for the stars shone, and the sea was nothing to cause us inconvenience, though the decks were wet with scud, and there was a moaning in our top-hamper that foretold heavier weather.

The *Comet* stood along within half pistol shot of us under a reefed mainsail and jib, so we might hang together. We could make her out clearly, skimming along as easily as the deep-sea birds that follow craft for days in mid-ocean, remaining always a foot above the waves. She was as silent as though she sailed without a crew, with no figure showing on her decks except that of the helmsman. Not a sound could I hear from her above the complaining of our mast, the screaking of the boom and the gun carriages, and the gushing rush of the waves along our sides. Yet I knew her people were on deck, as were our own, armed with cutlasses and boarding axes, the sharpshooters ready with their muskets, and all of them lying under the bulwarks or sprawled around the long guns.

When we had held our course for two hours, there was a hoarse half shout of "Sail ho!" from the bow. In the same instant I heard the same half-stifled call from the deck of the *Comet,* and as if she had been nothing more substantial than a fog she sheered away and was gone in the gloom.

I saw the bulk of a smallish vessel on our lee bow. We came up on her fast. I caught sight of the light from her binnacle and made her out to be a small brig. We hauled a little away; then ranged alongside. There was a shout from the man at the helm of the brig. With that Jeddy clapped his hands, and our boarders came out from under the bulwarks and went over the brig's side and into her waist, fast and silently.

There were four men on the brig's deck, unarmed and with no thought of attack, so when Jeddy led a boarding party of ten toward the stern and Rowlandson led another ten toward the bow, all with cutlasses swinging, there was no opposition and no noise save another shout or two and a little thudding of feet on the deck.

In five minutes Rowlandson's ten boarders were back again. The brig came about, according to plan, and the two of us bore off to the southwest, all without a shot being fired or a flare kindled to give the alarm.

For fifteen minutes we drove back on this course, keeping the brig close under our lee; then, having put five miles between ourselves and the convoy, we hove to once more and settled the business.

The brig proved to be the *Star of the Indies,* Fagin, master, two six-pounders and a crew of nine, from Jamaica for Liverpool, laden with rum, sugar, and fresh fruits. Also she had two thousand dollars in specie, which we promptly seized. Having no time to waste, I proposed to the captain that if he would put his men to work transferring a part of his fresh fruit to the *Lively Lady,* receive on board our prisoners, and engage to sail northwest for two days, so that he would be in no likelihood of picking up the convoy again, I would transfer one third of the brig to him and one third to Captain Lubbock, who had told me of the convoy, and one third to the remainder of the prisoners and his crew and set them all free. Otherwise, I told him, I would take him and his men prisoners and scuttle his brig to boot.

I thought, when I was done speaking, that the captain would jump down my throat in his eagerness to accept; and two hours later we were once more on our way to the northeast, free of prisoners and keeping a sharp lookout for the *Comet.*

A little after half-past ten we made out a sail on our weather beam and were sure we had again come up with the convoy. When we found this craft to be another small brig, we fell away from her, wishing bigger game. We were soon rewarded by sighting a large ship, and without more ado ran under her lee and ordered her to wear immediately and head southeast, or we'd sink her. This was the plan made between Captain Boyle and myself—that I should run my second prize off to the southeast while he ran off to the northwest. Thus if one of us should be pursued by the convoying sloop, the other would have time to strip his prize.

Instead of obeying our order, the ship held on her way, firing a gun. We heard no wail from the shot; so she may have fired it to warn the others. At this 'Lisha Lord rapped out a quick order to the musket men, as we had agreed. A crackling of small arms sent pale flashes against her sails and the smoke wisps that still clung to them. There was a crying-out on her deck, indicating that Moody Haley and Moses Burnham had poured their fire into the helmsman.

"Wear ship!" I shouted again, "or I'll blow you to pieces."

She came about slowly. Ahead of her a blue flare blazed in a ship's bows, revealing faintly luminous mainsails, topsails, and topgallant sails against a wavering background of blue light. Two miles to leeward another blue flare shone out; and then a third, almost a mile away. There was no way of telling whether they had been set off out of fright at hearing the gun, or whether Boyle had swooped down on another of the convoy and so put all of them into the tremors.

Now a strange thing happened when we had run this ship five miles to the southeastward and hove her to; for when I boarded her I found a person I had known before; and though I had no thought of meeting an acquaintance, I felt no surprise at the encounter any more than as though I had expected it.

The ship was the *Lord Startham*, James Houie, master, from Kingston to Falmouth, 407 tons, 10 guns and eighteen men—or what had been eighteen men; for our musketry fire had killed the helmsman and wounded the first mate. She was laden with sugar, rum and indigo, and carried 8,250 English pounds in specie. Not liking the groans of the first mate, poor man, who had been shot through the lungs, I sent back the boat to bring aboard our doctor, Jotham Carr, ordered the indigo to be swayed up from the hold for transfer to the *Lively Lady*, and rapidly proceeded to an examination of the ship's papers, knowing the sloop-of-war might come down on us at any moment.

I discovered there were three passengers aboard, one of them a Mr. Sanderson, manager of a sugar plantation in Jamaica, and the others his wife and her maid. I had no liking for this; for there was no place on our sloop for women, nor had I any desire to encumber myself with prisoners.

"Have these people brought here," I said to the captain, for whom I had little sympathy because he had kept on his course when I hailed him. "I think they should have something to say concerning their disposition."

Sanderson proved to be a young man with a pleasant dignity about him and a look that struck me as vaguely familiar. With him came his wife, a pretty blonde girl of a washed-out appearance, as though she had stood too long in tropical rainstorms, and behind her a maid whom I could see but dimly in the light of the whale-oil lamp, which swung in figure eights with the uneasy rolling of the ship.

"I'm sorry for all this," I said to them, wondering where I had seen Sanderson before, "but I hold a commission to take, burn, sink, or destroy all enemy craft, and this ship must be sunk. Now, I can do either of two things, and because of Mrs. Sanderson I'll let you say which it shall be. Either I can take all of you as prisoners to my sloop, which is small and uncomfortable, and destroy this ship; or I can stand by you till morning, run you within sight of the convoy, and set you afire. Then the sloop-of-war will take you off, or you can go in your boats to one of the other vessels. There's some danger in the first course, for nobody can tell when we'll be fired on ourselves. As for the second course, if you go aboard a merchantman, she may quickly be captured herself, so you'll have it all to do over again."

When I said this my eye caught a movement of the maid behind Mrs. Sanderson. I stared hard at her and saw she had a gray, reminiscent look. Her face seemed to soften a little from its grimness, as though she wished to smile but couldn't quite decide on it. I knew then I had seen this grim gray woman in a field near Saco. Her name, I remembered, was Annie; she had given Jeddy and me a glass of wine at the behest of Lady Emily Ransome. It seemed a queer thing, the thought that flashed through my head when I recognized her; for it was the thought that this was quite right and proper: that the whole affair had happened this way before, which of course it hadn't.

Having glanced at me, she looked quickly down at the cabin floor again. It occurred to me it might be well to wait before seeming to recognize her, lest the Sandersons annoy us with questions and make it more difficult for me to do what I had to do. Also she put other thoughts in my head: thoughts of Lady Ransome's hoity-toityness: of how she had looked with my knife clasped tight in her hands, cutting her initials on the old beech tree: of my miniature of her, which, as it happened, I had in my breast pocket even now. It happened, too, that I had a thought to speak to Annie alone.

Before the Sandersons could answer my question, young Jotham Carr came in at the cabin door. "Captain," he said, "the mate's dead."

"Well," I said, looking at Houie, "I'm sorry to hear it. It would never have happened if you hadn't been so injudicious as to run from an armed vessel at night."

"Captain," said Sanderson, "we'd be obliged to you if you'd let us remain on board this ship to-night. I'd prefer not to trust my wife to a small boat in a choppy sea."

"Very good," I told him; "and how'll you feel if it comes on to blow a gale and you have to get off in it to-morrow?"

He stared at me without speaking. I strove hard to fix my mind on the colting I had received aboard the *Gorgon*, for I had no more love for the business than Sanderson had.

"My wife has been ill," Sanderson said. "I'm taking her home in the hope she'll recover."

There it was: what I had dreaded. If I have learned anything about war in the little I have seen of it, it's that you mustn't think of the enemy as human beings, like yourself, but as some sort of devouring monsters capable of doing any wicked deed: that you must think of everyone as nothing more than worthless playing cards or chessmen, to be tossed away or crushed or destroyed so long as advantages are gained and battles won; otherwise there seems to be nothing worth fighting about. Yet in spite of knowing all this I had let Sanderson mention his wife's illness; and on top of everything I had been such a fool as to listen to him.

"Well," I said, thinking hard of how I could learn more about Annie without seeming to ask, "your wife will probably be all right, with the sea voyage and all. She's fortunate to have a woman to look out for her. I should think it would be hard to get such a woman in the Indies."

"Oh, we'd never have got her in the Indies," he said. "I wrote to my sister in England, and she sent her out to me."

"Oh, did she!" I said weakly, for his mention of his sister in England, coupled with Annie's presence, had made it plain to me at last why I had found a familiar look about him. It was because his sister had married Sir Arthur Ransome.

I strove to decide what should be done, and the more I strove, the more I regretted my misfortune in encountering such people as Sanderson and his blue-eyed ailing wife. For a moment I considered sending for Jeddy, knowing he held himself merciless where Britishers were concerned; but I could see it was a matter I must settle myself.

"Well," I said at length, watching Sanderson carefully to see whether he might not give me reason to be harsh with him, "I've heard that turn about is fair play, and if this is so, I must remind myself that a few weeks before this war broke out I was taken from my brig by a press gang from the crew of the *Gorgon* sloop-of-war and whipped for nothing except to gratify the spleen of her captain, and be damned to him."

Sanderson twisted up the corner of his mouth and looked at me out of eyes the color of smoke, so that I stared at him in a sort of confusion because of the memories of Lady Ransome that crowded my brain. "All Englishmen aren't like that," he said.

"Probably not," I admitted, "but since England filled her ships for this war out of jails and poorhouses, the Englishmen that Americans see are worse than anything we've ever been able to imagine."

"I've heard so," he said. "It's a great pity."

"Oh," I said, "there's no use going over and over all this! If you and the captain will give me your word to keep away from the convoy and make no further effort to join it, I'll turn you loose with your cargo. But I wish a paper signed—a paper saying it's done because of Mrs. Sanderson, and for no other reason, and stipulating that half the sale price of the cargo belongs to her."

"Sir——" said Sanderson in a choked voice; but I had no time to listen to further talk.

"Is that agreed, yes or no?" I asked.

Since there was nothing else for the captain to do, he agreed.

"Very well," I said gruffly to him in response. "You'll step into Mr. and Mrs. Sanderson's cabin and draw up the paper instantly." As he seemed to demur and cavil, "Instantly!" I repeated sharply. "I mean the three of you!"

They obeyed me, and I turned to Annie, who seemed about to follow. I frowned, to cover an unreasonable embarrassment. "You'll remain here," I said, and I fear I looked foolish. "You're not needed in the drawing up of such a paper, I take it."

"No, sir," she returned meekly, leaning against the table and swaying with the slow rocking of the ship. "You have something you wish to say to me, sir?"

I stared at her sternly. "No, I haven't."

"You didn't wish to ask——"

"Well," I said negligently, "I seem to recall having seen you. I seem to have seen you in attendance on Sir Arthur Ransome at——"

"No, Captain," she said quietly, "upon Lady Ransome."

"It may be; it may be," I returned. "I suppose they were both quite well when you last saw them? They reached home safely?"

"Quite safely," she said. "They went straight to Ransome Hall, near Exeter."

"Exeter?" I asked. "Oh, yes: they went to Exeter. But this ship is outward bound from Jamaica. She—they left home again, possibly."

"It was I," she said, looking down at her feet. "I was not to stay there long myself. We were home in May, and in June Lady Ransome sent me to her brother's wife in Jamaica."

"Oh," I said, "to her brother's wife! Indeed!"

She glanced toward the door of the Sandersons' cabin, which was just off that of the master, in which we stood. "Yes, Captain."

I stroked my chin. "You've been long in Lady Ransome's service?"

"Since she was twelve years old, Captain." Suddenly she gave a hiccup and went to sniveling and catching her breath, most distressing.

"I can't see how she could let you go so far away, if she thought so highly of you," I said.

"It was over something that was lost."

"You mean something belonging to Lady Ransome?" I asked. "Something she thought you'd stolen?"

"Oh, no, sir! It was S'Roth! This thing was lost, and I was the last one to see it; and S'Roth was angry and kept saying I should take better care of m'lady's things."

It seemed as though I might burst in this small cabin, what with the heat and all. "Did he nag at her?" I asked. "Did he nag at his—at Lady Ransome?"

"Oh, sir," she cried, "he's a devil! He's forever peering and prying! He kept at m'lady and kept at her about it, and kept at her to get rid of me and get somebody who could be trusted not to lose valuable things, and at last he said I'd have to go."

I could see Sir Arthur's thin, pale face before me and hear his whining voice chewing at his words and pushing them up against his teeth.

I stood and simmered for a while, rolling Annie's revelations through my head. Talk, I knew, would remedy nothing; my best procedure was to let well enough alone and hold my tongue. Yet I could not bring myself to drop the subject, not until I had asked Annie one more question; so I coughed and cleared my throat, and finally said to her: "What was it she lost? Was it—was it a piece of—was it a piece of jewelry?"

At this Annie nodded violently and burst into a storm of tears, so that it would have been difficult for me to question her further, even though I had wished to.

Somewhat uncertainly, I fear, I watched her and thought of many things to say but didn't say them. Instead, I finally broke out with, "Well, it's too late to mend matters now," and I added, not quite knowing what I meant myself: "A present's a present and couldn't be returned without insult, so stop your sniveling!"

Upon this, much befuddled in my mind, I strode out to the main deck and gave a great many orders in an angry voice. Among them was one to Jeddy, which he heartily misliked—to take fifty gold sovereigns from the specie kegs and carry them to Annie.

Seeing he was averse to the task, and being a little clearer in my mind, I took the sovereigns myself and went below. Truth to tell, I could not leave the ship until I had seen Annie once more. She was sitting in the cabin where I had left her, staring down at her folded hands.

"Now, here," I said, dropping the sovereigns in her lap, "I don't understand this. I can't wait around here all night listening to hints. Do you understand?"

"Yes, sir," Annie replied.

"Well, then," I said, "well, then—ah—you say there was—that is to say, you could see that this man—this gentleman we were speaking of—you could see he wasn't always—ah—pleasant?"

"Yes, sir."

"Well," I said, impatient at her slowness, "speak up! Don't beat about the bush!"

"Oh, sir!" Annie said, "it was a great mistake, and such a pretty little thing, always gay and happy; and now sour looks if she so much as laughs at anything! She'll be old and bitter while she's still a baby."

"Old and bitter!" I repeated, recalling how Lady Ransome had bound up my head in Arundel, and how I had felt her soft arm against my cheek. "I won't—a man can't—there must have been some help for it!" I looked up at the whale-oil lamp, jerking at its chains with the wallowing of the ship. I thought it burned dimly. The reek of it seemed to irritate my eyes and throat. "You can always get—I mean, couldn't anybody help—couldn't you help her? Couldn't you do anything?" I may have shaken the cabin table overstrongly, for I heard the mahogany crack.

She looked away from me thoughtfully. "I?" she asked. "I? What could I do? Now, you——"

"I?" I asked. "What could *I* do?"

"I think," she said, moving uncomfortably, "I think she'd like to see you again."

"See me?" I demanded. "Why should she want to see me? How could she see me when my country's at war with England?"

"And will you be fighting forever?" she asked.

I thought the matter over and over, but I could make next to nothing out of it except that it would be well if I did what I could to see that this war of ours was as short as I could help to make it.

* * *

It must have been one o'clock in the morning when we finished loading the indigo and specie aboard the sloop and hauled away

from the *Lord Starham*. Toward morning the east wind that had
threatened us the night before died completely, and we lay and
wallowed on a turbulent gray-blue sea. On the following day the
breeze came up again from the west, and we moved along in search
of the convoy, without finding it. During the night, however, we
heard the sound of guns and guessed that the *Comet* was at them
again. Early the next morning we found them, twenty-seven sail,
huddled together so close that from where we watched them they
looked as though a skysail could have been thrown over the lot, barring one, which hung in their rear, so that I knew it was the *Comet*.

While we watched, one of the convoy put about and started back
toward the single sail, all very small and distant to the eye; and we
heard guns, though we were too far off to see the smoke, even.

It seemed plain to me that the *Comet* was harrying the convoy
for the deviltry of it, and that the *Turnstone* was seeking to chase
her away or get within striking distance of her. If Boyle wished to
play that game, I thought, I could do nothing but help him; and
with that I crowded on all sail and moved off to the westward; then
bore north; and in two hours' time we had run well ahead of the
convoy and were bearing down on its weather bow.

The *Turnstone* was still playing at long balls with Boyle, and I
hoped to reach one of the convoy before she could return; but it was
impossible; for when the convoy sighted us they ran together like
frightened quail and fired guns, whereupon the cruiser put about
instantly and returned to them.

We lay off, a little out of gunshot in case the *Turnstone* took it
into her head to let drive at us with her long guns; and while we lay
there, studying the convoy and picking out the craft that looked most
likely as prizes, Boyle did a thing I was glad to have seen, so that
if ever I could have a fast enough craft, I might some day find myself
in a position to profit by the lesson.

He bore off to windward of the convoy, which was closely
bunched, with the sloop-of-war herding them along in the rear, and
then came running along toward us, as pretty a sight as ever was.
The masts of his graceful craft seemed to bend and give like willow
branches and to thrust her along by their bending, as a strip of
whalebone, pressed against a slender board, might spring it through
the water. The *Comet* came close up under our lee; and Boyle, affable and dapper, clung to a stay and waved his hat.

"You'll dine with me, Captain?" he shouted.

I nodded.

"Pray put about," he called. "I'll be back in half an hour."

We payed off and watched him. He stood past the convoy; then tacked suddenly and shot across its bow. With that the *Turnstone* moved out from behind the merchantmen and set off after Boyle. But Boyle, having rounded the head of the convoy, hauled his wind in a flash and slipped down the opposite side, having put the entire fleet between himself and the sloop-of-war; and to us it seemed, and was indeed the fact, that the *Turnstone's* movements, by comparison with those of the *Comet*, were like those of a clumsy, flustered crow attempting to escape the agile dartings of a kingbird.

While our crew, and our officers as well, for that matter, stamped their feet at the bulwarks, shouting with laughter and waving their caps at this display of speed and agility, the *Comet* rounded to and shot alongside a fine large ship. What happened then we could not see, except that the *Turnstone* labored slowly around the head of her clumsy charges. Before she had rounded them we saw well what it was that had occurred; for the *Comet's* head payed off again, and she flew on her way down the convoy's lee side, while from the deck of the ship at which she had stopped there rose a pale wavering haze of smoke—a haze that grew thicker as we watched; then suddenly billowed out and puffed upward, enveloping the mainsail, topsail, and topgallant sail in a pillar of smoke and flame. We could see the *Turnstone* come up with the burning vessel and heave to, so the crew might be picked up, and all the while the *Comet* foamed along behind us, as swift and innocent-looking as a teal duck skimming the surface of a marsh.

She drew abreast, so close we could see the rings in the gun tompions and the gold key dangling at the end of Captain Boyle's watch fob as he stood by the wheel, beaming at us and feeling tenderly of his small mustaches.

He lifted his hat debonairly as our crew manned the rail to cheer him.

When I stepped aboard the *Comet* a few moments later he said apologetically, "I hope I haven't made you hungry, Captain! I'm some minutes late; but dinner's waiting in my cabin."

XIV

I<small>T WAS</small> on the fifteenth of December that the *Lively Lady* came through the teeth of a blow into the Bay of Biscay, got under the lee of the land, and made the mouth of the Loire; and I know of nothing that had ever looked more welcome to me—barring our own oblong patch of farmland in Arundel—than the calm surface of the river, the bright green islands in it, and the small stone houses on the low-lying banks.

We had clung to the lee of the convoy until a gale of wind blew up from the northwest, whereupon that had happened which always happens with a convoy: it had been scattered by the blow, some heaving to, some scudding under bare poles, and some setting a few rags of sail and holding their course as best they could. While they were thus scattered we captured, in two days' time, a ship and two brigs without the firing of a gun; and it was with the last of them that our trouble started.

The brig *Loyal Nancy* was laden with 146 puncheons of Jamaica rum and some mahogany; and we took out her crew and burnt her. The brig *Hesperides* was laden with rum, sugar and coffee, and 2,300 English pounds in specie; and we took out her crew, used her as a target, and sank her. The ship *Rose of the West* was laden with 320 hogsheads of sugar and 90 seroons of indigo, the latter having a value of $18,000.

This *Rose of the West* was a handsome ship of 400 tons; and after we had taken the indigo from her with great difficulty because of the roughness of the sea, I gave orders to burn her, though I regretted the destruction of so staunch a craft. Before my orders were carried out, Rowlandson Drown, with three of the men, came to me. Rowlandson, his dark gray face pushed forward by his thick bull neck, looked mulish and lowering.

"Captain," Rowlandson said, "there's been some talk among the men about the destruction of these vessels. It seems to us as how it might be possible to make a dollar out of this ship if she was handled different."

"How would you propose to handle her, Rowlandson?" I asked,

fearful that I had overlooked something, and desirous of getting as much prize money as could be got.

Jeddy thrust in a contemptuous oar. "He wants to make chairs out of her and raft 'em ashore."

"Go ahead, Rowlandson," I told him. "Let's hear what's on your mind."

"Well," he said, "it appears to us we must be close to some port or other after all this sailing. We could put a prize crew aboard that ship and run her in."

"No," I told him, "I won't do it, Rowlandson. We came out intending to man out no prizes, and we're not equipped for it."

"Couldn't you spare four men?" he asked.

"No," I told him, "I'd have to send a navigator with them. I can't spare them, anyway. We've got barely enough men as it is."

"We could sell that ship for forty thousand dollars!"

"You could if a sloop-of-war didn't take you prisoner, which it probably would, and if you got to port, which you probably wouldn't. I won't do it."

"A dollar's a dollar!" Rowlandson grumbled. He stood looking at me, gray-faced and glum, but I shook my head.

"It isn't safe," I told him. "What I'm doing is best for all of us."

In spite of his dissatisfaction and that of a good part of the crew, when we slipped into the yellow waters of the Loire we had a cargo aboard that weighed little but was almost as valuable, we later learned, as those brought in on the first cruises of the *True Blooded Yankee* or the *Comet* or the *Grand Turk* or the *Governor Tompkins,* or the *General Armstrong* or the sloop *Polly* out of Salem, or the *Harpy* of Baltimore, privateers that made enormous sums from the beginning, and harried the British until the very mention of their names was enough to cause a flutter in the insurance rates.

* * *

We found Nantes a good town, as Captain Boyle had told us, though there was an air of depression and sorrow to the place, and unusual numbers of womenfolk. For every man that met the eye there were three women—all on account of the millions of men that Bonaparte had slaughtered in the making of his vainglorious wars.

There was infinite detail to the sale of our cargo, which had to be done slowly by French agents; and after that there would be the figuring of shares and the refitting for another cruise, so I left the crew aboard the sloop and went to take lodgings at the Golden Eagle Inn—L'Aigle d'Or: a tall, narrow building facing the Place du Com-

merce, near where the small river Erdre flows through the city and
into the Loire.

Captain Boyle had told me that all American captains patronized
L'Aigle d'Or when they were in Nantes, because the proprietor, M.
Marcel Solbert, had spent several months in America and learned
what he believed to be English. M. Solbert met me at the door and
immediately proved that he thought he spoke our tongue.

"Ah!" he said, clasping his hands in front of him like a woman.
"Ah! Gentiman, you are *capitaine*, eh? Ah, *oui!* Gentiman, you live
Philadelphia, no? I have work wiss *livres* in *maison de livres de mon
ami*, M'sieu le Comte Moreau Saint-Méry in Philadelphia, eh?"

He took me to my room, a narrow room with windows opening
on a courtyard smelling peculiarly of stables, soapsuds and cheese
rind; and when I came down I met three other American captains,
all waiting impatiently in Nantes until their cargoes should be sold
—Captain Dawson of the letter-of-marque schooner *Ned* of Baltimore; Captain Troutman of the privateer schooner *Lion* out of Mar-
blehead, and Captain Hewes of the privateer *Leo* out of Boston.

Through them I found agents—the Latour brothers: polite men
with bushy whiskers large enough for squirrel nests—and thought to
settle down to wait for our rich booty to be turned into money; but
there was such an air of discomfort about the country, what with
Bonaparte's terrible battles and the ghastly news of the death of four
hundred thousand Frenchmen on the steppes of Russia, and the con-
scriptions that were forever taking place to provide more men to be
slaughtered, that none of us could rest easy.

We set out again in February to chasten the British, believing
that when we were back from our cruise the Latours would have
settled our affairs. Yet I think I would have done better to stay on
shore: for we were twice chased away from prizes by British frigates; and when the cruise was over the men, headed by Rowlandson
Drown, were grumbling louder than ever, demanding a larger vessel
and crew so we could man out our prizes.

When we were back in Nantes, furthermore, I found the Latours
had disposed of our cargo to such good advantage that I dared not
tell the crew for fear their newly acquired wealth would make them
unwilling to risk their skins in fighting; since every ordinary seaman's
share now amounted to something better than twenty-four hundred
dollars. Consequently I kept my own counsel, banked the money
with the Latours, refitted the sloop; and early in May, when the hawthorns were pink-and-white clouds against the rich green of the
swelling fields, we slipped down the Loire again and stood off to

the northwestward on a cruise that, for general cussedness, would have been difficult to beat.

We ran straight into one of the hellish westerly gales that blow into the Bay of Biscay with hurricane force, kicking up such seas that a sloop the size of ours is stuck against the face of one of them like a fly against the page of a book; and we, clinging to our canted deck, must look upward to the crest of the wave and downward to the trough of it, with no horizon at all save that furnished by our own wave and the next one to it.

The gale seemed bent on wringing the *Lively Lady* as a woman wrings a towel, twisting the stern in one direction and the bow in another. We were obliged to heave-to under a double-reefed mainsail, nor did one of us dare move without a leg or an arm hooked around something, lest we be snapped through the air like a whip lash.

Fearing for Pinky, I tied him tight in a blanket and corded him to the roof of the cabin, where he hung with head protruding and whiskers a-bristle, barking passionately when lamps were broken from their fastenings and every loose object sent flying from one side of the cabin to the other. After four hours of this a tremendous sea came down with a roar in the wake of our starboard shrouds. It seemed to me we were gone; but the sloop struggled gradually upright, and I found the force of the blow had broken one of the top timbers and split open the plank-sheer, so that I could look directly down into the hold.

Knowing one more like this would leave us clinging to splintered spars in the cold green surges that towered around us, I sent Jeddy and 'Lisha Lord and Cromwell and Rowlandson Drown to cut loose a spare boom. This we spanned with a piece of new four-inch rope; and to the bight of the span I had them fasten our small bower cable. The other end of the cable we fastened to our mast. Thereupon we threw over the boom, paying out sixty fathoms of cable, and at once the sloop came head to the wind, riding as easily as a mallard; for the boom not only acted as a floating anchor, holding us in place, but it broke the ragged crests from the seas and forced them to march at us in a more orderly manner, instead of rushing from every direction like becrazed things. Thus it gave us a chance to nail tarred canvas over our broken plank-sheer; and we rode out the gale without further injury.

Following this we gave chase to a ship, lost her in the darkness, cruised two days in search of her, picked her up again, and lost her for good during the night. We sighted a brig and hove her to, only to find she was an ancient craft, in ballast and not worth sinking, so we let her go. Then we lay and creaked in a calm for two days, a hot, steamy, uneasy calm, smelling of newly caught fish, after which we suffered from light and variable airs that left us wallowing here and there like a drunken seaman.

We were well over toward the coast of Cornwall one dismal morning when the lookout sighted two craft in the southwest. We made all sail in chase of them, and when we discovered that one was a ship and the other a small xebec—a xebec being a three-masted craft with square sails on the foremast and lateen sails on the main and mizzenmasts—it seemed to us our luck had taken a turn for the better.

When we came up with the ship, she hoisted English colors. It seemed strange to me that she should be so slow a sailer, for she had the appearance of smartness; so we hoisted American colors, bore up and gave her both long guns, hulling her near the water line. I thought for a moment she had struck, for she lowered her ensign. The men set up a roar; but there was something about her I misliked. She kept a small yellow flag at her main, which seemed contrary to good sense; then, in merchantman fashion, hauled up her mainsail slowly and clumsily backed her maintopsail.

I shouted to 'Lisha Lord that something was wrong and immediately wore ship, passing into her wake. When we were in a raking position, 'Lisha and Pendleton Quint gave her both long guns, and we could see the distant cabin windows go out as the grape and the round shot went in.

The gun crews stood with open mouths, waiting for her to come into the wind in token of surrender. Instead of that, she wore; and as she wore she ran up her ensign again. Ports flew open along her gun deck, and we saw she was a heavy sloop-of-war, disguised by closed ports and by having a tier of ports painted on a strip of canvas stretched over the channels, so to look like a merchantman.

"My God!" 'Lisha shouted. "It's the *Gorgon!*"

Her side disappeared in a white cloud, above which we could see her sails spreading, fast, as no merchantman ever set them.

The round shot from her broadside went over us, wailing like giant sea gulls, and there was the clattering hiss of passing grapeshot, a most unsettling noise.

I heard a grinding thump from the waist. When I looked along the deck I saw a round shot had caught poor black Sip, the brother of Pomp, and taken his hip away. He lay there looking first at the great raw hole in himself; then up at Pendleton Quint; then back at himself again, with a terrible look of anxious surprise on his face.

Pendleton jumped over him and sighted his gun, careful and delicate, as if sighting at a distant goose. He pulled the lanyard, and the
smoke blew down across us, setting us to coughing and filling our
eyes with moisture. When it blew away, Jotham Carr had got Sip
out from under the feet of the men, so they could load with no
interference.

We made sail upon the wind and left her very fast; but fast as
we left the *Gorgon*—if indeed it was the *Gorgon*, as 'Lisha Lord said
and swore—it was nothing to the quickness with which Sip left us.
He lay in the scuppers for a time; for Jotham Carr refused to let us
move him, saying it would be no use and would only hurt Sip. He
smiled a gray smile up at me. "Gosh," he whispered in his flat Maine
speech, that seemed to me so strange to come from a black man's
lips, "smoky wind, Cap'n Dick—good troutin'—Kimball's Brook—le's
go fishin'—to-morrah——"

So Sip went home to Arundel; and I, remembering it was I who
had persuaded him and Pomp to leave their little cabin on the high
land above the marshy banks of our river, wished myself back where
I could hear the red-winged blackbirds chucking and whistling in
the bayberries at the edge of our creek—where I would never have
to smell gunpowder again.

*   *   *

It was the devil's own work to hold the men in hand and get the
Lively Lady out of the Loire again that autumn. The amount of our
prize money had leaked out and been magnified in the leaking; and
so sure were the men that they were close to having the wealth of
merchant princes that I was hard put to it to make them remember
our country was still at war. They let slip no chance to remind me
they were set on sailing in a larger vessel than the *Lively Lady;* and
I knew it to be true that the increasing wariness of the British made
it advisable for privateersmen to use larger craft, heavily armed and
manned. None the less I knew the *Lively Lady* was a lucky boat,
whereas God alone could tell what our fortune might be if we
changed.

Finally I got her to sea again, and the cussedness of this cruise
was greater, even, than that of the preceding one.

Again and again we were robbed of prizes by the alertness of British cruisers; and once a fast British merchantman struck her colors
to us toward dusk, let us slip alongside her, then ran up her colors,
opened fire once more, cut up our rigging so that our mainsail came
down on the run, and finally escaped us in the dark. To cap it all,

while we were cruising off the Spanish coast, we found ourselves one dawn in the midst of the whole British fleet supporting Wellington's armies. We tacked like a fly dodging a broom, got some holes in our sails and one through our hull, and to escape had to throw over our carronades, so that the only guns left to us were our two long eighteens.

When, therefore, we saw the islands of the Loire again, the men were glum and dark and truculent, and I was no less gloomy than they.

*   *   *

There were new faces in the narrow front room of L'Aigle d'Or when I came into it on a dark night in early December, though Captain Hewes was still there, a bottle of Vouvray before him and a stranger sitting across from him—a stranger whose hat perched precariously on the side of his head.

Hewes pushed a glass of Vouvray into my hand before I could unbutton my jacket. "We needed you," he said. "Dawson sailed for home, and Troutman was captured; and France has too many Frenchmen in it for our taste. Captain Hailey and me, we're getting lonesome."

"Hailey?" I asked, looking quickly at the stranger.

"You hit it!" Captain Hewes laughed. "He's the one: captain of the *True Blooded Yankee,* out of Brest."

Now there was no American seaman who hadn't heard wild yarns of the brig *True Blooded Yankee,* though she had been privateering only since late in February or early in March; but, accustomed as I had become to hearing fantastic tales of our privateersmen, I didn't believe the tenth of what I heard about the *True Blooded Yankee,* any more than a grown man believes fo'c'sle rumors of the *Flying Dutchman.*

"Well, sir," I said to Captain Hailey, "I'm glad to meet you and find you're flesh and blood and not some sort of corposant that's been fevering the brains of the British."

Hailey laughed and lifted his hat, replacing it on the opposite side of his head, tilted at the same dangerous angle.

"Why," he asked. "What have I done now?"

"We heard you'd captured an island in the Channel and held it two days," I said.

Hailey scratched contemplatively at the corner of his mouth. "That wa'n't quite so," he said.

"Well, it didn't sound reasonable to me," I told him.

"What happened," Hailey said, "was that we rammed a wreck off the Irish coast and had to careen ourselves somewheres and fit two new planks; so we picked ourselves a nice island and took it and put the natives to work. There was an armed schooner that thought different, but we mounted our long guns on shore and sank her."

"How long did you hold it?" I asked, goggling at him.

"Heh, heh, heh!" Hailey said. "Six days!"

Hewes raised his eyebrows at me. "He took nine towns in Scotland and Ireland and held 'em for ransom; and he went into one harbor and burned seven vessels. He came home with two hundred and seventy prisoners and a four-million-dollar cargo, in addition to the prizes he manned out."

"Oh, here, here!" Hailey protested. "It wa'n't four million dollars!"

"How much was it?" I asked.

"Gosh, I don't rightly know," Hailey said. He checked on his fingers. "There was twelve thousand pounds of raw silk, eighteen bales of Turkey carpets, twenty boxes of gums, a hundred and sixty dozen swan skins, twenty-four packs of beaver skins—oh, gosh! Say three million and a quarter, or three and a half, or so. I'm going up to Paris now to see Mr. Preble. He's owner."

"Well," I said, "you made a great haul!"

Hailey hitched forward in his chair. "I tell you, I've got a fast brig. She's *fast!* And I got a crew that won't be took. They'll outshoot and outfight anyone."

"Why will they?" I asked. "They won't outshoot and outfight my crew, man for man!"

"Yes, they will," Hailey said. He tilted back in his chair with an air of confidence. "Yes, they *will!* We couldn't pick up enough Americans; so Preble, he had some hokus with the French, and we searched the prisons for seamen: American—English—anybody that wanted to chance it."

We stared at him in silence, and he smiled at us.

"Was you ever in a French prison?"

We shook our heads.

"No," he said, "and you don't want to be. These men of mine, they wanted to get out, and they don't want to go back. And the English among 'em, they don't want to be took. If they're took they're swung from the yardarm quick. Quick! *Real* quick! Why wouldn't they fight? I've got a big crew, two hundred of 'em; and you never saw anybody shoot faster and straighter than they shoot, when they have to. I've got a fast brig, and there ain't anything going to get away from me when I start out after her; not *anything!*"

I began to see why the *True Blooded Yankee* had become such a terror to the British, and I wondered how I would like a crew taken out of French prisons; but before I could make up my mind, I heard someone running along the flagstones that edged the river.

There is little running in French towns on dank December evenings, when all good Frenchmen are snugly sealed in steamy kitchens; so we fell silent and looked toward the door, where M. Solbert, his hands cupped around his eyes, had pressed his forehead against the glass to see who it was that pelted so unceremoniously beneath the silent elms of Nantes.

The rapid footsteps came closer. M. Solbert fell back suddenly from the door, and in that moment it opened. Tommy Bickford stood before us, blinking and peering about the room. There was a smudge of soot on his cheek and a charred hole in the front of his pea-jacket.

He came to me. "Cap'n Dick—the sloop! She burned!"

He made a quick little bow to Captain Hailey and Captain Hewes, and smiled at me uncertainly.

"Did she burn to the water?" I asked.

"Yes, Captain."

"How'd she catch?"

Tommy looked at Captain Hailey and then at Captain Hewes. "Speak up!" I said. "I think I know. They set her, I'll bet! They saved my papers and the long guns, didn't they?"

"Yes, Captain: they saved pretty near everything."

"Then they set her," I said. I turned to Hewes and Hailey. "They wanted something bigger, so to carry more men and man out prizes."

Hailey laughed dryly. "I can tell you where to find the extra men," he said. "I can show you all the nicest jails in France."

So there was I, who wished to shorten the war, left without a vessel. I thought of the miniature in my pocket and stared at Hailey, while it seemed to me clear that I'd have most earnestly preferred his jailbird crew to my own simple downright fellows from home.

The brig I got to take the place of the old lucky *Lively Lady* I bought from a fox-faced Frenchman, Robert Surcouf: she lay in the basin at La Rochelle, and we were three months reconditioning her. Privateering was no new venture for her: the fox-faced Robert Surcouf had sailed her and fought her years before against the English —sailed her and fought her in such a manner as to bring him undying fame. Her figurehead had been a white shrouded woman of wood; and Surcouf had called her the *Revenant*, which means the *Ghost;* and always, in Surcouf's hands, she had disappeared like a wraith from the fastest British frigates that hunted her. But six years before, rich from the taking of prizes, Surcouf had married and given his wife his word that he would fight no more; and being determined that the British should never touch her, yet wishing to have her somewhere within reach, he had dismantled her and laid her up, a dismasted hulk, in La Rochelle.

It took a power of persuading and 4,000 English pounds to get her from him; and on top of everything I was obliged to sign a paper that I would never allow her to fall into the hands of the British. Having gone that far with him, I brought my crew from Nantes to work upon her, and they did it with a good will too; for not a man of them but could see, under the lumber and the pigsties and the steep-roofed penthouse with which she had been disguised and disfigured, her beautiful run and great breadth of beam.

"Fifteen knots!" Surcouf had bragged. Yet when I saw her made fit for the sea again, I doubted that he had bragged at all. We rigged her as she had been rigged when Surcouf had sailed her—as a taunt-rigged brigantine: square-sails, that is, on her foremast only, and high-masted. Her mainmast was a handsome tapering stick; her upper spars drew out into topgallant, royal and skysail masts that seemed as slender and fragile as the new wands that spring from a willow stump in June. Her shrouds and stays, beautifully fitted and served with hide wherever they lay in another's chafe, were so few in number that a landsman would have deemed her as sparsely rigged as two fishing poles, and therefore useless.

Our two faithful long guns stared grimly from their ports amidships; and sixteen carronades, which had come with the brig when I bought her, were lashed snugly on their slides.

Her decks were scrubbed; the bolts and rings in her high and solid bulwarks shone clear and bright. Except for her riband she was painted a dull green, against which her copper shone like newly minted gold. We gave her a black streak, set off from the green by stripes of gilding; and I went down over the bows myself with Rowlandson Drown, bent on making her figurehead into something that would keep me from forgetting I must do whatever lay in my power to help make this war a short one.

We cut away the shroud from the head and body of the corpse Surcouf had built, leaving a tight braid of hair around the brows, and making the shoulders smooth and sweetly rounded: then fashioned a snug little dress that flowed back into the cutwater. The lips and the eyes I carved myself with my jackknife; and when she was done we painted her carefully, the face a creamy ivory with a faint flush to the cheeks, the lips a brilliant red, and the hair a copper color, like that of a copper bolt chafed by the rubbing of a rope. The dress was a beautiful shimmery green with shadows and high lights, so that a breeze seemed to be whipping it around her.

When she was finished, one evening early in March, I walked down to see how she would look in the moonlight, and Jeddy went with me, and Davy Maffett, captain of the privateer brig *Rattlesnake* out of Philadelphia—the same Davy Maffett who had sent prizes valued at one million dollars into Norway during the winter just past, and as daring a captain as ever sailed.

We stood on the quay of the basin, the odor of drying fish nets in our noses and St. Nicolas Tower bulking against a moon of burnished silver. Davy Maffett looked and looked at the figurehead and whistled a little. Then he crossed the quay to a near-by tavern and returned with three bottles of sparkling white wine. We popped out the corks, and Davy held up his bottle toward the green-clad figure under the bowsprit. It gave me a strange tightness in my throat to see her there, smiling a faint, tremulous smile, as though she well knew what we were doing but was too much of a lady to look around at us.

"Here's to the *Lively Lady*," Davy said. "May all of 'em want her but none of 'em catch her!"

"The *Lively Lady!*" we shouted, and drank; and that was how we rechristened her.

*   *   *

One hundred and twenty men she carried, but I had not taken all of Captain Hailey's advice, though I had taken some. All of the hundred and twenty were Americans, and I think the last ten of them to arrive in La Rochelle were the roughest and wildest of the ten dozen.

They came in charge of Alley McAlley of the old crew, that little Irish tailor from Arundel who had signed with us because of his admiration for Jotham Carr, who had cured him of the itch. He had picked up an intelligible jargon of French and had been combing the coast towns for stranded fellow countrymen of the right, rough sort. With them he also brought, sewed into the waistband of his trousers, a letter given him in Nantes by Captain Jacobs of the Baltimore letter-of-marque schooner *Kemp*.

It was from Captain Boyle; and when I saw his name written at the end, he flashed into my mind, dark and handsome and polite, standing on a carronade, his *Comet* slipping over the waves like a flying fish and he waving his hat at me.

"ESTEEMED SIR AND FRIEND," the letter said, "*by good chance I have fallen across my brave friend Captain Jacobs, of the letter-of-marque schooner* Kemp, *Baltimore, and by him I send you my wishes for good health and success. Until the fifteenth March I shall hold station about one hundred miles west of the Scilly Isles, to intercept vessels bound into the English Channel or the Irish Sea. If it suits your wish and convenience we can keep company there or thereabouts. If not, I will run for Nantes on the fifteenth March, hoping to have a snail or two with you before refitting for another cruise. I am in a new brig,* Chasseur, *sixteen long 12's, and she is able to sail a little. If you come out, be so kind as to hoist a pair of blue pantaloons to your main peak, so there may be no mistake, and I will run up a green silk petticoat with ruffles. I am in great hopes of encountering you, and trust that if you come out, you will bring a few bottles of sparkling wine and a cheese or two. I have a partiality for the white Roquefort cheese, though any cheese will do. The more powerful the better. Accept, dear sir, the assurances of my distinguished regard.*

"THOS. BOYLE."

I read it again to make sure of the date and the cheese. "Get your men aboard," I said to McAlley. "We were only waiting for you."

I touched my breast, feeling that little oval of mine under the outer cloth; and I bethought me of how Captain Boyle rounded the convoy, burned a British ship, and came blithely to have me for dinner with him. I thought, too, that in Captain Boyle's company I might at least help a little to shorten this war.

"Get your men aboard," I said again, "I'm going to buy some cheese and wine to take to Captain Boyle on his *Chasseur* a hundred miles west of the Scillies."

*   *   *

It was late in the day, with a cold westerly wind seeming to hold up the sun in a smutty sky the color of a newly blacked eye, when we rounded the point on the northerly side of the harbor and dropped our pilot.

We knew the brig was very fast, for there was a lift to her, almost like that which I felt as a child, when I swung in the long rope swing hanging from the high oak on the far side of the creek in Arundel—a lift that caught my breath and filled me with the exultant sensation of being about to soar on and on, into another world.

The harbor of La Rochelle is a pleasant harbor in ordinary times, and as safe as any harbor anywhere; but in 1814 it was bad because of the manner in which blockading frigates and sloops hid themselves behind the shoulders of Ile de Ré, and pounced on Americans coming out of shelter.

We were a quiet lot as we bore to the north, past La Pallice and toward Breton Pass, the seventeen-mile sound separating the Ile de Ré from the mainland. There were lookouts at the mastheads; and I had put 'Lisha Lord in the larboard fore chains and Cromwell in the starboard fore chains to con the brig. Jeddy and Cephas were driving the men, clearing the decks of the litter that covers them when a craft first puts to sea, and so keeping them occupied; but they were as quiet as the rest of us, for until we were clear of the narrow channel, and the greenish half light had thickened into a comfortable blackness, there could be no feeling of security in the mind of anyone.

This presentiment of danger was justified as we slipped past the eastern end of the Ile de Ré; for the two men aloft shouted, "Sail!" sharply and simultaneously. A second later 'Lisha bellowed, "Cruiser in the lee of the island!" and in the same moment I saw her topsails dimly—topsails with such a tremendous high hoist that they could belong to nothing but a frigate.

I remember saying to myself, "To hell with this!" for due to the narrowness of the channel, we couldn't possibly escape a broadside if we held our course. We went about, then: almost we spun around, as if some vast hand had taken the brig by the bowsprit and turned her on her heel. I heard laughter from the men in the waist, and a whoop or two, and knew they were laughing with delight at her swiftness.

We slipped back along the eastern tip of the island in the gathering gloom. I find it hard to make clear the feel of swiftness in a vessel. It is a little like that which comes into the body of a runner at times—a quick consciousness of lightness and suppleness, as though running were no exertion, and could be continued indefinitely. Our sloop had been a fast craft; but there was no such feel to her as to this brig, which seemed to pour herself over the waves without effort, adjusting herself to irregularities in the water like an otter gamboling in the rapids of a fast stream.

She moved, it seemed to me, with a soft rush, a tireless swoop, a smooth unchecked flight, devoid of bumpings and squatterings such as mark the progress of slower craft. I have watched kestrels come into the wind and hang there motionless, except for a little shivering of the wings: then turn without effort and soar away on a straight, effortless flight, very rapid; and it was like a soaring kestrel that the *Lively Lady* seemed to move.

There was still light in the west when we hauled our wind to pass out along the southern side of Ile de Ré; but the light was dim and faintly greenish, which was fortunate for us. Against this dying paleness, as we opened the island, the lookouts made out two more sail, two miles off our starboard bow, running down with the wind on such a slant that they were bound to intercept us. I could feel in my bones they were British frigates or sloops-of-war, and I knew they must have learned there were American privateers in La Rochelle and so been sent to blockade the port.

I had no love for this situation. Our canvas was new and bright; and since they had surely seen us I knew they would separate, one edging in toward the Ile de Ré and the other off toward the Ile d'Oleron. I also knew that if either of them passed within gunshot of us, which was likely, we would get a broadside that might wing us and leave us swinging in circles on the water like a wounded duck.

How long it was before darkness hid those two sail from us I cannot now recall. It may have been two minutes; it may have been four; but to me, watching this beautiful brig slash over the waves like a frightened swan, it seemed like an hour out of a sleepless night.

I shouted for lanterns and called 'Lisha Lord aft to step a mast in the longboat; and while he worked at it with his men I sent a seaman part way up the foremast ratlines with a lighted lantern.

When it was dark at last, a thick gray dark, we came into the wind and hung there. 'Lisha lowered away the boat, lashed its tiller, made fast a lighted lantern to the masthead, scrambled back on board, and cast her off. He shouted, whereupon the man in the ratlines doused the lantern he was carrying. The empty longboat bobbed away from us toward the Ile d'Oleron, the lantern bright at its masthead. We watched it a moment, then wore ship and stood back toward the Ile de Ré.

We may have been a quarter mile off shore when Jeddy spoke and the men jumped for the topgallant clew lines and the fore clew garnets. They worked as though bawled at by the Bull of Bashan; yet I had to strain my ears to catch Jeddy's muted whispers. "Peak and throat halyards! Jib downhaul! Rise tacks and sheets! Let go! Clew up!" I heard him whistle a shrill little whistle between his teeth and add, "Settle away the main gaff, you!"

In another two minutes' time we were slipping along with every inch of canvas furled, as dark and silent as a deserted brig, so that an enemy vessel would be obliged to run us down, almost, in order to see us, and would, in such case, shoot by us too fast to bring guns to bear.

There was a creaking as the head yards were squared: then we bore up before the wind and lay there, listening. There was a small moaning of the breeze in the rigging, and a slatting somewhere above us, and the lap, lap, lap of the waves against our bends. Far off to larboard we could see a pinpoint of light, blinking and blinking; then disappearing for a second; then blinking and blinking once more. We watched it and watched it, until it seemed nearly gone: only a spark now and again. We peered for it until moisture ran from our eyes and lay cold on our cheeks; and as we peered there was a flash like sheet lightning seen through a rift in a cloud: then a thud, as though someone had dropped a weight far down in our hold. We saw two lights, one close under another, rising, and knew one of the cruisers was hoisting her signal lanterns. Immediately, farther away, two more lights went up. With that I snapped at Jeddy to make sail. Jeddy shouted, and the crew sprang up from under the bulwarks, cheering and whooping; for like the rest of us they knew the cruisers had gone too far afield after our longboat to locate us again—that there was nothing now between us and the open sea, and that, once free of the land, no British cruiser ever built could overtake us.

In four minutes' time our sails were set and drawing and we were running to the northwest, all clear.

XVI

IT WAS early March still, a blustery bright day, and we were casting around in a circle west of the Scillies when we made out a sail on our weather quarter, coming down on us fast. When she proved to be a brig, we bent on the pantaloons—a pair belonging to Cephas Cluff, who was large in the bends and with next to no tumble-home about him—and ran them up. Instantly a billowing green ensign of some description went to the brig's masthead; and Cephas, watching her through the telescope, said, "There's ruffles on it!"

"The Irish navy!" Jeddy shouted; and since we were delighted to encounter Boyle again, we combined business with pleasure while waiting for him to come up, hove over a cask, circled it, and banged away at it fifteen times with our lee battery, thus giving him a salute of fifteen guns.

This brig of Boyle's, the *Chasseur,* was as beautiful a vessel as it had ever been my fortune to see. She was brigantine rigged, like the *Lively Lady,* but with a lighter bowsprit and foremast and more of a rake to her sticks, so that she seemed to me to have a quicker and more elusive look than the *Lively Lady*—the look, almost, of a slender girl running hard, her head back and her stomach thrust out before her.

When we had fired the fifteen guns, we tacked twice and came back onto the *Chasseur's* course, slipping along beside her not fifty yards away, so close we could see the patches in the mainsail where the passage of a bushel of grapeshot had been repaired, and the wind-blown hair of the grinning crew that lolled, close-packed, over the hammock nettings to watch us come up, and the fluttering ruffles on the bosom of Boyle's shirt. He stood on one of his long twelves, clutching the main shrouds and waving his bell-topped gray beaver at us.

"Very kind!" we heard him shout. "Too many guns! Hope I can live up to the compliment!"

He looked around at his helmsman, making a little circular movement with his hand. The *Chasseur* hauled her wind and ranged closer. We could hear the crackling and whipping of the green silk petticoat at her main peak, the patter of the foam clouts skittering from beneath her raking bows, and the babble of her crew as they talked and laughed.

"Delighted you came out," Boyle called over. "Did you bring the cheese?"

I nodded.

"I'll come aboard for dinner when it's dark," he said.

He did not, however, for the day turned gray and dirty, and the wind shifted into the northeast. In the afternoon it stiffened to a gale, so that both of us lay-to under double-reefed mainsails. That night it eased up, and by morning the wind had come around into the south, and there was a light fog that began to burn off around ten o'clock. When it lifted we saw a sail to the southwestward; and since Boyle was the nearer to it, he hauled his wind in chase, while we bore on toward the northeast.

Toward noon we made out a column of smoke in the southwest and concluded Boyle had found his chase to be a small craft of little value and so set her afire. A little later the shreds of mist in the northeast cleared away still more, and we made out a large ship off our lee bow, heading in a southeasterly direction—a magnificent, freshly painted, high-sided vessel, bearing all the earmarks of a merchantman. When she ran from us, as she soon did, we knew we were right and so piped all hands to quarters.

We came up on her fast, and I could see she was armed with stern chasers. Therefore I kept off and sailed past her, sending extra muskets and loaders to Moody Haley and Moses Burnham and the rest of the sharpshooters in our tops. Then I came down on her bows, wore across them in a raking position, fired a gun, and shouted to her to heave-to. Instead of this she attempted to wear in order to give me a broadside. This she could not do, because of our speed; for, seeing what she was about, I came up into the wind very sharp and crossed her bows again, wearing immediately afterward. Even then she would not strike, thinking perhaps that because I was moving straight away from her I was running. Therefore I turned once more and ran back to windward of her. As we came up, 'Lisha Lord shouted to the men in the tops, and they opened on her with muskets. We saw man after man go down at her guns, so that when her broadside let off it was ragged and useless, and the shot passed around us and over us. Also two men in succession were shot down at her wheel, and an officer on the quarter-deck slipped to his knees, clutching at his shoulder. Immediately after, a man ran out from the cabin hatch and hauled down her colors, and she slowly hove-to, at which we came about and ran up to leeward of her, with our crew shouting so triumphantly and stamping so delightedly at their good fortune as to drown the slatting of the reef points against the main- sail. Nor was my own pleasure any less than theirs, for we had suf- fered no damage whatever in the encounter, and the *Lively Lady* had outsailed her bulky antagonist as readily as my little dog Pinky runs in circles around a cow.

I boarded her myself, to see what disposition to make of her peo- ple as well as what manner of prize crew to put into her; and I had no sooner stuck my head above her bulwarks than I hankered for her myself, because of her cleanliness and her broad, scoured decks, splotched here and there with the red stains that had resulted from our musketry fire.

Even before I made a move to take possession I began to plan how I could have her for my own some day.

Five men were laid out in the shelter of the main hatch, and the remainder of her people, gathered around them, glowered at us as we came over the side. The officer who met us, a young man, seemed to expect harsh treatment; for his lips were pressed tight together and his face was pale.

"Captain?" I asked him.

He cleared his throat. "Second officer. The first was shot through the shoulder. The captain went to his cabin when—when we struck."

"Lower away your longboat," I ordered, "and send your men aboard my brig. What is this ship?"

"The *Pembroke*, West Indiaman," he said, getting a little color back in his face, "London for Port-au-Prince."

"Well, get your boat away. I'm putting a prize crew aboard."

I left Jeddy in charge of the deck and went to the cabin. I had heard about the richness of big West Indiamen, but I had never been aboard a wealthy Londoner before; and here was one indeed. She was 540 tons: a roomy, comfortable ship; and when I stepped into the cabin, I was staggered by what I saw. Two silver lamps were hung on long silver chains; and beneath the lamps was a dining table, covered with gold brocade weighted at the corners with silver tassels. Behind the table rose the rudder case, carved and colored to represent a close-packed stand of bamboos; and these, at the top, branched out in feathery green fronds, all carved out of wood, which spread interlaced across the ceiling. Behind that, in turn, were the stern windows, hung with blue brocade. The cabin walls were paneled with gray wood, some of the panels filled with mirrors edged in gold, so that the bamboo of the rudder case was reflected back and forth. Doors let into side berths, three doors to a side; and in a recess

stood a piano colored gray to match the cabin panels. There was a
scarf, a green scarf, across the piano bench; and it seemed to me I
caught from it a singular delicate fragrance.

A sallow-faced man sat at the table, his chin sunk on his chest,
staring at a handful of papers that lay before him. When I came
in he rose and bowed, a quick, angry bow, as though he would rather
be whipped than do what he was doing.

"Captain," I said, "I must ask you to take whatever personal belongings you require and go at once aboard my brig. Do you have
passengers?"

"You have the authority for this, no doubt?"

"A commission from President Madison, sir, to Captain Richard
Nason of the private armed brig *Lively Lady*."

What answer he made I cannot say, for at that moment one of the
cabin doors swung open.

I stared and stared at what I saw; for beyond the open door,
swaying to the uneasy motion of the ship, stood a slender girl, a girl
in a green silk dress, her pretty arms bare to the elbow, and her hair,
tight braided around her head, the color of a copper bolt chafed
bright by rubbing. As for her face, it was the same as that on the
miniature I had carried in the pocket of my shirt, for fear of losing it,
ever since the distant day when I sailed from Portland in the *Neutrality* to carry foodstuffs to the English in Spain.

Just then it did not seem to me so necessary to shorten this war.

XVII

IF EVER I saw a man in a rage so powerful that he was on the verge of being poisoned by it, it was Sir Arthur Ransome when he learned he must leave his comfortable West Indiaman and go aboard a crowded brig not half the size of the vessel he was leaving. I was in a hurry to man out the *Pembroke* and send her on her way to Nantes, for I had learned she had been driven from a convoy by the gale of the day before; and there was no knowing when a fast frigate might come prowling down in search of this fine fat chicken that had straggled from the flock.

But say what I would to Sir Arthur, I could not hurry him in his preparations. He stood by his berth, quite helpless, asking his wife in his whiny voice where he had put this and where he had put that. He would pick up a thing and stare at it helplessly: then hand it to her to hold, looking like a baulky horse; and with each passing moment he seemed more and more impatient with her, though she had only tried to help him.

At length I asked her if she was ready to go. She said at once, without looking at me—and indeed, she had not looked at me at all except when she opened the door of her small cabin—that she was. At that, unwilling to endanger our crew or our prize by further delay, I called to Jeddy to send down Gideon Lassel and Seth Tarbox. When they came, I told them to enter Sir Arthur's cabin, take every movable thing except Sir Arthur, and dump the whole in a blanket. This they did, regardless of Sir Arthur's angry protests. Then Gideon threw the loaded blanket over his shoulder, and Seth took Sir Arthur by the back of the coat and pushed him on deck. I sent Lady Ransome after them and followed her out myself; and as we went we could hear Sir Arthur expostulating with Seth, telling him to take his hands away.

They tumbled him into the boat and jumped in after him; whereupon Jeddy and I handed down Lady Ransome, and I gave Cephas Cluff his final orders: to head for Nantes and sell the *Pembroke* to the Latours for one hundred francs, so she might lie safe at her French quay, and be readily repurchased when all danger of seizure was past. Also I wrote the Latours, giving Cephas authority to draw on them for funds and live aboard the *Pembroke,* keeping her neat and ready for sea, until I should come for her.

No sooner had I gone over the side than the *Pembroke* slipped off to the eastward, toward Nantes.

Raging as Sir Arthur was, he was silent in the boat—not, I felt, from good sense, but because it was a part of his scheme of life to show no feeling publicly before menials; and it was as a menial, I knew, that he regarded me. At all events, he sat stiffly on the thwart beside Lady Ransome, staring over my head at nothing. I was glad of this for two reasons, one being that if he had opened his mouth, the boat crew, being in high spirits over the taking of the *Pembroke,* would have mocked him in some dreadful way, since nothing seemed to strike them as being as laughable as the speech of an Englishman; and the other being that it kept his eyes from encountering the figurehead of the *Lively Lady* as we came down on her lee bow, although he was a dull man about some things and might not have seen it even though he looked directly at it.

I could have wished, even, that Lady Ransome had been less curious about her destination; but as luck would have it she cast a glance over her shoulder at the brig when we were less than ten paces from her dolphin striker; and as a result she looked squarely at the figure Rowlandson Drown and I had fashioned and painted with such care in the harbor of La Rochelle—at the copper-colored hair, the brilliant red lips, the bare pink arms and the shimmering green dress with the look of being whipped back by the wind into the duller green of the cutwater.

With lips a little parted, she stared and stared; and I, watching her, had the singular impression that only a few days had passed since I first saw her sitting in a field near Saco, with my little dog Pinky on his haunches before her; but I had no heart to dwell overlong on this strange feeling, for when she turned from the figurehead, her eyes met mine in a glance so level that it appeared almost to have something of enmity in it.

I think Sir Arthur would have resumed his arguing as soon as we set foot on deck, had I not sent him, with his wife and Captain Parker, to my cabin until the brig was squared away toward the south on the lookout for the *Chasseur,* and until the wounded first mate was comfortably stowed in one of the side berths off the gun room. I had the feeling that I had done something wrong, nor was this feeling lessened when I went into my cabin and met the accusing gaze of Sir Arthur and Captain Parker and saw how Lady Ransome refused to look at me and stared at nothing from the stern windows.

"Well," I said. "I regret this had to happen to persons I know, but war's hard on friendships."

Sir Arthur whinnied, a short, angry whinny. "Friendship!" he exclaimed.

"Oh, well," I said, feeling sorry for them, "it's hard on everything, and since we must live on this craft for some time, I'd like you to know I don't relish making prisoners of people who have been in our house and eaten our food."

With that I went to logging them, and so discovered from Captain Parker that Sir Arthur was on his way to Jamaica, where he had been threatened with the loss of vast sugar lands through litigation. It came into my head, when I learned this, to ask Lady Ransome whether Annie had come safely to England in the brig in which I had placed her and the Sandersons; but when I looked up at her I thought I saw apprehension in her eye and so said nothing.

"Just what do you mean, may I ask," Sir Arthur said, when I had put away the log book, "by saying we must live on this craft for some time?"

"Why," I said, "I mean just that! I can't set you adrift in an open boat, and I think you'll agree that the water's a trifle cold for swimming."

Sir Arthur stared at me along his nose, an unpleasant look such as he might have given to a servant. "I warn you," he said, "that you'll be held to blame for any harm that comes to my wife or myself or any of our property, and that you'll be treated like any other pirate when you're taken, as you must be."

"Well," I said, "no harm's going to come to any of you if I can help it, so make your mind easy on that point. And since you bring up the matter of blame, I'd like to ask your captain what was in his head when he allowed this lady to remain in the cabin and refused to strike his colors to me."

Captain Parker moved uncomfortably in his chair but made no answer.

"Captain Parker is an experienced navigator, in whom we have the utmost confidence," Sir Arthur said. To me his voice sounded finicky and unpleasant.

"In that case," I told him, "I can only remind you that if my brig hadn't been faster than anything Captain Parker had ever seen, I'd have been justified in raking you through your cabin windows, which is something I don't like to think of."

They stared at me without speaking.

"There's another thing," I said, as calmly as I could. "It seems to me it's a little singular to choose this time to travel, even in a convoy and with a captain in whom you repose confidence."

"Oh, indeed," Sir Arthur said. "Indeed! Words fail me to express my gratitude for your interest in my personal affairs! It would doubtless mean nothing to you to know that a fair part—a very fair part— of the island of Jamaica is at stake in our lawsuit."

My answer was both gruff and awkward. "I don't see," I said, "why you should bring a lady along."

"Don't you?" Sir Arthur asked quickly, his face the color of fresh putty. "That's truly unfortunate!"

Lady Ransome bent her head over her clasped hands and spoke for the first time, her voice so low and husky I could scarce hear it. "A lady that has to be watched," she whispered, "would need to be brought along."

Sir Arthur turned on her. "Hold your tongue!" he said quietly. "Is this any place to discuss our private affairs?"

Into Lady Ransome's eyes came a foggy, wavery look that set me off on another tack, talking more loudly than I might otherwise have spoken. "Now, here!" I said, "if you'll give me your paroles to do nothing that can damage or hinder this brig or its people, I'll try to land you in a safe port."

There was venom in Sir Arthur's glance. "And what if I don't choose to give my parole?"

"Well, sir," I said, "if you won't give it, I'll have to demand it. The lady must be put ashore."

At that Captain Parker gave his parole, as did Sir Arthur, and I sent for Tommy Bickford to help make them as comfortable as was possible in our cramped quarters.

Late in the afternoon we fell in with the *Chasseur* again; and when Boyle, standing in his main chains, shouted gaily at me to tell him what I had been doing, I thought it best to lower a boat and go aboard the *Chasseur*, so my passengers might not hear me spreading their affairs to the world.

I told Boyle about Sir Arthur and asked him to join me for supper so I wouldn't feel like a voiceless fool when Sir Arthur became talkative over his wine and favored me with his rudeness. Boyle laughed. "Since when have you been voiceless under such conditions?" he asked.

Not wishing to tell him it was because I didn't want to hurt Lady Ransome's feelings, I contented myself with saying I became voiceless because Ransome persisted in addressing me as though I were a groom or a scullery boy. Boyle nodded thoughtfully. This, he said, should amuse rather than anger me. "His wife," he said, "has thick ankles, no doubt, and a raw, carroty look, like so many English-women."

My reply, perhaps, was overwarm. "Not at all! She's rather good-looking."

"Indeed!" he said, "and what's the color of her eyes?"

"They seem to be green, but in reality they're a sort of smoke color," I told him; whereupon he turned from me to open his chest of old Madeira. I saw he was smiling, and wondered whether I had made a mistake to admit knowing the color of her eyes.

I thought many times that evening that if I had sat alone at supper with Sir Arthur and Lady Ransome and Captain Parker we would have been a glum and silent gathering; but men from Baltimore are prattlers, seeming to talk for the pleasure of hearing the sound of their voices, which are soft and slurry, doubtless from living in close proximity to Negroes.

Boyle had no sooner come into the cabin, with his white teeth, his clear, sallow skin, his gentle politeness and his soft, warm voice, than Captain Parker brightened up, and Sir Arthur took a reef in his chin, so that his nose came down out of the air and left him looking like any normal human being, while Lady Ransome smiled for the first time since I had seen her open the door in the cabin of the *Pembroke*. Indeed, no woman could have helped smiling if Boyle had bowed over her hand as he bowed over Lady Ransome's, saying as he did so, "This repays me, ma'am, for being a sailor! We get to thinking there can be nothing in life but lobscouse and dirty weather, and then Heaven sends us—" he straightened suddenly and looked earnestly at her—"and then Heaven sends us a pair of eyes the color of smoke in the swamps of Maryland."

He looked around at me, as if to make sure I heard what he said, whereat I flushed as red as the turkey cover on the table.

"Lud 'a' mercy!" Lady Ransome cried with an air of unbelief, "you're never from America, sir, speaking such poetic nonsense to me."

"Now your ladyship is paying compliments," Boyle said, "whereas I was telling the simple truth! Tell me, now, what part of England you think I come from, if I'm never from America, as you say?"

"Oh, not England!" Lady Ransome exclaimed hastily. "I meant I didn't know American men spoke—I didn't know they were in the habit of——"

Boyle chuckled, and there seemed to me to be little pinpoints of mockery in his eyes. "It's a large country, Lady Ransome," he said.

"Our products vary widely. Now in the North we have the Province of Maine, where the people never speak for fear of committing themselves to something; but farther to the south we have Maryland, where we're trained from childhood to fall in love at first sight continuously throughout our lives."

"You're speaking now of the training of maidens and ladies?" she asked, "or do you mean your gentlemen would never fall in love unless trained to? If you mean the latter, your ladies must all be perishing of broken hearts, I take it!"

Captain Boyle laughed lightly. "No, ma'am; it's only our own hearts that break, and that without any training."

Sir Arthur cleared his throat with what I considered unnecessary loudness. "Are you the captain of a privateer, Captain Boyle?"

"I have that honor, sir," Boyle said. "The *Chasseur* of Baltimore; sixteen long 12's."

"Do you ever find men of standing serving as captains of privateers?" Sir Arthur asked almost genially—due, probably, to the rapidity with which he had tossed off his wine.

"Never, sir!" Boyle assured him quickly, "only a lot of scamps like Captain Nason and myself. Some of our privateer captains have been downright notorious." He rolled up his eyes at the ceiling and went to checking off names on his fingers. "Truxtun, Porter, Biddle, Decatur, Barney, Perry, Murray, Rogers, Cassin, Little, Robinson, Smith, Hopkins . . . terrible low fellows all of them; but they reformed and entered the navy, as I have the greatest fear you already have the displeasure of knowing, sir."

He sipped his wine smilingly, and then went on: "Now, let me see: Captain Nason wants to send you to England, and he said something about taking a small brig and turning her into a cartel for you." He raised his glass toward Lady Ransome and drank the remainder. "It seems to me I wouldn't advise a cartel. She might be taken by another American before reaching port. As you doubtless know, our government pays a bounty for each prisoner, and you might possibly be taken to America."

"But we're nearly in the English Channel!" Captain Parker protested. "There can't be Americans in the Channel, my dear sir!"

Boyle raised his eyebrows at me. "Had you understood the Channel had been cleared of our privateers?" he asked.

"No," I said. "We're in it already, and Captain Hailey of the *True Blooded Yankee* is fond of cruising in the Channel when he isn't holding towns for ransom in Scotland and Ireland. The *Scourge*, the *Rattlesnake* and the *Grand Turk* are Channel cruisers, and there are seven or eight others standing off and on the coasts of Great Britain, though they may not be in the Channel at the moment."

Captain Boyle shook his head sadly at Captain Parker. "I fear, sir, your mind has been less on the war than on other matters—or, possibly you've listened to unreliable information."

It was Lady Ransome who finally said she was quite sure Captain Boyle's advice would be worth following, at which Captain Boyle bowed and flashed his white teeth at her. "That's kind of you, ma'am," he said, "and I appreciate it. I must tell you, too, that you can have complete confidence in Captain Nason's judgment, for though he's young and a great believer in Maine taciturnity and not committing himself to anything, he's as good a seaman as ever I kept company with."

The fiery heat of my face was not cooled by the somewhat discouraging silence that followed these words of Captain Boyle's; and at length, in desperation, I quickly swallowed a glass of wine and said it seemed to me the best thing to do would be to run to the Channel Islands, which were a little out of the beaten track, and set our prisoners ashore on one of them. From here, eventually, I said, they would get passage to England in a government sloop or schooner, and would be safe with English folk meanwhile.

"There!" Boyle cried. "What did I tell you! A perfect arrangement!"

The others, however, had nothing to say, but sat and pecked at their supper.

At length Sir Arthur observed dryly that after Captain Boyle had boasted of the manner in which Americans were making themselves at home in the Channel, it seemed not unnatural to hope his party might be landed in Plymouth harbor.

Captain Boyle smiled at him as sweetly as a newly wakened babe smiling up into his mother's face. "Where our privateers go," he told him softly, "depends a little upon the reward in prospect. When they risk themselves out of kindliness, they must take some account of numbers. You are three, and Captain Nason and I have a hundred men apiece to consider. Those two hundred, Sir Arthur, might be willing to venture their skins for a prize worth the good part of a farm to each of them. But I think they'd mislike Plymouth harbor as the scene of a Christian deed performed without even the prospect of being thanked for it."

Lady Ransome raised her eyes to mine for a moment; then dropped them immediately.

"Ow," Sir Arthur said at length. "Remarkable, your speaking of thanks, Mr. Boyle! Attacking us without a word of warning when we were harming nobody—that might be defined as somewhat cowardly, mightn't it? You put it all as a wholly commercial matter, you and your men, as I understood you to say, thinking only of how much money's to be made out of it. If you're to do a brave act, there would first have to be a calculation of the pennies to decide how many of them your bravery may be worth."

For my part, I could have wrung his neck, so deep was my resentment of his words; but Captain Boyle seemed undisturbed.

"Yes," he said, "I've heard that before; but as it just chances, I've always heard it second hand. Not before has it been said to me directly. I feel a little unfortunate that it's thus spoken at last by a captive; but since we're so happy as to have a lady with us, I'll explain these matters more fully than I would ordinarily do. Thus you may be able, hereafter, to state the case properly."

Captain Boyle rose, walked to the stern windows, drew aside the curtains and peered out. "A fine starry night," he said. With that he returned to his chair, and, as he came, fixed the back of Sir Arthur's head with a hard, level gaze.

"Well, now," he said, "this is the way of it. Most people in this world seem to be in the position of doing things for money. Your kings and our presidents; your doctors, lawyers, generals, admirals and ship-builders; your poets and your writers of books: all these men earn a living by what they do; and by stretching a point you might say it's a commercial matter with them. Why, I've even heard it said your great families in England marry oftener to gain a few acres of land or a sure addition to their incomes than for love."

He paused and looked shyly at his fingers, the most harmless-looking gentleman I had ever seen, and I was astonished to discover that Lady Ransome was as white as the linen at Captain Boyle's wrists, and that Sir Arthur's leathery, dust-colored face had gone a muddy red.

"Yes," Captain Boyle went on gently, "we're most of us money chasers in this world, though some of us chase it more grimly than others, and others chase it because they're whirled along with the chasers.

"Now, you gentlemen may or may not be aware that in the American navy there are only seven frigates and fifteen sloops-of-war to cope with your tremendous fleet of eight hundred men-of-war; but this is a fact. It's also a fact that many hundreds of Americans—many thousands of them—are eager to do battle with a nation that has so flouted and insulted their country as has England."

Captain Boyle leaned forward and looked wistfully into Sir Arthur's face. "What's to be done in such a case?" he asked. "These men are seamen: all their lives they've known nothing but the sea. They're lost on land; and the ways of landsmen are beyond them. They'd be worthless in an army; and besides, they've no quarrel with England on the land. It's on the sea that England treads on our toes and denies us the right to be our own masters; and it's on the sea that Americans wish to fight for free trade and seamen's rights and no impressment."

Captain Boyle, it seemed, could not sit still. He rose again from his chair to stand with his back against the oak rudder casing, swaying as the brig, rising to the lift of a wave, swooped with it and lowered herself gently to the bosom of the following wave.

"What can these people do who want to fight you?" he repeated, looking from Captain Parker to Sir Arthur. "There's no room for 'em in our navy, on our few small government vessels. What am I to do when I want to fight you? I'm a navigator. I can work a brig or a ship, and work her well. I can fight her. Shall I go as a common seaman on one of our twenty-two government craft, where my knowledge of seamanship will be lost? What are the rest of us to do?"

Captain Boyle's voice fell almost to a whisper, so that I leaned forward for fear of losing his words in the slight screaking of the rudder and the lapping of the water against our sides. "You have a vulnerable spot, you English," he said. "It's your merchant fleet. We're striking home, Sir Arthur Ransome, when we send the price of flour in England to fifty dollars a barrel—to sixty dollars a barrel."

"Ah, yes," Sir Arthur said. "And getting the sixty dollars yourself, Mr. Boyle!"

Taking a handkerchief of gray silk from his breast pocket, Boyle smoothed it between the palms of his hands; and as he did so he lowered his head and looked into Sir Arthur's face as intently as though there were nothing else worth seeing in all the world. "I think I've made myself quite clear," he said. "I beg, therefore, you'll indicate in some way to me that you've labored under a misapprehension."

Sir Arthur met this intent look now bent upon him for a moment or two only; then lowered his eyelids and glanced aside.

"Oh, I've no doubt it's a fair enough sort of fighting, according to American ideas," he admitted.

Captain Boyle bowed gravely, resumed his seat, and lifted his glass to Captain Parker, then lowered it. "On second thought, Captain," he said, "I can't ask you to drink with me to the fortunes of war just at present."

"No," Parker returned gruffly. "And they wouldn't be what they are for us just now except for the damned laziness, saving Lady Ransome's presence, of our damned blockading fleet that's supposed to hold your privateers inside your own ports. How you get by them I'm damned if I can see, saving Lady Ransome's presence again."

"Oh, but it's the simplest thing in the world!" Boyle said. "We back out."

"Back out?" Parker repeated, with a kind of hoarseness. "Back out?"

"Let me explain it," Boyle said winningly, and turned to Lady Ransome. "You see, ma'am, your people have a heavy blockading fleet cruising up and down before the entrance of every harbor in America, so we come out stern foremost: that is to say, backwards; and your people look at us carefully and think we're going the other way. So they don't bother us. Sometimes we have to back halfway to the Scilly Islands; but, after all, what could be simpler?"

Captain Parker sputtered, grunted, and seemed to be swearing internally. Lady Ransome said, "La!" and looked purely scornful, whereupon Boyle lifted a protesting hand toward her.

"You'll not betray me, ma'am," he said, "for giving this information to the enemy—I'm afraid I must regard your husband and Captain Parker as enemies; but I'm sure they'll be honorable and not betray the secret. Doubtless you know yourself, ma'am, that Sir John Borlaise Warren had it published in England how well he holds the Chesapeake blockaded; but as a hundred and fifty American privateers are constantly passing in and out of those lively waters, Sir John could only be excused on the ground that he sees nothing but their sterns and therefore thinks they're all inside."

When he had said this he sat staring at Parker. His face had suddenly become as blank as a clam shell. His eyes seemed turned inward, and his lower lip sagged, so that he looked to be gone entirely from us. Then, as abruptly, a little glow appeared upon his cheek. He came to life, smiling, and turned to me.

"Blockade!" he said. "Why, what fools we've been, Captain! Warren's in America, blockading us; and we're here, so why shouldn't we blockade them?"

"Blockade who?" Sir Arthur asked.

"The British!" Boyle cried, striking his fist on the table. "Captain Nason, we'll blockade England."

"Good!" I said.

Captain Boyle clapped his hands softly and rubbed them together. He slid from his chair to walk up and down the end of the cabin, beaming delightedly at me, as though I had done something mighty pleasing. "Pencil and paper, Captain!" he said. "Pencil and paper! This blockade must be effected at once!"

I went to my dispatch box for writing materials; and thinking all eyes were on Captain Boyle, I stole a glance at Emily Ransome, only to find she had looked suddenly over her shoulder at me. It was the same level glance she had given me once before; but now I saw no enmity in it; for when she turned quickly away, her face and throat flushed hotly red. I fumbled in my dispatch box as though my fingers were turned to thumbs.

I forgot, almost, what I had come to get; I heard but dimly the voice of Captain Parker, plainly outraged by Boyle's remarks. "It seems to me, Captain Boyle," he said, "that what you say is in extremely poor taste!"

Boyle stopped abruptly in his pacing. "Poor taste, Captain?" he asked, as if he doubted his ears. "Surely you didn't say poor taste!"

Captain Parker made a sound like an outraged goose. "Such a thing's impossible of accomplishment," he said, "and you'd never say it to our naval officers; so it must be said for the purpose of irritating us, who are helpless here in this cabin."

"Why, sir," Captain Boyle said, and I thought he spoke regretfully, "I'll ask you to pardon me if I've irritated you. That wasn't my intention." He raised his eyebrows at Lady Ransome. "Have you found my words irritating?"

"I find them pleasantly fantastic," she said, smiling at him.

Boyle shook his head sadly. "Not fantastic," he said. "They're meant more soberly. Why, here—" he turned to Captain Parker— "it's not half as impossible for me to blockade England as for Sir John Borlaise Warren to blockade America. And I question your judgment, my dear sir, when you tell me I'd never say such a thing to naval officers. I'm quite willing to say it to anyone." He seemed struck with a new idea. "I shall *insist* on saying it to everyone! You shall carry my proclamation to London, Captain Parker, and post it in Lloyd's Coffee House!

"Take it down for me, Captain," he said, seeing I had brought pencil and paper. "Take it down! We'll make three copies, so all Great Britain may be warned."

Thereupon, with a mocking spark in his velvety brown eyes and the gentlest of smiles playing about his lips, he wandered around the table, dictating to me, seemingly oblivious of the rigidity with which Sir Arthur and Captain Parker sat in their chairs.

"At the top," he announced, "the word 'Proclamation,' printed large, and flanked by American eagles with ruffled feathers, if you're any hand at drawing eagles: if not, we'll get along with American ensigns. After that, in red ink, the word 'whereas,' large and italicized, and with that we can start." His voice rose a little and became flat and monotonous. "*Whereas*, It has become customary with the admirals of Great Britain, commanding small forces on the coast of the United States, particularly with Sir John Borlaise Warren and Sir Alexander Cochrane, to declare all the coast of the said United States in a state of strict and rigorous blockade without stationing an adequate force to maintain said blockade;

"I do therefore, by virtue of the power and authority in me vested, possessing sufficient force, declare all the ports, harbors, bays, creeks, rivers, inlets, outlets, islands and seacoast of the United Kingdom of Great Britain and Ireland in a state of strict and rigorous blockade."

"Ow!" Sir Arthur protested.

Captain Boyle held up a warning hand and continued his dictation: "And I do further declare that I consider the force under my command adequate to maintain strictly, rigorously, and effectually the said blockade."

"Adequate!" Captain Parker protested. "Two small vessels *adequate!*"

"Why not?" Boyle asked. "Look at Warren!" He nodded at me and resumed his flat, monotonous dictating voice: "And I do hereby caution and forbid the ships and vessels of all and every nation in amity and peace with the United States from entering or attempting to enter, or from coming or attempting to come out of, any of the said ports, harbors, bays, creeks, rivers, inlets, outlets, islands, or seacoast under any pretext whatsoever. And that no person may plead ignorance of this, my proclamation, I have ordered the same to be made public in England.

"Given under my hand on board the Private Armed Brig *Chasseur*, THOMAS BOYLE, Commander."

Captain Boyle came and looked over my shoulder. "I date it as from my own ship, as more fitting and proper, if you'll pardon me, Captain Nason. Have you it all?"

"I think so," I told him, pleased to see Sir Arthur looking at me sourly. "In reference to the supposed British blockade of America, it might be nearer to the truth if you inserted, before the words about stationing an adequate force, the words 'without possessing the power to justify such a declaration.'"

"My dear Captain," Boyle said, starting back wide eyed, "the proclamation would have verged on the inaccurate without such a phrase. I thank you a thousand times for the suggestion! Pray make it so!"

With that, smiling graciously upon us, he caught up his hat and swept a quick bow to Lady Ransome. "Charming evening," he told us. "I shall hope for others before the blockade ends."

XVIII

IT WAS thick as pea soup in the Channel on the following morning:
thick and choppy; and it seemed to me there was trouble in the air;
for Pinky lay in my bunk, his head hanging across my legs and his
beady black eyes wide open, now elevating one bushy yellow eyebrow at the stern windows, then twisting the other toward the door
of the cabin, and between times growling faintly deep in his throat;
so in the end he drove me to dressing and going on deck at an early
hour.

I could make out nothing in the fog. Pomp, standing his trick at
the wheel, his face like polished ebony from the wetness of the air,
jerked his head to larboard and said he had caught a glimpse of the
Chasseur's topgallant sail half an hour earlier. There was no breeze
to speak of; only light airs from the west that left us wallowing and
creaking in the oily cross-seas, with steerageway but little more; so
from our reef-points and top-hamper there was a slatting and whacking reminiscent of a hailstorm on a barn roof. The suggestion of a
barn, indeed, was one that came to me readily, because of the barn-
yard flavor of our waist, where there were sheep pens and crates of
fowl.

One of the men brought me a cup of coffee, stout enough to hold
up a nail, and I mooned idly over it, with that early-morning numbness of eye and brain which often accompanies changeable weather.

Pinky stirred himself between my ankles, where he was resting,
and peered out around my leg. Feeling his stub of a tail begin to
thump, I looked around myself and saw Lady Ransome had come
on deck, a dark green kerchief bound around her head like a
Spanish fisherwoman's, and her fur cloak wrapped tight about her.
I gawked at her, my cup half raised.

"Well," I said, staring. "Well—what are you—where——"

"Is it hot?" she asked, looking at the cup.

"Yes," I said, holding it before me as if waiting for someone to
throw a marlinspike at it.

"Let me have a little," she said, and took it.

"Wait; I've been drinking from it. I'll send for more."

Even while I said it, she drank what was left, watching me over the rim as she did so. I couldn't, for the life of me, think of another thing to say, and only stood looking at her until she put the cup back in my hand, which was still half open in mid-air.

"What would your aunt Cynthy say if you gave her coffee like that?" she asked. "What do they put in your coffee? Rusty iron?"

"It seems to me," I said, "it seems to me you look thinner than when I saw you in Arundel."

She seemed almost to study over her answer. "How is your mother, Captain Nason?"

"She's very well. She helped me with this sloop. No: this is a brig: she helped me with the sloop I had before this."

"When did you see her last?"

"Why, only a short time ago. Last fall. No: it was longer ago. A year ago. No: it was over a year ago: it was a year and a half ago."

Speech deserted us, and we stared at the tide streaks always to be found in the dirty gray water of the Channel, which has as many cross-currents as one of our marsh rivers within a few minutes of flood.

Only the night before, it seemed to me, there had been scores of things I wanted to say, if I could catch her alone for a moment. Yet now that I was alone with her, and she surprising me by seeming to be in a friendly mood to boot, my brain was as muddled as a plate of lobscouse. Nothing would rise to the surface.

"There are sticklebacks in England," she said at last. "They live in the ditches. In London I found a print of a woodcock flying with one of its babies held between its knees, as you said. Has your head hurt since that day?"

I told her it hadn't, and wondered why I had to be so dull and stupid.

"I suppose you've helped other girls cut their initials in the beech tree," she went on. "Better carvers than I. La, how crooked my letters were!" She laughed a gay little laugh, though it seemed to me she laughed overlong. "I fear you're always following after the women."

"No, I'm not," I said, hoping my voice sounded stern and truthful.

"Why," she said, "there's one under your bowsprit at this moment. Aren't you afraid she's leading you on, Captain Nason?"

"Leading—leading me on?" I stammered. "She was a ghost when we got the brig. She was pale—she looked entirely different."

"And you had her changed afterward, Captain Nason?"

"I changed her myself," I said. I intended my words to have no double meaning, but I thought she eyed me strangely.

We stared at each other. She stooped suddenly and picked up Pinky, pressing her cheek against the top of his head.

"I saw your brother," I told her awkwardly. "A pleasant young man. I saw Annie too. Did you see Annie?"

She nodded. "You said nothing to my brother about knowing me?" she said.

"No, I didn't. Did you?"

I knew she hadn't because of her sudden interest in adding to the roughness of Pinky's eyebrows. "Why was it you said nothing to him?" she asked.

"I don't know. Maybe because we're at war. No: I don't know why. Perhaps for the same reason I didn't tell my mother about your picture."

"What picture?" she asked, wide eyed.

"Why," I said, wishing I had held my tongue, "the one you—the one Annie——"

"Where is it?"

I fumbled under my coat and had to rip the button from the pocket, so clumsy were my fingers. I got out the picture at last and unwrapped the silk handkerchief from it. I glanced at it before I gave it to her. Certainly, I thought, she had grown thinner, and there was a look in her eyes that had never been in them when I first knew her, and that was not in the eyes of the miniature—a look I have seen only in the eyes of prisoners.

She gazed steadily at it, turning it between her fingers: then, before I realized what she was doing, she dropped it inside the collar of her dress.

"Here," I said, "here!" and I found myself with my hands stretched out toward her, as if to snatch it back again.

"There's been a deal of trouble over this, Captain Nason."

"But," I said, "it's—I've carried it—you can't——"

"Where did you find it?"

"It was in my coat when I sailed. It had slipped through a hole in the pocket. I've never let it out of my hands. It brings me luck!"

"Luck! Lud! It brought me more talk than was ever caused by the Great Plague! Now there'll be no more of it." She hummed a tune under her breath.

"You mean you'll tell your husband you've found it, and he'll stop talking?"

She nodded, without interrupting her humming.

"Stop a minute," I said. "Shall you tell him how I happened to have it? And where I was carrying it?"

"Of course," she said, looking abstractedly at the masthead.

"Well," I told her, "if you've been talked at till you're sick of talk, as I suspect you are, I'd give the matter more thought. I think it would be safer with me. It's brought me luck, and I'll try to see no harm comes to it."

The man at the masthead shouted, "Sail on the larboard beam!" The fog, I saw, was lighter; much lighter; but still there was no breeze to speak of.

Peer into the fog as I would, I could make out nothing.

There was confused shouting near the forecastle. 'Lisha Lord came aft to say the lookout had caught sight of a craft with two royals when the fog lightened for a moment. How far away, 'Lisha said, he was not sure. A mile; maybe less: maybe more.

"Was he sure of the two royals?" I asked him. If there were two it couldn't be the *Chasseur*. She was a brig-schooner like ourselves and carried only one.

"He says two," 'Lisha insisted.

We peered to larboard, but the fog hid what lay beyond us. We could see it drifting like smoke above the water, with little rents and alleys in it, as though it were being pushed aside, here and there, by objects invisible to us.

While we stared and stared into that blank gray wall, our mouths open and our muscles tight from our anxiety to sharpen our senses a muffled, cottony thud struck our eardrums like a ghostly finger pressed against them. We seemed to float in a thick, motionless world—a world without breath or life; and as we waited so, a burst of cavernous thuds tumbled on each other's heels irregularly, like the distant barking of two monstrous dogs.

I knew on the moment what had happened, as surely as though I had looked through the curtain of fog and seen it. The *Chasseur* had blundered into an enemy craft of some sort; and what would happen to her, with no breeze for maneuvering, God alone could tell. In no other way could the matter be explained, and our duty, as I saw it, was to find out whether it was indeed so. There were two ways, I knew, of finding out. I could send away our boats loaded with boarders; or I could run out the sweeps and move the brig herself in range. Since the *Lively Lady* moved easily, I figured she might be swept up almost as quickly as the boats could be manned and got away and rowed to an attack: also I felt that our guns would be needed, and if I depended on boats, the guns would be useless.

"Get out the sweeps, clear the waist of lumber and pipe to quarters," I told 'Lisha Lord.

He ran down the deck. Irrelevant thoughts popped into my head, such as that 'Lisha was from Bath and as smart-looking an officer as could be found on any British man-of-war, and that we were lucky to have him to point our guns. The brig was a turmoil of running and shouting, with the shrilling of the bos'n's whistle threading through it, as is always the case in a sudden call to quarters; and over everything continued the hot, sepulchral roaring of the guns, pressing thick, moist air against our faces.

Jotham Carr ran past, to turn my cabin into a hospital, Tommy Bickford at his heels to stow my dunnage and bring me my fowling piece. The thought of the fowling piece put Sir Arthur into my head, so I caught Tommy by the arm and turned to Lady Ransome, who had been wiped from my mind by the thudding of the guns. From the waist came a disquieting baa-ing and cackling, as the men hove the livestock over the bulwarks; but there was a faint fixed smile on Lady Ransome's lips, a smile that would stay there, once she had put it on, it seemed to me, even though the whole world fell to pieces around her.

"Go with Tommy," I told her. "Get your husband and Captain Parker. Tommy'll take you below, where there'll be no danger. Don't be afraid."

"I'm not afraid," she said.

I knew there was something I wanted to ask her, but there were too many things on my mind, such as how these other vessels might be lying, and whether 'Lisha had kept shot hot in the galley, as he had spoken of doing. She stared at me over Pinky's head, and while I was trying to remember what I wanted to say, I saw Captain Parker step on deck. Behind him was Sir Arthur, weak looking and the color of the little sponges that grow in the rock pools of Arundel, near low-water mark; so I knew he had been made ill by our wallowing in the calm. As they appeared a burst of gunfire stopped them in their tracks.

Parker shot a quick look at the fog that hemmed us in; then peered at the men casting loose carronade slides, tricing up ports, manning the sweeps, and running like ants with shot, powder, water pails, rammers, and muskets.

"Look here," he said, stepping up to me, "what's happening here?"

"Nothing you need worry about. Go below with Lady Ransome."

Sir Arthur's face was green. "Ow!" he said. "I can't permit this."

I remembered, then, that I had wanted to speak to Lady Ransome about the miniature; but now it was too late.

"Take your husband below," I told her, "and be quick about it.

Keep the dog. He'll be company. Don't let him loose. He likes the
guns."

She nodded, a bright nod, and went away with Tommy, the two
Englishmen following her, and Pinky peering back at me from around
her arm.

Moved by the sweeps, the brig was swinging to larboard, toward
the hoarse bellowing of the guns. I told myself we must see the vessels soon, since they could see each other; that it was the Ransomes'
own fault, getting into this trouble; that if they hadn't wanted trouble, they should have stayed in England, where they belonged; that
I hadn't lost a man so far, only poor Sip; that my mother would say
that what I was doing was all right, if she were here. That's the way
of it with me, I'm sorry to say: When close to trouble, I can only
think small thoughts that have next to no bearing on the matter in
hand.

A spout of water shot thirty feet in the air off our starboard quarter, giving me a picture of how they lay, broadside to us and two
cable lengths ahead. The gun crews, silent at their stations, pointed
and whispered when they saw the spout. We swept off to larboard
again, so we could come up under their bows or sterns, in a position
to rake. I felt movement in our topsails, the beginning of a light
breeze. In the same moment the lookout shouted again, and as he
shouted we saw them dimly, their top-hamper showing through the
dissolving fog, their hulls hidden, except for patches here and there,
in layers of smoke.

We came around more, until we lay broadside to them, our bow
to the westward. They were pointed northeast, a pistol shot apart.
The nearer one was a ship-rigged sloop-of-war, a corvette, with British colors at her peak. Her foretopmast was cut through at the head,
its spars and gear lolloping from the cap in a tangle. The mizzenmast
trailed over the counter, with the jagged stump of the mast rising
from the wreckage. Through the smoke we saw her people hacking
away with axes to clear the decks.

Yet there was life in her, and plenty of it. The *Chasseur*, dimly
seen through the smoke, seemed a ragged wreck of the swift brig
that had skimmed the waves beside us on the day before, though I
well knew that a vessel, though apparently cut to pieces, could be
nobly patched by a skillful crew in an hour's time. Her main-boom
was shot through, her foretopgallant yard was broken in the slings,
and her bowsprit dangled in splinters and festoons from her stem.
Her sails were riddled and shredded from the passage of grape and
round shot, so I knew the Britisher's gun crews were shooting too

high. In the moment when the two craft became clear to us through
the thinning fog, a man pitched over the side of the *Chasseur's* maintop, hung by a knee; then sprawled downward to the deck, turning
slowly in the air and vanishing in the smoke.

"Get at them with muskets," I told Jeddy, "whenever our people
can shoot without hurting the *Chasseur*. I want no gun fired till we
can rake."

The breeze died again, and the guns roared thunderously, almost
in our ears. A little futile spattering of musketry set in from our tops.
The men were under the bulwarks, stripped to the waist; for even
in cold weather there is a feeling of greater security if no coats or
shirts hamper the arms or shoulders, and if belts are pulled tight
at the waist to ease the shrinking in the stomach that comes with
fighting.

Our eyes burned and watered with the fierceness of our peering,
for there's no time to meditate when creeping into position within
easy range of an enemy, waiting for the gunfire you know must come.
And creep we did; for though the men drove the sweeps through
the water until it whirled and sucked, we seemed to lie motionless
in the oily chop, except for the lifts and lurches of the brig as the
waves had their will of her. Yet we moved; for there was a sheep
pen clinging against our side, with three half-dead sheep in it; draggled, wretched, staring-eyed beasts that blatted and blatted as the
cold Channel chop slapped unendingly at them; and this pen moved
slowly backward from our waist.

We had swept a little beyond the Britisher before she opened fire.
It may be that between the men needed to work her guns and muskets against the *Chasseur* and those who chopped at her tangles
of spars and cordage, she had no men to waste on us, or she may
have hoped to force the *Chasseur* to strike and then engage us.
Whatever the reason, we were nearly ready to turn again and sweep
under her stern when she let go her starboard battery.

There was a whirring and rattling of grapeshot above us as the
smoke jetted irregularly from her side, a small downrush of severed
tackle, and the rasping shudder that comes from being hulled with
solid shot. I moved forward to reassure the men, but they stayed
where they were, those at the sweeps pushing hard; the men under
the bulwarks lying tight, some with their arms over their heads to
guard against splinters, and some with their faces screwed around
toward the quarter-deck, grinning.

I could see the Britishers ramming home charges at the starboard ports. We would have two minutes, I knew, before the next broadside: maybe three, and maybe even four. I could make out officers on the quarter-deck as the smoke drifted away; and I wished, as I had never wished for anything in my life, for a breeze to drive us around under her stern so we could rake them off.

'Lisha Lord moved from gun to gun in the waist, tinkering with them, almost like a woman prodding at her hair, striving to get it just so. Suddenly he straightened, whirled, and jumped for the quarter-deck.

"By God!" he shouted, "it's the *Gorgon!* It's the damned old *Gorgon!*"

She let off at us again, as though in protest at 'Lisha's words. We felt the push of air against us, and a hellish clattering and whirring all about us, so I knew she had pointed her guns better. To this day I cannot kick a gray-winged grasshopper from the dune grass of Arundel in late summer without feeling my heart turn over in my breast; for their whirring is like that of flying wood splinters ripped from masts and yards and bulwarks by round shot. I could see splinters pass in a shimmery yellow mist, and felt a quick ache in my left shoulder, where a small splinter had driven into me, point first.

The men at a starboard sweep were sprawled on the deck, knocked there when the sweep was shattered by a round shot. Our foretopmast swayed, then buckled with a sound of rending timber, and hung loose and draggled. A man toppled over the edge of the foretop, twisted in mid-air and clung by his hands. I saw Moody Haley reach down, clutch him by the back of his shirt, and heave him back into the top. One of the men crawled out from beside a carronade. Blood gushed in spurts from his neck. He reached the musket stand by the main hatch, pulled himself to his feet, then fell again and lay still, a black stream moving slowly from under him.

Jeddy hustled a new sweep to the starboard sweepers, and Rowlandson Drown bawled at his men to cut away the foretopmast. I pulled the splinter from my shoulder, thankful when it came out easily from the bone, and told Pomp to put over the helm.

"All ships look like the *Gorgon* to you," I reminded 'Lisha. Automatically I figured that if nothing happened to us we would be in a position to rake in three minutes.

"Like hell they do!" 'Lisha said, his voice shaking as if with cold. "That's the *Gorgon!* I thought it was the *Gorgon* when I got a look at her through the fog! Now I know it! Look at her maintop netting, made in diamonds! That's mine, by God! I made it!"

It was in diamonds, as he said; and as I peered at her, wrapped in smoke and littered with her tangled top-hamper, it seemed to me I could recognize, on the quarter-deck, the burly figure of Captain Bullard-Jones.

Smoke gushed from her starboard battery once more. "One—two —three!" 'Lisha counted, above the howling and rattling that followed the discharge. "Three! They can't bring the others to bear!"

"Give 'em a gun," I said. "Keep it away from the *Chasseur*." I thanked God, as 'Lisha jumped for the long gun, that the *Gorgon* had been able to bring only three to bear; for these three had left a ragged, furry hole in our mainmast, shattered the bottom of our longboat, and stretched Rowlandson Drown on the deck; while something, though there was no way of knowing what at the moment, had happened to our steering gear. The wheel had whirled suddenly in Pomp's hands, throwing him to the deck with wrists half broken.

I saw Jeddy run to Rowlandson and pull at his arm, looking at his face; and from the way he let his arm drop and turned away I knew Rowlandson was dead.

'Lisha worked at his gun, squinting and squinting. The deck jerked as he fired, and in the same moment the sternmost gun of the *Gorgon's* starboard battery, struck fair on the muzzle by 'Lisha's shot, kicked backward and exploded.

The crew of the long gun leaped like jumping jacks, sponging and loading. "Load with one shot!" I heard 'Lisha tell them. "There's a hot one goes on top."

He ran down the deck toward the galley, slapping at the gun crews. "Steady as a rock!" he shouted. "We'll never have no such gun platform again! Right into her guts, boys!"

We crept in and crept in, closer to the *Gorgon's* stern, but slowly: as slowly, almost, as the moon comes up beyond the brown rocks of Cape Arundel. Her masts, wrapped in a tangle of sails, spars, shrouds and running rigging, drew closer together as we brought them in line, and up through them rose white wreaths of smoke from her guns; for still she hammered at the *Chasseur*, and still the *Chasseur* hammered back, though the roars of both had a labored, weary slowness.

'Lisha ran from the galley, behind him two men with pails.

I saw a long gun emerge from one of the *Gorgon's* stern ports and slowly come to bear on us. My muscles were tight as barrel hoops, and I wanted to crouch behind the bulwark for a second—for half a second even—to do anything except stand and wait.

'Lisha Lord shouted to the gun crews of the long guns. They

dumped the shot from the pails into their guns, and 'Lisha ran for the forward carronades.

The *Gorgon's* stern gun bellowed at us. It was langrage—old iron and bolts and pieces of kettles and nails—and it screamed around and over us as though the sky were filled with angry cats.

'Lisha's first shot went through the cabin windows of the *Gorgon*. His second smashed her rudder. Our men came up cheering from behind the bulwarks, all a-drip from waiting. They cheered and swabbed and cheered, and last of all 'Lisha ran to the long guns loaded with hot shot.

Perspiration dropped from Jeddy's chin as he shook his fist at the *Gorgon* and screamed at her, in a shrill, cracked voice, to strike her colors.

The long guns roared out of a welter of white smoke. Aboard the *Gorgon* we heard a muffled, anguished cough, as though some great hulk of an animal had coughed in deathly sickness. The smoke lifted; the cough died; then rose immediately into a roar. The wreckage of her mainmast and mizzenmast reeled; and up from her midship section sprouted a bell of planks and cordage and men and gear, a bell that blossomed into a mushroom of smoke and suddenly climbed up and up into a flame-shot column, in which moved black, broken objects, turning slowly as they mounted.

A strange silence came down upon us and on all the sea as well. It was silence, and yet not silence; for in the distance there was a rushing noise from within the column of smoke that still mounted upward from the *Gorgon*, until it seemed to hang over us like an enormous maple tree in full leaf. We heard a rasping and creaking from our damaged top-hamper, and a sickening moaning from a wounded man in the foretop.

"Lower away the boats," I told Jeddy. There was a walloping splash hard by our counter, and thumps here and there on our deck, followed by a rush of falling fragments, hurtling down at us from the sides of that cone-shaped cloud.

The hull of the *Gorgon* had opened out like a melon suddenly dropped on the ground, but now her bow and stern came upright again. The opening seemed about to close; then slowly and wearily widened once more; and the bow and stern, wavering and groping as though feeling their way beneath the surface, settled deeper and deeper into the gray water of the Channel until it came to us suddenly that they were entirely gone: that there was nothing left of the *Gorgon* but a welter of planks and broken spars and splintered fragments, with heads here and there among them, and over them a vast, ever spreading umbrella of smoke. From those heads among the wreckage there rose a faint, thin piping, like the distant calling of young frogs such as we hear in Arundel on warm nights in the spring of the year.

XIX

THE men were knotting and splicing the rigging, plugging the shot holes in our hull and nailing lead over them, and making ready to fish our wounded masts and spars as soon, almost, as the boats had been lowered away; for they knew, as well as I, that the English Channel was no place in which to waste time celebrating a victory, especially when we were helpless as a shark with his tail cut off. We would be fit to maneuver, I knew, in a half hour's time if there was nothing to worry us but our masts and spars and rigging; for no seamen in the world are so quick and handy at repairing ship as are American seamen. But in addition to our top-hamper we had our rudder to consider; and when we came to look at it we found we had no rudder at all, the rudder post having been cut by a shot, and the whole machine having wrenched away. Thus we couldn't move until we made a false sternpost, or preventer sternpost, reeved a rudder of plank to it, fixed it in place, and fastened the false rudder in turn to the main chains by guys and tackles. This is the devil's own job, and we laid out the necessary gear on the quarter-deck, to save time and trouble; and into this turmoil came Sir Arthur Ransome and his wife and Captain Parker.

I think there is some good in most men, at least in those brought up among decent people, although some Englishmen seem to take pains to discourage Americans in that belief. To me Sir Arthur Ransome seemed to be such an Englishman; and I wondered where I could stow that green-faced nuisance before he offended my crew with one of his ill-considered remarks, and so got himself thrown overboard. Even as I did so he came to me, radiating offensiveness. "Look here, Nason," he said, in that whiny voice of his that set my teeth on edge.

"*Captain* Nason to you," I told him, feeling savage from anxiety as well as from the discomfort in my shoulder. "For God's sake, hold your tongue till we've put ourselves in order!"

"Ow!" he said, stiff and contemptuous, "Lady Ransome asked——"

"She's not hurt?" I snapped, conscious that the very thought made the deck seem to lurch beneath me.

"She wishes to be of assistance to your surgeon in the cabin," he said, staring at the clotted splotch on the shoulder of my shirt, so that I was reminded to put on my coat again. "I couldn't myself: very squeamish stomach on the water."

I thanked him as well as I was able. The cabin, I told him, was no place for a woman; and we could somehow make out by ourselves. I never had any doubt that Sir Arthur Ransome thought me a boor; and just then he was no doubt entirely right, though I tried to console myself by thinking he had never had to supervise the making of a preventer sternpost and rudder.

The fog was growing steadily lighter. Directly overhead was a patch of blue sky. The cat's-paws were steadying, so I knew we would soon have a breeze from the west. The boats were coming back from the wreckage of the *Gorgon;* and men were swarming in the rigging of the *Chasseur* like snails on eel grass. Her bowsprit was in place once more, though the bobstays and shrouds were not set up; a new foretopgallant yard had been swayed onto the cap, and the main-boom had been fished. I tried to make out Boyle through the glass but couldn't find him.

Jeddy came over the side while we were reeving guys through the preventer sternpost. "It was the *Gorgon,*" he said. "Those people from the *Chasseur,* they say they'll make you King of Maine when we get home."

"Well," I told him, "I'd rather have their rudder, so we'd be sure of getting home. How many did you pick up?"

"Seventeen. The *Chasseur's* boat got about thirty."

"Any officers?"

"No; only seamen and petty officers."

"Any wounded men?"

"No; they sank."

"Is Boyle all right?" I asked him.

Jeddy looked at me thoughtfully. "They got hit pretty bad, I guess; but Boyle, he only got a bullet through that gray beaver of his."

I think the thought of Rowlandson Drown lying on the deck came to both of us at the same time, because Jeddy coughed and cleared his throat and said we couldn't all be lucky; then turned away quickly to attend to the *Gorgon's* men.

A patch of sunlight showed on the water near us. Ripples lapped against our side, and it occurred to me that if my luck were what it should be, the fog would have held on and the breeze held off for another hour.

"How long, boys?" I asked the men rigging the tackles on the rudder.

One said twenty minutes; another an hour. A man screamed in the cabin, so I knew Jotham Carr must be taking off an arm or a leg. It came to me that he lacked practice in such matters: that it would be better for me to help him than to stand on deck with nothing but my thoughts to keep me company. I had no more than started for the cabin when I saw the *Chasseur* wear to the north before a light westerly breeze. I thought Boyle was coming down to see what he could do for us, and I was wishful of seeing him; but it seemed strange he should wear to the north when we lay southwest of him.

I saw him crowd on his studding sails, holding steadily to his northerly course; and so rapidly did he leave us under this press of canvas that even while I gazed blankly after him, the figures on the *Chasseur's* quarter-deck faded to specks and then to pinpoints.

Jeddy came and stood beside me, looking after her. "Well——" he said. "Well——" And with that he launched into a string of curses that he never got out of any book, not even one of Tobias Smollett's. It was in the midst of his cursing, when he had become so involved and fanciful that the men at work on the rudder sat back on their haunches to stare up at him, that the man at the masthead shouted "Sail!"

Jeddy stopped abruptly. The men flew at their work again. We made out the sail, far to the northward, beyond the *Chasseur*. I realized instantly that the *Chasseur* had seen it first and set off at once to intercept it; and I thought to myself that this is the way of it, often, when a friend seems to go off unfaithfully on other affairs, so that we curse him and soon thereafter lose him as a friend.

What the sail might be we couldn't tell. It looked to me like a ponderous craft. I had my suspicions, and they were such as to give me an empty feeling in my stomach and a coppery taste in my mouth; for I had no desire that our cruise should end here in the gray waters of the Channel, with us caught like a rabbit lurching and squeaking in a trap.

I could see Boyle holding straight for the sail, and knew he would do what he could; but I also knew we must make a try at helping ourselves. If she should indeed be an enemy, as I suspected, she might turn off in pursuit of Boyle if only she could see us under way. It was this, I was sure, for which Boyle was hoping.

The hole in our mainmast had been fished, and a new topmast swayed up, fidded, and stayed; so that nothing stood between us and safety except our rudder. Due east, if my reckoning was good, lay the Island of Jersey, largest of the Channel Islands. With a light

westerly breeze, provided we were able to maneuver, we could turn
the Ransomes adrift close to the island and be safe on the Norman
coast in the little harbor of Carteret or St. Germain-sur-Ay before
sundown.

I thought about it; then called Jeddy and 'Lisha Lord to the quarter-deck. The *Chasseur* was hull down, but the strange sail, which
she had not yet reached, showed the tops of her bulwarks above the
water. We needed no word from the man at the masthead to tell us
that a ship of this size must be a seventy-four—a ship-of-the-line;
and since America had no war craft larger than a forty-four-gun
frigate we knew she had to be a Britisher.

"Well," I said, "we'll try steering with the sweeps, unless somebody knows a better way. If we can keep before the wind for five
minutes she may run off after Boyle." They said nothing, but stood
staring into the north. As we watched, the *Chasseur* hauled her wind
and went off to the northwest, to windward of the seventy-four. We
peered and peered, hoping to see the seventy-four go off on the same
tack after her, though we knew no seventy-four ever built could sail
half as fast as the *Chasseur*.

"Some of these seventy-four captains," 'Lisha said, "they ain't so
bad. Either they're moss-backed old pigs, not fit for eating or killing
or anything else, or they know their business."

There was a dull, distant thud, more of a throb in the air than a
thud; then another; but the seventy-four came straight on. 'Lisha
grunted. "Threw a couple thirty-six pounders at random! He knows
his business."

"Get out the sweeps," I told them. "Run 'em through the stern
ports."

We made sail and wore around. As we came before the wind the
sweeps seemed almost to hold her steady. She got fresh way rapidly,
held on her course for half a minute, then yawed suddenly to
larboard.

"Starboard!" Jeddy bawled. The men at the sweeps pushed hard
at them. The *Lively Lady* shivered a little, wallowed back toward
her course, hung for a moment, then yawed again and broached to.

The seventy-four may have been three miles off; but so accurately
was she pointed that if she kept on as she was, her stem would slice
us neatly in two, unless we could take ourselves out of her path. The
Chasseur had come about and shot past her to windward, and now
wore across her bows once more. Boyle, we knew, was armed only
with long twelves, whereas the seventy-four must carry thirty-six
pounders or forty-two pounders: consequently it was clear to us that

there was nothing more for him to do. Yet he would not give up. He hove a shot at her as he passed her bows: then tacked twice in quick succession, letting off a gun each time, though he could no more hurt the lumbering hulk that surged contemptuously on her way than a woodpecker could hurt the side of a house.

Rowlandson Drown's assistant had been a gangling young man from Quincy in Massachusetts, one James Combs. At Rowlandson's death he had become ship's carpenter; and it was he who straightened up from the rudder, shouting, "Get her over." With 'Lisha Lord and Jeddy climbing around and among them like two inquisitive cats, the men put this rough machine overboard, then lashed the upper part of the preventer post to the brig's sternpost, and bolted the two together to keep the false sternpost from rising up or falling down. There were men under the stern, working half submerged, with one or two entirely under water at times.

Seeing that his attempts were useless, evidently, Boyle had left the seventy-four and was coming down on us under a cloud of sail. Behind him the seventy-four, less than two miles distant, towered upward like an iceberg, glistening white and no less pitiless and dangerous.

The men worked at the tackles like figures in a nightmare, slower than anything I had ever seen; and I was so desirous of getting free of this enormous black-stemmed vessel and the triple line of guns along its side that I was hard put to it to get enough air into my lungs. I stood silent, my hands clenched tight in my pockets and the nails biting into my palms. The machine was done at last, so that Jeddy set up a shout from larboard and 'Lisha from starboard.

With two men handling the larboard tackles and two the starboard tackles of our makeshift rudder, the *Lively Lady* wore slowly around. She made as though to yaw; then held steady and slipped more and more rapidly through the water, to the south, straight away from the seventy-four. She was a mile off by now, a tremendous big ship, making the *Chasseur*, close astern of us, look like a pilot boat. As we picked up speed she fired a gun. Jeddy laughed and waggled his fingers at his nose. "Growl, you black bitch!" he said; and indeed there was a look about her of a big black dog showing white teeth at us, in a rage at having a dinner snatched from her jaws.

The *Chasseur* came up under our lee, her crew swarming along her bulwarks and high on her ratlines, bawling and hurrooing at the top of their lungs, and waving their hats and hands until the whole brig seemed aflutter. Boyle was perched on his aftermost long gun, but his bell-topped beaver was not on his head, so that he did not make us one of his fine sweeping bows. Instead of that, he reached up his hands, tightly clasped together, and shook them at us without a word. It occurred to me he might be feeling the same tightness in his chest and throat that I felt—a tightness that came from knowing him to be safe and grateful for our help—and so be averse to attempting any speech.

He dragged out his gray silk handkerchief, blew his nose violently; then smiled and nodded at me. I thought he was about to say something; but even as I cupped my ear with my hand I saw him cast a quick glance at our foretopmast and stand staring at it, his mouth half open. At the same moment I saw the heads of all his crew swing upward as if drawn by one string, so that every eye on the *Chasseur* was fixed on our foretopmast.

I needed nothing more to know that we were done: not even the ripping, splintering crackle that followed immediately as our new foretopmast gave way two thirds below its head and toppled to leeward; nor yet the second crash following close on the heels of the first when the foremast, weakened no doubt by the break during the engagement and by this additional strain, broke off close to the deck.

A hissing groan went up from the decks of the *Chasseur* as she shot ahead of us, and as we veered around, dragged by the wreckage. There was a queer, absent-minded look on the faces of our crew and of Jeddy and 'Lisha as they stared at the wreck of the foremast, almost as though they watched a cat sleeping on the deck or some similarly harmless and familiar spectacle.

Boyle, I saw, intended to speak us once more. He came into the wind, then wore around, starting to circle us. The seventy-four, still a mile astern, lumbered relentlessly on her way. I turned my eyes from her, knowing I would see enough of her before the day was done.

"Work fast," I told Jeddy. "Get out boarding axes and cut all rigging. Lower away the boats. Get the prisoners on deck and into the boats, and the wounded too."

Boyle ran under our stern, his crew as silent and watchful as though we were strangers.

"Do anything!" I heard him shout. "Anything! Prisoners? Can I take prisoners? Any belongings? Can I take anybody? Anything?"

There was the least possible chance that one boatload of people had time to pass from us to the *Chasseur*.

I turned to look at the Ransomes and Captain Parker. There was a smug look about Parker and Sir Arthur, for which I could not blame them; but Lady Ransome's face I could not see, because she was sitting on the deck, with Pinky still in her arms, and was too busy with him to notice me.

"No, indeed, thank you," Sir Arthur said, in answer to my unspoken question, and I remember how mislikable I found his pronunciation of "thank you," which was "think yaw." "No, indeed! We'll stay where we are!"

I waved to Boyle to go on. "Stand by," I called to him, "until the *Lively Lady's* gone. I don't want her taken!"

Boyle nodded vigorously; the *Chasseur* slipped away into the south; and to me her departure seemed like that of an old, dear friend, so that my heart was like lead.

The seventy-four was close on us: no more than a half mile away. Our prisoners were on deck and our boats in the water, and Jotham Carr was seeing to bringing the wounded from the cabin. There was only one thing left to be done. Since I wished to be sure it *was* done, I warned Jeddy not to strike our colors till I returned; and with that I ran forward and down into the carpenter's quarters.

There was an old roundabout jacket belonging to Rowlandson Drown lying on the bench, where he had dropped it less than ten minutes before he was killed. I picked it up and hung it on a nail and tried not to think about it as I poured varnish over the shavings and worked with my phosphorus bottle and a match to get a light.

The drenched shavings burst into flames with a roar, and I fled back on deck pursued by a blast of heat that singed my shirt. The seventy-four, hove-to at pistol-shot distance, was like a black cliff, bristling with guns. Her bulwarks, rigging and ports were a-swarm with men—as many as can be found in Arundel and Cape Porpus put together.

At the sight of me, Jeddy pulled down our colors with such eagerness that I knew the seventy-four had been threatening to throw a shot at us if it was not done speedily.

I looked around, but could see nothing else that needed doing. Lady Ransome sat in the stern of the longboat, still with Pinky in her arms. Beside her sat her husband, his blanket full of belongings at his feet. I sent them away; then shouted up to the gold epaulettes shining above the gaily painted taffrail that we were on fire and needed boats. After that, as well as I could for the growing heaviness in my head, I took my last look at the *Lively Lady*.

They wasted no time getting us aboard, for a burning privateer is no welcome neighbor to any ship. Knowing the customs of our captors, I thought they would put us in that stinking, three-foot-high den in the bows known as the cable tier, and leave us to rot in the dark on the slime-covered coils of the cable. I have no doubt that if this seventy-four had been one of the ships used for transporting American prisoners, we would have received the same inhuman treatment suffered by thousands of captured Americans during the war; but it had fallen to our lot to be taken by the *Granicus*, Captain Wise commanding, and this Captain Wise was as pleasant and as easy to be with as any of our own great captains. Why Decatur and Perry and Lawrence and Hull and MacDonough should be quiet, companionable, polite, pleasant, thoughtful men, and the greatest of our fighters to boot, and why our incompetents should have been selfish blusterers, I do not know; but that was the truth of it. The captains I have named would not, I have heard men say, permit their crews to be whipped for offenses, and this was also true of Wise; but throughout the entire British navy of more than eight hundred ships there was hardly an officer who would not tie up any member of his crew for the smallest infraction of discipline and see his back chopped into bleeding mincemeat. I say here, in no spirit of rancor, that British naval officers, taking them by and large, were more cruel and brutal than can possibly be realized by persons who are sheltered in peaceful homes, and sleep securely on soft beds under warm blankets; so to find myself in the hands of a man like Wise was as great a surprise as to drop a hook among a school of sculpins and catch a fat beefsteak.

We were paraded before him as soon as we were aboard. He stood at the quarter-deck rail, staring down at us, a thin, tall man, possibly fifty years of age. His hair was crinkly brown, heavily shot with gray; and he had a habit of half closing his eyes before he spoke, so that he seemed about to deliver himself of an angry remark.

"I'm told," he said to us gruffly, "that the prisoners aboard your brig were well treated, and I'm a believer in turn about. I'll therefore put you to lodge on the orlop deck, and you'll be in charge of your own officers until you pass out of my control and into the hands of the Transport Office. I expect orderly conduct from you, even though I've heard that such a thing is seldom found where American seamen are concerned. Until I'm disabused you'll receive the same rations issued to the people of this man-of-war."

He turned on his heel; then swung back to us again. "I'd like to see your captain in my cabin."

When I stepped forward he nodded curtly, spoke briefly to a young officer near him, and walked off without another word. Tommy Bickford would have followed me with my duffel bag; but a red-coated marine took it from him.

I cast a final look around as I mounted to the quarter-deck of this towering vessel. Back under our lee, a smudge of black smoke pouring from her forward hatch, lay the *Lively Lady*, forlorn and untidy, her foremast dragging in the Channel chop; her mainsail lying half over the side, slack and useless, like a broken wing. A mile to the south I saw the *Chasseur* slipping toward the southeast. Even as I looked she hauled her wind and stood back toward us again, so I knew there would be no better days in store for the poor hulk we had just left. Boyle would sink her if she didn't sink herself. I tried to remember, watching her, when it was I had brought the cheese to Boyle; but I could only remember it was long, long ago.

The young officer spoke to me, sharp and haughty, ordering me to follow; and I stumbled after him with a slack and gone feeling, as though my legs and brain were stuffed with straw.

The captain's cabin in one of these British seventy-fours is a palace by itself, rising from the rear of the quarter-deck like a rich house set down at the end of a village green; and I, entering it, felt myself shabby, with something of mendicancy and disgraceful misfortune about me.

The young officer rapped at a paneled door and stood aside for me to pass in, looking as though he wished me the worst luck in the world. I entered a low-ceiled room that seemed enormous, larger than our living room in Arundel, and stood before this tall, thin, crinkly-haired captain. He had laid aside his great cocked hat and was sitting at a polished table with a hand on either knee and his lips pursed as though he intended to clap me in chains for life.

"I've been told, sir," he said, without preamble, "that you purposely set fire to a prize."

"No, sir; I did not."

"I have the word of an Englishman for it!" He eyed me coldly. "I have his word you shouted to the commanding officer of the privateer brig that annoyed me so determinedly before I came up with you. You told him to stand by until your vessel had been destroyed."

"I didn't strike my colors until after the fire had broken out," I said.

"Then you set the fire?"

"Yes, sir."

"Then in effect you set fire to British property; for you had no means of escaping and were as good as captured."

"It wasn't a prize till I struck my colors," I repeated, feeling dull and numb. "You might have blown up."

Despite my hair-splitting, he gave me a courteous reply.

"So I might! So I might! I never thought of that!" He compressed his lips again and made a flirting motion with his hand. "That's no reason, however. If you destroyed a prize with no greater justification, I shall be forced to take steps. I'll be forced to make representations to the Transport Office."

There was a dull roar far astern, like the muffled rumble of a nearing thunderstorm, and I knew I would never set eyes on the *Lively Lady* again. Something seemed to go from me, so that I could hardly stand on my feet before this captain, who suddenly appeared to me more powerful than any man I had ever met. I saw he was waiting for me to speak.

"Well," I said, "there was no way out of it. I passed my word."

He frowned. "Come, come, Captain! You'd better tell me the full tale. And let me have your name, while you're about it."

"Nason; the *Lively Lady,* eighteen guns and——"

"Yes," he said, flirting his hand again, "yes, yes! Wise is my name: *Granicus,* seventy-four. Now, Captain Nason."

"Well," I said, "there it is." For the life of me I couldn't remember what he'd asked me.

Captain Wise eyed me closely. "So you passed your word, did you?"

"Yes. I couldn't get the brig till I passed my word she shouldn't fall into the hands of the British. I passed my word, and so I got her."

"Indeed! And to whom did you pass your word?"

"Robert Surcouf," I said. "Fox-faced man. Damned French pirate. Asked double what she was worth and made me give my word to boot."

"Was that Surcouf of St. Malo?"

"Yes. Surcouf. Look out for him. Had to have her, and he traded close, damn him. There's worse people than Yankees, and you can tie to it."

"And where did Surcouf get her?" he wanted to know. It seemed to me his face had come loose from its fastenings, for it appeared to slip sideways: then waver back into place.

"Get her?" I asked. "He built her! The *Revenant.* Meant *Revenge,* Jeddy said. He's a crazy little fool. She never meant *Revenge.* She's a ghost. I mean she *was* the *Ghost.* I took her out of the grave, Captain, and made her the *Lively Lady,* but now she's a ghost that's laid for good, green dress, red hair and all."

With that, feeling somewhat upset because of the throbbing in my shoulder, I laughed at the thought of the ghost that had been laid—

laughed till the tears ran down my cheeks and till I had to hang to the table. Then I found myself in a chair, drinking a glass of brandy, and heard Captain Wise at the cabin door, passing the word for the surgeon.

"Well, well," he said, "well, well, well, well! So that was the *Revenant!* Well, well, well! I should have you shot for that, my boy! Well, well, well, well! The *Revenant.*"

I might have fallen asleep from the persistence with which he repeated himself and the regularity with which he nodded his head as he sat staring at me, if the surgeon had not come in, a man both pompous and obsequious, followed by a pimply-faced assistant smelling of medicines.

"Now," Wise said, "anything wrong with you? Get hurt this morning?"

"No," I said, not liking the looks of the surgeon. "Nothing. Nothing at all."

The surgeon's assistant had my coat off and whipped the shirt over my head before I could down the last of my brandy.

"Pretty!" the surgeon said, looking at my shoulder. "Sweet as a daisy. Very finely cushioned by the deltoid muscle." He prodded me with a forefinger like a red banana. "Hm! Hard! Surprised the splinter didn't bounce off! Take out half a pint of blood and he'll be better than ever!"

He bled me, as I knew he would; for these navy surgeons bleed a man for everything under God's heaven—for headache, toothache and footache; for burns, frostbites, loss of memory and even loss of blood. Whenever they don't know what to do, they bleed their patients; and since they seldom know what to do they're forever bleeding someone. Yet I must admit that when he had taken a cupful of blood from my arm I felt relieved.

"How'll he do for dinner?" Captain Wise asked the surgeon, while the assistant helped me on with my shirt.

"Admirably," the surgeon said. "Ten minutes' rest and he'll be fit to eat a sheep!" He went away with his assistant, wheezing mirthfully like a porpoise clearing his nose of a vast accumulation of air and water.

"Yes," Captain Wise said, "a bite of dinner'll do you no harm. It'll occupy your mind and improve my own. I've heard monstrous strange tales about Americans, but I've had few opportunities to speak with them."

The wheezy surgeon was right; for after I had stretched myself for a time on the berth in the small gun-deck cabin in which I was stowed by the captain's orders, and had freed myself of blood and powder stains and struggled into the clean clothes Tommy Bickford had stuffed in my duffel bag, there was a stiffness in my shoulder; but the blackness that filled my brain after the blowing up of the *Lively Lady* had fallen away, as the tide falls on our Arundel beaches, though now and again a black wave came out of the receding tide and lapped at my brain once more, as I suppose must always be the case whenever a tide goes out.

Sir Arthur and Lady Ransome were in the captain's cabin when I went to it, and Captain Parker as well; and I cannot deny feeling bitter when I saw how they had become gay and light-hearted and inclined to toss scraps of gaiety to me, whether I wanted them or not.

"Ow, Captain," Sir Arthur said, as I came toward them, "we owe you an apology, I fear, for making you a trifle late for your appointment at the Island of Jersey."

I smiled as pleasantly as I could.

"Jersey!" Captain Wise exclaimed. "Weren't you getting a little deep in enemy waters?"

Sir Arthur laughed spitefully. "You'd not have thought so, Captain, if you'd heard Mr. Nason making free with our Channel, no longer ago than last night! You'd have thought the place was full of his friends! He was talking, even, of blockading Great Britain!" He stared at me. I looked from him to Lady Ransome and felt a sudden tightness in my breast to see her bend down her head as if to hide the wave of color that mounted suddenly into her face.

"I think that was Captain Boyle," I said. "It's Captain Boyle who intends to blockade you."

Captain Wise made a mildly explosive sound in his throat. "I've heard of him!" he said. "In the Indies. The whole British navy has heard of him. It wasn't Boyle—why, by God, sir, of *course* it was Boyle who squittered around me like a petrel! So that was Boyle! I nearly ran off after him when you got under way this morning. Why, I'd as soon expect to mash a flea with my best bower anchor as catch that gentleman!"

He led the way to the table and, when we were seated, looked at me sharply. "Your brig, now," he said. "How did she sail with Boyle's brig?"

"About the same," I told him. "Under favorable circumstances we did fifteen knots."

He shook his head wonderingly. "I can't account for it. Boyle's vessel was American built, I take it."

"Yes. Baltimore built."

"We can't build such vessels," Captain Wise said, "and if we could, we couldn't sail 'em."

Sir Arthur widened his eyes slightly. "Don't you think it possible, Captain, that Americans brag a little faster than they sail?"

Captain Wise studied Sir Arthur carefully. "No," he said at length, "no, I regret to say that doesn't explain it. We've taken a few of these fast American vessels, but had the devil's time trying to use 'em. We're afraid of their long masts, so we shorten 'em. We strengthen the hulls and find we have tubs."

"And may I ask, Captain Wise," Sir Arthur asked, "whether or not you've ever been in America? You appear to display a peculiar tolerance for its people. Ah—they shoot birds sitting!"

Captain Wise coughed. "Then I wish to God, sir, they'd be as thoughtful of us and wait till we sit!" He turned to me. "You people are different from us on sea, and I've heard you're more so on land. Yet most of you are only two or three generations out of England. How do you explain the difference, Captain Nason?"

I think I got red, and I know I spoke foolishly; for what came upon my tongue were only the stock phrases of our politician orators. "I think it's the air of liberty we breathe that makes us different. Our fathers won our freedom from British bondage; we cast off the shackles——"

Suddenly I stopped, remembering in what plight I stood myself at that lamentable moment, and seeing that the others thought it strange I should speak just then of freedom and the casting off of shackles.

Captain Wise coughed again; not even Sir Arthur looked at me, and the air seemed heavy with discomfort. It was Lady Ransome who spoke; her voice was low, and her eyes hidden by her lashes.

"Freedom," she murmured. "Yes, Americans seem to love freedom; and what will so many of them do when they're in our prisons?" She spoke the last word in so faint a voice that it was scarcely audible.

I stared at the table, unwilling to trust myself to look at her. Her husband laughed comfortably. "It's to be feared, my dear," he said, "that you've asked a question Mr. Nason will unfortunately soon be able to answer. Fortunes of war, fortunes of war!"

Lady Ransome didn't look up, and Captain Wise cleared his throat. "I was thinking about your little dog, Captain Nason. Lady Ransome tells me the dog she brought aboard is yours, but is nevertheless English. My thought was this: for a time American prisoners in English prisons were allowed to keep dogs, but there got to be too many of them, and someone gave an order they should all be killed. I'm afraid there was great lamentation: rather hard on the poor men, because seven hundred of those little comrades of theirs were destroyed on one day. Too bad, too bad!"

He assumed an air of gruffness that deceived no one. "Too bad, of course! Ah—since your little dog's already in Lady Ransome's custody and seems happy with her, it might be—you know your own business best, of course—Sir Arthur being a sportsman—ah, I thought it might be well if Sir Arthur could persuade you to—ah——"

"I'd consider it a great honor," I said, "if Lady Ransome would accept my dog: a great honor and a great relief, for to have him killed would be worse than——"

"No," Sir Arthur interrupted promptly. "The dog has points; I've noticed him, but I shouldn't want to be indebted. I don't mind purchasing the dog for my wife; but no gifts! No gifts!"

Lady Ransome looked up; her hand was at her throat, flat against it, so I could see the little indentations in the smooth skin over her knuckles. Yet the fingers seemed almost to flutter, as if she were about to make a gesture toward me; and I wondered, if her impulse carried, what that impulse would be.

"Of course," I said to Sir Arthur. "However it's done, it's a favor to me. Make the price whatever you like."

"Ow!" Sir Arthur said, "I never make an offer. *You* make the price, you know: if it's reasonable, I accept: if not, I won't, eh?"

I have no doubt, as I have said, that the man tried always to be just and fair; yet to my way of thinking he could do and say nothing gracefully.

"Would two pounds be too much?" I asked.

"Ow, not in the least," Sir Arthur said. He drew a wallet from his breast pocket, took out three bits of paper, and tossed them across the table. "I think he's worth all of three pounds, you know!"

I picked them up and put them in my pocket, unmindful of his manner in my relief at Pinky's safety.

"That's right," Captain Wise said, "that's right. You'll find use for that before you know it."

There was a knock on the door, and the captain's polite young secretary entered and bowed. "Land, sir," he said. "Wembury Point."

"Plymouth!" Sir Arthur said. "We're nearly home, eh, Nason?"

At the word "home" I turned to Lady Ransome sharply, as though she had spoken. She was staring full at me, almost haggardly; and for that moment it seemed to me, strangely, that we were actually speaking to each other, though I could not have said what the words were or even what they meant.

Suddenly she sprang up. "Plymouth?" she cried to Captain Wise, "Plymouth? But that means—Dartmoor!"

"Yes," he said, and he seemed ill at ease. "I—that is—well, really, there's nothing to be done about it: you'll go to the depot at Dartmoor, Captain Nason."

XX

THE harbor of Plymouth is cup shaped, with deep green hills rising abruptly from it; and because of the persistent rain that fell as long as I stayed there, it gave me the feel of a large green funnel that was gathering all the misery in the world and pouring it down my neck.

We moved up, in the early morning, past a partly finished breakwater between the sound and the inner harbor; and I, thinking to myself that I must, if possible, have a final word with Lady Ransome before I was taken ashore, set out to go on deck, only to find myself stopped by a red-coated marine on guard at the cabin door.

"Captain's orders," he said, barring my way with his cutlass. "Prisoners to be took to the berth deck for disembarking."

I backed up and sat on the edge of my bunk, half desperate with disappointment. I had watched and watched, the night before, and vainly tried for a word alone with her, for I couldn't forget the little movement of her hand at her throat. It had seemed to me, the more I thought of it, that there was something she wanted to say to me but couldn't. Later, half asleep in my berth, I could have sworn I heard her voice in my ear: not a dream voice, but a living voice, saying nothing of importance, but saying it so distinctly that I started up on my mattress, dry throated and my heart pounding fit to push my ribs apart.

The marine shuffled his feet outside the door and coughed. "Captain's orders," he repeated. "Prisoners to be took to the berth deck for disembarking."

"Now?" I asked him.

"Yerss," he said.

There was nothing for it but to go, so I picked up my duffel bag and followed him into the bowels of the ship.

Our men were peering from ports at the slanting drifts of rain that tinged the green hills of Plymouth with a bluish haze. They were guarded by so many marines that I thought there must have been a mutiny, though I soon found this to be the custom of the British where American prisoners were concerned.

Tommy Bickford took my bag. "Where we going, Cap'n Dick?" he asked.

Jeddy and 'Lisha Lord pushed up close to hear the answer. When I told them Dartmoor, they blinked, as a dog blinks at a threatened blow.

We came to anchor in that portion of the harbor known as Hamoaze, and no time was wasted getting boats into the water and us into them, so that the *Granicus* might be relieved of the burden of feeding us. As we lay in the boats and cutters, sopping up rain like sponges, I stared and stared at the quarter-deck of the *Granicus* and at the cabin windows, unwilling to admit I had looked for the last time on the face of Lady Ransome, and her hair like rubbed copper, and her smoke-colored eyes that had silently asked me for God knew what. But in return for all my staring I saw only rivulets of rain water trickling from the galleries, and an occasional scowling face peering from the after ports.

They put us ashore in the drizzle; and even at this hour in the morning we found ourselves surrounded by drunken sailors out of grogshops, trulls with voices like knives, old women carrying jugs of ale and baskets full of cakes, fried eels and boiled sheep's heads; by Devon farmers in corduroy breeches, red vests that dropped half down their fat thighs, and little tight brimless yellow caps like the scooped-out half of a pumpkin.

Some pitied us and others didn't. "Look at 'em!" a trull screamed, pointing at Jeddy and me, "look at 'em, sayin' they're Amairicans, when there ain't nobody as don't know Amairicans has red skins."

The English sailor with her looked at her gravely, raised her chin with his forefinger, and hit her fair on the jaw. She went down in a heap in the mud. He swayed on his feet, wagging his head at us drunkenly. "Sportsmen!" he said. "Tha's what we are! Treat prisoners like sportsmen even if they *be* a lot o' blasted rebels!"

Our escort of a hundred moon-faced Devonshire militiamen started us off at last, up the steep streets of Plymouth and away from the sour smell and the mud. As we went, Plymouth seemed more than ever like a funnel; for a piercing wind roared down the abrupt roadways, rain beat into our soggy garments, and brown driblets of water wriggled from foothole to foothole in the claylike mud.

I expected, when we reached the top of the hill, to march off on a level to wherever we were going. Yet when we had toiled up we found the top was only the beginning of another range of hills, somewhat less green than those near the ocean; and when we had labored up the second range we found a third before us, brownish and sad looking, drenched with rain, and wreathed in ragged veils of fog. Beyond the third was a fourth, and beyond the fourth, a fifth; and through all the length of that sullen, interminable day the hills mounted before us, so that the road was like a never-ending river of mud pouring down from some monstrous reservoir high up among the dirty scud of cloud and mist and rain.

The color of those hills changed gradually from brown to gray, and then to a dark gray; so that the country was as somber as it was chill and watery. There were no trees or shrubs on that vast expanse of rolling countryside, and no houses—only here and there, at wide intervals, a hut that seemed to shrink into itself at the threatening hills that frowned upon it. As we went higher there were patches of snow, and a biting dampness to the air such as I have never felt on any ocean.

We plodded upward all that cold wet morning, and in the afternoon we came to the longest of those long hills, its top lost in a driving gurry of snow and rain. There were stupendous granite pinnacles and knobs jutting from its dingy surface as though an angry God had pelted it with the leavings from the rest of the world.

There was a confused babbling before and behind us, and I caught the word "Dartmoor." Jeddy pulled at the sleeve of the moon-faced Devonshire militiaman beside us. "Is this Dartmoor?"

The soldier looked at us stolidly. "Dartymoor be oop," he said thickly.

It seemed to us the hill would never end; but we topped it at last and found ourselves looking off at a country faintly like that through which we had already mounted, and yet unlike it. It was more gigantic, as though we were seeing what we had already passed through, but seeing it magnified and distorted by weariness and hunger, or by a sick man's dream. The ground before us swept off into a broad valley, and then up to tremendous remote heights, treeless and houseless, and dotted here and there by fingers and spikes of granite, small-seeming things in that enormous expanse. The road, empty of all life and unsheltered by any tree or house from the drive of the rain and snow-laden wind, stretched off ahead of us like a dirty string.

The valley and the distant hills were almost black, except where snow lay on them; and what was more, the drab soil around us, when I poked at it with my fingers, was not good clean dirt, but a slimy black peat, unhealthy and decayed.

"Dartymoor," the soldier beside us said, and I thought there was complacency in his voice. Certainly there was pride in the gesture he made with his musket toward the dreadful land that faced us, though how any person could look at it except with horror was beyond me; for if ever a place looked like an abode for devils and lost souls, it was that swarthy, sinister moor.

We were like blind insects, it seemed to me, crawling and crawling up the roof of a great black barn: insects that might be blotted from the face of nature with little exertion and no regret.

They gave us no rest, these pie-faced Devonshire soldiery, but drove us on, across the somber hills, past up-thrust granite arms that seemed to threaten us; up and up, and down and down, and up and up again; and late in the afternoon we came to a wretched square stone house, rising from pools of water in which sad ducks paddled. Beyond it we saw another, and beyond that a bend in the road and a downward path to a shallow, desolate valley where there were more houses.

Beyond the houses, sprawled against a dingy hill slope, lay a circular mass of granite; a sort of giant millstone.

We stared at it and stared at it, lurching drunkenly down the slope like mud-caked scarecrows; but if any man of us had a thought in his head, either fearful or otherwise, about that dark and hulking prison, he kept it to himself.

XXI

THE shape of that miserable place, as I have said, was vaguely the shape of a monstrous millstone or cartwheel. The outer rim of the wheel was a stone wall a mile in length and twelve feet in height; and thirty feet from it was the inner rim of the wheel: a similar wall, twelve feet in height as well. Around the top of each wall was stretched a wire to which bells were hung, and if any part of the wire was touched, no matter how lightly, the bells set up a clangor; and every guard in hearing came running with his loaded musket.

Projecting from the inner rim at intervals were loopholed bastions; so when the guards ran into the bastions and up the steps with which they were supplied they could sweep the entire prison yard with their muskets and cut down any person who might be striving to mount the wall.

This enormous tilted cartwheel was divided into equal parts by a high stone wall running through its center. On one side of the wall were offices, guardhouses and storehouses. On the other side were the prison buildings, seven of them, each one shaped like a huge New England barn, but their walls built entirely of stone, and all of them pointing inward to a common center, like clumsy spokes in this vast wheel. The seven buildings were again divided, three being in a yard by themselves on one side of the semicircle, and three in a yard on the other side; and in between, standing alone and walled off from the three to the right and the three to the left, was the odd prison, Prison Number Four, which was the deepest and darkest in the place, barring the Cachot or Black Hole itself; for it was in Number Four that those Frenchmen who were known as Romans lived, and King Dick and his court, and all the Americans who had been captured up to this time.

The high wall that separated the prison half of the cartwheel from the other half was pierced in the center by a high barred gate, and the gate led from the prison half into a market place, a hundred feet square, which might be regarded as the hub of the wheel.

We were driven like sheep beneath a stone archway in the outer wall, taken in hand by a detachment of bare-kneed Scotch soldiery, and herded down through the inner gate and into a small stone house that stood on our left, near the hospital. Our clothes were soaked and covered with mud. There was mud in our hair, even; and some of us could not stand upright because of the blisters on our feet.

They wrote our names in a book, giving us numbers: putting down our rank, when we were received, where we were born; our ages and statures and appearance; the shape of our faces, the color of our hair and eyes, the marks on our bodies—all the things that would help them catch us again in case we escaped.

While we stood waiting for this wearisome duty to be completed there was a shouting of sentries outside, and a stir and bustle among the clerks who were taking our names, and with that in came a florid-faced, hook-nosed man with a high chest and thick upper arms and curly brown hair, dressed in the uniform of a naval officer. This man was Thomas Shortland, captain in the royal navy: agent for prisoners of war at Dartmoor; and we were not long in discovering what thousands of Americans already knew—that if ever a man deserved to burn in hell, it was Thomas Shortland.

I was sure, as soon as I looked at him, that he would have a touchy temper; for this is something, I have found, which often accompanies curly brown hair.

"My God!" Shortland exclaimed angrily to one of the clerks, "what's Pellew thinking of to send me this number of men! A hundred of them, and there's already nine thousand in the prison!" He stamped up and down; and I knew, from the look of him and the rage he was in, that to attempt to speak with him about getting a parole would be doing all of us a disservice.

"Give these men hammocks, blankets, and mattresses," he snapped. "Yes, and mess equipment. You, Hawkens: see they get mess equipment, and spun yarn for slinging their hammocks."

They brought us our bedding: a hammock of fair quality, a mattress about an inch in thickness, stuffed with something that felt like wet wadded newspaper, and a blanket that might have held out wind if it could have been tarred.

When the clerks were done with us we shouldered our bedding and limped into the rain, to find our bags waiting. We picked them up, whereupon the Scotch soldiers marched us through still another gate and down across the empty square market place, which would have been the hub of the hulking wheel to which I have likened the prison. We could see the square front of Number Four Prison ahead of us, with dim lights shining from its six end windows: windows that gave it the look of glaring at us out of ancient, rheumy, hating eyes.

The soldiers pushed us through iron gates at the far end of the market place, and a warden led us between two strong walls, up to the face of the building and around a corner to an entranceway. He fumbled at the door, rattling a key in the lock. There was a stale, sour smell around us, in spite of the bitter wind that whipped the raindrops through our sodden garments.

When the door creaked open, a volcanic blast of noise and fetid air surged out. "Git along in!" the warden shouted. "'Urry up! Don't tike the 'ole bloody night!"

I don't know how I had come to think of Dartmoor as a place of small stone cells in which manacled men lay eternally on the floor, groaning. This was how I had thought of it; but now that the iron-studded door had closed behind us I saw there were neither cells nor manacles. If there were groanings, they were completely lost in a deafening hubbub of gabbling, laughing and hurrooing, shot through with scraps of song, shrill whistlings, and a clatter of iron against iron.

An enormous room lay before us, with colonnades of slender posts extending from floor to ceiling along the length of it, as though hundreds of small schooners, stripped of standing and running rigging, were moored close together, not only along the walls, but down the center of the room as well. Thus it had the look of the most tremendous stable in the world, with stalls for hundreds of horses; but instead of horses between the masts or posts or stanchions or whatever you wish to call them, there were men squatting around kettles in groups of six, eating, drinking, laughing and shouting; men sewing at garments, or searching themselves for vermin, or reading in books and newspapers, or playing games, or busy at pursuits that were mysteries to us. Among them were flickering candles whose yellow beams seemed to make their garments and their faces yellow, but to cast no illumination whatever on the remainder of their prison. Thus the masts or stanchions vanished into the upper murk, and the yellow company was outlined against a wall whose swartness glittered strangely, though it was not till later that I saw the glitter was caused by the reflection of the candles on moisture that trickled unendingly down the face of the dark stones.

The pressure of the men pushed me into an alleyway between the stanchions, an alleyway that ran the length of the building. The men in the stalls, most of them clad in sleazy roundabout jackets, saffron yellow in color and stamped back and front with the black TO TO of the Transport Office, never so much as raised their eyes. We dragged ourselves wearily a little farther down the alley, and then a little farther, helpless and friendless, but ever hopeful of finding a spot where we might squeeze in and rest.

It seemed to me that every inch of floor space in this great prison house was occupied, and we doomed to wander through laughing, yelling prisoners until too exhausted to move farther.

Yet we were strangely succored, and by one who aimed to persecute us, as is sometimes the case in this life. Jeddy Tucker, suddenly dropping his bag and hammock at my feet, reached silently for a gangling, saffron-colored figure hunkered on the floor, searching his body for vermin like a yellow monkey.

When Jeddy pulled him to his feet, I saw it was Eli Bagley, whom we had last seen heading to the westward in his crazy brig, hopeful, like Columbus, of reaching the American continent.

He stared at us open-mouthed for a moment; then burst into malevolent laughter. "Gol durn ye!" he said to Jeddy, and his wandering gaze included me as well, "they got ye!"

He was a miserable object, dirty and with no shirt beneath his yellow roundabout jacket; and when I looked into the stall in which he had been squatting I saw men no more savory-looking than Bagley.

He laughed again, excitedly. "I thought you wouldn't never get took! By gorry, I wished you was here last winter, when we didn't have no clothes nor fires nor nothing."

"Where can we hang these hammocks?" I asked him.

"You go to Tophet!" he squealed, his lantern-jawed face a fiery red, and his chin whisker trembling with rage. Then he grew calmer, as though realizing we were all Americans together. "Well," he said, scratching himself uncertainly, "well——"

"Go on, Bagley," Jeddy urged him. "We never did anything to you that you didn't deserve."

"You belong up on the next floor," he said, peering at us sharply. "All your people are up there. Go on up them steps—" he pointed to a long flight of stone stairs opposite the doorway through which we had entered, stairs that ascended into the darkness in which the ceiling was shrouded—"and when you've clumb 'em, ask for King Dick."

He pressed his nutcracker lips tight together, then doubled over, slapping his knees and cackling.

We shouted to the drabbled, mud-smeared men who stood crowded in the alleyway behind us, staring at the tumult and movement of this vast cavern of a prison with the yellow pinpoints of countless candles reflected in their eyes. They turned and made their way up the stone stairway, looking, as they mounted that steep slope, bent beneath the burdens of their bags and hammocks, like the picture in the Bible that my mother brought from England in her sailing days—the picture showing the building of the Tower of Babel.

Jeddy and I climbed the stairs last of all to find our crew huddled close together at the top. I saw there was trouble brewing; for the huddled men had lowered their bags and hammocks to the floor and were hitching at their trousers and sleeves, as men do when on the verge of using their fists.

When we pushed through them and came into the front rank, we saw we were in another vast stable-like room, no different from the one on the lower floor. Similar rows of stanchions extended as far as we could see in the gloom, and candles made innumerable golden points through its dim cavernous length. Yet there was a difference; for it had a ranker smell to it, a smell something like that in the den of a fox; and above all else the prisoners were different. On the floor below they had paid no attention to us, so that we felt alone and forgotten, and therefore helpless. Here, on the other hand, there were faces turned toward us wherever we looked: thin, mean, pockmarked faces that made quick movements, like animals watching in the deep forest, raising and lowering their heads as though to catch our scent.

They were ugly faces, gray-looking even in the yellow light of the candles, and gaunt. Some of these unsavory folk were clothed, and badly clothed, in yellow rags or grayish rags; whereas others wore nothing except pieces of cloth twisted around their loins.

It was easy to tell from the look in these men's eyes that we weren't welcome, and I knew we would do well to get away quickly, since we were in no condition to fight—not even to fight naked scarecrows.

"I want King Dick," I said. "Which is King Dick?"

A voice among these watching faces said something in French. They were all Frenchmen, I saw, and bad ones, too, if it's possible to tell anything from a man's face. A squatting, half-naked figure close to us rose on hands and knees. A knife was tucked in his right hand so that the blade extended halfway up his bare gray arm. He snarled at us, using a word I had never heard before.

"Shut your mouth!" Jeddy cried. He threw his clothes bag at the half-naked man, knocking him in a heap. He followed the bag like a cat, dragged the man to his feet and drove a fist into his windpipe, so that he sprawled to the floor and lay there. Jeddy snatched up the knife which the half-naked man had dropped, and recovered the clothes bag at the same time.

The rest of the ragged men scrambled upright and glared silently at us. Most of them, I saw, had knives; and I quickly decided that if blows were to be struck, we had best strike first. The thought had no sooner passed through my head than I heard a shrill, high voice, far away and beyond the circle of snarling French faces, shouting querulously, "Frawg! Frawg! Frawg!" With that the angry Frenchmen sank back as if they had been puppets, deserted by their guiding hand. The anger vanished miraculously from their faces, and they cast only occasional glances at us from the corners of their eyes.

The distant shout of "Frawg!" was picked up by other voices, all strangely high. It occurred to me suddenly that these were the voices of Negroes.

We became conscious of a bustle not far from us: a scurrying and hustling. Figures approached between the stanchions, one a towering, giant figure. As it came close enough to be lighted by the feeble yellow candlelight, we saw it to be that of a gigantic Negro. He wore a bearskin hat, so that he seemed eight feet tall; and in his right hand he carried a long club, like the handle of a boarding pike, but thicker and gnarled. His face was a soft, sooty black, like the black on the bottom of a kettle, and his head seemed too small for his enormous body, rather like a melon balanced on an up-ended long gun. Yet his mouth and eyes made up in size for the smallness of his head; for his mouth stretched all the way across his face, as though slashed with a knife; while his eyes, possibly because of their whiteness against the sooty black of his skin, had the appearance of china door-knobs set on swivels.

On each side of this tremendous man, as he bore down on us with eyes rolling from side to side, were two smaller Negroes: one a scowling, bowlegged, ape-like man in a bright green coat reaching nearly to his heels—a personage whom we came to know later as the Bishop; and the other a worried-looking darky with a peculiar habit of constantly looking behind him. The worried-looking one, we afterward found, was known as the Duke because he claimed to have been one of the secretaries of the Duke of Kent.

The towering black man and his two attendants came to a halt over the Frenchman who had been hit. He still lay where he had fallen, clutching at his throat.

"Heah!" the huge Negro said in a plaintive, light voice, poking the Frenchman with his stick and rolling his eyes over us, "Wha's goin' on heah? Who stirred up all 'is whuppus?"

I took the knife from Jeddy and tossed it beside the Frenchman.

"I was told to come up here and ask for King Dick," I said. "These Frenchmen figured on stopping us."

He stared at me solemnly. "Who?" he demanded. "Who tole you? 'At's me! Ah'm King Dick. Ah'm King up here. Who was it tole you?"

"Bagley," I said.

"Bagley? Ole Goat-whisker Bagley? Ole Bone-face Bagley?"

I nodded.

"You an' him friends?" he persisted.

Jeddy pushed up to him like an impertinent sparrow. "Friends!" he exclaimed. "How could we be friends? We know him too well! Hell, if he knew how to sail, he'd captain a slave ship!"

King Dick peered at him carefully, then dropped his head suddenly on one side, half closed his eyes, and giggled as though a finger had tickled him. Jeddy laughed, reaching up to slap this black hulk on the shoulder. King Dick gave way to immoderate mirth, opening his mouth until it seemed like a yawning cavern in his face; while his two henchmen viewed us somberly. His laugh eventually died, and he scanned us again with glittering roaming eyes.

"'Ese Frawgs," he said, "'ey doan' want no moh white folks messin' up 'is prison! 'Ey was fus' heah, an' 'ey get snippety when 'ey's crowded."

He turned and shook his stick at the Frenchmen, silently hunkered over mysterious pursuits. "You Frawgs!" he shouted at them, "you keep 'em stickers away fum mah sight, or you'll get youahsefs into a buckus 'at no Frawg ain't never seen nothin' like!"

He turned and waved his club over us benevolently. "Come on, you white folks," he said. "'Scuse mah delay, but we been havin' trouble wif ouah society in 'is place, so we gettin' picky an' choosy!"

XXII

I HAVE the vaguest of recollections of my first night in Dartmoor Prison; because when I was sure my men would have food and a place to sleep, I seemed to move in an ever thickening haze of drowsiness, a haze that pressed against me as heavily, almost, as water; and when my head dipped beneath its surface, as it often seemed to do, I knew nothing, though it appeared I was able to walk and talk and even eat a little while so submerged. I recall passing hordes of half-clad Frenchmen, and coming among more black men than I had ever seen together except in the West Indies. Above all else I remember the tumult; for none of these prisoners were sitting quietly, but were engaged in trades and traffickings, tending small shops, crying their wares, peddling their products, crowding around gaming tables, or operating miniature restaurants and coffee stalls. All of them, black or white, perpetually watched the movements of King Dick, so there was no doubt about the high position he held.

He led us to the rear of the building, where one of the stalls between the stanchions had been set off from the others with strips of canvas. In this stall was a large armchair, its frame brightly gilded and its back and seat upholstered in red plush. Before it was a table at which sat two white boys dressed neatly in blue roundabout jackets, duck trousers, and varnished black hats.

King Dick took Jeddy and me into the stall with him, the Bishop and the Duke entering close behind, as a matter of course; and indeed, unless he sent them on errands they were always trailing him like a double shadow cast by two strong lamps. As soon as he entered, the boys leaped to attention. They, he carelessly explained, were his seckataries.

He threw himself on his red plush throne. "Heah you, Namiah!" he said to one of the seckataries, "you go git Jesus Fenton an' Pigtail an' Goose Huck an' Ayun-Haid. I want 'ose boys come a-flyin'!"

Namiah darted away.

"You, Albert," he said to the other, "you go tell Chickenfoot he doan' sell no more beer, seppen to mah frien's, 'nen git 'at plum gudgeon man an' 'at lobscouse man an' 'at freco man, an' tell 'em I say come a-runnin' wif ev'y las' scrap in 'eir kids."

He nodded and winked at us as Albert hurried off on his errand. "Ain't nobody sells no beer in 'is yah Number Foh, on'y me!" He had the proud, aloof look of the man who has reached a position of affluence and power and is telling how he did it. "You lemme 'lone in 'is prison long enough," he said confidently, "'an I'll buy it right off 'ose English white folks."

Negroes, singly and in pairs, pushed up to the opening in the front of King Dick's stall to stare at us with glistening eyes. King Dick rapped the cement floor sharply with his gnarled stick. "You, Jesus," he said to a pale Negro with thin lips and a Spanish look about him, "you git on up in 'at cock loft an' tell 'ose Frawgs in mah boxin' 'cademy Ah needs 'at space to-night. You tell 'em not to make no muckus 'bout it, lessen 'ey lookin' to git sent to Plymuff wif 'ose odder Romans."

He explained the matter to us quickly. "'Ose Romans," he said, "'ey never wore no clo'es a-tall, jus' gamble, gamble, gamble, wussen any white folks in 'is world. Ain't nobody can't stan' 'em, so we sen' 'em down into Plymuff, so's 'ey kin live in a hulk, all by 'emse'fs. But, mah lan'! We's gitten mo' of 'em ev'y day. Looks lak 'ey's allus somebody gotta be Romans!

"You, Ayun-Haid," he continued, turning back to his henchmen and addressing a Negro whose close-cropped skull had a hard, metallic look to it, "you cut out sixty of 'ese new white folks an' take 'em up into mah 'cademy in 'at cock loft an' show 'em where 'ey hang 'ose hammicks. You an' Jesus stay wif 'em. You heah me? You stay wif 'em, an' doan' go 'way till 'em hammicks is all hung, lessen you want mah fis' bounced off yo' pan!" He flirted his stick at Iron-Head, who at once scurried among our men, gathering his flock together.

King Dick rose from his throne and addressed them tersely and to the point. Even in my half-conscious state I could feel, in this enormous, smiling Negro, an air of assurance and authority that would have done credit to the quarter-deck of a 74-gun ship.

"'Ey's close to 'leven hund'ed men in 'is Number Foh Prison," he said, "an' room foh 'bout th'ee hund'ed; so you do like Ah tell you, else you won't fin' no place to hang yo' hammicks, not a-tall. Ah's King in 'is Number Foh, an' Ah likes good white folks; but bad white folks, Ah takes an' bends 'eir jaws roun' into 'eir eahs! You go 'long up, an' Ah'll sen' up somepin foh you to chew on."

Seating himself, he went on with his orders: orders to Goose Huck to take one Frenchman from each of the center stalls on the second floor and bid him sling his hammock under the beams at the side of the building; then to empty six stalls entirely and scatter the occupants among the places made vacant by the single removals; orders also to Pigtail to follow Goose Huck and instantly report any insubordination on the part of the Frenchmen.

"'Em's mah odors!" he reminded Goose and Pigtail. "You tell 'em Frawgs Ah wouldn't do it, seppen it's gotta be done, an' if 'ey make huckuss 'bout it——" He pushed out his tremendous black fist, then flicked it forward, twisting it as he did so, and somehow it had the look of a projectile that would pierce six inches of oak plank.

It was about then that my senses began to slip from me for a minute at a time. In no way could I keep my ears or eyes open. I heard King Dick's voice saying, "Heah, white boy, bite yo' teef on 'is plum gudgeon," but what became of the plum gudgeon I would never have known if Jeddy had not told me, when he roused me on the following morning, that I had swallowed it in my sleep. King Dick himself, Jeddy said, had peeled off my coat, found my shoulder swollen, and so had slung my hammock in his own stall, lifting me in his arms and placing me in it as easily as though I had been five feet tall and no bigger than Emily Ransome.

Jeddy shook his head as he stood peering into my hammock. "What beats me," he said, "is the stuff this black elephant knows. I was going to call Jotham Carr to doctor your shoulder; but the King said no. He got out a chicken bone and a feather and a piece of horsehair. Then he tied the feather onto the bone with the hair and stuck it under your shoulder and said it would be all right in the morning. How does it feel? You can't cure anything with chicken bones, not that I ever heard of."

I looked at my shoulder. The soreness was gone from it, and there was a ragged shred of cloth protruding from the puncture where the splinter had entered. After I had drawn it out, the wound looked no worse than a flea bite.

"Well," I said, "he took a shine to both of us, and a good thing he did!"

King Dick came hastily into the stall while I was donning my still-damp clothes. "Slip yo' cable!" he said in his plaintive, high-pitched voice, slapping his black paws together with a smack like a longboat coming down with a run on still water. "Git yo'se'f six white folks togevver foh yo' mess, 'nen go 'long down an' git raidy to count out in messes. New men come in, prisoners allus count out."

Our mess of six included Tommy Bickford, 'Lisha Lord, Jotham Carr, and John Cromwell. We joined the throng in the rear of the prison's first floor. After we had stood there a while, jammed in with a thousand filthy Frenchmen, Negroes, and ragged, starved-looking

Americans, the doors were opened, and we filed into the rain-swept prison yard. Every sixth man got the number of his mess on a ticket, and the ticket holder, in turn, received a day's rations for his mess from the prison cooks—two loaves of brown bread, a chunk of beef weighing three pounds, including bone and gristle, and a handful of vegetables.

Number Four Prison had looked evil enough the night before, with its pale eyes glaring through the rain; but in the gray light of early morning its appearance put a weight like an eighteen-pound shot in the pit of my stomach. Some of the feeling may have been caused by the sour stench of the half-naked Frenchmen who slunk through the crowded yard in twos and threes. Some, certainly, was due to the perpetual drizzle of cold rain, and the barren hills we dimly saw beyond the outer walls—hills blackened as though by fire. Most of all I think I was oppressed by the granite barriers that hemmed us in; for I now perceived that the reality of escaping over those towering walls would take more study than I had ever given any problem in navigation.

We had been in the yard less than five minutes when Jeddy spied a man with whom he had drunk a pitcher of ale at the Ship Inn in Salem when we went there to buy the North River sloop that became the *Lively Lady;* and in three seconds he had his arm across this man's shoulder, the man's name being Josiah Pettengell, a master's mate; and the two of them were as thick together as though they had married sisters.

Because of this we were soon surrounded by a dozen Salem men, a few in decent coats and breeches such as we ourselves wore, but most of them in strange saffron-colored roundabout jackets and trousers, marked with the broad arrow and the letters T. O. The jackets and trousers were undersized, as if made for children, so that their wearers looked half starved and forlorn.

They shook their heads dubiously when told how King Dick had found us places to sleep.

"You want to watch them blacks," Pettengell said; "they'll steal the nails out of your shoes if you ain't careful. They was scattered all over the building when we first come here; but they got to stealing so much, they was put all together up on the second floor."

"I notice the stealin' ain't stopped," one of the Salem men said. "Them niggers was awful handy to blame anything onto."

"They treated us all right," I told Pettengell.

"Maybe they think you got money," he said, "and aim to gamble it out of you. You better move down with us as soon as some of our Frenchmen die off. They die off pretty fast."

"Well," I said, "for a while we'll stay where we are. What's the matter with those Frenchmen up on the second floor?"

With one accord the Salem men looked over their shoulders, as men do when asked for information on odious topics.

"They're the fellers that took the place of the Romans," Pettengell said. "Give 'em time and they'll *be* Romans." He spat on the ground. The others followed his example.

"What's a Roman?" I asked, having wondered about it since hearing King Dick mention them.

"Bad Frenchmen," Pettengell said. "Bad! By God, we don't know nothing about being bad, alongside those fellers. I've shipped with tough ones, but I never see nothing like those Romans. They never wore no clothes."

"At night, you mean?" I asked.

"Hell!" said one of the Salem men, "not *never!*"

"They'd freeze," I protested.

They laughed. "Look," Pettengell said, "they was as hard all over as the sole of my foot from sleeping on stone floors without no bedding nor nothing. They slept nested against each other to keep warm. They rolled over on orders, all together, and never got took sick. They never had nothing the matter with 'em."

"No smallpox even," one of the others said.

"Hell," someone said, "that was because they'd all had it before they was weaned."

"No, it wa'n't," Pettengell said. "They never got typhus, nor colds, either. They was the healthiest folks ever I see, and the worst."

"Murder, you mean?" Jeddy asked.

"Murder!" Pettengell said. "Murder wa'n't nothing! By God!" he made a hissing sound, expressive of disgust, and the others growled assent. "You wouldn't believe it," Pettengell said. "There ain't nothing in the world as bad and dirty as a bad Frenchman, and the percentage of bad ones is awful high."

The others told what they had seen these Frenchmen doing, publicly and unashamed, and the telling made my stomach quake like a shivered topsail.

"What's the chance of escaping?" I asked, "or don't you ever think about it?"

"Escaping!" Pettengell said. "We don't think about nothing else! Listen!" He tapped me on the chest. "Until last month we ain't had anything in here. We ain't had *anything!* Nobody had no money.

Most of us didn't have no clothes, only the rags we wore when we was took. The British wouldn't give us clothes. Our own government wouldn't send us clothes. Our own government wouldn't send money. You heard about Beasley yet?"

I said I hadn't.

"Reuben G. Beasley?" Pettengell persisted. "Ain't you never heard the name Reuben G. Beasley?"

We shook our heads.

Pettengell's lip drew up like an angry dog's. "Reuben G. Beasley," he said, "is American agent for prisoners of war in England." He broke into bitter profanity. "When we was dying off like flies with smallpox, he came up here and wouldn't see but one of us for fear of catching it himself. Stood and talked to one man out of all our hundreds, holding a perfumed handkerchief to his nose, and saying, 'Oh, mercy! What a confounded stench!'" Pettengell made his voice high and lisping, like a silly woman's. "That's the only time he ever come to Dartmoor; and him the American agent! When we wrote that we were starving and freezing and herded in with Frenchmen out of cesspools, he never answered our letters. When we had to lay on the stone floors of this prison with typhus and pneumonia, Beasley let us lay and die."

He eyed us furiously, and we stared back at him, wondering if it could be true.

"Well," he went on, "that's why we ain't made any escapes. It wa'n't till last month we got clothes out of Beasley—these damned yellow rags—and a prisoner's allowance: five half pennies a day. We're rich now. Two and a half pennies a day, we get: nigh onto seven shillings every four weeks. We can buy tools. We can keep shops and make money. We can have a quid of tobacco every day or two. Give us time and we'll show you some escapes!"

There was a movement among the prisoners in our section of the yard, and I noticed there were fewer than when we had come out. Pettengell looked around. "Market's open!" he said; and with that he and his yellow-clad companions hastened away.

Jeddy laughed defiantly. "Well," he said, "that sounds pleasant, don't it!"

I left him to prowl among the French, well aware that in a short time he would know near everybody and everything worth knowing, and went back myself into Prison Number Four to see King Dick, as I had been told to do.

I could see from the activity among the Americans in our prison house that work was no hardship to them, but a Godsend. The hammocks had been triced up against the stanchions, setting off each stall or bay from the one beside it; and in nearly every bay was a group of men at work: three or four, and sometimes even the full population of the bay, which was six.

From the seriousness and diligence with which they labored, they might have been making jewelry or tapestries that would bring them thousands of dollars in wages: yet the majority were cutting soup bones into small pieces that would serve as planks in the fashioning of ship models—models that might take six months in the making. Some were plaiting straw into baskets and boxes; others were manufacturing lobscouse and plum gudgeons in kettles over small stoves.

The first and second floors, however, were quiet by comparison with the third; for the gambling tables on the third floor were already open, and the vendors of coffee and tea were shouting their wares. At the far end a Negro band practiced wild and tuneless music, rich in ragged drum-beats and wailing discords; and in another quarter Negroes rehearsed a play that had a sound of Shakespeare, but a Shakespeare grandly mangled.

I found King Dick holding court in the space which, I learned, he had reserved as a boxing academy; for he taught boxing when free of his royal duties. He was seated on a green-topped table that I was to know later as the Bishop's altar on Sunday, the royal judgment seat on weekday mornings, and a Wheel-of-Fortune table during afternoons and evenings. On one side of him was the Duke and on the other the Bishop, both glowering darkly at an abashed Negro who stood before King Dick. There was something of a crowd in attendance, mostly black men; while stretched on the floor at the outer edge of the crowd was a Frenchman in a soiled yellow Transport Office suit. As I came up, the Frenchman struggled to a sitting position and felt his jaw in a gingerly manner, moving it from side to side as though doubtful of its security.

King Dick poked the abashed Negro in the chest with his stick.

"Ah give you warnin' two weeks back, Ashmodeus Jones," he said, in a high, almost breathless voice. "Ah tol' you not come pussuckin' aroun' nat' t'eater wif so much beer in yo' stummick. Din' Ah tell you, Ashmodeus?"

The eyes of Ashmodeus rolled spasmodically in search of succor. He was manifestly unable to answer.

"Tha's what Ah done," the King went on, prodding the culprit with his staff, "an' how you foller mah odors? Ah had a complaint las' night fum Clerphus Lapp 'at when he was a-mekkin' a speech to Ot'ello, playin' he was Des'emona, an' all painted nice an' white, you

was a-sittin' in nat t'eater wif anodder stummick-full of beer, jes' awful drunk, an' bus' right out a-laffin' an' a-laffin' so's he's 'bliged quit
bein' Des'emona an' holler 'at you be th'owed out. 'At's what you
done!"

"Ah wa'n't drunk," said the culprit feebly.

"Ah s'pose," the King said, in a faint, reedy, skeptical voice, "Ah
s'pose you din' have no beer a-tall? Ah s'pose not!" He flapped one
huge flat foot against the door, in time with the ragged drum-beats
of the Negro band.

"Nuh-nuh-nuh, Ah had two li'l' mugs," Ashmodeus said fearfully.
"Ain't nobody goin' git drunk on two mugs beer."

King Dick rapped his gnarled stick on the floor. "'At's what you
say, Ashmodeus! 'At's what ev'y drunk man say. Nex' time you see
someone git drunk for th'ee-foh days, you ast him how much he put
into hisse'f, an' he say he had a glass or two—jes' two li'l' glasses!
'At's what he'll say! Hyuh, hyuh, hyuh!" He laughed darkly. "What
Ah say is 'at you was drunk, else you wouldn't go lussuckin' aroun'
nat t'eater, yellerin' an' bellerin' when Des'emona right in a purty
speech. 'At's what Ah say! 'At's judgment nis co't!"

"Amen!" said the Bishop in his deep, booming voice.

"Judgment nis co't," the King went on, rising to his feet and adjusting his enormous bearskin hat upon his small head, "is 'at you git
yo' jaw wiped. Nen you keep away fum 'at beer an' outen nat t'eater
lessen you want git wiped th'ee-foh times, all togedder."

The eyes of the waiting audience widened expectantly. Ashmodeus looked over his shoulder like a hunted animal, saw no way
of escape, and sought to hide his face behind his arms. King Dick
made a quick movement with his huge left fist, a movement that
caused Ashmodeus to jerk his hands convulsively toward his stomach,
as if to protect it. With that King Dick's vast torso rolled to the left,
and his right arm came up a short distance. Ashmodeus's head
snapped back. His body became rigid and elongated. He seemed
to float upward from the floor, as though drawn by a wire, and in
the next instant he fell with a lummocky thud on the cement-covered
floor, jerked his right knee weakly, and lay still.

"Co't's adjourned!" King Dick said. He turned indifferently from
his admirers, leaving them to dispose of the insensible Ashmodeus
in any way that suited them, and came to me.

"Wheah's 'at li'l' Feevolus?" he asked.

"Jeddy?" I asked. "He went around looking for someone he knew.
What's a feevolus?"

"Li'l' bird," King Dick said faintly, yet shrilly, making what he may

have considered a bird-like motion with his tremendous big hand.
"Li'l' pickety bird, li'l' quickety pickety bird." He flirted his hand
vaguely and led me down the center of this long attic, bright by
comparison with the ground floor, which was a dank and gloomy
cave; brighter even than the second floor; but there were pools of
water on the cement underfoot, showing that the roof leaked. There
were stanchions in sections of it, as on the other floors, except at the
two ends, which were airy open halls. At one end I could see a rough
stage—doubtless the theater where Clerphus Lapp, painted white to
represent Desdemona, had been enraged by the drunken laughter
of Ashmodeus Jones. At the other end, toward which King Dick was
leading me, were tables encircled by prisoners both black and white.
As we came closer, my ears told me that the white patrons of the
tables were French as well as Americans.

The tables were arranged in a rough circle, in the center of which
were two barrels of beer on wooden trestles, and two smiling black
men waiting for customers. From the players rose a shrill and perpetual gabble, an occasional bellow of "Keno!" and a peculiar ear-
piercing shriek, that sounded to me like "Rit! Rit! Rit!" All this
uproar, somehow, seemed a fitting accompaniment to the wailing discords of the black musicians.

King Dick signaled imperiously to one of the beer guardians, who
ran out from behind his trestle.

"Gim us 'ose stools, Shellac," he said. He beamed on me engag-
ingly. "Had yo' breakfas'?" he asked. When I shook my head he
added to Shellac: "Gim us 'ose stools, 'nen tell 'at Gawge Washington
Dinwiddie bring 'ose fritters ovah heah, 'nen bring us two mugs 'at
beer an' wipe 'at foam off 'em. Ah doan' wan' no foam 'is mawnin'
or any odder mawnin', you heah me, Shellac?"

"Yarsuh!" Shellac said. He shuffled rapidly away, to return immediately with two rough stools and two brimming mugs of beer. We
were approached by a small, bowlegged Negro, shrieking at the top
of his lungs and peering at us over the pile of puffy fritters that filled
his tray. His monkey face was distorted by strange twitchings resulting from the trilling half scream, half whistle with which he cried his
wares, "Frrrrrit! Frrrrrit! Git yo' frrrrrits!"

King Dick rapped the feet of the fritter vendor with his gnarled
stick and eyed him severely. "Heah, Dinwiddie! Doan' mek all 'at
noise when you see me talkin' business wif a frien'! Ah kain't think
about nuffin' wif all 'at whussickin' goin' on!" He reached forward,
engulfing a dozen fritters in his gigantic hand. "He'p yo'se'f," he said
to me. "Ah got credit wif Dinwiddie." Dinwiddie smiled a weak,

monkey-like smile; and when I had taken four of the fritters he tip-toed away, a withdrawn look about his rump, as though fearing to be called back.

King Dick stared at me out of doorknob eyes, popped two fritters into his cavern of a mouth, and washed them down with a draft of beer.

"Ah doan' mek frien's easy," he said at length. "Less you meks, less you loses." He studied his beer mug thoughtfully. "Ah heahs what you done to 'at ole Bagley; an' Ah heahs 'at li'l' boy Tommy call you Cap'n Dick. Ah doan' like Bagley; an' Dick's *mah* name, too; so Ah guess Ah's oblessickated to be frien's wif you."

"Well," I said, "we need a friend, God knows."

He nodded solemnly.

"'At li'l' Feevolus, he tol' me you figgerin' on gittin' out 'is ole prison."

"I've got to get out!"

He closed his eyes wearily. "Whuffoh you want to be like all 'ose white Americans? Allus pussuckin' roun' bout gittin' out! Whyn't you hol' yo' tongue an' be good white boy?" He washed down two more fritters.

"Don't you want to escape?"

He laughed. "Mah lan'! Ah guess Ah doan'! Ah's mekkin' money, an' Ah's keeping odor in 'is ole prison."

"Keeping what?"

"Odor," he said, chewing his fritters. "Wif mah club an' mah fis'. You seen me keepin' odor jes' now. 'Ese prison folks, Cap'n Shoatland an' 'em, 'ey's obleeged to me foh keepin' odor, an' if Ah wants to git out, Ah gits out. Ah gits out any time an' stays out th'ee houahs, foh houahs, sem houahs! Come sunny days, Ah puts on mah blue clo'es an' goes into Princetown; 'at's whah Ah goes! Whuffoh Ah want to escape, wif plenty money, an' bein' King of 'is ole Number Foh, an' goin' ovah to Princetown when Ah feels lak dussuckin' aroun' a li'l'?"

He leaned forward suddenly and closed his huge fingers around my biceps. "Mm, mm!" he said. "Kin you hit?"

I said I could hit as much as was necessary to keep a brig in order.

"Stan' up," he said, "an' take a whup at mah chin." He rose to his feet, a towering, smiling figure, and held out his chin invitingly.

"What for?" I asked.

"Ah want to see kin you hit," he said, and I saw he meant it. "Hit hahd as you kin. Ah ain't goin' to feel it."

I took him at his word and drove my fist at his velvety black jaw.

To my surprise it slipped out from under the blow, so that I missed and nearly lost my balance, though I felt my knuckles graze his cheek.

He caught me with an arm like a jib boom when I staggered forward. "Mm, mm!" he said in a hushed, faded voice. "You kin almos' hit, on'y if you go lashin' out wif yo' right fis', you ain't never goin' get nowheres." He stared at me thoughtfully, caressing his cheek with fingers the size of marlinspikes. "Heah!" he said at last, "Cap'n Shoatland say 'is French war goin' be ovah one of 'ese days, 'nen all 'ese Frawgs, 'ey goin' back to France; an' all 'ose Americans in Plymuff an' Chatham an' Stapleton, 'ey comin' up heah. How you lak Ah learn you how to hit, 'nen you be king in anodder prison when 'ey all filled up wif Americans?"

"I wouldn't do it if I could," I told him. "I don't want anything except to get out."

"Ah show you plenty ways mek money," he said hopefully.

"I've got some."

He nodded, tapping his stick on the floor. "Yarse," he said. "Ah wouldn' say nuffin' about it. Ah doan' know nuffin' about you escapin', but effen Ah heahs somepin', Ah tells you or 'at li'l' Feevolus."

He popped the last of his fritters into his mouth and upended his beer mug against his broad, flat nose. "You talk French?" he asked me then, and I suspicioned from the restlessness of his doorknob eyes that he had a reason for asking.

"A little."

"'At ain't enuff," he said, and I was sure, then, he knew something he was unwilling or unable to tell me.

He studied the narrow skylight that stretched the entire length of the slant-roofed cock loft in which we sat. "Ain't no use not wukkin' in 'is ole prison," he said at length. "Folks 'at does nuffin', 'ey goes bad. Frawgs, 'ey git to be Romans. Americans, 'ey git to be Rough Alleys."

"Rough Alleys?" I asked.

"Yarse," he said. "Rough Alleys. Fellers 'at won't wuk an' won't keep 'eyse'fs clean, on'y gamble an' steal an' go mussuckin' aroun' mekkin trouble."

"Why do they call 'em Rough Alleys?" I asked.

"'Cause 'at's what 'ey are," he said. "Rough, an' belong in alleys."

Not until later, when I knew more French, did I discover that the Rough Alleys, who caused such grief among us before we were finished with Dartmoor, got their name from the French word *raffalés*, a term applied by French prisoners on English prison ships to those among them unfit in dress, person, and manners to associate with folk who made any pretense to decency. "Whyn't you start wukkin' on French?" King Dick continued. "'At ole Gin'ral Le Feeber, ovah in Prison Number Sem, he give lessons in French, an' talk clear an' nice, not all yockety, yockety, yockety, lak mos' Frawgs."

"Number Seven?" I asked, to make sure.

"Yarse; Sem," he said.

He warned particularly against gambling, declaring it was a curse, not only to his old Number Foh, but to all the other prisons as well, inasmuch as prisoners who became addicted to gambling would sell their clothes and even their daily food ration in order to gamble.

I asked him how they lived if they sold their food rations.

"'Ey picks up 'at ole swill behine 'ose cookhouses," he explained. "Doan' you gamble, an' doan' you let none of yo' white boys git started, not lessen you want to see 'em runnin' aroun' wifout no shirt nor nuffin'."

Keno, he said, was not particularly bad, but Faro and the Wheel of Fortune, which he said the Frawgs called Roulette, were sure poison.

"If they're so bad," I asked him, "why have 'em? You could drive them out if you wanted to, being King."

He let his head sink on his shoulder and giggled weakly. "Whuffoh I wan' do 'at?" he asked. "You ain't seen 'em Frawgs ovah in 'em odder six prisons! 'Ey'd tek money offen a li'l' baby what hadn' had nuffin' to eat foh a week! Whuffoh Ah let 'ese folks in ole Number Foh go ovah an' frow 'eir money at 'ose Frawgs? You t'ink 'ey stop gamblin' effen Ah frow out Faro an' Wheel o' Fortune! Nawsuh! Not no moh nan 'ey stop drinkin' effen Ah say ain't goin' be no moh beer in Number Foh! Ah keep 'ose gamblin' tables right heah whah no-body starts no russickin wivout Ah knows it!"

A shrill outcry rose from a near-by table. "Lookit 'at!" King Dick said. "Go on down git yo' dinner!" He strode swiftly to the table, his bearskin hat towering above the excited players.

"'At ain't nobody's fault on'y yourn!" I heard him shout. "Effen you goin' gamble in heah, do yo' gamblin' wifout no hussuckin'!" He drew two yellow-clad figures from the milling throng and made what looked to me like gentle jabs at them, jabs that traveled about six inches. Yet both gamblers bounced from his keg-like fists: bounced, fell violently to the floor and lay still.

There was, I could see, much to be learned about Dartmoor Prison; and as I hobbled down to our bay on the second floor I thought to myself I would have plenty of time in which to learn it.

XXIII

Wʜᴀᴛ it was about our life in Dartmoor that weighed heaviest on us, I find it hard to say. At one time I think it was the stench of the place—the bitter-sweet, flat, choking odor of unwashed bodies and fragments of food and hidden filth; for though some of our bays were scoured daily, others were given only a hasty sweeping—what Arundel housewives call a lick and a promise.

Again I think it was the cold; for the windows had no shutters, only iron bars, so that the bitter winds, the daily rains and snows, and the penetrating fogs that curse Dartmoor for nine months in every year poured in on us day and night. At other times I think it was our despairing rage at the wrongs inflicted on us by our jailers —inflicted not because we had committed crimes, but because we had fought to protect our country and our homes from conquest.

It may have been the lack of certainty as to our fate: we might, for all we knew, be kept in this dripping stone tomb for the remainder of our lives, unless we could escape; nor was this a groundless fear; for on every side of us were Frenchmen who had rotted either in the hulks or in Dartmoor for eleven long years, forgotten and forsaken by their country, their families, and their friends.

It may have been the myriads of fleas that lurked in cracks of the floor or folds of our hammocks, creeping out in the night to raise rows of welts on our bodies, welts that kept us awake and in torment with their burning and itching. Lice I don't mind. They are clumsy slow creatures, and any man who takes the time and trouble to be clean can keep them from his clothes and often escape them entirely. Fleas are different. They are too quick to be easily caught, and cleanliness is no guard against them.

It may have been the threat of disease—of smallpox, pneumonia and typhus—that hung over us constantly; or the clamminess that soaked up into us from the reeking floors; or the manner in which our wardens and guards taunted and jeered us. God knows they got back more taunts and jeers from the Americans in five minutes than their thick British wits could think up in five days, but none the less we brooded over their lying tales of American defeats when we had gone back at night into our prison house, and wondered and wondered whether, when we returned to our homes, we would be doomed to spend the rest of our lives paying taxes to keep a half-witted prince regent in women, liquor, and gambling funds.

In our own prison and the other six, prisoners had set up schools for the teaching of every subject under the sun. There were classes in navigation, knitting, tailoring, barbering, fencing, dancing, French, German, Spanish; in cooking, mathematics, boxing, painting, wood carving, Latin, Greek, chess playing, and the use of the globes; in gambling, even, and theology and violin playing.

I cannot remember all the things taught in Dartmoor; but for the expenditure of a penny an hour I truly believe a man could have instruction in any known subject, so that the prison was as good as a university, provided a man was hearty in his desire for knowledge. And to a man who lacks that desire, no university is better than a prison.

*   *   *

The Frenchman whom King Dick called Gin'ral Le Feeber proved to be General Le Febvre, an officer who had served with General Rochambeau in the French expedition to Santo Domingo. Like many other French officers, he was no longer admitted to parole, because of the frequency with which his paroles had already been broken.

He was a tall, thin man, and under his eyes were dark pouches that seemed to match in shape the enormous drooping mustaches that curved down like sickles on each side of his mouth. He had strange ideas, telling in one breath how he had broken his parole, and in the next speaking of his honor, eagle eyed and fierce; then caressing his mustache and boasting how he had got three girls with child during his stay in the parole town of Wincanton. Yet I liked him. He seemed not only kind, but even honorable, as that term is understood by most. I am sure I could have left money with him and had no penny of it touched, unless he was starving; and I know he would have seen France in hell before he lifted his sword in behalf of any Bourbon king, though he would have marched alone with Bonaparte against all the cannon in the world.

He made us welcome when we told him why we had come, and stood proudly before us, a huge cocked hat on his head, and holding under his arm, pressed against his coat of fine black broadcloth, a cane made of bone rings fastened together and polished.

"Yes," he said, speaking English well enough, "this king of yours, this king of Number Four, he is not appreciate'. There is nothing like him. He is a leader; and like all leaders, he finds out the affairs, both great and small, and places them together, do you understand, to discover the cause—the drift—the pattern. Perhaps he has told you something new, this king?"

We watched him silently, because we knew nothing, except that King Dick must have had a reason for sending us to Le Febvre.

He shrugged his shoulders. "Nobody knows nothing," he said, "but I feel here—" he struck his breast with his clenched hand—"that things in France are bad—bad! Yet if things are bad in France there may be a wind to blow good to us, eh?" He pulled at his sickle-shaped mustaches and peered at us sharply. He rolled an eye toward the next bay, where two Frenchmen were playing chess with a set of bone chessmen; then glanced up at the barred window overhead, through which the Dartmoor fog drifted in wisps that vanished at once in the gloom of the prison.

"You desire to speak French, eh?" he said finally. "Whence does it spring, this desire?"

"King Dick put it in my head," I told him. "He told me to learn French so to keep myself busy."

His eyes seemed to search the air above and beside me; and as they moved from point to point, they swept repeatedly across my face, never lingering but always returning. At length he smiled. "Yes," he said, "I teach you all the French you need. You find my French very useful; useful, but expensive. Maybe you find it cost too expensive."

"How much does it cost?"

"Five pounds each man."

There was something here I could not understand; but I sensed that this general, like King Dick, knew something we didn't. He had something to sell, and we couldn't afford to go without it.

"Five pounds!" Jeddy exclaimed. "I got some French already! I couldn't use more than a shilling's worth."

"Five pounds is all right," I told the general. "Five pounds apiece. When do we start?"

The general smiled grimly at Jeddy. "Truly!" he said. "Say me some French, so I see about your accent."

"Well," Jeddy said, "I speak the pure Nantes French. Maybe you don't know that brand, but it takes me in and takes me out." He cleared his throat, stared round-eyed at the general, and spoke up boldly: "*Mon Dieu, mon général, commez vous portez vous? Il est très méchant aujourdui, n'est pas; il fait plouit tout le temps.*"

The general seized his head in both hands and rocked it. The face of one of the chess players appeared suddenly around the canvas screen that separated the bay where we stood from the next, stared blankly at Jeddy, and withdrew as suddenly as it had appeared.

"Dear sweet mother of God!" the general said. "*Il fait plouit! Il est très méchant aujourdui!* What horror! If this is the true Nantes French, then I know at last why the citizens of Nantes were treated so badly in the Revolution. *Il fait plouit!* Ah, my God! My God!"

"What's wrong with it?" Jeddy asked.

"As well ask what is wrong with England!" the general groaned. "It is all wrong! The gouvernment, the people, the prisons, the houses, the women, the dress, the speech—all, all is wrong. So it is with your French."

He turned to me. "You speak the pure Nantes French also? Speak something to me, so I know the worst."

"Mine's canal French," I told him; and with that, speaking stiffly, since I have never felt free in foreign languages, I said: "*Je vois depart de cette prison ici.*"

The general glared at me, breathing heavily through his nose. He drew a folded silk handkerchief from his breast pocket, flung it open, enveloping us in a wave of violent perfume, and dabbed at his brow.

"Look now," he said, when he had folded most of the odor back into the handkerchief and placed it in his bosom again, "you are strange people, you Americans, laughing and mocking at all things, but doing it stiffly, without unbending. Being mockers, you fear others will mock you. Therefore you do not speak easily."

"General," Jeddy said, touching him lightly on the chest with the backs of his fingers, "with a quart of brandy in me I can say anything in French."

"But certainly!" the general cried, flicking Jeddy's chest with his finger tips in turn; "the stiffness is relaxed by the brandy. For a moment you forget yourself! That is the truth. Therefore we find a way to make you forget yourself so that you speak easily, even without the use of brandy, eh?"

There were chairs in the general's bay: chairs and a chest; and attached to stanchions were two paintings, one of a naked woman and one of a woman not quite naked, but almost, so that the place had quite an air. The general drew our chairs close together.

"You know how we do this?" he went on. "We make you become other persons. No longer are you Americans when you come here to study with me. You become French persons—new persons. Thus you forget yourselves and your fear of being mocked, and talk like Frenchmen, waving the hands, raising the eyebrow, lifting the shoulder, curling the lip. You see? Ha, ha!" He bunched his fingers, kissed their tips, and tossed the kiss toward the picture of the almost naked woman.

The thing seemed reasonable. At least there could be no harm in trying it; so I nodded.

"Good!" the general said. "We start this minute." He tapped me on the chest. "You are Jean Marie Claude Decourbes." He repeated the name slowly, raising his shoulders and opening his eyes wide, so that he had a look of almost childish innocence. "Jean Marie Claude Decourbes. *Mais oui!*" He leaned forward and stared searchingly at me. "Who are you?"

"Jean Marie Claude Decourbes!"

He shook his head. "Shoulder!" he criticized. "Lift the shoulder! You are surprised I ask you! Everybody know you are Jean Marie Claude Decourbes—" his voice rolled sonorously—"enseigne de vaisseau de la Marine Impériale de France! Raise the shoulder! Use the face! That is what a face is for—to show what passes behind it. You droop the eyelid and raise the chin one sixteenth inch: you are insult because the name is not known. You raise one eyebrow: you are patient with an ignorant man. You raise two eyebrows: you are surprised an intelligent man should not know. You see? Use the face! Why did God give you the face? Not to be blank toward all the world, like the sheep or the goat, *hein?* But to speak silently to women of things that cannot at the moment be said in words! To mislead the enemy! Very good! Who are you?"

I drew down my mouth and raised my eyebrows. "Jean Marie Claude Decourbes," I protested.

"Damned if it ain't!" Jeddy said.

From his breast pocket the general drew out a small mirror. He breathed on it, wiped it on his sleeve, examined his face in it first on one side and then on the other; then handed it to me. "Look in this and say to yourself one hundred times who you are. Jean Marie Claude Decourbes, a seaman of Provence. Never forget. You are Jean Marie Claude Decourbes!"

He turned to Jeddy. "Give attention, small one! You are Felix Berthot, Capitaine du navire *Ma Mie* de Nantes. Who are you?"

Jeddy lifted his shoulders until his head seemed almost to sink beneath their level, drew up his eyebrows and splayed out his hands. "Felix Berthot!" he plaintively declared, and anybody with half an eye could see from his gesture that he considered the general both rude and ignorant for asking.

The general rubbed his hands together. "Good!" he said. "It marches!"

Before we left the shelter of the dripping stone walls of Number Seven I had learned not only that my name was Jean Marie Claude Decourbes, but that I was born in St. Rémy de Provence, that my parents were Agathe and Antoine Decourbes, that I had one brother and five sisters, that I had been captured by the British frigate *Garonne* in the year 1809. Jeddy, being more flexible with his face and hands and shoulders, had delved deeper into his private life, and was taking pride in having wed a woman of Morlaix during the year 1804 and in being the father of two daughters.

Having arranged to return on the following day, we crossed the stone-flagged yards, slimy from dirt and the unending moisture of the Dartmoor mists. Swarms of yellow-clad prisoners were walking, gabbling, yelling, playing childish games and working at various pursuits while waiting for their noontime soup to come from the copper boilers of each prison's cookhouse. Something about the tumult dulled my sense of individuality, and suddenly it seemed to me that I was no longer Richard Nason, but was indeed Jean Marie Claude Decourbes, and that I had truly been shut up in this dank and sour-smelling prison since the year 1809. Yet this day was the fourth of April, and we had been where we were for less than a week. I was moved to wonder how we would feel about it if we had been there for years, instead of for a day or two. There came a time when dates meant little; but this date of April 4th was one that will never slip me, any more than will some of the dates that closely followed.

*   *   *

We had no sooner reached our bay and set out our plates and cups in preparation for the coming of Tommy Bickford with the bucket of soup than King Dick passed, attended by the Bishop and the Duke.

He grinned at me languidly, but went on without speaking. Yet he had no sooner vanished into his own bay, with the Bishop and the Duke popping in after him like two dogs popping into a cave after a bear, than he reappeared again alone and came lightly down the alley to me.

"Heah," he said faintly, wrinkling his forehead until the lines on it looked like the depth lines on a chart, "you an' Feevolus been ovah to Number Sem to see 'at old Gin'ral Le Feeber?"

I said we had.

He made a slight movement of his melon-like head: a movement that seemed to indicate he wished to see me alone.

Even as I got to my feet my heart began to pound against my ribs like the strokes of a gunner's sponge. I knew as well as though he had written it out that somehow he was bringing me the news I had known I must have ever since I sat in the longboat in Plymouth harbor, peering vainly through the slanting curtain of rain at the dripping stern windows of the *Granicus, 74.*

I walked with him away from our bay. "'At old Gin'ral Le Feeber," he said, turning a lackadaisical eye on me, "he'll learn you moh French 'an anyone."

I could hardly speak until I had gasped a lungful of sour prison air. "You've got something for me," I said, when I could talk without choking.

"Yarse!" His black paw half opened before my face, and I saw a square of soiled paper resting against his pink palm. I took it from him. "White man come into 'at market 'is mohnin', sellin' aigs. He ast Agnes foh somebody 'at knowed 'em Americans; an' Agnes, she sent Clerphus Lapp foh me." Agnes, I knew, was the pretty vegetable seller from the near-by village of Tavistock, who came each day to the market. "Ah wouldn' tell nothin' to nobody, 'f Ah was you," he added darkly. "Don't do nobody no good, seppen to give 'em somep'n to talk about."

The note was printed roughly in pencil:

"Please be selling something in the market one week from to-day that will be 11 April."

It was unsigned, but I needed no signature to tell me who had sent it.

"Wipe 'at look off yo' pan," King Dick said severely. "Doan' go lookin' 'at way lessen you want somebody follerin' you roun' to see effen he kain't git to know about somep'n wuff sellin'."

I showed him the message.

"Whah 'is lady comin' fum?" he wanted to know.

"What makes you think it's a lady?"

He chuckled a fluty, hysterical chuckle. "'At ain' no way answer King Dick! Whuffoh you got 'at li'l' sizzicky look in yo' eye effen 'tain't a lady? Mebbe you git 'at look foh an ole man wif whiskers, huh? Nossuh! Naw SUH!"

"Well," I said, "I don't know for sure, but I think you're right, and I want to sell something in the market a week from to-day."

"'At ain't no trouble," he assured me in his weakest, weariest voice. "What you want to sell?"

"Anything," I told him. "I want you to buy something for me; something that'll let me into the market: something a lady'd like to buy."

He nodded. "'Ey's some nice li'l' ships finishin' up ovah in Number One," he said. "Hund'ed gun ship, foh feet long: make a nice li'l' present foh a lady."

"No," I told him, "that's too large for a lady."

"Nice li'l' frigate ovah in Number Five," he said. "No bigger'n mah han'." He opened his gigantic fist and stared admiringly at the vast spread of bone and sinew. "Got a lady foh a figgah-haid."

"That's what I want," I said. "Get it for me, and tell the man to paint the figurehead with a green dress."

*   *   *

I think I might have sickened from impatience if my waiting had not been leavened by the news that came into the prison on the ninth day of April and sent the eight thousand Frenchmen into a shrieking frenzy.

Because most of these Frenchmen had been in Dartmoor since 1806, which was the year the prison was built, they had found means to circumvent their jailers in the matter of newspapers. The British tried to deprive the prisoners of all news, but French newspapers and English too were delivered to the Frenchmen neatly baked in loaves of bread.

When these loaves came into Prison Number Seven on the morning of April 9th there arose such an uproar from the prisoners that the soldiery came out of the barracks on the run.

Frenchmen poured from Number Seven like a swarm of hornets, and the din brought other swarms from Number Six and Number Five. The uproar swelled and swelled until gamblers, Negroes and half-naked French came tumbling down from the second floor and the cock loft of Number Four. It spread to the yard beyond us, where the gray bulks of Number Three, Number Two and Number One crouched with noses pointed at a common center, like three enormous mangy cats glaring at their prey.

We ran to the covered walk along the wall between the prison yards and the market place; for it was only along the walk that we could pass from the yard of Number Four into the others. When we entered the yard of Numbers Seven, Six and Five, there were four thousand yellow-clad figures in it, weeping, embracing and kissing, as Frenchmen so often do. Somewhere among them started the song that goes, *"Allons, enfants de la Patrie, Le jour de gloire est arrivé"* —a song that sends quivers along my spine. Others ran about in a frenzy, shouting *"Vive l'Empereur!"* *"Vive la France!"* in strange, cracking, trembling voices, or stood helplessly in their grotesque, pinched-looking yellow suits marked with the broad arrow of the criminal and the staring letters T. O.—stood with tears trickling and trickling from their eyes as if there would never be an end to their weeping.

We watched them in silence, wondering what ailed them, while the soldiers on the walls lowered their muskets to stare round eyed. At length General Le Febvre and another man came pacing toward us, watching their excited countrymen out of eyes that seemed too hard and old for tears.

General Le Febvre nodded curtly. "You know about this?" he asked, gesturing toward the yellow-clad thousands.

We shook our heads.

His features were rigid, in spite of what he had said to me about expressing the feelings through the face. "It is done," he said. "The wolves have pulled down the lion. Bonaparte is finished, and the Allies have taken Paris. Now the wolves have nothing more to fear, and we shall go back to our own country."

He stalked off with his friend, his eyes as tragic as those of a man who has lost all he loves; and it was plain to be seen that the butcher Bonaparte, who cared no more for him than for a fly crawling on the wall, had held as much of his heart as had France itself.

"To our own country!" Jeddy repeated, echoing the general.

It dawned on me, then, why the general had insisted and insisted until we had almost come to believe it ourselves, that Jeddy was Felix Berthot and I Jean Marie Claude Decourbes, enseigne de vaisseau de la Marine Impériale de France.

XXIV

THE market square of Dartmoor Prison was a busy place, even under the worst of conditions, for all the petty shopkeepers among the
prisoners were in constant need of replenishing their stores of tobacco, pipes, needles, thread, awls, boots; pots, pans, and pails; butter, eggs, cloth, coffee, tea, beer, rum, meat, fish, soap, and God
knows what-all. But on this eleventh day of April it was busier than
I had seen it in my short stay—busier, I think, than it had ever been.
Not only were patches of blue sky showing now and again through
the low-lying fog bank that hung perpetually over the prison when
rain was not falling, so that the market folk were out in full force;
but the news of Bonaparte's defeat had brought French *émigrés* by
the score to congratulate their countrymen on the end of their imprisonment, and to seek supporters among the old soldiers—supporters for the king who was now to be hoisted back on the throne
of France by the English.

Against the side walls of the square were rails to which were tied
the donkeys of the market folk who had ridden in from Tavistock
and Widecombe-in-the-Moor and Moreton-Hampstead—donkeys that
added to the turmoil by bursting into brays so mournful that they
might have been an embodiment of the hopelessness of all the nine
thousand prisoners.

The market folk were ranged behind long trestle tables set in a
double row down the center of the square, while the Jews occupied
the choicest positions, close against the barrier between the market
place and the prison yards, where they could easily carry on their
traffic in obscene toys with the French prisoners, giving smuggled
brandy and dirty books in exchange for the toys. To get these places
they scrambled for them at the opening of the market, while the
prisoners pressed against the railings and cursed them for the manner in which they crowded the women out of the way, sometimes
even oversetting them and trampling on them in their anxiety to
snatch the most desirable places.

On that morning, truth to tell, I saw none of them; I had eyes for
nothing save the main entrance to the market from the moment
when the double sentries at the gate, seeing the small frigate made

of bone that I carried, admitted me to the mud and deafening racket of the great square.

I can hear now, as though I still stood waiting among them, the howling of the Jews, the bellowing of the Devonshire wood and charcoal and poultry sellers, and the wild, coarse voices of the fishwomen, in particular of a terrible old woman with stringy gray whiskers, who wore a fisherman's boots and jacket and a dragoon's forage cap, brimless, and boasted of a wide knowledge gained in unsavory ways. She seemed to be at my elbow with her screaming. Move as I would, her voice sliced perpetually into my brain, making an agony out of the waiting that was a torment in itself; waiting that seemed to hover on the edge of eternity.

It came to an end when, above the heads of the yellow-clad French prisoners at the entrance, I caught sight of a small three-cornered hat, like the one my father wore as a captain in the last war. I could not see her face, what with the guards at the gate, and the elbowing countrymen and French émigrés; but something about the hat told me it was hers, so I was prepared to see her and armed against the making of any sign of surprise. I had it in mind, as soon as I caught sight of her, to go closer to the gate, so she might have less distance to walk through the black mud that covered the entire market square; but when she had come far enough through the gate to let me make out her face, I saw she had seen me at once, and I forgot about the mud.

The yellow-garbed scarecrow Frenchmen swirled around her, offering their small wares, and I feared it would be necessary for her to stop and speak with them; but they fell away before her and she came straight to me, a half smile on her lips.

I looked at the frigate I had brought her. My hands were shaking, and I knew I must be careful not to break it. When I lifted my eyes again I saw that her green riding habit was spotted with mud. There was a dab of mud, a small dab, on her cheek, which seemed to me almost as white as the face of the figurehead on the Lively Lady.

"It has a green dress," she said, then. "Is it for me?" She drew a deep breath and added uncertainly, as if she had half forgotten it, "Richard?"

I nodded, being in two minds what to say in reply, and so saying nothing.

"May I see it?" she asked. So faint was her voice that I barely heard her, what with the screaming of the fishwomen, the braying of the donkeys and the yammering of the crowd. She took it from me.

With the little frigate gone, I felt freer to think about saying something; so while she studied it, I coughed and said, "I knew you'd come."

She seemed lost in contemplation of the toy. I was conscious of a movement beyond her. When I looked more carefully I saw a small, thin, bowlegged man, and behind his shoulder the head of a dog that stared at me and moved his nose as a dog will when uncertain. It was my dog Pinky; and in the moment I saw him he leaped outward and was snubbed by a cord fastened to his collar, so that he swung in mid-air, scratching and scrambling. I ran to him and found he had leaped from a small wooden seat, like an inverted bracket, strapped against the bowlegged man's back, near his waist.

As soon as I got him in my arms he spread himself against my chest to root at my neck with his cold nose.

"Well," I said, when I had my hand around his muzzle, so he could only lie against me, snorting and jerking his head in an effort to free himself, "what's all this?" I was speaking to Lady Ransome, but she had turned away and gone to look at the donkeys tied against the high granite wall.

The bowlegged man grinned and touched his hat. "'E wuddn't 'a' fell off, sir," he said, "for anything 'ceptin' 'is marster. 'E's rid there for near a fortnit nah, sir, like a bloomin' lamb. 'E's a grand little dog with the 'ounds: tikes to it like a cat to a 'erring. Reg'lar little lion, 'e is!"

Lady Ransome came back to us. "He's safe with Captain Nason, Mark," she said. "Unleash him and leave him." She drew another deep breath. "Look after the horses, Mark, and I'll come out soon."

He touched his hat and slipped the leash from Pinky's collar. "Please to remember, m'leddy," he said, "them horses got to walk back, and this moor ain't no place after dark."

She made no answer, so he touched his hat again and went spraddling toward the entrance, the little bracket sticking out from his back as though he were off for a load of bricks.

She looked up, as if waiting for me to say something.

"What's the sense of having him ride on that shelf?" I asked, though I didn't care why he rode on it.

"Because that's how we carry them," she said, moving her shoulder impatiently. "When a terrier's what he should be, he'll never give in, but runs with the hounds till he wears his pads to the bone; so we carry him on what you call a shelf till the fox goes to ground."

"Then what?"

"Then," she said, "he's tossed off, so he can go down after the fox and fight him out." She looked at me quickly from the corners of

her eyes. "Lud 'a' mercy!" she added, "I think you must be studying
to be an Englishman, so you can spend your life talking about dogs
and horses." She raised the little frigate above her head, studying its
delicate bone planking, and again there came into my mind the
thought of her pressed against the old beech beside our mill creek in
Arundel, laboring to carve her initials on it. It seemed strange to me
that with all this turmoil surging around us I should be conscious of
nothing but peace.

"I knew you'd come," I said, forgetting I had told her this already;
but it seemed she had forgotten it as well, since she said, "Did you?"
without ceasing her study of the frigate.

"Yes," I said, and could recall not one of the things that at some far
day in the past I had planned to say to her.

She looked at me quickly, then slipped off her gauntlet, undid a
button in the front of her long-skirted riding coat, and brought out
a small package. "This is yours, Richard," she said. She placed it on
the deck of the little cruiser so I could take it without being seen. "I
didn't—I don't know—I've wished I'd never taken it from you."

I knew what it was; and I stared at it, lying there. It seemed to
me I had wanted this miniature back more than I had ever wanted
anything.

"Don't you wish it?" she asked, in her soft, husky voice.

There was almost a breathlessness to her laugh when I snatched
it up and buttoned it into the pocket of my shirt, where it seemed to
lie against my breast like greatly needed armor.

"I've hated it," she said, "ever since I took it from you. You said
it brought you luck; and when you lost it, you lost your luck as
well."

"No," I said, "we sank the Gorgon."

"Oh, yes," she said, "but after that! Dartmoor!"

"Well," I reminded her, "you're here, and I've got it back. That's
luck."

"I'd have given it back before you—before you fought," she said,
"or on the Granicus, but I couldn't. There was never a chance." She
stamped her riding boot in the mud. "That awful Captain Parker!
That awful Captain Wise! They never left me alone!"

"Was that what you meant when Sir Arthur bought Pinky and you
made a motion with your hand?"

"What motion?"

"Why," I said, "you had your hand at your throat; don't you
remember?"

She put her hand to her throat, staring at me.

"Yes," I told her. "Like that. You moved your fingers a little. There was a look in your eyes—I thought you wanted to say something to me."

"La! How could you remember a thing like that?" She put her hand on Pinky's head; and Pinky, twisting suddenly, brought our hands somehow together. The unexpectedness of it gave me a start, and I couldn't blame her for hurriedly making adjustments to her hair with the hand that had touched mine.

Embarrassed, we stood and looked at Pinky.

"Well," I said, when we had been silent overlong, "that night on the *Granicus,* in my berth, I'd have sworn I heard your voice close by my ear. When I tried to go to you in the morning I couldn't. The sentry wouldn't let me. I wanted to see you. I wanted—I wanted——"

"Yes," she interrupted me. The huskiness was in her throat again. "I—I wanted you to have the miniature. I wanted you to know I felt badly, Richard. It was our fault. It was my fault. You'd be free now if—how could I know you'd—I'd never——"

"Look here," I said. "Put these ideas out of your head! It was the fog. It was the fortunes of war. Nobody can tell what'll happen in war times. If Rowlandson Drown had stopped to hang up his jacket before he came on deck, he mightn't have been killed. Our mast might have been more stoutly fished, and we'd have got clean away. But Rowlandson wasn't to blame for not hanging up his jacket."

She raised her eyes to mine. They seemed to swirl like the swift water of the Arundel River on an August day.

"Don't cry here," I said. "Look at the green dress of this figurehead. It seems years ago that I first saw your green dress. It's a beautiful color—green. Do you remember telling me I couldn't pronounce the name of my own home?"

She smiled tremulously. "Of a Rundle!" she whispered. "I've learned a lot since then."

"What have you learned?"

"Oh, la! I've learned Baltimore gentlemen are taught to fall in love at first sight, and why beech trees are planted in America."

My thoughts skipped about, evading me. "Did you ride from Exeter this morning?"

"We were away before sun-up," she said. I had a sudden picture of her, small and gallant in her saddle, outlined against a golden sunrise.

"For God's sake," I begged her, "tell me things I want to hear. The day'll be gone before you know it."

"What shall I tell you?"

"There's something wrong with you. I see it in your eyes. You're thinner. Your eyes are hurt all the time. If there's—if there's something in your life you can't bear——"

At that she stood straighter and seemed haughty. "I think you misunderstand," she said. "I came to-day to let you see your dog again and to ask if there's anything I could do for you, because I had your acquaintance in America."

"Well," I said sadly, "there's one thing you didn't learn. Somebody should have told you an American can't be made to feel like a whipped dog by calling him 'my good man.'"

"What do you mean?" she asked. "How could I call you 'my good man?' I'd never say it."

"It was in your voice," I told her. "You were kicking me out of your way for saying something you thought presuming and too intimate."

She stamped her foot. "Don't you dare! Don't you dare! *I* kicked you out of my way! *I!*" She stopped and looked at Pinky. "No," she added, softly, so softly that I held my breath for fear a word might escape me, "no, Richard."

"Well—" I said—"well——"

"It's only that you don't understand the English, Richard. I've had the thought that you think hardly of Sir Arthur, but he's a fine honest man and a just man. He's kind to animals, and religious, and it's a great honor to be his wife." I thought she flushed a little. "He's a believer in Joanna Southcott. The newspapers are full of her prophecies, and he's gone up to London to see her."

"Has he?" I said feebly. Then, in spite of me, I laughed, and perhaps the laugh was unpleasant.

"Please be kind to me," she said. "I've ridden a long way to see you, and now there's so little time!"

I fear I laughed again, and more unpleasantly, but I was ashamed of it. "I'll be kind in the way you mean," I said. "I'll make no words to trouble you."

At that her under lip trembled; she was all compassion. "Strange, isn't it?" she whispered. "Strange I should be asking you for kindness, poor prisoner!" Then she went on, speaking low and rapidly, "I can't be very kind to you; I can only do what I can: that's to bring your dog to see you and tell you a friend thinks of you, Richard. Your friend would help you get away if she could."

I looked down at her little boots that were sinking in the mud. "I'm afraid you mustn't stay much longer in this cold."

She laughed ruefully. "The cold's nothing, but there are pixies on this moor, and everybody says you mustn't be caught on it after nightfall."

"What in God's name is a pixie?" I asked her, and regretted the words as soon as they were spoken. "Don't tell me! I don't want to know what a pixie is! Tell me something I can think of in this damned prison! How do you live? What do you do all day? Who do you talk to and what do you talk about?"

"No," she said, "there are things I must ask. Do you know it was two years and three weeks ago to-day that I came to your house in Arundel?" She pronounced it "a Rundle," like one of our Arundel people. "I've often wondered what the winters are like there? Is there a sweet smell to the air always?"

"Wait," I said. "How can I——"

"There's something I must say to you, Richard," she said. "This little boat——"

"It's a frigate."

"I know," she said, "I know, Richard. Some other time. You can teach me these things some other time. I want to know them. But this little boat: I must speak about this little boat. You bought it, didn't you?"

"Well," I told her, "that's one thing to be thankful for. My mother made me promise to carry money in a belt whenever we chased a sail, and by the grace of God it hasn't been taken from me. The little frigate is nothing. It'll remind you of American sailors."

She nodded and looked at me strangely, and in some way I knew she had next to no money with her: that the horse-faced Sir Arthur allowed her to have none.

"Now," I said, "here's something. No letters go out of this prison without being opened. Can you write my mother for me?"

"I've written already," she said. "I'll write her again."

"Tell her I'm well. Tell her I'll be home again some day—perhaps sooner than she looks for me."

"Ah, I hope so!" She leaned close to me, bending her head over Pinky's. Then, tousling him with her fingers, "Listen," she whispered, "I've wrapped a map in your package. It's forty miles to Exeter. There are press gangs at Plymouth and Teignmouth, and a watch is kept at Tor Bay; but Mark Tate, that man who carried Pinky, is a good man. He'll do anything for me. He takes his beer at the Goose with Three Heads, near Ransome Hall, almost in Exeter. It was Mark who brought the letter here. If you can reach him——"

"No," I said quickly, and in as low a voice as hers, "I'm planning with a Frenchman. I think it'll come about that way, through France:

through France; but you know how I thank you, and I'll keep the dear map, as I keep the little picture."

At that I think she was disappointed, and yet glad I had better plans than hers. She sighed. "I fear your friend is useless to you, Richard."

I made bold just to touch her hand. "You haven't told me what you do all day and what you——"

But at that I saw the man Mark Tate close by us.

"Beggin' pardon, m'leddy," he said, shooting an apologetic glance at me, "but it's gettin' on in time. This moor ain't no place after dark, m'leddy, an' we'm near to forty mile to make. Hard going too, m'leddy, the first of it."

"Yes, Mark," she said. "Take Pinky. I'll follow in just a moment; in just a moment, Mark."

He took the dog from me, touched his hat, and spraddled away. Pinky, squirming in his arms, got his forepaws on Mark's shoulder and stared back at me, his brow wrinkled and his ears held high. He whined sharply.

She fumbled with her gauntlet. "I suppose I may never see you again."

"That might be," I said.

She gave me her hand. It was as cold, almost, as a bit of ice.

I wanted to say more to her. It seemed to me we were standing there together in the mud, waiting for me to find words to say to her; but I could not even speak a farewell, and only formed "Goodbye" with my lips.

I swallowed hard and tried again. "Emily!" I said. "Emily——" But I could get no further.

She turned a little from me, and my eyes clung hungrily to the picture of her that was within them—her little figure straight as a lance in her three-cornered hat and her wide-skirted coat and her riding habit looped up on her hip, out of the way of her small muddy boots.

"Ah, thank you," I whispered. "Thank you!"

She drew her hand from mine, smiled as though we had met for a moment on the street; then turned and left me.

XXV

THERE were prisoners packed against the railing between the prisons and the market place on the morning of the twenty-first of May: prisoners peering from the end windows of every prison house, and crowded on the prison roofs; for on that day the first draft of Frenchmen, five hundred of them, passed through the iron-studded gates and down the road toward Plymouth; and if there's a sight to make a man sick and desperate, it's to see others march away to freedom while he stays behind.

We had pressed ourselves against the market barrier, Jeddy and I, to watch them hand in their hammocks and blankets and become their own masters after years of living death; and there was one I shall never forget. He was a thin, stooped Frenchman with gaping holes in the knees and elbows of his yellow Transport Office suit, huge flapping bare feet, and a crust of dirt down the front of his jacket. He came up to the guards, breathless, like a fluttering, frightened bird, to tell them his hammock had been stolen—though I think, from his looks, he had sold it for money with which to gamble.

The guards pushed him away, for the rule had been made that no prisoner could go free until his hammock was turned in. He came scuttling out past us and dashed for the prison to hunt for it, or to beg one from another man; but soon he came hurrying back again, so wild looking that I almost thought I could hear his heart thudding with terror beneath his ragged yellow jacket. We saw him run to the guards; and by this time the last of the five hundred were crowding through the gate; but the guards struck at him and drove him off, for he had no hammock.

Panting like a frightened dog, this tattered Frenchman went down on his knees. I saw he had an open knife in his hand; and even while I wondered what he wanted of a knife, he stabbed the blade into his throat and fell over on his side, pushing the blade away from himself, so that his throat opened out in a spurt of blood. He sat up and looked at us, dazed like, holding his throat together with his fingers. Before the guards could come out and pick him up, he had fallen back on the ground with no blood in him.

So only four hundred and ninety-nine Frenchmen crowded out into the wet Dartmoor fog, some of them weeping and some kissing the handful of soldiers that escorted them down the long hill. My heart was both glad and touched with envy by the secret knowledge I had that among them were more than twenty Americans who, being able to speak French, had answered to the names of dead Frenchmen.

The prison records had been badly kept at the time of the small-pox epidemics; and many prisoners who had died were not marked down as dead. For years, General Le Febvre told us, the Frenchmen had drawn the rations issued to these dead men and sold them, and drawn clothes and shoes in their names and sold those; and now, having no further use for the names, they sold the names as well.

The names of Felix Berthot and Jean Marie Claude Decourbes, we learned, would be called at the same time as Le Febvre's name, probably in the third draft.

The second draft of a thousand men was released on the twenty-fifth of May, and fifteen Americans escaped with them. The third draft of a thousand went out on the last day of the month; and something had alarmed the British, so that they were watching. General Le Febvre was in this draft, and Felix Berthot, and Jean Marie Claude Decourbes.

We had let our beards grow for three days, on orders from General Le Febvre; and when the draft was called we took our hammocks and bags and went out past the sentries and into the market place, wearing the patched yellow rags we had bought from Frenchmen.

The general, waiting for us, herded us along.

"Remember," he whispered, "you care no longer for these guards. There must be no apprehension! They are nothing to you—dogs under the feet! You are free men! You understand? You are Frenchmen, freed by the Peace! No man can stop you."

We watched the Frenchmen ahead of us pushing up to the gates at the far end of the market place, eager to be gone from the mud and fog and dripping walls of Dartmoor. Clerks at the gates took the names of those who passed out, checking them off in a ledger.

It is waiting, as every man knows—waiting and thinking of what is to come—that causes more trouble than almost anything in the world; and it was to shorten this waiting that I turned to look for the last time on the angry stone faces of the seven prison houses. For a moment I had the illusion that they were faces indeed, grotesques that gnashed their teeth at us. Upon the roofs stood lines and clusters of prisoners, following us hungrily with their eyes when we trooped through the gates; and other prisoners were pressed against the iron barrier at the far end of the market place, as we had been pressed to watch the first draft go out.

The front row was hunkered down like monkeys, so those behind could see over their heads; and as my eye ran along this crouching, ape-like line, it was caught and held by a weazened, malevolent face that had been gone from my mind for weeks; a face I had seldom glimpsed since the night of our arrival, when its owner welcomed us to Dartmoor with a snarl and sent us up the stone stairs to what he doubtless thought would be a pummeling from King Dick.

It was Eli Bagley who crouched there, glaring furiously at us as he had glared at me when I called him from his berth in Halifax harbor, and later when I had taken his sailing master from him and sent him wallowing off on a trackless sea with his brig full of British supplies. I turned away with a cold feeling behind my ears; for we had forgotten Bagley in making our plans to escape. If I had remembered him, I would have contrived to have him held inside Number Four until we were well out of the way; for I would have known he would make trouble for us if he could.

The general prodded me, and I turned to see Jeddy, just ahead, attempting to embrace and kiss the clerk, though hampered by his hammock and bedding.

"Hey!" the clerk exclaimed, disgusted. "*Allez vous en!* Save them kisses for somebody as wants 'em! Wot's yer name, yer little grasshopper! *Nom! Nom!*"

"Felix Berthot," Jeddy said, bursting into the set speech so carefully taught him by the general. "Ah, my friend, how I have a heart swollen with joy because of my wife Marie and my two beautiful daughters and that beautiful Morlaix——"

"Ah, the hell with *cette belle* Morlaix," the clerk said roughly, pushing him ahead and fixing me with a hard eye. "*Nom!* What's your *nom?*"

"Jean Marie Claude Decourbes, m'sieu," I said, drawing down my mouth and lifting my two bundles an inch.

"Gord!" the clerk said to a brother clerk who stood beside him, "wouldn't you think they'd name one of 'em Jack or Jim for a change!"

He flapped over the pages of his ledger and ran his finger down one of them; then looked at me impatiently. "Where from? "he asked.

I smiled and nodded, saying, as the general had told me, "*M'sieu désire?*"

"Oh, Gord!" he said. "*De quoi? De quoi?*"

"St. Rémy de Provence," I said, pushing the sounds up into my nose and letting them die there, as taught by the general.

"All right! Go ahead and good luck to you, Frenchy. *Bon chance!*"

I hurried away, and heard the general break into an instantaneous flux of French that must have fairly engulfed the clerk who had questioned me.

Before we knew it, almost, we were through the arched gate and out on the slippery road. The long line of Frenchmen stretched so far down the hill ahead of us—the hill at the bottom of which lay Princetown—that the head of the column was lost in the mist that had come to seem as much a part of Dartmoor as her fleas and the bells on the wires around the walls.

I had long looked forward to the day when I should find myself on the outer side of those iron-studded doors; but now that the dream had become a reality I felt only a profound depression at the thought of Eli Bagley glaring hatefully from behind the bars of the market place.

I told General Le Febvre about Bagley: how we had first taken his boat in Halifax harbor; then punished him on the edge of the Gulf Stream.

The general turned and looked back, up the hill toward the prison walls. There were four guards at the end of our long column. Strung out behind the guards were baggage wagons, loaded with our duffel bags. The road itself was a trench cut in the slippery black peat of the moor; and we could see at a glance there was no way for the two of us to scramble from it unseen.

"Holy name!" the general said, tugging at his mustaches. "Sweet Jesu! here is an affair out of hell!"

We looked desperately for drains into which to crawl, but there were none: only the barren river bed of a road, slimy with mud. We looked for thickets in which to hide, but the land was treeless and grassless: a desolate rolling expanse, with fingers and humps of granite thrust up through it here and there, but all of them far removed from our line of march. There were no houses: nothing—only the vast stretch of black moor, to which spring had brought a faint swarthy green, such as comes over the face of a Negro afflicted with seasickness.

"Well, now," the general said, "I think of nothing!" He struck his forehead with his hand. "Holy God! There must be a way! If we could get to Plymouth——"

Jeddy laughed a fierce short laugh. "Plymouth!" he cried. "We'll never reach the halfway mark!"

We looked behind us again, fearing to see a messenger posting after us; but there was nothing in that slot of a road, only the four guards and the baggage wagons.

"Here," Jeddy said desperately, "have these friends of yours start a fight, General. Everyone'll climb on the bank to watch it, and we'll climb up with 'em and hide somewhere till they've gone on."

"It's no good," I told him, and my mouth was dry, as though stuffed with cotton. "Look at these yellow suits! We'd get nowhere in 'em! We couldn't hide for five minutes, not even on Dartmoor."

"Truly," the general said, "you must do better than that!"

"Oh, for God's sake!" Jeddy said, "let's fight our way through 'em!"

"It would do more harm than good!" the general protested, staring helplessly around like an owl revolving his head in search of food. "Instead of ten days in the Cachot they give you one month—two month."

I looked back once more and saw a dim figure approaching through the mist. My stomach pitched down and came slowly up again, as it always does when hope departs. We walked on in silence. To me the gabbling of the Frenchmen in front and behind us seemed like sounds that were no part of our life, as the lapping of water under my cabin windows has often sounded between waking and sleeping.

We heard a voice, then, shouting blandly in our rear, "Ah gits mah beer 'is mawnin'! Mebbe Ah bus' open one li'l' bahl, 'count of all 'ese Frawgs gittin' out f'um under foot!" It was King Dick. When we looked around, we saw him towering above the four guards in his bearskin hat and smiling down at them as though they were his benefactors.

They cursed him affectionately. He flapped his ham-like hand at them and came on, singing happily and grinning from ear to ear at the marching Frenchmen:

> "When Ah sees mah Lawd on Jedgment Day,
> Ah's go'nter say, 'Lawd, Ah's heah to stay:
> Ah kin fry yo' fish; Ah kin scrub yo' floh:
> Ah's pow'ful handy wif a twenty-foh!
>
> "'Ah needs you, Lawd, an' you needs me!
> Ah's a bestest gunner 'at ever you see!
> Ah kin pivot 'at gun; Ah kin shoot him right:
> Ah kin blow ole debbil clean outa sight!'"

I made ready to hail him as he came abreast of us; but when his eyes met mine, I was warned to silence by a fleeting expression of almost Satanic ferocity that momentarily contorted his face and was instantly gone. He paid no more attention to us than as if we were strangers; but he lowered his voice and sang a third verse of his song in a half whisper:

> "'Ere's somebody lookin' foh folks Ah knows:
> Devonshuh Ahms is safe, Good Lawd!
> Git inside quick: git into 'at attic!
> An' doan' git out till Ah gits to 'at attic!"

He quickened his pace when he had finished, and broke into a fourth verse; and before he had reached the end of it he was forging rapidly toward the head of the column—like a frog through a goose, Jeddy said.

*　　*　　*

Princetown, named for Britain's dissolute prince regent by the pig-headed Englishman who built it, Sir Thomas Tyrwhitt, lies half a mile from the gate of the prison. More than once I have longed to change places with the prince regent for five minutes for the sole purpose of hanging Sir Thomas Tyrwhitt for naming such a town after me—and God knows he deserved to be hanged for persuading the British government to build Dartmoor Prison on his property.

We reached the Devonshire Arms in a sweat of apprehension for fear we would be overtaken before anything could be done to help us. The line of prisoners had halted; and the officers of our guards were standing expectantly near the door. As we came up, King Dick emerged with a barrel of beer clasped in his arms, making no more of it than of a bolster stuffed with feathers, and grinned a grin that threatened to split his head in two parts.

"Heah!" he shouted, "doan' ev'ybody stan' jus' nussickin' roun'! Git a-hol' 'is ole bahl while Ah gits a hawse!" The prisoners surged forward, forcing us toward the inn. They seized the keg and drew it toward the middle of the street, while King Dick went back indoors. We flattened ourselves against the front of the inn, near the door, and clung there, which was not difficult, since all the others sought to be near the barrel.

A carter in a rusty top hat and a long smock emerged from the inn carrying a stout wooden horse; and two boys, very important, followed him with a bung starter and a basket of earthenware mugs. We could hear King Dick, inside, laughing his oily, chuckling laugh.

"Ev'ybody gits mah beer!" he insisted heartily. "Ev'ybody's gotta taste mah beer!" He herded out an old man and a small girl; then stood like a colossus before the door, his arms benevolently spread. We edged ourselves along until we were behind him.

"Whoo!" he shouted. We heard the thumps of the bung starter, followed by the gush of beer and the slushy chuck as the spigot was driven home. Jeddy dodged through the door, and I after him. We stood in the stuffy, beery dimness of the inn's taproom, holding our breaths and listening for a cry of warning; but we heard nothing save the happy, thirsty babbling of the Frenchmen.

We looked at each other; then, at a slight sound, stared hastily around. In the doorway facing us a girl stood—a buxom, red-cheeked girl in frilled cap and short-sleeved dress. She nodded and turned away silently, evidently expecting us to follow. We tiptoed after her, and she led us up three flights of stairs; then stepped aside to let us enter a smelly attic with two pallets in the corner.

There was the sound of a slap and a scuffle behind me as I crossed to the dusty small window.

"Doan't 'ee be a zany!" the girl said.

"Bot you are so beauty-fool, *ma chérie,*" Jeddy murmured.

"You Frenchies!" she exclaimed, and tittered. "They's cloaze under the beds, carters' cloaze. Boots be under pillows. Lay youmselves on they beds, and doan't forget ye're droonk. They's rum oonder they washstand, and if any o' they guards coom oop, zee as how 'ee's droonk raight!"

She scuffled with Jeddy; then left us. We tore off our saffron-colored Transport Office rags and scrambled into the carters' garb that lay neatly folded beneath the mattresses: leather breeches, red vests to the thighs, long dust-colored smocks, and worsted stockings that pulled over the knees. Under the pillows were enormous boots and rusty battered top hats, such as every Devonshire wagoner wears, so we knew we weren't the first escaped prisoners to make use of this attic.

"For God's sake, be careful!" I told Jeddy, as I laced the heavy shoes. "Don't make that girl angry! We're not a half mile from the prison!"

"Angry!" Jeddy whispered, raising his pale eyebrows. "She let me kiss her! If you can kiss a woman she'll never blab!"

The tumult in the street subsided. When we peered from the small dusty window we saw the barrel of beer had been lifted to the back of one of the baggage wagons and had started off toward Plymouth, with prisoners and guards trailing alongside. We became aware o' distant noises below us, and stretched ourselves on the two beds with the rum bottle between us. Our retreat was invaded by the perfume of frying bacon and of coffee—genuine coffee, such as we hadn't tasted in months.

"Probably the bacon's rancid," I told Jeddy.

He removed his top hat, lay back on his bed, and stared dreamily at the rough timbers of the roof. "Do you know how much of that rancid bacon I could eat?"

I couldn't answer for the moisture in my mouth.

"Well," he said, "I'd start off with two fry-pans full: big fry-pans. I'd eat it out of the pans. I'd shove the bacon on one side and push slices of bread into the bacon fat, and first I'd take a bite of the bacon, and then I'd take a bite of the bread. Then I'd have 'em cook me another fry-pan full, and drop six eggs into the middle of the slices; and when the eggs were half done, I'd stir 'em all up together and eat 'em with a spoon: a big spoon."

We heard a rasping sound, like that of sandpaper passing over wood with quick, regular strokes. We looked up to see King Dick in the doorway. He had mounted the stairs in his stocking feet as softly as an enormous black cat, and the rasping noise was his stifled laughter.

"Mah lan'l" he said in his faint, high, plaintive voice, "heah Ah gits mahse'f all whuffussed up 'bout you white folks, an' heah you is lyin' in bed lak 'at ole prince region an' not whuffussed over nuffin' seppen bacon!"

"How did they find out?" I asked him. "It was Bagley, wasn't it?"

"Ain't no way tellin'," he said. "'Ese infohmers, 'ey's foxy, so's 'ey won't be tattooed wif T. R. on 'eir forruds foh bein' traitors."

"Can we get away?" I asked him.

"Yarsel" he said. "Yarse SUH! Ain't nobody goin' look in 'is ole inn, account it bein' so close 'at ole prison." He stared at us innocently, then drooped his right eyelid slightly. "Ah gits all mah beer heah," he added irrelevantly. "Two bahls weekdays; foh bahls on Sadday; six-sem bahls on pay days."

He took a bundle from under his woolly black jacket and handed it to Jeddy. It held a loaf of bread and a wedge of cheese.

"Nawsuh," he said, "ain't nuffin' goin' happen to you long's you doan' try go buckussin' aroun' Plymuff or Teignmuff or Tor Bay. 'Is li'l' gull downstays, she goin' lem you know when ev'ythin' raidy tonight, 'nen you git up ovah 'at ole moor—up ovah 'at *high* moor. 'At road, she doan' run nowheres seppen Exeter, soon's you git stahted up. Effen you's still agoin' in daytime, ack lak you's drunk an' doan' know nuffin'; 'at's how 'ese Devonshuh folks acks when 'ey's natural."

My heart turned over in me at his mention of Exeter.

King Dick rolled his eyes at us. "Ain't nobody goes out on 'is moor night-times! Not nobody! Ah wouldn't, lessen Ah had to, an' Ah ain't never goin' to have to. 'Ey's ha'nts on it."

"Haunts hell," Jeddy said somewhat thickly, because of the bread and cheese in his mouth. "How do they know there's haunts if they don't ever get out where the haunts is?"

King Dick chuckled. "'At's all right foh li'l' Feevolus lak you," he said, "sayin' Haunts Hell; but me, Ah stick in 'at ole prison! Ah ain't goin' puckussin' roun' wif no pickies. 'At's what 'ey call 'em: pickies. 'Ose pickies, 'ey holler 'nuff to whuffle yo' haiuh raight offen yo' haid; so effen you sees anyone on 'at ole moor, jes start a-pickeyin' yo'se'fs."

Jeddy contorted his face at King Dick in a horrible grimace. The King stared at him, fascinated, then drooped his head on his shoulder and giggled weakly: the giggle of a brainless, foolish young girl.

He straightened his bearskin cap, looking, in that dim attic, like a tremendous, overwhelming black djinn out of the Arabian Nights.

"Effen you needs money——" he said, then hesitated.

"I've got some," I told him. "What about this?" I pointed at our clothes.

"'At ain't no 'count," he said.

Jeddy shook his fist at him. "You old rascal!" he said gruffly. "If I wasn't busy I'd get up and knock your old head off!"

This black mountain of a man stared soberly at us, while I fumbled for words to tell him how I felt. In the midst of my fumbling he stepped backward and left us without a sound; and to this day I have never found the words for which I sought.

XXVI

We came down from the cold, black hills into the warm, green, neatly hedged valleys of the Teign and the Exe, gawping and gawking at everything we saw as though we had never before set foot outside our native Dartmoor. When hailed or questioned, as we sometimes were, we stared as in a daze, scratching our heads and hanging our mouths so wide open that bats might have flown into them. This acting served us well, for it occasioned no surprise; and folk never persisted in their questioning after seeing the witless countenances we turned upon them.

The town of Exeter lies against a ridge above the river Exe; and the Goose with Three Heads Tavern crowds close to the road which joins the town to the pleasant fertile moorland behind it—the moorland that is the beginning of the steep ascent to the wretched heights of Dartmoor.

By dint of pretending to get ourselves drunk on Exeter spring beer, dark and fruity and smooth, and by lying in the field opposite the inn with one eye glued always on the front door, we caught bowlegged Mark Tate spraddling down the road for his evening's quart or two. Wishing to show myself no more than was necessary, I shouted at him from the field where we lay, "'Ey, Ma-ark Ta-a-ate."

He stopped, peering in our direction. "'Oo the 'ell's that?"

"Zhut 'ee va-a-ace an' coom 'ere!" Jeddy growled.

He took a step toward us, uncertain in the late English twilight, so I stood up and faced him.

"Well," he said, offended at such familiarity from a mud-stained wagoner, "of hall the blooming gall! I ain't tradin', an' ain't buyin' an' ain't got no time to waste to-night, neither."

He turned toward the tavern, but I got him by the arm and shook some sense into him. "Stow your clack!" I told him. "Look at me and remember where you saw me last." I took off my carter's hat and ran my fingers through my rumpled hair.

He thrust his small face close to mine, then fell back and swept me with a horseman's eye.

"Hods!" he exclaimed. "How the 'ell—get back in the field, ye wild man, before somebody suspicions something!" He pushed me back, and we jumped the ditch to where Jeddy sat.

"This is Jeddy," I told him, "my second mate."

"Aye, I heard about him! He's the little feller that got into a fight in Ameriky and got carried home, all bloody, on your shoulder." He scanned us, scratching his chin.

"So ye done it!" he said at length. "I dunno how ye got away, but ye certainly done something! What ye goin' to do now?"

Jeddy gave him a confidential answer. "We're going to send you for a five gallon can of beer and six feet of sausages," he said; and when we had done this and were seated in the soft, sweet-smelling grass, washing down sausages with long draughts of mellow spring beer, it seemed to me that we must be near the end of all our troubles and that there could be little more that was cold and cruel in a warm and pleasant world.

"This Exeter ship canal," Mark told us, "she takes boats up to nine-foot draft, and we can get you aboard one of 'em, if ye give us time—only we'll near have to buy the bloody boat, prob'ly!"

"How far is Ransome Hall from here?" I asked.

He studied me for a time. "All right," he said. "Blummy if I don't do it, though it'll mean a lashin' o' trouble if I'm cotched!"

"What do you think it'll mean for me?"

He laughed sourly. "Hods!" he said. "Ye don't know Sir Arthur! He does what's right, even if he has to cut the ears off everybody in the world but himself!"

"I know him as well as I want to," I said. "Why work for him if you feel that way about him?"

"Work for him!" he said violently. "I wouldn't work three seconds for the damned old sharkskin! Me, I work for Leddy Ransome, same's I used to work for her old man. The money comes out of his pocket, but by rights it's hers. By rights he ought to pay her everything he's got, just for living with him! If she got what she deserved for doing that, blam it, she'd be richer'n the Duchess of Portsmouth!"

"You used to work for her father?"

He sucked at the can of beer and nodded. "There was the nicest old feller in the whole damned county of Devon. The nicest old feller and the worst Faro player! He'd go into the Regimental Club or Sadler's or the Boot and Bit, pour down four bottles o' port and get himself into a game of cards with some red-faced old buck as never took nothin' but toast and water before playin'. When he got

through there wouldn't be a gorrammed horse in the stable or a gorrammed dog in the kennels!"

I had heard tales of the gambling among the English, and of London gaming clubs such as the Cocoa Tree Club, White's, Boodle's,
and the Thatched House, where it was no uncommon thing for an
English macaroni who imagined he was playing the gentleman to
lose five thousand pounds, or even his home, in a single evening's
play. I had heard of these things, but had thought of them, always,
as impossible tales out of a book. Yet here was Mark Tate sitting in
a field in Devonshire, wagging a sausage at me, and telling me how
Emily Ransome's father had been saved from the Jews and the
debtors' prison: saved because Sir Arthur Ransome had taken over
his broad acres and his daughter at a higher valuation than could be
got from the Jews, since the Jews would make no offer on the
daughter.

"There's gambling clubs in Exeter, is there?" Jeddy asked.

"*Is* there!" Mark exclaimed pityingly. "There's gambling clubs
wherever there's gentlemen."

"*Is* there now!" Jeddy said thoughtfully. "And do they play the
Wheel of Fortune at any of 'em?"

Mark laughed shortly. "*Do* they! *Do* they, when there ain't no man
can play it without leaving his money behind? I'll love a duck if
they don't!"

"And where's Lady Ransome's father now?" I asked, while Jeddy
chewed contemplatively at his sausage.

"Dead," Mark said. "Shot himself. Lost some more and blew off
the back of his head with a load of duck-shot. Nicest old feller that
ever lived, too: always pleasant. Pity he hadn't learned earlier that
he couldn't play cards, so he could 'a' hopped the twig before Miss
Emily had the snaffle hooked on her!"

*   *   *

Late at night, when there was no more passing on the road, Mark
led us back in the direction from which we had come; then bore off
to the right, through a stone gate and into a grove of trees as black
as the inside of a powder barrel. We caught the scent of newly
turned earth; then the smell of stables; then the perfume of newly
sickled lawn grass; and while the odor of lawn grass still hung
around us Mark steered us off to the right again, and we felt ourselves close to a building. When Mark had pushed us through the
doorway and lighted a candle, we found ourselves in a cottage little
bigger than the cuddy of a Quoddy boat. There was a bunk in the

wall, like the bunk in a cabin, and a fireplace in one corner with a kettle hanging before it. To the right was another room, smaller by a foot or two, which might also be called a kitchen or a bedroom, depending on however one's fancy happened to run; for it had another fireplace; but also it had a bunk in the wall and an outer door facing in the opposite direction from the one by which we had entered.

It was good to sleep on real beds again, after the hammock mattresses of Dartmoor, which might have been stuffed with clam shells for all the comfort we took on them. Our ears, it seemed to me, had scarcely touched the pillows before morning had come and Mark Tate, bowlegged and alert, was tugging at us to get us up again.

"You keep to the back room," he said, pitching my clothes at me, dragging me from the room in which I had slept and pushing me in with Jeddy. "Front room stays open: back room stays locked. Lock both doors an' don't let a yip out of you! Don't open nothing, only for me or Leddy Ransome! They's water in the pail in the corner, an' a razor under the window, an' bread in the cupboard over the fireplace."

He spraddled from the cottage. Jeddy stared resentfully after him; then fell back on his bed and took on the aspect of a dead man—as I might have done if it had not been for Mark's hint about Lady Ransome. With this in mind I could neither stay still nor get a decent breath into me. I set to work brushing off each piece of my wagoner's dress, though there was no way of making it look like anything but what it was; and I was slow indeed at my dressing, what with taking my miniature from my pocket to stare at it, and listening at the door, and peering from the small back window at the wide expanse of meadow stretching off among clumps of towering oaks, elms and beeches, to lose itself eventually in a warm, golden haze.

It was too regular for my fancy, this spread of English park; for I have a liking for our rough New England meadows, swelling and rolling among solid masses of pines, birches and maples, or for flat marshes threaded with twisting silver ribbons of salt creeks, or even for ragged dunes, green and gold against the blue of the sea. Yet knowing what I knew and expecting what I expected, I said to myself that this little part of England, soft in its golden haze, was more beautiful than any piece of land I had ever seen.

I waited and waited in this low-ceiled room, sitting down and jumping up a hundred times, and wishful of going out into the warm June sunlight where I would feel less stifled from the thumping of my heart. She might, it crossed my mind, have gone to London. She might be ill, even; and at this thought I was in despair for fear I might have to go away without seeing her.

I recalled, at last, what Mark had said about bread; and when I found it I remembered how I would go along the Arundel beaches, between voyages, to shoot plovers or yellowlegs for aunt Cynthy's pies, and how I could never sit down among the dunes to take a mouthful of food without having a flock of yellowlegs come flying along just out of gunshot; and I, my mouth clogged with food, unable to whistle them down within range. Thinking this, I cut off a slice of the bread and found it white and sweet, and so cut off another, and then another; and while I was biting at the third, I heard a clattering of claws in the next room: the clattering my little dog Pinky makes when he hastens eagerly around a room in search of something, alert and stepping on his toes.

I stopped and listened, my mouth half full of bread, and my heart pounding fit to choke me. I heard Pinky blowing at the cracks beneath the door—blowing, and then sucking the smells of the cottage into his black nose. He scratched at the door and whined; then barked three times, sharp barks, impatient and peremptory. A moment later I heard Emily Ransome's voice, soft and husky: "Sh! Stop it!"

I jumped to the door, opened it, strode across the threshold, and closed the door behind me. I think I would have had my arms around her in spite of the bread in my hand and the mouthful I could not swallow if Pinky had not leaped against my chest and set up such a squealing of delight that I knelt down and took him up for fear his outcries would bring someone in on us.

When I had his head under my elbow, he lay and blew against my ribs, fluttering his tail with pleasure. I stared up at Emily. She stood looking down at me, a queer half smile on her red lips, as a person smiles at the memory of some pleasant far-off happening that comes dimly into the mind. She seemed to me as beautiful as she was kind.

"You should never have come here," she said, looking intently into my eyes. "You should never——" She broke off and glanced around the room; then looked back at me again. "No, that's not true! I'd have felt—I'm glad you came! There's nothing I can do, but I'm glad! I've thought of you often. I thought—I thought——"

"Well," I said, "there was no end to my thinking of you." I reached for her hands, but she lifted them quickly to her throat and clasped them there, as I had often seen her do before.

"Why do you say that, Richard?" she asked. "It's useless to say it!"

"I say it because I want to say it—because I have to. Why, if you didn't wish to hear it, did you bring back your miniature?"

"Yes, I know. It was wrong; but you said it had brought you luck. I thought—I thought you might have need of it."

"Need!" I said. "Need of it! I'm afraid of wearing it out, taking it from my pocket and looking at it a thousand times a day."

She moved to a small woven rug near the fireplace and sank to her knees, facing me.

"I suppose," I went on, "it's useless to say that, too."

She nodded.

"You don't mind hearing it, though?"

"La!" she said with that queer half smile on her face, "I don't hear such things often enough to know whether I mind or not!"

"Well," I said, "that's easily remedied if you've no objection to hearing the truth about yourself—how your eyes are smoke-colored; how I see them in every mist and cloud, and in the sunlight and the dark, for that matter: how your lips are——"

She rapped her clasped hands against her knee. "Richard, it's no good, none of this! The more you say the more you'll want to say, and I won't listen. I've heard you boast how Americans keep their word; yet you want me to go back on mine!"

"Oh, for God's sake," I said, "that's entirely different!"

"Oh, of course!" she said, smiling ruefully, "it's entirely different since it's you who want it. If anybody else wanted me to forget my vows, it would be terrible, wouldn't it?"

"No, it wouldn't," I said; but when I saw the look in her eyes, I admitted she was right. "Yes," I agreed, "and the reason it would be terrible is——"

"No," she said. "No! You're my friend, and I'm yours, so——"

"Friend! I'm no friend of yours!"

"Yes, you are, and that's all you are, and I must do what I can to get you safely away. I've talked to Mark, and he says——"

A shadow fell across the window. Pinky jerked his head from under my arm, his whiskers and eyebrows sadly rumpled, and growled a ferocious, rumbling growl that set his body to vibrating like a halyard in a gale. I moved back against the closed door, and my hand behind me fumbled at the latch; but I had been too rash in the coming out. Emily rose to her feet as the front door opened quickly. There stood Sir Arthur, a fowling piece held easily in the crook of his elbow, and on his gray, horse-like face a look that seemed to me to have more of satisfaction in it than anything else. The fowling piece, I saw, was cocked.

"Ow!" he said, peering at me along his nose, "I was right! Here you are, where you're not wanted! You've a genius for it, on my wahd!"

He cast a glance over his shoulder. "Stay there!" he called to somebody beyond our sight. "I'll whistle when I want you!" He stepped in, shut the door behind him, and leaned easily against it, cradling the fowling piece in his arms. He looked from me to Lady Ransome, breathing heavily; while Pinky growled deep in his throat and blinked his eyes, knowing I would slap him, which I did, though gently.

"Countryside has word of your evasion from Dartmoor, Nason. Great bargain, really, that cur of yours! Saw him rooting about Tate this morning, and it came to me like that—" he snapped his fingers —"that he must have caught a rather rank scent, eh?" I watched him with some curiosity, wondering that he showed so little anger. "Had a feeling it was you he was snuffing for."

He lowered the right hammer of his fowling piece: then cocked it again, so it clicked sharply, twice, in the silence of that small room. "Fancy you finding your way here, of all places! One would think you'd been directed!"

"No," I said, "it was an accident."

"Indeed!" he said. "More of a misfortune than an accident, I dessay!" He cast a calculating glance at Lady Ransome. "They never come singly, eh, my dear? Here's Tate, I mean, running to you about this fellow! It's my money he takes, and one would think it might enter his mind that I have the fahst right to know what's going on. I'm afraid we must let Tate go, eh? Not the thing for him to have done at all!"

"Please, Arthur," she said, "please don't blame Tate! It was only that he—well, I think he wanted to do what he could for a poor man in trouble."

Sir Arthur threw up his head, like a horse freeing himself from an undesired hand. "Curious!" he said, "so much sudden sympathy! I fear Tate must be given in charge for aiding and abetting, my dear!"

"You'll give Tate in charge?" Emily asked. There was no huskiness now to her voice, but a peculiar soft clearness that made it seem louder than it was. "Might that not involve your wife if Tate should tell the truth and say he did it for her?"

Sir Arthur looked at her; there was a spark in his eye, not a hot one—it was the gleam of the icicle. "You should have thought of that yourself, I fear, Lady Ransome. There might indeed be some such embarrassment for you."

"I see," she said, "and Captain Nason goes back to Dartmoor?"

He shook his head with an amused ruefulness. "Captain! Captain! Captain! Don't you think we've had a little too much of captaining for a species of hybrid, half inn-yard hostler, half petty pirate? It seems to me high time we had done with all your captaining, Lady Ransome!"

She stared at her hands, front and back, as though she found something strange about them. "So you'll send him back to Dartmoor!" she said. "What did he do for us when he had us at his mercy, as you have him now?"

"Oh, dear me!" Ransome said. "Do you expect me to argue? I confess I'm surprised, for I pay you the compliment of saying you've seldom lacked intelligence. I think, my lady, you understand very well that your present position doesn't entitle you to the grace of argument from me."

At that she seemed to become quickly a little paler. "My present position? My present position? What do you call it, Sir Arthur?"

"Precarious," he replied lightly. "At least precarious. I put it to you: what's the position of an imprudent lady with whom an enemy of her country finds a patently agreeable refuge? And doesn't the question present itself: by what means and by whose encouragement does this enemy of her country reach the lady's presence? I take it she must have connived. Ah, yes, indeed! 'Precarious' appears to be the accurate word."

She raised her hand to her throat. "That is, you put your wife in the precarious position!"

"I! I put her? Tut, tut, my child! How can I put a lady where she has most deliberately and carefully put herself?"

Emily had begun to breathe fast and audibly. "So you'll do it!" she said. "This is what we've come to! You'll do it because I've been merciful and grateful!"

He uttered a sound like the sour echo of an indulgent laugh. "I do it because you've been 'grateful'? It would be too much to suggest that our language contains such words as 'duty' or 'honor' or 'law'? But I fear it's discourteous to remind you of what you yourself have so long forgotten!"

At this I took a step toward him in spite of the fowling piece which he shifted to a readier position as I moved. "You might remind yourself of the word 'honor,'" I said. "You can't speak to her like that!"

Emily turned to me, and suddenly she was weeping. "I don't care!" she cried. "I'm thinking of your going back to that horrible place, the mud, the cold, those terrible men in yellow clothes——"

Sir Arthur interrupted shrilly. "How well you describe it, Lady Ransome! Now we have it indeed! So you've been there!"

She turned to him. "Yes, I went!" she sobbed. "I did go, Arthur! I wanted to help him. I want to help him now. There's no harm in that! There's no harm in that and none to you. There's never been any harm to you in anything I did; and there never will be in anything I do. Couldn't you just let him go now? I'll never see him again. Couldn't you——"

"Disgusting!" He threw the word in her face with the most fierceness I ever saw from him. For the moment it seemed that something like a real passion mastered the man. "Disgusting! You make this show of yourself before me! Do you think I've been blind? Do you think I was blind in America? You little fool—you shameless little fool! Falling in love with an inn-yard lout; throwing yourself at him! And then, when he turns pirate, letting him make calf's eyes at you before my face! Sneaking off to coddle him when he's in jail for his thieveries! And now, when he's skulked out of his cell to you, begging for him! Begging for a damned dirty Yankee runaway thief! My God! What a paramour for Lady Ransome of Ransome Hall!"

I had heard as much from him as I could endure. "Open that door!" I said to him. "Open that door!"

Then, as I moved toward him, he poked the muzzle of the fowling piece at me, but I was quick, slapped it aside and took it away from him.

I opened the door myself. There were three workmen grouped around it, listening, all of them with guns. I smashed the muzzle of the weapon against the floor, so that the barrels were bent, and threw it into a corner.

"This man is an escaped prisoner from Dartmoor," Sir Arthur said. "If he makes a move, kill him!"

Then he spoke quietly over his shoulder to Emily. "Go to the house and remove everything that is yours," he said. "Pray be careful to take only what belongs to you!"

XXVII

THEY put me in Exeter jail; and I had been there three days before I got a word out of the man who brought me my hard bread, thin soup, and water—tepid water that must have been standing in the June sun. When he did speak in answer to my questions, I found his lingo difficult to understand.

"Noa, noa," he said. "Us bant agoin' vur tew zend ee backalong tew Dartymoor dreckly minit: not till us cotches tha body as wuz wi' ee. Zir Arthur hiszel, 'e yerd at tha Hall fra Dartymoor az they wuz tew or ee. Tuther must be a urnin' tha moor. When us cotches tha body an' ast tha tew or ee lockit up yere, than'll be time tew zend vur sojers as tew such bad bodies can be trustit wi'."

I had a gleam of hope for Jeddy, since he was still at large, having had the good sense to lie hid in the back room of the cottage until they had taken me away.

"Well," I said to the warder, "you may not catch the other bad body; he's not so bad, by the way, and neither am I."

" 'Ess shur that ee is!" the man said, and shook his head mournfully at me. "A bad, bad, bad body thee'rt! Zim they do zay in Exeter town az how they'm a purty bobbery an' stirridge at tha Hall, an' her leddyship put oot, an' banned fra' a' the gert vokes, an' gude vokes tew, an' a' on account ov a bad, bad body fra Dartymoor. 'Ess fay, thee'rt a bad, bad body, man!"

That was all I got from him; he called me a bad, bad body a thousand times, I think; for I lay in Exeter jail two months, until mid-August, before they took me back to Dartmoor.

Dun-colored clouds were caught against the barren face of North Hessary as we made the final ascent from Princetown to the depot gates; and the wisps of fog that drifted across the top of the seven crouching, staring prison buildings seemed less like fog than like the prison smells rising perpetually from the yawning, never-shuttered windows.

In his office Captain Shortland, with his crinkly brown hair and his ruddy, jovial face, beamed at me in a manner to make me think again of the grinning, big-nosed Punches I had so often watched on the streets of Nantes, strutting on little shut-in stages and blithely whacking friends and enemies alike with great clubs.

"Hah!" he said, moving his head forward and back and lifting his shoulders at the same time, as vain men so often do to improve the set of their coats, "so you've come back to us! Good! Good! I almost like to have my boys try it, out in the great world; for they all come back—ah, most of them: hah, hah!—to more permanent quarters!"

"Do you mean the Cachot?" I asked, knowing only too well the Black Hole was the penalty for those caught in serious crimes and attempts to escape.

He smiled, a pleasant, regretful smile. "Yes," he said, "the Cachot." He picked up some papers from his desk. "This is a rather serious business, you know. Not the usual case! No, indeed: not the usual case! One thing on top of another!"

I waited for him to say what he had to say, thinking helplessly, as I had thought from dawn to dark during the past weeks in Exeter jail, of Emily Ransome.

"At all events," he went on, "you'll have company. Four other Americans. They tried to burn a prize; so we were forced to give them duration."

"You were forced to *what?*"

"Duration. Serious offenses, you know! Not as serious as yours, but serious enough."

"Do you mean you're putting me in the Cachot for the duration of this war?"

"That's it! I knew you'd be sensible about it."

"Wait a minute," I said. My brain was in a muddle. There was no escaping from the Cachot, I knew. It was a stone coffin. There would be no way in which I could get word from Emily; no way in which I could get word to her; and God alone knew when the war would be over.

"This Sir Arthur Ransome——" I said.

"You've got it!" Shortland smiled. "There was the burning of the *Lively Lady*, and the escape by impersonating a Frenchman—of course, you'd only get ten days in the Cachot for attempting to escape; but you see there was also breaking and entering and the destruction of property at Ransome Hall. Ransome's laid information against you for the whole affair. Nothing else to do, you know." He cleared his throat. "I'll send you in."

"Just a minute," I begged him. "Give me a hearing on this. I haven't had a trial."

"Why *should* you have a trial?" he asked. "We have Ransome's word—and Ransome's a gentleman, you see."

"Oh, my God!" I said, "there isn't a Negro in Number Four whose word wouldn't be honester! The man's working out a personal spite on me! I claim a right to be heard!"

"I've heard enough!" he said, and the geniality vanished from his face.

"No," I said. "Wait! There was no breaking or entering at Ransome Hall. And since when has it been a crime to escape from a war prison? I gave you no parole! Nobody asked me for a parole! I was captain of a privateer of eighteen guns and entitled to parole, but I asked for none. Why shouldn't I try to escape if I get the chance? Wouldn't you?"

He stuck out his jaw and blinked his eyes, and all at once the dangerous temper of the man was on his face. Captain Shortland had the record of an officer brave to rashness, a hot fighter; but his nature was brittle, and never was more than a thin cracking lacquer over the anger that seemed always smoldering underneath. "Look here," he said, "your second officer escaped with you—Tucker. Where is he?"

"How should I know where he is?"

"Well, somebody helped you get away, and when you went, Tucker went too. Now you tell us where you last saw Tucker, and who helped you, and I'll see what can be done."

"Why, then, you *can* see what can be done, can't you! My God, Captain, get me a hearing, will you? You can't put me in the Cachot like this!"

Shortland's face turned wine color. "You damned Yankees," he said, lowering his head like a bull and half whispering the words, "you think you own the whole damned earth! You keep this place in a mess with your damned screaming and complaining and bellowing for your rights, until ten of you are worse than a million Frenchmen. Let me tell you, you haven't *got* any rights here! And you're no judge of what I *can* do and what I *can't* do! I've got orders from the Transport Office to put you in the Cachot for duration, and that's where you go!" He raised his voice to a bellow. "Mitchell! Mitchell!"

The chief clerk popped in at the doorway.

"Oh, for God's sake!" I said. "Let me write Pellew! Let me write the American agent again—Reuben Beasley! I wrote him twice from Exeter, but he may have been away. Let me try once more!"

Shortland shouted with mirthless laughter. "Beasley! If you wait for an answer from Beasley you'll stay in the Cachot forever! He

never answers letters! Not from Americans! Wouldn't you like to
write the prince regent? Take him out, Mitchell!"

He left the room, slamming the door behind him. Mitchell gave
me a blanket and a truss of straw, and turned me over to a sentry,
who led me down across the empty market place, dismal in the light
of flickering lanterns. The dim, ogre-like face of Number Four glowered at us as we came to the barred gate that cut off its yard from
the market. The sentry drew his bayonet along the bars with a clatter
and turned to look appraisingly at me.

"We'm a-gettin' all the 'Merricans this side o' hell," he said. "Won't
be none o' 'ee left to foight, soon, I'm a-thinkin'."

A turnkey came in answer to the racket of the bayonet against
the bars, and the two of them led me to the left, along the covered
walk, and finally out into the space between the circular inner wall
and the high fence of iron bars. The Cachot stood snugly between
the inner wall and the iron fence, looking, because of its granite sides
and arched roof, unpleasantly like a tomb. As we approached, a
squat figure came out from behind it and peered inquiringly at us.

"Here's another, Carley," the turnkey said. "Duration for this one,
too."

The squat man came close up to me. "Duration, hey? Holy bones,
you must be bad! You must 'a' spit on an admiral!"

The sentry and the turnkey laughed and left us. Carley took a key
from his pocket: a huge key fastened to him by a chain. "Anyways,
'twon't be as if yez were alone, with four in for duration a'ready,
and ivery wan av ye'er four thousand felly citizens fixin' to git
throwed in with yez for attimptin' to brek out av the dippo. Mary
help us all if thim four thousand divvles iver gits over the fince!"

A hoarse voice hailed us from the Cachot. "Mike!" the voice said,
"let that poor boy come to bed! He'll be gettin' his death o' cold,
standin' on that damp grass!"

Carley turned the key in the lock, dragged the iron door outward,
pushed me in with a sweep of his arm, and swung the door shut
with a clang.

I was in a dark room, smelling powerfully of damp straw, latrines
and dirty bodies. There was a slit of dim twilight in the door, where
the wicket was half open; and high up, on opposite sides of the room,
were two other small openings into the dusk of that August day:
openings smaller than my hand. There was no other light in the room,
and the darkness was like dark wool against the eyes.

The hoarse voice spoke up. "I don't seem to recall your face,
though you have a kind of familiar look."

There was a spatter of laughter from the interior of the room.

"Jesse Smith of Stonington, Connecticut," the hoarse voice went on. "That's me! A reformed Federalist that's seen the error of his ways. Who might you be?"

"Richard Nason," I told him. "Arundel."

When Smith spoke again his voice seemed almost respectful. "Got your straw with you?"

I said I had, and immediately felt him take me by the arm.

"We got a few choice positions vacant," he told me, urging me forward. "Being last in, I took the one farthest away from the door. That's the nicest when you're last in, because it's the only one you'll get. How'd you like a nice empty space next to me, only a little further removed from the door?"

"Fine!" I told him, heartened by his folly.

He pulled the truss of straw from my shoulder, and I could hear him breaking it open. "You want to take your bearings damned careful if you have to get out of bed in the dark," he warned me, "because this is an awful easy place to get turned around in. If you get lost, you might be five or six months finding your bed again."

The other men snickered. It seemed strange to hear their laughter coming up from the floor. Being unseen and unidentified, they were unreal, like ghosts.

"Wasn't you in command of the *Lively Lady* when she sunk the *Gorgon?*" Smith asked.

"It was the *Chasseur's* fight," I told him. "We only got there at the end."

Smith rustled my straw. "There you go!" he said at length. "All smooth and soft, like corn stubble after a frost. Lay down a minute before supper and let these other jailbirds do some warbling for you."

I followed his advice, grateful to him for his flow of talk. One of the other men coughed and cleared his throat.

"Simeon Hays: Baltimoe," he said softly. "Privateer *Surprise* of Baltimoe. We-all heard about the *Gorgon*. That must 'a' been a right amusing lobster-boiling. Jim Rickor, of 'Nappolis, he's over beside the doe. Next him is 'Lisha Whitten of Newburyport, and across from Jim is John Miller. All *Surprises*. John, he used to be an Englishman, but he don't like 'em no moe, so he's an American."

"Strange he don't like 'em!" a new voice said.

Smith spoke up again. "Meet Obed Hussey," he said. "Another of them Maine Federalists."

"Jesse," the new voice protested, "that ain't right, not even in fun.

I'd ruther you called me what you call the lobster-backs than be called a snivelin', English-lovin' Federalist!"

"Well," Smith said to me, "you prob'ly get the general idee."

"Supper!" a voice near the door said suddenly. The wicket slid wide open.

Smith took me by the arm and led me to the door, where each of us received a tin cup of cocoa and a quarter loaf apiece.

"Drink it where you are," Smith said. "If you try to walk round with it you might drop it, and you wouldn't get no more."

When we had given our cups to Carley and gone back to our straw again, I knew I could have eaten five loaves of bread instead of a quarter loaf, and topped off with something substantial like a sizeable platter of salt fish and pork scraps and one of my aunt Cynthy's lemon pies as a sort of stopper on it.

"Can't we get more than that?" I asked.

"That's more'n we're supposed to get," Hays said. "The bread, that's fixed up for us by the prison committees. They give the money to Carley, and he buys the bread. We ain't supposed to have that much to eat. You get kind of used to it, though. Your stomach shrinks."

"Your brain don't shrink, that's the hell of it!" Jesse Smith said. "You get to thinking about baked beans and brown bread, or a nice clam chowder with sliced potatoes and onions in it and pork scraps floating around on top." I could hear him swallow hard.

"Or hash," said another voice.

"There goes 'Lisha Whitten with his hash!" Smith said bitterly. "Can't you talk about *nothin'* but hash?"

"I like hash," Whitten said. "You take a nice hash chopped up plenty fine with boiled potatoes and raw onions, and brown her——"

"Listen," Smith said harshly, "do you s'pose anybody in this Cachot don't know as much about hash as you do? We never mention food in here without you have to go to work and drag in that hash of yours. Hash, hash, hash, hash, hash! That's all you can think about: just hash!"

My mind seemed like a pond that is, as our Maine people are given to saying, working. The consciousness of Emily Ransome completely filled my head, yet other thoughts seemed to rise through that consciousness as air bubbles rise from the bottom of a working pond. They rose and vanished, leaving behind the deep and unchangeable consciousness that occupied me. I could hear Jesse Smith telling about the new tunnels the Americans were digging—tunnels large enough to let all of the five thousand American prisoners escape at one time; and simultaneously I could wonder and wonder unceasingly what in God's name had happened to Emily: where she had gone and with whom; and whether she was comfortable, with enough to eat.

"They're going down twenty feet," Jesse said, "straight down from the floors of Number Four, Number Five, and Number Six! Then they're going to level out, bring 'em together, and dig for the wall."

He told how every American in the prison had been sworn to secrecy; how an arrangement of lamps and small wooden windmills, revolved by hand, had been invented to keep the air pure in the tunnels; how the excavated dirt was concealed from Shortland and the turnkeys by being fed, handful by handful, into the streams that run through each prison yard for washing.

"They're down there now," he said, "pecking at that damned yeller gravel an' bringing it up in their pockets and shirt tails." He stopped suddenly, and I knew he had remembered some of us were in the Cachot for duration; so that no tunnel could lighten our troubles.

One of the men near the door burst into a racking, interminable fit of coughing. Another went to snoring lightly.

There was this much to be said for the Cachot, along with the many things to be said against it: it seemed to act like a drug on most of us, so that we slept easily and heavily in it, despite the roughness of its granite floor and the brutal chill that fingered at our bones both night and day.

* * *

I had my first look, the next morning, at our tomb and those who shared it with me. By the faint light that filtered through the two hand-sized slits I could see that our granite box measured six paces by six paces, and maybe fifteen feet high. The floor was made of enormous blocks: the walls of smaller ones down which there was a perpetual trickle of moisture. There was a small pile of straw for each man, and at the end opposite the door a wooden bucket for a latrine. To one side of the iron door was a shelf, and on it a bucket of drinking water. Attached to the shelf by a piece of spun yarn was a half gourd for a drinking cup. We had the clothes we lay in, and our coarse prison blanket for a wrapping and a couch. In the room there was nothing else.

The door was of iron, with an eight-inch wicket in it. Toward night Carley would open the wicket a little, so we could look out without standing on each other's shoulders. At eight in the morning Carley came in with our breakfast: a cup of hot cocoa for each of us, and a quarter loaf of bread apiece, though the bread was not supplied by the British. Seemingly the smuggling of it to us was known and winked at. At the same time Carley would carry out and empty the bucket, renew our drinking water and look at us to see whether we were sick. At noon he brought us a bucket of soup. At night he brought us cocoa and bread again. Usually he brought it at six o'clock in summer and at four in winter, though he made the supper-hour later on days when other prisoners were sent to the Cachot. He did this so the new men wouldn't have to go supperless to bed. He was a kind-hearted man; and while he could do little because he had been threatened with punishment if he was caught smuggling food or liquor or newspapers to us, he did whatever he could.

Smith explained the workings of the place to me when we had heaped our straw in piles after breakfast and covered them with our folded blankets. He was a studious-looking young man with a long mop of straight black hair that came back over his ears and hung to his coat collar behind. If it had not been for his manner of closing his eyes after saying something particularly grave, and then opening them slowly and rolling them at his hearers with an air of simulated intolerance, he would often have been suspected of being serious, which he seldom was in my hearing.

"You got to keep busy in this place," he said, "and you can't keep 'em busy unless you drive 'em. They'd rather lay and brood. On account of that, we elect a captain and a first mate every week. Me, I'm captain this week, and Obed Hussey, he's first mate. Obed ain't a bad first mate."

Obed Hussey, I saw, was tall and broad shouldered: as fine looking a boy as would be encountered in a month of Sundays, except for the beard on his face and the raggedness of his clothes.

"Mr. Hussey, prepare the race track for the first race!"

Jesse explained while Obed Hussey busied himself in spreading his blanket in the middle of the Cachot floor. "We run a series of louse races. That's one way to keep 'em busy. Every man supplies his own louse; and anybody that claims not to have one is supplied by the nearest contestant. That prevents shirking. The winner gets held up to the window to report on what's going on outside. Losers have to let the winners stand on their shoulders. It's a good idea to have your races early and late, before and after market, when there's plenty in the yard to report. Between times you got to make 'em take exercise. They don't let us out of the Cachot to exercise; don't let us out for nothing except sickness, and you got to be awful sick to be took to the hospital. If you catch jail fever, they won't let you be took to the hospital till you're mottled with it, and that's pretty late. In fact, it's too late."

"Race track prepared, Captain Smith," Obed said.

The men rose reluctantly from their piles of straw, spectral gray figures in that dim tomb, and approached the blanket, on which Obed, with a bit of lime, had drawn seven narrow alleyways.

"You got yourself a louse?" Jesse asked me.

I told him I had come in clean.

"We'll fix that," Jesse said. "Rickor, give Cap'n Nason one of your best bugs. Don't give him none of them half-growed ones, neither! Give him a good big one, so's he'll have a chance with the rest of us."

Rickor, a tired-looking, stoop-shouldered man, searched himself carefully: then handed me an active gray insect.

The men knelt in a circle around the blanket, holding their entries at one end of the alleyways.

"Are you ready?" Jesse asked.

The others growled expectantly.

"Go!" Jesse shouted.

The seven entrants were dropped on the starting line. They moved jerkily and indecisively on the rough surface of the blanket.

"I snum!" Hussey said. "I got another putterer! I ain't had a fast one in a week!" He poked at his entrant with a straw, baulking him in his effort to go in the wrong direction.

"Whitten!" Jesse shouted angrily, "you're blowing on yours!"

"I ain't neither!" Whitten protested. "I got to breathe, ain't I? I wasn't doing nothin' but breathing."

"Breathe through your nose, then," Jesse said.

My entrant tacked first to starboard, then to larboard, as if in search of a safe haven; then stood still.

"What do you do when they stop?" I asked Jesse.

"Hope and pray," he replied. "They can't be touched when resting."

My insect conquered his suspicions and moved rapidly ahead.

Simeon Hays set up a shouting and snapped his fingers furiously. "Move yo' laigs, Gray Ghost!" he cried. "Come on, you li'l' gray rascal!"

His louse, a long slender one, forged across the finish line.

"That's the fifth time in three days you came in first, Sim," Jesse Smith said sourly. "Either you're tempting that insect with some kind of food, or you're holding him over on us. Lemme see you execute him right now."

Simeon obligingly cracked him between his thumb nails.

Last of all Obed Hussey glumly herded his entry across the finish line with a straw, picked him up and examined him carefully; then destroyed him.

"I declare," he said, "there's something plumb contrary about these animals of mine! If I could do it, I'd be almost tempted to clean 'em out, lock, stock, and barrel. Come on, Sim!"

Simeon Hays mounted easily to Obed's shoulders, hooked his fingers over the sill of the small slit near the ceiling, and peered out through it. The rest of us went back to our blankets.

"It's kind of foggy up back," Simeon reported, "but you can see the hills the other side of Princetown. They's a man on a donkey on the long road, 'bout two mile away, heading north by east. Looks like a flea carryin' a littler flea. They's four Rough Alleys huntin' in the swill box back of Number One cookhouse. One of 'em's found something. Looks like a turnip! They's about two hundred men in sight. They got a Keno table pitched between Number One and Number Two. They's seven fellers playin' ketch with a ball made out of spun yarn . . ."

The rest of us lay back on our blankets in the gray gloom, striving to see into the prison yards with the eyes of Simeon Hays. It seemed to me that the world of which he spoke was a foggy, unreal world of specters and pixies. I took my miniature from my pocket and unwrapped it, holding it in the crook of my arm so I could study it unseen. The lips, I thought, moved as if to whisper to me; but in the Cachot there was no sound save the slurred Baltimore speech of Simeon Hays, telling us the few things he could see and understand of the infinitesimal happenings behind Prison Number One.

XXVIII

In the Cachot every man, I think, found his sharpest suffering from a different source. My own was the intolerable pressure of my incessant wondering: where had Emily gone, and how were things with her? What did she suffer, and what did she suffer for me? I think mine was the sharpest mental anguish there. For most of the other men, what they bore physically was enough to be busy over. Added to their special ills, we had a common bitterness in the scantiness of our food and light. Perhaps the darkness was the hardest to bear for most of us; there was never any light in that place save what filtered through the two small barred windows. Yet there were some among us who seemed most discomfortable because of the skimpiness of the rags they wore. One man would talk whimperingly an hour at a time of a fine suit of clothes he had once worn. Another bragged over and over of a beaver coat his father had given him on his fourteenth birthday; and there were others whose speech dwelt eternally on the diseases to which the Cachot, as well as the whole prison, exposed us. They would shiver and pretend to knock on wood as they spoke of jail fever, smallpox, and a violent pneumonia that set the lungs to crackling. Some found it most horrid—and indeed this was a thing oppressive to the soul—that for weeks on end we might have no more news of the world and of the movement of life upon our planet than did the very dead in the churchyard. The earth seemed to have closed over our heads and to lie heavily there.

It was not until October that we had word of how the war went, and then what we heard was horrible. Carley told us, doubtless not realizing what he added to our sorrows; for, as I have said, he was as kind as he dared be. He told us how the British had landed from their fleet in the Chesapeake and marched up to Washington, with Mr. Jefferson's militiamen running before them like frightened rabbits; and how they had put the torch to the library in Washington, to the Capitol, to the President's House, and to many public offices, as well as to the navy yard.

There was no racing on the blanket, and not even any looking out through the slit in the wall on the day after we heard that.

Perhaps it was a month after this when a New Bedford man, consigned to the Cachot for ten days, came in with news he had from a fresh draft of prisoners just brought to Dartmoor from the sea. Thus we learned how American privateers were being built in ever greater numbers and destroying more British commerce than at any time since the first two months of the war; and how British merchants were demanding the war be stopped before they were ruined. Even a hoarse and racking cheer went up from that dismal place when we thus heard of the greatest of all the privateering feats of the war: how the American privateer brig *General Armstrong* lay in Fayal harbor, neutral waters, and how she was unrightfully beset by a British sloop-of-war, a frigate and a ship-of-the-line, and fought off four hundred men, who came in boats to take her, destroyed most of them, and then was sunk by her own captain, who reached the shore safe with all but two of his men.

Through that chill autumn we gradually hardened to the increasing cold and dampness and so kept our health. Those who came in for ten-day stretches, however, having been accustomed to the use of hammocks and to better food and to exercise, developed troubles in their lungs from sleeping on the cold granite and quickly became fit subjects for the hospital.

The chief surgeon was a man named William Dykar, who had served in America with the British in our war for independence. He was an old man, violent tempered and opinionated, like so many officers who reach high positions in every army and navy; and he would visit no sick man in the Cachot because it was his belief that Americans could never be trusted to speak the truth and claimed always to be sick so to escape. Therefore sick men could get no treatment in the Cachot; though if one of them, on being released, was unable to stand, Carley would call a sentry and take him to the hospital, where too often he died. Therefore I say, after due thought and consideration, that this William Dykar, chief surgeon of the depot at Dartmoor from 1809 to 1814, was a deliberate and cold-blooded murderer.

It was toward the end of October that a seaman from Townsend, Maine, one Jesse Field, was put in among us. Beyond the fact that he had attempted to escape, and in so doing had lain full length in freezing mud against the wall of Number Seven Prison for a matter of six hours before being discovered, we could find out nothing from him, for he was weak and shaken with violent chills. He lay all that day on the straw we gave him, since he had been sent in without any; and on the following morning we saw there was a sort of brown crust on his lips and teeth. It looked to us like typhus. When Carley came with the breakfast, therefore, I told him to go again to Dr. Dykar and ask him for the love of God to give an order for this man to be taken to the hospital before all of us came down with the disease.

"I been meanin' to tell yez," Carley said. "Dykar's out! They t'run him out!"

"Who's the new man?" I asked. "Is he a real doctor, or a murderer, like the other?"

"Yez'll soon know!" Carley said. "His name's Magrath, and he's one of the salt of the earth—a descendant of the Irish kings."

We went back to watching Field and to cursing our jailers for their heartlessness. Before we knew it, almost, there was a rattling at the door, which swung back and revealed Carley standing at the side of a tall, thin, one-eyed man. He stood staring in at us, his mouth pursed up and pushed to one side and his left hand feeling at his face as if he sought a beard that wasn't there.

"How many of you in here?" he asked suddenly. His voice was deep and pleasant, with none of the snarl in it we were accustomed to hear from Dartmoor officials.

I came to the door and told him.

He looked me up and down. "Anything wrong with you?" he asked.

I told him there wasn't. "It's a man that came in yesterday: Jesse Field. He looks like jail fever."

"Hm," he said. "I'll trouble you to wrap him in his blanket and bring him out where I can see him."

Hays and I made a blanket snug around Field and brought him out. It was the first time we had been in the open air since August. The sky seemed huge and brilliant, even though heavy with gray clouds; and the air had a queer, piercing smell to it, as if drugged.

We put Field on the ground. The new doctor pulled down his eyelid and looked into his eye, then peered into his mouth.

"Call four sentries," he said to Carley. "This man goes to the hospital at once."

"Sor!" Carley said, "I'll have to be havin' an order. I'll run to the office and ask kin I have wan."

"No, you won't!" Magrath said. "You'll run to the nearest sentry! Who are you to talk about the office when I can see with half an eye you have a decent heart in you? Get along!"

He turned back to us. "Let's see this hole you live in." He walked into the Cachot, lowering his head as he passed through the door. We stayed behind, eager to have the air as long as we could.

He was pale when he came out, and there were beads of perspiration on his upper lip. "How are the vermin in there?" he asked.

"The fleas are bad," I told him, "but we keep the lice pretty well under control."

"We could do better with 'em if we had some light," Hays said.

"You have no light?" Magrath asked incredulously. "You mean you spend your lives in the dark?" The other men in the Cachot came to the door one by one, then edged, blinking, into the open, staring up at the sky and at their own raggedness.

"We're not allowed to have candles," I told him. "This is pretty brutal treatment, Doctor. If I'd ever caught one of my men treating a dog like this, I'd have knocked him into the scuppers."

Four sentries, militiamen, warmly dressed in long hooded overcoats, came up and looked wonderingly at us. I would have paid well for one of their overcoats if I had had the money, but Exeter jail had left me with only seven dollars.

"Take this man to the hospital on your muskets," Magrath said. They stood there for a second, uncertain. Magrath snapped his fingers, and they moved, then, to obey, though they were clearly reluctant.

"What are you in for?" he asked me.

"Four of these men are in on a false charge," I told him. "They're in for duration. So am I. There's more reason to what they charge me with, but I'm guilty of no crime. I'm guilty of nothing but trying to escape."

There was a commotion in the prison yard on the other side of the tall iron fence that separated the Cachot enclosure from the prisons. Prisoners shouted and ran toward the pickets. We saw Captain Shortland, followed by a militia officer, hastening toward us.

We watched him coming, stocky and strong; and the prisoners in the yard shouted in time with his footsteps, "LOB ster, LOB ster, LOB ster!" By the time he reached us he was red and angry.

"Good-morning to you, Captain," Dr. Magrath said.

"Who let these men out?" Shortland demanded. "Carley! Carley! What in hell do you mean? Put these men where they belong!"

"My fault, Captain," Dr. Magrath said. "I had a report: a case of jail fever. These men, if you'll permit me to say so, Captain, should be looked after more carefully."

"*Looked* after!" Shortland said. "What in God's name do you mean? I was told to put 'em in close confinement. Should I button 'em into lace nightgowns and send 'em to bed in my guest chamber?"

"Indeed and indeed, Captain," Magrath said, "you've little leeway in carrying out your orders! Aye! What I have in mind, Captain, is that these men, after all, are prisoners of war, and I have a fixed conception of a prisoner of war. He's a man held in trust: a man for whom an accounting must be rendered when the war's over."

Shortland laughed, a sharp, mirthless bark. "Good God, Doctor," he said, "let's not have trouble at the very beginning! You know what orders are! These men are where they belong! What good is close confinement if you make it a damned lawn party, eh? These men get exactly what they deserve! Here, you, Carley! Push 'em back in the Cachot!"

Carley fussed around us like a kindly old woman, saying, "Now, byes! Now, byes!"

Magrath went on talking to Shortland in his deep, soothing voice, and we hung back against Carley's insistent pushing so we might hear as much as we could.

"Quite so, Captain," he said, "but we don't have to change close confinement to something worse, eh, Captain? Sleeping on granite, now, in this climate! There's nothing like this in all England. Did you ever try sleeping on granite, Captain?"

"No, by God!" Shortland shouted, "and until I do what these men have done I never expect to!"

"Not that, Captain!" Magrath protested: "You don't mean that! These men served their country, as I understand it. Nothing about that to deserve granite beds in winter, eh? I doubt you'd have been pleased, Captain, when you were first lieutenant of the *Melpomene* —hah, hah! There's a many of us remember that cutting-out party of yours, Captain! Suppose, instead of cutting out the *Avanturier* and winning the rank of commander you'd fallen into the hands of the French and they'd clapped you into a black hole? Left you there with no light, and wet granite for a bed, eh?"

Shortland made a contemptuous sound in his throat. "Punishment's not punishment unless a man knows he's being punished!" he said. "Every damned one of these Americans is determined to get free! If we don't punish 'em we'll have 'em all breaking out and terrorizing the country."

"Ah," Magrath said, "I had Americans at Mill Prison before I came here. There isn't one of 'em that'll give up trying to get free because you put 'em in the Cachot when they fail. No, no! Nothing gets anywhere with 'em but kindness! The harder you are on 'em, the worse you'll find 'em. They're not Frenchmen, Captain."

"You're wasting your breath, Doctor," Shortland snapped. "I know how to handle my men!"

Magrath twisted his mouth and fingered his chin. "Yes," he said mildly. "That must be true. But let's look at the medical end of it, eh? I tell you, Captain, I don't like this African smallpox that runs about here, nor this violent pneumonia. They're like deadly poisons if not treated quickly and treated well. I must ask to be allowed to keep my eye on these men, or the guard may slip the wicket some fine morning and find all of 'em stiff as a sternpost."

They turned toward the Cachot, as if already it had become a charnel house; and when Shortland saw us still crowded in the doorway, holding it open against Carley's efforts to push us in, his face took on the look of badly cooked beef.

Before he could speak Simeon Hays shouted to Magrath: "Feed him some calomel, Doctor! His liver ain't what it ought to be!"

With that, not wishing to cause trouble for Carley, we gave ground, and the door clanged shut on us once more.

Now, whether the doctor's suggestions had some effect on Shortland, or whether the doctor himself was responsible, I don't know; but one November evening—a cold, dark twilight, when we were lying silently on our piles of straw, which had grown so shredded and mouldy that they were less like straw than like dusty chaff— Carley rattled the door and pushed open the wicket.

"Here, byes!" he said. There was exultation in his voice. "I got a present for yez!"

I got up quickly, stumbling over Hays, and went to him.

"Don't nivver say I ain't give yez nothin'!" he said, handing me a piece of candle, an acid bottle, and a bundle of sulphur-tipped spunks for dipping in the bottle.

"Who are they from?" I asked.

"I dunno nawthin' about it," he said. "When yez finish with that, I'll get yez more; but pay attention to this, for the love av Mary! Whenivver yez use it, stuff the windys full of straw so the light won't show."

I doubt there are many folk, barring the blind, who know what it is to spend the greater part of their time in the thick dark. There is little I can say about it save that all of us dreaded the coming of night more than we had ever dreaded anything. Miller, the Englishman who had turned American, got the horrors one November evening. He burst out snuffling and groaning and hiccupping like a child, declaring he couldn't live another day in the place, and saying there were bells ringing in his ears, piercing his brain like knives. He carried on to such a degree that Hays and I crawled over and got our hands on him, lest he knock out his brains against the floor.

That one small point of yellow flame, almost absorbed by the dark walls of the Cachot, turned our misery into what, by comparison, seemed gaiety; for when the candle was kindled, our minds took fire from it as well, so we were able to speak, instead of lying silent and helpless. If we wished to move we could do so without stumbling over a man's legs—which was a serious business, because our legs were thin-skinned from scanty food, close confinement and perpetual dampness. Above all we could occupy ourselves by lying around the candle as the spokes of a wheel radiate from the hub and engage in the making of hair bracelets, this being an art in which Jim Rickor had perfected himself when he should doubtless have been working at something that is known as "more useful." Because of this I have ever since been loth to say what is useful and what isn't.

Since our hair had not been cut for months—nor our beards shaved, for that matter, nor our clothes washed, nor clothes or shoes given to us to replace the rags in which we lay—we were able to pull long hairs aplenty from our own heads for the making of bracelets. These, we hoped, would serve a double purpose; for not only did they occupy our hands, but Rickor claimed they were sovereign remedies against rheumatism. Therefore we made them prodigally; and each one of us had hair bracelets on his wrists and ankles, and hair rings on his fingers, while Rickor made himself a collar, an inch and a half wide, with a neat cravat, all woven out of hair.

With the coming of December we had a fruitful subject for conversation. The month had no sooner started than Carley told us there was a rumor through the prison that American commissioners and British commissioners had met in Ghent, in Holland, to discuss peace, and were close to arriving at a decision. Thus, suddenly, we began to hope. For months we had thought of nothing in the morning except how to get through the day, and at evening how to bear one more night. But now we had rosy and heart-stirring dreams that Peace might come at any moment to free us from cold and filth and aching bones, as it had come to free the Frenchmen. Every visit of Carley's was an adventure: he might, we thought, have news; and whenever he came to the wicket we held our breaths for fear we might lose a word.

Our hopes rose and fell like a fire. Jesse Smith came back to us on the ninth, swearing that if he hadn't known us in the early days of our imprisonment, he'd have taken us for haystacks because of the length of our hair and beards. He had been caught trying to scale the wall, he said; and when we asked him why he had tried to escape with Peace imminent, he laughed sardonically.

"Peace!" he said. "If there's to be Peace, why are the British fitting out an expedition to capture New Orleans? They don't know when they're licked! They don't know yet that we licked 'em in the Revolution! You got to lick 'em three times before it counts, and we've only licked 'em twice, so far!"

Sick at heart, we told him to hold his tongue, and set him to making a hair bracelet, loaning him our own hair for it. I can hear him now, commenting on his first bracelet.

"Hair bracelets!" he said. "My God! If the folks at home could only see me now! What if this should ever get to be known in Stonington, Connecticut! I can hear 'em, pointing at me and saying, 'There goes Jesse Smith, that was captured by the British in the war and suffered horribly, making hair bracelets! Wounded, too, he was: cut his finger on a hair!'"

But rumors of peace persisted, and so, too, did the attempts to escape, as we knew from men who were daily thrown in the Cachot.

A part of the fever to escape, it seemed to me, was due to the approach of Christmas; for Christmas is made much of in our province of Maine as well as in all New England; and as December dragged by, on snow-laden wings, our thoughts and our speech turned continually to our homes, so that we were filled with a powerful longing for them. There were times when it seemed to me I could smell, even through and above the stench of the Cachot, the odor of roasting goose, the sweet scent of spices on apple sauce, the faint mellow perfume of cider, the fragrance of mince pie. In my imagination I could see the frost figures on the windows of our large front room and catch the smell of the house: a scent of dry pine wood and cinnamon and soap and smoke, mixed with a faint trace of hay and sea air.

Christmas was a dark day, and we burned our candle all the morning so we could see to work on our hair bracelets; and Carley, instead of opening the wicket to give us our soup, unlocked the door and swung it open. Behind him we saw the doctor, tall and thin and one-eyed, wrapped in a heavy brown overcoat dusted with fine snow. From under his coat he drew a small bundle.

"Well, gentlemen," he said in his deep pleasant voice, and he wasn't being sarcastic, either, though we were the wildest and raggedest looking men, I do believe, that ever in the history of the world had been called "gentlemen," "well, gentlemen, I wish you many, many merry Christmases—in your own country."

"We wish you the same, Doctor," said Simeon Hays. "We wish you the same, in this country or any other."

"Yes," the doctor said, clearing his throat, "yes. I appreciate that very much. Are you gentlemen quite well?"

"Why," Simeon Hays said, "considering the amount of wine we drink and the number of rich seegars we smoke, we're tollable, Doctor—tollable. Our appetite ain't too good: probably there ain't one of us could eat more than one cow, unless it was an awful small one."

"I see," the doctor said. "I wished very much to bring you something to read, gentlemen, but like most other things, that seems to be forbidden. I've brought you a small plum pudding, and Carley has a full ration for you today instead of the regular two-thirds ration. I deeply regret the plum pudding is so small, but I'm forced to say that gentlemen who've been on two-thirds rations for months are almost better off with no plum pudding at all."

He gave the bundle to Simeon Hays. Carley, overcome with emotion, rattled our bowls against his pail of soup with as much noise as though building a new wing on the Cachot.

I fished two clusters of hair bracelets from behind my pile of straw and handed one of them to the doctor. "Doctor," I told him, "we couldn't figure what to give you for a little remembrance, so we left it to each man. Oddly enough each man decided that the most useful thing would be a hair bracelet. We want you to take them as meaning we're grateful."

The doctor took the lot and examined them, smiling queerly. When he spoke, he seemed to find difficulty in expressing himself. "Why, gentlemen," he said, "this is a—this is a—I'm sure I shall never—this is a most unexpected——"

"From his childhood he's always hankered for nothing on earth so much as a hair bracelet," Simeon Hays enlightened us in a hoarse whisper.

Seeing the doctor had no desire to make a longer speech, I handed the other cluster of bracelets to Carley.

"Timothy Carley," I said, "these are for you, with thanks for past kindnesses."

"Oh, holy Mary!" Carley said, snuffling childishly, "I'm as proud of 'em as I'd be of the Garter!"

"Why, you wicked, blasphemious old man!" Simeon expostulated, very ladylike; "*whose* garter?" With that, being half starved as usual, we went for our soup.

Dr. Magrath cleared his throat. "I have one other little gift for you, gentlemen. It's only a bit of hope, so to speak; but there's worse gifts than hope. You may be quite certain that before this month is over there'll be a peace treaty signed between England and America."

We stared at him. I know that I, for one, had such a pounding in my throat that I had trouble in downing my soup; for the face of Emily Ransome came so suddenly into my mind that an enormous hand seemed to clutch at my heart and squeeze it.

Magrath smiled a lopsided smile at us, blinking his one blue eye; then the iron door clanged shut behind him.

"Well," said Simeon Hays, holding up a spoonful of soup. "Here's to Christmas and freedom!"

*   *   *

Magrath had been right, for on the twenty-ninth day of December word was cried through the prison that on December 24th, in Ghent, the commissioners of England and America had signed a treaty. The war was over!

Peace! Nothing to do but for everybody to go home, kiss his wife and family or his sweetheart, and go back to the counting house, or begin milking the cow or hauling the nets again.

Peace! Nothing to do but throw the prison gates open. Nothing to do but open the door of our hell, the Cachot, and let us walk forth free men.

No, it was not like that. It was with the very signing of peace that the climax and worst of our Calvary began.

All the world knows that the St. Bartholomew of Dartmoor Prison came after the Peace had been signed.

XXIX

In the Cachot we innocently thought night after night that with the coming dawn Shortland would throw open the iron door; yet the days and the weeks went by, leaving us no better off than we had been before the Peace. January came down on us with a howling blizzard, and the short, bitter cold days dragged so slowly that we came to seem to ourselves like old, old men. Things that had happened a week before were lost, almost, in the dust of distant ages.

From overmuch lying on the granite floor we had sores on our legs and hips and shoulders. Some of our sorry company were given to periods of moaning and sobbing that made me shiver and retch. For days on end Simeon Hays sat huddled in his blanket, hugging his knees, staring at nothing out of hollow eyes, making no sound except to grind his teeth. I turned more and more to my small picture of Emily Ransome, to look at it and stay my spirit with its loveliness; and when I did, my fingers shook and seemed to me more like claws than the fingers of a human hand.

Magrath came frequently to see us, but his visits were short because, apparently, the sight of us distressed him and he could do nothing to help us. Whenever he came we always asked about the Peace; but he could tell us nothing except that it could not be genuinely regarded as a peace until the sloop-of-war *Favorite* had carried a copy of the treaty to America, and until it had been ratified by President Madison and brought back again to England.

"Look here," I said to him one morning, late in January, "these men are losing hope. I can't make 'em work any more."

"Why not?" he asked.

"Well," I said, "I can handle one of 'em easily, but together they can beat me. I no longer have the heart to hit 'em."

He nodded and left us. That afternoon he returned with Shortland; and the five of us who were for duration were brought from the Cachot and lined up before the commandant and the doctor.

I was blinded by the glare of the open sky reflected from the snowy ground, and it was a little while before I was able to see the true fearsomeness of Hays and Rickor and Whitten and Miller, who were emaciated and horrible-looking.

Shortland and Magrath stood and eyed us silently, Magrath tall and pale and one-eyed, and Shortland broad shouldered and curly haired and red-faced, looking like Punch and smelling so strongly of rum that he made my mouth water. Shortland looked inquiringly at Magrath. "Well, what's wrong with 'em? They look like any of these damned tricky Yankees, so far as I can see."

Magrath stepped up to me and felt my upper arm. "Would you mind holding out your hand?"

I held out my hand. It seemed almost transparent.

Magrath thanked me: then stepped back beside Captain Shortland. "Captain, these men must be clothed. They must have fresh air each day. They've got to have half an hour of exercise in the open. I'll help you do your duty, but I won't connive at murder."

Shortland's face grew purple. "Why, by God, Magrath, what do you mean!"

"What I mean," Magrath said, and he spoke as pleasantly as though offering an opinion on the weather, "what I mean is that these men are sick. Hope deferred maketh the heart sick, Captain. They're not only sick; they're being starved to death. Surely your eyes are as good as mine."

Shortland dug his heel in the ground angrily. "These men are criminals!"

I heard Simeon Hays, beside me, mumbling in his unkempt beard, and took him by the wrist to keep him quiet.

Shortland took a quick step toward him. "What's that you say?"

"You're a hell of a captain," Simeon said dispassionately.

Magrath moved between Shortland and us. "Captain," he said, "these men are unstrung from cold and poor food and living in the dark. They feel an injustice has been done them, and I must confess to having the same feeling myself. They've been brooding over it. You must make allowances for them."

"I'll show 'em——" Shortland began savagely.

"I beg of you!" Magrath protested. "This is all beside the point! I've made up my mind. What I ask is little enough. If you find it impossible to agree, I shall be obliged to pursue the matter through other channels—at once."

"Of course," Shortland said sourly, "of course, if they'd give their paroles not to——"

"Just a moment, Captain!" Magrath broke in. "My opinion is not contingent on these men's paroles. They've got to be clothed and have exercise, whether they give paroles or not."

Shortland glowered, his lips pressed tight together so that he looked more than ever like Punch. Then he turned to Magrath with a frank and pleasant smile. "Well, well!" he said, "we mustn't be too hasty. I think I see your point of view—yes, indeed! I'll give it careful consideration, Doctor: careful consideration."

"That's a very generous spirit, Captain," Magrath said. "Under the circumstances, any undue amount of consideration would be inadvisable. Ah—you'll let me know to-morrow morning, eh?"

Shortland whirled to look for Carley. "Put 'em back!" he snapped, jerking his thumb at us. And off he stamped through the snow without another word to Magrath, while the prisoners behind Prison Number One, gathered at the iron picket fence that separated us from the yards, began to chant, in time to his footsteps, "LOB ster! LOB ster! LOB ster!"

*   *   *

Four days later Carley brought us five prison suits of coarse blue cloth, and new prison shoes made of felt with wooden soles. In the middle of the morning of that same day Carley unlocked the iron door and called the five of us into the narrow enclosure between the inner stone wall and the iron picket fence. There were five sentries drawn up in a line, waiting. At a word from Carley they went to pacing along the enclosure, twenty-five yards one way; then twenty-five yards back to the Cachot again; and we, like five sheep, or like five merchantmen under the convoy of five sloops-of-war, paced beside them.

The Americans came running from the yard of Prison Number One when they saw us, whereupon Carley warned us that if we attempted to talk with any other prisoners our exercise would be immediately stopped. With that he went over and stood by the iron picket fence to speak to the constantly growing crowd.

"Yez'll have to spread the word," he shouted to them. "Any attempt to talk to these byes in here and they'll get no more exercise. Look at 'em all yez want to, but don't say nawthin' to 'em!"

They liked Carley, we could see; they must have known he would do whatever he could for us; so they said never a word to him or to us: only stood pressed against the iron bars, looking and looking at us; and above their ceaseless gabbling we could hear other prisoners running across the cobbles of the prison yard to see this strange new spectacle: men who had been buried alive since midsummer.

Up and down we paced by the side of the sentries, and it was hard to tell which helped us most: the stretching of our legs in the open air, or the sympathy we could feel coming out to us from the restless, silent, strangely dressed crowd of men beyond the iron pickets.

Every day thereafter we were taken out and marched up and down by the side of the sentries for half an hour; and every day the men came from all the yards to watch us. King Dick was there on the second day, his bearskin hat towering above the men beside him. His black face was expressionless; but whenever I looked at him I could see his enormous white eyes, round as china doorknobs, rolling from side to side, and from the ground to the top of the twelve-foot iron pickets and back again: examining, I knew; estimating; calculating.

Because of the walks and the warmer clothes, and the decent feel of them against our bodies, we got back our self-respect and went to making hair bracelets again, and to holding our races, which we had given up.

It was on the morning of February 6th, a Monday, that we heard Carley gabbling to someone outside, very amiable and friendly.

When the door opened, Jesse Smith stood there, his hands on his hips, grinning down recklessly at Carley; and with him was another figure, a smaller one. Behind Jesse, a rolled blanket on his shoulder, peering and peering in an effort to penetrate the darkness of the Cachot, was Tommy Bickford—pink-cheeked, smiling, brown-eyed Tommy Bickford, whose father had taken my father on his shoulder when the Congress galley fought the whole British fleet at the Battle of Valcour Island and carried him wounded but safe to shore.

Carley pushed them in, looking hard at Smith before he swung the door shut. "Holy Mary!" he said. "Don't yez nivver do nawthin' but try to escape? There ain't nobody can say yez don't know what yez want! Yez'll be a great man, Mr. Smith!"

Jesse ignored him and pushed Tommy Bickford toward me. "There he is," he said. "Your eyes'll get used to it in a minute. Edge over."

I caught Tommy's wrist and drew him down on my heap of matted straw.

"Cap'n Dick," he said, "Cap'n Dick——" His voice broke.

"That's all right, Tommy," I told him. "I'm glad to see you; awful glad! What on earth have you been doing, Tommy, to get yourself put in this place?"

"Nothing, Cap'n Dick," he said. "Honest, I didn't do nothing! Only made out to escape."

"Well, you must be a born fool, Tommy, with good clothes and good food and good treatment, trying to——" I stopped. It came to me, suddenly, that he had made the attempt so he could be put in the Cachot with me.

"I only made out to, Cap'n Dick," he said, grinning at me.

"Who put you up to it? King Dick?"

"No, sir. King Dick, he thought mebbe he hadn't ought to let me do it on account of the way you might talk to him when you got out. He said you'd make a turrible yukkus, but I told him you wouldn't."

"When I get out?" I asked.

"Yes, sir. King Dick, he said if he could get word to you about getting out, you could probably get out."

The mere thought of escaping from the Cachot brought a moisture into the palms of my hands and a trembling into my knees. "The trouble with that, Tommy, is that if I should try it, the others wouldn't be allowed to take exercise any more."

"No, he meant all of you, Cap'n Dick, he meant you and the other four gentlemen."

Simeon Hays crawled over beside me and leaned on his elbow, staring at Tommy. Elisha Whitten and Jim Rickor and John Miller sat up on their blankets as if pins had been thrust in them.

"Go ahead, Tommy," I told him. I was proud to have the others see him sitting there, neat and pleasant and smiling, and to have them know our town of Arundel could produce a boy like Tommy Bickford.

"Cap'n Dick," Tommy said, and it was easy to see he was as excited over what he had to tell us as we were to hear it, "King Dick says these militia soldiers are turrible thick-headed: thicker-headed than any of the colored gentlemen in Number Four. He says they come from Somerset, up north of here, and he says a donkey's awful intelligent and thoughtful compared to Somerset militia. He says he's watched their eyes when they do sentry-go with you gentlemen, and every time they turn round, their brains keep right on travelin' for as much as a minute almost."

"He's right, by Jiminy!" Simeon said. "They're thick, and they're mean."

"Yes, sir," Tommy said. "And King Dick says any folks that have been treated the way you gentlemen have been treated can pull themselves up to the top of that iron fence; and he says the time to do it is when these Somerset lobsters turn around on their beat. He says they ain't thinking of nothing when they turn around, and it's awful hard for 'em to start thinking."

"Tommy," I said, "that fence is twelve feet high."

"Yes, Cap'n Dick," Tommy said. "That's what King Dick figured.

THE LIVELY LADY

But the cross bar between the pickets is only ten. King Dick says you can get your hands on the cross bar; then he and the others can push their hands through and shove you up."

I looked at Simeon Hays. He nodded. We looked at the others. They sat silent and motionless, staring at Tommy.

"You can do it, can't you, Cap'n Dick?" Tommy asked. It was less a question than a proud statement of fact, delivered by way of setting all doubts at rest.

"Yes, I can," I told him, not wishing to disappoint him, and wishing, also, to give the others as much confidence as possible. "Of course I can get over—of course we can get over; but when we get over, what do you think Shortland will be doing?"

"King Dick says for you not to worry about nothing but getting over," Tommy said. "King Dick says you'll be looked after. He says if you get out of here they'll never get you back in again."

Simeon Hays wiped the palms of his hands on his jacket. "When did he think?" he asked. "What day was he thinking of?"

"Why, to-day," Tommy said. "He'll be waiting there, to-day, right where they turn, down at the bend." He pointed at the door of the Cachot, and it seemed to me, as I turned my head to look where his finger was pointing, that I could see open country: the marshland along the creek behind our gray house in Arundel; the silvery-green pines that rise beyond it in unbroken ranks.

"Tommy," I said, "we can't do it to-day. Carley's responsible for us, and he'd get the blame. Carley's been pretty good to us, Tommy —the only one that has, barring the doctor. Shortland would have him flogged, and it might kill him."

Tommy's under lip sagged.

"Carley goes to mass on Sunday," I told him. "He's a papist, and he has to go to mass; but that's six days off."

"It don't make a mite of difference," Tommy said, smiling and eager again. "King Dick said he'd wait there every day until something happened. He'll be there Sunday. He'll be there, Cap'n Dick! All you got to do, the day you want to try it, is to kneel down on one knee and tie your shoe when you come out of the Cachot."

"Tommy," I said, "you're a good boy."

* * *

Every day our exercising was watched by a larger and larger crowd, until it seemed to us there must be a thousand men crammed into the little piece of yard behind the tall stone haunches of Prison Number One, all of them following our every move as we marched up and down, up and down, beside the sentries. Every day King Dick was there, pressed tight against the iron railings, but behaving in a casual manner, as though he had more interest in the weather or in the tall Negroes who accompanied him than in any of us.

It was best, it seemed to me, to have the thing over as soon as possible; and so we planned, on Saturday, that when we came out on the following morning, we would walk to the end of the beat with the sentries, walk back to the Cachot, then go to the end once more and take an extra two steps when the sentries turned. With the second step we were to break for the picket fence, a matter of eight paces from our line of march.

It was chill that Sunday morning. When we heard the rattle of the key at the door Jesse Smith slapped each one of us on the back, saying, "Don't never let me see none of you again!" Tommy Bickford, who was hoarse with a cough, touched me on the arm and said, "Good-bye, Cap'n Dick. I'll be out on Wednesday with Mr. Smith."

A sour turnkey named Parker unlocked the door for us, and we went out, blinking, into the cold February air. The prisoners were close against the iron pickets, watching for us. When we appeared they murmured among themselves, sounding like a calm sea fingering and lapping at a seaweed-covered ledge.

I went down on my knee and fumbled with my shoe. It seemed to me the murmuring stopped.

"What you come out here for?" Parker roared at me. "Exercise or not?"

I jumped to my feet and fell in behind Miller. In front of him was Hays. In front of Hays were Whitten and thin Jim Rickor.

I was chary of looking straight at the silent crowd that stood behind the pickets, for fear Parker might see guilt written on my face; but I snatched a hasty glance at their watchful ranks and caught sight of King Dick, fixing his tall bearskin hat more tightly on his head and working his arms somewhat, as though to free them of pressure. His head was thrust forward, and his eyes, which ordinarily had the look of china doorknobs, were small white slits in his black face.

Parker, lounging against the corner of the Cachot, jingled his keys and stared lackadaisically at the silent crowd of prisoners watching us. I could see we had nothing to fear from him; for whatever was to happen would be finished before he knew it had begun.

I looked at the heavy-lipped, heavy-eyed face of the militiaman beside me and saw he was indeed as slow witted as King Dick had said. He was the very man, I hoped and believed, to stand stock-still with his musket on his shoulder and just stare at me for some precious seconds when he saw me run.

When we were abreast of King Dick we turned and marched again toward the Cachot. There was a slight swaying motion among the men near our huge black friend. I breathed deep, to ease the thumping of my heart. From the tail of my eye I saw King Dick shouldering himself free of those beside him. We turned at the Cachot and trudged back again.

I looked at the top of the pickets. The cross bar, high on the fence, was higher by two feet—by three feet—than the crown of King Dick's enormous bearskin hat.

I heard Hays clear his throat and knew how he felt, stuffed full and blown up with waiting.

My head was rigid on my neck, like the ball on a newel-post. I should, I felt, have set the attempt for later, when we had become more limber. My knees were stiff; my legs seemed like bean poles— thin and brittle and quite useless.

The sentries turned. The bright bayonet on the musket barrel of the man beside me swung slowly as he wheeled. I looked away from it: fixed my eyes fiercely on the ground. I took one more step, listening. There was nothing. I took another, turned sharp to the left and moved somehow toward a wild roaring that seemed to hold me up and engulf me. There was a vague, tossing movement before me, and I was conscious of a whining close by my shoulder, a whining I knew was made by Hays, straining to reach his goal. Yet I could see nothing with clearness except the towering pickets rising from a turbulent human sea and bound top and bottom by endless cross-pieces of iron.

I felt myself leaping at the upper cross-piece—leaping and reaching. I could see my fingers rise toward it, slowly, as a gull's beak rises toward a fragment of biscuit tossed from the stern of a vessel. They caught it and clung.

I could feel the hands of prisoners lifting my legs and feet. I was pushed up and up, though how I got over the top of the pickets I don't know. I only know I did, and then pitched forward and down into a turmoil of struggling, squirming men.

Hands clutched me anew. I was dragged rapidly through the crowd. I struggled for a footing and got one at last; and as I ran, I saw King Dick had me by the shoulder of my jacket with a huge black paw. He was clinging to his bearskin hat with one hand and whisking me along with the other. There were prisoners running ahead of us and on each side. We were the center of a rapidly moving mass of men in which it was almost impossible to distinguish individuals.

This throng surged abruptly against the rear of Prison Number One and swirled around it, leaving a narrow alleyway. I went up the steps and through the door behind King Dick. The crowd poured in behind us, quiet no longer, but shouting and cursing with excitement.

I was in a chair, then, and a man was daubing lather into my beard. In front of me towered King Dick, huge and black in his woolly suit, staring watchfully from one end of the building to the other.

I drew a deep breath. "Whew!" I said, "that was close! Did they get out? Did all of them get out?"

King Dick laughed a sudden nervous laugh, but instantly fell serious. "Nemmine 'at!" he said. "Keep yo' pan quiet till 'at beard gits shaved! Mah lan', Ah never see so much haiah, not on nuffin' seppen a goat!"

The barber's razor dragged at my tender skin as though it had the teeth of a cross-cut saw.

"Ah doan' want no cuts on 'at pan," King Dick warned him. "'Member what Ah tole you!" He looked around at the prisoners who filled the alleyway, gabbling and laughing. "Whah's 'at artis'?" he demanded.

"Right here, King," a voice said. I looked under the barber's elbow and saw a slender man crouched on the floor beside King Dick, a box held tenderly against his breast. The beard at length was gone. The barber passed a towel hurriedly over my face, and immediately the slender man opened his box and went at me with breathless care. I could see that the box contained a black powder, and that he was applying it with a rabbit's foot.

"We's raidy!" King Dick told the watchers. "Git away to bofe ends."

They hurried off, part of them to the front of the building and part to the rear. The slender man rubbed my neck and chest with the rabbit's foot.

"'At's enough!" King Dick said. "Cain't be too pinnicky, not 'is minute! You come on ovah to Number Foh."

He took me by the arm and hurried me to the back door. "Doan bovver wiv no one," he said. "Keep a-lookin' down, like you's a mad nigrah!" Fifteen or twenty prisoners sauntered out ahead of us. Others came out beside us, and still others in our rear. Surrounded by these stragglers we wandered to the covered way connecting the yards. There was a commotion among the sentries. The prison yards were filled with Americans, packed around the gates, moving aimlessly in excited clumps, hooting at the soldiers. We came safely to Prison Number Four and sedately mounted the stairs leading to King Dick's domain.

King Dick pushed me into his throne room, dropped heavily on his red plush throne, and eyed me thoughtfully.

"Namiah," he said to his seckatary, who stood waiting the royal orders, "go git a basket o' plum gudgeons an' foh mugs of beer, wivout no foam on 'em. 'Ey's goin' to be a war roun' heah, an' we better git ouahse'fs raidy."

XXX

Rᴵᶜᴷᴼᴿ, Whitten and Miller had not attempted the barrier. Hays had got over, and within half an hour was as well swallowed in the crowd as I was myself. Captain Shortland, raging, had promised heavy punishments to the guards if we got clear of Dartmoor: not only that, but he swore to have us back in the Cachot and see us rot there.

There have certainly been larger wars than this war of six thousand unarmed, imprisoned Americans against red-faced Thomas Shortland and his regiment of thick-witted Somersetshire militia, but I doubt that there have been stranger ones.

The prison houses buzzed like beehives after our escape, and acquaintances came hurrying to see me on the second floor of Number Four to tell me how the governing committees of the prisons had refused to deal with Shortland and had ignored demands that we be given up; how even the Rough Alleys, headed by men we knew only as Sodom and Gomorrah, were fighting him and the militiamen with all the obscenities to which they could lay tongue; and how the bulk of the prisoners, simple seamen from New England and New York and the Chesapeake, were determined to give him no satisfaction.

It was on the day after our escape that King Dick came to me, chuckling. "'At ole Shoatland," he said, "he's goin' bus' his bazoo effen he gits much moh lip offen 'ese white boys. Mm, mm! 'At ole Shoatland, he's pow'ful mad!"

He had, King Dick said, closed the market, thinking to bring the prisoners to terms.

"Mah lan'!" the big Negro exclaimed, "what 'ose white boys call him an' call 'ose Som'set m'litia—ooh! Meks yo' yahs bu'n when you heahs it."

I could hear a derisive howling from the yard outside and from the lower floor of the prison house: the howling of hundreds of men; but King Dick would not let me go to a window to see what it was.

"Rest yo'se'f right yah," he said. "'At old Shoatland, li'l' buhd tol' him 'at one of you's hidin' in 'is prison, 'an he's goin' drive ev'ybody out so's he kin suhch it!"

"Maybe I'd better get in the hole?" I said, for King Dick had a movable slab in his throne room, and underneath it a royal storehouse for his money bags and private rum supply; and this was my hiding place when searchers were near.

King Dick shook his head. "Ain't nobody goin' out, not till 'ey gits raidy," he said.

The howling grew louder; and as we watched the staircase at the rear of the long hall, a mass of shouting, laughing prisoners came pouring up onto our floor. Hard on their heels was a squad of Somersetshire militia, pursuing them with bayoneted muskets at the charge.

The prisoners came past us, leaping, whistling, turning handsprings, roaring with laughter; and behind the angry, red-faced militiamen pressed another howling, capering mob. Thus escorted, front and rear, the militiamen shambled the length of the alley and vanished down the stairs at the far end, only to reappear immediately up the stairs opposite those which they had descended. At the top they turned in seeming desperation on those who followed them; their march reversed itself, the pursued becoming the pursuers. The place, it seemed to me, was full of squads of frantic militiamen, all of them preceded and followed and hindered and jostled by contemptuous prisoners.

Eventually King Dick tucked me snugly under the slab; the militiamen were left in possession of the building and allowed to search, while the prisoners packed the yard outside and cursed them for bloody library-burning lobsters and worse.

Later that day, when the black paint on my face had been renewed, we watched from a window to see the rioting in the yard.

There were men employed to light the lamps in the yards and market place, and when these men came in among the prisoners, they were promptly seized. Thereupon a company of militiamen was sent to the yard of Number Four Prison to push the prisoners into the prison house at the points of bayonets; and I truly believe any old woman would have known more than to send a small body of troops among reckless men at such a time. Resentful of the bayonets, the prisoners sought to pry up paving stones to use as weapons. We could see the soldiers cocking their muskets; and at this the militia officers came out in front of their men and ordered them back to the market place, in spite of the shouts of Shortland, who stood on the covered walk overlooking the yard, bawling God knows what to prisoners and soldiers alike. Thus the prisoners were conscious of

defying Shortland successfully, and the Somersetshire militia could
see they had been flouted by unarmed men.

*   *   *

I was in a fever to be free of the prison. To find myself out of the
Cachot, rightfully a free man, since the war was over, and with every
right to go in search of Emily, yet to be held here and to be a fugitive
within the walls, was sheerly maddening. I was troubled, as well, by
the news Jesse Smith brought when he was released from the Cachot
and hurried to King Dick's domain in Number Four.

"By God!" he said, when he had looked hard at me and made sure
it was I beneath the black paint, "I damn near died that morning,
waiting to see if you'd get over!"

"Where's Tommy?" I asked him.

"Well," he said, "I was coming to that. I been kind of dreading
this. That's an awful nice boy, Cap'n Dick! Gosh! Seemed as if he
wouldn't talk about *nothing* but Cap'n Dick!"

"Say what you mean," I told him. "Are you trying to tell me
Tommy's sick? What's the—— He hasn't got the smallpox?"

"No, it ain't the smallpox. He—by gracious, I never *seen* a nicer
boy!"

I waited for him to go on. He cleared his throat and ran his fingers
through his hair, matted from his ten days in the Cachot. I could
smell the stench of the place, as if a gargantuan polecat had bedded
down with him; and the sweat came out on me at the thought that
violent, worthless Shortland could have sent a boy like Tommy
Bickford, worth a million Shortlands, into that terrible granite box.

"That night," Jesse went on, "after you'd broke out, he had a little
cough, and a chill that wouldn't let up. He shook and he shook, and
he couldn't get to sleep. First we thought he was excited on account
of you, because he kept talking about Cap'n Dick. Cap'n Dick this
and Cap'n Dick that, and some lady or other!" He coughed and
cleared his throat and looked at me apologetically. "No offense,"
he added.

"No," I said.

"We—well, we fixed him up with extra blankets, but when he went
out of his head and began thinking you were back with us, along
toward morning, we suspicioned what it was."

"Did you send for Magrath, Jesse?"

"We sent for him when Carley brought breakfast."

"Did Magrath say it was jail fever?"

"He didn't say anything," Jesse said uncomfortably. "Just picked him up in his arms and walked off with him."

"Well, Jesse," I said, "he's a good boy. There never was a better. I'd like you to get cleaned up and find out about him. I'd like you to go just as quick as you can. His father saved my father at the Battle of Valcour Island."

"Sho!" Jesse exclaimed. "Did he, now!"

"Yes," I said. "Go see Magrath. Tell him I'll come over any time it'll help Tommy. You tell Tommy he needn't worry: I'll wait for him."

We waited for tidings of Tommy in the midst of a turmoil such as I had never heard or seen before; for Shortland sent message after message into the prisons, demanding this and demanding that, so that the criers were forever crying this madman's proposals up and down the aisles, and the prisoners were perpetually howling their hatred and contempt for what he proposed; and the yards outside the prison were in a tumult all through the day because the sentries and wardens were being mocked by every prisoner in sight.

At the end of a week this violent and foolish man, finding the prisoners determined to defy him, opened the market once more. Thereupon the prisoners, realizing they had beaten Shortland, celebrated their victory.

Instead of stopping their gambling at a reasonable hour, they kept it up all night; and there was riotous drunkenness and uproar on all sides, in spite of the efforts of the cooler-headed to keep order.

It was early on a March evening that King Dick came hurriedly to his throne room to stand between the stanchions, his melon-shaped head tilted over on his huge shoulder as if listening to the shrill clamor that rose from the bottom floor of the prison.

"Here!" I said. "What's the matter? Tommy isn't worse, is he?"

King Dick took off his bearskin cap and ran his huge, banana-like fingers across his forehead.

"Mah lan'!" he said. "Mah lan'! 'At's too close for mah pleasure! 'At ole ship *Favorite,* she better git in here wiff 'ose raffication papers, showin' we's free men, else 'ey git 'eirseffs jibbited up wiff bayonets!"

"What happened?"

"'Ose sentries was fixin' to lock 'em dohs when Ah come back fum 'at ole hospital," he said, "an' one of 'ose Som'set m'litia, he up an' jibbits his bayonet into one of 'ose white folks—jibbits him in his laigs an' in his back an' in his rump, so's he's all bloodied up! Mm, mm!

Mah lan', 'at ain't no way to ack! Ah doan' lak 'ose ole bayonets, no SUH!"

"What was he jabbed for?"

"Not for nuffin'," he said. "He hadn't done nuffin' nor said nuffin'."

"I don't believe it," I told him. "An armed man wouldn't bayonet a prisoner without reason."

"Ah heahs you," King Dick said calmly. " 'Ese Som'set m'litia boys, 'ey bayonet 'em wiffout no reason, 'cause Ah seen it! Mm, mm! 'Ose white folks is mad! Me too! Ah's mad; on'y Ah wants sompin to fight wiff, effen 'ere's goin' to be jibbitin' wiff bayonets. Effen Ah ain't got nuffin' to fight wiff, Ah moves out. Lissen 'ose white boys! Mah lan'! Lissen now: wha's goin' on now? Lissen to——" He broke off, for in the yard outside was suddenly set up a wild yelling. We could see prisoners at the far end of our floor pushing against the windows to look down at the tumult.

"Lissen! Lissen to——" King Dick began again, but he never finished, for the prisoners at the windows broke away and ran for the staircases, shouting, *Favorite! Favorite!* At the same time the staircases leading down from the cock loft were filled with men, all racing for the open air.

I saw Jesse Smith free himself from the scrambling throng and swing his arms at me. *"Favorite!"* he bawled. "She's in! When you going back to Arundel?"

* * *

In that very moment the hopes of six thousand men, legally entitled to freedom, rose to a happy height. Jesse Smith was laughing deliriously. He actually began to dance, and hugged me like a bear, trying to make me dance with him. "Old Stonington, Connecticut!" he shouted, when I had pushed him off. And for half an hour thereafter he seemed unable to do more than splutter with delight and shout the three words over and over: "Old Stonington! Old Stonington, Connecticut!"

To have told any of these six thousand men then that he would be in Dartmoor more than seven days longer would have brought on an immediate fight, I think. Not one of the six thousand could have dreamed that Reuben Beasley, the American agent in England, would not have ships to carry them home in a week's time.

That night I washed the black from my face, and the next day went boldly and openly to the hospital to see Tommy Bickford. His curly brown hair had been cut close to his head; and he looked shriveled into himself from the burning of the fever, so that he seemed like a skeleton beneath the bedclothes.

"Well," I said, "how you feel, Tommy?"

"Good," he said, and moved his lips a little, as if he tried to say my name, but hadn't the strength.

"Well, Tommy," I said, "you're a good boy. I wouldn't have let you go into that Cachot, Tommy. Don't you ever do anything like that again."

"No, sir," he said.

"You hurry up and get fat and strong," I told him, "so we can start together when the time comes."

He nodded, fixing his eyes on my face as if to see whether I had any plans I was keeping from him. "That lady come back?" he asked.

"No," I said. "I've had no means to hear from her or from Jeddy Tucker."

I took her picture from my pocket, unwrapped it, and held it up for him to see, thinking it might do him good to look at a face not covered with stubble, or grooved from starvation, or gray from being penned inside dripping stone walls. His eyes fastened to it and clung; so I propped it against a fold in his blanket.

"Tommy," I said, "I want you to put some flesh on your bones. We're liable to be out of here almost any hour, but now I won't go till you go with me."

I felt a hand on my shoulder and looked up to see tall, thin, one-eyed Dr. Magrath.

"Well, well!" he said. "This is an unexpected pleasure!" He stooped over and picked up Tommy's wrist, seeming not to notice the miniature of Lady Ransome.

"Time for a little sleep, Tommy," he said. He lifted an eyebrow in my direction, so I got up to go.

"Eat your soup and get fat," I told Tommy again.

I took back the miniature and went out with Magrath. There was a strange, unpleasant, unclean smell in the stone-walled corridor.

"Can't you get him out of here, Doctor?" I asked.

Magrath drew his fingers down the blind side of his face, as if to free himself of a cobweb.

"Look here, Captain," he said, "do you think it's quite safe for you to be out in the open like this?"

"But we're at peace!"

"Yes," he said, "but you're still in prison, and some people can't distinguish between a man who happens to be in a prison and a criminal. I'm having hard work to get your friends released from the Cachot."

That was the truth of it: the war was over, yet from morning to night the Somerset militiamen glowered at us over the walls; their bayonets winked at us in the watery sun that occasionally peeped through the rain clouds and fog banks of late March. The war was over, yet the bells still hung on the wires; and each night, at sundown, sentries manned the fire steps while turnkeys herded us into our prison houses and locked the doors on us. We were at peace with the English, yet the criers cried through the prisons a notice from red-faced, hook-nosed Thomas Shortland that any man caught attempting to escape from the depot would be punished by being locked in the Cachot for ten days.

Thus the deferred hope of these six thousand penniless and half-starved men threw them into a desperate rage that grew deeper and more bitter from day to day; and after a week had gone by with no prospect of relief or release for any man there began to be talk of how we could overpower the guards, break the gates, and march in a body to Tor Bay or Teignmouth. This talk, we learned, was carried somehow into the market place and spread among the farmers and merchants of Princetown and Tavistock and Moreton-Hampstead. Men from those towns moved their families into Plymouth for fear the country would be overrun by six thousand angry Americans. The guards on the walls were doubled.

I think I alone had cause for gratitude; for Tommy Bickford was gaining weight; his talk was beginning to sound as though there might be a trace of blood and muscle in him after all, and I made trip after trip to the hospital without being discovered by Shortland.

"Be careful, Cap'n Dick," Tommy warned me after one of my visits. "I'd feel safer about you if you'd kept on your paint, I think. Maybe you'd better turn blackamoor again."

I laughed at him then; but half an hour later I had a shock and thought for a moment that perhaps he had been right.

"You go on up to Cap'n Shoatland's office," King Dick said, meeting me at the top of the second-floor stairway in Number Four. "You go on right up there. King Dick and Shoatland, 'ey bofe say so."

"What!" I gasped. "What!"

But the big black man laughed and reassured me—though he mystified me too. Visitors for me waited in the office; the commandant himself had agreed to let me go and come, and he had added the words "in spite of past offenses."

"Who is it?" I asked.

"Ah doan know," King Dick said and giggled. "Whyn't you go fine out yo'se'f? Sooner you hurry, sooner you'll know. Ain't Ah tole you——"

So far as I know he may have finished his question. If he did, it reached only the empty air where I had stood when he began it, for I took his advice and hurried.

From the door of Shortland's office I stood and looked back, down the hill and across the market place to the seven prison buildings crouching at the bottom of the slope, like seven cats watching me patiently, as if secure in the knowledge that still I could not escape them. Then I knocked on the door and went in.

Shortland, red-faced and hook-nosed, was crouched behind his desk. Opposite him sat a slender gentleman in blue broadcloth, accompanied by a fashionably-dressed lady, plump and pretty and fair-haired. The man jumped up when I came in, and looked hard at me; and I remembered his eyes. Like those of Emily Ransome, they were the color of smoke in the swamps of Maryland.

"Why—" he said—"why—the man I wanted—why, what's happened to you? I mean, you may not remember me: Sanderson, my name is."

"Yes," I said, "I remember Mrs. Sanderson and you very well—very pleasantly." I licked my lips to take the dryness from them and steadied myself. "Your sister," I said, "your sister——"

"Yes," he said. "Where is she?"

"Where is she?" I asked. "Where is she? Don't you know where she is?"

"No," he said. There was a look in his smoke-colored eyes that wrung my heart with the memory of how Emily had put her hand to her throat when Sir Arthur had offered to buy my dog Pinky.

"Wait," I said, "wait a minute. You've heard from her, or you'd never have come to me."

"She wrote and told us," Mrs. Sanderson said. "We came home as soon as we had the letter."

"Yes," Sanderson added, "but in the letter she said you would know everything."

I turned from them and looked at Shortland. He stared back at me with hard, round eyes; and his thoughts were easily read. He would have taken infinite pleasure in having me triced up and catted.

"Letters and messages have come for me in the past seven months," I said. "Where are they?"

He answered as quickly as if I had asked him the number of guns on Nelson's *Victory*. "There's nothing for you. No letters or messages." His hawk-like glare was fixed on my face; his barrel of a chest stuck out like a pigeon's.

"No letters or messages in these seven months? Did you say there have been no letters for me, Captain?"

"That's right!" he said, "that's right! You understand me now."

He turned to Mrs. Sanderson. "These Americans give us a deal of trouble," he said, seeming to speak merrily and confidentially. "It appears we can't do anything to suit 'em."

I looked at the knuckles of my right hand and wondered at the whiteness of them; at the way these long months of darkness and dampness and bad food had made knuckles and joints stand out like knobs. What Shortland told me was impossible; but there was no way of knowing whether the letters had been appropriated by prison officials, or whether they had been sent to Sir Arthur Ransome, or what had happened to them. I knew the man was lying: I could see it in the defiance of his eye and catch it in his overready answers. Yet there was nothing to be gained by bandying words, and I told myself I must go easy, take it gently.

"Seven months!" Sanderson said. "Where have you been for seven months that you couldn't ask about letters?"

"Buried alive," I said, "but that's over now. Your sister: she wrote you a letter. Where did she write it from?"

"There was no way of telling. It was handed to the captain of a 74 in a Portsmouth gambling club."

"In a gambling club!" I said. "Who—not by——"

"No," he interrupted, "by a gentleman: a gentleman who had won money from the captain. When the captain was stripped clean, the gentleman gave back his money and the letter with it, asking that it be delivered; and in the course of time I received it."

"Well," I said, "she must have been afraid Sir Arthur might find her, I think." I looked at Shortland, sitting puffed up and angry behind his desk, eyeing me closely as though wishful of snatching the thoughts from my brain; and I made up my mind I had said almost enough.

"I think so," Sanderson said. "Aye, I think so."

Mrs. Sanderson snuffled suddenly, then dabbed at her eyes with a wisp of a handkerchief and smiled up at me mistily.

Sanderson coughed. "It took us aback at first, the things she wrote about you. Excited—a little wild—but under the circumstances—ah —I dare say quite genuine—ah—her happiness and all that! Ah—we're here because we'd like to be friendly."

Mrs. Sanderson nodded in agreement. "We'd like you to know it's understood," she said gently. "We're taking her side, of course. Yours too, Captain."

"We've come to you first," Sanderson said, "because we couldn't find her in the three days since we landed. Unhappily she hasn't any relatives but me, and no family friends to turn to. It might be you could help us find her, and, at any rate, we've come to take you out of prison. We'd like to do that for your own sake, Captain. We found out we can free you; and we'll sign the papers now if you're ready to go with us."

I looked from him to Shortland, doubting I had heard correctly.

"Yes," Sanderson said, "it's a new ruling of the War Office. Any American prisoner must be released at the request of a British subject, or of the captain of an American merchant ship; and at his release he receives a passport from Captain Shortland."

"Nothing has been said to the prisoners about this," I said to Shortland.

"I dare say," he returned coolly. "It's quite possible there's been an oversight on the part of one of the clerks."

I looked at him for a time, wondering whether his cruelty to help-less people was due to a poison in his veins.

"Well," I said after a little, "I dare say it's an oversight you can easily correct. I hope there's been no such oversight about my letters."

He started up behind his desk, his face fixed in the same queer, hook-nosed grin that Punch affects when about to thump his friends to death with his great club. "You—you damned—you presume——" He stopped, suddenly conscious of the intensity of our scrutiny, and sat behind his desk again, breathing heavily. "These Americans!" he said to Mrs. Sanderson, with that same pretense of confidential amusement. "There isn't one who doesn't feel competent to govern this prison."

Sanderson turned to me. "We'll take you out now?"

"I'm sorry," I said. "I can't tell you how happy I'd be to leave this place."

"You mean there's some reason you can't leave?"

"Because of a boy from my town," I told him. "He's a good boy—the best boy I ever knew. He almost sacrificed his life to help me, once; and many years ago his father saved my father at the Battle of Valcour Island. I promised him I'd not go away without him."

"Bring him with you," Mrs. Sanderson said eagerly. "We'll be

happy to have him. There are two of us, and we're allowed one prisoner apiece."

"He's in the hospital," I explained. "He's had typhus. The doctor
says he's to rest quiet for two weeks more."

"Two weeks?" Sanderson said. "That's the eighth of April. Then
we'll come back for you and your friend on the eighth of April."

"Thank you," I said. "His name's Tommy Bickford. When you see
him, I think you'll be glad you're taking him away from such a place
as this."

"We will indeed," Sanderson assured me. "We will indeed! I wish
we could take all of you!"

Shortland laughed. "You don't know 'em as I do! If you did I doubt
if you'd let 'em within pistol shot of you or your wife."

The Sandersons ignored him. "The eighth of April, Captain
Nason," Mrs. Sanderson said as she gave me her hand. "God send
we have good news for you, too, on the day we take you and your
friend out of Dartmoor."

XXXI

THE effigy of Reuben Beasley had been hanged, torn down, and kicked into the gutter by the furious men who were still prisoners because of his laziness and inability. No longer did these men in patience toil over their ship models of bone, or weave hats and boxes of straw; they drank and howled and sang desperately.

The night of the fifth of April was the worst of all, because of a sudden whim of the officials to offer us for rations the stale hard biscuits saved through the winter to guard against famine. The Rough Alleys set up an eery yelling at sundown, broke open the gates into the market, and charged up the market slope, howling for bread. There they stayed for hours, in the dim light of the market lamps, their clamor dying to confused rumbles and rising to angry roars.

By morning we heard that all the towns on the moor were in a panic over the ferocity of the Americans. It was a morning strange and memorable for its warmth and sunniness—two things I had seen so seldom on Dartmoor as to count them miracles. So began the blackest day that I have ever known.

*   *   *

I did not think it a black day as I walked slowly along the front of the market place in the early afternoon with Tommy Bickford. "One more day," we both said, time and again. "One more day, and then it's the eighth!"

Tommy was neat as a pin in a natty blue seckatary's suit presented to him by King Dick. Dr. Magrath had given him his discharge from hospital care two days before, telling me to keep him in the sun and walk him a little at discreet intervals, and with that had coughed, stroked his cheek, bidden us good-bye, and stalked away, as good a gentleman as I ever saw.

"One more day and then it's the eighth," I said, for the hundredth time, I think, as we walked along the front of the market.

Tommy touched me on the arm with a thin hand to which the life was returning. "One more day, and then it's the eighth, Cap'n Dick!"

After a time we strolled into the yard that held Prisons Five, Six, and Seven. Here we lounged, following the sun around the buildings, and we sat on the warm ground while Tommy half dozed, roused himself to murmur, "One more day," and half dozed again.

When the chill of sundown settled on us I roused him for a final walk before we should go in, and as we stood up, he murmured, "One more day," and his face wore his old-time look of seeming pleased with everything and everybody.

The yard in which we walked—that of Prisons Seven, Six, and Five —was shaped like a segment of pie. The curved crust of the pie was formed by the two outer walls and the inner barricade of iron pickets; one edge was the wall that divided us from our own prison house, Number Four; and the other edge was the wall, part masonry and part iron fence, that separated us from the barracks and the market place. We walked, therefore, along the curved iron pickets from the barracks walls to the Number Four wall, then back again, taking it slowly and having a care not to be bumped by ball players and skylarkers.

The sky was taking on the pale green color that I have seen only on Dartmoor on the few clear evenings I knew in that dismaying country: a green color that throws a strange illumination on the swarthy hills. The militiamen detailed to light the lamps in the yards were making ready, I saw, to come through the gates.

There were four sailors tossing a ball near the barracks wall as we came down to it. While we watched them, the ball struck one man's finger tips and flew over the wall into the barracks yard. The men stood there shouting for their ball like four dogs barking at a squirrel up a tree; but no ball came back to them, and one of the men pried at the stones of the wall with a sharp stick. As we looked, two of the stones fell out. The man stooped down and picked at the opening; then peered into the hole and again bellowed for the ball.

From the direction of the market place I heard a shouting no different from what we had heard a score of times every day. Then, from the sentry walk at our left, a Somerset militiaman bawled words I couldn't distinguish; words that he repeated and repeated, and that other sentries along the wall picked up and repeated as well.

It sounded like, "Ear coamin drool Ear coamin drool" and it dawned on me suddenly they were shouting "They're coming through!" The voices sounded panicky. I began to fear the sentries were imagining we had begun at last the attempt they had so often heard we planned.

"A little more," I said to Tommy, "and those fools'll think it's come

—think we're all going to make a breach in the wall and escape in a body."

I had no more than spoken when a sentry's alarm bell clanged; then another and another. In the distance, among the buildings at the prison entrance, the big alarm bell set up a clamor, spilling brazen notes in nervous, irregular, rapid bursts, as if it, too, were stricken with senseless panic.

The Americans near us were doing nothing—not even those ball-players who had picked at the wall: they stood where they were, staring about them in the gathering greenish dusk as if to discover the reason for all this bell ringing.

I took Tommy by the arm, and we moved along the covered walk toward the yard of Number Four. The big alarm bell clanged as if a dozen men were hauling at the rope; and all the other bells in the world seemed to be jangling from the walls. The shouting I had heard from the direction of the market place was echoed in other sections of the yards; the air was filled with the sound of bells and the ragged, excited outcrying of human voices. I could see prisoners running behind us from Number Seven and Six and Five: running toward the covered walk, I knew, to see why the alarm was ringing.

"How do you feel, Tommy?" I asked.

"Good, Cap'n Dick," he said. "What they doing, do you suppose?"

I swung him along, not daring to urge him too much, but eager to get into our own yard and into Number Four, where we would be away from all this running and yelling and bell ringing.

We came to the end of the masonry wall at last and could look through the iron pickets into the market place. What I saw I didn't like. Militiamen were tumbling through the gate at the upper end; and close to us, not ten paces from the iron fence, a file had already formed: a close-packed, red-coated line of men whose faces seemed to me to have caught some of the sickly greenish light that filled the western sky.

What was worse, the gates broken two days before were broken again; and there were prisoners in the market place: a hundred, maybe; maybe a hundred and fifty. Hundreds more were crowding up to the shattered gates, so that those who were already in the market were pinned where they were—in the front by the Somerset-shire militia, and in the rear by a constantly increasing crowd of hooting, yelling prisoners.

Worst of all, I could see the stocky, broad-shouldered figure of Thomas Shortland standing at the end of the file of militiamen: standing there, sword in hand, signaling to other militiamen who were spilling through the upper gate and running down across the market square.

Knowing what I knew about Thomas Shortland, I stooped and took Tommy Bickford in my arms, swung him up against my chest, and ran for the yard of Number Four. When we reached it, it seemed full of prisoners clattering up the slope toward the market gates, all strangely pallid in the greenish twilight, and shouting to know what was happening.

Behind me I heard Dr. Magrath's voice, deep and soothing, urging the prisoners back into their yards.

"Now, gentlemen!" I heard him say. "Now, gentlemen! None of us wants trouble! Just drop back in the yards, gentlemen, so there'll be no chance for misunderstanding!"

With Magrath among the men, I thought, there would be no violence if it could be averted; so I set Tommy on his feet and looked back at the market place. I could see Magrath's head above the prisoners and above the militia. I could see, too, what Magrath could not see: that the prisoners in the market were being pressed harder and harder by those striving to be a part of a confusion that must have been as unfathomable to them as it was to me.

"Keno!" someone shouted. The cry was taken up by others. "Keno! Keno!" It was the battle-cry of the Rough Alleys.

"Now, Tommy," I said, "there's Rough Alleys mixing in it. We'll keep on going."

He smiled, though I knew he had no wish to go, and he limped down the slope beside me, dragging his leg. The men, still running toward us, dodged around us and kept on running.

"Come on and fight, you lousy lobster-backs!" someone shouted.

"Lobster-backs! Lobster-backs!" they howled. A roar went up behind us.

I heard Shortland's voice—a voice I could never mistake, because of the rasping, hurried, overwrought tone that came into it when he was excited and angry, and unbalanced because of his anger. "Get back!" he shouted. "Get back there! Push 'em back! Charge! Charge!"

A shrill cry went up, a pallid, discordant cry that blended, somehow, with the green light in which it seemed to me we moved, all of us, like shadows on a Stygian shore. I knew, on the instant, we had come to the end of all the misunderstanding and mistreatment heaped on us; knew the hatred which had smoldered for so long had burst at last into hot flames.

Knowing Tommy could move no faster, I picked him up again,

casting a look over my shoulder as I did so. The close-packed prisoners were struggling to escape from the market place into the
security of the prison yards. From the outcries that pierced the com-
parative silence which followed the first discordant howl it was clear
enough that the Somersetshire militiamen were paying with bayonet
thrusts for the insults they had received.

"Please not to bother about me, Cap'n Dick," Tommy said. "I can
make out all right." He was a good boy, always. I made what speed
I could toward the lowering face of Number Four.

I heard, then, what I had been waiting for—Shortland's bullying,
raging voice. "Damned Yankee rascals!" he shouted. "Fire!"

Then, for a moment, there was no sound except that of scrambling
and scuttling and running. There was a curious fearfulness to the
sound, as to the frightened rush of mice in the walls of a house.

"Fire!" Shortland shouted again, more loudly. "Fire, God damn it!
Fire!"

Then came a single musket shot, and after it a shrill tumult of yelling. The next instant the green twilight was ripped and slashed by
a musketry volley: a ragged volley that echoed and roared among
those gray stone walls and tall prison houses as though it had come
from carronades.

The shrillness of hundreds of voices suddenly became piercing. Everywhere there were men running as fast as they could; and I ran
too, but heavily and slowly, because of the weight of Tommy
Bickford.

There was another volley of musketry fire, and another and another; then, horribly, firing came from the encircling walls. Spurts
of flame stabbed the dusk all along the great ring about us. We
seemed to be the center of a whirling confusion, a crashing, screaming dizziness, almost as though this great granite millstone of ours,
in a final convulsion of cruelty, had come alive to whirl us down the
barren slopes of Dartmoor to destruction.

A black man, running close beside me, tripped, staggered, and
regained his feet. When he started forward once more his leg bent
at the thigh like a piece of rope, and he fell on his face, struggling
to drag himself forward with hands like black claws.

The reports of the muskets seemed in our very ears, as though the
soldiers had come out of the market place into the yards to pursue
us fleeing, unarmed people.

"What they shooting for, Cap'n Dick?" Tommy asked me. "Isn't
the war over?"

We had come close up to the front of Number Four. All around us were running prisoners, converging on the entrances. Dimly I could see that those around the doors were jammed, tossing their arms and shouting. Figures burst from among them as if popped out by the press. "Locked!" I heard them screaming. "The door's locked!"

I saw Jesse Smith come out of the jam. He stopped and motioned; then ran forward and got his hands on me, pulling me to the ground. A musket exploded almost in my ear. Men ran past and over us, yelling. They had muskets, and one of them laughed wildly, stabbing at Jesse's prostrate form with his bayonet.

They were Somersetshire militia, all of them. Beyond us they halted and fired into the mass of men who still struggled before the locked doors. Two of the prisoners pitched downward and lay still. The others broke and ran, leaving some who limped and crawled away. Jesse was digging at the cobblestones with his fingers: but the stones were immovable, cemented in place by the black Dartmoor muck.

Against the end of the prison sat a man holding his shoulder, his hand a smear of blood. One of the militiamen stopped before him, loading his musket, whereupon the man, John Washington, a prize master from the Baltimore privateer *Rolla* and a peaceable good fellow, held out his bloody hand to him as if to show he was hurt. At this the militiaman dropped the ramrod back in its socket, cocked his piece, held the muzzle against Washington's face and fired.

"Oh, God!" Jesse said. "Oh, my God!" We tore and tore at the cobbles with our fingers, but could do nothing with them.

One of King Dick's seckataries, a fine-looking boy named Jackson, fourteen years old or thereabouts, who had been impressed aboard the British cruiser *Pontes* but had given himself up rather than serve against his own country, ran out from the shelter of the doorway of Number Four and raced around the corner of the building, evidently making for the rear door. He was an easy mark in his neat white trousers and short blue jacket. Four muskets spat at him as he rounded the corner. He rolled over and over, like a shot rabbit: then sprawled on his face.

More soldiers were coming from the market place. Behind us I heard Shortland's voice, yelling words I couldn't distinguish. "Quick, Jesse!" I said. "Get Jackson before they load again." Jesse ran for the small sprawling form at the corner of the building; while I got my arms under Tommy, swung him up against my breast and followed. I set off down the cruel long length of Number Four, expecting each moment to hear the crash of muskets at my back.

Jesse Smith was ahead of me. Beyond him, now that we were unprotected by the towering front of Number Four, were the points and slashes of light made by the muskets of the sentries on the walls as they sniped at the defenseless men beneath.

We turned the lower corner at last, so close to the walls that I could feel, I thought, the heat of the musketry fire blazing in our faces. Yet we were fortunate and escaped the bullets, which we heard flirting past us and smacking against the rear of the prison.

The door stood open, by the grace of God. I followed Jesse Smith up the steps and into the prison, my legs like lead and my lungs aflame.

I set Tommy on his feet and looked about me. There were no lights in the prison, but in the darkness I could make out that the floor was covered with men, lying full length with their faces turned toward the entrance.

There was a clatter of feet outside. Two more prisoners raced up the steps and threw themselves, panting, on the floor.

"Look out!" one of them said. "They're a-comin'!"

The door moved to close, but before it did a group of militiamen stood enframed against the outer green light. With no word of warning they threw their muskets to their shoulders and fired among us. The door slammed shut, leaving the militiamen outside upon the steps.

I heard Tommy cough, a distressed, bubbly cough; and I felt his hands slide down me as he slipped to his knees. "They shot me, Cap'n Dick," he said in a faint, surprised voice.

"Hold on, Tommy," I said. "Nothing'll hurt you with me here."

There was the sound of a long breath from him—a difficult breath, as if a pillow was pressed to his face.

"Tommy!" I said, so frightened that I felt close to suffocation from the pounding of my heart. "Where did it hit you, Tommy?"

There was no answer from him. "Tommy!" I said, louder; then I shouted his name and got my hands on him. I found the hole. It was under his left shoulder. My hands came away sticky. He was dead.

When the candles were lighted there was a Somersetshire militiaman pressed into the corner of that crowded room. He had come in the yard at dusk to light the lamps and had been carried into the prison with the first rush. We sat with our dead and wounded and watched him for two hours before Magrath came to take the hurt to the hospital. With them the doctor sent the militiaman, for though no man had touched him, he was mouthing and tittering like an idiot.

XXXII

Thus I lost my dearest friend and came alive myself out of the massacre in Dartmoor Prison. America bears the pain of April the 6th, 1815, and England bears the shame of that day. To my mind what Britain did less than three months later at Waterloo loses its glory because of the red smear she put upon her flags so short a time before at Dartmoor.

There were Englishmen who knew and bitterly rued the crime of Shortland. The kindly Sanderson was one of these. When he came to take me away on the day after the "one day more" that Tommy and I had talked of so happily, Emily's brother shook my hand but said not a word to me until we were beyond the walls. Then he cursed Shortland and Dartmoor and the government, and his wife cried.

"My dead friend and those others," I said, "are part of history now. May justice be done to their memory there, though justice be unknown in the land where they suffered. The Peace has reached them at last."

Mrs. Sanderson cried harder at this, and to regain my own composure I had to comfort her.

"You brought me news?" I asked a little later, as the carriage took us easily toward Plymouth, down those long, desolate hills up which had toiled thousands of leaden-hearted Americans. "You've learned what has become of Emily? You can put me on my way to her?"

Sanderson set his lips together in a tight line and stared off across the fortress-like hedgerows that guard the roads of Devon.

"Let's have the worst of it," I told him when I saw the look on his face. "I'd like to get it over with. Is she—is she——"

"I think the worst of it, Captain Nason," Mrs. Sanderson told me, "is that we can get no trace of where she went after she left Portsmouth. She vanished into thin air."

"We could have told you more, two weeks ago," Sanderson said. "When we first came to take you out of prison we didn't tell you because it seemed you were bearing all a man could, and we decided not to add to the burden upon you—not to tell you all we knew until you were out and free to move. Captain Nason, there was a good reason for my sister to vanish."

I drew a deep breath. "By vanish you mean hide—you're telling me she had to hide from someone who followed her?"

"From more than one who followed her," Sanderson said bitterly. "No, it's not what you're thinking, Captain. We'd been to Exeter before we saw you, and the place was all too busy mouthing the pitiful story."

"Sir Arthur Ransome——" I began.

"Sir Arthur Brute!" Mrs. Sanderson interrupted. "Sir Arthur Beast!"

"I suppose he thought he was within his rights," Sanderson said. "I suppose he fooled himself into thinking his revenge was 'justice.' The man is of a petty but viciously vindictive nature. We heard he spoke of 'avenging outraged honor' and of being an Aristides for law and justice. Ah, well, his vanity was on the raw!"

"What did he do?" I asked huskily.

"You see," Sanderson explained, "you see——" He coughed and tried again. "There's nobody who'd believe any of it—we knew it was only vindictiveness. Ah—he charged Emily, you know—an ugly fellow at bottom, I really think—he brought charges the authorities had to take cognizance of, whether or no. I assure you, Captain Nason— ah, that is, we don't want you to think——"

"Why, sir," I said, "I think you and Mrs. Sanderson are the kindest of people."

"Well," Sanderson went on, "he charged her with—he charged her with—he charged he found her with you."

"I hated him, always," Mrs. Sanderson assured me.

"Even more desperate in the eyes of the law than his charge on the personal account," Sanderson continued, "he laid an information against her for aiding and abetting the escape of an enemy prisoner; and there, of course, he had her; for she was trying to help you, and was caught in the act, as you remember he had witnesses to prove. If she'd been taken on that information there'd have been no possible defense, nor any way for her to save herself from a term of imprisonment."

"Well," I said, after a few moments, "God knows I was sure there was good reason why I'd heard nothing from her."

"Yes," Sanderson agreed, "it was as good a reason for lying hid as you could find; though I think that if we could get word to her that we're in England she might come out of hiding."

I wrestled with the matter for a time. "Portsmouth," I said at length. "You spoke of Portsmouth?"

"Yes, she had a small white dog when she left Ransome Hall; and it was through the dog that the police traced her to Portsmouth."

"Of course!" I said, brooding over it. "Of course; and it was from a gambling club in Portsmouth that the message came to you!"

"Yes," Sanderson said, frowning in puzzlement. "There's a strange thing, now, isn't it!" He looked thoughtfully at the neat thatched cottages that lie along the green hill slopes behind Plymouth, into which our carriage was clattering. "When the police went to her lodgings to arrest her, she was gone, and her dog too. The police learned then that her lodgings had been taken and paid for by a gentleman known as her brother; and all of them—the man, his servant, Emily and her dog—departed together as suddenly as they had come. The police investigated further and found that the man calling himself her brother had opened a small gaming club. On the evening before he disappeared from Portsmouth with Emily he fought an English naval officer and hurt him badly."

"So," I said, "they fled together from Portsmouth?"

"Yes—they did," Sanderson replied uneasily. He frowned more deeply. Discomforting embarrassment seemed added to his distress, and he evaded my eye. Then he looked up at me plaintively, and his expression became one of amazement; for by the grace of heaven I had suddenly found the courage to laugh.

"Over what had the gambler and the British naval officer fought?" I asked.

Sanderson stared at me. "Why, I ascertained that the officer had referred slightingly to the Scotch renegade, John Paul, who fought in your navy under the name of Jones. The officer spoke of him as a traitor and pirate; and with no word of warning this small impostor, whoever he was, slapped the officer's face, then seized him by the ears and pounded his head on a Wheel-of-Fortune table with such force as to ruin it."

"Are you sure of that?" I asked, puzzled. "Are you sure the officer didn't speak flatteringly of Jones?"

"We read the information laid against the man," Mrs. Sanderson said. "It was sworn that the officer referred to Jones most disparagingly. I recall he used the words 'renegade Scotch toad' and 'murdering Judas' just before the man claiming to be Emily's brother attacked him so violently."

Her husband continued to stare at me; so I said to him, putting my hand on his knee: "Give me a little while to think, and I'll tell you why I laughed, my dear good friend."

So they were quiet, and I *did* think. By the time we had arrived at the Duke of Cornwall hostelry, on the high land looking out over Mill Bay to the main harbor of Plymouth, I was satisfied I knew a part of what had happened.

"It *is* good news you brought me, after all," I told them, when the porter had left us alone in the Sandersons' big room, from the windows of which we could look across to Drake's Island and Mount Batten. "All the while that I spoke with Emily in the front room of Mark Tate's cottage there was a good comrade of mine lying in the room behind us: Jeddy Tucker, a man she knew; and he wisely stayed hidden while I was taken away to Exeter jail. I was sure that if he could find means to be of service to her, he would. He's a shrewd fellow and a true good heart. Now I know what he did. He was quick at cards and all kinds of gambling; and it had to be by gambling that he put money into their pockets—his and Emily's and Mark Tate's, who must have acted as his servant. Well, now what hinders us from following them?"

I went to the window and looked out at the blue salt water. It had been more than a year since I had felt it under me, or seen it even; and the year had seemed longer than all the other years of my life. There were war craft at anchor in this safe, cup-shaped haven, and merchantmen moving in and out. I longed to be among them with the quarter-deck of a stout vessel beneath my feet and a fair wind filling my topgallant sails.

"Following them!" Mrs. Sanderson echoed. "How can we follow them when none of us knows where they are?"

Before I could answer, my eye caught sight of a brigantine riding at anchor off Eastern King Point—riding as gracefully, among the squat, heavy merchantmen and war craft, as a slim sheldrake among a host of clumsy gulls. She was drying her sails, from which I knew she was newly arrived in port. There was such a rake to her tapering sticks that she had something of the look, even at rest, of a slender girl straining eagerly forward, running, her head tilted back and her stomach thrust out ahead of her upper body; and I stared at her, forgetful of my friends for the moment.

Mrs. Sanderson touched my arm. "Did you mean what you said?" she asked. "You know the man who took her away—you think you know where he'd go?"

I turned from my study of the brig. "I think so," I said. "Before I was taken prisoner I sent a prize into Nantes: a fine West India-

man, the *Pembroke*. She was in charge of Cephas Cluff, my first
officer; and my orders to Cephas were to lie in Nantes until I should
come there myself to get the ship and our prize money from my
agents. If Jeddy took Emily from Portsmouth to escape the police,
there's only one guess as to what he would have done. He'd never
have let her come near Dartmoor, for fear she'd be taken; nor would
there have been any safe place in England, after that, for either of
them. But it was easy enough to go to France; for then Bonaparte
was still in Elba, and France and England were at peace; and to
France they'd have gone: to France and to Nantes and to the *Pembroke*, where they'd be among friends."

Sanderson laughed abruptly and huskily.

"If they're anywhere," I said, "they're in Nantes. They're in Nantes,
and it's to Nantes that we'll go!"

With that I laughed too, clapped Sanderson on the shoulder, took
him by the arm and pulled him from his chair. "How soon can you
be ready?" I cried. "How soon?"

"My dear captain!" he protested, "how can we do any such thing?
No English vessels can be found to carry us into a French port, now
that we're at war again! What's more, even if you yourself have
means to sail for a French port and arrive there, my wife and I are
English and couldn't accompany you while our country's at war with
France. But I see no means for you to go yourself, Captain Nason.
I fear we must wait until Boney is cornered once more and put where
he'll no longer torture all the world."

What he said was true; the wind dropped out of my sails, and I
stood staring dismally from the window. "Another war!" I groaned.
"We must wait for the end of another war!" Then for a time we
three were quiet, cogitating gloomily.

A murmurous sound intruded on our silence. At first I thought it
came from out of doors; but presently I recognized it as the voice
of a man talking in the next room. I listened idly: it became more
audible—a gentle, winning voice that seemed to have in it a note of
deference and yet a tone of assurance.

"Why," I said, "why who——" and with that I went near the closed
door that shut off our room from the next. The voice became distinct
to my ear. "Oh, do you think so?" it said, "do you really think so!
That is very kind and thoughtful of you, sir: very gracious and very
handsomely said!"

I turned to look again at the brig lying off Eastern King Point. A
faint breeze caught her shivered sails, bellying them a little and
dimly revealing, on her mainsail, the patches where the passage of

a bushel of grapeshot had been repaired. At her mainpeak a flag stirred idly. I saw it to be the Stars and Stripes. "The *Chasseur!*" I cried. "The *Chasseur!*"

And with no more explanation than that to my two friends, I hurried from the room, ran to the door of the adjoining chamber, and went in. At the far end of the room was a table. At one side of it sat a red-faced, fat Englishman; and at the other a gentleman, neat and handsome in a brown broadcloth coat and pale-colored trousers buckled under his boots. On the table between them was a gold-headed cane and a gray beaver hat apparently in no respect different from the one that had been shot from the head of a warm friend of mine upon a certain conspicuous occasion. I saw the gentleman stroke his small black mustache and heard him say to the red-faced Englishman, "But it's *not* extravagance, if you'll permit me the correction, sir—not at all! If we're free with our money we'll find it easier when we wish other prisoners released; and after all, my dear sir, we can't even be sure of civility from most of your compatriots unless we—I hope you don't mind my mentioning it—unless we pay well for it."

I cleared my throat, for the sight of him moved me.

Captain Boyle rose to his feet and raised his eyebrows, striving to see me clearly in the dimness. "Whom have I the pleasure——" he asked politely, and I saw him dart a suspicious glance at the red-faced Englishman.

"A passenger for your packet boat," I said, with a gruffness in my voice that was due to no desire to disguise it.

"My packet boat!" he exclaimed. "You've been misinformed, I fear! I'm not in the passenger-carrying business, sir."

I cleared my throat again. "I think you might be," I said. "I think you *would* be, if——"

He came forward quickly; stopped; then stepped close up to me and dropped his hand on my shoulder. "Why—" he said, and there was a thickness in his speech that somehow brought moisture into my own eyes—"why, I've been planning—I came here to ask for your —why, yes! I think I *would* take a passenger for any port this side of hell, or the other side, for that matter, if Captain Nason wished to go there!"

*   *   *

It was not until the *Chasseur* was at sea that I told this gallant friend of mine why I had asked him to carry me to Nantes. Then, in his pleasant cabin and across his damask tablecloth, I told him everything, even why the *Lively Lady,* lying deep within the closure of the waters we traversed, bore upon her prow a figurehead—now, alas! encrusted—that when he saw it had hair the color of rubbed copper and was gowned in shimmering green. I told him, too, how Jeddy Tucker, who had so often fought upon our native shores and upon shipboard, enraged by any word of admiration for John Paul Jones, had contrarily fought the British naval officer in Portsmouth for referring slightingly to that same John Paul Jones.

When I had finished speaking of this strange action of Jeddy's, Captain Boyle's eyes danced; then he became graver, looking at me intently. "Splendid!" he said in a low voice. "I think it's a sign. I think it's one of the many signs—signs that the great thing is done."

"What great thing?" I asked.

"The greatest thing in the world for your country and mine," he answered. "Before we fought England this second time we were not a nation. We were a few millions of individuals, scattered into arguing, backbiting groups—towns and communities and separated jealous states; every man for his own section; every section for itself. Now your Jeddy Tucker fights for the good name of an American hero because he can bear no tarnish put upon a national brightness; and that spirit is everywhere among us, because we've found out that we're America. Not many men know better than you what suffering the war has brought, Captain Nason; but history must say it has done a great task, and that Dartmoor was worth the price. We're a nation at last."

XXXIII

THE *Pembroke* lay at a dock on the lower end of the Isle Feydou, huge and towering in the pale night mist that drifted down the Loire from the vine-clad hills above it; and I, standing close under her high sides, called softly up to the watch on deck to know whether Cephas Cluff was aboard.

"He might be, an' again he mightn't," the watch drawled. "Depends on who wants him."

Cephas himself spared me the trouble of answering by appearing above the taffrail, broad of beam against the starlight beyond.

"Come down here," I said to him. "I want a word with you where we won't be heard."

"Land o' Goshen!" Cephas whispered, staring fixedly at me. "My land o' Goshen!" He moved quickly and lightly to the companionway and came over the side; then held to my hand with his great rough fist and breathed heavily. "It's you!" he said. "Where's the others, Cap'n? Gorry, we been afraid you wouldn't never come! Aye, we mighty near believed you wouldn't never come!"

I stood and looked at him, afraid, almost, to ask the questions that boiled in my mind.

He nodded at me. "They're aboard," he said. "They been living there. She's in the captain's quarters. Jeddy said you'd want it that way."

"Is she—how is she——"

"Good!" Cephas assured me emphatically. "Food's a thousand percent better since she came aboard. Ain't nothing gets by her!"

"Well," I said, "as soon as we settle with the Latours we'll clear for Plymouth and pick up the rest of the crew. Captain Boyle's tending to it for me."

I ran up the companionway, leaving Cephas breathing heavily behind me, and went aft to the cabin. The door to the captain's quarters stood ajar, and beyond it I heard voices. I listened, my heart thumping fit to burst.

I recognized Jeddy's impudent tones. "Box-hauling," he was saying, "is a piece of seamanship you use to claw off a lee shore, provided you got plenty of hands aboard. Say you've reached for a point in a heavy gale and find you ain't going to make it, account of wind and sea and currents; there ain't time or room to tack, so you box-haul her. Here she is, coming into this point here. The spoon's the point and the fork's the wind."

"I can see it quite plainly," a voice said—a soft and husky voice that set the blood to pounding in my head, "and it's not necessary for you to tip her like that. You know how I'd feel if she were broken."

"I'll thank you not to tell me that again, ma'am," Jeddy replied brusquely. "Now, ma'am, having her in that position, you got to turn quick—turn her on her heel. All right: you clap your helm a-lee, haul up your mainsail, brail up your mizzen and mizzen staysail, square the after yards, let go the fore tack, sheet, bowlines and lee braces— be so kind as to point 'em out, ma'am."

"Here and here and here," said the soft and husky voice.

"Correct, ma'am," Jeddy said. "Then you brace the head yards sharp aback, haul over the weather jib and foretopmast staysail sheets, and she pays round off on her heel—and there you are, ma'am, free of your lee shore and headed for open water. Now, what was it she done to get there, ma'am?"

The soft voice answered him in the tone of an obedient child saying her lessons. "The main and mizzen topsails lying aback gave her sternway, and when the larboard side of her rudder pressed against the water in backing, it helped her head to cast to larboard."

I opened the door softly and went in. At the long gold-covered table beneath the silver lamps sat Emily and Jeddy, their backs to me and their heads close together over the small bone frigate I had last seen in the dreary market place of Dartmoor Prison. Beyond them rose the rudder case, carved and colored to represent a close-packed stand of bamboos; and because of the swirling in my head at the sight of Emily, the carved green fronds that branched above her seemed to sway and flutter in a silent breeze.

"So there we are," she said, looking at Jeddy, "free of our lee shore and headed for open water." Then her eyes descended to the little frigate; her head bowed and her figure drooped. "Headed for clear and open water," she said sadly. "Ah, if we were! Do you think we ever will be, Jeddy?"

There was a faint growl, and my little white dog Pinky came out from behind the rudder case, walking importantly on his toes, to stand peering doubtfully at me. Emily, seeing him staring beyond her, looked up into one of the paneled mirrors. Her widening eyes met mine. With a fluttering hand she set down the frigate, and even before she turned to me I could see in those dazed, widening eyes of hers all I had ever hoped to have of life.

"Free of our lee shore," I said unsteadily. "Free of our lee shore, my dear, and headed for clear and open water."

THE END

AUTHORITIES

On privateering, seamanship, and the War of 1812: ABBOT, WILLIS J., *American Merchant Ships & Sailors*; BOWDITCH, NATHANIEL, *New American Practical Navigator*; CHAPELLE, HOWARD IRVING, *The Baltimore Clipper*; CHAPIN, HOWARD M., *Privateer Ships & Sailors*; CHATTERTON, E. KEBLE, *Sailing Ships & Their Story*; CHATTERTON, E. KEBLE, *Ships & Ways of Other Days*; COGGESHALL, GEORGE, *History of the American Privateers*; DAVIS, CHARLES G., *Ships of the Past*; ESSEX INSTITUTE, COLLECTIONS OF THE, Vol. II, No. 2, *Private Armed Vessels Belonging to Salem During the War of 1812*; ESSEX INSTITUTE, COLLECTIONS OF THE, Jan. 1901, *Account of the Private Armed Ship "America" of Salem*; JAMESON, JOHN F., *Privateering & Piracy in the Colonial Period*; JOHNSON, CHARLES H. L., *Famous Privateersmen & Adventurers of the Sea*; LEVER, DARCY, *The Young Sea Officer's Sheet Anchor*; MACLAY, EDGAR S., *History of American Privateers*; MAHAN, *Sea Power in Its Relations to the War of 1812*; PEABODY, ROBERT E., *The Log of the Grand Turks*; ROBBINS, ARCHIBALD, *Journal of the Loss of the Brig "Commerce"*; ROOSEVELT, THEODORE, *Naval War of 1812*; SCOTT, MICHAEL, *Tom Cringle's Log*; SHERBURNE, ANDREW, *Memoirs*; STATHAM, COMMANDER E. P., R.N., *Privateers & Privateering*.

On Dartmoor Prison, and on conditions in England and France at the end of the Napoleonic Wars: ABELL, FRANCIS, *Prisoners of War in Britain, 1756-1815*; ANDREWS, CHARLES, *The Prisoner's Memoirs, or Dartmoor Prison*; BROEMEL, P. R., *Paris & London in 1815*; COBB, JOSIAH, *A Green Hand's First Cruise, & Five Months in Dartmoor Prison*; HAWTHORNE, NATHANIEL (edited by), *Yarn of a Yankee Privateer*; LOLIEE, FREDERIC, *Prince Talleyrand & His Times*; PALMER, BENJAMIN F., *Diary of (at Melville Island & Dartmoor)*; RECORDS OF ARUNDEL PRISONERS, *Registry of Prisoners of War (Dartmoor Section)*, Public Record Office, London; THOMSON, BASIL, *The Story of Dartmoor Prison*; VALPEY, JOSEPH, JR., *Journal of (in Dartmoor Prison)*; WATERHOUSE, BENJAMIN, *Journal of a Young Man of Massachusetts . . . at Dartmoor*.

*   *   *

The descriptions of the *Chasseur* and the second *Lively Lady* are based on Model 986 in the Louvre Marine Museum—that of the brigantine *La Gazelle*, 18 guns, built at Bayonne on the plans of M. Marestier and launched in 1822. Marestier studied Baltimore clippers in America for the French navy; and *La Gazelle* is believed to be the only existing model that accurately reveals the lines of the best Baltimore clipper privateers of the War of 1812.

*   *   *

The author gratefully acknowledges the generous assistance of Mr. Booth Tarkington, Mr. Howard Irving Chapelle, Commandant Edward Hubert of the Louvre Marine Museum, Mr. Henry Dawes, secretary to the American Ambassador to the Court of St. James, Mrs. Marion Cobb Fuller of the Maine State Library, Captain William H. Gould of Kennebunkport, Me., Mr. J. Templeman Coolidge, Mr. Irving R. Wiles, and the Library of Congress.

CAPTAIN CAUTION

TO
L. T. R.

I

Capt. OLIVER DORMAN, of the armed merchant barque *Olive Branch,* of Arundel, ten guns and twenty-five men, stared calculatingly upward, quadrant in hand, his gray fringe of chin whisker seeming to point accusingly at the towering spread of canvas that half filled itself in the faint, hot air currents of the doldrums, only to go slack once more, as though every sail, from the vast courses to the small and distant royals, had sickened beneath the violent glare of the August sun.

What he saw seemed to leave something to be desired; for he fell to whistling soundlessly, and peered, as if hopefully, along the barque's broad deck, which wearily canted itself to every point of the compass in succession as the glassy surface of the ocean rose and sank in bewildering disorder. Heat waves shimmered upward from each of the five larboard carronades, and, more faintly, from the deck itself. Between the starboard carronades, the crew, barefooted and stripped to the waist, languidly worked at making spun yarn. They were screened from the sun by the foresail, as well as by a strip of sailcloth stretched from the foremast to the starboard ratlines; and as Captain Dorman eyed them, a seaman rose listlessly, dropped a bucket over the bulwarks, drew it slowly back and poured the water on his head and shoulders. Having done so, he gazed doubtfully into the bucket.

"It appears to me," he said, and so faint were the noises of the barque in the oily calm that his voice came clearly to the quarter-deck—"it appears to me like as if somebody left a dead fish in this ocean."

Captain Dorman sniffed the air, as brackish, indeed, as though it rose from a dying sea. He grasped a spoke of the wheel and moved it a little against the grip of the helmsman, as if to feel the vessel's pulse; then turned abruptly toward the taffrail, where his first and second mates were busy on the day's reckoning with quadrant and latitude tables. Close by them, but sheltered from the sun beneath a patched skysail that served as an awning, sat a girl whose smooth black head was bent over a long and narrow book. She gazed from under arched brows at the serious face of the tall first mate; then moved a shoulder impatiently beneath the thin gray silk of the Chinese jacket that buttoned tight around her throat and fell nearly to the knees of the gray silk trousers below it.

"What do you make it, Dan?" she asked.

The mate plucked at the shirt that clung wetly to his broad chest. "Wait. I'll go over it once more."

She nodded pleasantly. "That'll make four times you've been over it, Dan. It's just as well we haven't had a breeze for a week or two; because if we had, you'd be going over it till suppertime."

He smiled at her. "I might," he admitted. "I aim to miss St. Paul's Rocks, and it's safer to miss 'em on purpose than by accident."

Captain Dorman moved beside them, mopping his face and wrists with a blue bandanna. "Now, Corunna," he said, "you tend to the book and let Dan'l tend to the sights."

She tossed her head impatiently. "I can take a sight quicker than Dan. I don't see he's any handier to do things simpler and quicker than anybody else; and your telling me again that he is, won't make me believe it. Just because he's bigger than all of you together, you think his judgment's better than mine, but if I can't shoot the sun in half the time Dan Marvin takes, I'll eat the quadrant."

"Maybe so," Captain Dorman agreed. "Maybe you can. You've had lessons from me and Dan'l and Noah and everybody else in Arundel that knows how to take a sight. I'd be ashamed to own you as my daughter if you couldn't take one as quick as any man. Only it just happens that what sights are took for this barque are took by me and Dan'l Marvin. We don't trust nobody's sights but our own. The only reason we trust to your handwriting in the log book is because none of us attended the Misses Hubbard's Academy for Select Females in Waterville. No doubt you can write rings around us, Corunna; but it don't seem to us we need any help in navigating."

He thrust out his under lip and nodded severely at Daniel Marvin, as if to imply that this was the proper way in which to handle a select female—brusquely, that is, and with little or no mincing of words.

Then he coughed, glancing at a slip of paper in his hand. "What did you get, Dan'l?"

"South 4°; 29° west," Marvin told him.

Corunna Dorman lifted a shoulder in silent protest, but dipped her pen in the ink bottle between the tips of her Chinese slippers, bent her black head above the log book and, with delicately upheld little finger, wrote across the top of the page the words: "Remarks on board, Tuesday, August 4, 1812."

"That's what I make it," Captain Dorman said. "How'd you make it from St. Paul's Rocks?"

"I figure we're a good day's run from 'em, Cap'n Oliver, even with a decent breeze."

The captain hastily corrected a figure in his reckoning, nodded profoundly and tossed his paper overside. "That's about right, Dan'l." He handed the quadrant to Marvin, who replaced it in a triangular green box bearing, in white letters, the words "Elihu Marvin, Arundel, 1791."

Captain Dorman pursed his lips in sour contemplation. "Well, my mind's made up! There's something wrong. We ain't sighted a craft of any kind since we put into Pernambuco for water! Even the southeast trades, they've up and cleared out on us before their time. 'Tisn't natural!"

He raised his chin and moved his head, dog-like, as if striving to locate a scent. "There's a little air from the south'ard," he said to Noah Lord. "Get those yards squared around. We'll go off to the northeast."

Even as the second mate shouted the orders that started the half-naked crew from under the shelter of their strip of sail and set them to hauling at the heavy yards, Marvin stared doubtfully at Captain Dorman; and so, too, did the others; but the only one to speak was his daughter.

"Northeast?" she asked. "Have you changed your mind about going back to Arundel?"

There was something like bitterness in Captain Dorman's reply. "Northeast is what I said, and good reason too. We're a hundred and eight days out of Canton—a hundred and eight days!" He brandished a finger before Marvin's nose. "What you think your father would have said about a craft that took a hundred and eight days from Canton to St. Paul's Rocks? He wouldn't have called it a craft; he'd have said it was some kind of vegetable!"

"We had bad luck, Cap'n Oliver," Marvin protested. He, too, raised his head and moved it from side to side, sniffing the hot and brackish air; and as he did so, the captain and the second mate followed his example, so that they seemed like puppets moved in unison by a single hand.

The captain's puckered lips became less sour. "I knew it," he said. "She's coming." In the direction toward which the three men stared, there was a faint darkening in the pallid expanse of sea.

"That shows you," Captain Dorman continued. "For a hundred and eight days we've done what we ought to do, and got nothing for it but a foul bottom. I reckon there's enough weed on us to fertilize Boothby's farm. As for the crosses we've had to bear, it's a sin and a shame!"

On the upthrust fingers of his left hand he ticked off additional complaints. "Tail of a typhoon off China; tail of some kind of a dod-rotted disturbance off Chile; druv back and druv back and druv back when we tried to round the Horn; blown two hundred miles out of our course off the Falklands; and now just laying here and rotting like a dead whale; and all because we always done what we was supposed to do! What I say is, it's high time I do different! High time!"

"Bad luck's bound to change, Cap'n Oliver," Marvin said. "She never stays anywhere forever; and I say let her go of her own accord. If we try to get away from bad luck, she's apt to move the same minute we do, and in the same direction. We might never get rid of her. Let's wait one more day, Cap'n Oliver."

"Wait!" Captain Dorman growled. "Wait! If we wait another day, we'll send down roots. . . . Hey! Look here, Dan'l!"

He seemed almost to prance on the quarter-deck as the sails filled. Over the weather rail drifted a breath that had a perfume of the sea in it instead of the flavor of water laden with decaying things. The *Olive Branch* ceased her purposeless heaving and forged slowly ahead.

Captain Dorman sat himself beside his black-haired daughter, casting, as he did so, a somewhat dubious glance at the neat darns in the knees of her gray Chinese trousers. Daniel Marvin, staring down at father and daughter, found a singular resemblance between them—such a resemblance as might result from the labors of a Chinese craftsman if, having rough-hewn the kindly, rugged likeness of the captain, he should make another smaller carving, smoothing every line, rounding every contour, and making finer every feature until he had obtained the graceful figure of Corunna Dorman.

The captain turned his eyes from Corunna to Marvin. "You see, Dan'l," he said, "there's years when there's a southerly breeze over toward the African coast, contrary to Nature. Things being contrary to Nature up to now, we might catch it and move north on it till we meet up with the northeast trades. We might do worse than touch at the Cape Verdes for a breaming; then run for home with a clean bottom."

Marvin nodded impassively, raised his chin to the faint breeze and ran his hand along his neck to clear it of the moisture that made it as bright as the mahogany rim of the wheel. "I'll take the quadrant below," he said. "You through with the log, Corunna?"

She looked hard at him, but spoke to her father. "Dan thinks he knows better, father," she said. "He's getting the Marvin look around his ears." She laughed lightly. "If Dan owned the *Olive Branch*, he'd show us some sailing. I guess Dan never heard that the longest way 'round is oftentimes the shortest way home."

"Now, now!" Captain Dorman protested. "A man's got a right to his opinion, Corunna. Eli Marvin wouldn't 'a' been so eager to have Dan'l come along with us as mate if he'd thought we'd try to hammer his opinions out of him; and if Dan'l goes as master of his father's brig next voyage, maybe he *will* show us. . . . Speak up, Dan'l, if you got anything to say."

Marvin shook his head. "It's not for me to say, Cap'n Oliver. It's only that I got a feeling against going off our course." He hesitated. "I woke up quick last night, as if there might be a change coming."

"'Twon't do, Dan'l," Captain Dorman said. "If there'd been a change coming, I'd 'a' woke up myself. And there's no use fretting about going off our course! The way things are, we haven't *had* any course since I don't know when; and now look at us!"

The four of them peered to windward. The breeze, though faint, had freshened. The sickly pallor of the ocean had given way to something that lacked only a little of being sparkle. Astern of the *Olive Branch* stretched a long fold as if the water had been pale blue silk, caught on a bolt under the barque's counter and drawn into a ridge by a giant lying hid beyond the sea's curve.

Corunna Dorman closed the log book with a snap, picked up the ink bottle and rose to her feet, a sturdy, strong-shouldered figure. "It doesn't make any difference!" she said. "Not to Dan! This breeze has no business being here—that's what Dan thinks! . . . You'd rather lie in a calm, wouldn't you, Dan, than enjoy a breeze careless enough to be where it wasn't expected?" She turned and went to the cabin, pausing at the companionway to look superciliously at the three men and exclaim, "Shark-fin soup!"

Captain Dorman shook his head, seemingly baffled. "A woman gets to be a terrible nuisance on a vessel, 'specially in hot spells and calms. Every voyage, for the last three years, I've sworn I'd leave her ashore next time; and by gracious, so I would, if her mother was alive. Trouble is, there ain't anybody to leave her with. Most folks would try to make her feel like a scarlet woman because of knowing there was times when she wore those Chinese unmentionables of hers!"

"If you'd left her ashore," Marvin said calmly, "you wouldn't be getting shark-fin soup."

"No," Captain Dorman agreed uncertainly.

"It appears to me it might be more of a nuisance to leave her ashore than to have her aboard."

Captain Dorman eyed his mate blankly, his lips pursed in a soundless whistle. Marvin, silent and respectful, moved a broad shoulder suggestively toward the cabin. The captain emerged from his revery, cast a quick glance at the towering square sails on the main and foremast, ran his eye over the crew, gathered now around their mess kids between the starboard carronades, sniffed once more at the faint hot breeze; then, followed by Marvin, he scrambled down the companionway to his dinner.

II

By midafternoon the breeze still held, and the *Olive Branch*, with a bonnet laced to her gaff topsail and studding sails set on her main and foremast, held steadily on her course to the northeastward. At the break of the quarter-deck sat Corunna Dorman, her head bent over an intricate piece of needlework which pictured, in brilliant wools, the Holy Family seated beneath a fig tree and contemplating with what may have been suspicion the distant spires of Jerusalem.

Up and down the weather side of the quarter-deck paced Daniel Marvin, his blue-striped shirt and his bell-bottomed duck trousers, disreputable from countless washings, whipped against him by the hot winds from the northwest. When he turned at the break, an arm's length from Corunna, her eyes flicked upward at him, only to fall again to her work as he wheeled at the taffrail. He watched the sky; he watched the sea; he watched the helmsman. He watched the crew, forward, washing their garments by dragging them overside, attached to ropes. He studied the soft pitch, oozing, in spots, from the deck seams; he watched the set of the topgallant sails and royals; he watched the barque's wake, flowing out behind her, in small, endless folds. He watched everything, it seemed, except Corunna and her needlework.

Not even when she whispered, "Dan!" as he prepared to wheel for his monotonous journey to the taffrail did he look at her, but only turned once more as if he had heard nothing.

At his next approach she stretched a hand toward him and spoke his name less softly. The hand, he saw, held a long needle, pointed firmly at his knee, and at no great distance from it.

"Ma'am?" Marvin asked. Moving to the rail beside her, he scanned, as if in eager inquiry, the swirling depths beneath.

"Ma'am!" Corunna said bitterly, but so faintly that even the helmsman could have caught no more than a murmurous sound. "Ma'am, indeed! You'd be careful not to commit yourself, wouldn't you, even if Gabriel was blowing his horn?"

Marvin's eye traveled from the water to the peak of the mizzen sail and back again, passing lightly over the face of the helmsman—a Maine Indian as tall, almost, as Marvin himself, and clad in knee-length trousers so voluminous that they had the look of a short fringed skirt. "Shipboard's shipboard, Corunna. There's always somebody to see what's happening. Plenty of time after we get ashore. And there's Cap'n Oliver: I wouldn't want him to have hard thoughts of me. A little patience never hurt anybody."

She drove her needle through the canvas background of the Holy Family and wrenched the yarn after it with such violence that it seemed to hiss. "You weren't worrying about what anybody might see that night off Rio." When Marvin remained silent, she looked up at him quickly and found him smiling.

"What's more," she persisted in a tone as peremptory as it was quiet, "you weren't delivering any lectures on the necessity of being patient—not *that* night! I don't even recall you making mention, that night, of waiting till we got ashore. And I don't seem to remember being addressed as 'ma'am'—not once! What was it you called me that night, Dan? I hope it hasn't slipped your memory!"

"It was dark that night, Corunna."

"Dark!" she exclaimed. "Of course it was dark! Does it have to be dark to make you stop behaving as if I had yellow fever? That's the way you've acted ever since!" She thrust her needle recklessly through the center of the Holy Family, rolled the needlework together, reached up to the bulwark and swung herself quickly to her feet. Something about the heel of her Chinese slipper seemed amiss, for she half turned to look at it; and in so doing her fingers, seeking support, caught at the hand with which Marvin held to the rail. Her arm pressed, as if by accident, against his side.

He stepped back to scan with sudden solicitude the spread of canvas above him. "Mind your helm, Steven!" he said sharply to the tall Indian. "Keep the upper sails full."

"You did it again!" Corunna whispered, when he turned to her once more. "A body'd think you'd be poisoned if you touched me! Didn't it mean anything to you—that night off Rio?"

"Don't be foolish, Corunna. We can't always have what we want as soon as we want it, and it's better we shouldn't."

"You mean you've changed your mind!"

"No," he said, "no. I don't mean that. I don't change my mind that easily."

"You do!" she insisted. "You have! If you haven't changed your mind, you couldn't keep away from me! You'd want to touch me, every chance you got!"

"So you find, do you, that all of us act alike?"

He laughed when she set her fists on her hips and stared up at him as if scorn at his words had robbed her of speech. "The way I figure it, Corunna, is that I'm sure enough about myself, but less sure of you. It's a long way home, and I'd dislike to have it said I'd taken advantage of a lady who's inclined to be hasty in her judgments."

"Hasty!" she exclaimed. "Hasty! I?" She drew in her breath slowly, almost as though it had been driven completely from her by his charge. "You seem to think I'm hasty because I'm able to make up my mind! Well, let me tell you this, Dan Marvin: It might be better for you if you had a little more of what you call hastiness in place of the patience you're forever preaching about! Patience! The Lord deliver us from your kind of patience, that won't let you do what you want to do till everything just suits you—so that you never do it because you die of old age before you're suited!"

Marvin glanced quickly at the Indian helmsman; then moved a little away from the angry girl.

"Hasty!" she exclaimed again, moving after him. "Who are you, I'd like to know, to pass judgment on my hastiness? Doesn't that just prove that you think you're better than the rest of us? You think your family's better! You think you're better because you invent new ways of doing things—yes, and because you're sizable enough to whip any man that might think to stand out against you. That's it, Dan: You're stuck up, like all the Marvins! They've always been stuck up; always thought they were better than anybody in Arundel, ever since your aunt Phoebe marched to Quebec, and since your father helped that French duke to buy land from General Knox." She stamped her foot, seeming to flatten beneath it all persons of title as well as all Frenchmen.

Marvin shook his head. "I never noticed it, Corunna. Seems to me my father makes more of knowing your father and Steven Nason and this man's father"—he moved his head slightly toward the Indian helmsman—"than of having done Talleyrand a good turn. If he's stuck up, maybe he's stuck up on account of being first mate on your father's brig when he was young."

She fell silent, fingering the stitches that held together a rip in the shoulder of her Chinese jacket. "I suppose," she said at length, "that if these things were bright and new, you might——"

The helmsman interrupted her. "Dan'l," he said, "seems to me I caught a sight of suthin off the weather beam."

Marvin swung himself over the bulwarks and into the mizzen ratlines with an ease and lightness that belied his height and breadth of shoulder. Halfway up he stopped and stared off to the southeast.

"What is it, Dan?" Corunna asked.

"Get your father's glass," he said. "Tell him there's a sail to windward, and the wind's dropping."

She did as he ordered; then mounted the ratlines after him to sit on the crosstrees, clinging to his knee, while he focused the glass on the thick blue haze in the south, a haze so hot that it boiled and rolled like smoke.

Far below them, her father moved to the rail and looked upward, his round face, fringed with whiskers and gray hair, seeming to be balanced ludicrously atop of little more than a pair of shoes.

"What you make it out to be, Dan'l?" he shouted.

"Three sail," Marvin called down to him. "They must have caught a southeasterly breeze. One of 'em's headed straight for us. The other two, they're pointed more to the eastward."

Marvin lowered the glass and peered astern, past the limp, flapping expanse of the gaff topsail. The folds of the wake had flattened into the oily, silvery surface of the sea—a surface touched here and there by the small rufflings of vagrant airs. Ahead of and high above him, the staysails and the square sails on the mainmast hung limp and draggled; while from among them came a thousand slappings and lollopings as the staggerings of the barque in the renewed calm set blocks and sails and sheets to bumping and lamenting in mid-air.

He went quickly down the ratlines, leaving Corunna to follow or not, and gave the glass to Captain Dorman.

"Any sign of a breeze?" the captain asked.

Marvin shook his head. "Only the one the stranger caught."

Captain Dorman adjusted the glass and leveled it. "First sail we've sighted in a dreadful long time! Seemed as if every seaman must have gone ashore and got himself the cow and garden he's always talking about." He growled and grumbled to himself as he watched the distant vessel, whose topsail, topgallant sail and royal were now visible from the deck of the *Olive Branch*, though the sails and yards and masts wavered and quivered in the heat, almost like reflections dimly seen in agitated water.

"What you make of her, Dan'l?" the captain asked suddenly.

"I think she left the other two sail on purpose to have a look at us."

Captain Dorman passed the glass to the second mate, who stood silently beside him. "Let's hear what you think of her, Noah."

Noah Lord studied the oncoming vessel deliberately. "Brig: full sail," he announced. "Pretty heavy sparred, she is. Pretty high hoist to her topsails, seems to me."

Captain Dorman's lips were pursed, and there was a gray cast to his face that may have come from the stifling heat that had again enveloped the barque. He made two turns the length of the quarter-deck, and in that time seemed to arrive at a decision. "Yes," he said, "they look high to me—high and heavy. Get out the sweeps! We'll sweep 'round and get to moving, so to take advantage of that breeze when it reaches us. No sense lying here like a bump on a log!"

The second mate ran forward, shouting to the crew as he ran, and in a minute's time six twenty-four-foot oars had been thrust through the sweep holes between the gun ports, and the sweating men were working the *Olive Branch* around to the northwest.

"Who'd 'a' thought," Captain Dorman said to Marvin—"who'd 'a' thought we'd strike anything off here? And I guess there ain't much doubt about her being something, with topsails that size! She ain't a merchant vessel; she's got some men aboard." He looked around him uneasily. "The Britishers, they'd be sticking to the West Indies—they and the yellow fever. It just don't seem reasonable to strike a thing like this, off in the middle of nowhere! There's something about it I'm taking a misliking to." He laughed with what may have been intended for carelessness, but to Marvin it seemed to be nervousness that impelled the captain to draw the folds of a blue bandanna handkerchief across and across his palms. "Some day, Dan'l, we may have to fight somebody, so's to remind 'em we got a few rights on their ocean."

Marvin nodded soberly. "We might," he said, "if we ever get half enough ships to do it, but it doesn't look as if we ever would."

Driven by the sweeps, the barque rocked slowly to the northwestward. The brig, now astern, moved steadily closer and before her the silvery blue of the ocean was darkened by the breeze that bore her on. The eyes of the three men moved constantly from the approaching brig to their own upper sails. At last the main topgallant sail and royal bellied a little, then slapped the mast.

The captain drew a deep breath. "There it is," he said. "Now we'll get it." The topgallant sail and royal filled again, and the topsail and the huge course seemed to come to life.

"We'll keep 'em sweeping," Captain Dorman said. "With the sweeps and the breeze, maybe we can show her a clean pair of heels. God knows what she is, but it don't seem likely she'd leave two other craft, just for a friendly call on us." He went through the motion of whistling silently. "We can't afford to take risks," he added. "She might be a Spanish privateer, or one of those damned Frenchmen from the Indies. They'd as lief cut our throats as eat a mess of greens, Dan'l! We'll have to load and double-shot the guns, my boy. Everything I've got on earth is in this barque! If the worst comes to the

worst, we can cut up her rigging and get away when she hauls off
to repair the damage."

From the brig, so close that her white streak was visible, wavering
raggedly in the heat waves, there grew a small white blossom that
bloomed and broke and drifted off in pale streamers, all in a moment's time. Down the wind there came a heavy thud, as if some
vast horse, enraged, had driven a steel-shod hoof against a fragile
wall.

III

From the main hatch, Marvin, superintending the casting loose of the guns, as well as the bringing up of powder bags, six-pound shot, tubes, fuses and all the lumber that was necessary to the operation of the *Olive Branch's* small batteries, could hear Captain Dorman laying down the law to his daughter. "Go below," he told her, "and put off those heathen trappings. Get yourself into proper female dress; then hunt out a safe place below the water line, where you'll be off my mind."

Marvin had to listen hard for her answer; for her voice was low, with more entreaty in it than defiance. "One place is as safe as another," she told her father, "and I want to see what happens. I've been on the *Olive Branch* almost half my life since I was born in Corunna Harbor, and I never yet found a place safer than this quarter-deck. I'm not afraid of that brig. She's not as big as we are, and I don't believe there's anything to be afraid of, but if I have to be shut up below, where I can't tell what's going on, I'll die! I'm as much interested in this barque as you are! If there's to be any fighting over her, you'll need everybody you've got, and I want a hand in it."

As if overwhelmed by her flux of words, Captain Dorman looked desperately aloft and then astern, where the brig, thrusting thin white ribbons of foam from under her heavy bowsprit, was little more than a mile away. He signaled to Marvin, who ran aft, pausing only long enough to remind the panting men to load with wads between the shot unless they wanted their guns to burst.

"Now, here," Captain Dorman told him, "she's faster than we are, though she wouldn't be if we had some of the sculch off our bottom. Anyway, she's bound to come up with us; and if she fires on us, there's got to be steps taken. We've run up the American flag, and she ain't got no right to fire on us, no matter who she is. If she does, she's a pirate, entitled to be treated as one. We're peaceable folks, going about our business. If she fires on us, we'll keep on going till she starts to yaw again, to bring a gun to bear; then we'll veer and come into the wind clumsy and slow, as if we'd given up. We've got just the breeze for it, Dan'l! There we'll be, Dan'l, helpless-looking as an old scow; and so she'll close with us. When she does, we'll fire with the upward roll and chop her masts and rigging to pieces."

Noah Lord nodded; but Marvin, his lips pressed tight together, stared silently at the oncoming brig.

Captain Dorman moved close to him. "Dan'l," he said, "nearly every cent I've got in the world is in this barque and her cargo. Maybe I did wrong to risk so much. I won't say as to that. What's done's done. If I get this barque home safe, I'll be a rich man. If I don't, I won't have a penny, and neither will Corunna. No pirate's going to stop me, not while I've got the say. I know what you're thinking. You're thinking what's going to happen if we don't chop her to pieces. Well, Dan'l, we got to, that's all. 'They cry unto the Lord in their trouble, and he bringeth them out of their distresses . . . he bringeth them unto their desired haven.'"

"These guns haven't been fired in a year," Marvin said slowly. "The men can't lay 'em or serve 'em properly."

Corunna came close to her father, a sturdy figure in her jacket and trousers of gray silk, and stared at Marvin with what seemed to be almost oriental placidity. "They're going to be fired now, Dan, even if I have to fire them myself."

Marvin seemed oblivious to her words. "Why," he said thoughtfully, "there *is* a way! There *is* a way to lay 'em properly! I never thought of it before! We could hang a pendulum—a gangway pendulum—if only we had the time."

Captain Dorman sighed, a quivering sigh. "If only we had the time, we wouldn't need a pendulum, and we wouldn't need guns, either. Now, Dan'l, Noah and I, we'll tend to the two after guns. Take Steven off the wheel and put him on the bow gun, and you lay the two 'midship guns yourself. Wait for me to fire, Dan'l; then cut her up in the tops."

He stepped to the break in the quarter-deck and shouted to the sweating men who crouched close under the bulwarks. "Take it slow when you get your orders to veer," he said. "We figure on putting a fright and the fear of God into this craft, provided she needs it. When she's had her lesson, we'll clap onto the sweeps, get before the wind again, and be homeward bound as quick as you can say fish."

Behind them the brig yawed. To her mastheads rose the British ensign and pennant; and a moment later those on the quarter-deck of the *Olive Branch* clearly saw the orange flame that stabbed from the muzzle of her starboard bow gun, to be engulfed in the ball of white smoke that followed. There was a high thin screaming above the barque's weather beam—a screaming that ended when the shot, striking the water ahead of them with a thumping splash, sent a silvery cone of water high in air.

"British?" Captain Dorman cried incredulously. "Either 'tain't so, or she'll haul off when she sees we're willing to fight! They ain't so eager for war as all that!"

From the brig there came a hoarse shouting, indistinguishable above the small creakings of the barque. When the barque held on her course, another hail bellowed from the brig, following which her bow fell off again to larboard.

With that, the *Olive Branch* veered slowly to the westward. Less than a pistol shot away, the strange brig followed her example.

Marvin, tinkering with the elevation of his gun, saw Captain Dorman do the same—saw him prod and prod again at the quoin beneath the breech.

The captain stepped back to the lanyard, and in the same moment he seemed to twist and break and crumble—almost to fly to pieces with a thunderous roar. A burst of flame and smoke obscured the quarter-deck, and from the smoke came shouts and strangled cries. The captain's gun, Marvin saw, had burst.

As he ran toward the stern, he saw Corunna rise from her knees beside the heap of rags that had been her father. Behind her, Noah Lord moaned and clutched the bloody stump from which his lower leg hung by shreds and splinters.

She ran to the gun next to that which had burst, and it was there that Marvin caught her by the shoulders and held her. She strove to push him away, staring at him out of eyes as black as coals in her dead-white face. "The lanyard!" she whispered, in a voice that trembled and broke. "This gun hasn't been fired!"

"It's no good, Corunna! It's like breaking rock with your fists."

She struck him in the face and kicked at him. "Damn you!" she cried. "Fire that gun! Fire that gun! They've killed my father!"

He clutched the front of her gray silk jacket and dragged her, struggling and panting, to the mizzenmast. "Let go everything!" he shouted down the deck; and as he shouted, he slashed with a knife at the mizzen halyards and hauled down the American ensign that drooped from the mizzen truck.

She plucked at his arms and shoulders with fingers that scratched like claws. "You coward! You dirty damned coward!" she cried.

He caught her to him, pinning her arms to her sides, and looked at her quickly from head to foot. There were clots of blood on her paper-white face and her gray silk garments, but the blood, he knew, was not hers. Over her shoulder he saw that a boat had been lowered from the brig's after davits—a boat with a British naval officer in her stern sheets, and on her thwarts a dozen armed men. From near at hand there rose a steady moaning.

"Go to your cabin!" Marvin said. "Clean yourself and put on decent clothes! I want you back on this deck when that boatload comes aboard!"

She pulled against his arms like bent whalebone. It seemed to Marvin that her lips drew back from her teeth. "Damn you! Damn you! Damn you! You sneaking, cowardly turn-tail rat!"

He shook her as if she had been a folded staysail; shook her until her head sagged on her shoulders and her lips went slack. As suddenly as he had started, he stopped; her head fell back, and with the flat of his hand he struck her on the cheek. On her white face the prints of his fingers stood out with even greater whiteness.

"Noah Lord's bleeding to death!" he told her fiercely. "Get below, you little fool! If you've got brains, use 'em!" He dragged her to the companionway and thrust her into it. She stumbled and fell; then got to her feet and vanished toward her cabin.

Marvin ran back to Noah Lord, cutting loose and knotting the lanyard of his knife as he ran. He slashed the blood-drenched trousers from Noah's shattered stump, slipped the lanyard around it, pushed a belaying pin beneath the cord and rapidly twisted it until the cord, cutting deep into the leg, made an end of the crimson stream that flowed into the scuppers.

"Steven!" he shouted, his head bent over his sorry task, "Steven! Bring water buckets and a sail and two men!"

When, in five minutes' time, an English lieutenant in a wrinkled blue coat, soiled white ducks and a battered hat came over the side, a limp roll of canvas lay on the newly wetted deck, and Noah Lord, grayer than the rag of sail that covered the spot where his left foot should have been, was stretched motionless and seemingly lifeless in the shadow of the weather bulwarks.

The lieutenant was tall and young, with an air of having grown weedily in a space too small for him. His head was thrust forward, like that of a melancholy bird; his thin legs, half covered by soiled and shrunken duck trousers, gave him the look of a crane, stalking suspiciously at the water's edge. Marvin, watching him come over the rail, hitching at his sword to keep it from between his knees, was in doubt whether the redness of his face was due to the searing rays of the tropic sun, or to anger: but beyond question he was angry—

so angry, indeed, that he forgot to demand immediately the name, destination and port of departure of the vessel he had boarded.

"By Ged," he said with no preamble whatever, "I should have blown you to pieces and left you to sink, and be demned to you for a lot of filthy Yankees!" His boarding party of eight men, in glazed hats, and shirts and trousers that might once have been white, dragged their cutlasses over the rail to cluster behind the lieutenant and peer at the wrecked carronade-slide and the blood-stained heap of canvas in the scuppers.

Marvin eyed the lieutenant calmly. "This is the American merchant barque *Olive Branch.* Her papers are in order. The only filth you'll find aboard this craft is what you've brought with you. What's your authority for this act of piracy?"

"Piracy!" the lieutenant ejaculated. "Piracy! Why, you——" He gestured largely toward the hilt of his sword and frowned horribly. "His Majesty's cruiser *Beetle,* eighteen guns, and by Ged, sir, you're in luck, all of you, not to be shark meat this very moment. Why, demn you, sir, why didn't you heave to? You might have cost us a man! You're no better than madmen, all of you, always playing the fool—declaring war when you've nothing to declare it with, and now running from a cruiser that could knock you to driftwood with half a broadside!"

"War!" Marvin cried. "Did you say war?"

"A fool and deaf to boot!" the lieutenant said savagely. "D'you think it was a Maying party your clown of a Madison asked us to last June? A *conversazione?* My Ged! It's a pity all your carronades didn't explode, so to let a little light into you!"

Corunna Dorman stepped quickly from the companionway and walked between Marvin and the lieutenant, her arms, tight at her sides, hidden in the billowing folds of a thin black dress. She swayed a little, staring at the lieutenant out of eyes like black flints. Marvin, watching her apprehensively, saw that one of her hands, deep in a pocket of her gown, clutched something, he knew not what. Filled with a sudden fear, he grasped her wrist. "Easy, Corunna!" he said. "We've been at war since June. At war! We've been at war with England!"

She turned a somber glance on him. When he released her, she lifted sad eyes toward the boarding party from the British brig. Her hands, obscured no longer, were clasped before her. "My father——" she said, and on the word her voice broke and failed. "My father——" She drooped toward the lieutenant, and with that he caught and held her.

"Great regrets, mem!" he said huskily. He cleared his throat and laughed in a way that he may have thought pleasant. "Didn't expect the pleasure—ah, Ged! Frightful pity, mem! Not for worlds, eh? Do what we can!"

She freed herself from the lieutenant's arm. "We knew nothing of it!" she said. "We left Canton in May. What had we—what made you fire on us—what——"

The lieutenant laughed ingratiatingly. "You'll come aboard the *Beetle,* eh? Ged, mem, a pleasure! We're for the Azores with our prizes—a slaver and a Frenchman, mem; and now you, thank Ged!"

He turned to Marvin. "Get your men into boats and over to the brig. You've got five minutes to collect your dunnage. Don't take too much or we'll pitch it overboard."

He turned back to Corunna. "Sorry—sorry to cause you the inconvenience."

IV

Forty seamen and twenty scarecrow marines crowded close around the crew of the *Olive Branch* as they scrambled over the bulwarks and into the waist of the *Beetle* war brig, spurred on by the fractious voice and intemperate words of the *Beetle's* red-faced, thin-shanked commander, Lieutenant the Hon. Vivian Strope.

Lieutenant Strope himself followed hard on their heels, calling angrily for Mr. Benyon and Oddsly. Mr. Benyon, Marvin discovered, was a small pale child, attired in the white ducks, the glazed hat and the dirk belt of a midshipman. Marvin's discovery came about through being struck sharply in the small of the back and then brusquely elbowed to one side by Mr. Benyon in response to the lieutenant's call.

"Mr. Benyon," Lieutenant Strope said, "if any of you young gentlemen happen to know where there's a prayer book, bring it at once. There's an—ah—lady on the prize and we kent do a thing with her until we've fed the old man to the sharks in a manner to suit her! In this heat I couldn't remember a word of the burial service, by Ged, even if I knew the demned thing!"

The pale child saluted smartly and disappeared. His place was taken by the elderly, bald, disillusioned-looking sailing master in shrunken nankeen breeches and a gingham coat.

"Oddsly," the lieutenant said, "send ten men aboard the prize, with one of the young gentlemen in command—I think Mr. Jowkes. See to it, Oddsly, while I'm getting this Yankee overboard. They tried to fight us, Oddsly, the demned ruffians. Demnedest nuisance of all, Oddsly, is that one of 'em blew his leg off! Demned well wish it had been his head! Can't put him with the prisoners, demn it! See to it, and search the prisoners; then clap 'em in the hold. And just bear in mind, will you, that we've got to close with the other two prizes before nightfall?"

Clutching a prayer book that Mr. Benyon had brought him, the lieutenant scrambled down into the boat once more; while a detail of marines, under the eye of the sailing master, searched Marvin and the crew of the *Olive Branch,* removing from them not only knives but even belt buckles, coins and every metal thing.

"Smartly, now!" Oddsly told them, when this was done. "You'll go under guard in the main hold and we'll stow your dunnage where it'll be safe. You'll be allowed on deck in sections, starting as soon as the hatch comes off in the morning. Settle your differences peaceably if you don't want a bullet in your gizzards. We're overburdened with prisoners, and the guards have orders to take no chances—not with such ugly brutes as you Yankees. Step lively, now!"

He stared arrogantly at the dejected group of seamen and jerked a thumb toward the hatchway. Marvin raised a protesting hand. "Leave us our dunnage," he said. "It's not right to clap these men under hatches half naked, as they are. They'll need clothes."

Oddsly's reply was contemptuous. "No they won't! Not here they won't! This brig ain't Buckingham Palace! The state bedrooms were overlooked when she was launched, and you'll find your quarters somewhat restricted." He laughed appreciatively at his own facetiousness and swung himself down the ladderway at the main hatch.

Marvin, waiting for the men to follow the sailing master into the darkness below, cast a look astern. The *Beetle's* crew had mounted to the carronades and the hammock nettings to watch the *Olive Branch*, wallowing under the brig's lee, her slack sails a bright pink from the setting sun. Between the shoulders of the British sailors, Marvin could see small figures on the barque's quarter-deck, and as he watched, a gray lump fell from the larboard rail, half turned in mid-air, struck the water with a clumsy splash and vanished as if it had never been.

"'He bringeth them out of their distresses,'" Marvin quoted, thinking of kindly Captain Dorman and how he had come to stand close beside him, not an hour since, and speak of his and Corunna's needs. At the thought, Marvin laughed, but at the sound, which was more of a croak than a laugh, he licked his heat-cracked lips and passed his hand across his face, which seemed to him stiff. His eye ran quickly along the brig's armament—along the eight stubby carronades to a side, and the two long guns, twenty-four pounders, that had been run out of the larboard bow ports preparatory to raking the *Olive Branch* if the need had arisen. His shirt, drenched with perspiration, seemed to become even wetter when he contemplated what must have happened aboard the barque if those two guns had loosed their double loads of ball and grape at close range. He groaned aloud at the recollection of the words Corunna Dorman had spoken to him when, by his quickness, death and destruction had been averted. "'Sneaking, cowardly, turn-tail rat!'" he repeated to himself. The words reformed themselves in his hot brain and spilled

unbidden from his parched lips. "Cowardly, sneaking, turn-tail rat!"
he muttered. "Turn-tail, cowardly, sneaking rat!"

The voice of the sailing master roared at him from the hatch:
"Well, for God's sake! Are you coming along, or are you thinking of
taking a berth in the gun room?"

"Could I have some water?" Marvin asked hoarsely.

"Come down that ladder," the sailing master snapped, "or you'll
get a musket-butt behind the ear!"

Marvin descended the ladder hastily, stooped to avoid the beams
of the berth deck, and moved forward to a second hatch. As his
eyes became accustomed to the dimness, he saw, crouched on each
side of the hatchway, two grotesque marines, looking, in that hot
half light, like the guards of some dark inferno.

Out of a small square hole in the hatch protruded a ladder, and
from the hole there came the sound of many voices, and a stench
as evil as it was powerful.

"Down with you!" the sailing master said with what almost seemed
like enjoyment. "We'll be at the Cape Verdes before you know it."

Seeing that there was no help for it, Marvin laid hold of the ladder
to go down, but as he did so, a man rose through the hole in the
hatch to block his way. He had a thin face, long and palely yellow,
framed in lank black hair; a face that had, at no distant date, been
cleanly shaved, but that was now shaded by a growth of black stubble. As he rose higher on the ladder his garments were revealed to
be as darkly gray as a Quaker's coat. He glanced quickly at Marvin
from under an eyelid that drooped heavily, but spoke to the sailing
master in a hoarse voice that seemed to Marvin to have a singularly
pleasing resonance.

"I believe, sir," he said, "that unless you let some of us on deck,
you'll have a pile of corpses on your hands tomorrow."

"You know the rules, Slade," Oddsly said brusquely. "Nobody goes
on deck when we're hove to, or in chase of a sail. It's nothing you
can't stand. You mustn't judge white men by the blacks you've
carried."

Slade looked carefully at the sailing master, tilting his head backward as though to see him more clearly from under his drooping eyelid; and Marvin saw that the grayness of the man's shirt was due to
a crust of mud upon it.

He turned to Marvin then. "You're joining us, I think. Lurman
Slade, if you'll permit me, captain of the *Graceful Kate* brig."

"Slaver!" Oddsly said scornfully.

Again Slade tipped back his head to stare at the sailing master.

"You repeat yourself," he said. "I think this gentleman probably understood your first reference. He's not an Englishman!"

He smiled and nodded at Marvin, backing slowly down the ladder; and Marvin, after a final glance at Oddsly's grim features, followed Slade into a hot, foul blackness that seemed to rise about him like the steam from a witch's cauldron; then to close over his head as he descended.

He stood, Marvin felt—for in the darkness of the hold he could see nothing—on a tier of water casks that had been covered with a layer of mud, so that a second tier of casks might be placed in it and prevented, by its stickiness, from shifting. The stench of the place caught him in the throat and the pit of the stomach, as if those outraged organs fought silently against the unendurable; and the uneasy swaying of the brig seemed suddenly to sweep off into enormous arcs that momentarily threatened to become dizzying revolutions. He caught at the collar of his shirt and heard it rip in his hand; then, choking, he turned and fumbled again for the ladder.

A hand caught him by the arm. "No use to go up," Slade's hoarse voice told him. "The marines push you back. Lie down here between us. This corner of the hold is the officer's mess, anyway."

Dripping with perspiration, Marvin did as he was told, only to find himself wedged tightly between Slade and a hulk of a man whose outthrust shoulder, arm and hip had the feel of a seaweed-covered ledge. He groaned and heaved as Marvin pressed against him; but when Slade, leaning over Marvin, softly said "Argandeau," the hulk of a man was gone as quickly as though he had silently exploded. A moment later he spoke softly from above them: "Somebody call me?"

"I did," Slade said. "You'd sleep through hell, if you had to go there."

"Ah," the soft voice said, "you don't wake me to tell me about hell, I hope!"

"Why, no," Slade said. "I woke you so you'd give our guest some room."

"Ho!" Argandeau said. "So the Griffons took another! Soon we begin to be crowded, I think."

Against the dim light that filtered through the hole in the hatch Marvin saw Argandeau mount two steps up the ladder. "Mr. Griffon!" he called mildly. "Ho, Mr. Griffon! Rig the wind sail! I feel we are under way!"

A sentry's face appeared at the hatch. "'Oo the 'ell you calling Mr.

Griffin?" he demanded truculently. "We bloody well had enough of your Griffining!"

"Yes, well, you rig the wind sail," Argandeau said. "We choke to death here in this black sewer."

He came down the ladder, crouched beside Marvin and felt for his shoulder. "They are all Griffons, the English," he declared mildly, "with ugly, hairy faces like the hunting griffons of the Vendee. Similar as to whiskers, but less dependable and less aristocratic parentage. This ship of yours, what was she?"

"Barque *Olive Branch*," Marvin told him. "Three hundred and thirty tons, twenty-five men, ten six-pounders, of and for Arundel, from Canton."

"Six-pounders!" Argandeau exclaimed. "Good for nothing but shooting flying fish! Why you run from this cruiser? Don't you know she can knock you into fireplace wood?"

"I thought you were asleep during the chase, Argandeau," Slade interrupted.

"Ho," Argandeau said carelessly, "I hear in my sleep. I hear, even, that although you decide to fight and run, you do neither. Pfoo! Bang! And in one minute you are here, eh?"

Marvin cleared his throat. "Yes," he admitted uncomfortably, "yes. The only gun we fired blew up, and there was——" He checked himself. "There were important lives aboard. I don't mean my own particularly—I mean—I think—if there had been more time—I mean, I could have rigged a pendulum in the gangway. Even through the smoke I could have cleared her decks if I could have rigged a pendulum. With a pendulum we could have fired from an even keel, always. It was too late when it occurred to me—a pendulum——"

His voice died away. The silence that followed was broken by a faint, hoarse laugh from Slade. Marvin felt Argandeau's hand on his shoulder. "Yes, yes," the Frenchman said soothingly. "You have had an experience! I understand quite well! You rest now, and I speak to you of my *Formidable*. You say in English *Formidibibble*, I think, eh?"

"*Formidable!*" Marvin said wearily. "How did you come to call her *Formidable* when she wasn't?"

"No, no!" Argandeau murmured. "You be quiet. Do not speak of pendulums, or of anything, even. When word arrives in any port that Lucien Argandeau approaches in his *Formidable*, the ladies of that port, they flame with feeling! In every place—even in Martinico and Hispaniola—the girls cheer for the *Formidable* when she come, and weep for her when she go! For me they flame; for my *Formidable* they scream in exultation. She is gallant—swift like the frigate bird —swifter! Swooping on her enemies like the hawk, piff! In her I would fight any vessel, sailing in circles about those too large to take; laughing at them, ha-ha!"

"Yes, and here you are!" Marvin told him wearily. He buried his head in his arms and thought again of the words Corunna Dorman had spoken to him.

Argandeau was silent for a time. "I know what you feel, young man," he said at length. "You are sick, here in this cesspool. You think of your clean ship! You think of your home! You remember some sweet rabbit who has held you close—close! Your life drips out from you, here in the mud! You are all despair, eh?"

"I can stand it," Marvin said.

"Pooi! Of course!" Argandeau agreed. "On the sea, nothing is hopeless. We know that—we who have seen men washed from a ship's deck into eternity by a wave, only to be washed back again by the next."

"Got any water?" Marvin asked.

"They bring it to us soon. You listen, now. I tell you about Lucien Argandeau, because I have pleasure in speaking American, and I like very much your people. You notice my speaking of American, eh?"

"Yes," Marvin said numbly, "you speak very well."

"But of course! I am friends for three years with a beautiful rabbit from Boston. You know Boston?"

The words came slowly into Marvin's mind. "A rabbit? You were friends with a rabbit?"

"Ha-ha!" said Argandeau, "a stylish rabbit, very neat, very affectionate; a true angel, so that when she speak of returning to Boston, I say she go back to heaven."

"Oh, yes," Marvin murmured drowsily.

"Yes!" Argandeau sighed gustily. "I learn from the best of dictionaries—the sleeping dictionary. I have had a pocket full of them. *Epatant et pas chère, comme on dit, à Paris!* There is that about me, you understand, that is irresistible to rabbits! Now look: I tell you more about the brave Lucien Argandeau and his beautiful *Formidable*. In all the world, under my command, no vessel sail so fast. M-m-m-m-m-m! Like a bonito, she go Wheesh! Wheesh! Here, there, and then gone! Pooi!"

At the hatchway above there was a stir and rattling. A faint breath of air, still hot, but less foul than the nauseous steam that filled the hold, lightly touched Marvin's face, so that he knew a wind sail had been rigged. Argandeau's voice, droning out of a black void, fell soothingly on the ear. Marvin, dozing presently, dreamed that there were pleasant sounds, even in hell.

V

IN THE fetid hold of His Majesty's war brig *Beetle* there were close onto one hundred prisoners, forty-two of them Frenchmen from Argandeau's privateer schooner, thirty of them an unsavory lot from Slade's dark brig, and the remainder from the *Olive Branch*. Once a day one-third of all this sorry company were called from their filthy cavern, each man guarded by a marine with bayoneted musket. One by one, like dangerous beasts, they were herded and prodded upward, staggering and blinking, to the deck, where they were packed into a long-boat amidships and, ringed by sentries, allowed for a little time to rid their lungs of the effluvium that had poisoned them below.

So heady and so sparkling was the air, after their long breathing of noxious gases, that it mounted in them like wine, some becoming ill or dizzy, and others waggling their tongues as if, Argandeau said, they had been spliced with whalebone.

For two days the face of Argandeau remained a gray blur to Marvin—a gray blur from which emerged soft-voiced scurrilities concerning their captors, the English Griffons, and endless references to the rabbits—all of them rabbits of unrivaled beauty—who had succumbed to his charm in a hundred ports. Not until the second day after his capture was Marvin permitted to clamber up the ladder, preceded by Slade and followed by Argandeau and something more than a score of prisoners.

Accompanied by a marine as by a shadow, he went forward to the main hatch and emerged at last on deck. The sun beat down out of a pale sky, and the brilliance of its rays were so like an explosion in Marvin's eyes that he covered his head with his arms as he stumbled into the long-boat amidships.

"Excuse, please," Argandeau said. "I hold your arm because it is easy to fall against carronades or something when you come from that place."

When he could bear the light at last, Marvin cleared the moisture from his cheeks with hands that seemed to him strangely unsteady, and peered aft in the hope of seeing Corunna Dorman on the quarter-deck. The stern was screened from him, however, by the swelling belly of the main course; and as Argandeau pulled him down on a thwart of the long-boat, he turned to look for the first time at his new acquaintance.

He saw a man who seemed, by comparison with himself, almost short—a man whose shoulders sloped downward from his full throat as those of a bottle slope away from its neck; so that it was hard to say where his neck ended and his shoulders began. The shoulders sloped in turn into arms that reached almost to his knees. His ears were small and delicate as those of a child, and his short black hair grew in a widow's peak on his forehead with something of the appearance of a woolen wig.

All of him—face, hair, ears, arms, hands, shirt and trousers—was blotched and crusted with mud from the water casks on which he had lived and slept. All in all, there was that about him that suggested an ape strangely erect, but an ape none the less.

Marvin looked quickly at the other prisoners, who, urged forward by their guardian marines, were clambering into their long-boat, and saw that all of them were equally smeared with mud. He looked down at the hand with which he had rubbed the moisture from his eyes. That, too, was gray and mud-caked, and it came to him that his own appearance was no more agreeable than that of the others.

Marvin cast an eye aloft and around the horizon. The sultry breeze still held in the southwest. To leeward were a barque and a brig, and far back on their lee quarter, very faint, a sail. The barque, he knew, was the *Olive Branch;* the brig, therefore, must be Slade's *Graceful Kate* and the distant sail the *Formidable.*

"What's this craft doing without studding sails or royals?" Marvin asked. "It must be they're waiting for your schooner, Argandeau."

"Well, of course!" Argandeau said softly. "These are Griffons, sailing these vessels. Look there, at that poor *Formidable* so far astern she is no more than a small white flea! She sail twelve, thirteen knots, any day I have her. Put me on her quarter-deck and she run around this brig, pfoo! Like that! I am caught, it is true, but on a lee shore—yes; it is something that could happen to anyone, eh? To Surcouf; to Duguay-Trouin, even!" He glanced at Marvin. "Of course, I am not Duguay-Trouin, but be assured that if I had lived in the days of Duguay-Trouin, he would not have been ignorant of me!" He sighed pensively; then patted Marvin's hand. "Ask anybody in all South America, wherever you will. They tell you at once, 'But of course! Argandeau sail twice around Hispaniola while any Englishman trying to get from Dover to Calais!' Fourteen knots, whenever I take her out; but the Griffons, they cannot get more than eight, not ever. For me, she is a swan; for the Griffons, a dead skate. I tell you these Griffons do not know about sailing. They are nothing but mutton dealers and boot polishers, all loaded into vessels—nothing else! Nothing at all."

"That's right!" Slade said. "A lot of good stable boys were spoiled to make the British navy."

As if to prove Slade's assertion, tackles creaked behind them. Marvin saw the foot of the main course slowly rising. "Look there!" Argandeau laughed. "We take off more canvas, so to wait for my *Formidable*. I believe these Griffons cannot get even six knots from her!"

With the rising of the mainsail, Marvin turned again to the quarter-deck, which had become fully visible to the occupants of the long-boat. Forward of the cabin scuttle sat a woman, partly obscured by an awning; but from her dress of black silk and the brilliantly colored needlework that moved rhythmically in her lap, Marvin knew her to be Corunna Dorman. He half rose from his thwart: then, remembering the plight in which he was, sank back again.

Before Corunna stood Lieutenant Strope, though Marvin was able to see nothing of him save a pair of thin shanks protruding from abbreviated duck trousers. Yet they turned and postured, these legs, so that Marvin, in his mind's eye, saw Strope bending over Corunna in what he must have thought a position of fetching grace. From time to time, as the duck-trousered left knee thrust itself forward at a more acute angle, the rhythmic movements of the needlework were interrupted; and Marvin knew that Corunna's hands were idle so that she might more readily listen to the speeches of Lieutenant the Honorable Vivian Strope.

He stared around him with something approaching desperation in his eyes; and the sight of the noisome, filthy crew that filled the long-boat seemed to him, for all the cruel clearness with which the morning sun exposed them, as unreal as the solemn absurdities of a fearful nightmare. His glance fell on the tall Indian, Steven, and he thought, even while he noted the dead appearance of his copper-colored skin and long black hair where the gray mud had caked on it, that this was never the same Steven with whom he had so often gone into the marshes of Arundel to hunt black ducks, but a Steven out of a dream.

"You are shaking," Argandeau said. "I think it cannot be the wind, which is cooking my nose like an egg after the days I have ripened and grown white in the dark. I think it must be the sight of that rabbit there on the quarter-deck, eh?"

The Indian, catching Marvin's eye, put his hand to his chest. "Dan'l," he said, "I wish I could get me something for this ache."

Marvin rose to his feet and spoke to one of the marines who stood in a watchful circle about the prisoners. "Get an officer," he said. "I want to speak to the quarter-deck."

The marine stared blankly; then burst into a guffaw of laughter.

Argandeau whistled shrilly, close beside Marvin's ear, and gesticulated wildly. It was the infant midshipman, Mr. Benyon, to whom he gesticulated and whistled, and after a moment's hesitation the child pushed his way between the marines to stand staring palely at Argandeau as though staring at a strange animal in a cage.

"Your lordship," Argandeau said, while Mr. Benyon fingered his dirk and dropped his under lip, "your lordship knows how it is the custom on all civilized ships, that the people or the prisoners of the ship may at will present their complaints or compliments to the quarter-deck."

"Complaints?" the boy asked. "You want to make complaints?"

"Your lordship is a seaman," Argandeau continued, "and can recognize the barbarity that led one of these dog soldiers to do nothing but yell with laughter when my friend"—he placed his hand on Marvin's shoulder—"asked to speak with your noble commander."

The boy looked severely at the marines who towered about him. "That's no way to act!" he said. "Wha'd you want to laugh for? You ain't on this king's brig to laugh! You better look out, or I'll make you laugh out of the wrong side of your mouth!" He turned importantly and, like a petulant child, jostled the marines from his path.

"Sugar!" Argandeau sighed. "It catches them all, both little and great, if you know the sugar they prefer!"

Five minutes later Marvin was marched to the quarter-deck by a marine; and there he stood alone, as shabby a figure as could be found in any gutter, while Lieutenant Strope hung over Corunna, crooking first his left leg and then his right leg as he murmured to her. Rage grew in Marvin as he watched the black-haired girl, with her head bent low over her woolen Holy Family, and the Englishman who hovered above her—rage at an officer who could countenance such treatment of his fellows.

In spite of his rage, he had no eyes for Strope; he looked at Corunna, though she had no look for him in return. Yet, as he watched her, she stirred uneasily and flushed; then, while the lieutenant still addressed her, she stabbed her needle through her square of embroidered canvas, rose abruptly and went to the lee rail, to stand and stare at the three small sail that swam mistily in the blue haze to leeward.

The lieutenant peered after her; then turned sulkily to Marvin. "What is it you want?"

"Sir," Marvin said, "one of our men is sick. He needs looking after. I'd be obliged, sir, if he could have some attention."

The lieutenant thrust out his head, like a crane in a marsh pool at the sudden movement of a minnow. "Sick? What's the matter with him?"

"An aching chest," Marvin told him.

"Oh, indeed!" the lieutenant said. "What a pity!" He suddenly became bitter. "This is a war, you fool! We haven't the time to hold the hands of those with hangnails and bruised knees! A sore chest, for Ged's sake! D'you think I have so little fever among my own men that I must bother with malingering prisoners? Get back where you belong and take up no more of my time with your demned Yankee notions!"

"Sir," Marvin persisted, "the food is bad and the water's worse. We're choking, all of us, and the bread's solid with weevils."

"Well, what of it?" the lieutenant exclaimed, in a passion. "Do you think we can draw up to a bread shop in mid-ocean and lay in a fresh supply?"

"No," Marvin said, "but you could put us aboard one of your prizes, where we'd be able to breathe. Why, you feed your hogs better than we're fed; yes, and treat them better too."

The lieutenant's lips tightened and he laughed unpleasantly. "I wonder," he said, "what England would do without America to point out her shortcomings! Let me tell you this! You're like all the rest of your countrymen! You need a taste of the cat to improve your manners!"

There was a shout from the maintop. Losing all interest in Marvin, the lieutenant glared peevishly upward.

A seaman hung over the maintop nettings. "Sail on the lee quarter, sir!" he bawled. "Astern the French schooner!"

Strope thumped his fist on the weather rail. "Be demned and be demned to that French tub!" he cried in a reedy voice. "Turn up all hands and about ship! There's a sail in chase of the Frenchman!"

The waist of the brig straightway became a turmoil of thudding feet, shouted orders, the creaking of blocks and the shrilling of boatswains' whistles.

"Prisoners below!" the lieutenant added. "Get 'em under hatches and be quick about it!"

He went to the lee rail and placed his hand gently on Corunna's arm. She moved impatiently beneath his touch, and to Marvin there seemed to be a trace of moisture at the corner of her eye.

The lieutenant stared at her vacantly; then turned quickly and vanished into the companionway.

To Marvin, hemmed in by the turmoil of sweating seaman and grotesque marines, there was something crushed and forlorn about that figure on the quarter-deck—a figure that seemed to droop and waver in the blinding glare. In one small fleeting moment, he knew, he would be forced once more into the filth and stench of the *Beetle's* hold; and in his desperation he felt his heart must burst unless he could tell her how he grieved for her, and get from her in return just one word to cherish.

Hoping to be unnoticed in the tumult, he stepped beyond the mainmast. "Corunna," he said huskily, "Corunna——"

She turned a haggard face to him. Her drooping shoulders straightened. Her glance, hard and bitter, slipped past him to the mud-stained prisoners clambering from the long-boat; to the tall Indian, stooped with his wracking cough. Then her eyes stabbed sharply into his, and in them Marvin saw a look of terrible reproach and more terrible contempt—a look that said, as clearly as any words, "You did this! Coward!"

"Corunna——" he said again huskily.

The butt of a musket struck him between the shoulders. "Garn!" the marine cried furiously. "Garn below!"

Marvin stumbled forward, and Slade caught him by the arm. "Back to hell with us, eh?" the slaver captain said, and laughed. "You look like a man that's dead, and buried, too; but cheer up. There may be more than us in hell tonight, my boy! It's in my mind that something's coming down the wind and may be playing Yankee Doodle!"

VI

T<small>HE LADDER</small> had been drawn up through the square hole in the hatch, and around the hatch coamings were stationed four marines to make the security of the prisoners doubly sure. Below the hatch, in the blackness of the sweltering, reeking hold, there was a hubbub such as Marvin had never before heard; for the prisoners, tense from the lack of knowledge of what awaited them, screamed their hatred of British ships, British officers, British methods and British seamanship in language as foul as the air they breathed.

"If we had a belaying pin!" Marvin told Argandeau. "If we had anything at all, we might get ourselves out of this!"

"Ah, yes," Argandeau agreed, but with no conviction in his voice, "yes. And if we had a belaying pin, it would be myself who would be the first man to lead such a sortie. It would be unpleasant for the first three, four or five men who would ascend with me, but I would hearten them with my cries, and always they would say to themselves, 'Argandeau! Hah! Argandeau is with us,' and so——"

Marvin sighed deeply. "Well, we haven't any belaying pins."

"No," Argandeau agreed. "And so, since we have no belaying pin, would it not be better to go quietly to sleep?"

The bed of mud quivered beneath them, and from overhead there came an angry, muffled crash that set the thick, hot air to crawling on their faces. The cries of the prisoners died away, to be replaced by the noisy silence of a ship—the creakings and groanings of bulkheads, far-off thumps and rattlings, and above and through everything the chuckling and slapping of water against thin walls of plank.

"Now we find out something," Argandeau said softly. "The Griffons have spit out a pill."

"In that case," Slade said, "the stranger couldn't have run. She must have gone to work on your schooner."

"I fear it!" Argandeau said. "It would be like attacking a kitten whose leg has been broken—so easy!"

There was a quick change in the sound of the water that lapped against the brig's sides. The noise of slapping became a rushing swish; the vessel straightened, hesitated, seemed to hang motionless, and then tilted in the opposite direction.

"Yes," Argandeau continued. "What you say is true, Captain Slade. The stranger did not run. She awaited the approach of this Griffon's nest we're in: then she maneuvered. In no other way can our change of course be explained. If the stranger had not maneuvered, our English captain would have kept straight on. Yes, yes! And certainly the stranger would never maneuver against this brig unless he considered himself faster and better. No, no! If he were small and not confident, he would betake himself elsewhere, and in a straight line, without maneuvering! He would go quickly to a smaller tree in order to sharpen his claws." He sighed. "Observe, my friends, how the mind of a Frenchman is clear and logical, even in a moment of stress! I sweat with doubt and uncertainty: yet my imagination moves swiftly and unerringly, eh?" He grunted. "But none the less, I sweat! I, Lucien Argandeau, I am all brain and sweat! It is the waiting that causes the sweat, you understand: the waiting and the darkness, here in this Griffon kennel—this stinkpot. This waiting in a dark hole, I do not like! In the daylight, I care for nothing. I snap my fingers at a shipful of lions, pfoo! But to be caught so, in blindness! Bah!"

He rose suddenly from his place beside Marvin, seeming almost to bounce silently to his feet, and stood beneath the square opening in the hatch. "Yes," he said. "It must be that they have piped to quarters. And they have done something more. They have sent that rabbit from the quarter-deck. They have sent her below, to protect her from splinters and grapeshot. What a pity it is that I, Lucien Argandeau, am not free to comfort her! She is frightened; but the most frightened rabbit becomes calm, like a peaceful swan, when Lucien Argandeau comforts her. It is one of my talents—one of my smaller gifts."

Marvin and Slade rose from their places to stand close beside him. "How do you know they've sent her below?" Marvin whispered. "What did you hear?"

"I heard a rabbit!" Argandeau said. "That is something I make no mistake about, ever, because I have had great experience. I would not hear her unless she had come down the ladder."

"How did you know she was frightened?" Marvin asked.

"Rabbits are always frightened," Argandeau said calmly. "Also, this one is weeping, and she said to someone, 'Let me alone! Let me alone!' If you will listen, maybe you hear her."

"Hoist me up," Marvin said. "Let me climb on your shoulders."

"If you're thinking of trying to go up," Slade said, "you're mad! You'll get a bayonet in the face and they'll clap the grating on the rest of us!"

"Hoist me up!" Marvin repeated. "She's not frightened! Nothing ever frightened her. There's something here I don't understand."

They took him on their shoulders, steadying him by clutching his knees. He crouched just below the level of the hatch, listening. Beneath him the voices of the prisoners again swelled to a wild tumult of shouting. Marvin turned his head from side to side, striving to catch some sound from Corunna, but he could hear nothing save the cries of his comrades in misfortune, the lapping of the seas against the *Beetle's* bends and a rush of feet from the deck above.

Argandeau shook him impatiently by the ankle. "What you think you are doing up there? Picking coconuts?"

The words had scarcely left his lips when Marvin pitched sideways. The three of them fell in a heap. In the darkness of the hold the whole world seemed to reel and stagger. "Take care!" Argandeau said, and though his voice was gentle it almost echoed in the hold's dark stillness. "Guard yourselves! We luff to, and now will come something! Those who rest against the planking, move clear, unless you wish broken bones!" He quickly repeated the words in French.

Beneath them the brig steadied, only to burst at once into a paroxysm of gigantic jerkings and tremblings, accompanied by a thunderous roar. She had, Marvin knew, let off her broadside, which must mean that the *Beetle* had come to close quarters with her adversary; for he had seen that the bulk of her guns were carronades, useful only at short range. His muscles ached from the tightness that had come into them—a tightness that grew ever greater as he waited for the enemy vessel to let off her broadside in return.

Into his mind there came a picture of the Arundel marshes, empty and silent within their walls of spruce and maple, and of a marsh hawk dropping with outspread claws on a helpless animal that could neither fight nor run, and so lay flattened against the marsh, waiting. He thought, too, how for years there had been glib talk of war in the shipyards and taverns of Arundel and a hundred other towns; and it came to him that not one of those who talked had ever thought of such a war as this—a war in which men lay in the dark and hoped that death would pass them by.

"Do you think they sank her?" he asked Argandeau, and he hurried his words, to get them out before they should be smothered and lost in the crash of the stranger's guns.

"Ha!" said Argandeau, and to Marvin his voice seemed somewhat breathless. "Not with carronades! You know what I think?" He made a faint sound of protest in his throat, as though he found some slight discomfort in the caked mud on which he rested.

"What?" Slade demanded, and his voice trembled with irritation. "Say it, damn it!"

"What I think——"

Again the mud beneath them jerked and shook, and continued to do so irregularly, as though the brig had burst into a spasm of gigantic coughs.

Slade laughed harshly. "I should say they *hadn't* sunk her. That's random firing! That means the stranger's closing with us, and it's every gun crew for himself!"

"What I think," Argandeau continued gently, "is that this stranger has one large long gun, and is maneuvering to rake the Griffons with it."

There was silence again in the hold. Marvin pulled desperately at Argandeau's arm. "Hoist me up again," he said. "I've got to try to see—to try to see——"

Somewhere astern, Marvin heard a grinding smash, the sound of timbers violently rent, and the heavy roar of a long gun.

"Piff!" Argandeau exclaimed. "Close, that one!"

The sound of cries came into the hold, and the spongy spatter of musketry fire. Marvin rose to his knees, only to be thrown down once more by the clangorous shock of the *Beetle's* broadside. The long gun of the enemy vessel bellowed a second time, so close that it seemed to Marvin he could almost feel the brig's planking bend before it like a beaten drumhead. Prisoners scrambled and tumbled over him, to stand cursing and screaming beneath the opening in the hatch.

Argandeau grunted. "God be praised!" he said. "They are aiming that pill bottle at the deck, like wise men! I tell you this, too: If they come closer, they will give their pills by hand instead of from the bottle!"

In Marvin's throat there was a taste of brass, and his tongue seemed to him to lie as thick and lifeless in his mouth as the salt-hardened sole of a sea boot. What he was passing through, he told himself, could not be real; like evil dreams that he remembered, it had the semblance of something that would never end; of something so dark and so terrible that his strength and his wits had deserted him together, leaving him panting and palsied.

The brig lurched suddenly and pitched forward—a small movement by comparison with the hammer blows of her broadside; but to the *Beetle's* miserable human cargo it brought an even deeper silence than the guns had brought.

Argandeau caught Marvin by the arm. "They board!" he whispered. "They have turned on this brig and outsailed her, and they have laid her aboard at the stern. Ah, my God! Now I sweat indeed! Compared with this, my other sweating was no more than the perspiration of a flea!"

The uproar that arose on the *Beetle*'s deck came to them like the closer and closer raging of a storm. Above the continuous rattle of small arms they heard the howling of men, the shouts of officers, the shrilling of whistles, the beating of a boarding drum, and a rush of feet like the scuttling of innumerable giant mice.

And there was something more. From the opening in the hatch above Marvin's head there came a girl's voice—the voice of Corunna Dorman. To Marvin it seemed to weep and to implore, as if in a frenzy of fear.

"Here!" Marvin shouted. "Here!" He would have risen to his feet but for Argandeau's grip on his arm.

"Softly! Softly!" Argandeau said. "Something drop down in here! Who has that thing?"

He was gone, then, from beside Marvin, but through the continued uproar from above, Marvin could hear him calling: "Who has that? Give me! Give me!"

"It came through the hatch!" Slade told him, his voice shaking a little, as if from cold. "I heard it strike."

Argandeau's soft voice was close beside them once more. "This is something wrapped in the clothes of a rabbit!" he told them. "I tell by the odor! Ah!" He exhaled ecstatically. "Wait now; I am unwrapping! Ah! Ah! Knives—three knives! . . . Wait, now! . . . Four—five knives; one pistol! We have one pistol; five knives!" He took Marvin by the shoulder with a hand that trembled. "You know about throwing the knife, eh?" he asked.

"I never tried," Marvin said. "I'll stick to my fists."

"Fists!" Slade cried derisively. "What good are fists! Give me one of those knives! I've thrown a knife since I was a baby!"

"Now wait!" Argandeau said. "I am very fine with the knife—very well and very quick! You ask any man in Hispaniola!" He paused, seemingly to listen to an outburst of hoarse cheering from above. Hard on the heels of the cheering came another thunderous roar from close astern.

"Hear me now," Argandeau ordered. "Come close, all who can. I want the red man from the captured barque."

"Steven," Marvin said.

"I'm here, Dan'l," said a voice from the thick dark.

"Yes," Argandeau continued, "Steven and Aubert and Jonneau and Marvin."

Voices answered, close at hand.

"Listen, now," Argandeau said, "and see that this is told correctly to those who cannot hear. We have knives here. Four tall men will make a ladder, and we will go up and take this stinkpot from the damned British. You hear me?"

A rumble of voices answered him.

"Yes," Argandeau said, "whoever is trying to take this brig has been beaten off once, but will try again; and if you do not want to rot here in this hole, frying with heat and eating filth and choking, you will come up and help us. On deck there will be dead men, and wherever there are dead men there are weapons to be had for the taking. I go up—I, Captain Argandeau of the *Formidable!* When the English see me, they will be weak with terror! You understand? I go up first with Captain Slade. When we say come, step quickly on the shoulders of these four tall men, and there will be an end of this hell."

Marvin felt himself pressed against a group of men. "Lock the knees and brace the feet," Argandeau said. "Slade and I, we carry all the knives. Hold us at the height of your shoulders until we have drawn ourselves up; then push up the others. You understand? Throw them! Do not delay. Soon there will be the ladder for the remainder; ropes also."

"For God's sake," Slade protested, "stop talking!"

"Come, now!" Argandeau said. Again the vessel lurched and staggered forward. Far above them burst a storm of shouting and musket shots. Marvin hooked his knee inside Steven's, bracing his other foot against the flooring of caked mud. Slade, breathing heavily, stepped on their knees, then on their shoulders. Marvin saw his head against the dim grayness of the hole in the hatch, and beside it the bullet-head of Argandeau. They crouched there silently, steadying themselves; then rose upright together. Marvin felt Slade's feet press hard against his shoulder, and knew that he had thrown a knife. Immediately there was another quick pressure: then a sharp downward thrust as Slade leaped upward through the hatch.

A man fumbled at his arm, caught at his hair and went on up. Sweating, Marvin seized another, and another. There was a thudding overhead; the hatch came slowly off and the ladder slipped down past Marvin's face. Marvin threw himself at it and scrambled panting into the half light of the berth deck.

VII

Marvin, followed close by Argandeau, scrambled silently into the glaring sunlight and uproar of the brig's gun deck. A sweating marine, close by the hatch coaming, spat a bullet into the muzzle of his musket and turned, as he rammed it home, to stare wide-mouthed at the mud-smeared scarecrows rising in his rear. Marvin's fist struck hard against his jaw. His open mouth and eyes snapped shut; his neck stretched, rubber-like; his body rose as if to balance on his heels. Argandeau reached forward quickly, snatching the musket from his nerveless hands. The marine fell heavily beneath their feet.

On the quarter-deck a squirming throng of men struggled like animals packed tightly in a cage, howling and roaring as they fought. Jets of smoke stabbed from their pistols; cutlasses rose and fell spasmodically among them.

Over their heads was thrust the bow and long jib-boom of a towering schooner, the tip of the boom lodged and tangled in the *Beetle's* mainsail. At the schooner's main peak the American ensign fluttered in the burning southwest breeze.

Half-naked men ran like ants from the schooner's bow, cutlasses in hand, to leap from the high bowsprit into the dense mass beneath. In the rigging of the schooner were men with muskets, jerking about like jumping jacks as they fired and loaded; while the ratlines of the *Beetle* were filled with marines whose muskets spat smoke and pale flashes at the teeming deck of the enemy vessel.

At the taffrail, Lieutenant Strope held himself above the struggling men by clinging to the schooner's dolphin striker. Thus sustained, he thrust and hacked with a reddened saber at the men who hurled themselves, their faces contorted and their torsos adrip with perspiration, among the British seamen.

A marine, clinging to the foremast ratlines, spied the mud-stained horde emerging from the hatch and raised a faint, thin cry of warning. In the very moment of its utterance, Argandeau threw the knife that lay along the palm of his right hand. It passed through the ratlines with the swift flight of a swooping bird and buried itself in the glistening breast of the marine, who ceased his outcry to spread his arms apart and stare down in blank amazement at the knife hilt. So staring, he toppled slowly backward and vanished soundlessly below the bulwarks.

One man, and then another, turned from the press that swarmed and milled at the break of the quarter-deck, to stare in horror at the swelling array of prisoners; then, shouting hoarsely, pulled at the arms of their fellows. Marines leaped from the ratlines, wrenching at their cumbersome swords.

"Haul down! Haul down!" Argandeau shouted. Swinging his captured musket by the muzzle, he leaped toward one of the advancing marines and brought it against his head with such force that the wooden stock split.

Almost from between the legs of the advancing Englishmen darted the diminutive Mr. Benyon, clutching in both hands an enormous horse pistol. "No quarter!" he screamed. "No quarter!" He snapped the pistol in Marvin's face and, when it missed fire, strove to hurl it at him. Over-balanced in the attempt, he sprawled ignominiously on the deck. Marvin lifted him by the belt and tossed him backward, over the heads of the yelling prisoners.

"Haul down! Haul down!" Argandeau bellowed again. With the stockless musket he smashed the arm of a man whose cutlass was swinging toward his head. "We kill all! Haul down!"

Armed by now, the shouting prisoners hurled themselves on the English who, falling back before the sabers, gun rammers, muskets and belaying pins wielded by these mud-caked figures, were pressed into a mob so dense as almost to prevent the use of weapons.

"Haul down!" they roared. "Haul down!"

Empty hands rose in the air beyond Marvin. "Quarter!" cried an English voice; and the word was repeated here and there like the drops of a rainstorm; first slowly, then with a sudden burst.

There was a movement of the blood-red ensign at the *Beetle's* mainpeak. "She's struck!" Marvin cried. "Belay! She's struck!"

Beyond the upraised hands of the *Beetle's* men, Marvin saw the thin, stooped figure of Lieutenant Strope. His hat was gone, his face the color of canvas fresh from the storeroom. The single epaulette on the shoulder of his coat was shorn in two, and the arm beneath it hung useless. He shook the hilt of his upraised saber at the men who reached with eager hands for ensign halyards.

"No!" he shouted, in a voice that quavered and broke. "Put it back! I say no! I say no!"

A seaman on the bowsprit of the enemy schooner caught at a stay, swung forward and brought down a cutlass on the lieutenant's un-

protected head, shouting angrily, as he did so, "*Tais toi!*" The lieutenant slipped from Marvin's sight; and amid an ecstatic screaming
that seemed to him almost feminine, the British ensign came down
on the run.

Marvin turned quickly to push his way through the howling prisoners toward the hatch from which they had emerged, when he was
caught by the neck in an embrace so violent that he could think of
nothing save that there was further fighting to be done.

"Ah, ah, my brave child!" Argandeau shouted in his ear. "Don't
we make these Griffons wish they have not rubbed mud into the
beard of Argandeau, eh?" The Frenchman whirled him about, took
his face between two sweaty hands and kissed him on the lips. "I
see you hit that gentleman like a horse kick! I take you to fight with
me anywhere! Ha, ha! We serve the Griffons mashed and *en
brochette*, eh? You with the fist and me with the knife, no?" Holding Marvin by the shoulders still, he danced lightly before him; then
kissed him again with fervor.

Marvin pushed him away. "Where's Corunna?" he demanded.

"He means the rabbit!" Argandeau cried. "Why have you not told
me she is yours? Ah, but she is more pigeon! A true pigeon! You
know where we are this minute—now, if that sublime pigeon had
not helped us? We are down there in that stinkpot with mud in the
ear, and nothing to look forward to but mud in the other ear! Oh,
but Holy Christophe, Marvin, there is a pigeon whom I would be
willing to acknowledge as the mother of my children!"

He drew up his shoulders, then, and smiled affectionately. "Why
you look angry because I make a graceful compliment?" he asked.
"I tell you there are women who have sickened and died for lack
of one kind word from Argandeau! Not more than one hundred
times in my life have I paid such a tribute as I have paid to your
pigeon! In Hispaniola men go for miles to look with admiration at a
rabbit of whom Argandeau has been known to say that he would
be willing to acknowledge her as the mother of his children."

"We don't need to go into that," Marvin said.

As if to himself Argandeau murmured, "He means I may think
about his pigeon, but must never say what I think!" He shook his
head despairingly, then added, "You wish now to know the where-
abouts of your pigeon? Well, look there!" And he pointed to the
hatch where Slade, bending so low that his long black hair fell forward over his face, was at that instant helping Corunna to the deck.

"Why," Marvin said, with bewilderment in his voice, "why, he
didn't fight!" He stepped toward the two at the hatch, only to be

stopped by Argandeau once more. "Wait one little minute!" Argandeau ordered. "You do not please anyone by saying he did not fight, because he did. Oh, yes! He is very agreeable man with a knife; not complete artist, like me, but I think very good—very well!"

The tumult on the *Beetle's* quarter-deck grew louder and more shrill; and Argandeau, turning to cast a quick glance over his shoulder, stood staring at the man who picked his way almost daintily along the bowsprit of the victorious schooner.

He had an air of fragility to him, this man, that seemed to come less from his stature than from the snugness with which his cream-colored small clothes fitted around his slender waist and hips, and from the dark shadows beneath his black eyes. His face was palely brown; his head held high by the tall stiff collar of his fine blue coat.

"Look here at this!" Argandeau murmured, with a quality in his soft voice that turned Marvin's eyes from Corunna's flushed face. "Here is something wonderful! Out of this American schooner arrives one of the great men of France!"

Argandeau took Marvin by the arm and hurried him toward the quarter-deck. On the bowsprit, which hung like a suspended sword above the conquered British brig, stood the fragile, shadowy-eyed man, staring down at the howling, blood-stained throng who cheered him, and at the dead and wounded who lay among them and ringed them round. He spoke brusquely to those beneath, and at once dropped lightly to the deck to stand beside the body of Lieutenant Strope.

"This brave gentleman," he said in a penetrating, nasal voice, "is dead! Who commands here?" He looked sharply about him; then nodded slowly at the young officer who stepped forward. "I am Captain Diron," he said. "Private armed schooner *Decatur*, Charleston. I think I have been assisted in taking this vessel."

The young officer laughed abruptly, but there was no amusement in the sound. "If it hadn't been for that rabble," he said, moving his head contemptuously toward the vessel's bow, "we'd have cut you to pieces!"

Captain Diron studied him attentively. "Ah, yes!" he agreed. "No doubt!" The seamen behind him set up a growling, at which he abruptly wagged a finger in their faces. "Loysel!" he called. "Loysel! Be quick! Attend these English wounded and our own. Take what men you need! Mr. Safifth! Take charge of this brig and place her in order for the prize crew. Mr. Wasborn! Cast loose the schooner and lay her alongside."

Argandeau sniffed suddenly, and Marvin saw that although he

was smiling almost proudly at this brown-faced, fragile captain, there were tears in his eyes and wet smears on his mud-incrusted cheeks. At the sound of the sniff, the eye of the *Decatur's* captain fell on Argandeau.

"So!" Diron exclaimed. "You are the one!"

Argandeau lifted an eyebrow and shook his head. "With the help of these lion-hearted men it was nothing, Dominique! A lark hunt!"

Diron came quickly to him and kissed him first on one cheek, then on the other. Someone among the silent spectators laughed loudly.

Diron stepped back from Argandeau and swept the crowded quarter-deck with a hard black eye. "Get forward, those without business here!" he ordered.

The seamen about them thinned like smoke before the wind, and as they swirled and scattered, Slade moved from behind them, followed closely by Corunna Dorman. At the sight of her, Diron whipped off his hat, held it tight against his breast and bowed abruptly, with a questioning side glance at Argandeau. "Madame," he said, "your servant! I am most unhappy I do not know sooner that——"

"Yes," Slade said hoarsely. "Captain Argandeau might have mentioned her before." He pushed back his long black hair with a sweep of his hand. "We'd be down there yet if she hadn't brought us knives."

Argandeau smiled pleasantly at Slade. "Piff! You touch me! It should have been my duty to tell this thing with my first breath!"

Diron bowed again to Corunna. "Then you are a brave lady, I think. I have been in debt many times, but never to one so young and beautiful."

She made him the shadow of a curtsy. "Why," she said, "you'll owe me nothing if you get back the *Olive Branch* for me. Did you retake her?"

"That barque?" Diron asked. "She was yours, that barque?"

Corunna nodded.

Diron looked at Argandeau, as if seeking denial of Corunna's statement. Finding none, he glanced uncertainly around the quarter-deck. Two of the *Decatur's* seamen raised the body of a British sailor from the scuppers, swung it over the taffrail and let it fall. The splash seemed to put a thought in Diron's head.

"But such sights!" he cried. "They must be painful to a lady!"

"No, Captain," Corunna said quietly. "These people killed my father."

Diron held up a protesting hand. "It is necessary that I examine the papers in the cabin. You shall come there, where we can talk quietly." He turned to Argandeau. "Give me a few moments, my friend, and then we will speak fully together. I see now that it was your schooner we sank. Like a gourd, she was—so thin—and sailed by men who could contrive to foul her jib-boom in her own staysails! I am sad about this!" He patted Argandeau on the shoulders, kissed him again on both cheeks; then beckoned to Corunna and walked quickly to the companionway.

"Corunna!" Marvin said. "Corunna!"

She turned to Slade, seeming not to hear Marvin. "You'll come with me, won't you, Captain?" Slade, following her down the companionway, glanced up at Marvin from under his drooping eyelid with what seemed to Marvin like malicious mockery.

"Listen, my friend," Argandeau said, holding Marvin by the arm, "my *Formidable* is gone! Nowhere was there a craft so beautiful or so swift, and now she is gone!"

"It's too bad," Marvin said absently. "Too bad."

"I tell you, my friend," Argandeau said, "it is bad, yes; but not too bad. Nothing is too bad. If you lose a ship, you will find a better one. If you lose a woman, you have not lost the only woman there is. Look at me, eh? I am gay! That is why I am loved by my friends, by the rabbits, by everyone!" He pointed a foot delicately, flung up an arm and struck a pose. "We will visit now with my friend, Dominique Diron. For him, too, nothing is too bad. He is brave, like a lion; and why not! He has learned from observation! He served with me on the letter of marque *Superbe*. There was one time when we were surprised and attacked, Dominique and I, by two British cruisers. For three nights and two days we fight them off. We laugh and are gay. Ha! Ha! They cannot catch us—those two Griffons. We run the *Superbe* ashore and escape, all of us!"

"Yes, but this time they caught you," Marvin reminded him.

"Caught me?" Argandeau said. "Caught me? Who has caught me? Look at me carefully! 'Ah-hah,' you say to yourself, 'I behold Argandeau, who did not wish to remain caught, and therefore is a free man!' But come; we wash the mud from ourselves and go to see Dominique."

VIII

THE CAPTAIN'S CABIN of the *Beetle* was hot as an oven, and almost as small. Diron, his coat stripped off, sat before the center table, whereon was a litter of papers. Beside him sat Corunna; and when Marvin saw how Slade hovered over her shoulder, as if fearful that she might topple from her locker unless guarded, it seemed to him suddenly that this cabin was not less dismal than the hold had been.

Diron smiled affectionately at Argandeau. "You have arrived at the precise moment," he said. "You have not been presented to this lady, she has told me."

Argandeau bent his woolly, close-cropped head in a quick bow. "But I have had a gift from her, only today, that will make her live forever in my heart. No, I have not been presented to her, but I know her well; she is so kind that I shall never find time to say to her how kind she is."

Diron opened his mouth in a soundless laugh. "As you see, Miss Dorman, a dangerous man!" To Argandeau he added: "Thanks to me, Lucien, you shall have the opportunity to try; and for you it should be a good affair. This lady has kindly consented to take you and your crew to France, together with my wounded and the English wounded."

"To France?" Marvin asked quickly. "She has consented to go to France?"

"She has been so kind," Diron said. "The whole plan has come into my head like that, Lucien!" He snapped his fingers, glancing from Marvin to Corunna and back again; then addressed himself to Argandeau once more. "I thought for a time of taking you back to Charleston with me, Lucien; but the Americans, they do not have enough vessels of their own for privateering. For every American vessel there are a thousand American captains. But in France there are many vessels; fast ones—more vessels than captains. You assist this lady to go there, then, and maybe she assist you to get another vessel."

"Just a minute, Captain," Marvin said. "I don't understand this talk of France."

Corunna looked up at him angrily. "It's not necessary that you should."

Marvin drew a deep breath. "Don't talk that way, Corunna. What's France to us? Home's where we want to be."

Slade threw back his head to stare at Marvin from beneath his drooping lid. "You must have heard what the lady said."

"Just a minute, Corunna," Marvin persisted, ignoring Slade. "You can't afford to rush into anything like this. As I see it, the way to go home is to go home; and it's no good to say it isn't necessary for me to understand about it. It appears to me, Corunna, that I'm responsible for you. I've got as much right as anyone to know what you're planning to do."

"*You're* responsible?" she cried, rising to her feet, her hands clenched and her face colorless. "*You've* got the right? I'll have you understand that I allow no squeamish boy to be responsible for what I do or where I go. And of all men, you're the last I'd let question my decisions."

Captain Diron leaned forward in his chair. "It is all so simple," he said candidly, "that I think possibly you make a mistake not to tell the gentleman. It would be a pity if he smelled here a mystery where there was none!" He smiled gently at all the persons in the stifling little cabin.

"You see," he said, stretching out his hand, palm up, toward Marvin, "I have sacrificed a great deal to take the *Olive Branch;* for if I had not wished the barque for myself, I would not have fought this war brig, and so lost several men and suffered grave damage. It is not the business of a privateer to entangle himself with enemy cruisers. The odds against him are too great. You see that, I hope, sir."

Marvin nodded.

"Of course!" Diron continued, as frank and open a gentleman in his speech, Marvin thought, as he had ever heard. "Of course! Therefore, it seems to me only reasonable that I should ask a small favor from this lady in return for giving back her valuable property. After all," he reminded Marvin mildly, "title to the *Olive Branch* passed to the British when they took her, and to me and my crew when we retook her."

"The taking," Marvin persisted, "was not all on your side. Some of the taking was done by us, at some risk to ourselves. Meaning no offense, I must venture to remind you that our American courts might be more than sympathetic to this lady, if she should present her claim against yours."

Diron waved his hand languidly. "I find your reference to courts distasteful. There is a flavor of commercialism about it. It is difficult to remember, at times, that such a thing as chivalry still exists." He coughed deprecatingly. "Now this favor I have asked; in reality I have asked for nothing. In reality I have done a favor to the lady by suggesting to her how to act. Look here; there are British cruisers on your American coast as thick as bones in a herring. Your barque is slow; and if you run for home, you are nearly certain to be taken by a British frigate. But the nearer you come to England, the fewer English war craft you will see, for that has always been the custom of the English—to harry the enemy in his own waters. Captain Argandeau will tell you this is so."

Argandeau placed his knuckles above his eyes, with the forefingers extended. "I would be willing to sail into any English harbor this minute," he said, almost with indifference, "and make horns at the Griffons!" He wagged the forefingers.

"Of course!" Diron exclaimed. "With all the English far from home, therefore, your barque can run safely into a French port, where there will be a ready market for her cargo. And if, on the way, you should be overhauled, you will have enough men aboard to fight off a heavy vessel."

Slade nodded thoughtfully. "We'll have enough men to *take* a vessel, if we should feel like it—enough to take more than one, if they're not large ones."

Marvin stared at Slade and half rose to his feet, but sank back on his locker when Diron tapped him on the arm. "You see," Diron told him earnestly, "there will not only be the added safety of the route, but there will be these two fine seamen, Captain Slade and my friend, Captain Argandeau, to assist the lady with their knowledge and advice. Captain Argandeau, he knows the coast of France as he knows his own thumb."

"I know it better," Argandeau said. "There is no part of it that I could not recognize on the darkest night, which is more than I can say of this." He held up a grimy thumb and with it polished an imaginary spot before his eyes. "There is no port in all France where there are not at least several people related to me—" he stopped; then added, with an ingratiating smile—"by marriage."

Diron raised his eyebrows and held out his hands. "What more could one wish?" he asked Marvin. "I think it is great good fortune for the lady and for all of you that you encounter us."

"I admit it," Marvin said readily. "Still, there are a few small points that I might mention——"

"Yes," Corunna interrupted, "you might! Of course you might! But you needn't! I consider myself fortunate to have the advice of these gentlemen, and I've taken it!"

"Yes," Marvin said patiently, "but what's Captain Slade doing aboard the *Olive Branch?* He's got a brig of his own—a slave brig. That hasn't been destroyed, has it?"

"Mr. Marvin," Slade said a little ceremoniously, "I think I must ask you to use another tone of voice when referring to my occupation. After all, Mr. Marvin, John Paul Jones himself saw nothing wrong in officering a vessel on the Middle Passage."

"Is that an argument, Mr. Slade?" Marvin asked. "You can't make me respect the Portuguese by telling me that Vasco da Gama hailed from Portugal!"

Slade's voice was harsher than his words. "Any man who's had experience in these waters knows that it's doing a kindness to yonder poor black men to let them exchange the cruelties and sufferings of Africa for the comforts of a plantation."

Marvin looked hard at Slade; then turned again to Corunna. "Why is it he's deserting his own vessel to travel on ours? He's got owners, hasn't he?"

"He's traveling on the *Olive Branch* for good and sufficient reasons!" Corunna informed him. "I'll have you know that Captain Diron and Captain Slade are doing these things out of the kindness of their hearts, and to question them is outrageous!"

"I don't mean it so," Marvin said. "All I want, Corunna, is that you should give these things proper consideration. 'Tisn't in reason, Corunna, for Captain Diron to be asking favors of you for giving back the *Olive Branch*. She's yours anyway. He knows he couldn't keep the proceeds of her sale, because there isn't a prize court in America that would uphold him in it as long as you're alive to put in your claim."

Slade cocked his head on one side to look out from under his drooping eyelid. "A sea lawyer!" he exclaimed.

" 'Tisn't so much that I mind going to France," Marvin continued. "What I mind is seeing you deprived of your freedom to do as you like when you need to do it. Here you're hampering yourself with promises you don't need to make, and weighing yourself down with a lot of wounded men, and you're setting off for a strange country to sell your cargo—if you get there—in a market that'll skin you if it has the chance."

"You are speaking of the French markets?" Captain Diron

asked politely. "You have had unfortunate experiences with them, perhaps?"

"No," Marvin admitted, "but I never heard of a market that was in business for our benefit. There's another thing, too," he told Corunna: "You're entitled to hold any opinion of me that you wish, but you know my family, and you know that when your father needed help, he turned to my father, just as mine turned to yours when he needed anything. When all's said and done, Corunna, we're neighbors, and maybe that might still mean something to you. Now, I want no trouble with these gentlemen; but without meaning any offense, one of 'em's a Frenchman and the other's a slaver; and it seems to me, Corunna, that it's a strange thing when a girl from Arundel feels obliged to take advice from a slaver and a Frenchman —both of them gentlemen she never saw before."

"Pooi!" Argandeau exclaimed. "Now the slush bucket is kicked over!"

Captain Diron shrugged his shoulders. "This poor young man," he said, smiling at Corunna, "I think he does not know he is being so— what shall I say? We call it *gauche*. It is a fault of your countrymen, I fear."

"Oh," Corunna said, "it's shameful! To insult these gentlemen— how can you stand there and say such things of them—they, who only want to help me."

"Wait, Corunna!" Marvin begged her. "Can't you see it must be themselves they're helping? It *must* be! You're the only one who stands a chance of losing anything! Why, if Captain Diron was so anxious to help you, he could convoy you home, couldn't he, instead of sending you off to France, near to four thousand miles?"

"Of course," Captain Diron remarked pleasantly, "it might be disturbing for you if the young lady should be removed from your protection. I think it is possible you argue for your own benefit, eh?"

Marvin pressed his lips tightly together. "Couldn't you?" he persisted. "Couldn't you convoy us home?"

"You make me ashamed for you!" Corunna cried. "It isn't the first time!"

Slade's voice, it seemed to Marvin, set the chains of the hanging lamp to vibrating, so metallic was its harshness. "It's plain to see," he told Corunna, "that he considers himself your master."

Diron silenced him with a glance, and spoke courteously to Marvin. "Your question concerning a convoy, sir, is a fair one, but I have already answered it when I said that the *Olive Branch* is slow, and that English frigates are plentiful on your coast. You would hardly expect my schooner to engage a frigate. No schooner afloat would last five minutes, once she came within range of a frigate's guns."

"That's true," Marvin agreed, "but as you say, you fought the *Beetle* so you might get possession of the *Olive Branch,* and you must have ordered your prize crew to take her to Charleston rather than to France. Otherwise you would have made an argument out of it, I think."

Diron threw himself back in his chair, laughing heartily. "But you are suspicious, you Americans!" he exclaimed. "If you heard one of our French larks singing in the sky, you would say it was not a real lark."

"Well," Marvin said slowly, "I've never had much difficulty recognizing larks when I see 'em—or when I hear 'em. Some time ago I heard one of you gentlemen mention the fact that if the *Olive Branch* sets sail for France, she'll not only have enough men aboard to fight off a heavy vessel, but even to take a small one. That's a suggestion I'm able to recognize as easily as I recognize larks. It's a suggestion that the *Olive Branch* be used to make prizes of enemy merchant craft—or maybe of friendly ones." He looked hard at Slade, who tossed back his long black hair and coldly returned Marvin's gaze.

"If I'm not mistaken," Marvin went on, "that suggestion came from Captain Slade. He knows that none of us aboard the *Olive Branch* has a commission or a letter of marque entitling us to capture, burn, sink or destroy any enemy vessel. If we should attack one, we'd be in danger of being hanged at the yardarm—every last one of us. What Captain Slade suggested is piracy. While I'm in command of the *Olive Branch* I'll allow no such thing—and with Captain Dorman dead, I *am* in command."

Captain Diron placed his hand on Corunna's arm, as if to restrain her. "No, no!" he said. "You do not understand. Here on this table are the papers of Captain Argandeau, you see. Here is his letter of marque, my friend, for the *Formidable*. With these papers the *Olive Branch* will be the *Formidable* if she has occasion to attack any vessel, and still she will be the *Olive Branch* at all other times, eh?"

Corunna shook off Captain Diron's restraining hand. "Yes," she said, and to Marvin her eyes had the hardness of agates, "and you have forgotten that I am the owner of the *Olive Branch*. Therefore I have made myself captain, with Captain Slade as first mate and Captain Argandeau as second mate."

"What did I tell you about the slush bucket?" murmured Argandeau softly. "Two mules together could not more completely kick it over!"

IX

Cᴏʀᴜɴɴᴀ ᴅᴏʀᴍᴀɴ, impatiently pacing the weather side of the *Olive Branch's* quarter-deck, watched the last boatload of wounded rocking uneasily toward her from the near-by *Beetle,* escorted amidships by lazy-seeming sharks that rolled their eyes upward at the long-boat like affectionate dogs. The wounded who had already made the journey, twelve of them, were ranged close under the larboard bulwarks, where they might have the benefit of the steamy, sweltering breeze. All about them was piled the dunnage of the seamen who had come aboard and now clung to shrouds and ratlines to see the last of the *Decatur* and the *Beetle,* while the litter resulting from the capture of the *Olive Branch* still cumbered her decks and gave her an air of slovenly dejection.

Corunna, looking around suddenly, saw Slade smiling gravely at her, one eye half hidden by his drooping eyelid. There may have been meekness and modesty in the way he quickly lowered his glance, but there was little of modesty in his words or voice. "You're in danger, ma'am," he said, "wearing what might put to shame an empress and a bride."

She turned from him and peered over the taffrail. "I want somebody in the main chains," she said; "somebody with pikes or boat hooks to watch that boatload of wounded. The sharks'll have 'em over before we know it. I'll be obliged if you'll see to these things without having to be reminded of them, Mr. Slade."

Slade's exclamation seemed to have penitence in it as he jumped quickly for the vessel's waist; but quick as he was, Marvin was quicker. Almost as though he had heard Corunna's words, he came up the ladder of the main hatch, glanced at the approaching longboat, and at once swung himself around the main shrouds and into the chains, shouting for a sweep as he did so.

From Argandeau, at work with a crew on the wrecked carronade near by, there came a faint and abstracted humming.

> "Aux filles de bonnes maisons
> Comme il avait su plaire,
> Ses sujets avaient cent raisons
> De le nommer leur père,"

he sang softly. Corunna stared severely at his widow's peak of close-cropped hair; but seemingly he was oblivious to everything except the task in hand.

"Mr. Argandeau!" she said.

Argandeau straightened. "You need me, lady?"

"Yes," she said, "and I don't like the sound of 'lady.' You can call me Captain while we're aboard ship."

Argandeau bowed so deeply that his bullethead seemed lower than his knees.

"When these wounded men are aboard," she continued, "tell Mr. Slade to run up his jib and fore-topmast staysail and get under way. I want her kept north by west a half west. We'll pass to the westward of the Cape Verdes. Get the decks cleared and divide the men into watches. Then call the hands aft and send word to me. I want to speak to them."

"Yes, Captain," Argandeau said. "And Mr. Marvin? He is not an officer: therefore you let me choose him for my watch, perhaps. Then I give him lessons in many things." His gaze was candid. "When he has had a lesson or two from Argandeau, he will know how to throw the knife, how to be brave like a lion, how to make love so that every woman who sees him will pant for him." Modestly he added, "He has not had my advantages, poor fellow."

Corunna raised an indifferent eye to the clouds overhead. "I'm afraid Mr. Marvin must get along without your guidance for the remainder of this voyage," she said. "He's to be bos'n of this vessel."

"Ho-ho!" Argandeau said softly. "You put him where he must exercise that patience of which he is so proud, eh—nursing seamen and touching the hat to his betters! I think well! Very well!"

Corunna looked hard at him; then turned quickly and entered the cabin.

"Captain!" Argandeau murmured, skipping from the quarter-deck into the waist. "She is sugar cane! Captain Sugar Cane! With that to crunch, I would not recognize any other wife—not for a very long time!"

He swung himself into the main chains beside Marvin, who was splashing the twenty-four-foot sweep up and down beside the *Beetle's* long-boat as the last of the wounded men came over the side.

"Pull your front hair and say 'sir!'" Argandeau told him. "Maybe you think this is a French vessel, Mr. Bos'n, and that we are all equal, eh? All perfectly equal?"

Marvin stabbed with the long sweep at a gray shadow that flickered beneath the long-boat's stern. "Bos'n, eh?" he asked. "So she

decided to take me down a peg!" The sweep rose from the water as
lightly as a fishing rod, and fell again with a smack. "Well, it's all one
to me," he continued, "provided she gets me to a place where I can
do some damage to a little piece of England. I'm surprised she didn't
make me ship's cook, so she'd never have to look at me."

"If she had, my friend," Argandeau assured him, "it would be what
you deserve for saying to her that she must not do this and cannot
do that! That is something I learn about rabbits when I am six years
old and in love for the first time, or maybe the second. They are like
men, disliking to obey orders; and because they are built with nerves
in the brain that we do not have, they explode, Pfoo! inside the head,
when they are forbidden to do this or that. If they are timid, they
conceal the explosion; but later, when all is quiet, they take courage
and do what they have been forbidden to do. If they are not timid,
they snap the fingers in the face of those who forbid! Piff!" His
fingers clicked contemptuously beneath Marvin's nose.

A hoarse voice came up to them from the turbulence of the main
deck. "Isn't this a little early to begin criticizing a lady?"

Argandeau turned from Marvin and looked down into the upturned face of Slade. "Criticize?" Argandeau asked innocently. "I? I
criticize a lady? Never! I learn from ladies—learn only. I think, Captain, you might do the same to good advantage."

There was a rasp to Slade's laugh like the bite of a saw on wood.
"If I feel the need of lessons," he said, "I'll think about consulting
you."

"You will escape some trouble by doing it," Argandeau assured
him, "and you will also escape some trouble by getting this barque
under way and standing on quickly. The Captain, she told me to
tell you: North by west a half west."

"West!" Slade exclaimed. "You mean east!"

"East?" Argandeau whispered. "Is it east I mean? Now I am confused! She said west, I thought; but perhaps, as you say, it was east.
You must go quickly and ask her." He struck his forehead with his
hand. "My God, what horror if it should appear that Argandeau
could not repeat orders properly—that if he were told to raise the
ensign, he would let go the anchor instead! Oh yes! You must hurry
to the Captain and tell her it was not west, but east."

"We'll see about this!" Slade said. "Diron told her to make the Cape
Verdes!" His drooping lid seemed almost to close over his eye as he
stared up at Argandeau.

"Ah, yes!" Argandeau said thoughtfully. "Well, maybe she has forgotten what she was told. It is possible she does not realize that

Dominique intends to share the captaincy of this vessel with her, even after he has sailed away in his own schooner." He smiled innocently at Slade. "Perhaps," he continued, "perhaps you should go to her and inform her that she has made a mistake: that she is wrong: that her orders have not been to Dominique's liking. Perhaps, before it is too late, you should even send word to Dominique that he must come aboard once more and put his orders in writing, so they may never again be misunderstood by absent-minded ladies."

Slade peered over the bulwarks. The *Beetle's* long-boat, freed of her cargo, had pushed off from the *Olive Branch's* counter. A cable length away, the *Beetle* swayed lazily, her rigging filled with seamen busy repairing severed shrouds and stays; and behind her squat bulk the slender, raking masts of the *Decatur* towered high against the billowing pink clouds that hung above the streamy horizon. There seemed to be something of remoteness about the two vessels, despite their nearness, as though already they had forgotten the very existence of the *Olive Branch*. Slade ran his fingers through his long black hair, glanced uncertainly from Argandeau's face to the empty quarter-deck; then turned abruptly to the throng of seamen who were noisily sluicing from themselves the muck of their imprisonment in the *Beetle*.

"Set the jib and fore-topmast staysail!" he shouted hoarsely. "Man the lee fore brace! Slack away fore tack and stand by to swing the main yard!"

The *Olive Branch* fell off, the fore-topsail filled and she slowly wore into the northwest.

Corunna, Marvin saw, had come on deck, carrying a glass tumbler in her hand. She set it down carefully at the foot of the binnacle; then stood by the taffrail, staring back at the *Beetle*, her gray Chinese jacket and trousers dark against the glowing cloud banks beyond, and her smoothly combed black hair bound tightly in place by a thin red cord. Marvin jumped from the chains and ran aft. "Corunna," he said, "aren't you going to give 'em a gun?"

She turned slowly. "As bos'n of this vessel," she said, "I'll thank you to address the quarter-deck properly."

"Corunna," Marvin protested, "don't be like this, Corunna! You know there isn't anybody that——"

She moved away from him and glanced at the card in the binnacle. "Keep her so," she told the helmsman; then looked coolly at Marvin. "Give them a gun?" she asked. "It seems to me you're a little backward about guns! I think you'd better dip the ensign instead; that's more in your line."

He eyed her in silence, smiled faintly and moved to the ensign halyards.

She stamped her foot. "You think I'm pretending! You think I'm playing! Well, I'm not! I can sail this vessel as well as any man—better than most. I can fight the British as well as any man! Nobody hates 'em as much as I do, the murderers!"

Marvin, staring steadily at the masthead, carefully dipped the ensign three times, made fast the halyards and turned away. Forward of the main hatch he saw Slade, half concealed by the lumber amidships, staring at him; and the whiteness of that single eye seemed to Marvin to give the slaver's face a look of confident contempt.

Marvin turned back to her. "There's nobody like you, Corunna," he said. "You know how I feel about that."

"You had your chance," she reminded him.

He moved his hand vaguely. "You know how I feel," he repeated. "You're a woman, and women don't fight or captain vessels. There's something they haven't got, Corunna. They aren't hard enough, maybe. Maybe they do things too much from personal reasons. They're apt to be hasty, they're——"

She caught at his upper arm and half turned him toward her. "Let me look at you," she said solicitously. "I think it must be the heat that makes your head like this—all mixed and muddled. Why don't you put a little cool water on it, so not to hurt it permanently, trying to make it express all the things you don't know about women! Just belay all that, and step down to the main hatch and tell Mr. Slade to bring the men aft!"

She whirled and left him, to stand again at the taffrail, looking back at the brig and the schooner, already shrunken to the size of toys. Sighing, Marvin eyed the flatness of her back and the sturdiness of her shoulders; then went forward toward Slade.

For such a vessel as the *Olive Branch*, the throng of seamen who gathered at the break in the quarter-deck was as cumbersome as it was motley. There were a score of tall Yankees who had made up the original crew of the barque; another twoscore Frenchmen from Argandeau's schooner—short and swarthy men for the most part—and a jostling knot of shifty-eyed nondescripts from Slade's slaver. These last, Marvin decided, were sweepings from the foulest corners of the brown countries.

Sailors filled the waist of the barque from larboard to starboard bulwarks. They perched on carronade slides and clung to shrouds and backstays, scuffling and swaying and breaking into suppressed exclamations and hoarse, short bursts of laughter as they stared open-mouthed at the trousered figure of Corunna standing at the weather rail.

Slade pushed through them, mounted to the quarter-deck and spoke briefly to her, at which she advanced to the taffrail, set her hands on her hips and coldly eyed the grinning faces below.

"I'm the captain of this vessel," she said. "A few of you may have some difficulty getting that into your heads, but the sooner you get it, the better off you'll be. I've sailed in the *Olive Branch* for eight years. I know her better than any man alive, and I can get more out of her. I aim to bring all of you safe to land; and when that's done, I aim to fight the British for what they did to my father. I'd like all of you to bear in mind that if I hadn't brought knives and pistols to you, you'd still be rotting in the mud in the *Beetle*. I'll do the best I know how for all of you; and for your own good there's certain rules you've got to observe, whether you like 'em or not. Probably most of you won't like 'em, but this is going to be a healthy ship, and you'll do as I tell you.

"There's to be no fighting and no cursing. You'll get greens to boil in your food, and I want 'em eaten! You'll wash between decks every day, and you'll dry out, even if we have to build fires in the hottest spells. Mornings, weather permitting, you'll air your bedding; and finally you'll wash yourselves and your clothes daily, and put on dry clothes when wet. I aim to have no scurvy aboard this barque."

From the rear of the throng of seamen there came a shrill cater-wauling in no way different from the cry of an irritated infant, and hard on its heels rose a great burst of laughter. Corunna stepped up on the taffrail and stared hard at the most distant ranks of her audience.

"Silence!" Slade shouted hoarsely.

Corunna swept him with fleeting, angry eyes. "Apply that word to yourself, Mr. Slade," she said. "This is my affair!"

She dropped from the taffrail, ran to the binnacle and picked up the tumbler she had left at its foot. With it in her hand, she ran down from the quarter-deck and pushed her way through the throng of seamen until she reached, in the back row, a sallow, shambling sailor with black eyes that squinted at her with a hard defiance.

"I heard you yelping because your insides are out of order," she said. "I thought somebody's would be, so I made this medicine! Drink it!"

She pressed the glass, two-thirds full of a dark liquid, into his hand.

"Me?" he said contemptuously; but casting a glance about him and beholding only delightedly unsympathetic faces, he became uneasy. "I ain't got no trouble with my insides, and I ain't goin' to——"

"Drink it!"

"Lady," he said, "I ain't done nuthin'."

"Captain!" she said. "Not lady—Captain! And don't lie to me about your insides! I heard you! Drink it or spend a week in the black hole getting well! Drink it! Every drop you spill you'll get a day black hole!"

The seaman took the glass helplessly and drank. Movements of his throat denoted repulsion. With the last swallow he choked; then began to mutter protestingly.

Corunna took the glass from him and looked at him thoughtfully, while his fellows, puzzled, shifted and drew a little away from him. He pressed one hand questioningly upon his stomach and with an expression of misgiving turned and walked in silence toward the knightheads.

"My father had respect and obedience on this vessel," Corunna said to the staring crew. "So will I! Jalap and tartar emetic's what that man's got in him for his cure—jalap and tartar emetic, and he'd rather have the smallpox! It'll last three days, and there's more where that came from for any other man who thinks there isn't going to be discipline aboard the *Olive Branch*."

X

Oᶠ ᴀʟʟ the sea captains that Marvin had ever known, Corunna Dorman, he made sure, was the most unremittently exasperating. Often he watched her from the main topmast crosstrees, to which he climbed whenever the opportunity offered, not only because he feared that other eyes than his own might be slow to catch the distant glint of an enemy sail but also because he could view unseen, from this lofty height, the comings and goings on the quarter-deck.

There had been times when, between the owl-like twistings of his head as he scanned the horizon, he wondered whether Corunna's seamanship was a matter of chance or of design. He had seen her work the barque with her shining black head bent low over the worsted likeness of the Holy Family. Seemingly she never raised her eyes, except to give an order; and more than once, when she was tacking ship to gain an advantage from the shifting winds, he had leaned far out to watch her, fearful that she would either be too early with her commands, so that the vessel would not come round, or so late that everything would be caught aback and the barque put in irons.

Yet on each occasion Corunna, looking up from her bright worsteds, as if by chance, had at the precise moment called "Mainsail haul!" in a voice that came as clearly to his ears as though she stood beside him; and each time the ship had come about as smartly as a Baltimore pilot boat.

More exasperating than this to Marvin was the manner in which Slade followed Corunna about the deck, hanging over her when she was busy with her needlework, and almost seeming to lie in wait for her whenever she left the deck to go below. Marvin, gazing down from the crosstrees, came to think of him as a swarthy long-haired spider, watchfully sidling about the center of his web in expectation of the moment when he might pounce with certainty.

Yet Argandeau, coming to sit with Marvin on the crosstrees, found nothing exasperating in anything Corunna did and nothing repellent in Slade's activities.

"This pigeon of ours," he told Marvin, "she is different from all pigeons and rabbits. Out of the thousands and thousands of rabbits

I have seen, she is the only one who is able to seem always like a rabbit, even while doing the work a man should do. You have noticed this, dear Marvin—how a rabbit who engages herself to play like a man, or dress like a man, or exert herself like a man with the brain or the body, loses something out of herself, so that she is useless to look at? You have found it so, eh? In my early youth I discovered that I had no overpowering desire to gaze upon such a rabbit; and as for kissing—small choice between her and the binnacle!"

"I never noticed," Marvin admitted gloomily.

"But it is so!" Argandeau exclaimed. "Kiss one like that, and the next time you will ask for the binnacle! You must pay attention to women, and then you will see it is so! But with this pigeon of ours, she is somehow protected against that loss of something out of herself. I am conscious of her! I must restrain myself, so that I do not make myself desirable to her! I think it is possible that if I am not obliged to think continuously of other matters, very important matters—to think about how I shall get a privateer for myself when we are safely in France—I would give some thought to letting her be attracted to me. So little is needed. Pfoo!" He snapped his fingers. "Like that, I only need to let my consciousness of her become known to her!"

He peered earnestly to starboard and larboard, and glanced quickly at Marvin from the corners of his eyes.

"It is unfortunate," the Frenchman continued, as Marvin remained silent, "that I am unable to give my attention to this affair, if only to make it more difficult for Slade. I tell you, dear Marvin, I do not love him. Beneath that eyelid of his there is a look that means he is too easy in his mind about the future. I am not easy, and you are not easy, eh? Why should he be easy, this long-haired buzzard? Here is something worthy of our thought!"

Marvin laughed sourly and shook his head. "Corunna's from Arundel. She wouldn't consider a slave captain, not even if he was as handsome as George Washington. When the slave captain has a damaged binnacle to boot, she wouldn't look at him unless she had to."

"Pooi!" Argandeau cried. "You think beauty makes a difference with women? Or occupation? It makes no difference! I tell you it does not make so much difference!" Between his thumb and forefinger he plucked an imaginary atom from the air and tossed it carelessly from him. "It happens that I have been found captivating. I do not boast; I state the fact, claiming no virtues for it. These things are not talents; they occur! But it was not for my beauty that women of many countries have so frankly shown me their pining. It is because I let them feel my consciousness of them. Afterward, they find it impossible to keep me from their thoughts. Then, to gild those thoughts, I tell them magnificent lies of myself, and even more magnificent ones of themselves; for that is what rabbits prefer above all else. Ha! To make a rabbit believe you are a giraffe and she an eagless? 'Oh, rapture,' she sighs! I could be as ugly as those sheep in the pens amidships, but unlike them, I would have a perfume that would be intoxicating!"

Marvin scrutinized him carefully; then cleared his throat and resumed his study of the horizon.

"I tell you, dear Marvin," Argandeau continued, "it may be that you have had a thought to obtain this rabbit for yourself; and if it is so, you must be soon about it, because Slade is with her at all hours, telling her she is a great captain. In a little time she will consider him the wisest man in the world."

"What can I do?" Marvin asked. "I can't tell her she's a good captain, because it's against reason for a woman to be a good captain. Anyway, she thinks I'm a coward."

"Then tell her so!" Argandeau murmured. "Tell her you have been the greatest coward on earth, but soon will begin to be great because she inspires you. She is still a rabbit, you see, and must never be told the exact truth about anything. It is better that you do it than somebody else. Also, she is not a bad captain. I have seen worse. She is better than most English captains I have seen. It was a good idea she had, sending down the topgallant sails and royals, so that we are sure to see any dangerous craft before we can be seen ourselves."

"I see nothing good about the idea," Marvin objected. "If we wake up some morning to find we've blundered into an enemy vessel, we'll have small chance of escaping."

Argandeau laughed and swung himself down onto the futtock shrouds. "She is ready for such a misfortune also. She has many other ideas for our safety. You believe what Lucien Argandeau tells you, dear Marvin: Think less about how the rabbit will not do properly, and more about this Slade."

For a time it seemed to Marvin that Corunna's ideas would not be put to the test; for the *Olive Branch* came out of the blazing heat of the doldrums into the soft and pleasant cloudiness of the northeast trades, and slipped unmolested into the harbor of Las Palmas in Grand Canary Island for water, vegetables and such livestock as could be packed in her waist and between decks. From the Canaries she bore up, close-hauled, to the westward of Madeira; then set her course for the high shoulder of Spain and the Bay of Biscay.

It was in that vast funnel-shaped ocean lane, the narrow neck of which is Gibraltar, that Marvin, overseeing the dry holystoning of the newly washed berth deck on a cool October morning, heard a thumping of feet on the planks above him, together with a hoarse bawling for the bos'n.

Even as he swung himself over the hatch coaming his eye caught the gleam of a small white sail far away on the starboard beam; and from the look on the faces of the men who packed the bulwarks, staring first at the distant sail and then at the three figures on the quarter-deck, he knew as he ran aft that there was something about the sail that sat ill in the minds of all who had seen it.

Slade turned to him as he came to the break in the poop, lifting his head somewhat as though his drooping eyelid had shut Marvin from his sight. "Pipe all hands below," he said in his hoarse voice; "all but the original crew of this barque. They'll work the vessel, and the rest of 'em we'll put under hatches and batten 'em down. If we should be boarded, we'll keep 'em hid until the prize crew's aboard; then when we're well away, we'll off hatches, rise against 'em and retake the vessel."

Corunna, her telescope rested for firmness on a ratline, peered and peered at the distant sail as though Slade's words had found no lodging in her brain. Marvin stared from Slade to Corunna, and then to the far-off stranger.

Argandeau, close behind Corunna, spoke softly in her ear, eyeing Slade's back as he did so. "For such a cautious man as our bos'n," he said, "it might be that this plan would seem too dangerous."

Slade's laugh was as harsh as the scraping of a boat against a barnacled ledge. "Look sharp about it!" he commanded Marvin, and with that he turned from him to stand at Corunna's side once more.

Corunna lowered the telescope, glancing quickly at Marvin. "Why, yes," she said, "it might be, but it's got to be done, whether he likes it or not."

"Well," Marvin said, "I don't like it, and I'm not ashamed to say so. What will you do if she's a British cruiser, and she takes all of you aboard as prisoners?"

"She won't," said Slade quickly; "not if we don't fight her."

Marvin turned on him. "Why won't she? The British do any damned thing at all when they're at war! I never heard of anyone getting decent treatment from 'em unless their own ends were served by it!"

"Perhaps," Argandeau murmured, balancing himself on his toes—"perhaps this bos'n who is so free with his criticism is able to make a better plan, though I do not think so, because he does not have an intelligent look." He met Marvin's angry stare with the faintest lift of an eyebrow.

"There's nothing else to do but fight," Corunna said calmly, "and I somehow doubt that he likes to fight."

"Fight!" Marvin exclaimed. "How can we fight when we're too slow to board anything but a tub! What we might be able to do is scare 'em."

"Scare them?" Slade laughed contemptuously. "You'll make faces at them, no doubt!"

Argandeau nodded his head for emphasis. "Of all the people in the world," he said softly, "the English are the most cruel, but they are not easy to frighten."

"Maybe not," Marvin said, "maybe not; but I've never seen anybody yet that wasn't afraid of cholera!"

Corunna whirled to look at him, while Argandeau opened his mouth wide in a soundless exclamation. "Cholera!" she whispered. "Cholera!"

"Yes, cholera!" Marvin said. "What do you want to run from 'em for, once they've sighted you? It's as good as an invitation! Put about and run for 'em, and when we're within hailing distance, put me in a boat with two men to row and let me try it. If it doesn't work, you're no worse off than you'd be if you kept running."

"What?" Slade cried. "Why, she'd rake us with her bow guns before we had a chance to speak her."

Marvin studied him carefully. "It appears to me you're a little hasty in your judgment," he said. "She'll do nothing of the sort if we run down to her under half sail and at loose ends, yawing as if we had a sick crew and helmsman, and making signals of distress to boot."

Slade's laugh was as discordant as it was sudden. "It appears to *me*," he said, "that you're bound to have us taken!"

Corunna closed her telescope with a snap. "All hands about ship!" she said to Marvin. Marvin snatched his whistle from his pocket and went to blowing on it as if to blow the bean through the air hole.

Slade moved toward Corunna, who had taken her station at the weather gangway; but at the sound of a gentle laugh from Argandeau, he stopped. "Down with the helm!" she called. "Rise tacks and sheets!" With a creaking of yards and a slatting of rigging against fluttering canvas, the *Olive Branch* came about and bore off for the sail that now showed itself to be a ship with topsails so lofty that Marvin knew they could only be handled by the large crew of a war craft.

Half an hour later, the *Olive Branch,* with everything lying aback, lay wallowing in the path of the oncoming ship, a wretched slattern of the sea with the French ensign half hoisted to her peak. There was a helmsman at the wheel, but he hung across it, more like a sack of meal than a man. In the shadow of the mainmast lay two still forms, and on the quarter-deck a single dejected figure sat as if helpless on a coil of rope. Off her starboard beam bobbed a small boat, in which two men rowed, while two others huddled in the stern sheets.

The ship, a frigate of thirty-eight guns, came past the boat and rounded smartly into the wind, to leeward of it, her starboard bulwarks studded with gun crews.

The men in the boat gave way, pulling wearily toward the ship.

A blue-clad figure on the quarter-deck bawled at them through a trumpet. "What barque is that?"

Argandeau rose in the stern of the boat, holding to Marvin's shoulder. "*La Petite Citoyenne de Douarnenez!*" he called back, passing his hand weakly over his close-cropped head.

"Speak English!" bawled the holder of the trumpet.

Argandeau turned to Marvin, seeming to hold him in conversation, and the small boat came rocking closer to the tall black cruiser.

The Frenchman turned to the quarter-deck again. His face was pale, and there was an unnatural redness to his lips. "I ask you, please, you give us opium."

There was a running on the frigate's quarter-deck. "Halt, there! *Arretez!* Get to hell out of here! Get around under our lee quarter! Lee! Lee!" The man with the trumpet waved it violently.

Slowly the small boat rounded the high windows of the frigate's stern and came up under her lee quarter. On his feet once more, Argandeau lifted a pallid and imploring face to the taffrail above him. "Two men die this day," he said. "Five have sick, very much vomit! Maybe we all die unless we get opium!"

"Well, what is it?" the blue-coated man shouted, his voice somewhat shrill. "You got cholera on that barque? Hey? What you got—cholera?"

"I think yes," Argandeau said wearily. "You give opium?"

"Sheer off, there!" the blue-coated man shouted. "Yes, we'll give you opium and laudanum! Here, clap onto this line! Hurry up with that line, there!"

A slender rope fell across the boat. Argandeau, crouched in the bottom, caught it and slowly hauled it in. Fastened to its end was a package. He rose to his feet as if to thank the frigate, but already her sails were filling and those on her quarter-deck too occupied, seemingly, to listen. Listlessly the small boat turned toward the *Olive Branch*. The frigate slipped rapidly to the westward—so rapidly that the figures on her quarter-deck quickly shrank to featureless dots. Argandeau scooped up a handful of seawater and dashed it over his powdered face and reddened lips.

"Ha!" he said softly. "For a consideration I will give Monsieur Talma, of the Théâtre Français, a lesson in acting, eh? Now I think we know how to come safe to France."

XI

Racked by a southwest gale, the *Olive Branch* tumbled across the Bay of Biscay. In the cabin, Corunna, Slade and Argandeau bent low over a chart pinned to the cabin table and studied the ragged and inhospitable coast of France, while the bulkheads groaned and the hanging lamp plunged and jerked above their heads. Marvin, rewarded for his help in escaping the British frigate by the title of third mate, sat by himself on a locker.

"When I sail the *Formidable*," Argandeau said, "I come gaily from far countries; and Sweesh! I vanish into La Rochelle like an arrow, no matter what wind I have. I am indifferent to lee shores in my beautiful *Formidable*. Ah, ah!" He sighed heavily. "She mind me like a woman in the ecstasies of obedience to her first love. I have never been slow to make either vessels or ladies obedient."

"It was she, was it not, who went up in smoke?" Corunna asked dryly.

Argandeau made her a quick bow. "You interrupt!" he said. "I was about to say that I have not been slow to tell a woman what to do, once I learn what it is she wishes to do. Now I cannot tell what this barque wishes to do on a lee shore; and these lee shores of Normandy and Brittany, they are not affable. You look on this chart—how the head of Brittany thrusts itself out to sea! It is the head of a dragon, snarling at the ocean, eh? That is how she is, too—a snarler! Me, I would run into La Rochelle, but maybe you find it more comfortable to sail around the dragon's head and come in under the land at Roscoff or Morlaix. They have a drawback, those ports—they are close to England. For smugglers, that is good; for us, it might be bad."

"The closer to England, the fewer her ships," Slade said.

Argandeau raised his shoulder. "I hear Dominique Diron when he make that saying, and in return I make one of my own. Englishmen are where you find them. If it should be my business to fish for them, I would fish in any waters at all, and have better luck than those who say 'We will not fish in those waters, for the English never go there.'"

"I'd go into Morlaix," Slade remarked hoarsely.

"Morlaix is not bad," Argandeau admitted. "Me, I prefer Brest maybe, or Lorient, where there are guns to get under, eh, in case a frigate thinks she would like to come in to sit beside you. There are no guns in Morlaix."

Slade swept back his long hair. "But no frigate will ever make free with Morlaix," he said. "You couldn't get a frigate in there unless you floated her in on a raft."

"Do you know Morlaix?" Corunna asked Argandeau.

"Do I know it? In Morlaix I have five brothers-in-law—three of one family and two of another! To me it is like the face of my own neck, where I shave it each morning."

"And we'd have no trouble landing our cargo?" she persisted.

Argandeau laughed. "France and England, they are alike. Both countries are alive with thieves and politicians, which are the same things. Those who are not thieves or politicians are either smugglers, users of smuggled goods, fools or sailors. With a little money here and a little money there, you do as you like, eh?"

"Then it's to Morlaix that we'll go," Corunna said. She looked rue-fully at the elbows of her gray, water-stained Chinese jacket; elbows so crossed and recrossed by now with silken darns that they had the look, almost, of embroidered pads fixed to her sleeves. "And high time, too," she added, "unless I'm to do my sailing in a skirt with a band of grapeshot sewed to the bottom."

Slade touched her arm gently. "All the finery in France," he assured her, "can be no more beautiful than this."

She shook her head and smiled; and almost to Marvin's horror it came to him that there was a misty softness in her eyes that had not been there since the day her father died. He rose so noisily to his feet that both Corunna and Slade looked around at him in disapproval. "I'll go on deck," he said. "Somebody's got to be there if the rest of you want to talk dress all day."

Argandeau, following him on deck, laughed softly at him. "I think you are all alike, you Americans—without subtleness with your women! Look now what you have done! You have barked at this rabbit, so she will move her nose and sit where she is, to show you she does not wish to be barked at! To me it is a strange thing, dear Marvin, that any woman in your country consents to become married to an American man, when even your language of love consists of barks and growls, eh? We in France, we are subtle! We hunt always for the heartstrings of a woman, and we play softly on them, so that she is moved to do our will. You should learn from—well, I will not say from whom, but from someone whose words of love are like the whispering of spicy winds among roses."

"No doubt!" Marvin said bitterly. "No doubt! Slade must have taken lessons from a Frenchman!"

Argandeau looked condescending. "Perhaps. He does very well, too, though one would never mistake the little chameleon for the superb tree he strives to imitate. However, ladies are sometimes pleased with those little creatures, the chameleons."

There was anger in Marvin's voice. "You mean she's pleased with this one now?"

"Well, she's taking her time to listen to him. No?"

Marvin made no reply to this inquiry; and the two men, one meditative and the other moody, began to pace the quarter-deck in silence.

The *Olive Branch* had rounded Ushant and stood off to the eastward along the brown-spined nose of the cruel dragon's head of Brittany before Corunna came on deck again.

"Why not say it?" Argandeau said in a low voice to Marvin.

"Why not say what?"

"What you are thinking, my friend. Eh? What's that? Why, that I was right about that damned chameleon!"

It was late afternoon of a chill October day when the barque skirted the tumbled rocks of Roscoff and, with her bulwarks and rigging studded thick with sea-weary sailors, ran close-hauled for the high-banked estuary at the end of which lies Morlaix.

When darkness fell she lay at anchor three miles up the estuary. The stone walls of the Château du Taurau were far astern and the lights of the Happy Horse cabaret winked at her from the near-by shore. She was one hundred and forty-eight days from Canton and— as even Marvin admitted—safe at last.

Corunna, coming on deck the following morning, found Marvin bargaining with the bumboat men whose small craft, laden with horse-meat, water kegs and newly-caught marine delicacies such as mussels and squid, were clustered at the waist of the *Olive Branch* like squash seeds floating beside a segment of their parent squash.

Corunna gazed contentedly aloft and about her. The *Olive Branch's* yards were squared; a brilliant sun shone on the deck, still damp from holystoning, and on the brass-work at which the crew still scrubbed. The estuary lay glassy blue in the morning calm. At the small end of the estuary the town of Morlaix nestled peacefully at the bottom of a deep cleft in the green French hills—a true haven,

Corunna thought, from the trials and dangers of a troubled world.

Marvin, seeing her, came quickly to the quarter-deck. "If it's all the same to you, Corunna," he said, "I'd like to run out the sweeps and move a little nearer to the town. These boatmen say there's enough water closer in."

"What's wrong with this anchorage?" Corunna demanded. "Mr. Slade and I settled on it last night. Perhaps it isn't safe enough for you, but it is for us."

When Marvin was silent, she laughed scornfully. "You can't admit it, can you, Dan! Just because I'm a woman, you won't give me credit for doing what you said I couldn't do! You said I wasn't a captain; but I've brought this vessel safe to port, and no captain could do more. Yet you're too stubborn to acknowledge it!"

"No," he said slowly. "I'm not too stubborn. No man could have brought her in smarter, Corunna. Your cargo's safe, and there's no sick aboard. It's a miracle, almost."

"A miracle!" she cried. "Why is it a miracle? Why can't you admit it was seamanship, and be done with it? Mr. Slade says——"

"What do I care what Slade says!" Marvin interrupted. "He'd say anything! Common sense ought to tell you that! If he'd captain a slaver, he'd *do* anything too! Anything!"

It seemed to him then that Corunna's smile had malice in it. "Wasn't it you, Dan," she asked, "who jawed so much, not long since, about women doing things for personal reasons? Maybe you dislike Mr. Slade, Dan, because he's kind to me; not because he's a slaver. And after all, Dan, there's worse things than a good slaver! Why, think how much better off the negroes are in the Sugar Islands than they are in Africa, killing and eating each other."

"Yes," Marvin said. "I've heard that before. Slade told me. That's how I know he'd say anything. He'd say a squirrel was better off in a cage than up an oak tree, where it might get hit on the head with a limb! If he says you're a captain, he's saying it to curry favor with you! Where's your common sense?"

"What?" Corunna cried fiercely. "You'll see whether I'm a captain or not!"

"How'll I see that?"

"Listen and I'll tell you," Corunna said deliberately. "As soon as this cargo's sold, I'm outfitting a privateer against the English, and Mr. Slade said he'd be proud to serve under me!"

Marvin stared at her, his lips pressed tight together. "You'll not do that, Corunna!"

"Won't I? Watch and see!"

"Well," he said doggedly, "you can sail a ship, but you're not a captain! You're a woman, and you count on it! You're going into a venture without being willing to pay if you lose! You're banking on taking prizes without doing any of the fighting yourself; and if you're captured, you're counting on being treated like a woman, instead of being sent to the hulks like your officers and crew."

She swallowed twice and drew a deep breath. "What if I am?" she said at last. "What else can I do? What can I do when you talk to me this way? You wouldn't talk to Mr. Slade the way you talk to me, because if you did, he'd have a knife in you before you knew it. Just because I'm a woman I have to listen to you. Why shouldn't I take advantage of being a woman when I get a chance—especially against those that killed my father?"

Marvin stared down at his knuckles and slowly closed and unclosed his left hand. "Corunna, there's nothing so hard to answer as a woman's arguments, mostly because there's no sense to 'em. I could tell you that nobody's a proper captain unless he forever runs more risks than the men he leads; but you wouldn't listen to me. As for not being willing to talk to Slade, I think I can dispose of that argument, even to *your* satisfaction. I've been promising myself to say a few things to him as soon as we reached a safe anchorage, and it looks to me as if now was the time. Will you call him up here, or would you prefer to see me drag him up?"

"Dear me!" Corunna said. "Dear me! You're mighty brave all of a sudden, now that Mr. Slade has gone ashore."

"Gone ashore!" Marvin cried. "Why, how *could* he go ashore?"

Almost as though he had popped, like a djinn, out of the water butt, Argandeau rose suddenly from under the break in the poop. "Somebody saying Mr. Slade went ashore?" he asked softly.

Corunna looked from Marvin to Argandeau and back again. "Why, yes. What's wrong with that? I sent him ashore late last night, after you had turned in, according to plan."

"You sent him ashore?" Argandeau whispered. "I am sorry you have not spoken to me about needing something on shore at such an hour. I would have been honored to go, eh? And maybe, in spite of having some relatives by marriage here who have a mistaken opinion of me, I think I should have contrived to be back on the ship by now."

"Oh, there was no question of returning quickly," Corunna assured him. "Mr. Slade felt that the sooner we started hunting for a privateer, the sooner we'd be able to set out against the British."

"Ah, yes!" Argandeau said, almost happily. "Mr. Slade reminds you of this, and so you send him. That is very nice, but it is a little pity he would not speak to me before he go, because I might tell him where to look for this privateer. I am surprised, too, that he know Morlaix so well as to be able to ask confidentially about such an expensive vessel as a privateer."

"Not in Morlaix," Corunna said. "That was why we thought it best for him to land at night. Then he could be well out of Morlaix before daylight, so that no official would detain him, and reach Roscoff in good season. He has acquaintances in Roscoff, I think."

"Ah, Roscoff!" Argandeau breathed. "It is too bad, if he has acquaintances there, that he was so eager we come here rather than to Roscoff!"

"Well, land alive!" Corunna exclaimed angrily. "It's beyond me why you should make such a mountain out of a mole hill! Why shouldn't he have friends in Roscoff?"

"Why shouldn't he have told Argandeau?" Marvin demanded.

"Good reason!" Corunna declared. "He knew you hated him, and that you'd do whatever you could to hinder his attempts to help me. And so you would, both of you!"

"He set off to buy a privateer," Marvin said thoughtfully, "so he must have had a deal of money with him."

"To *hunt* for a privateer, I said!" Corunna told him.

"But he must have had money to go traveling," Marvin persisted. "You didn't have any. It's all tied up in the cargo. You'd be needing money to get the cargo ashore and buy supplies. Perhaps he had enough himself; perhaps even enough to lend you some."

"Is that your affair?" Corunna asked. She strode to the larboard rail and marched up and down the deck, staring sternly at the small white houses on the far bank of the estuary and the little brown-sailed luggers that were slipping slowly out to sea before the vagrant morning airs.

Argandeau laughed gently. "By now he is in Roscoff," he told Marvin, "and there is nobody in Roscoff except all of the best smugglers in the world, by which I mean all of the worst ones; so we will hope that someone take him for a spy and stuff him in a brandy keg."

XII

CAPTAIN SLADE in Roscoff, however, was far indeed from perishing, as the vivacious Argandeau desired, inside a brandy barrel; though it might well be of record that in his few hours of residence in that estimable town he placed within himself no inconsiderable quantity of the contents of such a barrel. His capacity was notable; no one who saw him could have guessed what he contained.

There was something disarming about his drooping eyelid; for when he tilted back his head to see the better, and smiled his quick and knowing smile, there was a look to him as though with the raising of the eye he lifted the curtain that hung before his mind, and permitted the world to gaze in on his sincerity and honesty. Even the hoarseness of his voice seemed proof of his candor; for on the face of it, no man would dare indulge in guile or fabrication in such rasping tones, lest his fraudulence be at once detected.

There was little indeed about the appearance of Captain Slade to inspire anything but amiability in those who saw him as he swung down the narrow streets of Roscoff on a warm October morning and entered the square that bordered the graystone inner basin. Clearly he was a somebody. There was distinction and urbanity in his bearing as he scanned the host of luggers, cutters and schooners that thronged both the inner and the outer harbors; and the rakish forward tilt to his fine beaver hat indicated a generous disposition and a well-filled purse.

It may have been the backward slant of his head that made him seem to inhale with pleasure the somewhat powerful odors of Roscoff; it may have been the stout cane held so carelessly beneath the arm of his light blue coat that gave him his air of harmless affability; but whatever it was that did it, there was that about him which drew a tolerant growl from the swarthy Frenchmen who sat along the basin's rim, scratching themselves and looking resentfully at the cloudless sky.

Moving thus in an atmosphere of honesty and good cheer, Slade eyed a tall and narrow tavern fronting on the basin—a tavern whose signboard was blazoned with a round red object bearing a faint resemblance to the face of King George III, together with the words

"Biftek Rouge." What Slade saw appeared to please him; for he swaggered jauntily through the door of the Biftek Rouge into a long room so full of men and of smoke as to give the impression that the floor itself was smoldering, and the men attempting to prevent a fire by sitting on it. The room buzzed with conversation when he entered, but as he stood by the small counter at the entrance, surveying the occupants, the buzzing died away and was succeeded by a heavy silence.

Slade laughed and cocked his eye at the fat woman in black who sat knitting behind the counter. "Brandy, madame," he said, smiling blandly at her small black mustache. "*Fine de la maison.*" He fumbled in the breast pocket of his coat and brought out a slip of paper. "You *savez cet homme ici*—Capitaine Henry Potter? Pottaire, eh?"

The mustached woman set a bottle and a tumbler before him; then studied the paper, front and back, without emotion. From a near-by table, a French sailor, gold earrings dangling on his cheeks and a canvas petticoat over his breeches, lurched forward to the counter and spoke quickly to the fat woman, who looked noncommittal, raised her shoulders to the level of her ears, and passed the slip of paper to him.

The Frenchman stared at it, scratching his nose. "No," he said at length, "that name means nothing in Roscoff."

Slade motioned to the fat woman for another tumbler, filled it for the Frenchman; then sighed and pondered, his lids downcast in vague regret. "Too bad!" he said. "Too bad! My friend Captain Chater told me Henry Potter worked regularly between Roscoff and Plymouth, and would set me across."

"You know Chater?" the Frenchman asked. He swallowed half his tumbler of brandy, shivered violently, and stared hard at Slade out of watery eyes.

"I knew him," Slade said. "He had the fever in Fernando Po. The damned fool wouldn't close his ports at night."

The Frenchman grunted. "Fernando Po!" he growled. "That is another thing, then! Strange Englishmen are not welcome in this town, but men from Fernando Po——"

Slade drew papers from his pocket, and as he waited for the Frenchman to examine them, he heard the humming and buzzing of the room mount again to its former violence.

The Frenchman pushed back the papers. "Yes, I will tell you. You know about Dunkirk?"

Slade shook his head.

"The Emperor Napoleon, he has turned over a section of the city to the English free traders, so that our poor country may take a few millions from the rich Goddams. All the time there are in that port five hundred sailors from across the ditch"—he jerked his head toward the Channel—"and if you go there, I think you find Pottaire." He finished his brandy, shivered again and pulled pensively at an earring.

"It's too far," Slade said. "Anyway, those that run out of Dunkirk wouldn't be going so far west as Devon; they'd be for Kent and Sussex. It's Plymouth I'm for."

Seemingly lost in thought, the Frenchman sniffed at the brandy bottle and pushed it toward the fat woman in black. "This Cousin Jacky is for export to England," he growled. "Spill none of it on your dress, lest it eat a hole. Give us a measure from the keg of '97."

Grumbling, the mustached woman produced a second bottle, from which the Frenchman poured two half tumblers.

"And," Slade reminded him, "I want to come back the same way in four days. I thought I'd pay in advance on this side, and leave the return money with madame here, to be paid when I come in again—paid with a hundred-franc bonus."

The Frenchman put an arm around Slade's shoulders and breathed heavily on his neckcloth. "Ah, but this is something we arrange at once. I am arrive here this morning, and I do not go back for four days, because every Englishman in the world either carries lace and Cousin Jacky, or wishes to buy it! There is the English of it for you! They make a law; then all of them work day and night to break it! Now there are so many of us that unless we take our turn, we bump into each other in mid-Channel! It is a hard thing for poor France that so many English should take the bread out of our mouths, no?" He patted Slade's shoulder and seemed to weep a little.

"It's tonight I want to go to Plymouth," Slade said.

"Yes, yes! But not Plymouth! Polperro, Yealm, Dartmouth, Cawsand, Looe—yes; every night there are luggers to those places, but not to Plymouth. Plymouth, it is too full of war vessels. Listen now to me. Here is what we do: Tonight four luggers go to Whitesand Bay, between Looe and Plymouth—two English and two French. I send you with an Englishman—Captain Vincent, cutter *Lottery;* he is very intelligent man. If there is something to be found out"—he raised his eyebrows suggestively—"by those fools in the army who are forever studying and daily growing stupider, Captain Vincent, he will deliver even a general anywhere in England in two days, entirely safe. You go with him to Whitesand Bay tonight and be nicely in Plymouth for breakfast; then in four days you come with a friend of Captain Vincent to Whitesand Bay once more, and we return here like two larks."

The cutter *Lottery*, laden with one hundred ankers of cognac, five hundred pounds of tea, seven thousand yards of lace and thirty bales of silk, ran due north from Roscoff on the night tide; and Captain Vincent, nursing the tiller of his swift vessel as easily with one hand as though he navigated a ship's dinghy in a canal, held Slade's gold pieces to the dim light of the binnacle; then stuffed them into the pocket of his breeches and cast a quick glance under the mainsail.

"You came to the wrong place for a Plymouth vessel," he told Slade, staring at him innocently out of clear blue eyes, "and if you wasn't a stranger, you'd 'a' knowed it. It takes money to shut up the Excise and Preventive officers in a port that size, and pay off a dozen revenue-cruiser captains to boot; and us little fellers, we ain't got it. It's only the big Scotch and French and Dutch and English companies that can pay that high for protection; and if we nose in on their preserves, it's a knife in the ribs or a bullet in the back, like as not, for those of us as does."

He spat over the side. "Of course, them that has to make port in all weathers, maybe they need protection; but Whitesand Bay is all I need; no questions asked and labor plenty. You'll see 'em turn out tonight, with four vessels unloading! We pay 'em well; and every farmer and shopkeeper and blacksmith in the town, they'll be out to help; yes, and the women and children and the parson. And why shouldn't they, when it comes to that? What right's a government got to say a poor man sha'n't have his tot of Cousin Jacky, if so be he needs it!"

"It's all the same to me where I land," Slade said, "so long as nobody throws me into jail for being American. Going on an errand of mercy, the way I am, I wouldn't want to be branded as an enemy and all that." He laughed. "I'm no more an enemy of England than you're an enemy of France, but we'd both be hard put to it if it came to explaining!"

Captain Vincent nodded, gazing round-eyed at Slade. "Aye," he said, "I was thinking the same. It's likely you'd have no trouble, with your head cocked up on account of your eye, and so looking important and mean, like an English gentleman. It's likely you wouldn't; only there's no telling—there's no telling." He brooded for a time. Then: "You said it was Bristol you were making for?" he asked.

"To carry poor Chater's watch and seals to his mother," Slade said.

Captain Vincent nodded. "If I was you, I'd make sure. Better be safe than sorry, 'specially if you can enjoy yourself doing it. It'll cost some money, but you'll find it'll be worth it, more ways than one—that is, unless you got objections to traveling around with a young female."

"It depends some on the female!" Slade tilted back his head to look at Vincent, and his teeth, as he laughed, were tight together, so that his laughter had more the sound of soft and eager breathing than of mirth.

"Well, I tell you," Vincent said, "this female's all right. She's young and she's sensible looking. Nothing flash about her, see; nothing to set people watching her all the time; nothing that'd oblige you to be fighting some young buck every few minutes to keep him from trying to cut her out; but she's sharp as a whip, and buffs better'n any female ever I see! Now, if you should get this female and take her around as your wife, she'd do all the talking, and nobody'd suspect you of not being an Englishman. Most Englishmen act tongue-tied when they're with their wives, anyway."

Slade cleared his throat. "I've had the same idea in mind for some time," he said frankly, "but I thought of visiting a house of entertainment where I could make a selection. I'm a little particular about my women."

"I'll tell you how it is," Vincent continued quickly. "There's plenty of females in Plymouth and Portsmouth and every other port nowadays, what with the men of the fleet to take care of, and the regular run of trade, and prisoners coming in to be looked after; but I tell you right now, you have to watch out for yourself! There's plenty in Portsmouth that'll stay with a prisoner fresh aboard a receiving hulk right out of the cable tier of a frigate, two shillings for a full night's work; but you know what happens if you take up with one like that!"

Slade laughed, a hoarse and racking laugh.

"Yes," Vincent went on, "but this female, she's nothing like that! There's admirals that've enjoyed associating themselves with this female, and haven't hardly been able to wait to get back off their stations so they could get hold of her society again. Admirals!"

The two of them chuckled.

"How's it sound to you?" Vincent asked.

"Not bad!" Slade said. "Not bad, provided she doesn't get to thinking I'm made of money. How much would I have to pay her?"

"I'll tell you how it is," Vincent said. "There was a few of us fitted up two houses in Plymouth—not the regular run, but high-class houses of entertainment. Some of the females we brought over from France for entertaining purposes, just the same as the Duchess of

Portsmouth was brought"—they chuckled again—"and some we found closer home; but they're all of 'em ladies, fit to be presented at Court, or to spend a week visiting in Buckingham Palace. Now, if this female goes stepping off with you, it hurts the profits, as you might say; so you'd better pay me enough to cover that end of it, and then you can fix up with her. Maybe she'd come too high for you. Whenever she puts in considerable time entertaining a gentleman, she has to have two new dresses, one for day and one for night, and five guineas a day. Too much, ain't it?"

"Well," Slade said, clearing his throat, "if she's as shrewd as you claim, she might be worth it. How much would cover the profits?"

"Oh, call it five guineas," Vincent said carelessly.

Again Vincent examined gold pieces in the light of the binnacle; and after that, in the lurching and swaying cockpit, he whispered busily in Slade's ear until, dead ahead, a score of blinking, wavering lights marked the tumbled rocks and the sheltered crescent beach of Whitesand Bay.

XIII

THE office of Admiral Sir John Duckworth, high above the dock-yard at Devonport, looked out over the bewildering marine activities of the Hamoaze to the lofty wooded slopes of Mount Edgcumbe, beyond which lay Whitesand Bay; and Admiral Duckworth himself, stocky and formal in his high-collared uniform coat and spotless nankeen breeches, stared from the window at the swarming waters below, in which shore boats, bumboats, ships' boats, and lighters of every description scurried like beetles among the frigates, line-of-battle ships, hulks, ships repairing, ships fitting and ships under sail. Behind him, the hoarse voice of Captain Slade filled the room with a ceaseless and not displeasing hum.

Admiral Duckworth turned from the window suddenly. "As I understand it," he interrupted, "you want one-half of the sum realized from the condemnation sale, if, as and when this barque is cut out from some port unknown. I tell you at once, my good fellow, it won't do! It's too much!"

Slade shrugged his shoulders. "That's as you see fit, Admiral." He coughed. "I've heard there are ways in which vessels are ships when they enter your prize courts and sloops when they come out—though, of course, that's none of my affair. And I know your prize money is often divided oddly. Why, I know a case, and so do you, too, sir, where a British admiral received four thousand pounds prize money from a single vessel, while the seamen on his ship were given two pounds apiece. Of course, that's none of my affair either, but it's been done, and done often, where your admirals were concerned; and what's been done can be done again."

Admiral Duckworth stared at him coldly, but Slade only laughed.

"It seems to me," the slaver continued, "that the circumstances should make some slight difference, too. Here's a vessel that will be fitted out as a privateer against you, under a Yankee captain that—meaning no offense—can sail circles around your fastest frigates and sloops-of-war. It seems to me it should be a privilege for you to nip this little enterprise in the bud, no matter how much it costs you—a privilege and a patriotic duty."

"Dear me!" the admiral said in a light voice. "Lessons in patriotism to a British admiral delivered by a Yankee merchant captain whose position is—let us say—equivocal? Interesting!"

Slade tilted back his head and smiled up into the red face above him. "Don't take me wrong, Admiral! Don't take me wrong! It only seemed to me I ought to mention the saving to your country, seeing that you've objected to my reasonable price for the information. Why, here, Admiral; this barque and her cargo will sell for thirty thousand pounds. That's fifteen for government and fifteen for me; and if you send a schooner to cut her out, her officers and crew would consider themselves made men if they divided five thousand among 'em. There's ten thousand left for government. Or call it five thousand, and make a fast sloop-of-war out of the barque. All profit, Admiral! But if you don't get her, what then? Suppose she slips out and takes four or five of your merchantmen, as she will! As she will!"

Slade clicked his teeth together and laughed his soft laugh that sounded like quick strokes of a brush against stone. "You'll have the shipowners buzzing around the Admiralty's ears, crying for their lost money and cursing the navy for a kettle of old goats and younger sons, and that's all you will have!"

Duckworth walked up and down the room, glancing angrily at Slade. "It's beyond me!" he said at length. "I've done some fighting against your people in my time, and it was generally the other way around. Usually it was our people that went running over to yours, because of all your wild talk of freedom; but here you are, wanting to sell your own shipmates!"

Slade seemed hurt. "No, no! You've got it hindside foremost, Admiral! The barque belongs to a poor, helpless girl with no mind for business. She's fallen into the hands of two unscrupulous rascals, Admiral. If they have their way, it'll be no time at all before the girl's stripped clean and deserted in a foreign port. They'll take her barque for a privateer, and they'll take her money from her on the plea of refitting. It's that, Admiral, that's set me off on this. I do hate to see an innocent maid so fooled and misled."

The admiral looked at him and laughed.

Slade sighed softly and rose from his chair, smiling somewhat ruefully. "Well," he said, "it's no matter! I see you don't take to the idea." Hat in hand, he moved toward the door.

"Half a moment," Duckworth ordered. "If we go in after this barque, are you sure she won't be tied up at a dock? Won't be unloaded? Are you sure a cutting-out expedition could get to her?"

Slade set his gray beaver hat on the floor once more. "I saw a French official before I came away. She'll be held at anchor, and won't break cargo until I return; and she'll cut out as easy as a rat hole out of cheese."

"Well," Duckworth said reluctantly, "we might arrange it."

Slade eyed the admiral thoughtfully, his drooping eyelid a pallid patch in his swarthy face. "You won't regret it! No: you won't regret it! And by the way, Admiral: there's one or two things I'd like to be sure of before the matter's considered settled. There'd have to be articles between us, stating clearly that I'm to receive one-half of the prize money resulting from the sale of the barque and her cargo, whose value is tentatively estimated at thirty thousand pounds; and that in case she's used for government service, I'm further to receive one-half of her value as decided by the prize court. Also an agreement that when the barque is cut out, the lady, if aboard, is to be set ashore before putting to sea. Also an agreement that the crew shall be taken for imprisonment to the hulks farthest removed from the port where the barque was captured. They're dangerous men, Admiral, and I want 'em put where there's no likelihood they'll cause the lady more trouble."

"Dear me! Dear me!" Grumbling, the admiral dropped down before his desk and scratched busily on a sheet of paper, while Slade watched him out of one black eye that seemed to glitter like a drop of ink in the sun.

The next morning this benevolent adventurer sat at an upper window of the *Swan* inn, tapping impatiently with a snakewood cane at his newly varnished boots. He cocked an eye at the curving streets of ancient Bristol and the forest of masts that edged the serpentine curves of the Avon as willows rim the banks of a meadow brook.

"Interesting, isn't it!" he said in his hoarse voice. "These English; they know how to do things! They put up a battery of church towers to catch your eye; and while you're busy looking at the towers, they run their slave ships right up to their own back doors."

He laughed the laugh that had the sound of bristles passing lightly over granite; then turned his head quickly. "Look here, my love! I've got business in this town, and I want you with me! Crowd on some canvas or you'll get something you aren't looking for!"

A small, brown-eyed, brown-haired girl came to his side, circled his head with a bare arm, rapped him lightly on the cheek with the back of a hairbrush and pressed his face to her bosom. "Now," she said, "don't tease!" She broke from him and went back to her prinking at a mirror; and Slade, watching her with a gleaming eye, was silent.

It was an hour later that the captain swaggered proudly from the narrow door of the *Swan*, his snakewood cane jauntily a-swing and at his side his lady, her small hand thrust demurely beneath his elbow; her eyes, sheltered by a snuff-brown bonnet, modestly cast down. It scarcely seemed that she could muster the courage to leave the side of her escort to ask even the smallest of questions of a stranger; but leave it she did; and while her apparent husband stood lost in admiration of the Norman tower of St. Peter's Church, she timidly begged a white-aproned wine merchant to direct them to Queens Square.

Then the decorous couple skirted the busy Avon, passed through the odors of wine, tobacco and leather that hung over the crowded High Street, and made their way into the quiet southern quarter of the city, where the squat brown houses of opulent shipowners were sheltered on three sides by the waters of the Floating Harbor. Here, while Captain Slade again seemed stricken speechless by the cold bronze scrutiny of King William III and his horse, or possibly by the sight of either the customhouse or the jail, his gentle companion hesitatingly inquired of a lofty footman where the residence of Sir Austin Braymore might be found.

It was not, indeed, until these two obviously estimable and virtuous folk had been admitted to the dim hallway of Sir Austin's home that Captain Slade regained his tongue; and the very manner of his regaining it was proof that he was pleased.

"Little devil!" he said, drawing his lady to him. "Every inch the bride! We came here as neatly as though we'd been brought up on the smell of fried eels!"

He peered past her at the elaborately carved love seat in the hall; then raised his chin, as if in haughty appraisal, to eye the cabinet in the near-by reception room—a cabinet of mahogany, carved delicately to represent a bamboo pagoda, rising to eaves that swept upward to still higher eaves, and thence to a stork at the top; a stork so graceful and so lifelike that it seemed poised above the cabinet, rather than mounted on it. Inside the cabinet were silver bowls and jars and milky plates, their centers blazing with heraldic designs in gold and blue and scarlet.

He bent his head to whisper close to the snuff-brown bonnet: "Make an excuse and stay out here. I'll see this gentleman alone; and after that, my love, I'll set you to playing the dear, fresh-wed little spouse once more."

A portly gentleman with a triple row of chins came heavily down the staircase, wrinkling his forehead at the couple below him. "Captain Slade and ma'am," he said politely. "The name is not—is not——"

Captain Slade seemed almost to stand on tiptoe, so far back did he throw his head to see Sir Austin clearly. "I came direct from Admiral Duckworth," he explained.

"So, so! So, so!" Sir Austin murmured. "From Sir John! So, so! Pray step back here, Captain."

He turned toward the far end of the hall, but before Captain Slade could follow him, his lady had swayed and gasped a little, and to the distress of Sir Austin and the captain, declared timidly and sweetly that the journey had been a thought too much for her: that she would sit alone, here in the hall, if only Sir Austin would have the kindness to send a servant to her with a thimble of Madeira.

"Of Bristol milk, ma'am! Not Madeira, but Bristol milk! That's the wine to bring the color back to those soft cheeks!"

He hurried to the bell pull, hastened for the smelling salts and bustled about for a cushion to slip beneath the feet of this delicate little lady; so that when he was finally alone with Captain Slade in the small white-walled room at the rear of the house, he was short of breath from his hospitable exertions, and wheezed a little as he sat wide-legged before his visitor in a large wing chair.

"So, so!" he panted. "From Sir John! Ha-ha! Difficult post! Happy to think he thought of me!"

The quick rasp of Captain Slade's laugh brought a look of puzzlement to Sir Austin's face. "It just happened," Slade murmured, "that your name didn't come up. No, your name wasn't even mentioned."

Sir Austin clapped his fat hands on his knees and stared in amazement. "Not even—not even—— Then to what, if I may ask, am I indebted——"

Slade turned his head and looked hard at Sir Austin from his one good eye. "Some little time before I saw Sir John, I ran into Fernando Po." He nodded brightly and added, "On business."

Sir Austin cleared his throat softly. "On business in Fernando Po? That is in Africa, is it not?"

Slade laughed a little harshly. "Seeing that the *Narcissus* was in the river when I was there, and that the *Venus* had cleared with six hundred and nine blacks three weeks before, you ought to know where Fernando Po is!"

He looked coolly about the small white room; got up, even, to scrutinize more closely the lady in the gown of shimmering brown whose portrait hung above a mantel of yellow marble—a mantel with a medallion chiseled by a master hand to show a dog, bone in mouth, staring at his reflection in a stream.

"H'm!" Slade said. " 'Lady, by Kneller'—best man you've got when it comes to white shoulders above a silk dress!" He sat down again and grinned into Sir Austin's still face.

"What happened," he continued, "was that Chater wouldn't close his ports at night. That's what you get for taking a man off the Channel and putting him on the Middle Passage. They know it all, they do, just because they've been able to run a few ankers of brandy past a handful of paid Preventive officers. Won't take advice! That was Chater! Wouldn't take advice! I told him what would happen if he didn't keep his ports shut, but he laughed, and it occurred!" Slade hissed jovially through his clenched white teeth, "He died of the fever."

Sir Austin drew a key from his pocket and fumbled, with helpless hands, at the lock of a mahogany cellarette that stood by his elbow. Slade leaned forward to take the key from the trembling fingers of his host. With a deferential smile he thrust it into place and raised the lid.

"Permit me," Slade said. He glanced mournfully at Sir Austin. "Your health, I fear, is not what it should be. It's the rich food, perhaps. Yes, it must be the rich food! A man your age can't be too careful about avoiding exertion or excitement. What can I give you, sir?"

"Brandy!" Sir Austin whispered. "A little of the brandy!"

Slade brought up a bottle with a fly-specked label, turned his head sidewise to examine it; then, puckering his lips in a tuneless whistle, he plucked two glasses from the rack. When he had filled one for Sir Austin, he sipped from his own, sighing gently as he rolled the liquor over his tongue.

"You'll be relieved to know," he at length continued, seeing that Sir Austin seemed content to sit silently, staring into his empty glass, "that I saved her for you. Yes, sir; I saved the *Narcissus!* When Chater was dying, the blacks rose, and if I hadn't been handy with a long knife, you wouldn't have any *Narcissus*. You'd have lost her, and everything with her—men, sails, spars, coppers and leg irons."

He shook his head reproachfully at Sir Austin. "You ought to give your niggers more space! There were ninety packed into the boys' room, and it was only thirteen feet, nine inches long. That's not enough—not for vessels as slow as your English tubs. Fifty days they take for the Middle Passage! You're bound to lose half of 'em when you pack 'em in like that! Sometimes it seems as though you English didn't have any sense at all! It's a wonder to me you're able to lay up a penny! Instead of suffocating so many, why don't you carry forty-five instead of ninety in your boys' room? They'd cost half as much, and you'd have next to no losses unless you struck bad weather."

"You don't know——" Sir Austin's voice failed him, so that he was forced to try again: "You don't know what you're saying!" He worked his lips from side to side, as if to free them of stiffness. "I won't listen to such things! I don't know what you're talking about!"

"No," Slade said, "I suppose not!" He brusquely drew a bottle from the cellarette and poured himself another brandy. As an afterthought he offered the bottle to Sir Austin, who seemed not to see it. "I suppose," Slade continued, "you also don't know what I'm talking about when I mention the *Narcissus* or the *Venus* or the *Delight* or the *Apollo!* Since you merely happen to own 'em, you naturally wouldn't have heard of 'em, or of what they're doing. That being so, I'll be glad to furnish you with something authentic. You'll doubtless be happy to hear the *Delight* landed four hundred and eighty blacks at St. Thomas on her last voyage, along with three tons of gum copal and twenty-two hundred double pawn cloths. That ought to mean fifteen thousand pounds in your pocket—fifteen thousand in addition to your profits in—ah—black ivory from the other three! Why, I doubt there's another slave trader in Bristol who can hold a candle to your fortune!"

He smiled in friendly admiration at Sir Austin, whose fat white cheeks seemed to be afflicted with spasms of trembling, as jelly shudders at a weighty footstep; and for a time they sat in silence, these two; Sir Austin clutching at his knees with plump white hands that shook and sweated, and Slade grinning up at the white shoulders of the girl in the portrait above the mantel.

Sir Austin, when he stirred, moved with the stiffness of a wooden man. His eyes were dull as those of a dead haddock. "Never!" he gasped. "It's not so! I deny it!"

Slade stroked his long black hair with the palm of his hand. "Before Chater died," he said, "I thought it might ease his mind to sign a writing for his family showing he wasn't in that business for himself. It mentioned he was working for you; and then—blast my absentmindedness!—if I didn't go and forget to give that paper to the widow!" His eye glittered. "But to remedy that, and to fix up poor old Chater's reputation, I've arranged that the writing shall be presented to Admiral Sir John Duckworth and other responsible officials on a certain date unless—unless——"

Sir Austin rolled almost drunkenly in his huge wing chair. "By God, sir! You must have—— Why, damn you, sir! Chater wouldn't have done any such thing unless you held a knife to his throat! I mean to say—— I beg your pardon! Yes, yes! He might have been crazed by the fever! Crazed; yes, yes! Crazed! This damned calumny—why, my daughter—but there's no one would believe such a slander—— What? Of a man that put a window in St. Margaret's and that bishops are damned glad to dine with?"

"Dear, dear!" Slade said carelessly. "I fear the bishops may be upset when they learn they've been dining with the owner of slave ships!" He rose to scan again the portrait of the girl in brown. "This your daughter? She's in society, I take it; but probably her position wouldn't be affected by anything that happened to you—ah—would it, Sir Austin?"

Sir Austin pressed his hands together. "The jail's just across the square, Captain Slade, and the sheriff's a friend of mine! I might warn you to have a care how you speak loosely of me in Bristol, or elsewhere. Do you think any man in Bristol could be brought to believe that——"

Slade waved his hand languidly. "And would they never believe it of such good Bristol citizens as Standish Trevor and Sir George Batt and Cottrell and Foster Penhallow?"

Sir Austin's breath made faint popping sounds as it broke from his slack lips, and Slade's eye gleamed with satisfaction. "They're on the list," he said suavely. "Those names are there with yours, and the names of their vessels as well." He cleared his throat. "You're slow to make laws, you British, but when you make 'em, you make 'em too severe, to my way of thinking! Of course, we've got a law against importing slaves into America—had it before you made your law, because of the way you were glutting our markets with blacks—but our law's nothing like as strong as the law you passed last year."

With his tongue he made clicking noises of commiseration. "To think it's a felony in England since last year! A felony to deal in dirty blacks, when everybody knows your cane fields can't be properly cultivated by anyone but niggers! Yes, sir; a felony, and punishable with transportation! Why, sir, it just doesn't seem within the bounds of reason that if that document should fall into Duckworth's hands, you'd be torn from your family and that daughter of yours, and transported to Botany Bay along with common thieves and drunkards and diseased women!" His shoulders shook with silent laughter. "It might be, in time, your family could join you out there, if you behaved yourself. I think your family'd be permitted."

Sir Austin looked at him piteously. "I suppose you want something."

Slade drew from his pocket the paper he had received from Admiral Duckworth, glanced closely at it, and handed it to Sir Austin. "I want two things," he said, "and considering I saved the *Narcissus* for you, it's little enough. I want fifteen thousand pounds advanced on that piece of paper, and I want a vessel. I want the fifteen thousand pounds in cash, and I want it tomorrow. And when I say I want a vessel, I don't mean any vessel. I mean a brig, a fast brig—a fast armed brig. She's got to have fourteen guns at least, and two of them long guns—long 24's. She's got to have quarters for a crew of a hundred and forty, and she's got to be trim and taut and ready for sea."

"Preposterous!" exclaimed Sir Austin, and he blew out the word as if it burned his tongue. "Why, where would I get such a sum and such a brig? How could I——"

Slade fixed his one good eye on him fiercely. "I've made myself clear," he said. "That's what I want and that's what I propose to have! You know it's worth that to you and Penhallow and Cottrell and Trevor and Batt to be saved from Botany Bay! You can tell them for me they're on the list, and the list will be in Duckworth's hands if I don't get what I want—the money tomorrow and the brig within a month. You know as well as I do that Liverpool has enough fast brigs hidden away to fight every sloop-of-war in the British Navy! Where would you get it, indeed! Who should know better than you that there were two hundred and fifty slave brigs out of Liverpool less than ten years ago? Two hundred and fifty! Go there and get one! You've got the money and you've got the influence! You own slave ships, and Liverpool was built on the profits of the slave trade. A man of your influence can get whatever he wants in Liverpool!" His laugh was like the rubbing together of two bricks. "Doesn't the sheriff come here to dinner? Don't you have bishops to dine?"

. . . When at last Captain Slade emerged from Sir Austin Braymore's small white-walled study, triumphantly rolling his glittering black eye from the Turkey carpets on the floor to the silver in the great pagoda cabinet, his modest little lady was asleep on the love seat in the hall, the tips of her brown slippers barely reaching to the floor and her lips parted as innocently and sweetly, in her childlike slumber, as the petals of a rose.

She opened her eyes as he gazed down at her; then, after a cloudy moment, recognition came back to her. "You're a sweet man," she said—"a sweet man to stand and smile at me so kindly."

"My dear, I wasn't," Slade told her as she rose and they moved toward the door. "I was smiling to myself to think how vastly I bettered myself in so short a time. Five days—why, it's genius!"

XIV

By FIVE DAYS Captain Slade meant the five since he had left the *Olive Branch* in the harbor of Morlaix, where that patient barque still lay with all her cargo, and a great deal of perplexity aboard her.

There were times when Marvin, eager to break bulk and see the cargo of the *Olive Branch* safe ashore, fell into such a rage that he talked bitterly to Argandeau.

"What's the matter with these Frenchmen?" Marvin demanded. "The crew of the *Formidable* went ashore long ago, and the English wounded have been safely put in jail, God help 'em, so that we're harmless enough; and we've shaken hands with a hundred officials and officials' clerks, and Corunna spends half her time on land, signing all the papers that anyone brings her; and we've paid money to every soul in Morlaix, I do believe! Everyone except the priest and the schoolmaster! Yet every day they think up another reason why our goods must stay under hatches! Why, they're worse than the Chinese, these Frenchmen!"

Argandeau raised his shoulders helplessly. "No, no!" he said. "You do not understand them. They have had many years of war, and many years of democracy, when every man claimed to be as good as every other man, but privately knew himself to be better; and now they have Bonaparte and a dozen spies to watch each one of them, so they must be careful, poor people."

"Careful!" Marvin exclaimed. "Do you call a thief careful when he makes you turn out the same pocket twenty times?"

"Eh, eh?" Argandeau cried. " 'Thief' is a strong word! The trouble is merely that some important man has not yet received what he should receive. He is afraid, perhaps, to tell us what he wants; or perhaps he is waiting to find out what all the others have received from us, so that he may be certain he will not receive less than any man."

"A body'd think," Marvin told him, "that we were their enemies, instead of helping them to fight the English. Don't they ever say what they mean? Are they always bowing and smiling and talking about friendship, and then doing everything they can to ruin us, like your idiot Admiral D'Estaing who talked so loud about helping us whip England in the Revolution?"

Argandeau examined him calmly. "I think you are excited, dear Marvin. It is true that D'Estaing was not a lion in battle and was something of a hen as a seaman, but if I had been in his boots, I would have won that little war for your thick-skulled countrymen in two weeks—maybe three."

Marvin reached over and caught Argandeau by the shoulder. "Of course! Of course! I am sure that it is so, my dear friend! How much easier it will be, then, for you to win an even smaller war with people even more thick-skulled!"

Argandeau lifted his eyebrows. "What is this you say, dear Marvin?"

"Go ashore!" Marvin exclaimed. "Go ashore and tell Corunna to stop signing papers; that you'll arrange this thing! We must make a start at landing this cargo today! I tell you I don't like lying here with no way of maneuvering, and not enough crew to fight off any gang of frog eaters that takes a fancy to come aboard. I don't feel easy. There's a change coming! If you're as good as you think you are, go ashore and make these Frenchmen stop squabbling over their pennies long enough to let us tie up to a dock and get our goods on land. Tell 'em we want less politeness and more friendliness."

Argandeau elevated his shoulders. "But we must be patient! These poor people will not understand if we are rude to them; and I am sure that when our little rabbit returns, she will have the permission to begin tomorrow or the next day to unload."

"So that's what you think, Admiral," Marvin inquired, with an ex-aggerated air of urbanity. "I scarcely knew you at first, but now you've finished speaking, I recognize the D'Estaing accent. How well I remember your skill at doing nothing, Admiral, when we needed help the most!"

Argandeau laughed softly. "Be quiet!" he said. "That tongue of yours, it is too busy! I'll do what you want! I'll see that rabbit of ours at the Hôtel de Ville in ten minutes and tell her I arrange to do what you wish, but only do it to save myself from the clacking of your voice."

Marvin watched him being rowed ashore. "Do not look so serious!" Argandeau shouted back to him. "Argandeau, he arrange everything! This afternoon you toss your cargo about, eh, and tonight we have fried eels and two bottles of brandy—maybe three! I bring them back with me!"

The boat moved in toward the wharves of Morlaix and the dismal-looking buildings of gray stone that rose steeply above them. Marvin, confident that Argandeau, brought at last to the point of speaking his mind to his countrymen, would be successful in his mission, went forward to the bow, where those that were left of the crew were dividing their time between the catching of eels and the exchange of hoarse pleasantries with the occupants of small boats engaged in the sale of onions, checked shirts, flatfish, apple brandy, red wine, lace and mussels.

With reluctance they abandoned their fishing, removed the hatch and fell to swaying bales on deck in preparation for the afternoon's unloading. Marvin, having put them to work, inspected the galley and the forecastle, examined the guns with a mind to having them scraped and repainted; then, still with the thought of painting in his head, went aft to the cabin to look for spots that would be better for a brushful.

The cabin was divided into two sections, and it was the smaller of these that Corunna still occupied. At its door Marvin hesitated, but only for a moment. There seemed to him, when he entered, to be something of Corunna about this small white room with its standing bedplace and its wide lockers—an air of sturdiness and crispness. Drawn over the bedplace was a patchwork quilt that almost glittered in the brilliance of its colors, and folded neatly on it lay her needlework—that worsted work of art representing the Holy Family gazing with suspicion at the towers of Jerusalem.

Marvin, touching it gingerly with his forefinger, smiled a little. From it there seemed to rise a faint fragrance of sweet grass and mallow, such as had come to him so often from the Arundel meadows on summer nights. He stared up at the ceiling and around at the white panels of this neat small cabin; then moved to the high locker against the after bulkhead—a locker with a Chinese courting mirror over it, and a swinging whale-oil lamp of pewter and copper, with small paintings of her mother and father on either side.

The painting of her mother, Marvin thought, would be Corunna to the life if, in place of the low black dress, edged at the neck with wooden-seeming lace, the portrait showed her in a stained and darned Chinese jacket with a collar that came high up around her throat and fastened with three jade buttons.

He slipped the oval frame from its hook. Through the tightly drawn black hair gleamed a white ear tip; the lips seemed to tremble on the verge of a smile; in the smooth column of the throat, as Marvin studied it, there was almost the beating of a pulse. He touched the pictured throat gently with his finger. The scent of sweet grass and mallow came to him again; and the face at which he looked softened and became charming, as had Corunna's on that night off Rio. He lifted it toward his lips, but before it reached them, he guiltily raised his eyes to his reflection in the mirror.

Reflected also in the mirror was the stern window, and through the mirrored window he saw, far down the estuary, a tall black schooner beating up on the rising tide from the Channel, close-hauled on the larboard tack.

He quickly hung the picture in its place, turned to the window and examined the rig and cut of the distant vessel. Despite the brisk-ness of the southwest breeze, she rode stiff in the water, heeling over so little that no part of her copper showed, if indeed there was cop-per on her. She was, Marvin felt, too large for a smuggler; and he knew, as well, that there was scarce a smuggler in either France or England but used either a lugger or a cutter in his trade in preference to a schooner.

She might, he told himself, be a French privateer; but it was doubtful, since her top-hamper was lacking in delicacy, to his mind, for such a vessel. Even at that distance he could see, from the spread of her ratlines, that she carried more shrouds and backstays than Diron and Argandeau would consider needful; and it was plain that she was rigged for strength rather than for great speed. Furthermore, she showed no colors, which seemed to him unusual for a vessel en-tering a home port after a cruise.

Vaguely uneasy, but more curious than uneasy, he took Corunna's telescope from the rack beside her bedplace and went on deck, where a score of bales had risen from the hold to clutter the amid-ships section. Increasingly uneasy, he mounted to the mizzen top and focused the glass on the schooner, which had come about on the far side of the estuary. She was pointing downstream from the *Olive Branch*, but from the set of the tide it appeared to Marvin that when the stranger next came about, she would be abreast of the barque.

Through the glass he could see guns on her deck, which was noth-ing strange; and her ports were closed, with no crews to be distin-guished near the guns, so that she looked peaceable enough. He was a fool, he told himself, to be disturbed over a harmless merchantman, running home, no doubt, with rum and sugar from Martinico; and with that he polished the lenses of the glass with a fold of his shirt and stared even harder at her.

From far behind him he heard a hail. A boat, he saw, was bobbing toward the *Olive Branch* from the direction of Morlaix—a boat with three men in it. As he looked, the man in the stern sheets rose to his feet, pointing and waving toward the oncoming schooner, and hailed again. Marvin saw, with a faint trembling in the pit of his stomach, that the man was Argandeau. What it was that he shouted, Marvin could not hear, nor did he need to hear.

His thoughts churned in his head, like wheels spinning in butter. "If I can pile her up on shore," he thought, "she's safe. If I try to run her ashore, but don't have time, I'm making it easier to lose her." He cast a quick glance at the schooner. To Marvin, the mile-wide estuary seemed to have shrunk in size; the white cottages on the far shore, so distant until now, must, he thought, have drawn near to stare critically at him. The schooner, pushing a milky wave before her, had swelled beyond all reason. Already half across the estuary, she seemed to tower above the crinkled water like a giant among schooners.

He jumped into the rigging. "All hands tumble up!" he shouted. "Get axes! Cut the bow anchor cable! Cast loose the main and fore-topsail!"

He rushed, spiderlike, down the ratlines; then leaped to the helm, putting it hard over and lashing it there. "Jib and fore-topmast stay-sails!" he shouted. "Crowd 'em on!"

The waist and bow of the ship seemed alive with movement as the remaining men of the crew scurried over the bales and into the rigging to get sail on her.

Slowly the gray walls and roofs of Morlaix moved to starboard; and the tall Indian, Steven, came up over the bows, in his hand a cleaver from the galley, so that Marvin knew the bow cable had been cut.

He called the Indian aft. "When they've got sail on her," Marvin told him, "wait till she points for the bank. Then cut the stern hawser and jam her ashore. Ram her in anywhere! Get there! No matter how!"

The tall Indian flicked the cleaver into the deck. It stuck there, quivering, handy to his grasp. "What is she? A lobster box?"

Marvin shook his head and vanished down the companionway. The *Olive Branch*, pushed by the southwest breeze moved slowly against the incoming tide, hesitated, as if caught on a sand bar, while the loosed sails shivered noisily but to no avail.

Argandeau scrambled over the starboard bulwarks. "Haul!" he snapped. "Haul those yards around! Never mind that schooner! Haul!"

He looked quickly over his own shoulder. The schooner was on them—so close that her long white jib-boom had the look of threatening the reluctant barque with a lashing; so close that Argandeau could see the moving lips of a whiskered seaman who leaned over the bows, a cutlass gripped in the fist that rested on the bulwarks.

The tall Indian at the helm jumped to the taffrail, slashed the stern hawser and hurled the cleaver at the towering schooner. The *Olive Branch* surged sluggishly toward the brown rocks that lay a half cable's length ahead.

"Dan!" Argandeau called. "Dan!"

Marvin burst from the companionway, spilling an armful of cutlasses on the deck.

"All hands aft!" he shouted, snatching up a cutlass. "All hands aft to stop boarders!"

"No good!" Argandeau told him. "We don't make it!"

"No!" Marvin shouted. "They can't do it! Hold 'em off!"

"No good, dear Dan," Argandeau repeated. "They cut us out. Look here, what they do!"

The schooner shot past the *Olive Branch's* stern, veering swiftly as she did so. Her bulwarks, Marvin saw, were packed with intent red faces, and as she veered, blue-clad men in shiny black tarpaulin hats swarmed into the fore and main chains and ratlines—twenty of them, thirty of them.

She slipped between the *Olive Branch* and the haven of brown rocks. Her broad walls of canvas hung over the barque, seeming to Marvin to cut off from the *Olive Branch* all sun and light and air. Then she closed in; and even while Marvin waited for the rasping lurch that must come when she laid the *Olive Branch* aboard, there was a growling call of "Boarders away!" from her stern. The bulwarks of the schooner spouted men, who hurled themselves into the *Olive Branch* like gargantuan blue locusts.

Argandeau caught Marvin's arm as a dozen British seamen converged on the quarter-deck. Two of them darted by Marvin. One went to the deck with the Indian; the other put the wheel hard over. Over the shoulders of the Britishers, Marvin saw that his crew, taken front and rear by the English, had dropped their weapons. Four of the seamen jumped suddenly at Marvin and Argandeau. A pistol butt struck Marvin's wrist and the cutlass fell from his hand.

The blue-clad Britishers, hitherto silent, burst into uproarious talk and laughter. "Easy as pickin' gripes!" one of them shouted. A sour-visaged officer, old enough to be an admiral, went to the *Olive Branch's* larboard rail and hailed the schooner's quarter-deck. "All clear, sir," he called to an elegantly uniformed youth who stood by the schooner's wheel. "Shall we run for the Nore?"

"What about the female?" the youth demanded pettishly. "Bring her up where we can see her!"

The officer turned on Marvin and Argandeau. "Where's the female that's supposed to be captain of this barque?"

Argandeau raised his eyebrows. "Female?" he asked. "How does it happen you think we are supposed to have a female captain?"

The sour-faced officer took a quick step forward and swung the flat of his cutlass against Argandeau's upper arm. "Where is she, you swab?" he demanded.

"She's ashore," Marvin said quickly. "Is Captain Slade aboard your schooner?"

"Slade!" Argandeau cried. "Ah, my friend! You've hit it! How else could these British have known we lay here worth the taking, and could be taken? How else would they have heard we have a female captain? Slade! Yes; Slade! But we shall not find him on their schooner! He would not risk that Argandeau, in chains, should yet find means to bite him to death!"

The sour-faced man turned to the rail to hail his youthful commander. "Ashore, sir! They say the female captain's ashore!"

The younger man laughed. "Ah, that's where the admiral said she was to be put! Nice of her to save us a bit of trouble! Sorry to miss her, in a way, what? First American that ever did anything right, to my knowledge! Sorry to miss a freak like that!" His voice became crisper. "Get right along," he called. "Take the barque to Sheerness, but not a foot farther, Cropsey. We'll go up to Chatham together."

The *Olive Branch,* manned by her British captors, sheered away from the schooner, which ran rapidly down the estuary ahead of them.

"Nah, then," said the sour-faced officer to Argandeau and Marvin, "we'll just clap you and your questions abaht Captain Slade into the cable tier! Captain Slade, eh? Well, if he's one of you hole-and-corner Americans, you'll probably meet up with him in the hulks, where all of you belong!"

XV

F<small>ROM</small> the courtyard of the *Queen of Scotland* tavern in the town of Morlaix there emanated at all times a powerful odor of badly cleaned stables, venerable wine casks and cheese; and when the sun appeared—as it infrequently did—above the chimney pots and jumbled tile roofs that surrounded the court, a singular penetrating fragrance of pickled herring rose in waves from the seemingly immaculate stone pavement of the court, and passed through the closed windows in the tavern as readily as though every window had been thrown open.

Since the sun shone brightly on this clear October day, and since, as a result, the fragrance of pickled herring was strong in every room in the *Queen of Scotland,* but particularly strong because of an opened window in the small fourth-floor room numbered "44," it seemed strange indeed that Corunna Dorman should sit huddled in a corner of that dim and cheerless chamber, staring fixedly at a knot in the floor—a knot around which the soft wood had been worn away by the restless feet of countless vanished guests.

From the roundness of her eyes, there seemed to be little doubt that she had seen all of the knot there was to see, but long minutes passed, and never once did she look up—not even when her black cloak, which hung in the center of a wall, moved jerkily and swayed from side to side, as if the evil spirit of the room, maddened by the smell of herring, had taken violent possession of it.

The cloak fell at last, revealing a small hole in the wall over which it had hung; and at its fall Corunna rose to pick it up and hang it over the hole once more. Having done so, she stood silent beside it, holding to the cloak's hem and staring with round eyes at nothing whatever.

She seemed, almost, to have lost her hearing as well as her vision, for when a light knock sounded upon her door, she still held to the cloak and stared fixedly into space. When, however, the knock was repeated and a woman's shrill voice called, "Open, please, lady!" she turned quickly to the door, dragged a chest of drawers from before it and snapped back the bolt.

The woman who entered was short and fat. Her fatness spread

outward from her bust, so that her shoulders had the look of being pressed upward by it, her eyes squeezed half closed by the surge of her enormous bosom, and her vast hips and thighs spread outward by the weight they carried. She breathed heavily and peered past Corunna into the room.

"You eat nothing! Why not you come down? I give bread and *chocolat,* and you need not think of *monnaie*—not yet."

"Yes," Corunna said. "Thank you. I think—I think I——" She stopped, swallowed hard, and contented herself with saying "Yes" once more.

The fat woman pushed past her into the room, jangling a cluster of keys attached to a brass ring, and stared at the large and elaborate bed. Her half-opened mouth had the look, in that enormous face, of a sort of buttonhole. She darted a quick, suspicious look at Corunna. "Don't you sleep sometime? You don't like this bed?"

Corunna reached out to her cloak and drew it to one side, revealing the hole beneath. "I slept in the chair."

By a movement of her eyes and upper lip, the fat woman gave the impression of raising her shoulders. She went to the hole, stooped a little and squinted through it; then, applying her lips to the aperture, she violently shrieked a veritable explosion of syllables. When she turned back to Corunna, she wagged her head solemnly. "Nothing! Think nothing about this! All rooms have these holes, and all men look through! What you expect?"

As broad and solid as a hogshead on two boulders, she stood and examined Corunna with scrupulous attention; but Corunna, again staring wide-eyed at the protruding knot, seemed oblivious of her presence.

"You don't know no way to get *monnaie?*" she asked at length. "You don't have no *bijou*—no ring, maybe?"

Corunna shook her head.

"You don't know some friend in Paris, no? In Boulogne? In Lorient? Maybe in Brest or Nantes, eh? In Brest and Lorient come many Americans in letters of marque. Maybe you go there, and you find a friend who take you in America, when you kiss him nice."

Corunna looked up quickly at the fat woman, opened her lips; then closed them again and fell to staring at her clenched hands.

The fat woman jingled the keys on the brass ring and dropped her voice to a confidential whisper. "Is here an *avocat* who is think you can get *monnaie* from the government in Paris because you bring wounded men here on that poor ship the dirty British had the audacity to seize from you. Eh! What a terrible thing for our beautiful city of Morlaix that those English should be so sly and so bold as to come into our very harbor in such a manner! Now perhaps the Emperor will give us some fortification worth something! *Hélas!* But it will not do you much good, poor little one! What you need, my child, is a protector. Come, you let me speak to our *avocat!* I will arrange it. You permit me to hint to him that you can be persuaded to go with him to Paris, and he will become eager. Oh, yes! When they are old, they are easily inflamed!" She placed a pudgy finger beside her nose and smiled craftily at Corunna. "It will be a good affair for both of us! He is good man—old and kind. I think he would be gentle, and you like his protection very much."

Far below them there was the sound of a slamming door, and of a stir—a throbbing pulse that somehow seemed to bring new life into the stale and tainted air of this ancient tavern.

The fat woman surged past Corunna and stood listening at the threshold. A burst of speech came up the darkness of the stairway, together with the noise of quick footsteps—footsteps that drew rapidly nearer.

The black bulk of the listening mistress of the *Queen of Scotland* shot through the doorway, plucked from her place by a violent hand, and where she had been stood Lurman Slade, slender and neat in his fine blue coat, his head thrown far back so that he might see clearly into the room, and a look of deep concern on his thin brown face.

"Corunna!" he cried hoarsely. "My poor Corunna!" He went to her quickly and took her by the shoulders. "My dear! I've been in a torment to reach you! If ever I'd known——"

He looked into her brimming eyes; then drew her suddenly against his breast, cupped her face in his hands and kissed her tenderly.

She drew a deep and quivering breath, like a child who has borne a heavy weight of suffering; then clung eagerly to him.

"You're here! You're here!" she said. "I didn't know—I was afraid—I thought you might never come! It was terrible! It was terrible! They were here, and then in a second they were gone!" She shook her head wearily.

Slade kissed her eyes and held her tight. "Never come!" he whispered. "You thought I might never come! I'd have come to you across the whole world, my sweet—my little sweet!"

She leaned backward in his arms to stare at the walls about her. "Why," she said, "it's been like an awful dream! Everything gone—everything swallowed up, and not a word from anyone! Not a word!" She shivered.

Slade took her hands in his and kissed them; then led her to the
one poor chair and knelt beside her. "My heart was like lead in me
when I left you," he told her softly. "Like a stone, it was! I could
hardly eat for thinking of you! I came to you on the instant the news
reached me. With all my heart in the search, I was seeking for the
ship that would be your privateer, happy that I was working for you.
Then, at a tavern in a little town I heard by chance of the cutting
out of the *Olive Branch*, and thank God I did hear! And so I am
come to you!"

"Yes," she said. "I'm glad you've come. I need somebody."

"Aye," he assented gravely, "you've needed somebody a long time,
Corunna—somebody that could protect you from your own simple
trust in people. I don't think you yet know," he added, "how the
barque was taken."

"Why, by the British!" she said, wondering. "They came in——"

"Aye, so they did," he agreed, looking at her pityingly. "In Roscoff
it's known how the British did it, Corunna. Aye, they know who
helped to do it! I blame myself! What a fool I was! I'm like you;
I'm not suspicious either, dear. I never dreamed he was anything
but a coward—a sulky country coward! He's a cumbersome lout, half
giant to the eye; and I was simple enough to think him an honest
one, all brawn and no cunning."

Corunna stared at him. "What do you say?"

"You ask me what I say, Corunna? I say what's incredible; much
harder for you to believe than for me, though I thought I knew him.
My dear, I sha'n't blame you if you can't believe it. I think there
was a time, before you knew me, when you liked him very well."

"Marvin?" she whispered. "Why, yes, I did!"

Slade touched her shoulder gently; he looked kind and wise and
good. "I knew. I understood, because from the first I understood you.
I knew you'd been very close to giving your heart to him, my dear,
and that but for some vital flaw, some ugly defect in his character
he'd betrayed to you, you would have given it; and so you'd have
been lost to me. Isn't that so?"

"Why, yes."

"I knew," he said in a low voice, full of pain; then smiled, as in a
lover's noble forgiveness. "Thank God that's past, and you *did* see
that defect. It's your having seen it for yourself that makes it easier
for me now to tell you how that base metal in him runs through the
whole fabric of his character, so that he could do what every man in
Roscoff knows he has done."

"Knows he has done——" she repeated uncertainly. "Lurman, you're telling me——"

"See here," he said. "I don't want to tell you. Do you think me a man not too proud to put a defeated rival in a false position?"

"No." She swallowed. "But Marvin—Dan Marvin! Marvin!"

"Marvin," Slade burst out bitterly, as if the truth leapt from his lips despite him. "Good God! Why, he handed over the *Olive Branch* to the British without a blow, either for you or for his ship! Without a blow! When he lay in the black hole with us, didn't he try to slip out to traffic with 'em? I never told you this before, Corunna, but he did! Why, you must have seen him currying favor with the commander of the *Beetle,* on the pretext of obtaining medicines for a common seaman! Medicines! Good God! I don't know what scheme he has, but you saw he was forever against anything that meant fighting the British. Oh, aye! The dog would ever keep his record clean with them! Forgive me if I'm bitter, but when I think what he's done to you, I forget you once held him for a friend."

"To me?" she said. "You think Dan Marvin would——"

"Corunna! Corunna! How did the English know just where to come and what to do? Why, my dear, there's not a man in Morlaix, aye, or Roscoff either, who doesn't know the *Olive Branch* was delivered to the British by her officers—and for a consideration. Do you think that Marvin couldn't have run the barque safe on shore if he'd had a mind to? Pah! You know better yourself! You're too good a seaman not to know. I wish to God I'd struck him dead at your feet, before he should have done this to you."

She rose suddenly and went to the window, where, square-shouldered and flat-backed against the pale October sunlight, she stared down into the noisome courtyard below.

"How could they know?" she asked faintly. "How could all these people know that Dan sold his soul to the English?"

Slade sighed, and his sigh seemed freighted with compassion. "Such things are always known, Corunna." He shook his head sadly. "Always, my dear."

"But he didn't want to come here in the beginning! He said the way to go home was to go home."

"Yes," Slade assented, "and when you overruled him, he was sour and sore, and now he's paid you for that overruling. You asked me how these people knew. Corunna dear, it's life and death to every smuggler on the coast to know what goes on in the British Navy to the last detail; and they *do* know, believe me! They know Marvin sold the *Olive Branch* to the English, and they know he'll not only get money in return but a British commission to boot."

"Ah, he wouldn't," she whispered.

"He'll have a commission from them if he wants it," Slade insisted, "and most of them here think he'll be a wise man to take it. Aye! They say he knows that America, with only fifteen cruisers, can make no stand against England with her thousand ships of war, so that England must win, and America be a colony of England's once more. That being so, Marvin will not only have money but he'll keep his lands in America, and be high in favor with the British as well." He shook his head and cocked his eye at Corunna. "Yes, he's a cautious man," he reminded her. "I think I've heard you speak of that, my dear; but now we both know, to our cost, it was something more than caution in him."

Corunna seemed to choke, looking down into the courtyard. "No!" she exclaimed. "No!"

Slade came close beside her. "My dear," he said softly, "we none of us know what's in a man's mind, and I could almost forgive him for turning against his country, if so be those are his principles. It's what he's done to you that I shall never forgive. To turn from a woman more beautiful than any Queen on her throne, and with the brain of a Decatur or a Nelson—that's what shows him in his true colors!" He touched her hand gently. "To think he left you here as destitute as any beggar in the streets! Left you here without a cent, without a ship, and, so far as he knows, without a friend!"

He turned her about, so that she faced him, and took both her hands. "Well, let him go! It's nothing to lose a vessel! It's nothing to lose money! If I had you, there'd be nothing in the world, no matter how poor I was, that would keep me from whatever it was you wanted and needed." He kissed her fingers.

"All my life I've paid no attention to women," he went on. "Now that I've seen you and felt the touch of your hands and the softness of your lips, I'll hate all women but you for the rest of my days."

She smiled faintly and shook her head.

"It's so!" he insisted. "Why, tomorrow we could set off for Paris; and before you can have bought yourself a dozen gowns, I'll find a way to get you a vessel, and have half of Paris at the feet of the fairest bride in all France."

His voice was that of a loving friend who brings a brave gaiety to battle the despondency of his beloved. Tears seemed about to rise in his eyes—tears of love and pity—yet he smiled upon her in a

valiant encouragement, and his hand came upon her shoulder with
the touch of a hearty comrade.

"Eh, Corunna? We'll up and at 'em! Here's a pair of us that can
look misfortune in the face. Now we're together, not all the bad luck
in the world—no, and not all the sneaking treachery of those we'd
love to believe in, neither!—ah, my dear, not all the evil in the world
can keep us down!"

Thus he swept her away.

XVI

It was not discomfort that weighed heaviest on Marvin, as the violent Channel seas racked and rasped him against the harsh coils of the cable in the airless, wedge-shaped den of the cable tier, nor yet the lack of humanity in the British who had him in charge, but the almost certain knowledge that it must have been Slade who had sent His Majesty's schooner *Sparrow* to cut out the *Olive Branch* from the harbor of Morlaix, and the even greater certainty that Corunna, by this sudden and overwhelming disaster, had been left penniless and friendless in France, with no person to whom to turn save Slade himself.

He groaned, ill at ease mentally and bodily, and prevented by the deck above from rising even to a sitting position. "You could have stayed there," he reproached Argandeau. "You *should* have stayed there!"

"You think too much about this, dear Marvin," Argandeau told him gently. "When those smugglers come running to me in the *Préfet's* office, doing me a kindness by saying that this schooner is a Griffon—a Griffon who had already cut out one other vessel from Morlaix and two from under the batteries of Dunkirk, and must therefore intend wickedness to the *Olive Branch,* what can I do, eh? You know who I am in Morlaix? I am the brave Lucien Argandeau! Can I say to them 'Pooi for your Englishman! I stay here and do nothing about him!' Can I say that? Not if I wish to remain the celebrated Lucien! No, I must say, 'Hah! The perfidious English! Lucien Argandeau will show them something that will make them laugh out of the wrong mouth! He will go out alone and dispose of them! Thank you very well!' Another thing, dear Marvin: There was a chance, eh? —a chance that if we were quick and fortunate, we could have got her ashore, so that this Griffon could have done no cutting out. Then your rabbit would have had money, and we could have shown the British some cutting out of our own!"

He was silent, and Marvin as well, so that they heard nothing in the darkness of their lurching, coffin-like inclosure save the smashing and rattling of the seas against the bows.

"To show the British something!" Argandeau whispered yearningly. "There is nothing else I want any more! Women and wine are pleasant, but I have had a large share—so large a share that to count the favors ladies have shown me—— Eh! Can a man count the glasses of wine he has had? Only the English are a flame in my head. Nowhere can I get money for a privateer except through you or your rabbit, dear Marvin!"

His voice was as soft as the murmur of a gentle wind among small leaves. "It was apparent to me that if your rabbit was deprived of the *Olive Branch,* she also lost the power of purchasing a privateer for me or for anybody else. Therefore I was obliged to devote my efforts to saving the *Olive Branch.* Observe the clarity of my thoughts, dear Dan! We French are logical above all other people; and when you say I should have stayed ashore to look after your rabbit, you are not logical! By the stomach of the Supreme Being, I did not even wait to go into the next building and tell her what was happening in the harbor. While there are Englishmen alive, I could not stay my feet! No, no! Argandeau to the fray! Well, it was done, and now I grieve about your rabbit. I am sorry we have not tossed a knife into Slade before he made this trouble, but I am sorrier that we have lost our chance to privateer. These English, dear Marvin, there is nothing in the world like them; and now I wish nothing in this life except to be in a fast vessel again, so that I can rip their seacoast from end to end!"

"Slade must have gone to Roscoff and crossed with a smuggler," Marvin murmured, seeming to have heard none of Argandeau's words. "If I'd got sail on her two minutes earlier—if those damned Frenchmen had let us haul in to the dock——"

"If!" Argandeau protested. "You are stuck full of 'ifs!' You will 'if' yourself into a sickness! You did everything very quick and with no slip. No man could do more. Duguay-Trouin, he could not have done more. Tom Souville could not have done more. My soul! Argandeau himself could not have done more! You dwell too much on this! You must sleep, eh? Sleep will wipe out the regrets that are false. You listen to me! In Spain, when I am younger, I learn Spanish from a Spanish lady, very beautiful. She teach me a proverb for everything in the world. 'An "if" in the mind is as bad as a *banderillo* in the hide of a bull,' she say. Also, she tell me, 'Two hours' sleep is better medicine than two hundred years of tears.' Whatever she wish to prove, she can prove with a proverb."

There was an end, at last, to the dizzy gyrations of the hole into which they were packed, and the prisoners, foul with the slime of the cable tier and sore from head to foot because of the bed of wet and stinking rope on which they had lain interminably, clambered weakly up the companion-ladders to find the barque hove-to under heavy skies in the lee of the crowded dockyard of Sheerness, at the mouths of the Thames and the Medway, and under the guns of two lowering forts.

The gray-faced officer watched them brought on deck; then, with a faintly sour smile, he warned them against shouting or the making of unnecessary noises if they wished to enjoy the benefits of the open air.

Doubtful concerning the quality of the smile, Marvin pressed forward. "With your permission," he said, "we'd like to take our private belongings with us—our clothes and some small articles."

"What articles are those?" the aged lieutenant asked.

"There's the picture of a lady in the small cabin——" Marvin said.

"No such thing!" the lieutenant snapped. "There's no picture of any kind on this vessel! If there was, it would do you no good to take it; there's no room for such trumpery on the hulks."

"Our clothes——" Marvin again ventured.

"Clothes!" the lieutenant exclaimed in disgust. "There's nothing I'd call clothes aboard this craft! Nothing but dirty Yankee rags! I suppose you'll be trying to say you had something wearable, and that these men of mine stole them! You'll be provided with clothes aboard the hulks, so let me hear no more drivel about your filthy duds!"

Marvin shivered. His muscles tightened until his back and his neck ached from the strain of them. Argandeau tapped him on the shoulder and sighed gently. "I tell you they are a flame in my head, these English!"

Two hours later, followed by the ironic cheers of the English seamen who had cut them out from Morlaix, they were packed into the waist of a government tender, with boarding nettings at both bulwarks and a squad of marines before and behind them; and thus guarded, they bore off to the westward, into the curving channel of the River Medway—a river with flat low shores and a wealth of mud banks from which there rose wisps of mist, smelling of decay.

It was near dusk of that gray October afternoon when the tender, rounding a wide bend in the river, came into an expanse of water so broad that it had the appearance of a lake. Ranged along the center of this lake, and bulking mountain-like above the flat expanse of water and the low fields beyond, floated fifteen structures that

seemed to Marvin to have the look of giant coffins, but coffins sadly
misshapen by pipes and platforms and warts and knobs that protruded from them in a thousand places and at a thousand angles.

"So there they are." Argandeau sighed. "There are the hulks, that
have been more terrible to France than any hell." He drew a deep
breath, and then another. "Breathe deep, dear Marvin, while you
can. There are Frenchmen in those coffins who have not breathed
pure air for six long years."

The tender drew abreast of the rearmost hulk. She was, Marvin
saw, the defaced and dirty remnant of what once had been a ship-
of-the-line—of what once had been more beautiful, with her tiers of
gun ports, her symmetrical sweep of hull, her glistening paint, her
towering masts, her web of rigging and her cloud-like spread of canvas, than any other structure fashioned by the hand of man.

Argandeau growled faintly in his throat. "Look!" he said. "Look
how she is old and sick, I think with leprosy, and so squats there in
anger, wishing never to move again! It is a sight to make a seaman
weep! They are cruel to everything, even to their ships, these
Englishmen!"

Pale vapors oozed from the countless pipes that were thrust from
the sides of the soiled and dreary hulks, vapors that coiled and
drifted downward like a mournful fog, so that the tender moved
along the melancholy fleet through an acrid veil of smoke.

She drew close to a hulk near the middle of the line; and to the
crew of the *Olive Branch*, silently staring from behind the boarding
nettings that had been raised between them and any possibility of
escape, came the shrill babble of unnumbered voices. A platform
encircled the hulk three feet above the water; and on the platform
two sentries rattled their muskets and challenged sharply.

"Tender *Primrose*, of Sheerness," bawled a hoarse voice from the
tender's stern, "wiv twenty-four Amairikins, cut out of Morlaix by
schooner *Sparrow!* Consigned to *Crown Prince* hulk by orders of the
Transport Office!"

High up in the lofty stern of this miserable vessel a window swung
open, and from it peered a face with a babyish look to it—a look as
though the person to whom it belonged had lived long, but never
grown up. The features seemed pinched together, as though the eyes
and nose and mouth, in infancy, had been seized in a ruthless hand
and compressed until they had become fixed.

"Are they washed?" this face called down angrily. "Have they had
a bath?"

"Yes, sir!" shouted the hoarse voice from the *Primrose*.

"Send them up!" called the angry voice. "But if they hadn't been, back they'd have gone to Sheerness! See you remember it, my man! You bring any more dirty Yankees to this hulk, and either you'll take 'em back to be washed, or wash 'em on your own deck!"

The *Primrose* swung against the landing stage, whence a long, canvas-sided companionway ran up to the high bulwarks of the *Crown Prince.* The boarding nettings were lowered, and the captain of the tender motioned the prisoners toward the hulk.

"You heard what he said!" he growled. "If you don't aim to be soused in the Medway with a rope round your middle, stick to it you been washed!"

They mounted the companionway, and the tall Marvin, coming over the top of the bulwarks at the head of the line of seamen, found himself looking down into an oblong space that seemed to him the size of the floor of a fair-sized barn. Beyond a loop-holed wall at one end rose a drab and dreary forecastle, from which smokepipes protruded like pins from a pincushion. Armed sentries stood behind the wall, and marines moved about on the forecastle itself, so that Marvin knew the forecastle belonged to those who guarded the prisoners. Beyond a similar wall at the other end rose the structure that had been the quarter-deck; and in his quick glance at it, Marvin saw it was still sacred to the ship's officers; for the pinch-faced man, dressed in a uniform too tight for him, stood silently at the break in the deck to watch the prisoners come aboard.

The space between the quarter-deck and the forecastle was a-swarm with men—more than Marvin had ever before seen packed into such a space—and from these men there rose an odor so strong and penetrating that it caught at Marvin's nostrils and his throat and sickened him.

The garments of these men were shredded and tattered. Through wisps of cloth showed skinny ribs: pipestem arms: bony shins and thighs. Such was the emaciation and pallor of this sorry crew that they had the look of skeletons who, by some devil's dispensation, had risen from the dead in rotted grave clothes for a reunion in this purgatory of the sea.

Yet there was nothing skeleton-like about their actions; for they posed and pirouetted when Marvin came down among them. They capered insanely before him, flinging their arms about, moving their shoulders, screaming unceasingly in shrill and womanish French. A thousand hands, it seemed to Marvin, were stretched forward to pat his back; to touch his arms: his shoulders. *"Les Américains!"* he heard them cry. *"Les braves Américains! General Madison brave homme! George Vasington brave homme!"*

There came into his head the thought that war made strange bedfellows, and that a common cause could unite men of widely different races. In that moment he felt a movement against his thigh, and as his glance dropped toward it, he thought he saw the flicker of fingers drawn back with the speed of light. He clapped his hand to his pocket; then turned quickly to the men from the *Olive Branch*. "Keep tight hold of your money!" he told them. "They got mine!"

Argandeau came close up beside him and spoke in French to the jostling throng around them. What he said was said softly, and took not long in the saying, but the words had the hiss of a whiplash. The ragged Frenchmen fell away before Marvin, so that a lane was opened through them. Suddenly silent, they stared at one another and at the Americans with eyebrows raised, and with hands and shoulders that protested their innocence more clearly than any words. Yet in their eyes Marvin seemed to see amusement, and even something of malicious mockery.

He scanned their faces sharply. Rage filled him at his loss, but in addition to the rage there was almost a sickness at the knowledge of his pennilessness; for without money, he knew, a corpse would have less trouble in rising from its coffin than he would have in escaping from this hulk to go in search of Corunna and of Slade.

An irate voice put an end to his attempt to find, among those pallid countenances, the face of the man who might have robbed him. "Here!" the voice shouted. "Here! Where do you think you are? Get back here where you belong!" It was the voice of the pinch-faced lieutenant; and, Marvin, recognizing a dangerous childish fury in the sound of the words, hastened through the jostling Frenchmen to stand close under the high poop on which the angry lieutenant stood.

He was, Marvin saw, a man approaching fifty, a plump man whose arms and legs were oversnug in an ornate uniform which had the air of having been made for a woman. His hands, resting on the carved rail before him, were smooth and white, and heavy with rings.

"Good God!" he shouted, stamping his foot angrily. "Twenty-four more! Over three hundred of you damned contrary Yankees aboard this ship already, and now twenty-four more of you wretched contentious creatures! You there—you tall man! What was it you stopped for? You spoke to someone! You've brought a letter to one of these prisoners! I won't have it! I'll put you in the black hole! I'll cut off your rations! I'll——"

"I've done nothing!" Marvin interrupted. "Nothing but try to find the man that picked my pocket."

The lieutenant, slack of lip, stared dully at him; then burst abruptly into laughter. "Listen to that, Sugden!" he cried, turning to a small man who stood humbly beside him, his eyes downcast and a long book beneath his arm. "There never was an Amairikin in this world that wasn't always talking about money or claiming he was badly treated! Pocket picked! 'Pon my word, Sugden, that's positively convulsing! Tomorrow he'll have something to say about the food. Tough meat, or weevily bread, most likely!"

Sugden laughed, a raven's croak, and looked, grinning, at Marvin. "Most likely," he agreed.

"I warn you now," the lieutenant told Marvin disdainfully. "There's no sympathy on this ship for whiners! Whine and escape! Whine and escape! You ought to have that motto on your flag along with the bars you've already put on it. One of you's worse than a thousand Frenchmen! I'll remind you now that those who try escaping from this hulk get the black hole! Don't forget it! Give your names to Sugden; then get over with the rest of your brave Amairikins and let them find room for you on the lower deck, if they can. If they can't, it's not my fault!" He turned and minced away.

Sugden set down Marvin's name, vessel and other matters in his long book. Another clerk tossed down to him a limp hammock, a bag of chopped rags and a blanket that had the feel of being woven from string. Behind him the Frenchmen were dragging hammocks from an airing-stage and disappearing beneath the hatches. He heard Argandeau supplying Sugden with astounding information— name, Lucien Argandeau; nationality, American; residence, Boston; wife, one wife; children, no children.

Before he could protest, he felt a touch on his arm and whirled to see a man no taller than a cabin boy—a spare young man with a face of extreme gravity and crinkly side whiskers the color of corn-silk after a frost. He wore an overcoat so long that it was near to dragging on the deck.

"Newton," he said, holding out his hand to Marvin. "Matthew Newton of Salem. Matt to some and Newt to others, but answer to both. Pressed aboard the *Poictiers 74*. Got put in here for not fighting. Enemy, I am. Dangerous enemy! Bad and dangerous! Now I'm President of the Lower Deck for a month. Come on forward." He nodded his head toward the bow. "We got a law—no Americans allowed aft of the main hatch when there's other Americans coming aboard."

"So you won't be robbed?" Marvin asked doubtfully.

"Oh dear, no!" Newton exclaimed. "We haven't anything to steal! It's so none of us'll lose his head and tell that fat snake Osmore what we think of him. If that should ever happen, he'd starve us to death, innocent and guilty alike."

He turned briskly and led them forward to the Americans.

XVII

THREE hundred and twenty-seven Americans, Newton told them, were already quartered in the lower battery of the *Crown Prince*, and now there would be three hundred and fifty-one to pack in with their hammocks, like herring into a barrel. Above them, in the upper battery, he said, there were three hundred and nine Frenchmen, privateer officers for the most part; while below them, on the orlop deck, slept another two hundred and sixteen of the Frenchmen, known as *Raffalés* and *Manteaux Impériaux*—men wholly lost and abandoned, who sold their very food and rags for money with which to gamble, and so went naked, except for single cloths which swarmed with insects, even as the imperial mantle of Napoleon swarmed with bees.

"So here we are!" Newton said. "We can't spread down onto the orlop deck, because no decent men could live within sight or sound or smell of the *Raffalés;* and we can't spread up with the officers and the bourgeois, because no American can get along with 'em." He eyed Argandeau and grinned. "No offense," he said. "Maybe somewhere there are better Frenchmen than those we've got aboard this hulk, but here there isn't one we can trust: not even the captains. They're mean, all of 'em, in small ways."

"No offense, to me," Argandeau said quietly. "I am a little tired of the French equality that is no equality at all, and the French liberty that gives Frenchmen no liberty except that of remaining in English prisons all their lives. For a time I shall try being an American—Lucien Argandeau, of Boston. These French, they are what you say because they believe that all is fair in love and war, and they can prove to you that life is nothing else—war and love. It is of course true that the French are, as they say, the most logical of all people on earth; but recently I have come to think that the simple truth is preferable to French logic."

Newton stared at him doubtfully, shrugged his shoulders and led them to the main hatchway. They descended its single ladder to the upper battery deck, where dim distances were filled with the up-flung arms of Frenchmen, hanging their hammocks; then went down another ladder to the lower battery deck, where the Americans, crouching beneath the massive planking of the deck above, crawled about with upturned faces, seeking the numbers chalked beside their hammock-hooks.

"It's too late for shifting hooks," Newton told them. "You'll have to sleep on the deck, between two lines of hammocks. You get a powerful lot of fleas down there, and it might be you'll be stepped on a few times, but you'll have better air. Tomorrow we'll squeeze these folks together, and you can sling your hammock amidships."

Marvin, close on Newton's heels, dragged his hammock as best he could through the shifting, jostling, noisy mass of men. Newton's hooks, he saw, were in a corner, near a barred porthole and a latrine; and even as Newton made fast his hammock-rope of spun yarn to the ceiling, a chain rattled loudly beside him. The port fell shut with an echoing thud. An angry roar of protest rose from the men around them.

"Drat 'em!" Newton cried. "You'd think they were afraid we'd chop ourselves in pieces and squeeze through the bars of the ports if they were left open after dusk!"

One by one the other ports along the lower battery slammed shut with a rattle of chains, and on that crowded mass of prisoners there descended a blackness that seemed to Marvin to thrust itself into his ears and press against his eyelids.

"Bring a light here!" Newton shouted. "There's twenty-four men got to sleep on the deck between No. 1 and No. 2 rows in the northwest quarter." A sulphur spunk flickered into blue flame near Marvin, then yellowed as a candlewick took fire.

"Get your hammocks in place," Newton urged the men from the *Olive Branch*. "Anybody caught with a light gets three days black hole on half rations, so all candles are doused if we have word from above that anybody's coming."

The hammocks, Marvin saw, formed a continuous layer of canvas between deck and ceiling, the edges of each hammock touching those on either side. Here and there, in this gigantic slit of a room, the dim light of a candle glowed palely. Stowed in their hammocks or squatting beneath them, the prisoners gabbled and shouted, the chorus of their voices striking on Marvin's ear like the muffled outcry of innumerable sea gulls.

"'Tisn't anything you can't stand," Newton told him, thrusting his head over the end of his hammock to look down at him. "When I was pressed onto the *Poictiers*, me being supercargo of one of my father's brigs and fresh out of Harvard College, I thought I'd die in a week, what with the terrible food, and the slave drivers they called officers, and the workhouse mongrels in the crew. But my goodness alive! I got fat on it! I'd have got fat on it even if the captain hadn't made me his secretary. Give a man fresh air and a little work and enough food to fill his stomach, no matter what the food is, and he'll get along."

To Marvin it seemed as though the air had suddenly been heated by a giant stove. It had the feel, he thought, of an animal's breath —the breath of an enormous beast that had preyed on carrion—and with the thought, a black depression filled his brain, so that the re-alization of his lamentable state came fully to him. In his mind's eye he saw Morlaix once more, cold and drab at the end of the narrow estuary, and as distant as those far-off Chinese cities that seemed less real than dreams. It was, indeed, like a figure in a dream that Corunna trembled in a sad perspective before him; a figure remote and small, and surely beyond the reach of one who lay, like these unfortunates, half clothed, half fed, and only half alive.

"I suppose he will," Marvin responded at length, becoming aware that Newton was contemplating him curiously.

"Yes, he'll get along," Newton repeated. "Now, you take these men here on this deck; they're in prison for nothing, all of 'em. Every last one of 'em, nearly, is in the same box I am. They were hauled out of American ships by British press gangs before the war broke out, and made to serve aboard British cruisers—hell-ships, they're called by some, and 'hell-ship' is the proper word for 'em. When the war came on, they said they wouldn't fight against America. That's all—just wouldn't lay a gun against a Yankee craft. For that they catted us, the bloody lobsters; whipped us like balky horses; chopped our backs to hash, and threw us into these hulks, so that we came into 'em feeling pretty bad—pretty bad!"

Newton laughed mildly. "If we were felons, we'd have better treatment. If we'd murdered our mothers, we'd be put in a prison ship, same as this; but we'd have more room and better food. The British never put more than four hundred criminals in a prison ship; but we're more than criminals. We're prisoners of war. We won't fight for 'em; so they jam as many as nine hundred of us into each hulk— us who never did anything to 'em."

He laughed a laugh so mirthless that it ended in a cough. "Not yet we haven't done anything to 'em, but some day we will!"

He stared down at Marvin unwinkingly. "I give 'em credit!" he said. "They did what they could to keep us just barely breathing. They underfed us, so they could make money out of our food; and they gave us no clothes to wear if so be our clothes wore out; and worst of all, they took our air from us at night; but it hasn't killed us—not any of us! We're alive, all of us!"

He studied Marvin's face intently, and seemed, even, to measure his great body with his eyes. "It's easy to see you've had enough air and plenty of victuals. You look as if you could stand some punishment—swim ashore, even!"

"Swim ashore!" Marvin exclaimed thickly. So heavy had the air become that Newton's hammock, dimly seen above him, seemed to have descended on his chest. The mere act of breathing had grown to be a labor, and there was a ringing in his ears—a ringing broken by short silences that must, he told himself, be sleep, but that seemed more like lapses into a poisoned stupor. He shook his head to free it of the rank fog that enveloped him, and into his mind came the sallow face of Slade, its drooping eyelid giving it an expression of malicious triumph.

"Swim ashore!" he repeated. "I'd swim a hundred miles to get to shore and to France!"

He moved to rise to his feet, but his head struck the bottom of Newton's hammock and he fell back again.

Newton disappeared, and his hammock sagged as if he had lost interest in the subject. "Well," he said, "sweet dreams! I'll see you in the morning."

It seemed to Marvin, staring up with hot eyes into the dark, that he was caught in a tomb. Through the web of noises that surrounded him he could hear Argandeau close beside him, squirming and scratching.

"In some circumstances it is a terrible thing to be too alluring," Argandeau sighed. "I think all the fleas upon this *Crown Prince* hulk must be females, because I do not believe that anybody else but me is receiving attention from any of them."

At seven in the morning, the ports were raised and the gratings removed from the hatches; and Marvin, shouldering his hammock and bedding, followed his fellow prisoners up the ladders to be counted. In the dusk of the day before, the French prisoners had seemed miserable, but the naked creatures who came up into the brilliant sunlight of that October day were purely horrible. To Marvin, waiting his turn, after the counting, to stack his hammock on the covered platform over the main hatch, they had the look of vicious and repulsive animals as they scuttled down the ladders again to their den on the orlop deck.

Newton came to him through the press of prisoners. "Here,"

he told Marvin, "come up on the forecastle. I want to show you something."

Marvin, drawing Argandeau with him, followed the small swaggering figure in the overlong greatcoat as it bustled forward and mounted nimbly to the high forecastle, from which a reek of smoke rose through a score of pipes. Four marines in threadbare scarecrow uniforms growled glumly at Newton as he stopped before them to strike an attitude that had something of the heroic about it.

"Ho!" one of the marines exclaimed. "'Ere's the bloomin' hactor! Well, we ain't got nuffin' for yer! No tobaccer; no ole clo'es; no needles ner thread ner nails ner nuffin'!"

Clasping his hands before him, Newton raised sad eyes to the speaker's face. "Pity!" he whispered. "Have pity on a pore unfortunate woman turned into the snow with her two tender children"—he gestured dramatically toward Marvin and Argandeau—"by an unnatural and inhuman father, with never so much as a sup of rum or a measly piece of twist to hearten them against the bitter winter winds! Ah, my children! My pore, pore children! Ah, the pity of it, to see them waste before my very eyes for lack of the barest necessities of life!" He seemed to sob and droop.

One of the marines snorted. Another said angrily, "We ain't got none, I tell yer!"

"Ah, say not so!" Newton cried. He drew himself erect and thrust a hand into the bosom of his greatcoat. "None! None! In all this broad demesne, no single piece of twist! No twist in all this royal throne of kings, this sceptred isle, this earth of majesty, this seat of Mars, this other Eden, demi-paradise, this fortress built by Nature for herself against infection and the hand of war, this happy breed of men, this little world, this precious stone set in the silver sea, which serves it in the office of a wall or as a moat defensive to a house, against the envy of less happier lands—this blessed plot, this earth, this realm, this England! No twist! Good God, no twist in England!" Passionately he struck his brow with his clenched fist, and staggered.

"Oh, 'ell!" one of the marines growled. He drew a fragment of rope tobacco from his pocket and reluctantly handed it to Newton, who examined it suspiciously, dusted it against the front of his coat, and suddenly bit off the larger part of it. He returned the remainder to the marine and, deaf to his hoarse outcries, herded Marvin and Argandeau to the starboard bulwarks.

"Now we're all right," Newton said. "Those lobsters won't bother us, for fear of losing the rest of their tobacco. Still, it's best to talk low and keep your eyes open."

The three of them stared out over the wind-swept waters of the Medway. Ahead and astern extended the long line of soiled and mis-shapen hulks, each one attended, as though it had spawned during the night, by a small fleet of vegetable and supply boats. Along the main channel of the river, between the hulks and the windmills and neatly hedged fields, moved brigs and ships and sloops, bound to or from the docks of Chatham.

Newton turned an uncertain eye on Argandeau. "There's some situations that require frank speaking," he said to Marvin. "Now I've got nothing against this French friend of yours; but what I've got to say is important; and if anyone should be careless enough to blab, it might be the death of us."

Marvin nodded. "What you've got to say can be said before Argandeau or not at all. He's here himself because of helping me try to stay away. If I get out, he gets out too."

"All right," Newton said hastily. "All right! That's understood. Now look here." He spat negligently at a passing supply-boat. "Opposite this hulk, on shore, is a village. See it?"

"We see it," Marvin said.

"All right," Newton whispered. "That's Jillingum, that village is. Spelled 'Gillingham,' but pronounced 'Jillingum,' the way they do here. To the right of the village there's two windmills. In line with 'em, and fifty yards off shore, there's a mud bank. See it?"

Marvin nodded.

"That bank runs all the way along this reach, out of water most of the time. Sometimes only a little out. Could you swim that far at night in cold water—real cold water?"

"Easy," Marvin said.

"The mud in those banks is like glue," Newton remarked. "You go into it pretty near up to your middle. That's the trouble with getting to shore—if you swim as far as the banks, you're pretty tired, on account of having to carry things with you; so when you strike the mud, you can't get through it, sometimes. Sometimes, when the ports are opened in the morning, we see men in the mud, dead. The British leave 'em there all day—two days, sometimes—so they'll be a lesson to the rest of us." In a thoughtful voice, he added: "The crows eat 'em."

The three men stared silently at the square green fields and the slowly turning windmills, toy-like against the clear sky.

"Well?" Newton asked.

"Well what?" Marvin demanded.

"Do you think you could get through the mud?"

"Why, I'd have to," Marvin said.

"Men have got through it, no?" Argandeau asked.

Newton nodded. "Three out of five got through it a month ago—Americans. Frenchmen have got through it, but mostly they were new men—privateer captains. Tom Souville got through it four times, and reached France twice, but he was captured three times and brought back."

Argandeau laughed silently. His close-cropped black head wagged gently from side to side. "Tom Souville!" he exclaimed. "When I am a young man in Calais, I have taught Tom Souville tricks in swimming. There is nothing Tom Souville can do that I cannot do."

They were silent again, staring at the distant and harmless-seeming gray thread of the mud bank.

"There's one more thing," Newton said at length. "How much can you fight?"

Marvin looked thoughtfully at his knuckles. "I don't rightly know. I never had to fight very hard. What I've had to do has come easy."

Newton felt of his upper arm and appraised him carefully.

"Well," he said slowly, "well, I'll tell you. I'll tell you just how it is. It's a hard job to escape from these hulks—a dreadful chore! 'Tisn't as if you just escaped whenever you felt like it; you've got to have money, and you've got to protect yourself from informers, and you've got to be prepared, and you've got to have the good will of the rest of the prisoners, and you've got to have the permission of the governing committee, and you've got to be relieved of your prisoner duties. Then, when all those things have been arranged, you're obliged to go to work and cut your way out. It's the hardest work in the world! If you laid out on a topgallant yard night and day for a month, trying to hand a sail that's stiff with ice, and never got it handed, it wouldn't be as hard work as getting out of these hulks, even after you've got the permission and the money."

"My money was stolen when I came aboard last night," Marvin said. "How much money does it take?"

"Wait," Newton said. "I'm coming to that. Now I'll tell you how it is: I want to get out of this place! 'Tisn't that I can't stand the bad food and the bad air and the bad clothes or the bad Frenchmen. These bad Frenchmen, they're a joke! They're so eager to take advantage of us Americans that all you got to do is to give 'em an inch of rope and they'll hang themselves. See this overcoat?"

Marvin nodded.

"That's a French coat," Newton said. "They think I'm easy because I'm little and look worried when I gamble with 'em. The Frenchmen aren't anything as long as you watch 'em—not anything! What I can't stand is wanting to get at these English and not being able to! Listen!"

He took Marvin by the upper arms and seemed to shiver in the grip of a violent emotion. "Do you know why they take so many prisoners and starve us the way they do? It's because half of England's fattening on our hunger and nakedness and cold. The more of us they capture, the fatter England grows. Seventy-five thousand of us, French and Americans together, and the contractors take money for clothes we're supposed to get, but never do, and for food that's never fed to us! The commander of this ship, the drunken hog, fought to get the job! It pays him seven shillings a day, but he'll be a rich man in three years, hunting foxes in a red coat and talking about filthy Americans! I was secretary to a captain, I tell you, and I know what I'm talking about! I've got to get out of here! I'll blow up if I can't fight 'em!"

"I don't blame you," Marvin said thoughtfully, "but if it's as hard to escape as you say, you'd be better off, wouldn't you, to stop talking about it?"

Newton gripped the high bulwarks of the prison ship and laughed exultantly. "Stop?" he cried. "Stop? Why, no! I've just started! I've been waiting for the right men! For the right men! It's my turn to go and you're the man I want to go with. You're strong and you're big. You'll make it, and if I go with you, I'll have no trouble. This man, too"—he whirled to poke Argandeau's arched chest—"he'd get through, and the Indian you brought aboard. There's nobody else aboard this hulk I'd risk it with. I don't think the others could make it. They're weak and hungry. Most of 'em are sick. Most of 'em have been in jail too long. You're different! When I saw you come aboard, it seemed to me you must be the man I've been waiting for ever since they threw me into this"—he laughed again—"this demi-paradise; this precious stone set in the silver sea; this England!"

Marvin looked quickly over his shoulder at the four marines, lounging at the forecastle rail; then stared intently at Newton.

The small man hitched up his long overcoat around him. "I'll tell you how it is," he said, and his crinkly yellow side whiskers seemed to quiver. "If you can lick a man as big as you are, and maybe a little bigger—if you've got the heart to take a pounding and give back better than you get—I can contrive for the three of you to have a chance to go. I can do it! There's only one stipulation, and that is that you take me." He shivered. "You're the man I've been looking for! Yes, sir, you'll make it!"

He hesitated, seeming to withdraw a little into his voluminous outer garment; then added, "Or you'll probably get killed trying."

Marvin drew a deep breath, but in spite of it, his voice trembled somewhat: "That's reasonable enough. Just show me who I've got to fight to get myself out of here."

XVIII

Two of the long wooden benches in the lower battery had been dragged into the corner where Newton's hammock hung at night, and so arranged that they protruded from the corner in a narrow V.

At the point of the V sat Newton, flanked on each side by five committeemen. Two other committeemen sat on the deck, ten feet in advance of the point of the V; and to Marvin, who waited restlessly near them, they volunteered the information that they were thus stationed as pickets to warn away such prisoners as might be tempted to intrude on the committee's deliberations.

Nor was their office an idle one; for the deck was crowded with men, arguing, yammering, whistling and singing; some of them cutting soup bones into miniature planks for the making of ship models; some weaving delicate boxes from fragments of straw, or carving dolls and chessmen from beef knuckles; others patrolling the deck ceaselessly, offering for sale a desirable sleeping location, the butt of a candle or a thimbleful of grease for use in a lamp; still others trying to sell their services for the repairing of shoes or the mending of clothes. Among them moved emaciated, half-naked Frenchmen, prowling restlessly in search of unknown matters, or soliciting patronage for the gambling tables in the upper battery.

"Sheer off!" the pickets growled to all of them. "Sheer off! Committee's in session for the good of the deck! Sheer off!"

Marvin, allowed inside the picket line by Newton's orders, heard Newton address the ten committeemen.

"There's several things to come before this meeting," he told them. "First is, what's to be done about getting some kind of answer out of the American agent? There's fifty-seven Americans next door to naked, and sixty-six without coats of any kind. By December there'll be two hundred without any clothes except rags so rotten that thread won't hold 'em together. Twelve hundred new prisoner suits were supposed to be delivered last month, the French say, but they say we'll never see 'em. Osmore and the contractors keep the money, and the clothes never even get made. If we can't get help from Beasley, we'll freeze, all of us."

"How many times has he been written to?" asked a sour-visaged man whose mouth was puckered as if from the eating of persimmons.

"The committees on this hulk have written him eighteen times since August fifteenth, Captain Taylor."

The committeemen moved restlessly on their benches, and it was Captain Taylor who broke the silence again: "If the contractor would buy back our fish allowance next fish day, we might get enough to put an advertisement in *Bell's Weekly Messenger*, requesting that he pay some attention to his fellow countrymen."

"That's all right," complained a man whose head and chest were enveloped in a hood of flour sacking, "only it appears to me this taxation business is getting kind of overdone. I don't feel like these men ought to be asked to give up any more food, not even those smoked herrings. They're about starved already; so starved that if they got took sick, with the doctor paying no attention to sick men, they'd die in a minute!"

"There ain't anybody can eat the fish, Henry!" Taylor objected. "The French, they say they marked some of 'em, so they can be recognized, and they been in use for seven years—delivered at three pennies and bought back for a penny."

"Maybe so," Henry admitted, and Marvin saw that his face had an unearthly whiteness to it—the whiteness, almost, of the belly of a flatfish. "Maybe so; only the next time we get 'em, you watch me eat mine! I'm getting so I can eat anything—even a newspaper that's been wrapped 'round a fish!"

"Yes," Newton interrupted, "and there's another thing. Our *Statesman* subscription runs out next week, and that means twenty-eight shillings a month for the paper and sixteen shillings a month delivery charges." He laughed bitterly. "Twenty-eight shillings a month! No wonder the English don't know anything. Knowledge comes too high! Anyway, we got to sell two days' fish and one day's bread to get that renewed, provided you want it renewed."

"Want it renewed!" one of the committeemen exclaimed. "We got to have it renewed. If there ain't any news nor anything to read, there won't be anything to talk about, and we might as well be dead."

"Newton," said sour-mouthed Captain Taylor thoughtfully, "how much of that sixteen shillings goes to Osmore?"

"Probably ten," Newton said promptly. "He might get fifteen. Even so, it's no use trying to do anything about it, because the one that tried to make trouble would get the black hole for two weeks. 'Tisn't worth it! Gosh! I'd rather give up all my fish forever than get two weeks black hole!"

"I move," said Henry, from the folds of his flour sacking, "that this committee communicate with Beasley in writing for the nineteenth time, and send a letter to the President of the United States saying that the American agent for prisoners of war in England does nothing to prevent said prisoners from being treated like some sort of weasels. I also move that enough of our fish be collected and sold by the president of this lower battery to obtain the *Statesman* for another month."

"You know there's no use writing to the President of the United States," Newton objected wearily. "There's no way of getting it out except through an escaping prisoner; and if it was ever discovered on an escaping prisoner, the whole committee'd get the black hole, and all the other prisoners would have their tools and trades seized and destroyed! I'd like to hear that motion restated."

Henry jumped to his feet, pulling at the flour sacking around his throat. " 'Tain't right!" he exclaimed, his voice shaking as if with cold. "My God, you can't starve men and trample on 'em and murder 'em like this, and keep 'em gagged while you do it! You can't, I tell you! You——"

"Henry!" Captain Taylor said sharply.

Henry's voice persisted, shrill and trembling, "They treat us worse than animals, the damned rotten skunks! They can't keep me quiet! There's some way to get help—there's got to be!"

"Henry!" Captain Taylor shouted. He grasped Henry by the arm and pulled him down on the bench, shaking him roughly. "You're elected committeeman to set an example to the rest of these prisoners. See that you do it!"

Henry drew a deep and quivering breath, and the committeemen stared at their travesties of shoes, a strange and silent gathering.

"Well," Newton said at length, "we don't need it put in the form of a motion. I'll get the *Statesman* and tend to writing to Beasley again."

He cleared his throat and rose to his feet, drawing his long, ragged overcoat tight around him. "There's one more thing, and that's the question of who goes next." He eyed the committeemen significantly; and they, coming suddenly to life, fixed their eyes eagerly on him.

"We're wasting time," he went on. "Everybody wants to be next and nobody's willing to recognize the claims of anybody else. Meanwhile the food and the grease has accumulated without any work being done—no work at all! First thing you know, some of the Frenchmen, they'll get through and get stuck in the mud. Then they'll double the boat patrol, and Osmore'll have the planking sounded four times a day instead of once. This business ought to be settled, and settled now. Somebody's got to get letters out of this place, so we can get some money, and I say we ought to agree on somebody that can do it."

"I was one of the first Americans aboard this hulk!" Henry exclaimed. "You know it too! I ought to have first chance!"

"Henry," Captain Taylor said kindly, "you're wrong about this! Your spell in the black hole was pretty hard on you—harder'n you thought for, I guess. I notice you going up the ladder mornings, and you blow like a porpoise when you get on deck. You haven't been getting near enough food, and you'd never even reach the mud bank."

"I tell you I would!" Henry said. "I'd rather die trying, anyway, than not try at all!"

"Yes," Newton said, "maybe you would, but we wouldn't rather have you! Now you listen to me! I say the thing to do is to turn this over to a new man, fresh aboard."

Captain Taylor shook his head, and from the look of his mouth he might have been eating chokecherries. "No," he said, "you figure he'd be successful because he'd be strong and well fed; but you don't want to forget that these men here in this lower battery have got something almost as good as strength—they're dreadful mad! They hate the British worse than anything on earth!"

"That's what I say!" Henry exclaimed. "That's what I been trying to tell you! I'm dreadful mad, and I'd be as successful as anyone!"

Newton stared thoughtfully from Henry to Captain Taylor, who quickly lowered his eyes. "No," Newton said, "that isn't the way I figure. The way I figure is that it would be easier for everyone to agree on a new man—a man they never saw before—and I figure he'd be quicker doing the work—doing the cutting. 'Twouldn't be so hard for him to drive himself as it is for us, who've been breathing poison down here every night."

"They wouldn't agree," Captain Taylor said.

"I won't agree!" Henry stubbornly insisted.

Newton crouched down between the benches and looked up into the thin and sullen faces of the committeemen. "I had word from Osmore yesterday," he whispered. "Captain Stannage and the rest of his friends are coming aboard Saturday afternoon to get drunk again, ladies and all, damn the blowsy sluts!"

"Osmore sent you word!" Captain Taylor asked. "I suppose that means——"

"Yes!" Newton exclaimed. "It means he'll bring Little White with him. It means he aims to have a couple more of us hammered to a jelly, just to keep his friends in good spirits. Osmore told me to make the usual offer."

The committeemen growled angrily, and Captain Taylor shook his head. "I don't like it!" he said. "It's a bad business, this Little White! I wouldn't mind if it was Frenchmen he jellied, but it goes against the grain to hear him howling his black laughter and see him smashing our people until they're no more than raw meat, and they submitting to it for the sake of a twenty-shilling note!"

Newton laughed confidently, and his crinkly yellow side whiskers seemed to bristle, so that he had the eager look of a small dog on the trail of game. "All right! But what if Little White got smashed himself when he set out to do the smashing? What do you suppose Osmore'd say, and Stannage, and those wenches of his that have been tittering at us and looking at us all summer as if we were foxes in a cage? How'd you like to watch their faces while their little pet gets some of his own medicine?"

The committeemen stared at him with eyes that suddenly glittered. Captain Taylor looked over his shoulder at the tall figure of Marvin, standing behind the two lookouts; then turned back to Newton with a sour smile. "So that's it!" he said. "Well, it's a thing we'd be powerful glad to see, all of us, and it might put heart into us, what's more; but it appears to me you're expecting too much."

"What if I'm not?" Newton demanded. "What if he can do it? Would you be willing he should be the next in line? Would you agree on him?"

"What you so anxious about him for?" Henry demanded.

Newton turned on him. "My land! Can't you see? He'd be fighting for the chance to get out, and for the money to take advantage of the chance!"

"Bring him over here," Captain Taylor said.

In response to Newton's call, Marvin stepped over one of the benches and stood between the two rows of committeemen. "Daniel Marvin, of Arundel," Newton said. "His barque was cut out of Morlaix by the *Sparrow* schooner."

The committeemen eyed him almost carelessly, as though their interest in him was slight. "Marvin?" Captain Taylor asked at length. "Marvin? Seems to me there used to be a Marvin out of Arundel in the *Talleyrand* brig, trading in Havana."

"The *Talleyrand* brig was my father's."

"H'm!" Captain Taylor said noncommittally. "Was your father cut out of Morlaix?"

"No, sir. I was aboard the *Olive Branch* barque. Captain Dorman was master—Captain Dorman, of Arundel. He was killed in the doldrums, trying to fight off a British gun-brig. His daughter took command of the barque and brought her into Morlaix. She's alone there now."

The committeemen, Marvin felt, had lost all interest in him, for their glances at him were few and furtive.

"Seems to me I heard tell," Captain Taylor continued finally, "that the *Talleyrand* brig was so named because your father helped Talleyrand to buy land from General Knox."

"Yes, sir."

"What reason you got for thinking you could beat this Little White if you ain't ever seen him?" Henry demanded suddenly.

Marvin stared down at his knuckles and worked his left shoulder under his jacket. "I don't know that I could. They say he's a good fighter, and heavier than I am. Well, I've thought about him, and I believe I've figured out a way to offset his extra weight. I've figured out a new way to fight. Still, I wouldn't be interested in trying unless I knew I wasn't wasting my time."

"Wasting your time!" exclaimed another committeeman harshly. "Why, there's a standing offer of twenty pounds to the man that beats Little White! Little White's boss, Stannage, who's a friend of Osmore, made that offer. Twenty pounds to any prisoner that does it—twenty shillings to him if he tries and doesn't."

Marvin nodded. "I don't take much pleasure in fighting," he said. "I wouldn't risk it if there was nothing in it but the twenty pounds."

Newton seized Marvin's wrist and raised his arm. "Look at his reach!" he told them softly. "It's the first time we've had a man aboard with a reach like that! It's nearly as good as Little White's!"

"If you knew you weren't wasting your time," Captain Taylor reminded him, "you say you'd be interested in fighting this Little White?"

"Yes," Marvin said.

"Whether you could beat him or not?" Henry asked.

Marvin nodded. "I want to escape from this hulk," he said. "I want to get back to Morlaix. If nothing stands between me and getting there except beating this Little White, he'll have to kill me to beat me."

Newton laughed, a laugh so nervous that it was almost a titter. "There it is!" he exclaimed to the committeemen. "What more do you want than that?"

"What is it you figure we ought to agree to?" Captain Taylor asked; then puckered his mouth sourly.

"Nothing unreasonable," Marvin said. "I want to be allowed to escape, and I want the right to pick the men that work with me and go out with me—if it ever comes to that. Three others I'd want to take, no more; and all for good and sufficient reasons. I'd expect all four of us to receive the usual supplies and protection while working."

"You mean nobody else would be allowed to use your cutting, provided you're successful?" Henry demanded.

"Not for three nights—not until we've had time to get clear."

"I don't agree!" Henry declared angrily.

"Oh, here, here!" Captain Taylor said. "That's fair! If they get away, we can pass men through the bulkhead to answer to roll call, so the four won't be missed; and when the three days are up, everyone can go that has enough money and food. If one of the four should be caught, nobody else would have a chance anyway."

"Well——" said Henry weakly. He looked helplessly from one committeeman to another, his face chalk-white in the flickering light that danced across the ceiling from the reflection of the sun on the crinkled water of the Medway.

"Gorry!" exclaimed a committeeman in dogskin trousers, one of the legs being made of the skin of a red setter and the other of the skin of a coach dog. "Gorry! I say yes—whether he beats him or not!"

"No!" Captain Taylor protested sternly. "Not unless he beats him! If he's willing to try under those conditions, I say yes, and so does Henry. You do, don't you, Henry?"

"Yes," Henry said reluctantly, "I guess I do."

A glance at the other committeemen seemed to satisfy Captain Taylor, for he nodded soberly to Newton and then rose from his bench to prod inquiringly at Marvin's biceps.

"In that case," Newton said briskly, "this meeting stands adjourned and I appoint the entire committee to demand a contribution of salt from each prisoner so we can get his hands in pickle with no loss of time."

XIX

The barge that drew up to the landing stage of the *Crown Prince* hulk at noon on Saturday seemed to blaze with color; for the oarsmen wore uniforms of blue flannel with the arms of the Stannages on breast and back in silver, gold and red; while in the cockpit sat Stannage himself, resplendent in a hussar's uniform, all gold and scarlet. Around him clung a group of damsels in silks, furs and feathers—damsels whose conversation seemed to Marvin, as he peered over the bulwarks at them, to consist largely of shrill laughter and shriller screams.

Between Stannage's knees crouched an enormous brown dog, thin and yellow-eyed, that panted constantly despite the chill wind that blew across the Medway, and cast longing looks over one side of the barge and then over the other. Close behind him stood a towering, smiling negro, whose noisy laughter ran like an undercurrent beneath the high-pitched merriment of the captain's gentle companions, and whose Eastern splendor dimmed the finery of the others. On his head was perched a vast turban of yellow satin, decorated with a tall plume held in place by a glittering bauble seemingly made of pearls and diamonds; beneath his short jacket of crimson satin a broad sash of gold cloth shone dully against the velvety black of his skin; and crimson satin trousers, voluminous enough, Marvin was sure, to make a dozen potato sacks, hung to his ankles, where they were fastened by tight gold bands.

"There he is!" Newton said. "There's Little White! What you think of him, Dan?"

Marvin shook his head. "Why," he said, "he looks like a handy man to have around a pivot gun or a galley stove, provided he got a rap from a belaying pin every few minutes to remind him where he belongs."

Newton nodded. "That's something he hasn't had in some little time. These people over here, they're all excited over Molineaux, the American negro who fought Tom Cribb. In consequence, they can't see a black man a little bigger than usual without thinking he's a fighter, and making a pet of him."

Cackling hilariously, Little White, evidently at his master's bidding, leaned over and took one of the damsels beneath the arms as though she had been a doll, held her for a moment over the side of the barge, so that she screamed and kicked like an excited child; then deposited her on the landing stage and spanked her briskly to start her up the gangway.

Stannage, a gaudy figure in his scarlet, fur-trimmed hussar's jacket, laughed as heartily at the playfulness of his dusky favorite as did any of the jeering prisoners that peered down at him from the bulwarks.

Marvin moved uncomfortably. "Why," he said suddenly, "this Stannage ought to have his face washed and be put to bed! He's only a child! He's never a captain—not at his age!"

"Oh, isn't he?" Newton exclaimed. "Well, he is, and he's more than a child! He's an idiot—the idiot son of rich idiots; so his family bought him a captaincy to get him out of the way. It's an old English custom! There's regiments over here officered entirely by idiots and children whose places have been bought for 'em. You can do anything with money in England; there's no place that's not for sale—church, state, army or navy."

Marvin laughed. "I guess they're not so bad as that!" he said. "If you're trying to make me madder at them than I am, you don't need to—not by lying about 'em."

"Lying?" Newton cried. "Lying? Why—well, wait till you know 'em! Lying! It was only a couple of years ago that the Duke of York was helping Mary Anne Clarke to sell any job in England to the highest bidder! The King's son and a bawd! It's no use having merit in England, not unless you have money along with it; and if you have no money, you're no better than a criminal! They pressed me into their damned navy, and I know 'em, and I'm glad I do, because it isn't Nature for people like that to win wars from people like us. That's mighty small consolation to a man who's buried in the hulks! Mighty small, but better than nothing!"

The boyish Stannage, looking petulant, came slowly and awkwardly up the companionway, dragging his enormous and reluctant brown dog; while Little White, crowding close behind with baskets, boxes and cloaks, rolled his eyes defiantly at the prisoners who watched him.

Argandeau, beside Marvin, sighed heavily. "It is well that I understand which is the master and which is the man," he said, "because if I did not, I might think that the smaller one was brought here by the black one for our amusement."

He watched the two gaily caparisoned figures mounting to the quarter-deck from the throng of emaciated, tattered scarecrows that packed the waist; then tapped Marvin on the arm. "In those baskets," he reminded him, "there is wine and fine food and yet more wine that they will be two hours in consuming. Two hours is no great time, so you must come now and have your dinner—two rotten carrots and a biscuit palpitating with weevils."

Marvin, climbing the ladders from the lower battery to the upper deck, mounted two hours later into a tumult so violent that the hulk seemed to shudder, as at the roaring of a storm—seemed almost to be sinking in a sea of sound.

The deck itself had become an amphitheater, and every exposed part of it, save for the quarter-deck and a square inclosure in front of the break in the poop, was massed with ragged, excited prisoners. There were prisoners clinging like ants to the two stubby signal masts; prisoners ranged in a triple tier along the high bulwarks; prisoners hanging like swarming bees against the face of the forecastle. All of them, wedged immovably in their places though they seemed to be, had freed their arms to shake a fist at the inclosure beneath the poop, so that the whole dreary hulk had the appearance of fluttering and vibrating, while from nine hundred throats there came an angry and derisive screaming.

In the center of the inclosure, set off by ropes from the close-packed prisoners who crouched around it, strutted the towering crimson form of Little White; and from the continuous rapid movement of his grinning lips as well as from the expression of rage on the faces of the prisoners closest to him, Marvin knew he was making game of them. From time to time he turned and looked up to the baby-faced hussar captain, standing at the rail of the quarter-deck with Lieutenant Osmore, and thence to the chattering women, who now sat comfortably, wineglasses in their hands, on either side of the hulk commander and their host. There was pride and almost admiration in the smiles they gave him; and even as Marvin, preceded by Newton and followed closely by Argandeau, forced his way from the main hatch toward the ring, a woman's gaily colored silk scarf floated downward from the quarter-deck and was deftly caught by Little White—caught and flaunted proudly in the faces of the howling prisoners.

At the sight of Marvin, crawling under the ropes of the ring with the small and heavily overcoated Newton, Little White ceased his posturing and stared intently at the tall American; then, catching his eye, he thrust out his lower jaw and grimaced horribly, his mouth spreading outward so that he seemed to have the face of an ape.

Marvin stared hard at him with a horrid fascination and shivered perceptibly, whereupon the roar with which the prisoners were greeting their champion's appearance became enfeebled with misgiving and died pathetically away.

On the quarter-deck two marines thumped on the drums slung at their sides. Lieutenant Osmore placed his right hand between the first and second buttons of his coat, frowned portentously and raised his left hand in a gesture of command. Over the hulk there fell an uneasy silence.

"You know the terms of this exhibition!" Osmore said in his shrill, domineering voice. "Captain Sir Rafe Stannage has kindly consented to permit his attendant—ah—White—ah—Little White—to display once more that art unknown to more—ah—effeminate, more cruel and more cowardly peoples—ah—the art sprung from British hardihood and love of fair play—ah—the art of pugilism!" He inclined his head to Stannage, who was staring as though baffled at a leather strap in his left hand; and from the throng of prisoners there instantly rose a roar—short, sharp and profoundly ironical.

"You know the terms!" Osmore repeated. "Any fighting or opprobrious remarks among the prisoners will result in two days black hole for the offenders. The rules of the exhibition will be Broughton's rules. Each round to be considered ended on the fall of one or both contestants After each fall, each man to be brought to scratch within thirty seconds or be deemed—ah—beaten. No falling without the striking of an honest blow. Challenger to receive one pound for his brave attempt, and if successful—ah, ha-ha!—if successful, twenty guineas!" Osmore chuckled and cleared his throat importantly.

"The challenger of—ah—White—of Little White—ah—is"—he drew a small paper from his coat and peered at it—"is one Marvin, of Arundel." He scanned the paper again, frowning, and repeated the word "Arun-del."

Stannage stepped to his side and looked over his shoulder. "Arundel? He's an Englishman?"

Osmore frowned severely down at Marvin, who stood patiently at one side of the ring, his ear inclined to the prolonged whisperings of Newton. "Arun-del!" Osmore exclaimed, striking the paper with his hand. "This says Arun-del! There's no Arun-del in America!"

Marvin nodded. "A-rundle, it's pronounced."

"Never heard of the place! Where is it?" Osmore asked.

"Where?" Marvin said, looking up at him thoughtfully. "It's no great distance from Bunker Hill and Saratoga."

A whisper arose from the men crouched at the ringside, a small dry titter that spread through the dense masses of prisoners as ripples spread from the dropping of a rock in a pond.

"Silence!" Osmore screamed, stamping his foot. "Silence!" He stared balefully from one side of the crowded deck to the other, until the unseemly tittering had died away. "Save your damned Yankee impertinence for another occasion or I'll clap you below hatches, all of you! You want to see this fight, and you'll behave yourselves or not see it! I'll say this, too: It's a lesson you need, all of you—you Frenchmen with your kicking and knife sticking—you Spaniards and Italians with your backhanded stilettos and daggers—you Yankees with your tomahawks and scalping tricks! This is to do you good! You people need all the lessons you can get in the cool courage, the restraint, the skill and the endurance with which the noble art of boxing has filled the breast of every true-hearted Englishman and made the British nation the mistress of the seas!"

There was a patter of applause from the young women seated at the quarter-deck rail.

Newton cleared his throat apologetically. "I'd like to ask a question, sir," he said. He stared up at Osmore from beside Marvin, as harmless as a downy chicken peering from under its mother's wing.

"Be quick about it!" Osmore ordered.

"We hope you'll not permit any of your Lancashire up-and-down fighting, sir," Newton urged. "We wouldn't like to see our man killed or disabled by kicking or gouging when on his back."

Osmore narrowed his eyes at Newton; then swept them quickly over the throng of ragged men beyond. There was a small trembling among them, and a sound like the vague shadow of stifled laughter.

Osmore's face darkened; he opened his lips as though to rebuke Newton; then seemed to cogitate. "Broughton's rules!" he snapped at length. "You heard me say Broughton's rules! Get your man ready! Surgeon Rockett has kindly consented to fill the difficult post of referee."

He read again from his paper. "Corporals Quigg and Spratt will act for—ah—White—for Little White. For Marvin, Newton and Argandeau."

Two red-coated marines popped into the ring beside Little White, who straightway leaped into the air, crowing like a rooster and shedding jacket, trousers, waistband and turban in a whirl of scarlet and gold. Beneath these garments he wore small clothes of the brightest green, fastened waist and knee with yellow bands. Above them his naked torso gleamed in the pale October sunlight like polished brown wood—wood in which knots and lumps swelled unexpectedly on shoulders, arms and back. His forehead sloped back abruptly from his broad flat nose, rising to a peak at the top of his head—a peak topped with a fuzzy semicircle of hair that had the look of a thick rope of crinkly black feathers extending over his skull and fastened to his ears on either side.

He continued to crow and leap as Newton helped Marvin to strip off his shirt, the huge brown hands flapping like wings against the green small clothes; and even his eyes, fastened on Marvin, were black and hard as those of a giant rooster.

Marvin, resting against the ropes between Newton and Argandeau, had the look of shrinking from his black antagonist. The pearly whiteness of his chest and arms might have been thought to be the effect of fear, and the long smooth muscles hidden beneath that gleaming skin seemed, by comparison with the knobby brown bulges of Little White, almost weak and helpless. Yet it was strange but true that whereas Little White seemed to have shrunk somewhat with the removal of his gaudy plumage, Marvin seemed to have become larger.

Down from the quarter-deck came the ship's surgeon, his chin held high by his black stock, and a huge watch clutched in his hand. He crawled beneath the ropes, poked Marvin in the chest with a finger like a marlinespike, stared curiously into the yellowish eyes of Little White; then stooped over with some difficulty and, on the deck in the middle of the ring, chalked a square with three-foot sides.

"Now," he said, "if you're ready, my lads?" He popped out under the ropes. His hand rose and fell; and with that Newton hustled Marvin to one side of the chalked square, while one of the marines ran with Little White to the opposite side, so that the four men hung in a knot at the center of the ring.

The shouting of the prisoners had fallen away to a breathless hum, and through the hum rose a hoarse voice, a voice so rough and rasping as to sound less like a voice than like the scraping of a file on the strings of some vast violin. It was the voice of Little White. "Kiss mah han'," he growled. "Ah kill Americans wiff it."

Newton and the marine ran back to their sides of the ring and dodged beneath the ropes.

Little White threw himself into fighting position. His left foot and his left arm were thrust well forward; his right arm guarded his stomach and lower chest; his upper body tipped back so far that if he had raised his eyes, they would have looked straight upward into infinity. Standing so, he laughed, a deep, roaring, hyena-like laugh;

for it was plain to be seen, from Marvin's posture, that Marvin was as ignorant of fighting as he was afraid of Little White. He had cramped himself sideways, his left shoulder turned in front of his body. His right foot, instead of resting squarely and flatly on the ground as a supporting platform for a blow, was poised on its toe, as, indeed, was his left foot as well. Both his knees were weakly bent, as though it was in his mind to turn at any moment and run like a coward from his powerful black opponent.

Roaring with laughter, Little White shuffled forward toward Marvin, who slipped off to one side. Roaring still, Little White shuffled after him, only to have his opponent slip off to the other side.

Nor was Little White the only one to roar. The deck of the hulk seemed almost to erupt with angry shouts of "Fight! Fight!" while Osmore, Stannage, the six women in their glowing silks and satins, and even the drummers at each side of the quarter-deck, hung far out over the rail to shout, "Fight! Fight!"

They moved around the ring, Little White shuffling forward and Marvin slipping off to left or right before him. Little White lashed out with a left-handed blow that cut a slit in Marvin's ear, and got from Marvin in return a veritable baby's tap—a breath of a hit, that touched Little White's eye and was gone, like a vagrant butterfly. Again, with the evident intention of ending the fight before it had fairly begun, Little White sprang forward, his fists driving like battering rams for Marvin's mark—that triangular-shaped patch beneath his ribs and above his belt. There was the crack of a hit, but it was the impact of a black fist against a forearm; the mark itself had moved away.

The prisoners groaned and hissed. One of them, close to Newton's corner, aimed a jab at the elusive Marvin through the ropes. "Stand up to him!" he bellowed. "Get out o' there if you can't stand up to him!"

Newton rapped the bellower sharply on the forearm with the edge of his hand. "Close your face!" he said. "Can't you see it's a new way of fighting?"

The near-by prisoners howled their disgust. "Be damned to a new way of fighting!" "It's a new way of running, and a rotten one!" "Make him show what he's good for!" "Make him fight!"

Minutes passed. Blood trickled from Marvin's ear; there were red welts along his ribs from the glancing blows of Little White's knuckles; but still he slipped off to one side or to the other, and shrank away before the black man's advance.

Anger had replaced Little White's hoarse hilarity. "Stan' still!" he growled, following Marvin's erratic twistings and turnings. "Isn't one of you Americans got bottom enough to stan' up to a fighter? Light somewheres, you dirty Yankee yaller bird, so's I can knock you half-way up to Lunnon!"

To Little White's amazement, Marvin laughed. "You can't fight!" he told the black man. "You can't even throw a cross-buttock."

Little White lowered his head and charged. To the prisoners, raging at Marvin's tactics, it seemed, and was indeed the case, that Marvin, at this quick movement, stood his ground instead of slipping off to right or left. As Little White's head shot past his body, Marvin's fist came up against his opponent's throat with a sound like the impact of a dead codfish against a plank. In another instant the black man's arms were around him and the first fall had gone to Little White with a cross-buttock.

Their seconds were on them as they sprawled to the deck, hoisting them to their feet and hurrying them to the ropes for a rest of thirty seconds. Argandeau held Marvin on his knee while Newton, gabbling in his ear to make himself heard above the din of the prisoners, sponged the blood from his face and chest.

"A thirteen-minute round!" Newton told him excitedly. "A thirteen-minute round, and you're barely scratched! You're like a Baltimore schooner sailing rings 'round a frigate! He can't touch you! Keep it up, Dan! Your way's the best way, no matter what these fools say! Don't listen to 'em! He can't fight! He's a flipper! I told you he was a flipper! He thinks he's fighting like Molineaux, but he isn't. He's just a big black chunk of sour beef! He hits at half arm and keeps his elbows close to his body, and he'll keep doing it until he thinks he's caught you! Then he'll imitate Molineaux again and try to chop you, and you've got him! You've got him anyway! That was a beauty—a beauty! Right in the whistle! Right in the apple! He thinks he's swallowed a hen's hind foot! Oh, oh! He's fat! He's puffy! And he thinks it was an accident! He thinks he ran into it! Look at him gulp! Look at him watch you!"

Marvin glanced across at Little White, seated on the knee of a red-coated marine while another marine dabbled water on the back of his neck. There was, Marvin saw, a soft smoothness to the black skin above the green small clothes, instead of the solid wall of corrugated muscle that should have been there; and the soft smooth surface rose and fell hurriedly. Conscious of Marvin's scrutiny, Little White blinked his small eyes, cautiously stretched his neck; then thrust out his mouth in an apelike grimace.

"Keep away from him!" Newton continued. "Keep out of his way until he's careless! Then you got him! Then you got him good! Remember what I told you!"

"Time!" the referee shouted.

Little White shuffled to the chalked square, falling into a fighting position so exaggerated that he seemed on the verge of tumbling backward. Marvin came less quickly to the scratch, and in the same cautious manner that had so enraged his fellow prisoners in the previous round—with his left shoulder thrust forward and his body bent as though he were torn with the simultaneous desire to advance and to run away.

Little White's hands revolved rapidly and he pawed the deck with an enormous foot. "Stan' up!" he commanded hoarsely; then coughed and cleared his throat and coughed once more. "Stan' up, you ole tabby cat!"

He lurched forward to hurl murderous blows at Marvin, who shrank before him, ducking and dodging. Again and yet again Marvin's left fist flicked out, touching Little White lightly at the corner of the eye, and so faint and ineffectual were the blows that the groans and the jeering of the prisoners changed suddenly to a burst of laughter. Even Little White laughed, though he coughed when he did so, and at the corner of his eyes a smear of blood showed bright against his brown skin.

"Jes' a moment and I gits you!" he said. His voice seemed choked and strangled, and when he had spoken, he wheezed. His shuffle became swifter; and as it did, there came a hesitation into Marvin's movements—a momentary catch, as though he had faltered in deciding how to turn.

Little White bellowed hoarsely; his right hand rose high above his head, and like a flail his long black arm swept down toward Marvin's neck. Instead of slipping away, Marvin moved closer. His right fist flashed upward to land upon the brown V below the ribs. The breath went out of Little White with a hoarse hoot. He tilted suddenly forward, so that his chopping blow lost its force and landed uncontrolled against Marvin's shoulder. Marvin's left fist drove once more against the negro's thick throat, partially straightening the black man, and once more his right fist whipped into the unprotected stomach that still quivered and jerked from the first unexpected blow. Little White clung to him with one arm—clung and fell backward, dragging Marvin with him; and the two of them plunged to the deck and amid a turmoil of frenzied shouting such as might have come from ten thousand madmen, rather than from nine hundred half-fed prisoners.

Newton, dragging Marvin back to his seat on Argandeau's knee, shook like a shivered sail; and his voice trembled even more than his hands. "You got him! You got him!" He rubbed the blood from Marvin's cheek and ribs, and laughed almost hysterically. "It worked the way you said it would, and you got him!"

"Time!" bellowed Surgeon Rockett, above the howling of the prisoners.

Argandeau pushed Marvin toward the chalked square; and as Little White, coughing and blinking, stepped warily to the other side, Marvin snapped his left fist toward the black man's face. The semblance of timidity and indecision was gone from him, and he had the look of one who has come to the end of long waiting. Yet this look went from his face quickly enough; for as he led with his left hand, Little White half turned, threw up his head and fell to the floor. In the same moment his second leaped at him, hustled him to his feet and dragged him back to the ropes.

Marvin, staring helplessly at Little White, felt Newton take him by the arm. "Wait!" Marvin said. He turned to the surgeon, who stood pompously outside the ring, staring at his turnip-shaped watch. "Wait! He fell without a blow! That's no fall! I didn't hit him!"

The surgeon looked up at him slowly. "You didn't what?" he asked.

"You heard me!" Marvin said. "I didn't touch him! Get him back here and make him fight!"

The surgeon laughed flatly. "You're a fine one to talk about fighting —you who did nothing but run for half an hour!"

"For God's sake!" Marvin shouted. "You——"

He stopped, staring at the pompous surgeon; then hurried to where Argandeau waited for him with outthrust knee.

Argandeau patted his shoulder, soothing him. "Remember; I have told you about these people!" he said.

The surgeon had gone to contemplating the face of his watch again. "A minute and a half he's given him!" Newton said. "Well, Dan; you do your best!"

"Time!" said the surgeon.

Marvin ran to scratch. Little White, breathing more regularly, glowered malevolently at him. Marvin grinned amiably. "You're licked, black boy! You're going to get hurt for playing tricks!"

Little White coughed and growled. Marvin slapped his outstretched left arm, a slap that tilted him forward; and as he tilted, Marvin's left fist landed wetly against his eye. Little White coughed and groaned. With hamlike hands he hammered Marvin's ribs. Marvin staggered and laughed; then rushed at Little White and drove him backward with a succession of blows to the stomach. He fell against the rope of the ring and bounced upright. When Marvin hit him in the throat and again in the stomach, he slipped to one knee and clung to the ropes.

"Foul!" he croaked hoarsely. "He bit me!"

Marvin caught him by the fringe of hair atop his head, dragged him to his feet and drove his fist against his throat. The negro fell heavily to the deck, made vague swimming motions with his hands, and then lay still.

"Foul! Foul!" shouted Osmore and Stannage.

The pompous surgeon popped through the ropes. "Foul!" he said, brandishing his watch in Marvin's face. "The man was down!"

"No foul! No foul!" screamed the prisoners.

"No!" Marvin shouted. "Both knees and at least one hand on the floor, or the man's not down, and you know it! They're your own rules! He's down now, but he wasn't when I hit him. Don't look at me! Look at your watch, you fat swab!"

He ran to Argandeau's knee. The marine came through the ropes and dragged Little White to his corner. A hundred hands fluttered over Marvin, patting his head, his back, his thighs.

A breathless silence came upon the prisoners while they waited for the passing of the thirty seconds at whose end, according to Broughton's rules, each fighter must either toe the mark once more or acknowledge defeat. Through this silence could be clearly heard the sound of Newton's hands, slapping and kneading Marvin's arms, and of his reiterated whisper—"He'll never make it, Dan! He'll never make it! He'll never make it! He'll never make it!"

The surgeon pushed the watch in his pocket. He leaned over to look at Little White; then stared venomously at Marvin. "Time!" he said slowly. "Time!"

Marvin walked to the chalk mark in the center of the ring. He stood there alone. In the opposite corner lay Little White. Marvin, watching him, saw one black eyelid flutter. The marine pulled at the negro's arm. He just lay there.

On the quarter-deck a woman screamed; and as if the scream had been a signal, the hulk became a bedlam of cursing, uproarious prisoners.

Newton, uttering unintelligible sounds, clambered through the ropes to throw his arms around Marvin's neck. Argandeau, tears streaming down his cheeks, embraced them both. "We win!" he blubbered. "Ah, my God! My God! I am excite! I choke! I die! We win! We win!"

Above them Stannage shook his fist at the prostrate form of Little White. "I've been sold!" he cried in his girlish voice. He leaned over the rail to point an accusing finger at Marvin. "You had no right to win! There was something wrong with it, but I don't know what! You don't deserve your twenty guineas, and I've a mind not to give them to you!" He stared about him indecisively, as if to seek support. Finding none, he fumbled in his pocket, tied some coins in a handkerchief and tossed them petulantly to Marvin; then turned suddenly to Osmore.

"Here," he said. "Where's my dog? I've been wanting to ask you all through the fight. Look at that!" He held up the empty strap and dangled it in Osmore's face.

Osmore stared at it blankly. "Your dog?" he asked. "Your dog is gone? When did you see him last?"

"After dinner," Stannage said. "One of the ladies was feeding him a sweet."

"What? You were foolish enough to let that dog run loose on this ship!" Osmore cried aghast. "I told you a week ago we had more than a dozen of these men sick from eating rats!"

Captain Stannage turned pallidly toward his six fair friends, whose sympathetically dismal exclamations pierced the air, yet went all unheard, lost under the thunder of cheering from the ragged deck below.

XX

ALTHOUGH an early afternoon sun slanted through the heavily barred ports of the lower battery, the entire deck was a turmoil of sound, and the noisiest portion of that cavernous place was the corner in which Newton's hammock hung at night. In that corner was a school of fencing in which three pairs of fencers lunged and panted, their blades rasping and their clumsy shoes a-clatter. In that corner, too, between the fencers and the ports, a dozen men from Kittery and Portsmouth worked with files and saws, fashioning tiny planks from soup bones. As they worked, they argued; and their arguments were deafening.

Behind this human screen four men were stretched upon the deck, close to the planking of the vessel's side. Sweat dripped from their foreheads and cut furrows through the grime that smeared their cheeks. Their breathing was labored and their work unceasing.

One, an Indian, drew a small bow backward and forward. The string of the bow was looped around a drill, a small drill made from a broken fencing foil.

Marvin, beside the Indian, held this rude tool tight against the side of the prison ship, pressed there by the bottom of a bottle. The bowstring, moving rapidly, turned the drill, so that it bit slowly into the oak.

Argandeau, strangely cramped, toiled with a saw made from a barrel hoop, joining the holes already drilled. The handle of the saw was a ball of rags; and the hand with which the Frenchman clutched it was bloody.

Between and beneath these three moved Newton, filling holes and cuttings with a mixture of grease and oak dust.

At two o'clock that night a bitter wind slapped the salt waves of Gillingham Reach against the bends of the *Crown Prince* hulk. The hulk strained at her moorings and rolled a little, as if uneasy with the stirrings of the miserable freight within her. A shivering sentry paced the narrow gallery three feet above the water. He came reluctantly from behind the shelter of the stern, peered with moist eyes at the distant lights of Gillingham, bawled a hoarse "All's well!";

then vanished silently, seeking the protection of the hulk's high galleries.

Out from the blackness of the misshapen vessel there sprouted a splotch of paleness—a splotch that lengthened into the naked figure of a man; a figure smeared with grease and humpbacked with a bundle lashed high on its shoulders. Almost like a wisp of wind-blown fog, it wavered outward from the hulk and disappeared. Three other figures followed, wraithlike, to plunge without a sound into the dark river. The sentry reappeared, snuffling. He peered quickly at the inky water and the bulging sides of the hulk. "All's well!" he droned, his voice trembling with the cold; then, huddled turtle-like in his greatcoat, he shuffled hastily sternward to escape the wind's shrewd blast.

The frigid chop of the Medway stung the faces of the four swimmers. The swift current wrenched at their legs and pressed like violent icy hands against their chests. Close together, they swam onward into the endless blackness that stretched before them and weighed them down. White gouts of foam rose angrily to leap at their twisted mouths.

A wave washed over Newton's head. His arms thrashed and the quick current bore him upstream. He cried a strangled cry, and choked. Marvin's voice was close beside him—a strained and harried voice: "Easy . . . almost there . . . almost. . . . Easy!" Newton groaned and moved forward slowly, half in the shelter of Marvin's great body.

The piercing wind flagged and lulled, leaped at them half-heartedly and lulled again. The angry chop lessened and slapped less fiercely at their numb lips. The water stilled; the current slackened—almost drew them shoreward. Marvin stood upright, caught at Newton and held him. He hung limp in Marvin's arms, coughed weakly and gagged. A smell of cold decay hung over them. There was a faint splashing near at hand. Half swimming and half crawling, Argandeau came up to them, with Steven close behind. In Marvin's arms, Newton groaned and coughed again. The other three stared, panting, at the dim and noisome mud.

Newton stood upright at last, swaying and shuddering in the shallows. Marvin eyed him, then turned from him abruptly and made for the shore. At the water's edge he sank knee-deep in ooze. Gripped by it, he lurched from side to side in a slow and clumsy caper. Laboriously he withdrew one foot and then the other; and with the effort there was a sound of sucking and the issuing of a stench, dank and horrible. He lost his balance, pitching forward against the foul gray slope. His arms, thrust downward for support, disappeared; and when he struggled to his feet, the arms were black with slime. His face was black, and his body as well. He threw himself flat on the bank and wallowed forward, spiderlike. Huddled on the slope, he gasped an order to Argandeau, who laid hold of Newton and hurled him roughly upward. Marvin reached backward, caught Newton by the hair and dragged him to his side. "Move!" Marvin told him hoarsely, his voice as thick as though it rose from muddy depths. "Move or you'll sink!" They squirmed and rolled on the yielding, quaking mud like two hurt animals.

Argandeau and the Indian floundered upward through the slime to lie, spent, beyond them. Marvin gained his feet, heaving at Newton's frail body. Argandeau reached back a hand, and between them they dragged and pushed their small companion over the crest of the slope and to the flat surface of the bank—a surface that shook like jelly and sucked hungrily at their naked bodies.

This trembling mass was soft as glue, seeming to have no substance. In it their feet sought vainly for a hold, and while they sought, the surface clutched their upper legs and drew them deeper.

Gripped by this noxious treacle, the four black figures reeled forward in a wavering and dreadful dance. Gasping, they wrenched themselves half free, only to sink again and on the instant strive once more for partial freedom. They groaned and sweated in the bitter wind. Mud filled their eyes and mouths, so that each one moved in blackness, seeing nothing and hearing only faintly the rattle of his labored breathing. They lurched and fell and rose; and with each move, the slime in which they groveled was vocal, seeming to smack its lips and slobber at their agony.

There was a flame in Marvin's chest—a flame that stabbed and crackled. Dark fears smoked upward from it, and the weakness of despair. Through its cracklings Newton's thin voice reached him—a voice shrill with terror. "Dan!" it called, "Dan! Wait! I can't—can't——"

Marvin floundered toward the voice and got his hands on Newton. "Stuck!" Newton gasped. "Can't make it!"

Panting, Marvin dragged at the smaller man, who retched. The mud held him. Marvin groaned and heaved, and Newton, struggling weakly, came slowly out. Marvin's legs churned in the stinking ooze. He fell backward in it, pitching Newton over him in his fall.

Here was the end, he thought. His leaden arms, reaching for support, found only slimy thickness, into which his weary legs and body settled. Cold sickness caught his throat. Small homely pictures of his youth swam slowly through his brain: Himself, a boy once more, bathing his scrawny body in a lamp-lit kitchen beneath his mother's watchful glance; a nest of helpless field mice on the hot Arundel marshes; a sweaty minister with uplifted eyes, droning hell and endless torment, and in a near-by pew Corunna Dorman, eyeing him aslant through fingers that devoutly screened her face. Up through these little pictures came the face of Slade, staring and smiling in sardonic mirth.

In desperation Marvin reared and twisted. Uncomprehendingly he heard a splashing near at hand. Fingers clawed his ear; clutched at his arm and slipped; then clutched again. Marvin wallowed forward, hung on a sloping surface and rolled heavily into the water of the lagoon that lay between the mud bank and the meadows of Gillingham.

The distant hulks bulked against the paleness of the coming dawn. In the heart of a haystack on a field in Kent lay four exhausted men, sick from their efforts, but for the moment safe.

XXI

A BLIND Hindu, his face shadowed by a soiled and bulbous turban and his bare brown shoulders protruding from the folds of once-white cotton in which he was swathed, sat by the dusty roadside on the outskirts of the small Channel town of Ramsgate, while his ragged attendant, a sharp-nosed, tow-headed youth, directed the attention of passers-by to the brown man's peculiar ability.

"'E kin mike fire wiff nuffin' but a bit o' string an' a toofpick! Couple o' coppers, friends, fer to see a sight you'll be a-tellin' your children abaht fer the next 'undred years!"

A few citizens of Ramsgate stood stolidly before the two, seemingly hopeful that the requisite pennies would be donated by others. Two sentries, evidently stationed on the edge of the town for the inspection of strangers, peered over the shoulders of the citizens.

A provision cart, laden with straw and live chickens, drew up, creaking. One of the slouching countrymen on the driver's seat tossed two pennies into the dust at the brown man's feet. The sharp-nosed youth seized them; then shook the Hindu's bare brown arm.

"'Ere!" he cried. "Git it aht!"

The brown man, fumbling in his cotton swathings, produced a small board, a pointed stick and a diminutive bow. Then, his sightless eyes staring over the heads of his audience, he looped the string of the bow around the stick and adjusted its point to a depression in the board. The bow moved rapidly; the pointed stick spun round. From the depression in the board rose a faint wisp of smoke.

The audience shifted and murmured. The horse of the provision cart, panic-struck, bolted forward into Ramsgate. The driver, shouting angrily, rose to his feet and sawed at the reins; but so keen was the interest of the audience in the smoke rising from the depression in the Hindu's board that not even the two soldiers turned to watch the bolting horse.

The horse slowed to a walk and stared around reproachfully at the driver. The cart skirted the sandy beach of Ramsgate and bore off toward the sheltering chalk cliff under which twoscore cutters, luggers and other small craft lay at anchor. Somnolent men in blue jerseys reclined against ancient docks and wharf houses, seemingly oblivious to both the cart and its occupants.

The cart came at length to a decrepit house in the doorway of which sat a whiskered man with bare feet. At sight of the carters he thrust a great toe through the meshes of a seine to hold it taut, while with his teeth and his two hands he set busily to work repairing a rip.

The driver, a tall man with knuckles strangely scarred, stared down at the net mender. "How's fishing?" he asked.

The whiskered man replied cryptically that there was a hole in nearly every net.

"I was told," Marvin said, "that a net mender by the name of Clay in Ramsgate was needing some poultry."

"I'm Clay," the whiskered man said. He withdrew his great toe from the seine and came to examine the hens in the back of the cart.

"Aye," he added, "them's 'ens, them is!" Under his breath he added with an air of finality, "Cost you ten guineas heach. Ten guineas to Calais."

"No, not Calais," Marvin said. "Morlaix."

Clay shook his head. "Calais, you'll go to," he replied sourly. "Calais, and lucky to get there." He snorted. "Morlaix! What you think we're running here? Blooming hexcursion boats?"

Marvin stared hard at the net mender and drew a deep breath. Before he could speak, Argandeau murmured quickly in his ear.

Marvin laughed, glanced appraisingly at the sky and vaulted lightly from the cart. "Calais it is," he said, "at ten guineas a man. There's two more of us on the edge of town—a brown man in an old sheet, doing tricks, and a boy leading him. Bring 'em in safe and we'll show you the color of our money."

It was close on to midnight when Clay put them aboard the lugger *Hirondelle;* and the captain, a squat Frenchman with legs so bowed a full-grown pig could have run between them without touching either, welcomed them politely and locked them in the lugger's tiny cabin.

To the four men, huddled in the dark, came the rattle of the lug sail rising. The *Hirondelle's* head fell off and the little vessel pitched uneasily in the Channel chop.

Argandeau fumbled at the cabin door. "Yes," he said, "this lock has four small fastenings. You bore beside them and we wrench it off—Pouff! Like that!" He snapped his fingers.

The Indian crouched beside him, and there began a sound of

gnawing—a sound so faint that it was lost in the screakings of the lugger's hull and the slap of water on her sides.

The cabin door banged open, and the four men tumbled into the cockpit. Three of them scrambled forward. Argandeau remained behind, smiling amiably into the lugger captain's horror-stricken face.

"A friendly visit, this," he ventured. "It is too cold and lonely in that cabin, eh? So we come out to suggest that you journey more to the southward, where it is a little warmer, perhaps."

"To the southward?" the captain asked incredulously.

"Truly!" Argandeau agreed. "To Morlaix. A beautiful town, Morlaix. You know Morlaix, perhaps? The women are beautiful to a degree."

"Morlaix!" the captain cried. "Why should I venture to Morlaix? You desire that I should lose my occupation? Name of a pig, but if I risk my beautiful *Hirondelle* on the long trip to Morlaix, I shall certainly do so!"

"If you fear to lose a situation," Argandeau told him sententiously, "abandon it. Always you will find a better one."

The lugger captain laughed bitterly. "A better one! I will be forced to become a Flushing or Middleburg man, carrying brandy to Ireland. To Ireland! My God, there is a dangerous affair!"

"Listen!" Argandeau said. He reached for the tiller and pushed it over. The lugger's head fell off and the little vessel ran more easily down the Channel. "Listen. You are a man of Calais, no?"

"Sacred heart!" the lugger captain wailed. "Calais, yes!"

"Yes," Argandeau said, "and you have then heard of Tom Souville, perhaps."

The lugger captain stared at him. "Heard of Tom Souville!" he exclaimed. "What do you think? Am I a dead man? Every man who is not a dead man has heard of Tom Souville!"

"Truly!" Argandeau murmured.

"Truly and truly!" the lugger captain agreed. "Four times that fox has escaped from the hulks. Four times he has cast foreign substances in the eyes of the British. Yes, I know him! Every man knows him! The English know him well! In his *Renard,* three days since, he has captured another English brig—a strong armed brig! You know this Souville?"

"Do I know him?" Argandeau asked. "Do I know my own nose? I think yes! We are like brother and brother together; like fish and potatoes!"

"Ah!" the lugger captain exclaimed.

"But yes!" Argandeau said. "You return to Calais and say to Tom Souville that you have done this for Lucien Argandeau, and he kiss you on both cheeks, like this!" He embraced the lugger captain and kissed him. "He will make your position more secure than Mont Blanc! That is something, eh?"

"That is something!" the lugger captain agreed. He crouched be-behind the gunwale and lighted a short pipe that smelled like smouldering hair. "That is something. With this wind, we reach Morlaix at sixteen o'clock, I think yes."

XXII

Tʜᴇ fat landlady of the *Queen of Scotland* tavern in the fish-scented town of Morlaix raised her thick shoulders and strove to widen her eyes above her fleshy cheeks. "Ah!" she exclaimed to the tall, roughly dressed man who stood before her high desk. "Ah, but I was sorry for that lady, you understand. She was desperate, poor little one! I knew; yes. Her back, it remained straight and beautiful; but me, Victorine, I knew! She was penniless and desperate! Indeed, yes! Not that I would have pressed her, ever! No! But I was sorry—yes, sorry—and then her friend arrived." The landlady sighed, and from the vicinity of her enormous bosom came faint creakings.

Marvin stared at her from under heavy brows. "A friend? She didn't have any! She didn't know anyone here!"

The landlady breathed heavily and pursed her buttonhole of a mouth. "Ah, but yes! It was a man—ah, very much! One with fascination in his face and in his movements. Oh, a very good friend of hers! He knew her well; for he had been with the poor little one on the ship before all the misfortune of that great loss. Then he had gone somewhere for a time." Her beady eyes peered out at him from rolls of fat. "To Roscoff—I do not know. It is no matter. He was a fine gentleman. His costume was rich! A fine coat! A fine hat! Ah—ah, all of the costume rich! And he paid well, that one!" Her eyes blinked eagerly at him. "He paid very well—very much!"

"You think she was glad?" Marvin whispered huskily.

The landlady's eyes flicked across Marvin's stained and wrinkled trousers and his broken shoes. "Yes," she said, "she seemed very fond of him, that poor little one. Oh, yes, very! And why not, eh? She had a figure, that one! A back so straight and flat I have never seen! No! She brought trade; I will not conceal it! There was a roundness to her that men came here to see. And this friend of hers, he had an air. It was something to be whispered to by that man, I think!" She shuddered softly. "They were a couple, that pair! Two cabbages, eh? I see them now, departing by the Paris coach. Me, Victorine, I would give one bottle of brandy to know the words he whispered as they left." Her laugh was oily and her eyes were hidden by the rolls of fat.

Marvin looked at her for one moment longer; then turned abruptly and walked to the door. He walked decisively, yet his steps were unsteady; and the landlady, watching him, ceased to laugh. Her piggish glance dwelt coldly on his back, and from her pursed lips there burst a contemptuous puff, like the breathing of a rolling porpoise.

Three men waited in the narrow street before the *Queen of Scotland* tavern. They stared silently at the grayness of Marvin's face as he came heavily toward them.

Argandeau cleared his throat. "My friend, you have learned something. You like to tell us what it is?"

Marvin nodded slowly. "Slade," he said. "It was Slade that did it —Slade that fixed us." He studied his clenched fist. "It was Slade," he repeated numbly. "He's got money—plenty of it."

The three men watched him, and when he was silent, Newton stirred uneasily. "The lady you spoke of," he ventured—"did you learn about her?"

Marvin lifted his eyes to the dull November sky; then lowered them moodily to Newton's face and slowly shook his head. "Nothing."

"You learned nothing?" Argandeau cried. "But it would be common news in Morlaix what became of her! Come; we go again and ask!"

Marvin eyed him. "Nothing, I said!" he repeated flatly. "Nothing! Henceforth nothing!"

Argandeau drew a long breath and nodded understandingly. "I see! I see! We cannot speak of her!" He lifted an eyebrow. "We cannot speak of her, and so we will not; but we can speak of Slade, eh? We can consider Slade!"

"Yes," Marvin said. "We'll consider Slade."

"Eh? And find him first?"

"Yes. I'm going to find him."

"Ah, when you find him," Argandeau said, "that will be something to enjoy." He pirouetted on the cobbles of the narrow street. "Where do we go to find him, my friend?"

"Paris," Marvin said.

"That is a city that *is* a city," Argandeau remarked. "Where is it in Paris that we shall find him?"

"I don't know," Marvin said. "I don't know."

Argandeau snapped his fingers. "Do not despair, dear Dan! Here in France there are men whose business it is to know many things. I think I can find a man to tell us of this Slade. You have heard of this man—Tom Souville of Calais? He is like to burst with the infinity of the things he knows! Come; we go quickly to Calais!"

XXIII

It was early morning when Argandeau led his three companions between the warehouses of the Quai de Kéroualle and out onto the egg-shaped cobbles of the dock itself, slimy from the cold drizzle that turned the buildings, the shipping and the harbor of Calais into a uniform dirty gray. Two vessels lay before them—one a tall and graceful schooner, and the other a small brig that squatted behind the schooner like a drab and dumpy mallard duck paddling ignominiously after a spotless swan.

At the edge of the dock, screaming shrill orders to the sailors at work in the brig's rigging, stood a plump, helpless-looking man in whose appearance there was no evidence of wealth, seamanship or profound knowledge. Yet this helpless-looking man was of necessity Tom Souville; for it was to him that Argandeau ran, and to him he spoke, bowing as handsomely, when he did so, as though clad in the finest broadcloth and satin, instead of the miserable shag trousers and striped shirt with which Clay had supplied him in Ramsgate.

There was something of timidity to Souville when he turned, at Argandeau's first words. His lips were slack; his eyes were wide; all in all he had the air of a person about whom there was little to fear and less to remember.

In the moment of seeing Argandeau, however, his face broadened and hardened in a thin-lipped grin, and he seized Argandeau by the upper arms, seeming almost to wrestle with him. As he did so, Marvin saw, over Argandeau's shoulder, Souville's eye flicker across him and his companions with the fierce scrutiny of a stooping hawk.

When, a moment later, he came to them, his eyes were wide and gentle and his smile diffident as he complimented them on their escape from the hulks of Chatham. "I do not need to ask how are you," he said. "You are happy men, alive and free where only a short time ago you were half dead and sealed in the tomb. I myself have known this feeling more than once. This rain seems not to be rain, eh? The whole world seems bright, and nothing too much for your efforts."

"I have told them this, Captain," Argandeau assured him. "Nothing is too much, if they have the great Captain Souville to direct them."

A look so vacuous as to approach imbecility swept over Souville's face and clung there until Marvin, nodding his head at the small brig, observed calmly that she was a tidy craft. "We heard you took her," Marvin said. "How did she sail with your *Renard?*"

"Good!" Souville said quickly. "Good! Not too good, but good! You know there is nothing sails with my *Renard*—not even any French schooner, and you well know that there are no vessels so fast as our French vessels. Therefore this *Challenger* sails well, but not so well but what I could sail a circle around her in any weather." He canted his head a little backward toward the harbor, his face as fatuous as that of a father indicating an adored child. "You have had an eye for my *Renard,* no doubt?"

"Yes," Marvin said, eyeing the tall schooner tied up beyond the brig's bows, "yes, she's a fine craft! If I could take out a craft like that, I'd make five million francs for her owners if I made a sou." He stared from her to the squat and clumsy brig. "I've sometimes thought, though, that this talk of the speed of French vessels is all my eye and my elbow. It appears to me I've seen English vessels that could sail with the best of French vessels, provided the English manned their craft with seamen instead of peasants and city boys."

"No, no!" Souville said amiably. "Look here at this *Challenger* brig. Her lines are not bad, but she is too narrow, and heavy beyond all need. Her yards are thick, like an Englishwoman's leg, and her bulkheads are like making a wineglass from a block of granite!"

Marvin nodded. "Yes, but this is not the only English vessel in the world. There was an English schooner came into Morlaix a month ago and cut out our barque, the *Olive Branch.* Now, there was a schooner!"

Souville smiled pityingly. "No, no! That *Sparrow* schooner, she is not much. In light airs, now, my *Renard* would leave her so fast she would seem anchored."

Marvin turned suddenly to Souville. "Why," he said, "here's a piece of luck! You must have heard the whole tale, or you'd never know the schooner's name. That was it—the *Sparrow!* If you know it was she that cut us out, you'll know what became of an officer who left her on the day she made port."

Souville's lower lip slackened, and into his eyes there came a blankness that was almost witlessness. "An officer," he asked. "An officer left her?"

A heavy silence descended on the little group of men—a silence broken at last by Argandeau: "There is something wrong here, my old friend," he said. "For some reason you guard yourself against us, and I think you know too much or too little."

He moved closer to Souville, making him a dignified half bow. "You suspect something, Captain; but I swear to you, by the friendship of our youth, there is no reason! These men are my friends, cruelly used by England, and more than eager to further the cause of France by doing England a hurt. This young man"—he flicked his finger tips lightly against Marvin's breast—"is a seaman, cautious with the peculiar caution of his country, and capable of inflicting great damage on an enemy. I have watched him—I, Lucien Argandeau—and I tell you that in one hour's time he thinks how to do things better and more quickly than they have ever before been done."

Souville raised his hands and let them fall helplessly. "I have heard only a little; so little that it is nothing. This officer, perhaps, had an eye partly obscured." He threw back his head, drooped one eyelid and looked quickly at Marvin, so that he seemed to peer out from under the lowered lid.

Marvin nodded, and Argandeau cursed softly in a foreign tongue. "You knew this man?" Souville asked.

"Knew him!" Marvin said grimly. "Slade set the English on us! What we wish is to know him better."

"So you had heard it?" Souville said. "How did it happen that you heard it?"

Argandeau laughed. "How does it happen you know there will be rain tomorrow? It is something you know. This Slade, he was our enemy. I, too, am sure—very sure—he sent the Griffons, the English, to cut out the *Olive Branch.* How he informed them, I do not know, but he went ashore the day we made port, and disappeared. The next thing we know, the *Sparrow* arrives, coming purposely for us. It is a strange thing, too, that the officials of Morlaix held us and held us, anchored in the estuary, refusing to let us break bulk. These Americans, they might have been enemies of France, from the way they were treated!"

Souville pinched his lower lip between his thumb and forefinger, squeezing a part of the seeming imbecility from his face. "Then you think there may have been a connection between this Slade and the behavior of the Morlaix officials? You think he might be an enemy to France as well as to yourself?"

Marvin nodded. "He was a slave captain, and slave captains cannot live except by bribery. He was an enemy to everybody and everything that would keep him from getting what he wanted;

and the thing he wanted most"—Marvin hesitated momentarily—
"was money."

Souville looked hard at Marvin and then at Argandeau. "All in
all, then," he said, "you consider him a dangerous man?"

Argandeau laughed angrily. "Dangerous! He should have a knife
in the back; or if you are too squeamish for that, he should be hustled
to Verdun and placed in the dungeons for the remainder of this little
war! Tell us where he is, my friend!"

Souville seemed suddenly enlightened.

"Ah, I did not understand," he said. "In wartime it is impossible
to tell. It might have been that you were in sympathy with the man.
Now you shall have everything from me, frankly and freely. We will
remove ourselves from this wet, eh, and go aboard my *Renard*, where
we can speak quietly over a bottle of the best brandy."

He turned abruptly, no longer anything of helplessness or indecision about him, swaggered to the companionway of the tall schooner,
and led the way over her side and to the after hatch. Marvin, bringing up the rear of the small procession, paused for a moment at the
bulwarks to study the bows of the squat brig beyond the *Renard's*
stern; then continued, whistling softly, downward into Souville's
quarters.

From the dark stains on the floor, as well as from the red paint
on the patched sheathing, Marvin saw that the *Renard's* barren cabin
had often been used as a hospital during engagements; and Souville,
rummaging in a chest for a bottle, while the others settled themselves on benches, replied volubly to Marvin's unspoken thoughts.

"You think there is small comfort here, eh? Well, that is so! My
Renard, she goes always on business; and the quicker the business
is done, the quicker we return home, eh? Therefore, I want little
here for the making of splinters; little that must be thrown overboard before an engagement; for any such throwing would take time.
In three months I shall have a larger vessel, with more comforts,
perhaps; but I am wise to keep my *Renard* clear and clean like the
boudoir of a young girl, eh?" He poured brandy into small glasses,
squinted through one of them, touched the glass to his lips; then
rolled his eyes ecstatically. "I drink your health and good fortune,
gentlemen! The Americans, they are our dear friends and brothers
against a common enemy."

"We came here to speak of Slade," Marvin reminded him.

"Yes, yes," Souville said. "Now I tell you! I see how you have suffered through this Slade, so I tell you everything! When this Slade
left your barque, he went to England, where he sold information

to the Admiralty for a large amount of money, perhaps fifteen thousand pounds; and he went then to certain merchants of Bristol who are engaged in the slave trade contrary to law, and threatened them with exposure unless they provided him with an armed vessel—a fast armed vessel."

Argandeau bounced from his bench, stamped twice on the floor, spat violently through a stern window and threw himself heavily on the bench again.

"An armed vessel?" Marvin asked slowly. "What sort of vessel?"

Souville shrugged his shoulders. "I have not heard, but probably a brig. The fastest ones are brigs. Later I shall know surely."

Marvin sighed gently. "Then he hasn't got it yet. Thank God!"

Souville shook his head. "No, and I am told that another month must pass before he gets it, but he had money from these Englishmen —a deal of money—and when he left England to return to Roscoff, he wrangled with the—ah—with the young woman who had accompanied him on his travels—a young woman who came to me with the tale. An interesting man, this Slade. He had promised to pay this young woman fifty pounds for favors received, but on leaving he would give her no more than twenty."

"There was a traveling companion, indeed!" Argandeau remarked.

Newton wagged his head in simulated admiration. "He'll bear watching, Slade will. He'd go far in politics or finance!"

"You say Slade returned from England," Marvin reminded Souville. "What then?"

"Why," Souville said, "then he went straight to Morlaix and to Paris. As soon as we had word from England of his activities, we traced him carefully." He frowned. "If only we had known two days earlier, we would have had him and there would have been one more enemy safe in the dungeons of Verdun! He moves quickly, this Slade of yours! Three days he spends in Paris; then he is gone, like a puff of smoke, back to England—back to his dear friends in Bristol. We have lost him, I fear. I hope it is not so, but I fear it."

"Back to England!" Marvin said. "He went back to England!" He groaned, and moved to the stern windows of the *Renard*, to stand staring down at the brig whose long jib-boom rose above the *Renard's* taffrail; then turned suddenly to eye the small and pompous Souville. Surprisingly, he laughed. "I'll tell you what I'll do, Captain: I'll capture Slade myself and make some money for you in the bargain, if you'll supply me with the means of doing it."

Souville looked at him blankly. "Supply you? I do not understand!"

Marvin set down his glass and tapped the table with his forefinger.

"Captain," he said, "you're playing a dangerous game with your *Renard*. She's fast, I know; but what happens to her, fast as she is, if you're caught by a frigate on a lee shore some foggy morning? At the worst, she's torn to pieces and you're killed. At the best, the English take her. Then you and your men go back to the hell of an orlop deck on a British hulk, and the fevers and bloody fluxes and black pneumonias that make the hulks as rotten as the meat they give you to gag on. You know what they are better than I do."

Souville smiled comfortably. "You talk like my wife."

"I drink to her wisdom," Marvin replied. "It's the truth. What's more, you'll catch a Tartar some day—somebody who knows how to shoot better than you do. Look at this brig you just brought in! Shot to pieces in her yards and sails and rigging, but not a shot in her hull! If you hadn't been able to take her by boarding, you wouldn't have got her at all. Isn't that so?"

"Never!" Souville declared indignantly. "It is not so."

Marvin rose again, went to the side of the cabin and rapped his knuckles against the sheathing. "An egg-shell," he said, "like so many French private vessels. Everything sacrificed to speed! A little bad luck, and she'd crumple under you. You wouldn't have got the brig if she'd shot straight and cleared your deck of boarders."

"But you would like to have this egg-shell of mine," Souville observed complacently.

"Ah," Marvin said, "but I've made a discovery that would make her safe! I've learned how to lie off at a safe distance and batter a vessel to pieces with a long gun. I've learned how to lay guns in smoke with a raw crew."

"And never miss, eh?" Souville scoffed.

"And seldom miss," Marvin said gravely. "That's the discovery."

"There is no way to do it," Souville said.

"Yes," Marvin insisted. "I've invented a way. It can be done with a pendulum—a gangway pendulum."

Souville, plucking at an end of his small mustache, seemed to mull over the word; then slapped his knee and laughed until his mirth ended in a spasm of coughing. "A gangway pendulum! A gangway pendulum, indeed! And what happens with your gangway pendulum? Perhaps your enemies mistake you for a clock, afloat on the ocean, and never beat to quarters until they are under your guns!"

"It's nothing to laugh about," Marvin assured him, "unless you're in the habit of laughing at something that will put money in your own pocket and at the same time damage England."

"A gangway pendulum!" Souville repeated, wiping the tears from his eyes. "And what do you expect me to do about this gangway pendulum?"

"I'm offering you the opportunity to benefit by it," Marvin said. "Sell me two-thirds of your *Renard* and keep one-third for yourself, and you'll have a prime investment."

Souville became instantly serious. "You have the money?"

"How much are you asking?"

"My *Renard* is a fortunate vessel," Souville said slowly. "If I sold her, I would require a good price. If it were not that I am building another, I would not consider it at all—not at any price. For selling two-thirds of my *Renard* I would require"—he contemplated the ceiling of the barren cabin—"I would require one hundred thousand francs, gold."

Argandeau whistled, a faint, long-drawn-out whistle, while Newton, clasping his brow, murmured, "She must be sheathed with silver!"

Marvin studied the knuckles of his left hand, scarred from his battle with Little White. "That would be possible, if one-half could be paid at the termination of my first cruise, and the other half——"

"No, no," Souville interrupted quickly. "I do nothing in that way! I know nothing about you or your seamanship! You pay me one hundred thousand francs in gold, and I gamble on you, because I am a friend of America and you are my brother in arms."

"But," Marvin said patiently, "I am offering you my gangway pendulum——"

Souville expelled his breath explosively and waved his hand before his face as if freeing himself of cobwebs. "It is something fantastic, this pendulum! I have heard of no such thing, ever, and to me it has no value!"

"I think you make a mistake," Argandeau protested. "My dear Marvin has said something to me of this pendulum; and if he says it has a high value, then it has a high value. I tell you he has a flair for making strange discoveries."

Souville sighed. "No, it is something I cannot consider. And now, my good friend, the morning passes and I must attend to the repairs on this small brig."

"One hundred thousand francs," Marvin said, almost to himself, "seems to me somewhat high for two-thirds of an armed schooner. I'll venture to say I could get a brig, and a good one, too, for a quarter of that sum."

"Of course," Souville agreed, "but she would not be my *Renard*."

"No," Marvin said, "but she'd be as good as this captured brig of yours—better. Yes, sir! I could buy a better brig than that captured brig for twenty thousand francs."

"It is possible," Souville admitted politely, "but the twenty thousand francs would have to be in money, and not in conversation about a gangway pendulum! And I think you will find that even though you have money, you will be obliged to pay at least twenty-five thousand francs. Certainly I would not sell this brig here for less than twenty-five thousand."

"You will insist on twenty-five thousand?" Marvin persisted.

Souville smiled. "Francs, you understand. Not pendulums."

Marvin walked again to the stern windows and studied the vessel carefully. "It's not a bad price, twenty-five thousand francs," he said. "Not bad, if you sell her as she is. Shall you sell her as she stands, long guns and all?"

Souville nodded.

Marvin drew his bench to the table, felt in an inner pocket and brought out a small heap of yellow coins. "You've sold your brig for twenty-five thousand francs," he said, "and I've bought her, and here's a little English gold to bind the bargain. I'll put Newton and Steven aboard today to take possession, and leave tonight with Argandeau to find the balance of the money. If you'll make out a bill of sale, these gentlemen can witness it."

Souville stared doubtfully at Marvin, then moved slowly to a small chest and fumbled in it for paper and quills. "You Americans!" he said. "I think you are becrazed! Can I believe it was this brig you desired from the first moment, and that you had no desire at all for my *Renard?*"

Marvin stopped in the counting of his gold pieces to look blankly into Souville's face. "You're laughing at me again!" he said. "I'm buying the brig only so you'll feel obligated to keep me informed of Slade's movements."

With the eye farthest removed from Souville he winked faintly at Newton; while Souville, frowning, pocketed the gold pieces before him and went to driving his quill with thoughtful delicacy across a flimsy sheet of pale blue paper.

When he had finished, Marvin took the paper from him and read it carefully. Then he drew Newton to the stern windows of the *Renard* and pointed to the clumsy brig.

"She's ballasted with rock," he said. "Her center of gravity's too high, and the sail she'll carry wouldn't make petticoats for my grandmother. Throw out the rock and ballast her with scrap iron. Her yards are stout enough for wharf piling. Sway 'em down and fine 'em out.

Scrape 'em till they bleed. Then she'll carry royals and skysails. Knock out the sheathing inside the bulwarks; it's no good except to make a splinter bucket out of her. Spend your money and spend it fast." He picked up his hat and eyed Newton warningly. "Trust nothing to chance. Be careful. Keep an eye on everything and be sure everything is right. We may have to sail into hell after Mr. Slade, and I want this vessel fast enough to make the trip without scorching herself or anyone aboard."

XXIV

M̲ARVIN, followed by Argandeau, came out from the avenue that tunneled through the forest of brown-leafed chestnuts, and stood staring across terraces and gardens to the gates of the Château of Valençay, and to the enormous pile of pallid stone beyond, looming against the blue November sky as dangerously as a cliff rising abruptly from a lee shore.

They studied the two round towers at either end of the château's long gray bulk—towers topped with shining rounded domes, so that there was a hint about them of gigantic warning lighthouses; then, having studied them, they fell suddenly to brushing their garments and arranging their cravats in the shelter of the lofty boxwood hedge that stood between them and the gardens of the château.

Argandeau sighed and shook his head. "It is possible that the thing may be accomplished," he said, "but not unless I tell them loudly that you are an American and therefore insane! You must remember the French do not do things in this way! They do not try to walk in to see a great man as if he were no more than a black cook in a forecastle! No! They write him a letter, and his secretary and mistress read it, and at the end of three months they may be promised an appointment which will not be kept. I tell you I think it would be well to have a letter written, in case this man is thrown into a rage because you come calling on him as if you were Metternich or Marshal Soult. I tell you he is a prince and a duke and a bishop, and nearly as great a man as Bonaparte himself."

"I'm glad to hear it," Marvin said. "He owes my father eleven dollars."

Argandeau examined Marvin carefully from head to foot. "Eleven dollars, now that we have spent everything on your clothes, is a great deal, and I wish we had it; but it is true that your clothes were worth the price. If you were older, with a red face and a puffy nose and a swollen stomach, you would look like a general or an admiral yourself, or a duke maybe. It is a pity you are not seeking help from a beautiful woman rather than from this great gentleman, who is able to talk anyone into thinking that black is white, or that it is possible to live without money. My Spanish rabbit, she had a proverb about such an affair. 'There are some men,' she said, 'who would not loan you fifty pesetas even though they were offered the Alhambra as security; but almost any woman, provided she is over ten and under ninety-eight, will lend you all she possesses on no greater security than a mouthful of lies about love.'"

Marvin rubbed the dust from his boots with a wisp of grass, carefully brushed the tight dark-blue trousers that were strapped beneath them, ran his finger around the inside of the high stock that rose above his frilled shirt, and examined his snugly fitting, long-tailed coat for blemishes. "Look here," he told Argandeau. "Look at me carefully. Be sure there is nothing about me to prevent this great man from listening attentively to what I say."

He placed his cocked hat a little on the side of his head, thumped his gold-topped cane in the dust of the road, rested one hand on his hip and stared almost defiantly at his companion.

Argandeau walked slowly around him. "It is perfect," he insisted. "Perfect! The seals of your watch, they look entirely real. There is nobody who would think the head of your cane was anything but gold. Also you carry this cane with an air, and the shoulders of your coat are narrow, so that you have a look of delicacy almost—nothing at all like a man who could put Little White under hatches in three rounds."

"Then try to find the door of this building and get me into it," Marvin told him, "so I can forget my clothes and do what I've come for."

He took off his hat, placed it, folded, under his arm, flourished his cane experimentally and glanced expectantly at Argandeau. Argandeau, however, seemed to have forgotten his existence; for he was staring, with eyes as large and round as plums, at the boxwood hedge that bordered the avenue.

Turning quickly, Marvin saw, above the clipped top of the hedge, a woman's face. In the very moment that he turned, an expression of annoyance crossed it, and it sank slowly from sight, leaving in his mind's eye a picture of black hair piled in a high knot, a pointed chin and large blue eyes beneath black brows as curved and slender as a bent hunting bow.

From beyond the hedge there came the sound of soft-voiced expostulation, followed by rapid protestations in the voice of another woman.

"Two rabbits!" Argandeau murmured. "One held up the other to look over, but let her slip."

"Sir from America!" called the soft voice from beyond the hedge. "It is the duke you visit?"

Marvin cleared his throat. "Talleyrand, ma'am."

"Yes," the soft voice continued. "You walk straight ahead through the great gates into the *cour d'honneur*. Across the court, on the right, is the *perron* of the vestibule. Do not go beneath the arch, or you will lose yourself."

"Thank you, ma'am," Marvin said. "I've been afraid I might not find him." He took Argandeau by the arm and set off up the avenue toward the imposing bulk of carved gray stone.

"Wait one moment!" the soft voice called. Then, closer to them, it added: "It may be you meet delay if you go to the vestibule. M. de Talleyrand is amused to see Americans, always; but he is here not often; and since you arrive on foot, the guards at the vestibule might neglect, you understand. The King of Spain, he is detained here, and so there are guards. Walk to the gates, therefore, and wait. I take you to another entrance, more quick."

"Thank you, ma'am," Marvin said again. He moved quickly to the opposite side of the avenue, drawing Argandeau after him. Argandeau skipped a little, and blew a kiss toward the sky. "Two rabbits!" he whispered ecstatically. "It was a proverb with my Spanish rabbit: 'Push Lucien Argandeau into a gutter and he will come out sweet with musk!'"

"You fool!" Marvin said. "You'd want to talk about women if you were caught in the breakers and next door to death! God knows what harm you've done us with your gabble! Get back to the inn and wait there for me!"

"But there are two of them!" Argandeau protested. "While you are engaged with one, it may be that I can secure the cost of our lodgings from the other. Have you forgotten that we have not one sou in the world? Not one sou among the pair of us?"

His protests, however, were vain; for Marvin, his cane swinging jauntily and his cocked hat somewhat aslant, went briskly from him toward the distant gates without a backward glance.

The two women came through an opening in the boxwood hedge, chattering to each other as if they could never find time to finish what they were saying; and to Marvin it seemed they were little more than girls, pretending, with youthful coquetry, to have forgotten he was to wait for them at the gates. Yet there was nothing of coquetry in the glance the black-haired girl turned suddenly toward him; only inquiry and something of puzzlement.

"The other," she asked. "He does not wish to visit the duke also?"

Marvin shook his head. "He came to keep me company. He went back to the inn."

"*Le Roi d'Espagne?*" she asked. "You are remaining at *Le Roi d'Espagne?* You will be uncomfortable, I think."

When he was silent, she turned from him and slipped her arm in that of her companion, saying over her shoulder: "You come with us, please. We take you to the tower, where the duke sits in the afternoon." She chattered a little to her companion, a round, brown girl whose brown hair was piled in a knot even higher and more pointed than that of the black-haired girl; then to Marvin, as if to put him at his ease, she said: "How far have you come?"

"From Calais," he told her. "From Calais since Tuesday."

"Then you have good horses," she said, "but I fear you break all your springs."

"No, ma'am. We came on foot."

The black-haired girl halted her companion and spoke rapidly to her; then stared at Marvin. "What is this you say? You walk from Calais to Valençay? And since Tuesday? Is it possible that a man can do this? I think no horse could do it!"

"No, ma'am," Marvin agreed, "but it was more important for me than it would be for any horse."

Again the black-haired girl spoke volubly to her companion, whereupon the two of them scrutinized Marvin as if in search of something about him that had hitherto escaped them. "It must be indeed important," the black-haired girl said. "Do you come direct from America to this place?"

"No, ma'am. From England."

"From England! But you are at war with—— Then I ask you, do you come direct to England from America?"

"No, ma'am. From China."

"From China? I do not know where—ah, *la Chine!* Ah-hah! Then it is important because you are *diplomatique,* eh? No! That is not so! If you were *diplomatique,* you would come here in a coach, and drive about this court with a great fracas, cracking the whip and blowing the horn and frightening the sparrows for two days! You cannot be *diplomatique!* But still the matter is important! Now I must think what it is so important as to bring a gentleman on foot from Calais to Valençay. Either it must be——" She stopped and eyed Marvin absently. At length, still silent, she drew her companion onward once more and, followed by Marvin, continued through the formal gardens that lay between the court of honor and the squat, round-topped tower in which the château ended.

At the angle between the tower and the main wall of this vast gray building there was a small door; and at the door the round, brown girl turned away, running lightly toward the main entrance. The black-haired girl looked gravely at Marvin. "Now you go in to see M. de Talleyrand. Perhaps you like better to tell everything to me, so that I help you with him?"

"Thank you, ma'am," Marvin said. "I wouldn't want to trouble you."

"But it is no trouble! Come; you tell me, and I shall see whether I have guessed correctly why your visit is important. Then I help you with the duke."

Marvin coughed. "I think, ma'am—no offense meant—that it would be better if I told Talleyrand himself. It's he that must help me."

She smiled faintly. "You are cautious, and it is no great fault to be cautious at the proper time. I think it would make a difference, perhaps, if I say to you that I am a member of the duke's household. It is possible you consider me a servant."

"No, no!" Marvin said. "I can see you're a great lady! But a lady can't—ah, that is to say, if I can't convince the duke, how can a lady convince him for me?"

The black-haired girl opened her eyes wide. "How? You do not seriously ask me how! Surely you do not think there is any wise man but knows he can do better at anything at all by taking the advice of a woman! Surely you know that any wise woman can persuade a man into doing whatever she desires!"

"That's no doubt true," Marvin admitted, "but it's my belief that for every wise woman there are fifty foolish ones who consider themselves wise."

He shot a quick glance at her, and found her smiling more broadly.

"And I am one of the fifty?" she asked.

"How can I tell, ma'am? You know it's important I should see Talleyrand, and still you keep me from him. Is that wisdom, ma'am?"

She shrugged, opened the door in the angle of the wall and preceded Marvin into a small vestibule, where she dropped her long brown cloak on a table. Marvin saw then that her yellow dress had next to no sleeves, and that, on one side, the skirt was slashed as high as the knee, almost as though a small staysail had been cut from it.

She arranged her hair, looking up at him from beneath her elbow.

"It may be," she said, "that the King of Spain is with him also—the one who was stolen by——" She wagged her head, frowned severely, thrust one hand into the front of her gown and the other behind her back, and puffed out her cheeks, so that she had a look of Bonaparte about her. "If he is there," she added sedately, "do not be disturbed by him. He is not much of a king."

She opened another door on the far side of the vestibule and went quickly into a circular chamber so large that for a moment it seemed to Marvin an empty blur of enormous pale carpets and gilded furniture heavily garnished with lions' heads. Out of the blur came a vast hooded fireplace, and windows opening onto an ancient and heavy cloister. Near the fireplace was a table at which sat a man with a face like parchment, his chin propped so high by a thick collar that he had an air of disliking the odor of the place. Yet his features were so placid as to seem lifeless, and his eyes peered out of the blank whiteness of his face like black paper pasted behind the eyeholes of a mask. In a reclining chair on the opposite side of the fireplace lay a swarthy, sulky-seeming young man, rubbing a finger moodily over the strings of a guitar.

The black-haired girl curtsied quickly to the gentleman at the desk. "Uncle Maurice," she said, "I have found this young man from America with something important to say to you: something so important that he cannot tell it to any woman—only to M. de Talleyrand himself—so I think it must be the most important thing that ever was known."

XXV

Talleyrand rose from his desk, smiling with an exquisite gentleness, but he did not move forward to greet his guest; and Marvin noticed that one of the shoes the great man wore was misshapen, as if the foot within it were crippled. The voice was rich and of a silken suavity:

"From America! I find this a great honor that a gentleman from your fine young country should come here to Valençay to see me— a great honor, and a surprise as well. Sit, please, and tell me who has sent you, and how do you learn I am here? It is almost never I come, and it is only four days since my niece and I set out to escape the turmoil of the Rue St. Florentin."

Marvin, uncomfortably erect in a small, hard chair, glanced from the smiling, mask-like face of Talleyrand to the black-haired girl, who had gone with the sulky man to stand beside a roulette wheel at a long window through which appeared the broad expanse of park, a dark belt of forest beyond, and, most distant of all, the little town of Valençay, its white roofs and Gothic church spire glistening in the afternoon sun.

"Why," he said, "nobody sent me. I came because——" He broke off and stared at the brilliant bindings of the books that encircled the room, and at the painted nymphs rioting on the ceiling. "It's a mistake, of course! We had a brig, the *Talleyrand,* named for a Frenchman who came to Arundel and was taken by my father to buy land from General Knox, years ago. I thought it was you; but surely it was never you who needed to buy lands in Maine!"

As if to himself and almost as an afterthought, he added: "And owed my father eleven dollars. It's not likely!"

Talleyrand lowered himself to a chair beside Marvin and looked intently into his eyes. "Eleven dollars?" he asked politely. "I have no recollection of——" He paused. "It is true, certainly; for no one would spuriously imagine the peculiar sum of eleven dollars; but it is strange that I—— Perhaps you remember your father telling the circumstances of those eleven dollars?"

"It was a wager," Marvin said. "You wagered that a certain Cap

Huff could eat no more than twenty-four ears of corn. He ate thirty-five, my father said, and so you lost eleven dollars."

Talleyrand nodded. "It is the truth! I remember it! After he had eaten the corn, he wished your father to wager me that he could also eat two pies of squashes. It all comes back! Dear me! Dear me! And you say I did not pay this wager?"

"My father said it was because of the buttered rum," Marvin said. "You went away early the next morning; and my father said any man might be forgetful in the early morning, especially after being free with the buttered rum. He said, always, it was worth more to him to be able to say Talleyrand owed him eleven dollars than to say Talleyrand had paid him eleven dollars."

"It was wisely said," Talleyrand agreed. "I hope your father is well? He found excellent land for me—excellent land—and so it was possible for me to live, selling a little here and a little there. Yes, yes, I remember; fools and wise men in America, they bought land at any price, anywhere! Tell me, your father is happy and successful?"

"He lost the *Talleyrand*, but now he owns another. When I go back, I shall take her out."

"You mean you will be captain of the ship?"

Marvin nodded. "Yes, and that's why I've come here."

"But of course!" Talleyrand exclaimed. "It is important that you return to America! I understand your eagerness, and I tell you that it can be arranged easily. You may be perfectly sure it shall be done."

"That's not it," Marvin said. He cleared his throat. "There's not time to go home. That is, the vessel I'd have if I went to America isn't the kind I want, and I want one now. I can do twice the harm to England if I can take out a vessel from France."

"Twice the harm?" Talleyrand asked. "I do not understand. If you sailed from America you would be more likely to discover unprotected British vessels, eh?"

"No, sir!" Marvin said. "It's in their home waters that they lack protection. You waste no time hunting 'em, for they're always to be found; and if you're cautious, you can surprise 'em where they least expect it."

"Now I see," Talleyrand said. "What you desire is a fighting vessel! You may depend upon it, I will assist you to this willingly. How much shall you wish to pay for this vessel?"

"No," Marvin said, "it's not only a vessel. There's another thing." Embarrassed, he glanced at the black-haired girl, to find her staring thoughtfully at him over the shoulder of her sulky companion. "If

I take out a private vessel from France, I'll need a commission, and it must be got from the American Minister—from Mr. Barlow in Paris. It's not only to get the vessel that I need your help, but to get the commission as well."

Talleyrand smiled almost sleepily. "But my interference is unnecessary, sir. You are—how shall I say?—you are perhaps overcareful in all this. Why do you not, my friend, go straight to Mr. Barlow and tell him what you wish? He is a gentleman and a poet, a trifle pompous and overcredulous, perhaps, but not at all a stickler for form. You will find him sympathetic, I am sure."

Haltingly, and with a kind of desperation, Marvin attempted to explain: "I wouldn't have come here if I could have seen any other means of getting what I needed. I must have someone to vouch for me to Mr. Barlow. I have no papers—they were taken from me by the British. I thought you might——"

"But even without papers," Talleyrand interrupted, "there were other seamen from your ship who can vouch for you—other officers? Were you the captain of the ship?"

"No, sir," Marvin said. "No, sir."

"Then who was the captain and where is he?" Talleyrand persisted.

"A lady was the captain. She thinks—she thought—it might be—that is, I can't let her——"

The black-haired girl moved to Talleyrand and leaned against his shoulder. "It was what I suspected!" she cried. "He had an air about him! I said to myself, 'This important matter has a woman in it.'"

"Well," Marvin said slowly, "I'll try to explain. You see, if I should go alone to Mr. Barlow, he'd ask about this lady, just as you have, and it might be he'd have learned from her—or from someone with her—that I'd been responsible for the loss of her ship to the British. Then he'd never issue a commission to me, and I could do nothing for her." He hesitated; then spoke haltingly: "You see—she's prejudiced against me—I think she's been told that I—that I—well, I think she was made to hate me."

The black-haired girl sank to her knees beside Talleyrand's chair. "Oh, the lady hates him!" she cried. "No wonder! Have you perhaps expressed to her your opinions concerning the wisdom of women?"

Talleyrand dropped an admonitory finger on her shoulder. "Of course," he told her, "you know everything about this affair, after hearing a few words; but I am older and duller, and there are still a few things obscured from me." To Marvin he added, "Now you begin, so that we may know about this lady you love, but who loves another gentleman who has been prejudicing her against you."

"That's not so!" Marvin protested. "That's not what I said, and it couldn't be true! She's hasty in her judgments, but she couldn't—she'd never——"

"Tell from the beginning," the black-haired girl insisted, leaning comfortably against Talleyrand's knee.

Before Marvin had finished his tale, the swarthy, sulky-looking Spanish king had ceased to turn his roulette wheel and had gone gloomily from the room, evoking doleful sounds from his guitar; and a servant had come to light the tall candles around the walls. When Marvin had finished, Talleyrand fingered his high stock and stared at the ceiling with expressionless black eyes.

"It is all quite plain," he said. "Not only must I intercede for you with Mr. Barlow, but if I do what you wish, I must purchase this vessel and intrust it to an untried captain, and all with no certainty for me of receiving any return whatever. Does this seem to you fair? To me it has the air of placing money carefully"—he dropped an imaginary atom from his finger tips—"in the ocean."

Marvin sat forward, balanced on the extreme edge of his chair. "No," he said. "You can't lose—not unless they sink my ship and kill me! If we have no luck, I'll pay it back after the war, with interest. But we'll—I can feel luck when it's close; every seaman that's worth his salt can feel it—we'll have my pendulum! You'll have the use of my pendulum! They'll never catch me while I have my pendulum! You'll have your money back ten times over!"

Talleyrand waved a white hand languidly. "It means nothing to me, this pendulum. You have thought about it; it exists only in your brain, eh? It seems to me a simple thing; so simple that our great seamen would have discovered it before now if it had value."

"Yes, it seems so," Marvin admitted, "but they haven't. Not even Nelson! Nelson said guns at sea aren't any good except at point-blank range, when they can't miss. He was wrong; but he's right, too, as long as guns are fired by guesswork, as they are now. Why, at long range, both the French and the English, all of 'em, fire with the roll of the vessel—as she rolls downward or as she rolls upward—hoping that one or two shots will be lucky enough to get home. A hit at long range is an accident today, unless a gun is handled by an expert rifleman; yes, and at long range there isn't one gun crew out of a thousand that could hit a mark the size of this château! With my pendulum there'll be no guessing about it. Every time I fire a long gun, I'll fire from an even keel, and I could hull this room four times out of five at half-mile range."

To Marvin it seemed that Talleyrand and his black-haired niece eyed him with as much of disfavor as disbelief. "I don't mean to brag," he told them mildly. "I've always looked for easier ways to do things, and almost always there's an easier way. It appears to me most people make things as hard for themselves as they can."

"Yes, I think it is so," Talleyrand said, "and I am interested in a part of what you tell me. I am interested to see how you are confident. You speak of England's great fleet as if it were nothing at all! It has destroyed our navy utterly—our fine, powerful navy—and yet it seems to be in your mind that a few men with a few small fishing boats can strike a blow at England that will be felt."

"And so they can," Marvin said. "So they can, provided their seamanship is what it should be. All that's necessary is to keep out of range of heavy war craft and sink the slow and clumsy merchantmen."

"Of course," Talleyrand admitted, "nothing else is necessary, provided, as you say, their seamanship is superior. When I was in America, I studied the inhabitants of your fishing cantons, and it was clearly to be seen that your fishermen are not to be compared with those of Europe, and that fishing in America is not a means of forming sailors and turning out strong and able seamen. It is a lazy calling in America, except in the case of the whalers of Nantucket."

"But we don't use fishermen on our merchantmen," Marvin protested. "We use seamen."

"But your seamen are fishermen first," Talleyrand said placidly. "I have been in your fishing cantons and written papers on the subject for our National Institute."

Marvin gripped his clenched hands between his knees. "Well," he said slowly, "we have many fishermen. We also have many merchantmen, and we've been forced to sail differently from the English merchantmen. They heave-to at night, most of them—send down their royal and topgallant yards and masts, even—whereas we crack on. Their ships are half manned with landsmen, because the navy steals their crews. We've had to be better seamen than the English, and so we are. You may depend upon what I tell you! If you help me with this vessel, you'll never lose by it. I'll—I'll make my father responsible in case I'm killed. I'll do anything—anything——"

Talleyrand, assisted by his black-haired niece, rose to his feet and stared with a faint, blank smile at the top of Marvin's head. "But of course I will help you!" he said. "Of course! Now I must think!" Again he scrutinized the ceiling on which half-clad nymphs cheerfully encouraged the advances of a disreputable satyr. "When is it you wish this vessel?"

"At once," Marvin said eagerly. "If I can't get to sea in two weeks, it might be—I might not be able——"

"Now let me see," Talleyrand interrupted. "I think it is best to do thus: Go now to your inn, and you will have word from me about this." The black-haired girl turned from him and went to stand by the window once more, idly turning the roulette wheel. "Yes," Talleyrand continued, "that will be best. There are things to be arranged."

Marvin hesitated. "If you could give me letters—to Mr. Barlow—to your bankers—I'd walk night and day to get to Paris with them."

Talleyrand's smile became indulgent. "No, no!" he said. "Nothing would be gained. The best thing is to wait patiently at your inn, and soon you will hear from me." He shook Marvin's hand warmly and limped with him to the door. "To have the pleasure of this visit is like a breath from America. Soon—very soon—we shall have the pleasure again, eh?"

The outer door opened and closed, and Marvin found himself standing in the angle of the towering wall.

When, a little later, he entered the main room of *Le Roi d'Espagne*, Argandeau bounced upward from the table where he sat over a brandy bottle with the inn's proprietress, a large woman with a black mustache.

"You have got it!" Argandeau exclaimed, looking into Marvin's eyes.

Marvin nodded. "I have the promise of it. He has promised everything."

"And it was all promises?" Argandeau persisted. "Surely he gave you the eleven dollars he owed your father!"

Marvin shook his head.

"Promises!" Argandeau exclaimed. "But I know these promises! Now it will be necessary for one of us to go back to see those two pretty rabbits that were behind the hedge."

XXVI

Tʜᴇ note that came to Marvin on the following afternoon was brought by a serving man in a green livery, and at the sight of the man and the letter he bore, Argandeau sighed softly. "Thanks to God!" he murmured. "The woman who owns this inn has been feeding us for love of me, but when she sees you have a letter at last, it may be she will be content to continue trusting us because of our prospects."

But the note contained no news of anything so definite as prospects; it did, however, cause Marvin to return anxiously to the spot where he and Argandeau had first come out from the avenue of chestnuts to find themselves confronted by the long gray walls and the squat round towers of Valençay.

As on the preceding day, he stood staring at the enormous mass of masonry and seemed to listen; then, apparently hearing nothing, he turned from the avenue, entered the edge of the chestnut forest and emerged on the leaf-covered grass of the château gardens. Even before he had left the shelter of the chestnuts he caught sight of her, swathed in a long gray cloak and sitting on a stone bench against the boxwood hedge; and it seemed to him, as he went toward her, that she eyed him with more indulgence than pleasure.

She nodded so that her black curls bobbed when he stood before her. "So you come back," she said, and to Marvin her eyes looked as round and guileless as those of a little child. "It must be you are no longer afraid you may be helped!" She gave him her hand; and Marvin, after holding it a moment, released it and coughed.

There seemed to be something of the schoolmistress about her as she wrapped herself more snugly in her gray cloak. "In America you do not kiss the hand of a lady?"

"Well," he said apologetically, "it is not—there are times—I mean, if we thought——"

She drew her hand from beneath her cloak, stared at it critically and again extended it to Marvin; yet, when he had taken it and bent over it, she drew it away from him as suddenly as she had brought it from under her wrap. "I must tell you at once," she said. "My uncle has changed his mind. It is impossible that he help you."

"Impossible!" Marvin exclaimed. "What do you mean? He said he'd help me! He *promised* to help me!"

She shrugged her shoulders. "There are things you do not understand."

He turned slowly to look at the thick tower of the château, with its outlandish rounded top. "Yes, that must be true," he admitted. "I do not understand how any man can make a promise and then break it for no cause." He rapped with his cane on the gravel walk. "I must see him again! He cannot break his promise like this!"

"It is no use," the black-haired girl told him. "In one little hour he departs for Paris, and it is quite, quite impossible that he should see you now."

"But there is no one else I can go to!" Marvin cried. "No one! There's no one in France who would lend me the money, except this man my father helped. If I could see him for five minutes——"

"But I tell you there are things you do not understand!" she insisted.

Marvin laughed. "I understand that I've lost two days through the promises he never intended to keep."

"Now you are bitter!" she interrupted. She patted the bench; and Marvin sat beside her, dropping his hat and stick on the gravel walk. "You do not understand Frenchmen, you Americans, any more than you understand women. My uncle, M. de Talleyrand, he would have helped you, yes, and gladly, if it had not interfered with his ideas of right and wrong."

"Then why did he promise?" Marvin said harshly. "Does he manufacture new ideas of right and wrong each day?"

She bent forward to look into his face, shaking her black curls so that a faint, penetrating fragrance rose from them. "Are there no promises broken in America?" she asked. "Here it is the custom; for if our great men said 'No' to everyone's demands, they would have poniards in the backs, all of them, in one day's time; and a great man with a poniard in his back is no better than a dead carp in the moat. So they say 'Yes' when they mean 'No.' If you had been a statesman you would know the truth of this. Maybe you do not have statesmen in America."

Marvin shook his head. "This is talk that means nothing, like your uncle's talk about American seamen. A broken promise is a broken promise, and nothing can change that. As for his ideas of right and wrong, they're probably no better than the papers he wrote for your National Institute on the fishing cantons of America. Fishing cantons! Good God!"

She came closer to him, so that Marvin felt the warmth of her shoulder through the sleeve of his coat. "No, no, no!" she said. "It is only that you do not understand, you Americans! Listen now, and I explain everything to you. My uncle, he loves France, but he does not love this small butcher"—she pretended to glower, thrusting her fingers into the front of her cloak and inflating her cheeks so that she had a look of Bonaparte about her—"this madman whose desire for power is hurrying France and all of us into one large grave!" She seemed to shiver, so that Marvin took her hand and held it in both of his.

"One month ago," she continued, smiling up at him, "this madman buried himself and his army in the depths of Russia—in Russia, and with winter moaning at his shoulder! Only this week we have had the news. He has burned Moscow! He has destroyed his shelter and his provisions, and the Russians are on every side of him: millions of them! He is audacious and imprudent and a madman; so it is inevitable that he and his army must sink, either beneath the numbers of his enemies, or beneath hunger, or beneath the snow. Already they are as good as buried. It is the beginning of the end. That is why Maurice has come to his château—to tell the Spanish king, who was stolen out of Spain and imprisoned here by the madman, that soon he can go back to his own country. Now you are able to understand it, eh? If my uncle helps you to go out on the ocean with a device that will be bad for England, then England might be longer in chopping off the madman's head and restoring peace to France."

"It's what I suspected!" Marvin said. "It's an explanation that doesn't explain. He'll help his brave allies, the Americans, if it suits his plans; and I'm his friend, unless it's inconvenient for him!"

"No," she assured him, "it is only that we, you and I, do not have great minds like my uncle Maurice. He is French, and the French people have ideas. You are materialist, thinking of the cost of your ship, but Maurice thinks above such things. He thinks of nations, moving against one another like a game of chess, and what is best to be done in each small move, you comprehend?"

"No," Marvin said.

"But you must! You speak of friendship! Do you think friends are common as herring? They are not! For poor people, perhaps, they are no more scarce than blue diamonds; but for the rich and powerful they are as rare as unicorns! My uncle Maurice has discovered that there is no man he can trust. Through one man he lost two million in the stock market; through another he lost his beautiful home, the Hôtel Monaco. Even by Bonaparte, for whom he had done everything, he was called a thief—a man without faith or honor! By Bonaparte!"

"It seems impossible!" Marvin said gravely.

"But it is true!" she insisted. "It was while that madman fought in Spain. His brother Lucien returned to France with millions and millions he had taken from the Spaniards, and Bonaparte said he had acted wisely. But when my uncle Maurice returned with only two little millions, this madman called him names, worse than a dog; worse than a pig! No, there is no man he can trust! From one woman, two women, perhaps, he can have sympathy and friendship. From a man, no! It is the same with me. I cannot trust any woman. I take pleasure in the company of some, certainly; but all of them—all!—they will say any bad thing about me behind my back, whenever it pleases them! If I want friends, I must find them among men—Maurice and my husband and perhaps one more, or two."

"Your husband!" he exclaimed.

She twisted quickly on the bench, drawing her hand away; then leaned backward to smile up at the expression on his face. "You see, I have told you there are many things you do not understand! When you are older, and have sailed your ship to many ports, you will no longer be like a little boy. Then, it may be, I would no longer offer to help you if you came hunting for assistance from my uncle Maurice."

She leaned toward him again; and again from her small pyramid of black curls there rose that faint and penetrating fragrance. "You see, I am telling you secrets. When you are in need of a lady's help you must appear helpless and far from home, and a little frightened, especially of her. Then she will feel at once that she must protect you, and see that you are made happy."

Marvin stared helplessly at her for a moment; then stooped for his hat and stick and rose to his feet. "I'll try to do better another time, ma'am."

"But you are obstinate!" she cried. "Never have I seen a man so obstinate! Can nothing make you believe that somewhere there is a woman wise enough to help you?"

"Why," he said, "I'm beyond help, if you've told me the truth. Your uncle won't help me, and there's no help for that, is there?"

She jumped from the bench and stamped her foot an inch from his own. "So you will walk back to Paris, because of your pride, penniless and helpless, and able to do nothing against your enemy, or for the lady he is stealing out from under your nose! Nothing, do you understand? Nothing! This Mr. Barlow, the American Envoy of whom you speak, he is not in Paris. He is not in France, even. He has been summoned to Vilna by the madman, and has gone to him. Like all the others, he has plunged himself into Russia and into his grave at a word from Bonaparte."

Marvin stared at his hand, clenching and unclenching it as though he found it painful. "Did you know yesterday that Mr. Barlow was not in France?" he asked.

She nodded. "Of course. And I knew more. I knew that a gentleman has recently come to Paris to act in place of Mr. Barlow. I myself know this gentleman."

"And so," Marvin said thoughtfully, "you let me go on thinking that Mr. Barlow was in Paris!"

She shrugged her shoulders. "It was not I who let you go on thinking. It was Maurice, who had his own reasons. Diplomats, you understand, consider it unwise to speak the truth or tell what they know. And who am I to disabuse you about anything, knowing that you believe there are fifty foolish women for every wise one?"

Marvin stared at her helplessly. "You know who it is that took Mr. Barlow's place? Who is it?"

She hesitated, her eyes on his face: then seemed to reach a sudden decision. "The gentleman's name is Barnet. He was the consul of your country in Havre. I myself know this gentleman. If I ask something of Mr. Barnet, he cannot refuse me." She came close to him and placed her hand on his shoulder. "But of course you think we women are foolish—all of us!"

He shook his head. "No: not all of you. If ever I had such thoughts about you, I made a mistake."

"Ah!" she said. "A triumph! The gentleman pays me a pretty compliment by saying he made a mistake! What, then, will the gentleman do?"

"Do?" he asked. "Do? I don't know what I'll do. I don't know. I'll try to think of something to do."

She made a sound of exasperation. "Almost I am tempted to do nothing for you, after all! If you need help so much, why is it you do not ask me for it?"

"It's not only a letter to Mr. Barnet that I need," Marvin said. "I've got to have money, and a deal of it. I'd mislike asking a lady for money, even if she could give it to me, and even if the lady had no husband or uncle to consider. It wouldn't seem—it wouldn't seem wise!"

"But I am not going to give it to you! First you must make it possible for me to get enough to lend you, and then you must repay my loan as you said you would repay my uncle—twice over—three times over!"

He was silent, studying her.

She laughed lightly. "You see, now, I am wiser than you have thought. You have thought, all this time, that I am impatient to give you what you need; but now you find you do not know, even, how you shall help me get it!"

"How I can help you get it," Marvin said slowly, "I have no idea, but you shall have a paper guaranteeing you 300 per cent profit on your venture—and I shall assume that you're as impatient for money as I am for a ship."

She sat on the bench again and looked up at him out of the corners of her eyes. "You are a nice young man—so nice that it would be easy to forget that one must be careful always about matters of business. Yesterday you told us of a pendulum. Of course, I know nothing of pendulums; but there was once an English gentleman who came here to see my uncle, and he spoke of your M. Benjamin Franklin, calling him one of those damned Yankees who could do anything." Her eyes twinkled. "It may be that he was right, and that there is something about Yankees that enables them to do more than other peoples. It might be that your pendulum is something new and wonderful. It might be, even, that you could invent other things if the need arose—that you could invent a safe manner of playing roulette. The thought came to me yesterday when I stood by the window and spun the wheel." She raised her eyebrows and sighed. "Here am I, obliged to play at roulette with my friends again and again each week, and each week the amount I owe is greater and greater."

In spite of the little smile that curled one corner of her lips, it seemed to Marvin that she was more than half serious in what she said. And after all, he thought, he *was* one of those damned Yankees.

He pondered on the structure of the gambling wheels he had seen aboard the prison ship. "I know little about gambling, ma'am," he said at last, reluctantly. "The Frenchmen on the hulks, they seemed to think a system does no good. That's what you're asking me to invent, isn't it? A system at which you can win? If that's it, ma'am, I'd better not waste my time or yours; for by the time you've won what I must have, the need for it will be over."

Again she jumped from the bench to place her hand on his arm. "But I seek only a method to keep me from losing! You said to my uncle that there is always an easier way to do things; so, if that is true, it is only necessary for you to play roulette a little, in order to

find an easier way for me to play it. Then I shall quickly save enough
for your ship, and I can give it to you even before I save it!"

"Play roulette a little!" Marvin exclaimed. "There are reasons why
I couldn't play roulette, even though it was played with buttons!"

"I know," she added hurriedly. She drew an envelope from the
front of her gown. "It is here! What Maurice owed your father, with
the interest for all these years, and a little more, too, since you are
doing this for me."

At the look in his face, she flirted her fingers airily. "But it is nothing to twist the nose over! Nothing! Maurice, he had intended to
return this to you, you understand, but affairs were pressing, so I
am doing it for him. Yes, it was his money."

She eyed him. "I truly think it was a part of the very money that
he brought home from Spain, as one brings home dust on his shoes
without knowing how or where it was acquired. And it is a favor
for me that you are doing with it—a favor! You must take it and go
quickly back to Paris. There you will visit No. 9 in the Palais Royal.
There are many gambling apartments in the Palais Royal, but No. 9
is the fashionable address. At No. 9 you study the wheel, morning,
noon and night, and then you make me a little system, eh? You make
me a little system, and I will come there soon—soon. If the system
has merit, you shall have what you need from me."

She pressed the envelope into Marvin's hand, nodding at him as at
an obedient child. Then her little smile seemed to harden and her
eyes to turn a paler, colder blue. "But don't forget—the money I lend
you in Paris for a ship—that's business. Three hundred per cent."

She laughed and added: "It's the kind of business I like; a chance
to get three for one, and the three to come suddenly! And what
would you? It's the spirit of the times—everybody playing with gold
and golden bubbles—and I'm a woman of the times. My husband
lost sixty thousand livres last week on the advice of a ballet girl. I
would like to show him how business should be done with a reliable
Yankee gentleman."

She glanced suddenly at the watch that hung from her neck.
"Heaven! It is already one hour, and I must depart with Maurice!"
She reached up, drew down Marvin's head and kissed him abruptly;
then ran lightly toward the château.

XXVII

T_{HE} turmoil that filled the high-ceiled rooms on the second floor of No. 9 in the low, dark-gray buildings of the Palais Royal seemed to pass lightly over Marvin, who sat at an end of one of the four crowded roulette tables. On one side of him was an aged harridan, her head swathed in a green turban from which rose a single ostrich feather; her cheeks were a hectic pink and her bared shoulders protruded angularly from a gown of a sickly yellow. On the other side was a girl as young as she was scantily clad; and the two of them stared frequently and invitingly at Marvin and the pile of colored plaques that he shielded beneath his big hands.

Close behind his seat stood Argandeau, resplendent in a long-tailed coat of delicate gray and trousers of a pale but brilliant blue; and the two of them whispered together, regardless of the crowd that surged around the tables—a crowd of officers, fops and women whose dresses, slit to the knee and even to the thigh, seemed about to, and sometimes indeed did, slip from the shoulders that held them precariously suspended—a crowd that screamed and chattered so shrilly as to drown in billows of clamor the staccato rattle of the roulette balls and the croupier's monotonous: "Make your plays, gentlemen and ladies. *Rien ne va plus.*"

"There it is!" Argandeau whispered. "Thirty-three! Four times this croupier has rolled it into the last dozen. He is in a groove! I say put it on the last eighteen, before he can escape from the groove!"

"The last eighteen," Marvin agreed, "but if we lose, we may be here the rest of the afternoon and all night as well!" He pushed twenty-five white plaques to a near-by section of the diagrammed table, rested his chin on his hand and stared up at the cluster of hanging lamps that burned dimly in the hot and smoky air. The ball whirred in the wheel, slowed, bumped against the nubbins, tripped on a slot and freed itself; then darted to its final resting place like a frightened mouse.

"Nineteen, red, uneven, last half," droned the croupier. He swept plaques from the board, reached over with his rake and knocked down Marvin's pile, counted it quickly and deftly pushed him an equal number of white counters.

"There is another finished," Argandeau said gently. "The four-teenth this afternoon! It is a good time to start another, eh? He is getting away from that last dozen, and soon I think he will roll it into the first eighteen."

Marvin, his hands cupped around his pile of plaques, rose in his place and looked uneasily behind him. At Argandeau's elbow he saw a small pyramid of black curls and a pair of blue eyes that stared innocently into his.

She nodded to him. "I am here, you see."

Marvin divided his earnings and handed a part of them to Argandeau. "Play carefully," he warned him. "What you win will go into your pocket, but what you lose must come out of it, also."

With that he relinquished his seat and joined the black-haired girl, who slipped her hand eagerly beneath his arm and turned him toward the curtained booths that lined the passageway between the roulette hall and the refreshment room. When the curtain of the inclosure she selected had dropped behind them, she made a pretense of fixing her curls and, as she did so, looked up at him from under her elbow.

"Now you are a little boy again—a sulky little boy. But it is not my fault. I came here as quickly as I could; not one moment sooner could I come!"

"You have no business here at all," Marvin said. "I believe every bad woman in Paris must come to this building."

She raised her eyebrows. "I do not know how to distinguish the good from the bad, and it would be interesting if you would tell me. It is the fashion to come here. You will see Madame de Staël here, and Madame de Senlis, as well as many of the laundresses, butchers' wives and cooks' daughters that Bonaparte has honored with titles. Ladies who come to our house for dinner come here to play; and some of them, I think, are quite, quite good, though I am not sure what you mean by 'good.' You are doomed to be an unhappy young man if you think that no woman is a good woman unless she has made no mistakes and had no desires, ever; and in case you wish that sort of good woman, you must be careful to marry a plaster saint out of a church."

"Well," Marvin said uncertainly, "well——"

She dismissed the matter with a movement of her shoulder. "You tell me now about our system. I have seen enough to know that you have discovered one."

Marvin drew up a chair to the booth's table and fumbled in his pocket. "I'm sure of one thing," he said, "and that is there's no system at all by which you or anyone else can be sure of winning." He brought out a thin packet of bank notes. "Still, it's possible to be lucky for a while. I've won enough to buy food and get new clothes for Argandeau; so here's the money you loaned me, over and above my father's eleven dollars, plus 6 per cent interest for nineteen years."

"Pouf for your 6 per cent and your nineteen years!" she cried. "Tell me how it was done!"

"Why," he said, "it's simple enough. Any child must quickly learn that his money will vanish like smoke at roulette, unless he plays the even chances—the black or the red, the odd or the even, the first eighteen numbers or the last eighteen. To stake your money on a single number is like throwing it in the fire."

"Sometimes it is possible to win on a single number," she said. "It is exciting, that!"

Marvin only laughed.

"To win by the even chances is too slow!" she objected, then.

"Of course it's slow! It's slow, and hard work; and you must be tireless, and keen in your judgment."

"You make it seem like a business rather than a game."

"So it is! So is everything else, if you want to win. I've been told there are some countries, even, where people make almost a business of love."

"Very well," she said impatiently. "We play on the even chances. What then?"

"Well," Marvin said, "when I studied the game I found that people met disaster most frequently from overreaching themselves. They'd become impatient, after many small winnings; so they'd bet largely and lose everything in two turns of the wheel. Therefore, it was necessary to find a method to prevent that—a method that would aim to win a small amount of money in a short time, and to begin again whenever the small amount had been won."

He set down some marks on a sheet of paper and she came and leaned against his shoulder, watching him. "For convenience," he said, "we'll say we're playing with plaques of one franc each." On the paper were five upright marks, close together. "Each of these marks," Marvin continued, "represents one franc. It might easily represent five francs, or ten, or a hundred, but we'll call it one franc. Suppose, now, that you start to play, having in mind that you wish to win five francs, and that when five francs have been won, you must start from the beginning to win another five. You have a line of figures—five ones—five one-franc marks. You must play, always, the figures at each end of the line. That is, you play a one and a one—two francs—and you play them, say, on the red. If you win, you receive two francs from the croupier, and you cross off the two end figures. That leaves three ones. You still play the numbers on each end—both ones. If you win, you receive two more francs and cross off the end figures. That leaves a single figure, which you play —one franc on an even chance. If you win, you cross off the last number and receive one franc. Then you've won five units—in this case, francs. If each unit had been ten francs, you'd have won fifty. So your venture is finished; your numbers are entirely crossed out. Therefore you set down five more ones and start over again."

She tossed her head. "And if I lose, I double, eh? That is no system!"

Marvin ignored her words. "Again you commence by playing the end numbers—two ones. You lose. This time you cannot cross out a figure; instead you must add the Figure 2 to your row of ones—a number greater by one than the last number. Then you play the two end numbers—a one and a two—three francs. If you lose you add the Figure 3 and again play the ends—a one and a three. If again you lose, you add a four, and play a one and a four. This time you may win; if you do, you cross off the one and the four, and play the end figures of those that remain—a one and a three. If you again win, cross off the one and the three, and play a one and a two; but if you should lose, add a figure larger by one than the last number not crossed off. When finally the numbers are entirely crossed out you'll again have won five units—five francs—so once more you write down your five ones for a new venture."

"Why," she said slowly, "I think there may be something in it. It seems simple, also." Her arm, resting on his shoulder, slipped around his neck, and with the impulsiveness of a child she pressed her cheek to his.

"Yes, it's simple," Marvin admitted, "but there's danger in it, none the less, as there is in almost everything that's exciting."

She withdrew her arm and stood a little away from him, arranging her hair and glancing at him from beneath her elbow.

"The danger," Marvin continued, "will come when you've lost repeatedly. There may come a time, then, when you're setting down larger and larger figures with each loss, and must stake thirty or forty or fifty francs on each play, again and again, in order to win only five francs eventually. It's not likely to happen often, but when it happens, I advise you to go cautiously—to stop playing entirely when your wagers, on a single game, have become as large as your previous day's winnings."

"Pouf!" she cried gaily. "Go cautiously, indeed! Come, we shall play your system and I shall show you there is no need for caution!" She seized him by the arm and tugged at him.

Marvin rose slowly. "Then you think you can win with this system?"

"But of course! You have won and I shall win!" She swayed against him, her blue eyes laughing up into his and her red lips a little parted.

Marvin put his arm about her. "Then you're satisfied with what I've done?" He lifted her and kissed her, kissed her a second time, and in the small and tawdry booth there was a moment of breathless silence.

At length she laughed softly. "We play now."

"It's what you wanted?" he persisted. "What you expected?"

"Yes, it is something new, and so easy that I cannot understand why nobody has discovered it before."

"Then there's still time today for you to go with me to see Mr. Barnet at the Legation; and with good luck I can be in Calais tomorrow."

"But we must play!" she protested. "Today you remain with me; tomorrow will be time enough to see this ambassador of yours."

Marvin shook his head. "There's my brig to be got ready. I've waited and waited until I'm near bursting from doing nothing. There were two American privateer captains in here yesterday, but today they've gone to Lorient, and tomorrow they're putting to sea. How do you think I felt, sitting here and elbowing all the—all the—well, sitting here in Paris when they were starting out to comb the Channel for British ships?"

"British ships!" she exclaimed. "I think there is something in your mind besides British ships."

He nodded. "There's the loan you're making me, and the 300 per cent profit I've promised to pay you on it. I've got that to think about, and other things as well." Seemingly as an afterthought, he added, "The sooner I get to sea, the sooner I'll be back with your gold."

"And the sooner you get to sea, the sooner you'll catch up with the lady who left you for another man, eh?"

Marvin took her hands in his. "A lady who has a husband of her own, and an uncle as affectionate as one I could mention, should never bother her pretty head about a lady I haven't seen for many a long week and may never see again." He kissed her almost roughly, threw back the curtain of the booth and drew her after him into the crowd that surged and gabbled between the roulette tables. On his way to the door, he tapped Argandeau on the shoulder and motioned to him to follow.

Argandeau clasped his forehead in despair. "It is against me!" he whispered hoarsely. "I am playing forty-two francs at one throw, and these buzzards have one hundred and thirty-seven francs of my money!"

"Leave it and be ready to start for Calais," Marvin told him. "We'll be on shipboard at this time tomorrow!"

XXVIII

THE outer room of the Legation of the United States of America was a small and dingy cubicle, presided over by a contemptuous lady with green eyes and hair the color of untended brass; and it seemed to Marvin, standing humbly before her with the black-haired girl beside him, that she was filled with the need of supplying the grandeur that her surroundings lacked, and of upholding, by means of haughtiness and pride, the dignity of the country that she thought she represented.

"Mr. Barnet is engaged," she told Marvin disdainfully. "You can sit down and wait"—she nodded her head toward an inner room—"but you should have come earlier. I think it's too late for him to see anyone else."

"But I must see him today," Marvin protested. "If you'll tell him it's important——"

The contemptuous lady eyed him coldly. "Leave your card, and it's possible you can see the secretary."

Marvin looked helplessly at his companion, who sighed gently. "I seem to recall," she said to the contemptuous lady, "that Mr. Barnet was brought here from Havre in order to act and to think on behalf of Mr. Barlow, who has gone to Russia. Perhaps I am mistaken."

The voice of the contemptuous lady was hard. "No, you're not mistaken."

"In that case," the black-haired girl said softly, "it will be interesting to the Minister of Foreign Affairs to learn that there is yet another who is thinking and acting on behalf of Mr. Barlow. He will be pained, I have no doubt, to know that the thinking for your great country is done in a room"—she touched a finger tip to the window-pane that overlooked the flickering street lights of the Rue St. Honoré—"where the outlook is so obscured."

"Obscured!" the green-eyed lady cried indignantly. "Obscured! I'll have you know that window was washed last week, ma'am!"

"In that case," the black-haired girl said, "you can doubtless see the advisability of going at once to Mr. Barnet, regardless of who is with him, and telling him that Comtesse Edmond de Périgord, Duchesse de Courland, must see him at once. At once, you understand!"

The green-eyed lady stared at her unbelievingly; then rose suddenly to her feet and hurried from the room. As for the black-haired girl, she made adjustments in the curls under her bonnet of yellow silk, glancing quickly at Marvin beneath her elbow as she did so—a way she had, and not an unpleasant one either, he thought. "You see," she said, "how often it is that even a woman may help a man."

The green-eyed lady returned breathless. "Please come in!" she gasped. "I wouldn't have—I didn't know——"

The black-haired girl stopped her with a gesture. "It is forgotten; but hereafter, for the sake of your countrymen, for whom I have great sympathy, I hope that the outlook from this room will be somewhat clearer."

The three of them passed through a large waiting room in which sat a strange figure of a woman—an angular, broad-shouldered woman who seemed to have no feet or legs, and whose face, bent over huge knitting needles that clacked and clittered, was screened from them by an enormous white headgear so constructed that sharp white wings protruded beyond her broad shoulders and shook with the violence of her knitting. Before her, on the floor, rested two empty boat-shaped shoes of felt, each shoe large enough to hold a healthy infant. At the sound of footsteps she looked up. Her face was long and brown; her eyebrows as bushy as newborn black ducklings; and from under them her beady eyes stared with a suspicion made more piercing by the sudden silence of her knitting needles.

Madame de Périgord tapped Marvin's arm. "See there!" she said. "A wounded grenadier, no doubt! It would be like this little butcher of ours"—she made a Napoleonic gesture—"to seize even the women to throw against the guns!"

The angular woman rocked mightily in her chair, and from under her black skirt two hamlike feet, covered with wrinkled white stockings, thumped to the floor and groped for the felt shoes.

Marvin and his companion left her groping, and entered a smaller anteroom, the anteroom of the Minister's office. The door into the office was open; and in the doorway, looking up into the face of a tall gray-haired man who was bidding her farewell, stood a bonneted girl whose dress of gray satin clung with unwrinkled smoothness to her flat back and slender figure. She turned, and as her eyes fell on Marvin, she seemed for a moment to flame into sudden radiance. Her eyes, deep in the shadow of her bonnet's brim, held sparks of light.

"Why, Dan!" she exclaimed. "You're—I'm——"

The tall man smiled. "You know this lady? You're just in time to wish her luck. A brave young lady, I tell her, to take out a letter-of-marque at such a time."

Marvin breathed heavily, as if incapable of thought or motion. "A letter-of-marque?" he mumbled. "A letter-of-marque?"

Corunna Dorman glanced from Marvin to the black-haired girl and back to Marvin again; and her face grew blank. "Why, yes," she said, "a letter-of-marque." She smiled gravely at the tall American beside her, bowed slightly to Marvin, and made as though to pass.

"Wait!" Marvin said. "A letter-of-marque. That means you're getting a ship for——" He stopped, seeming to swallow the word he had meant to speak.

"It means," Corunna said, "that Captain Slade helped me when I was deserted by everyone else."

"Slade," Marvin said thickly. "Slade."

"Captain Slade," Corunna said gently, "has been the soul of energy and generosity."

Marvin looked at her and said nothing.

"You must excuse me," the black-haired girl said suddenly. "I must not keep Mr. Barnet waiting." She smiled sweetly at Marvin. "When you have finished talking with this lady, you must join us quickly if you are to have your commission today." She went to Barnet and gave him her hand; then, as she passed through the doorway, she added over her shoulder, "Do not be long—Dan!"

"Wait!" Marvin said. "Wait!" But Barnet, bewildered, followed the black-haired girl into his office and closed the door behind him.

"So you're to have a commission!" Corunna said. "How strange! Are you getting one from America because the English wouldn't give you one?"

Marvin stared at her. "The English? What do you mean?"

Corunna returned his gaze steadily. "Oh, you can set your mind at rest! I haven't told anybody."

"Told anybody what?"

"How you brought down the English on the *Olive Branch*. I'll do nothing to stop you here." She made a faint movement of her hand toward Barnet's office. "I thought—I thought your own conscience would be punishment enough." She lowered her eyes.

"Brought down the English?" Marvin repeated stupidly. "How I brought down the English? I?"

She looked up at him. "You thought I'd never know, I suppose. You've forgotten how news spreads among sailors."

"News!" Marvin said. "Why, there never was a sailor's tale that wasn't a damned lie! Like barbers, they never get things right, and you know it! What is it you're trying to say? What is it Slade said, damn him! You couldn't truly think it was I——" He stopped, staring at her. "You do! By God, you do! You little fool! Slade told you, and you believed him! You little fool! You little fool!"

He checked himself suddenly, turned away from her; then turned back to face her and spoke more quietly: "I take it you're now Mrs. Slade," he said.

She looked at him with a steady eye. "Do you?" she asked.

"I wouldn't ask you the question, whether you are or not," he said.

"Wouldn't you?"

"Do you think I care?" he burst out. "Do you think I care on my own account any more? Well, I don't! I'll tell you what I care about: Your father was my friend, and that means I care about his daughter's safety. Yes, and that she isn't fooled by a pack of lies; so, husband or no husband, I'll speak out! Husband or no husband, you've believed a rat out of the swamps of Africa, and that's what he is!"

"He's kind and generous!" Corunna cried. "You can't say these things!" She knotted her bonnet strings. "Let me pass, please!"

"Then it's true!" Marvin whispered. "You're sailing with Slade!"

"No!" she said. "He's sailing with me! With me! He's a brave officer and a resourceful man, and as captain I'm glad to have him for a first officer! Let me pass!"

"I've got a vessel, Corunna," Marvin said. "You don't know what you're doing! There's a cabin for you on our brig, Corunna."

"A cabin! What for? For me to do needlework in?"

He was silent, gnawing at his lip and staring at her.

"That's your opinion still, I suppose?" she persisted. "A woman's judgment is too uncertain to let her handle a ship?"

"Why, yes! That's my opinion! It's my opinion that most women take chances at the wrong time and for the wrong reasons."

"Oh, dear me!"

"What's more," Marvin continued, "it's my opinion that most women don't believe what's told them unless it's as unreliable as their own desires. If I told you as much truth about him as he's told you lies about me——"

"What?" she cried. "You'd slander him?"

"Slander! Do you think it's never going to be proved how he sold the *Olive Branch* to the English?"

Corunna looked at him with the bitterest scorn. "He? Ah, that's your way out of it, is it? To try to put it upon him! Wasn't it Captain

Slade who led the men when they retook the *Beetle?* And where were you when it happened? The last man out of the hold! And weren't you in charge of the *Olive Branch* when the British cut her out? Don't you suppose everybody knew you could have run her ashore and saved her for me?"

Marvin's face was white. "Slade sold you out! He went to England and traveled the country with a common trull. He sold you out, I tell you, and divided the sale money of the *Olive Branch* with the English; then blackmailed merchants into giving him a ship!"

"Indeed! And how would it be possible for you to learn any such cock-and-bull story as this unless you'd had it from the English themselves? And why do you stop with blackmail? Why don't you tell me the poor man murdered little children?"

Marvin tugged at his neckcloth as though it oppressed him. "You've got to listen to reason! What chance do you think you'll have with a man like Slade?"

She laughed contemptuously. "You're all alike, you men! Each one of you pretends he's perfect, and that every other man is a monster! You slander Captain Slade, and at the very moment you do it there's a woman waiting for you! Who is she? And haven't I as much chance with Captain Slade as she has with you? I think I have! Oh, yes, I think I have!"

"Corunna," Marvin said slowly, "there's nothing I could do or say, ever, that would influence you. There never has been. Sometimes it seems to me you've always done and said the things that would make me feel most miserable. A thousand times I've wanted to take you by the shoulders and shake you for being so contrary, but I know now there's no use trying to make you do something you don't choose to do. When they put us in the hulks, Corunna, it seemed to me I'd have to pull up the decks with my bare hands to get back to you. Well, I've lost you. I could go to the Minister now with what I know about Slade, but I won't do it, any more than you'd go to him with what you think you know about me. I want to protect you, but I won't do it by force."

He waited vainly for her to speak. Then he said: "If you feel you've got to go on with Slade, go ahead. I've got one thing to ask—that you think it over for a few minutes right now. Either he's a traitor and a liar, or I am. Well, you've known me a long while, and him a short while, but he's fascinated you. I'll ask you to think it over and decide which you'll believe—him or me. That's all. I'm going into that room for the commission this lady's helping me to get. If you're here when I come out, I'll know you've changed your mind about Slade."

He looked at her expectantly, but since she made no answer, he walked past her, tapped lightly on the Minister's door and went in without a backward glance.

It was only a short time later that he came out with the black-haired girl, carrying with him a commission authorizing Capt. Daniel Marvin of the private armed brig *True-Hearted Yankee* to take, burn, sink and destroy all enemy vessels.

There was no one anywhere in the two outer offices except the green-eyed young woman, who was staring at the dirty windows.

XXIX

Tom souville, hunched over the table in the barren cabin of the *Renard*, counted a sheaf of bank notes; then looked up at Marvin and Argandeau and moved his small, pointed mustache so that he had the appearance of an astounded squirrel. "It is correct!" he exclaimed. "Correct! You have done it! It is bizarre—a *coup de théâtre!* You Americans! I have heard of nothing like it, ever! You say you will do a thing, and almost immediately it is as good as done!"

"Not always," Marvin said.

"But I say yes!" Souville exclaimed, jumping up and clasping his hands beneath his coat tails. "We have received, just now, an account of the privateering success of the Americans. It is something exotic! Something fantastic! The *Rossie* privateer took and destroyed fifteen British merchantmen in forty-five days; the *Decatur* took eleven in the same time; the *Saratoga* has taken eight; the *Comet* twelve; the *Paul Jones* eighteen; the *Mars* nine; the *Benjamin Franklin* six. The English, they are having a crisis of nerves!"

"My friend," Marvin said, "tell us the one thing we want to know."

Souville nodded. "I have found him. He is where you cannot get at him. He is in Dublin."

"Where I cannot get at him?" Marvin asked. "That depends! That depends! He hasn't bought a house there, has he? He isn't going to settle down, I take it." Thoughtfully he studied Souville's eager face. "If you should keep company with me in your *Renard*, don't you think it probable that in time we might find some rich prizes in unexpected places?"

"And I can have the use of your pendulum?" Souville asked.

"You're laughing at me!" Marvin said gravely. "You don't want my pendulum. Your *Renard* might be mistaken for a clock!"

"No, no!" Souville exclaimed. "I want it! I will try, once, doing things in the American manner. You let me use your pendulum, and I will keep company with you. I will do more; I will find you a crew of Americans, very fine; not drunkards or vagabonds, but strong men from jails, captured in prizes. In four days I find them, and that is none too soon; for this man you want to see, who is now in Dublin, I hear he will sail in eight days."

"Eight days!" Marvin breathed.

"Eight days," Souville repeated. "Look, you let me use that pendulum and I cancel your dock charges—one thousand francs."

"What else?" Marvin whispered.

"What else?" Souville demanded. "What else? Nothing else should be needed between two brothers in arms. It is for the glory of France, and so it should be given freely, eh? Ah, well; I will act as your agent here, free of charge, making sure that our thieves of officials do not strip you to the bone when you send in a prize."

"No, no!" Marvin said. "What else about Slade? Where is he going and what will he do?"

"What is it that you decide about the pendulum?" Souville persisted.

Marvin nodded. "I'll rig one for you. We'll sail together."

Souville sighed comfortably, seated himself on his chest and folded his plump hands across his melon-like stomach. "What else about Slade? Well, there is this about Slade: In Bristol he got the *Blue Swan* brig, an old slaver, very fast. Four long nines she carries, and eight twelve-pound carronades. She went out from Bristol at night, showing no papers before she left; and as she went, she collided with two merchantmen at anchor. Yet the whole affair was hushed at once, and the port authorities were like little children about it, wholly innocent and undisturbed." He raised his eyebrows. "That can have only one meaning, my friend. There is British official connivance in whatever this *Blue Swan* brig is doing." He nodded wisely, and Marvin stared bleakly from the stern windows.

"On the following day," Souville continued, "the *Blue Swan* appears in Dublin. There is scarcely one of these Irish ports where American privateers are not welcome. It is widely known, and with some reason, that so far as England is concerned, they are foreign ports; that if opportunity is given to their citizens, they would take joy in burning any English frigate and crucifying her crew. I think your Slade has gone to Dublin, therefore, to be joined by a friend to whom he does not wish to appear an English sympathizer." He twisted the points of his small mustache and stared at Marvin, who returned his stare with expressionless eyes.

"In fact," Souville went on, "I have heard from Middleburg, the port from which smugglers run to Dublin. Yesterday a diligence arrived in Middleburg from Paris, and the passengers embarked in a Dublin cutter—two females, one of them a——"

"I wish to hear nothing of that!" Marvin said.

"One of them a very fierce female, very large, who swears terribly in four languages; but the other, her mistress, a——"

"Nothing!" Marvin repeated.

Souville shrugged his shoulders and manipulated his mustache. "Of course," he resumed at length, "this obtaining of intelligence is less simple than is generally believed. It is thought that one man can put on false whiskers and find out everything in the world, but this is not so. No one man can find out more than a little about anything; so when we wish to find out about something, we take fragments of information from a man here, and fragments from a man there, and fragments from a woman elsewhere, and then we fit the fragments together in a picture, eh? Sometimes the picture is wrong, but more often it is right."

Marvin nodded. "I understand."

"Yes," Souville said, "and I think we have put together the fragments of the picture of this Slade. The English, as I have told you, are in a crisis of nerves over the exploits of American privateers, who are doing more outrageous things to British merchantmen than have ever been done. Not long ago they were saying that if America dared to fight England, there would be no American flag on any ocean in six months' time. And now behold! Throughout England there are terrible cries of agony at the incessant successes of these damned Yankees!"

Argandeau coughed. "We do what we can, we Yankees," he said.

Souville eyed him severely; then continued: "Already the British have persuaded some of your Yankee captains to carry information to Halifax concerning the movements of American privateers, but this is not enough. The process is too slow. What they need above all else are a few fast cruisers to work in company with a blockading squadron—cruisers that would seem to be American, you understand, and so would not be annoyed by other Americans they might encounter."

"Cruisers that would *seem* to be American!" Marvin exclaimed.

"There would be several good points to such a service," Souville continued placidly. "Such vessels would be under the protection of the English, and they could hoodwink the Americans; yet, if they saw fit, they could disguise themselves and pick up vessels here and there from either side—provided their captains were blackguards, quite regardless of honor; men desirous only of obtaining money, no matter by what means."

Marvin stared silently at him, his lips pressed tight together. Argandeau whistled softly.

"Yes," Souville sighed, "I think so. In eight days this brig of Slade's
—this *Blue Swan*—will be victualed and ready for sea. Her departure
from Bristol was connived at by the government, so she will somehow be on government service. She has a crew of seventy men—
which is too small a crew, as you know, to enable a vessel of her
size to man out prizes; and she has no coppers or leg irons aboard,
so that she is not going back into the slave trade. What is more, a
movement of government vessels has been ordered: A ship-of-the-
line from Plymouth to Dublin with orders for Havana by way of
Fayal; a frigate from Portsmouth to Dublin with the same orders;
and a sloop-of-war from Sheerness to Dublin, also for Fayal and
Havana. There is no reason at all for these vessels to proceed to Dublin—no reason except to make the acquaintance of your Slade and
his *Blue Swan*. Therefore, I say that he goes with the squadron to
assist in the control of your privateers. I say that, in addition to some
of the things we already know about him, he is a traitor! That, gentlemen, is the picture we have pieced together."

Marvin wet his lips and clenched and unclenched his hands as
though he felt a numbness in his fingers. "Fayal!" he murmured.
"Fayal! A neutral port!"

He got to his feet and looked from the stern windows at his narrow brig.

She was emerging, amid hoarse shouting, from a confused tangle
of men, gear and guns. New, slender and taunt royal and skysail
masts had been swayed up, fidded and stayed; and garrulous Frenchmen clung to ratlines, crosstrees and yardarms, reeving new rigging
and seizing on chafing gear under Newton's quick eye.

The prolongation of her masts had given her a new look—a look
of alertness. She was narrow still, and seemed, because of the absence of spring or rise in her deck, to lie as flat as a log in the water;
but she was clumsy no longer, for she rode with a new balance, having the look of being caught in a swift current and of straining at
the hawsers that held her to the slimy dock. Yet there was something
innocent about her—a look of helpless smallness—and although Marvin knew her to be three hundred tons and more, she seemed less
than a hundred.

Content at what he saw, he turned to Souville. "Find me the men
you spoke of," he said. "We've got to get to sea."

Souville stepped to the cabin door and shouted shrill orders into
the companionway; then turned questioningly to Marvin. "And
when we are at sea," he asked, "what then? For where?"

"Why," Marvin said, "we're for Fayal; but as a matter of precau-
tion, we'll look in first at Dublin."

XXX

A SMART breeze from the northwest whipped the *True-Hearted Yankee* fast through a warm ocean in which floated clots of yellow weed, and from which skittered shimmering fish that curved to left and right as if the threatening rush of her passing had given them wings.

Wedge-like, she sliced through the watery hillocks, urged onward by a press of canvas that towered upward into royals and distant skysails and spread outward into studding sails, so that the hull beneath seemed ludicrously small and helpless.

Yet there was no helplessness on her narrow deck; for the tall Indian, Steven, resplendent in the blue jacket and the crossed yellow belts of an officer of marines, drove two sweating gun crews at the laborious task of exercising long eighteen-pound traversing pieces. With the precision of machines the heavy cannon rumbled forward to the weather bow ports, the crews as silent at their hauling as the men of any king's cruiser. Boys ran beside them to place sponges, rammers and water buckets in neat piles abreast the trunnions. The two knots of men boiled around the carriages; to the eyes of the officers on the quarter-deck, they seemed to scramble like ants on sugar. Tackles were made fast to eyebolts; breechings were adjusted. With a rattle of chains the ports were triced up; the two long toms lurched forward, their muzzles disappearing through the bulwarks; quoins were rapped sharply into place. Smoothly the crews reformed in orderly alignment beside the guns.

The Indian struck an iron triangle. At the clang the gunners, squinting at their sights, shouted, "One! Two!" There was no count of "Three!" but in its place the linstocks of the gunners' mates slapped hard against the touchholes of the guns. "Boom!" bawled the gunners' mates. The gun crews made swift movements with rammers and imaginary shot; then snapped to attention. The Indian walked around the rigid crews, staring hard at them. Then he nodded. "Good!" he said. "You'll draw a gill extra, next mess. Count two after the pendulum strikes; then let 'em have it; and there ain't anything in reason between here and Fayal that we can't blow out of water!"

On the quarter-deck, Newton, scratching busily on a scrap of paper held against the triangular cover of a sextant box, whistled softly; then looked up at Argandeau, who leaned against the weather rail, scanning his features in a pocket mirror. "Twelve knots!" he exclaimed. "Twelve knots for twenty-four hours! Two hundred and eighty-eight miles in one day! That's sailing, mister! Two more days of that, mister, and we'll raise Fayal!"

Argandeau smoothed an eyebrow and returned his mirror to his pocket. "We will raise what?" he asked politely. "This place you mention—what was the name again?"

Newton looked at him coldly. "Fayal was what I said. You may have heard us speak of Fayal."

"Have I ever heard you speak of anything else!" Argandeau cried. "Fayal! Fayal! Fayal! Fayal might be heaven, it is so much in your hearts and on your tongues to be there! I have had Fayal with breakfast, dinner and supper since God knows when! I would like to think a little of the two well-laden Britishers that we took in the Channel, thanks to our pendulum, and sent back to Calais by Tom Souville, to add to our fortunes and the coffers of that beautiful rabbit, Madame de Périgord, but I cannot, no! I cannot hear myself think because of your clack, clack, clack about Fayal! I would like to meditate on the way this cautious Old Man of ours, this Captain Caution, of Arundel, took us into the very harbor of Dublin and removed an Indiaman from under the guns of the fort itself. Hah! There is something to think about, that, as well as how my dear Marvin ever earned the name of Captain Caution! But to you and the rest of you, all these things are nothing. 'Fayal!' you scream. 'Fayal! Fayal! Fayal!' You are like uncivilized people, or infants, taking pleasure only in anticipation." He sighed heavily, as if in despair.

The door of the companionway slammed shut behind them. The two men turned to see Marvin staring upward with a frown at the brig's upper sails. Argandeau lifted an eyebrow and softly withdrew to the lee rail.

"Two hundred and eighty-eight miles, Dan," Newton said. "That means Fayal day after tomorrow!"

Marvin rapped the bulwark with his knuckles. "And so to get us there," he said, and his accusing glance included Argandeau, "you pile muslin on her till she looks like a feather bed! Get in those studding sails and skysails! Can't you feel her dragging?"

Newton ran forward, shouting orders. Seamen swarmed from nowhere, as if by magic, and scuttled up the shrouds. The studding-sail booms came in; the skysail yards were lowered and their sails close-furled by men who seemed, like insects crawling on a ceiling, to defy the laws of gravity. The brig's deck took on less of a cant: the waves through which she sliced seemed suddenly to lift her and press her on.

"Just remember that," Marvin said severely, as Newton returned to the quarter-deck. "Any fool or Englishman can crowd on canvas, so that a vessel looks fast. What we aim to do is keep our lee rails out of water and go faster. Give her all she needs; not all she'll stand."

He took two turns at the weather rail, watching the gun crews housing the long guns amidships. "I've said it fifty times, but it'll bear repeating: This is a war we're in, and risks are the last things we want to take."

Argandeau laughed, and Marvin halted in his pacing to fix him with a questioning glance.

"Yes," Argandeau said. "Certainly yes! There were some of us who had that in mind, Captain Caution, when you ran into Dublin Harbor in daylight, and then snatched away that merchantman in the dark. There was no risk to that, of course; no more than picking up an alligator by the hind foot."

"I tell you there was no risk," Marvin said calmly. "We ran in and anchored with the British ensign set over our American ensign. There was nothing for the British to think except that we were a captured American vessel, running for safety from the French privateer that pursued us to the very mouth of the harbor. Every man in the fort could see Souville's vessel, and not one of them would ever think to look at us. You know yourself that if you do something openly with one hand, you can do anything you like with the other and never be caught at it, provided you do it quietly. To anchor under the guns of the fort was an extra bit of caution."

"Caution!" Argandeau whispered, raising his eyes to the sky.

"Yes, caution," Marvin repeated. "When they saw us do it, they knew beyond any doubt that there was no harm in us, and so gave us no thought whatever. There is no surprise so great as to do something you could not do if you tried to do it in the way you were expected to do it."

Argandeau moved his lips helplessly and shook his head.

"But Fayal," Marvin continued, looking at him thoughtfully; "Fayal is another matter. In Fayal we must be doubly cautious."

Argandeau raised an eyebrow and nodded understandingly. "Now you speak a language that has a meaning. You mean that in Fayal we must pick up *two* alligators by the hind foot."

XXXI

A NORTHWEST wind piled dingy clouds against the cone-shaped hills that rimmed the roadstead of Fayal with an amphitheater of green; and from the top-hamper of the *Blue Swan* brig, riding at anchor in the lee of Espalamaca Point, there came an uneasy moaning that seemed, to the girl who stood at the shoreward rail of the quarter-deck, too dreary and too shrill to be evoked by wind alone.

Despite her many days at sea, she had no eyes for the white houses nestling on the slopes behind her, half hidden in their vines and fruit trees; and she stared with a sort of fascination at the three war vessels that lay to westward, slowly swaying in the long swell from the tumbling waters beyond. Even though her hands were buried in the loose and heavy sleeves of a quilted Chinese jacket, not long out of a shop in the Palais Royal, she seemed to hug herself and shiver at the sight.

On the deck in the lee of the sternmost carronade sat an angular woman, her scow-like feet thrust out before her and her huge brown hands busily wielding knitting needles that seemed the size of boat hooks. As she knitted, she cast quick glances at the restless girl. "You get yourself sick with this worry," she told her at length. "Then you be no good when there is need to worry. What you worry over? Is it the shark that follows us about, looking up at us with one eye, like someone I know? He is like a kitten, merely playing. You are safe here, and soon you will be safe away—away from those damned *Anglais* with their goat whiskers. Brr!" She muttered to herself, and her mutterings were unpleasant.

"Yes, but we ought to be away now!" Corunna said, as if to herself. "Right now! If he hadn't been so kind—if he hadn't got this brig for me—I think I'd—I'd never stay here for such a——"

She fell silent, watching the distant group of officers on the high poop of the ship-of-the-line, and into her mind there came again, as there had come a thousand times before, the constant tenderness of Lurman Slade and his forethought in her behalf. It went back, this forethought, to the very day when she had arrived with Victorine in Dublin and had been installed by Slade in the captain's cabin of the *Blue Swan* brig. Victorine, grumbling in her suspicious Breton fashion at the manner in which Slade had eyed her, was stowing her mistress's Paris purchases in the lockers beneath the standing bed-place, when Slade had entered the cabin with a look of mock seri-ousness on his face to say that he had news—doubtful news—for her. A British frigate, he said, had just dropped anchor alongside.

She had sprung up in consternation; but when Slade, on that, had smiled, she sat down mystified. "You don't think, my dear," he had said, "that I'd have let you take the risk of coming to Dublin without guarding you against any possibility of harm! While we're on this side of the Atlantic, you're always in danger of capture and imprison-ment unless we play a game with the English—unless we spoil the Egyptians. That's what we've done, my dear! I've hoodwinked them, gammoned them, told them this and told them that; and the upshot is they've given me a letter-of-marque, the poor fools! A British letter-of-marque, so that they're bound to protect us until we're ready to bid them good day! Let their frigates anchor where they will; they can't harm *you*, my dear! You'll only need to let me act as captain when they're about." He had laughed and patted her hand, and added, "I'd like to see their faces when we take French leave!"

It had disturbed her; yet she would have been ungrateful, she knew, to protest an act intended only for her safety; and so she had admired him for his resourcefulness and cunning. She had admired him still when, later, he returned to say that he had made a master stroke—arranged, even, to sail as far as Fayal with a British squadron. "With half the distance covered," he had chuckled, throwing back his head to see her more clearly from beneath his drooping eyelid, "we're as good as home! I'll claim a reward some day"—his eyes gleamed hotly—"for the way I've taken care of you! Some day, and soon!"

At the sound of a barking cough from Victorine, he had turned and left her, and Corunna had heard him shouting at the crew in sudden anger; but she told herself that what he said was true: He had taken care of her, and for what he had done she must be truly grateful. Yet beneath her gratitude had stirred a vague disquiet—a disquiet that had persisted during the long voyage to Fayal in the company of the hated Britishers, and that had grown even stronger when Fayal was reached at last, and the *Blue Swan*, despite a favor-ing wind, still lay at anchor within pistol shot of the squadron leader.

Ill at ease, she stared around her at the towering hills of Fayal—hills that seemed, for all their soft greenness, to threaten and im-prison her.

Only half conscious of the hoarse gabble of the woman Victorine, she stood on tiptoe to peer for the hundredth time at the quarter-deck of the ship-of-the-line, to which Slade had been rowed an hour since. "It's part of the game," he had told her, laughing softly at her protests, "part of the game. For your sake, I've got to do what I can."

Victorine emphasized her words with agitated jerkings of her knitting needles. "Who but Victorine should know the ways of men—little Victorine, yes, who has married five of them—five! One I lost at Trafalgar, and six would have married me the next day. Six out of the forecastle of the *Glorieuse*, where I had resided for nine months! Name of a name of a name, but I know them! Here and there you find good ones, perhaps—I think so—but never among the smooth ones—the ones who softly say soft things. They are like soap, the soft ones, slipping out from under the hand and vanishing for a moment; and the first thing you know, another has picked them up to use. Hah, yes! I know them, those smooth ones; fragrant and firm, at one moment, but always softening and changing when exposed to the water of flattery. Soap, they are! This gentleman of yours, he is soft and smooth. I have watched him with you. He is gentle, yes. Ah, well; I know him! It is with *you* he is gentle. With me he would not be so gentle! I have seen him look at me. When he has the chance, he thinks to himself, he will give me a kick—Poom!—and little Victorine will pop through the hull of this vessel like an eighteen-pound shot. That is what he thinks. He has no love for me, that one! I am in his way! If it were not for little Victorine, says that piece of soap to himself, he would be alone with you when he is with you, and much happier for the freedom to try to make free with you. Hah! Hah!" She laughed darkly. "Ah, well! I have no fear! Better men than he have thought to kick Victorine through a bulkhead, but you can tell by looking at me that I have never even dented one." She rubbed the instep of one vast felt shoe with the toe of the other.

"Hold your tongue!" Corunna said absently. Her glance shot suddenly seaward, caught by a movement at the edge of the perpendicular cliff of Espalamaca Point. From behind the cliff moved the staysails and jibs of a high-bowed vessel. Even before her foremast hove in sight, Corunna knew from her slowness and clumsiness that she was a merchant craft; while from the tautness of her rig, when her fore and main masts came into view, Corunna said to herself that the vessel was a brig, and American. Yet the girl was only partly right, for a stubby mizzenmast followed the main from behind the steep headland; the vessel was a barque, not a brig, but undoubtedly

American; for at her mizzen truck an American ensign whipped smartly in the breeze.

Corunna stared blankly at the flag; then made a sound of distress with her tongue against the roof of her mouth. A cloudiness filled her eyes, as if the far-off scrap of bunting had put it there. "Well, I declare!" she cried. "I'll be switched! The poor fools ought to know better!" She stamped her foot angrily and pressed white knuckles to her lips, seeming to hold her breath.

As if in answer to her thoughts, the barque appeared to hesitate at sight of the four war craft lying close inshore. A small and clumsy crew shook out and sheeted home the topgallant sails that had been handed preparatory to anchoring, and at the same moment the barque hauled her wind and stood off, running to the southward across the harbor mouth. The American flag dropped from the mizzen, and in its place rose the British flag.

Again Corunna stamped her Chinese slipper on the deck. "Oh," she cried, "what's the man thinking of? He's lost his mind!"

She crossed to the other rail to watch the attempt of her clumsy and guileless countryman to escape the trap of his own making; and she knew at once, from the heaviness of the strange barque's movements, that she must be an easy prey to any who pursued her.

A boat, she saw, had pushed eagerly off from the hulking ship-of-the-line to windward. It bobbed toward the *Blue Swan*, and Corunna recognized her own jolly-boat, with Slade in the stern sheets.

Victorine scrambled to her feet. "Soap!" she grumbled. "Here comes your Mr. Soap! Me, just now I prefer the company of the octopus I have saved for your dinner!" She padded to the cabin hatch, her huge felt shoes slapping the deck with something like disgust.

Slade waved gaily to Corunna, his head tilted far back to let him see clearly with both eyes. "Call all hands!" he shouted down the wind. "All hands to make sail!"

Without any word from her, a boatswain in the bows set up a piping, and by the time Slade had rounded into the lee of the stern and come aboard, a part of the crew were casting loose the topsails; while others, at the capstan, were heaving the brig short.

"What's this?" she asked sharply.

Slade chuckled and turned to look at the slow barque, forging steadily southward toward the steep slope of Guia Head. "Why," he said, "we're ordered in chase. You saw him, the poor fool! Running in with his colors set, and losing his courage when he saw us lying here! Such stupidity I never saw! He could have come in and been safe, but he lost his head and ran, the poor fool! Gave himself away into the bargain; and then thought to deceive us, like an ostrich!" There was a furtiveness to his laughter, like quick movements among dry leaves.

She stared at him; then a slow comprehension dawned on her face and she laughed delightedly. "And because we're fastest, you persuaded them to send us out alone! Well, it was worth waiting for, to go like this!"

She looked once more for the strange barque; and as she looked, its topgallant sails merged with Guia Head's sharp outline and vanished.

The topsails of the *Blue Swan* were sheeted home; the topgallant sails set over them. Amid a shouting and a clattering, the anchor was catted. The brig's head fell off to the southward and she slipped rapidly toward the troubled steel-gray expanse of open sea.

It was only ten minutes later when she rounded the headland behind which the barque had disappeared, and hauled to the westward, but in that short time the barque had set her royals and put an unexpected stretch of tumbling water between herself and her pursuer.

Corunna laughed again. "She's faster than we thought! Trust an American to be faster than she looks!" She wrapped herself more snugly in the folds of her quilted jacket and looked uneasily at Slade. "By nightfall she'll be as safe as we."

Slade, watching the distant barque from a carronade slide, muttered beneath his breath, jumped to the deck, walked quickly forward and snapped an order to the gun crews by the foremast. A whistle blew long and shrilly, and at the sound the men scattered, running to their stations.

White-faced, Corunna caught at the arm of a running boatswain's mate. "Here!" she said. "Tell Mr. Slade I want him!"

The boatswain's mate stared at her. "Quarters!" he said, and ran on to the cabin hatch.

Slade came slowly back, stepping from side to side to give free passage to heavily laden powder boys, and Corunna went to meet him.

"What are you doing?" she demanded. "I'm in command of this vessel, and I'll have no orders given from my quarter-deck without my sanction! By what right did you order these people piped to quarters?"

He laughed gently through tightly clenched teeth. "Why," he said, "you know as well as I that we're bound to play a part—to play a part."

"To play a part!" she cried. "What part is there that we need to play when we're free from the British? What have you manned those guns for?"

He tipped back his head and looked at her along his nose. "You're excited," he said. "You forget that barque yonder doesn't know what we are. She might take it into her head to let fly at us. Surely there's no harm in self-protection." He took her arm and pressed it.

She wrenched herself free. "Self-protection! Do you think I'm blind? We'll alter our course two points, and then she'll know we're peaceable!"

His voice was low and husky: "Don't be impractical, my dear. This crew of ours—they think they're on an English vessel; and why shouldn't they? Just bear in mind they're English themselves. We'll have to handle them carefully, Corunna, or they might turn against us. In time we can swing them to our side; until then, it's best to let me handle things in the way that'll benefit us both. We'll have to show 'em it's to their advantage to follow our judgment."

"They're not English!" she said. "They're Irish! There's Americans among 'em, too, of a sort! What do you mean—in time we can swing them to our side? You're lying to me! You're trying to squirm out of something! I'll—I'll put you under arrest in your cabin!" She drew a deep, quivering breath and shivered, as if with cold.

He shook his head sorrowfully. "I was afraid of this," he said kindly. "I owe it to you and to the men themselves to do what I'm doing. Why, here's what seems to be a division of authority, my dear —you with your papers that they've never seen—papers that might be forgeries, for all they know—and me with what they take to be an honest letter-of-marque from the British Government. You can see yourself that it's a dangerous situation unless it's handled properly." He turned from her suddenly and swung himself into the ratlines to look forward at the fleeing barque; then nodded his head at the helmsman and motioned a little with his hand. The brig yawed to larboard.

"Give 'em a gun!" he shouted.

"No!" Corunna screamed. "No!"

The brig lurched. Her bow seemed to rear. The starboard bow gun crashed ponderously. A billowing cloud of white smoke hid the *Blue Swan's* bowsprit, then eddied down wind as the brig came back on her course. Slade, peering through the smoke, snarled at what he saw.

Corunna reached through the ratlines to clutch him by the ankle. "My God!" she cried. "You're not firing on them! They're Americans!"

He looked down at her through the shrouds, and his expression was one she had never seen. "This is a man's business!" he told her harshly. "There's a fortune in it for us! A fortune! I'll ask you to go below if you're afraid of seeing something that might disturb you."

Again he motioned to the helmsman. Again the brig yawed, and again the bow gun thundered. From the foretop there came a thin shouting—a shouting that spread to the *Blue Swan's* decks. The gun crews capered joyously among the guns, and powder boys leaped with excitement.

"By God!" Slade shouted. "Her mizzenmast! It's down! We got her! We got her!"

It was as Slade said, although such gunnery seemed a miracle. The distant barque had fallen off her course, and over her counter trailed her stubby mizzenmast.

"You rat!" Corunna said. "You rat!" She tugged at Slade's ankle. He laughed and stepped to the bulwark, but she caught at him again, so that he lost his balance and sprawled to the deck.

He scrambled to his feet, his face yellow. "Here!" he said. "What the hell you think you're doing?"

"You skunk," Corunna whispered. She seemed, in her rage, to have grown near to the height of Slade himself. "You damned skunk! You damned dirty slave-driving skunk! You damned——" Her breath failed her. She struck at him with her clenched fist.

Slade laughed his rasping laugh. He turned to the third officer, who watched them curiously. "The lady's excited," Slade said. "The firing's unbalanced her. We'll put her below!"

She fought silently, but Slade and his man had her. They dragged her to the cabin ladder. "Get down there!" Slade said. They lifted her from her feet and swung her through the hatch. Slade scrambled down the ladder after her and jerked her to her feet in the dimness of the companionway.

"It's a good time to have it out with you, Corunna," he said, "just because there isn't any time for it. I've coddled you along to keep you with me, because up to now you could have got away, if you tried. But now you can't! This brig's mine, not yours; and I do what I want to with it and with everything on it! I'll drop the play-acting, but I'll treat you well if you'll be sweet."

She struck at him.

The door of the captain's cabin swung open. In the doorway stood the woman Victorine, tall and angular against the stern windows behind her.

She looked at Corunna's face and instantly stabbed at Slade with the two long knitting needles in her left hand. He gasped and clutched at his thigh. Then Victorine dragged Corunna across the threshold into the bright cabin. The door slammed in his face and the bolt shot home.

The two women heard his fist crash against a panel of the door, and after that they thought he laughed. "To hell with you this little while!" he said, and scrambled up the ladder to the deck.

XXXII

It was a brig, and American, Corunna had thought at first, that she had seen creeping around Espalamaca Point into Fayal Roads; and a brig was what it had been, an hour earlier, when it lay hove-to so far at sea that the lesser peaks below Fayal's high cone were misty nubbins on the water's edge.

"We'll take no chances," Marvin had said to Argandeau and Newton. "Rig the false mizzenmast, and stretch canvas over the ports and hammock nettings. Then we can round the point with a cable dragging and see what's before us with no danger to ourselves. One of them might come out in chase if we're cautious about it. With us as slow and harmless as we'll seem to be, it won't be the big ones that come out, either. It might be the sloop-of-war, and it might even be——"

"Stop!" Argandeau shouted. He clenched his fist, extended his first and little fingers, and with their tips touched the nearest carronade. "Be cautious! You must touch metal—so—when you give tongue to your desires, lest they turn sour!"

Marvin stared at him. "Metal?" he asked. "Wood's better. It's handier." He turned to look at the island, coldly blue against the gray sky. "If nobody comes out," he added, "we'll take our bearings and come back at dusk." He drew a deep breath. "We'll come back at dusk and see what's to be done." He struck his hand against the taffrail. "Rig the mizzenmast! Run the long guns to the stern-chase ports. Cover the ports with the jolly-boat and get a screen around the guns. I want her high in the bow, and clumsy-looking!"

So the *True-Hearted Yankee* brig had become a barque, high-sided and cumbersome; and thus disguised she had labored in from the sea, a weary traveler seeking peace and rest in Fayal Roads.

As she passed the point and opened the broad bay rimmed with white houses set on slopes of dusty green, Marvin cast a quick glance aloft and then along the vessel's narrow deck. Above him, a handful of sailors crawled lazily about, handing the topgallant sails. Before him, from quarter-deck to bow, a double row of men were ranged inside the bulwarks, wedged tight between the carronades. It was no scurvy crew that Marvin eyed, but quiet men, neat in brown uniforms from France. Satisfied, he turned to the harbor.

"There they are, Dan!" Newton said; and his voice, like his pale whiskers, seemed to tremble. "There they are! Four of 'em, and one of 'em the *Blue Swan!*"

Argandeau drew his small mirror from his pocket and examined his face anxiously. "That brig," he said, "she would be easy to approach in the dusk, eh, Captain Caution? I think we make a pleasant call tonight, and so I must shave, perhaps."

Marvin walked to the wheel. "That brig," he said to the helmsman. "That brig——" He coughed and cleared his throat. "The brig beyond the three war craft! Get her in your mind."

The helmsman stared straight ahead. "I got her."

"Get her so you can find her in the dark," Marvin told him.

"I got her," the helmsman assured him.

"All right," Marvin said. "Bear off and on and off again; then point for Guia Head. It's steep-to. Allow for a two-knot on-shore current and don't waste any time getting around the head. Straighten her out when she points due west, and hold her parallel to the coast."

"Due west," the helmsman dutifully repeated.

Marvin turned to Newton. "Haul down the colors and run up the British ensign. Shake out the topgallant sails. Remind 'em not to hurry." Newton ran forward.

"Take in the cable?" Argandeau asked. He kissed his hand to the war vessels close inshore.

Marvin shook his head. "Let the cable alone. Let it alone." Into his mind there came the face of Captain Dorman. "'They cry unto the Lord in their trouble,'" Marvin murmured. "'They cry unto the Lord in their trouble, and he bringeth them out of their distresses . . . he bringeth them unto their desired haven.'" He looked quickly over his shoulder, as if he thought to find an old friend near at hand.

Overhead, the topgallant sails dropped from the yards and were sheeted home. The vessel wallowed uncertainly in the heavy swells that thrust themselves beneath her and passed onward to the accompaniment of complaining gurglings from her bows—of gurglings and angry hissings, as though she protested at the trailing cable that restrained her.

A head came over the edge of the maintop and stared, open-mouthed, at the quarter-deck. "They're going aloft!" it cried. "They're going aloft on the brig!"

Marvin seemed not to hear. His eyes were fastened on the little spouts of foam that rose slowly from the foot of Guia Head and seemed to cling for a time against its rocky sides.

"We take in the cable?" Argandeau asked softly.

"Take in three fathoms," Marvin said. "No, take in two fathoms."

"It's the brig," Newton told him. "She's coming out alone."

Marvin nodded.

Argandeau passed his hand caressingly over his chin. "So it is the *Blue Swan* after all! Better I go now and shave."

Marvin looked at him.

"You think I don't need it," Argandeau said hastily. "Ah, well, I remain here where all can see how I am gay! They will speak of it in later years. 'Lucien Argandeau,' they will say, 'he stood there in the shadow of that great rock, but more magnificent than the rock itself, because he was gay in the face of danger.'" He scanned the bulging slope of Guia Head that towered above them; then cast a quick glance over his shoulder. "Now she comes," he told Marvin. "She is a brig indeed, that *Blue Swan!* She moves fast! What you think—we take in that cable?"

"Take it in and coil it down," Marvin said. "Don't hurry, but when it's done, crowd on the royals and call the men aft. I've got a word to say to them."

Released from the drag of the heavy cable, the vessel seemed to hasten forward with the surges as if impatient to reach the calmer water beyond the head. She rounded steadily beneath the dark bulk of the overhanging cliff; and as she rounded, the cliff edge, like a drawn curtain, abruptly cut off from Marvin's gaze the white houses of the town and the tall brig that followed.

With the setting of the royals, she seemed to slice knifelike through the waves, in no respect different from the fast brig that had accompanied Tom Souville's *Renard* to sea, save that her false mizzenmast swayed precariously in its fastenings forward of the wheel; while strips of canvas, stretched around the bulwarks, added to her apparent height.

Marvin stood silently before the false mast while the crew, herded by Newton and the Indian, Steven, pressed aft to crouch amidships. He looked over his shoulder at Guia Head, falling fast astern. There was no vessel in sight.

Marvin stared down at the brown-clad men before him. "You know what we're up to," he said. "We're probably going to fight the brig that's in chase of us. It may be some of you don't like the idea of standing up to a vessel that isn't a cargo vessel. If that's the case, it may make you more peaceable in your minds to know she's got

specie aboard. To the best of my knowledge, she's carrying fifteen thousand English pounds. That's seventy-five thousand dollars.
What's more, I propose to divide one-half of that fifteen thousand
pounds among the crew of this vessel, provided the proper discipline's observed and she's taken as I want her taken. That'll mean
over four hundred dollars apiece to each one of you, just for this
one engagement."

"Yow!" screamed a seaman in the rear of the throng. A pleased
rustling and whispering swept over the remainder of the crew.

"The commander of that brig," Marvin went on, "is an American,
and as bad as they come. I think he's a traitor, bent on mischief to
all true-hearted Americans. We'll soon know. If he fires on us, there's
no doubt about it. Anyway, he's the man I'm after. I don't want him
hurt. I want all gun pointers to keep their fire away from the cabin
and quarter-deck of that brig. Restrict yourself to her rigging, so far
as possible. That's why you've been told to load with chain and bar
shot. Keep your sights on her bow and foremast. There'll be a penalty
for each time she's hulled aft of the mainmast—a penalty of one thousand dollars deducted from the amount to be distributed among you.
So you'll do well not to fire until your sights are free of smoke and
you can see what you're aiming at. You've got the pendulum, and
there'll be no excuse for hitting her too far aft. Make sure you hit
her, too, unless you want to spend the rest of this war starving and
freezing on a British hulk! That's all. Get forward and keep yourselves below the bulwarks, where you won't be seen by those in the
tops of the vessel in chase."

He turned again to look back at Guia Head. As he looked, the
Blue Swan's jibs and squaresails popped suddenly into view from
behind it, almost as though a puff of smoke had shot from its foot.

"Pooi!" Argandeau exclaimed. "Here am I, ready to be gay, and I
find nothing to be gay about!"

"You'll scarcely have time," Marvin told him. "On the chart there's
three small islands close inshore, halfway between Guia Head and
the western point. We're nearly there. I don't want to pass 'em. Drag
the cable again, and keep the islands on our beam. If necessary,
drop a staysail under the bow."

"Good!" Argandeau cried. "We set the stage, eh? Ah well: you can
count on Argandeau to push over the scenery on him!"

A dozen men payed out the cable, and once more the vessel labored slowly in the choppy seas.

"Look! Look!" Argandeau said. "She blows out a bean, I think!"

Astern, the *Blue Swan* yawed; a fleecy ball of white burst from her bow. The distant explosion jarred the false mizzenmast in its lashings.

Argandeau opened his mouth wide in a soundless laugh. "Close!" he said, jerking his thumb contemptuously to larboard. "Close as last Friday!"

The *True-Hearted Yankee* creaked and labored onward, her officers and crew caught in a frozen silence. Under the bulwarks the men stared white-eyed at Marvin, who in turn stood staring patiently at three small islands close against the low and rocky coast.

Closer now, the *Blue Swan* yawed again and fired a gun. The ball skipped past them to windward, whacking against the swells.

Marvin came suddenly to life and clapped his hands together. "Cut the mizzen!" he said. "Cut it on the larboard side and pitch it over the starboard counter, where it'll drag and be seen from the brig! Down with the helm and point for the islands! Keep the cable dragging! Rig the pendulum! Take in the royals!"

Men scuttled crab-like over the decks, keeping their heads below the level of the false bulwarks. They slashed at the preventer stays of the stubby mizzenmast and tumbled it over the taffrail. The crews of the long guns crouched beside their pieces, growling among themselves and freeing the falls of the jolly-boat, which hung low from the stern-davits, screening the stern-chase ports.

Forward of the mainmast, at its foot, three men set up a padded iron tripod from the apex of which hung a bar tipped with an inverted gong of polished brass. At the level of the gong, and straight beneath the apex of the tripod, they made fast a small steel ring. This done, they stepped back, letting the iron bar swing free. It oscillated. The vessel rolled, and the bar, swinging off to one side, caught for a moment against a leg of the tripod; then swung downward. The brass gong touched the small steel ring, and the vessel echoed to its clang. The men under the bulwarks made motions of sponging and ramming. The tall Indian caught the pendulum and held it still.

"Set all guns at point-blank range," he shouted, "and keep your ears open for changes!"

The *Blue Swan* was close at hand; as close, almost, as the small islands near the shore; so close that the white foam beneath her bows was reflected in her bright copper as her forefoot lifted, giving her the look of being sheathed with gleaming ice.

Marvin, staring at her with such fierce intensity that the northwest wind whirled moisture from his eyes, felt Argandeau take him by the arm.

"You see who I see, standing on a carronade?" Argandeau asked him softly. "Look how he tips back his head! And his long hair; I can see it blowing!"

"Yes," Marvin said. "Yes. They can't get inshore of us now. They wouldn't dare. They'd strike the rocks. They'll have to run past our guns!"

From the small figure on the *Blue Swan's* quarter-deck there came a hoarse shouting, indistinguishable above the wailing of the breeze in the top-hamper. Marvin, sighting at the onrushing brig along his own starboard taffrail, shouted, "Pendulum!"

Behind him the gong clanged and quickly clanged again.

"Now!" Marvin shouted. "Let go! Cut away the mizzen! Cut the cable! Strip off the false canvas! Drop the jolly-boat! Fire when the pendulum strikes! Brace around the yards!" He went to the wheel and seized it.

The deck of the *True-Hearted Yankee* boiled with men. The bow of the *Blue Swan* lay dead astern. The jolly-boat pitched downward with a whirring of falls. The pendulum clanged. With the clang, the guns at the stern ports bellowed, and the brig seemed to leap ahead, forced forward by the recoil of the guns. A thick cloud of white smoke enveloped her stern and her lower sails.

Marvin spun the wheel. "Long guns to the larboard bow ports!" he said.

Coughing and cursing, the men wrestled with the long guns, hustling them from the smoky quarter-deck and running them forward through the clumps of seamen who hauled at tacks and sheets.

A gun roared from the *Blue Swan*, lying hid beyond the smoke cloud; and another followed. Grapeshot screamed and rattled high in the rigging of the *True-Hearted Yankee*. A severed rope plumped down at Marvin's feet.

The *True-Hearted Yankee* shot ahead, clear of the smoke. On her larboard beam, the *Blue Swan* yawed from side to side, her bowsprit dangling from a snarl of ropes and splinters, and her long jib-boom dragging beneath her bows.

The pendulum clanged; two carronades roared flatly from the *True-Hearted Yankee*. The *Blue Swan's* main course split apart and flapped raggedly in the wind.

The pendulum clanged again. Three more carronades flung jets of smoke toward the damaged brig. The *Blue Swan's* bulwarks, near her foremast, crumpled into splinters. Her shrouds and backstays parted and curled upward like scorched string. The foremast itself swayed forward; then, with a crackling that came faintly to the shouting gunners on the *True-Hearted Yankee,* fell slowly backward, the yards and sails stabbing and tearing at the slender spars and straining canvas of the raking mainmast.

In the time it takes a small white cloud to pass across the face of the sun, the *Blue Swan* had become a shattered and unmanageable hulk.

Newton looked across the rail. "'Captain Caution!'" he said, and laughed. "He waltzes across a harbor mouth filled with British guns —enough guns to blow him and his ship and all of us to China! And right on top of that he takes this brig just like machinery, and not a hair of our heads is hurt—and not many of theirs, either, for that matter. Yet there's Slade and his brig and his men at our mercy, on account of Captain Caution!"

XXXIII

THE *True-Hearted Yankee*, her topsails thrown aback and her pendulum clanging slowly in the long swells, lay under the lee of the shattered brig; and Marvin, boarding the *Blue Swan* with the tall Indian at the head of a dozen brown-clad seamen, armed with pistols and boarding axes, found her decks thronged with a crew already beginning to be drunk and hilarious from the contents of a looted spirit locker.

On the quarter-deck, Slade, four officers about him, laughed hoarsely at the sight of Marvin and drank from the pannikin in his hand. He threw back his lank hair with a sweep of his head and spoke from the side of his mouth to his officers, who moved uncomfortably.

Marvin stationed six men at the break of the deck and motioned Steven to the cabin with the others; then spoke quietly to the group of men around the binnacle: "Where's your captain?"

Slade stepped forward. "There's no need of all this rigmarole," he said. "Go ahead and get it over with."

Marvin's reply was almost pleasant. "You're captain, are you?" He glanced at the other officers and spoke more to them than to Slade. "Properly handled, you should have had good cruising in this brig." He looked placidly at the *True-Hearted Yankee*, where round-mouthed guns seemed to stare in amazement at what they saw.

"Properly handled?" Slade asked. He drank again from his pannikin. "Handled with damned Yankee trickery, do you mean?" He laughed and turned, as if for admiration, to his officers.

Marvin stood silent, watching the drunken crew that cursed and stumbled amid the wreckage in the *Blue Swan's* bows.

"Well," Slade said in a voice suddenly quiet, "what about it?"

There was no sign that Marvin heard the words. He stood motionless with head a little bent, and seemed to listen.

Steven's head and shoulders appeared above the cabin hatch. "We can't find the specie," he said. He pitched a bundle of clothes to the deck, scrambled after it and turned to help Corunna through the hatch. Behind Corunna crawled Victorine, an angular figure, a cord made fast across one shoulder and between her knees, so that her voluminous skirts were drawn upward into bunchy pantaloons, beneath which her vast felt shoes fumbled for a foothold.

Marvin seemed not to see the two women. "You can't find the specie?" he asked the Indian thoughtfully. "That makes it awkward! Awkward!" He clasped his hands behind him and moved closer to Slade's officers.

"Ordinarily," he said pleasantly, "I'd take you gentlemen aboard and give you fair treatment, but under the circumstances it wouldn't be safe. You see, the people aboard my brig know about this man who calls himself your commander. They know what he is. They know he's a thief, a blackmailer, a liar, a turncoat."

Marvin's face grew sterner. "They'd be bound to hang him without a trial," he told the silent officers. "It might even be they'd get out of control some night and do it. If they did, they might take you as well, knowing you'd carried out his orders, and I can't have that. I can't have that!"

Slade threw back his head and folded his arms; there was a kind of pride, not braggadocio, in his attitude. "Go ahead," he said quietly. "Go ahead and get it done."

There was no flaw in his gameness; he expected no mercy and asked for none; but there was a barely perceptible quiver to Slade's mouth, and beneath the tranquillity of his voice something like a broken breath of sound, a tremor more felt than heard; and it disturbed Marvin. He looked at Slade again gravely; then turned to the officers.

"In spite of what I've been saying, I did mean to take this man home for trial, and I hoped to see him hanged, as did three of my friends here. I think they'll back me up in what I'm going to do about it now."

He cleared his throat, then went on: "Well, we've got him down, and we aren't going to do what we intended. He's lost his ship and everything else, thank God; and I guess it'll be enough for us if he goes back to England with you. If any of you like him, I guess you'd better keep him there, because if he's ever taken by any American ship, or sets foot on American soil again, it won't be good for him. I guess it's enough for us, if we ever think of him again, to know he's in England with nothing but his reputation as a traitor to make a living out of."

Slade looked at him incredulously. "You mean you're letting me go?"

Marvin laughed. "If that's what you call it," he said, then spoke once more to the officers. "Now you can see why it's awkward. For the reason I've told you, I can't take you as prisoners, nor do I propose to leave this vessel while it hides the specie of this man you call captain. It's hidden somewhere in his cabin, for there's nowhere else he'd dare to hide it. Therefore, gentlemen, I'll have to ask you to get yourself as far into the bows of this vessel as you can get. I'm going to put a match to your magazine and blow up the cabin and the specie with it." He turned to Steven. "Break open a powder keg and lay a train to it."

A stocky, red-faced officer coughed nervously and addressed him in the thick speech of Devon. "The specie kegs," he said, "are stacked in the rudder case, high up."

Slade laughed and tossed his empty pannikin over the side.

Marvin nodded to Steven, who turned and hurried below. He considered Corunna then. "I think," he said, "it's safe enough in case you wish to remain aboard this vessel. I'll have to set her afire, to make sure she's destroyed, but the guns you've heard will bring out the sloop-of-war to see what's happened. She'll be out pretty soon. But even if she doesn't come out, you're close enough to shore to get there with no trouble."

She looked at him, her knuckles pressed against her lips.

He hesitated. "In case you wish to be taken off——"

She only continued to look at him, but he thought her eyes were fierce with disdain.

"She will go," Victorine said. "Put her in your boat and take her to your ship."

"But if she doesn't want to——" he began.

Victorine pushed her red and furious face almost against his. "She will go!" she screamed. "Put her in the boat and take her to your ship!"

Steven came through the hatch with a specie keg in his arms. "Seventeen of 'em!" he said. He thumped it down on the deck.

Marvin smiled and looked back toward Guia Head.

"Put 'em in the boat," he said. "The sloop-of-war's coming down on us. Throw over the guns and set this vessel afire in the bows."

But it was the Indian who came to Corunna and Victorine. "Now, ladies," he said, "we're going home."

The *True-Hearted Yankee*, under a cloud of sail, bore to the northwestward past the rounded peak of Castello Branco Point. Marvin, at her taffrail, watched the sloop-of-war haul her wind toward the burning brig; then spoke to Newton, who stood beside him, eyeing him with proud affection. "I want Argandeau!" he said. "I saw him run forward, when we came aboard, and jump down the fore hatch. He's got no business going below at a time like this. Send for him. Tell him I want him."

It was a full five minutes later when Newton returned, pushing Argandeau before him. At the mainmast Argandeau balked and crouched, like a startled fawn, casting timid glances at the cabin hatch. Marvin stared at him, puzzled. "Where've you been?" he demanded. "What ails you?"

Argandeau wiped his forehead with his sleeve and spoke humbly in a thick voice:

"Captain. I am not gay!"

"Aren't you? What of it?"

"Captain, I ask permission to spend all daylight hours for the length of this voyage in the hold."

"What?"

Argandeau shivered. "Captain, you have heard me speak of rabbits, perhaps too much and too lightly. The one called Victorine was formerly pleasanter to the eye, as you will believe, since it could not be otherwise. At the time I speak of she was—an acquaintance of mine."

"Was she?" Marvin said calmly. "Well, I can't have women interfering with work aboard this vessel. House the long guns and make all snug. A little ordinary caution, now, will get all of us safely back to France and fortune."

"All of us?" Argandeau turned a tragic face upon him. "A little ordinary caution? It is in that manner that one speaks when it is not himself who is in danger, but only a friend! My captain, you would not be so philosophic if you had ever been loved by a volcano, and even made the miscalculation of being wedded to one! I would not admit it publicly, but it appears that one of my marriages was with this artillerist! This great grenadier! This Stromboli of a Victorine! It is my simple confession—I am not perfect—and I am at your mercy."

"How is it possible for Argandeau to fear a woman?" Marvin asked. Then he quoted almost the selfsame words that Argandeau had once said to him on the deck of the *Olive Branch*. "You in France, you are subtle! You hunt always for the heartstrings of a woman, and you play softly on them, so that she is moved to do your will."

"Ah, my God! My God!" Argandeau whispered. "I spoke as a Frenchman! I am an American now—a true-hearted Yankee. I know nothing of women, and wish to know less!"

Marvin stared hard at him. "All right, stay below during daylight unless you're needed," he said, and went below himself.

Marvin rapped on the door of the captain's cabin. Victorine opened it, knitting needles in her hand; and Marvin, looking beyond her, saw Corunna rise to stand with her back against the table, facing him.

"Well," he said gravely, "we're glad to have you aboard, you and your friend." He glanced at Victorine. "I think I've seen you before. The knitting looks familiar."

"And why not?" Victorine demanded. "I have carried these needles for protection since the good God knows when, knitting all day, and at night pulling out what I have knitted."

"For protection?" Marvin asked.

Victorine wagged her head. "Hah, but you were right! I knew you were right when you spoke rudely to this cabbage here"—she stabbed a needle toward Corunna—"in Paris."

"Yes," he said, "it was in Paris that I saw you."

"As I say," Victorine continued placidly, "I know! Me, I know! What we females need is not compliments, but truth. Of my husbands, the most successful with me spoke truthfully to me; and I, to keep him quiet, pretended to an adoration for him that was somewhat more than I felt. Thus we adored each other! Ah, yes, he was the best of them all!"

Marvin glanced quickly at Corunna, but she was staring through the stern windows with hard, uninterested eyes at the towering blue cone of Fayal.

"Well," he said awkwardly, "if there's anything you need, either of you, you'll let us know. I thought you might like—I just thought I'd say that Steven found your sea trunk aboard the *Blue Swan*. It's here. I'll send it down to you. This is the captain's cabin you're in, but you won't need to think of that—I mean, I'll steer clear of enemy vessels while you're—well, I only mean you're welcome to the cabin."

She looked at him, and in her look there was disdain and anger still. It seemed that somehow he had been guilty of something, or that Corunna thought so; and he felt, as he had felt before, that he could never please her.

He moved to the door, then, and fumbled with the latch. "Well," he said, "it may be a month before we can set you ashore. We can't control these winter winds. You may find it hard—that is, if you'd rather not have me—if you'd rather not speak to me, Corunna, your —your lady here could bring me messages about anything you'd like us to do—like us to do for your comfort." He pressed the latch and hesitated, looking across the cabin at them. Victorine slid a sidelong glance at him above her knitting, but Corunna, examining the elbow of her Chinese jacket, might already have forgotten his existence. So he went out.

From Fayal the *True-Hearted Yankee* bore up to the northeastward. For two days Marvin, busy with the discipline and welfare of his crew, caught only fleeting glimpses of his passengers; for they, it seemed, came to the deck when he was in his own small berth, or working with his charts.

He had the thought, late on the second day, that they might find it easier if he should let them hear, as if by accident, that he would keep the deck at night, leaving it free for them at earlier hours. With the thought, he went on deck to find the brig rushing along a plain of black and silver beneath a moon so brilliant that it had the look of being closer than the distant mastheads. By its light he saw that his thought to remain in his cabin by day and to emerge only when darkness fell would not please Corunna; that here, once more, he could not please her.

In the moonlight he saw three figures leaning against the rail under the swelling main course. Two were women; and to his astonishment the third was Argandeau—an Argandeau who gestured with fearless grace toward the far horizon, and murmured with such fervor that his words poured from him with the sweet cadence of an endless lullaby.

"They must have seen me," Marvin sighed; for Argandeau's murmurings were suddenly silent; and after that the female figures, moving to the clack of knitting needles, left Argandeau and vanished down the hatch. Argandeau came to him, then, to stare with painful innocence at the moon.

"Wasn't it you," Marvin asked him, "who begged permission to stay in the hold?"

"Not forever!" Argandeau said reproachfully. "Did you hear me use the word 'forever'? Is it not necessary for a human being to come up at night?"

He moved closer to Marvin. "I must tell you! A strange thing happened! Strange, yet freighted with relief and consolation. Last night I was yonder, and suddenly she was behind me, full of recognition. Well, I took upon myself the calm of Socrates before the hemlock! A ship is a place where a man cannot run limitlessly with Stromboli in eruption pursuing on felt slippers at his heels! My friend, you await my narrative of the crisis! I will not keep you in suspense! My poor captain, Stromboli is extinct!"

Marvin looked at him. "Extinct?"

"Extinct! My once volcano! Flat as a dead fish! It can scarcely be credited, but when she saw me, she laughed; and what do you think she said to your pigeon? She said, 'It's that old Argandeau, an old rascal I used to know!' That was all she said of me; and we had a nice conversation, the three of us. You heard me, no? We spoke of the ocean and the moon and where is the best cooking in Paris. It's incredible! Even as I talk I must pinch myself and pinch myself!"

He took his cheek between his thumb and forefinger, and wrenched it. When he had released himself, he said carelessly, "Your pigeon does not talk much any more. I think she is sad."

"My pigeon!" Marvin exclaimed. "Don't call her that again! She's hated me a long while."

Argandeau rested his cheek on his hand and stared at the moon. "M'm! I think you have something on your mind. I think so. I think I have had the same thought. In the hold these past two days, sitting in a corner of the carpenter shop and also concealed in the bread locker, I have been able to give more than a little thought to the matter. I have wondered whether that rabbit is Mrs. Slade. I have had the thought also that it is something she will never freely tell you; also that a sure way to find out nothing at all about it is to ask her. The temptation to ask will return and return, stronger one year than another, no doubt; but I would not ask. No, I would not ask."

"No," Marvin said uncertainly. "Well, I won't have——"

"No," Argandeau repeated. "No! As for hating you, I think so. Yes indeed, I think she hates you; and why not? I ask you why not? For one thing, you have proved yourself right and her to be wrong; but that would not be the chief reason for her hate. No. The chief reason would be that it was not you who took her from the *Blue Swan.* I tell you there will be times when that hatred will be remembered at moments that will make you leap with surprise, like a fish."

"I *did* take her from the *Blue Swan.*"

"No, that is not correct. That volcano—that extinct volcano—she *made* you take her."

Marvin struck the bulwark with the flat of his hand. "How the devil did I know? How should I have known what she wanted?"

"And there you are!" Argandeau cried. "That is what she hates you most for! For not knowing! For not knowing she wasn't Mrs.

Slade! For that, and because she had found out she was wrong about everything!"

Argandeau looked at him pityingly. "You think, perhaps, a woman will run to a man and tell him she has been wrong? That would be a fine beginning, eh?—for a woman to say she has been wrong, so that forever after he would be able to say to her, 'Hah! You were wrong about that thing, back there fifty years ago; therefore you are wrong about this matter here and now!' A wonderful affair, that, since it would reappear all the rest of your lives, causing bitter words and bitterer thoughts! No, no! It is too much to expect a woman to admit being wrong at the start, when all women know that to make such an admission is like placing a club in the man's hands—a club with which he will surely thump her—Piff—like that, when he is at a loss what else to do! Yes, yes, my good friend; you must expect her to hate you—yes, and bitterly! You must understand this! It's never the pigeon that is wrong; it's you—you entirely!"

Marvin shook his head, puzzled. "If she hates me, she hates me. How can I help it if she hates me? You don't think, do you, that I want her to hate me? I'm not anxious to have anyone hate me, least of all that—least of all—well, I don't like to have her hate me. I never hated her. The fact is—well, the fact is I never could help liking her. Even when we were children in Arundel."

He looked astern, over the dark waters, as though he hoped to see, far off, the little town beside the narrow river.

"I'm glad for her sake," he went on, "she didn't marry Slade. I never thought she would. But I don't know what to do—what to do about it, or about her—I don't know at all. I can't help having been right; I don't feel like taking any blame for that. She *has* been wrong all this time, and there's no other way to look at it."

Argandeau gazed long and steadily at the moon. "No," he said dreamily. "No! Of course there is no other way to look at it. No other way at all. Nor can you ever change her hate for you; of course not! Still, that pigeon is a guest on your vessel. She is in your charge, even; so you might, perhaps—it is a small thought, this one, and of no value, doubtless—you might do what you could to make her feel better."

"Why," Marvin said simply, "I would! I'd be glad to! But I don't know how! She takes no pleasure in anything I do or say!"

Argandeau raised his eyebrows, a moon-struck picture of exasperation. "But there is nothing easier! Go to her and tell her!"

"Tell her what?" Marvin demanded, equally exasperated.

"Tell her you've been wrong."

Marvin just looked at him; and from his look, it was clear to Argandeau that Marvin thought him off his head.

Yet Argandeau's words recurred to Marvin in his bed that night, and he thought about them. Indeed, he lay awake, turning them this way and that in his mind; and at last he struck upon a matter concerning which he might have been at least a little wrong. He had, as he recalled it, told Corunna she would never make a proper captain of a ship. That, he admitted, might have been an overstatement; for certainly she could come as near being a proper captain as any woman could. His words, perhaps, had been a little rough, tinged with incaution. Hazily, before he slept, he knew he owed it to Corunna to explain those words.

Thus it happened that at noon the following day it was the captain himself, instead of Newton, who came to the cabin for the log book. He hesitated before the cabin door, and almost turned away; but at length he cleared his throat and knocked; then dropped his hat and fumbled for it on the floor, and was still groping for it when Victorine's voice called, "*Entrez!*" When he had found his hat, he coughed and knocked again and immediately entered.

They were at the table, both of them, engaged in unraveling the last product of Victorine's needles, and at the sight of him they stopped and stared.

"I wanted to see—that is—you know, the log book," he said with an air of choosing his words carefully.

The two women looked at each other and then back at Marvin; and it was Victorine who took the log book from the rack beside the door and placed it in his hands.

He took it gratefully. "I didn't want to disturb you," he said. "I only thought I'd get the log book." He coughed, examined the cover of the book with apparent surprise; and then, with a sudden desperation, he said to Corunna, "I've been thinking things over, and I thought I'd tell you I believe I've been wrong about—about——"

She looked at him strangely. "Wrong?" she asked. "About what?"

Unexpectedly to himself, as if by a God-given inspiration, he said the right thing. He heard himself saying, "About everything!"

At that she seemed to change before his eyes. No sailor woman stood there, hard and hating him, but a soft-eyed girl, drooping, gentle and on the point of tears.

"Ah, no!" she said in a shaking voice. "You were never wrong about anything, nor ever will be!"

Beneath the noonday sun the *True-Hearted Yankee* sliced, close-hauled, into the teeth of the northeast trades. Under the watchful eye of the Indian, Steven, two gun crews trundled the long guns toward the bow, racing, amid the hoarse exhortations of twoscore brown-clad seamen, to win the gill of rum that would reward each member of the winning crew.

On the quarter-deck, Argandeau walked twice around the cabin scuttle, staring at its shining frosted glass as if beneath it rested some rare treasure he had helped to find. As he walked, he skipped and muttered.

"What's that you say?" Newton asked.

"It should be put in the log," Argandeau declared. "In the log, certainly!"

"Not today it shouldn't," Newton said. "The captain's writing the log today. He took it to the cabin. You'll have to wait until tomorrow. Is it the race you're so anxious to get in the log, or what?"

With his thumb and forefinger, Argandeau pinched Newton's cheek ecstatically. "That I am gay once more, my small good friend! That I am gay again!"

* * *

Below them, in the bright cabin, the captain smiled down upon the golden square of sunlight that lay across the log book's open pages. The ink was wet upon the ancient words that he had written:

And so ends the sea day; all well on board the good brig True-Hearted Yankee, *of Arundel. God Save the United States of America.*

THE END

For the aid so freely given him in the writing of this book and the obtaining of information on seamanship, gunnery, ship-design and the Gangway Pendulum, the author is profoundly grateful to

Anna Mosser Roberts

Booth Tarkington

R. E. Gould, *Anson, Maine*

W. H. Stone, *Patton, California*

Howard Irving Chapelle, *Assistant Editor, "The Mariner"*

Harry A. McBride, *Department of State*

P. V. H. Weems, *Lt. Commander, U. S. N.*

Holden C. Richardson, *Capt., U. S. N.* (*Retired*)

Marion Cobb Fuller, *Maine State Library*

The Library of Congress

ARUNDEL

"When I think of the thin, tinny novels which tumble from the press today, to be forgotten within a few months, I feel that *Arundel* is a permanent contribution to the literature of this country. I go around telling people to read it; but I despair—until they have read it—of making them realize its quality. It seems to me like a perfectly splendid plum pudding! No, I think it is more than that; I think it is brown bread, and roast beef, and beer! It is *the real stuff*, and while I congratulate the author upon having written it, I congratulate all of us novel-reading folk even more heartily. How anybody can lap up whipped cream when he can get *Arundel*, I don't understand!"

—MARGARET DELAND

PRINTINGS

First published .... November 18, 1929
Revised, replated and reprinted .... June, 1933; October, 1956
U.S., 1931 twice; 1933 twice; 1934 four times; 1935; 1936 three times; 1937 three times; 1938 three times; 1939; 1940; 1941; 1942; 1943; 1944; 1945 twice; 1946; 1947; 1949; 1953; 1955; 1956
Braille, Library of Congress .... January, 1934
Family Reading Club .... November, 1956
Doubleday Dollar Book Club .... December, 1956
International Collectors Library .... April, 1958
England (Bodley Head) .... September, 1936
Germany (Holle & Co.) .... October, 1936
Germany (Buchgemeinschaft) .... January, 1937
England (Readers Union) .... December, 1938
Sweden (Bonniers) .... March, 1939
Denmark (Aschehoug) .... November, 1939
Italy (Mondadori) .... September, 1940
Armed Services Edition .... May, 1945
Spain (Janes) .... May, 1946
France (Editions de la Paix) .... Details unobtainable
Czechoslovakia (Borovy) .... October, 1947
Arundel 300th Anniversary .... June, 1953
German Book Society (Koch, Darmstadt) .... January, 1955
England (Collins Fontana) .... September, 1956

RABBLE IN ARMS

"*Rabble In Arms* is magnificent. In both the beauty and the horror of his story, Kenneth Roberts reaches supreme heights and can defy comparison with any author that ever lived and wrote in any language I ever read in the original or in translation. They talk big talk of Tolstoi, Victor Hugo, Stephen Crane and a few others, but I put Kenneth Roberts up with the best of them. He is a great author who has actually written great novels."

—RUPERT HUGHES

PRINTINGS

First published .... November 2, 1933
Reset and replated .... June, 1957
U.S., 1933 twice; 1935; 1936; 1937 three times; 1938 twice; 1939 twice; 1940; 1942; 1943; 1944; 1945; 1948; 1950; 1953; 1956; 1958
Braille, Library of Congress .... January, 1934
Talking Books, Library of Congress 1945
Illustrated Edition .... October, 1947
International Collectors Library .... November, 1955
Family Reading Club .... June, 1957
Doubleday Dollar Book Club .... April, 1958
  Reprinted .... September, 1958
Germany (Holle) .... October, 1936
Germany (Book Society) .... January, 1937
England (Collins) .... January, 1939
Australia (Collins) .... January, 1939
England (National Library for Blind) .... March, 1939
England (World Books) .... April, 1940
Italy (Mondadori) .... June, 1941
Czechoslovakia (Borovy) .... July, 1941
Sweden (Bonniers) .... February, 1945
Spain (Janes) .... September, 1946
Republished Czechoslovakia (Odeon) .... January, 1949
Republished Sweden (Bonniers, Folkbibliotek) .... May, 1955

NORTHWEST PASSAGE

"Towering above all else in the swirling 700 pages of *Northwest Passage* is that indestructible giant, Robert Rogers, a prodigious creation, a character bristling and sounding with life, a vivid portrait for your literary gallery. *Northwest Passage* will give you three novels' worth of entertainment."

—CHARLES LEE, *Minneapolis Journal*

PRINTINGS

First published .... June 25, 1937
U.S., 1937 fifteen times; 1938 eight times; 1939 four times; 1940 three times; 1942; 1943; 1944; 1945; 1946; 1947; 1948; 1950; 1952; 1954; 1956; 1957; 1959
Book-of-the-Month Club .... July, 1937
Braille, Library of Congress .... September, 1937
Talking Books, American Foundation for Blind .... January, 1949
International Collectors Library .... December, 1958
England (Collins); Book Society; Daily Mail Book-of-the-Month
                                                  January, 1938
Australia (Angus & Robertson) .... February, 1938
Sweden (Bonniers) .... April, 1938
Germany (Paul List) .... September, 1938
Denmark (Jespersen) .... September, 1938
Norway (Cappelens) .... October, 1938
Finland (Kirja) .... November, 1938
Holland (Torrentrans) .... December, 1938
Japan (Mikasa Shobo) .... December, 1938
Italy (Mondadori) .... March, 1939
England (Foyle's Book Club) .... May, 1939
Hungary (Revai) .... May, 1939
Czechoslovakia (E.L.K.) .... June, 1939
Continent of Europe (Albatross Giant) .... June, 1939
Poland ("Roj") .... July, 1939
Rumania (Ciornei) .... November, 1939
France (Editions Stock: 338 printings) .... February, 1940
Brazil (Companhia Editora Nacional) .... July, 1941
Spain (Janes) .... June, 1946
Yugoslavia (Athenaeum) .... Details unobtainable
British Broadcasting Co., 8 instals .... July–Sept., 1947
Czechoslovakia (Podrouzek) .... January, 1948
Sweden (Bonniers, Folkbibliotek) .... November, 1953
Germany (Europäischer Book Club) .... March, 1953
England (Collins Fontana) .... November, 1953
Italy (Mondadori) 4 Vol. Pavone Edition .... January, 1955
Yugoslavia (Kosmos, Belgrade) .... May, 1955
Finland (Otava, Helsinki) .... December, 1956

OLIVER WISWELL

"The story of the Royalists in the American Revolution has never been adequately told in fiction form. Now, after 160 years, Kenneth Roberts has undertaken this herculean task in *Oliver Wiswell*. No one excepting a man of Mr. Roberts' stature as a writer could lay before us the case of the American Royalists. It takes industry and unending research to accomplish the bare skeleton of such a book; it takes a high form of imagination, finished technique, and courage to carry the task to a successful conclusion. Yes, courage; for even after the passing of centuries, old prejudices still persist and cloud issues. It requires something greater than good writing and technique to hold up for examination a lost cause, and turn the dead past into a living present. This Kenneth Roberts has done. He has given life to people who were only names on a page of history, and summed up a case for Americans whom we had forgotten were Americans."

—INGLIS FLETCHER, *San Francisco Chronicle*

PRINTINGS

First published .... November 22, 1940
   Reprinted twice before publication
U.S., 1940 twice; 1945; 1946; 1948; 1952; 1957
Braille, Library of Congress .... January, 1941
Australia (Angus & Robertson) .... January, 1941
Sweden (Bonniers) .... February, 1941
Switzerland (Humanitas; Zurich) .... April, 1941
Brazil (Companhia Editora Nacional) .... July, 1941
England (Collins) .... August, 1943
England (National Library for Blind) .... November, 1943
Czechoslovakia (Thalia) .... May, 1946
France (Editions de la Paix) .... September, 1947
Spain (Janes) .... May, 1949
Italy (Mondadori) .... September, 1949
Switzerland ⎫
Germany ⎬ (Diana; Zurich) .... November, 1953
Austria   ⎭

LYDIA BAILEY

"*Lydia Bailey* is a rich, long, never lagging book, triumphantly ranging over half the world and more than half of human hopes and follies. It shows Kenneth Roberts' special power of bringing the past to full and unforgettable life; and in its anger at political selfishness and stupidity it has a harsh, barbed meaning for today. If 1947 produces a better novel, it will be a notable year for American fiction."

—WALTER HAVIGHURST, *Chicago Tribune*

PRINTINGS

First published .... January 2, 1947
U.S., 1947 three times; 1956; 1958
Literary Guild .... January, 1947
Braille (Library of Congress) .... June, 1947
Book-of-the-Month Club .... July, 1947
Braille (Clovernook; Library of Congress) .... January, 1948
Argentina (Rueda; Spanish) .... October, 1947
Brazil (Instituto Progreso; Portuguese) .... November, 1947
Norway (Cappelens) .... December, 1947
England (Collins) .... January, 1948
Australia (Collins) .... January, 1948
Sweden (Bonniers) .... May, 1948
Switzerland (Diana; Zurich) .... June, 1948
Denmark (Aschehoug) .... June, 1948
Holland (Breughel) .... August, 1948
Finland (Aura) .... October, 1948
France (Editions de la Paix) .... November, 1948
Hungary (Konyvkiado) .... December, 1949
Spain (Janes) .... July, 1950
Italy (Mondadori) .... November, 1952
England (Collins Fontana) 1954
Yugoslavia (Kosmos; Belgrade) .... May, 1955

BOON ISLAND

"Once you've read this powerful story, the barren rocky island will become a part of your inner consciousness. You'll never forget it."

—W. P. BURNETT, *Saturday Review of Literature*

"*Boon Island* is one of those experiences in reading which, like *Robinson Crusoe*, *The Journal of the Plague Year* or *The Admirable Crichton*, can never be forgotten. It is a book you feel in your bones and in your stomach. Kenneth Roberts has added a dimension of his own to the old theme of men against the sea."

—BRADFORD SMITH, *New York Herald Tribune*

PRINTINGS

First published	January 2,	1956
Reader's Digest Book Club	April,	1956
Book-of-the-Month Club	August,	1957
England (Collins)	September,	1956
Denmark (Aschehoug)	September,	1956
France (Denoël)	November,	1956
Sweden (Bonniers)	January,	1957
Argentina (Jackson)	February,	1957
Mexico (Cumbre)	February,	1957
Italy (Mondadori)	July,	1957

TO BE PUBLISHED

Finland	Werner Soderstrom
Germany	Diana Verlag

THE BATTLE OF COWPENS

"The last work of the late Kenneth Roberts is a small volume that looms big in the mind and heart of this nation. For the *Battle of Cowpens* was really the turning-point in the American Revolution, when Morgan's rough and ready raiders took on Tarleton's veteran troops in a South Carolina meadow and in less than an hour showed the way that Yorktown would go. This is a diorama of the battle done with the unfailing skill of Roberts at his best though his last. It is a gem of historical re-enactment."

—Charles A. Wagner, *New York Mirror*

"With scrupulous fidelity to fact, Mr. Roberts has illumined one of our 'greatest hours' and given it dimension, significance and literary immortality."

—Alice Dixon Bond, *The Boston Herald*

Published .... April 3, 1958

OTHER BOOKS BY KENNETH ROBERTS

TRENDING INTO MAINE (published Little Brown, 1938: Doubleday, 1944)
"Kenneth Roberts takes you into the kitchen, sits you down by
the stove, hands you a doughnut, and stuffs you full of Arundel, Maine
traditions, Maine smells, Maine people, the hardships of soldiering,
the pleasures of ducks' breasts, the bravery of sea captains' daughters."
—E. B. WHITE, *Saturday Review of Literature*

MARCH TO QUEBEC (published 1938: revised 1940)
"Bringing together, in *March to Quebec*, the journals of the Quebec
Expedition is an exceedingly valuable contribution to the Americana of
the Revolution. . . . Many have been practically inaccessible. . . .
Only a few libraries in the country have them all, and he who would buy
them for himself would be obliged to spend a large sum of money and
wait for a year or so before some dealer in rare books could accumulate
all of them." —*Boston Evening Transcript*

MOREAU DE ST. MÉRY'S AMERICAN JOURNEY (1793–1798)
(published 1947: a translation by Kenneth and Anna Roberts)
"Here is a cross-section of a nation in the process, to use Moreau's
apt phrase, of being born." —*New York Times*

I WANTED TO WRITE (published 1949)
"The record of the reading, the assimilation, the eternal tracking
down of details, the enormous correspondence, and the starts and stops
of a historical novel in progress. Here is the reason why it took three
years to write *Oliver Wiswell* and five years to complete *Lydia Bailey*.
Here is what you go on doing, once you have learned to write."
—*Atlantic Monthly*

HENRY GROSS AND HIS DOWSING ROD (published 1951)
"In October, 1949, Henry Gross dowsed a fresh-water dome at
Clayhouse on a map of Bermuda, an island on which no potable spring
water supposedly existed. The Clayhouse well was drilled and, on April
27, 1950, flowed 44 gallons a minute, a daily 63,360 gallons 'wasting its
sweetness on the desert air.' . . . It is the greatest Bermuda story ever
told." —PARK BRECK, *Mid-Ocean (Bermuda) News*

THE SEVENTH SENSE (published 1953)
"*The Seventh Sense* is Roberts' answer to the volleys of his critics
—the account of the first year's operation of Water Unlimited Inc.,
whose aims are to insure an adequate supply of water for the world's
people, and to obtain for Henry Gross a steady income."
—ALAN NASH, *Rochester Times-Union*

WATER UNLIMITED (published 1957)
"The earlier books [*Henry Gross and His Dowsing Rod* and *The
Seventh Sense*] convinced me of the authenticity of Roberts' reports,
and of his theories about the circulation of subterranean water. . . . I
recommend this volume and the two earlier ones to any person not
blinded by unshakable prejudgments as offering a major contribution
to the world's vital need for water resources."
—EDMUND FULLER, *Chicago Tribune*